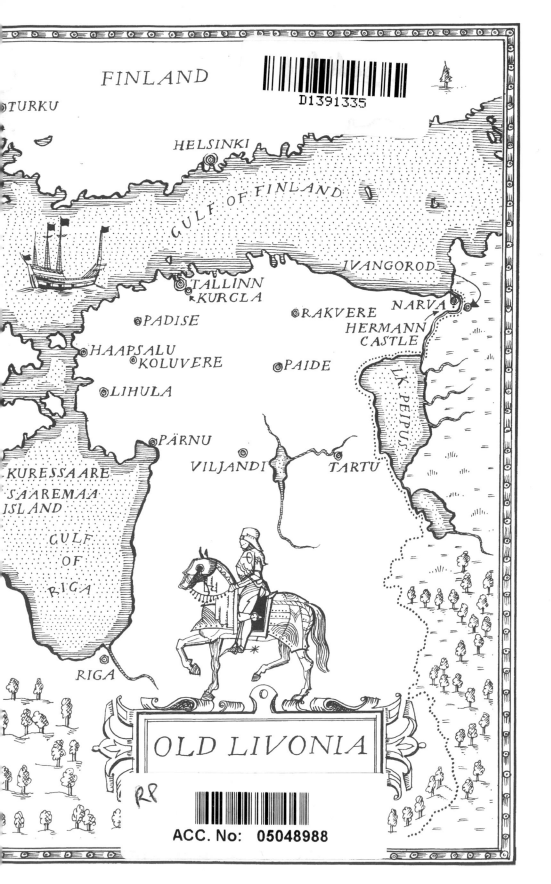

FINLAND

TURKU

HELSINKI

GULF OF FINLAND

IVANGOROD

TALLINN
KURCLA

NARVA
RAKVERE
HERMANN
CASTLE

PADISE

HAAPSALU
KOLUVERE

PAIDE

LK·PEIPUS

LIHULA

PÄRNU

KURESSAARE
SAAREMAA
ISLAND

VILJANDI

TARTU

GULF
OF
RIGA

RIGA

OLD LIVONIA

THE ROPEWALKER

Jaan Kross in English translation

The Czar's Madman (1992)
Professor Martens' Departure (1994)
The Conspiracy and Other Stories (1995)
Treading Air (2003)
Sailing against the Wind (2012)

BETWEEN THREE PLAGUES
Volume 1. The Ropewalker (2016)
Volume 2. A People Without a Past (2017)
Volume 3. A Book of Falsehoods (2018)

JAAN KROSS is Estonia's best-known and most widely translated author. He was born in Tallinn in 1920 and lived much of his life under either Soviet or German occupation. He won countless awards for his writing, including The National Cultural Award, The Amnesty International Golden Flame and France's Prix du Meilleur Livre Étranger, and played a key role in developing Estonia's consitution. He died in 2007.

JAAN KROSS

THE ROPEWALKER

VOLUME ONE *of*

BETWEEN THREE PLAGUES

THE STORY OF BALTHASAR RUSSOW

Translated from the Estonian by
Merike Lepasaar Beecher

MACLEHOSE PRESS
QUERCUS · LONDON

First published in the Estonian language as *Kolme katku vahel* by
Eesti Raamat, Tallinn, Estonia in 1970–80
First published in Great Britain in 2016 by

MacLehose Press
An imprint of Quercus Publishing Ltd
Carmelite House
50 Victoria Embankment
London EC4Y 0DZ

An Hachette UK company

The translator wishes to acknowledge the generous support received from the Cultural
Endowment of Estonia and its Traducta translation grant programme.

ISBN (HB) 978 0 85705 694 8
ISBN (TPB) 978 0 85705 456 2
ISBN (E-book) 978 0 85705 457 9

10 9 8 7 6 5 4 3 2 1

Designed and typeset in Cycles by Libanus Press
Printed and bound in Great Britain by Clays Ltd, St Ives plc

CONTENTS

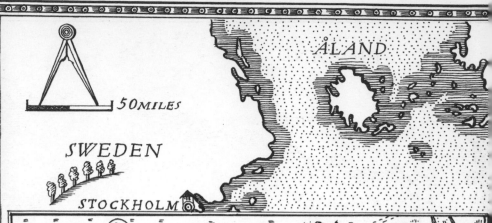

ÅLAND

SWEDEN

STOCKHOLM

TALLINN

1	BISHOP'S HOUSE & OLD MARKET	8	APOTHECARY
2	ST NICHOLAS' CHURCH	9	DOMINICAN MONASTERY
3	DOME CHURCH	10	VIRU GATE
4	TOOMPEA CASTLE	11	TOWN HALL
5	TALL HERMANN	12	NUN'S GATE
6	ST OLAF'S CHURCH	13	GREAT GUILD
7	HOLY GHOST CHURCH	14	GREAT COAST GATE

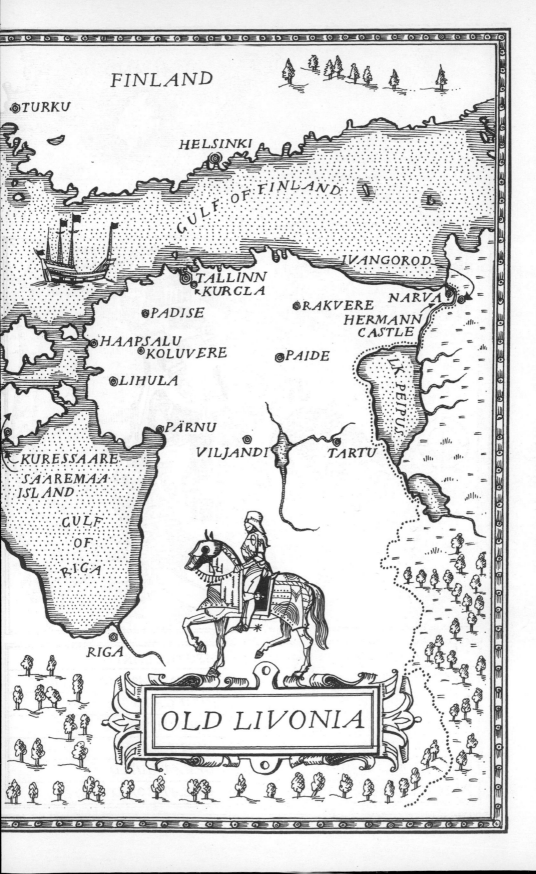

Translator's Acknowledgement

I am deeply grateful to Kristiina Ross and to Tiina Randviir for their always thoughtful responses to the many queries I sent their way in the course of preparing this translation.

Translator's Introduction

Between Three Plagues was written and first published in Soviet Estonia in four volumes, appearing one volume at a time in the decade from 1970 to 1980. It was the first of Jaan Kross' many historical novels and the most expansive and ambitious of them. Unlike anything previously written in Estonia, it is both a vivid tapestry of historical personages and events and a searching, engaging portrayal of an individual life – a novel in the grand tradition of nineteenth-century European and Russian novels, combined with a *Bildungsroman*. Its subtitle is *The Story of Balthasar Russow*. Russow (c.1536–1600) lived in Old Livonia (the territory of present-day Estonia and Latvia). He is the author of a remarkable work: the *Chronicle of the Province of Livonia*, in which he recounts the history of Old Livonia from 1156 to 1583. Russow wrote the *Chronicle* during the Livonian Wars, which spanned the years from 1558 to 1583, and this twenty-five year period is its focus. Old Livonia was a battleground for warring powers, with Russia, Sweden, Denmark and Poland–Lithuania scheming and battling for dominion of this small corner of northern Europe. It was a terrible, turbulent time. As armies besieged and bombarded towns and ravaged the countryside, repeated outbreaks of plague and periods of famine devastated the populace. Russow was witness to it all, taking notes on everything he observed and everything he heard as he gathered information for his *Chronicle*. Central to Kross' narrative is the story of how Russow's *Chronicle of the Province of Livonia* came to be written. Jaan Kross has described it as "the first classic of Estonian literature".

Kross considered *Between Three Plagues* his major work, with the greatest degree of identification between the main character and himself. In the memoirs that he wrote near the end of his life, he quips that he has asked himself: "Would I have undertaken that work if I had not come from the same part of town as my main character?" Kross did in fact see Russow as a kindred spirit, due in part to a serendipitous overlap of geographical and biographical details: they both spent a quiet, idyllic childhood "on the same spot of earth", in the fishing village of Kalamaja, outside Old Tallinn; both saw their worlds shattered by war in their twenties; both had peasant relatives in the countryside and experienced the rift between townspeople and countryfolk. And both were writers in a society where there were dangers for writers. Kross saw Russow as a man with a mission: to record the truth of the historical events in Livonia at a time when the people of that land knew very little about their history, when it was dangerous to talk about historical truth, as it was for Jaan Kross when Estonia was part of the Soviet Union. Kross spoke about his interest in Balthasar Russow thus:

I was moved by what he attempted to do: he sought to become an educated person, in the sense of that word in his time, a time when the sum total of educated Estonians could be counted on ten fingers. And another thing: he wanted to preserve the truth, as he saw it, of course. And this is something that no-one with his background had ever attempted in this land . . . Furthermore, I saw an obligation and an irresistible opportunity to learn more about our sixteenth century – which was not very familiar territory for us. And this, like all fictional works based on historical topics, promised another opportunity for me to test my skills, to experience the kind of thrill an athlete feels before a sporting event. Take, for example, that old Roman dance, which was executed among swords set upright, their hilts fastened to the floor. The imagination of a novelist writing historical fiction has to dance a similar dance among the swords of the facts set into the floor of history. And the author must perform his dance – be he Clio's half-sister or half-brother – without getting bloodied by the swords . . .

Between Three Plagues was written at a dark time in Estonian – and Russian – history. In Russia, Khrushchev's Thaw was beginning to congeal, but the loosening of censorship that had occurred during the Thaw seemed to be holding and, as Jaan Kross put it, was "asking to be tested". The opening up of Soviet cultural life that was to be brought about by Mikhail Gorbachev in the 1980s was not yet conceivable. Estonia was ruled by functionaries loyal to the Soviet system. Independent Estonia as a nation with a history of its own was only a memory. Its blue–black– white flag was banned from public places and prohibited in private homes. This was the context in which *Between Three Plagues* was first read. The novel was was enthusiastically received. There were print runs of 32,000 for each volume, followed in the mid-eighties by two more editions.

A review in 1980 by the Estonian literary scholar Mall Jõgi, entitled *Jaan Kross, Chronicler of the World*, provides a sense of the importance of Kross' writings to his compatriots, and of what he had achieved in the 1970s with his historical fiction. In addition to this monumental novel, he had written short stories and novellas about other figures from Estonian history. Mall Jõgi writes:

> In the span of ten years, Jaan Kross has added to our bookshelves an entire little library of Estonia's past. He has significantly influenced the understanding of the history of his country and changed it in many ways: he has replaced the picture before him, of the greyness and dreariness of a long, dark night of serfdom, with a colourful carousel – replaced dry facts with intriguing events, dull sophistry with spirited thought, shadowy figures with living beings. And he has done it in a way that everyone reads him with pleasure: pupils and teachers, casual readers and the literati, engineers and historians. They read and begin to see history as a something living, fascinating, progressing.

Jaan Kross had opened a window onto Estonian history and introduced his readers to memorable characters from their collective past. Although the events recounted in *Between Three Plagues* would not have been familiar to all Estonian readers, they were played out on a stage known to virtually the entire populace. The streets and towers and walls of Tallinn, as well as the surrounding countryside, the locations of battles, castles and other towns – were all familiar territory. The story of Balthasar Russow's life is a vividly told, compelling story about a boy of peasant background who becomes Estonia's first historian. Moreover, he is depicted as one of them. Russow's *Chronicle* was what first piqued Kross' interest in him, but documentary information about its author was sparse, and "everyone at the time, in 1963–64, thought Russow was German, historians too, even though he was born in Tallinn and was considered somewhat strange by fellow Germans because of his gruff criticism of men in power and his strangely benign attitudes toward the town's Greys". It was the evidence of Russow's Estonian roots unearthed by historian Paul Johansen that confirmed Kross' decision to write *Between Three Plagues*. Readers delighted too in finding parallels with their own time and its tribulations in some of the events depicted in the novel, events "sufficiently disguised in 400-year-old costume", as Kross put it, to elude detection by censors.

History and Fiction: Facts and Imagination

What intrigued and gratified Jaan Kross when writing historical fiction was the opportunity "to conjure the reality of the past – in a real sense, an imperishable reality – back to life". He formulated rules about the relationship between facts and invention in an historical novel. 1. The details of the novel's setting must be specific and accurate (including the details of daily life). 2. The coordinates of the great sweep of historical and political events must also be true to historical facts. 3. The writer is free to imagine plausible scenarios for his characters. In the case of Balthasar Russow's life and times, Kross observed that there was "the right amount of concrete information and the right amount of space for the imagination to spread its wings".

Much is unknown about the historical Balthasar Russow, but there is some documentation, and Kross used all available records. Balthasar Russow was probably born in 1536 and died in 1600. He graduated from Tallinn's town school in 1558, studied in Stettin (1558–62) and Wittenberg (1562–63), paid a brief visit to Bremen in 1563, returning then to Tallinn, where he became the pastor of Holy Ghost Church and where he lived until his death in 1600. There are records of his three marriages, of an argument with his father–in-law, and of the houses he lived in. On record, too, are the denunciations of his *Chronicle* by German gentry objecting to what they called Russow's "heinous lies and slanders" against the nobles and his "unacceptable" expressions of sympathy for the peasants and the Greys (town-dwellers of peasant extraction). Russow's *Chronicle* was for Kross an invaluable source, compensating for the sparseness of other documentation, for "it had to be – as every work is – a hidden picture puzzle of its author".

Almost all the characters in *Between Three Plagues* are historical fig-ures – whether cited in the *Chronicle*, in history books, or in archives. For some there is ample documentation, others are no more than a name in a registry. The only significant figure in the novel who is entirely fictional is Epp, Balthasar's first and enduring love, a peasant girl who works on his aunt and uncle's farm. Kross created her, he said, "to embody the nostalgic pull of the ancestral past – something so strong in Bal's consciousness and subconscious, that it had to be repre-sented by a concrete figure". A recurrent theme in Jaan Kross' fiction is that of divided loyalties and the struggle to define one's identity – to determine where one belongs. Balthasar is torn between loyalty to his country relatives – whom he sees as part of himself, yet whose way of life he cannot embrace – and his desire to take advantage of the opportunities afforded in town: an education, a chance to achieve something, to become someone – opportunities not open to his relatives. It distresses him to realise, when still a scholar at the town school, that he has begun to look upon his country kin and their lives with a sense of pity and to view the life of the prominent, wealthy doctor in whose town house he lives with a kind of envy. In his heart he remains conflicted. But what he is ultimately able to give to his people, whom he has had to leave behind, is their history.

As for the setting of the novel, "the sixteenth-century context of Tallinn was right there and sufficiently colorful". And Kross made the most of it. Tallinn is a commanding presence and so vividly delineated that critics have identified it as a "main character". A longtime resident of Tallinn told me of seeing Jaan Kross' tall, lanky figure roaming the streets in the 1960s and 1970s, head thrown back, stopping here and there to peer at the buildings of his hometown, seeming to fix in his mind the details of its roof-lines and doorways, its steeples and towers rising above its medieval walls, perhaps peopling the streets with figures of that earlier time in order to conjure onto the pages of his book the scenes that he saw in his mind's eye. A traveller to Tallinn today could walk into the town of the novel. The buildings and streets of Balthasar Russow's time are largely still there. The house Russow lived in – the Bishop's House, identifiable by the fresco of the bishop high on its peaked façade – still stands at the edge of the Old Market. The Town Hall, where the councilmen debate the fate of Russow's *Chronicle*, commands the marketplace as it has since the beginning of the fifteenth century. Looking across Town Hall Square, one can see the steeple of Holy Ghost Church, where Russow was pastor. And not far away, still standing, is St Olaf's Church, believed to have been built in the twelfth century. From its steeple stretched the long rope on which the visiting Italian acrobats performed the heart-stopping, spellbinding feats described in the opening pages of the novel.

Narrative Devices and Prose Style

In both subject matter and prose style *Between Three Plagues* was a revelation and a new literary experience for its first readers. Kross' prose is idiosyncratic – inventive, ruminative, highly descriptive – varied and vivid in both narration and representation. It is in some respects a realist novel, yet Kross employs several modernist literary devices – interior monologues, dream sequences and hallucinations, and alternating narrative voices and perspectives – which serve to reveal and dramatise the inner lives, the observations and judgements of his characters. Kross subscribed to the concept of "emotional memory" that informs Konstantin Stanislavski's method of training actors to summon in themselves the emotional responses and behaviours of the characters they portray. "My main effort," he said, "has been to get as close as possible to my characters, to inhabit their skin, and to act as they would have acted. As I imagine it, of course . . ." Kross' descriptions of the scenes his characters inhabit are realistic and striking in their concrete detail. His powers of visualisation are extraordinary, and his goal is to enable the reader to "see" what he sees, to enter the setting that his words create. His careful attention to detail stems from a sense of what for him was an "obligation" to the reader: "If an historical novel is to summon a reader into the world of the past, it should be credible – as concretely imaginable and immediate as possible."

Jaan Kross' prose is not spare. Critics have remarked on his long – sometimes very long – sentences, written in a kind of ornate, baroque style, with their many subordinate clauses, elaborate descriptions and historical and literary allusions. Kross explains: "The historical subject matter of my novels demands longer sentences in order for my language to be more in tune with the modes of speech from the past . . . Some examples of the style of the *Chronicle* are reflected in the novel." Furthermore, the interior monologues are in effect a "flow of thoughts, and best represented by a flow of words" that do not necessarily form complete sentences, but wander, with the pauses and breaks and changes of direction characteristic of the process of thinking.

A narrative device that Kross adapted from old chronicles and some eighteenth- and nineteenth-century fiction is the synoptic heading that introduces each chapter. Most of them are written as a single long sentence, approximately like this: In somewhat archaic, quaint, metaphorical language, the all-knowing, sometimes coy, narrator gives a cryptic account of events to come, as he muses on politics and history, eternity and fate, and moralises, philosophises, makes judgements on characters, pronounces verdicts on outcomes, and comments upon the process of narration and the rules of drama (even remarking, at times, on what he had intended, but was unable, to describe in the chapter).

Censorship and Compromise

"The conflict between literature and power is a reality of life in a repressive society," according to Kross, and "was the inescapable atmosphere in which people lived during the Soviet period . . . writers of course were more aware of it than most others . . . The very existence of it presupposes an unequal power relationship: there are those who control and those who are controlled . . . In such societies there have always been people who resist in order to define, at least for themselves, an identity, and to assert some measure of autonomy."

The central theme in Kross' historical novels was identified early by the Estonian poet Jaan Kaplinski: "Kross brought the new theme of moral compromise to Estonia's historical novel. Under six centuries of foreign domination, benign or otherwise, we simply sought strategies of survival and tried to remain decent, to maintain our identity. Compromise is the great Krossian theme and this is true to our historical reality." To those who viewed compromise as lack of principle and criticised it as capitulation, Kross responded: "Dear comrades, it is also a compromise that we write any books at all, given that we know censorship exists . . . I have never written in order to show how to make compromises, but always about how, despite the circumstances, to survive with one's integrity and identity intact." Later he added: "Actually, I would very much like to see someone examine my texts for the theme of compromise-as-weapon."

Kross found ways to speak the truth without incurring repercussions, and ways to compromise without damaging his integrity. He has described how he and his wife, Ellen Niit, a prolific and beloved poet, attempted to define for themselves the parameters of the possible:

> Ellen and I represented the possibilities of what we could write in the 1960s by drawing two circles. One circle contained things that should be written. The other, those things that could be (were permitted to be) written. Examining these circles, it became clear that they weren't entirely opposed, and with some effort, they could be brought closer until they touched – at first at one point, and as they began to overlap slightly, the area of overlap became larger . . . so that there was room to place quite a few things in it. This, at a time when conditions of censorship were such that one final consequence could have been to give up writing entirely.

The censor's shadow loomed over every creative mind and original work in Soviet Estonia. Jaan Kross has voiced his ideas in essays and interviews on the subject. The question was not whether to make compromises but how to determine the limits of compromise and how to avoid compromising oneself. Although Kross spoke with admiration for those fellow writers who, in order to avoid having to shape their writing to appease the censors, abandoned original work entirely during the Soviet period, he chose a different path. Censorship played a role in determining his career as a writer. He was a celebrated poet before becoming a novelist. Having been arrested in 1946 for "bourgeoise recidivism", he wrote poetry and translated Russian and German poets in Gulag camps and Siberian exile while serving his sentence. After his release and return to Estonia in 1954, he inspired many young poets with his innovative, highly original themes and free verse. By 1969 five collections of his poetry had been published to great acclaim. But when Moscow censors pressured a local cultural periodical in Estonia to denounce Kross' poetry as "decadent" and "insufficiently Bolshevik", he made a decision. Faced with the prospect of having to comply with the prescriptions and proscriptions of censorship, he abandoned poetry and turned his attention to the historical novel. "History would allow me to write obliquely of the present and play with paradox and ambiguity." He described his relationship with the censors as a game of hide-and-seek. "I have, like every other writer who wrote during the time of Soviet rule, done half the work for the censors myself." Kross later remarked that he had done some of his best writing under the constraints of censorship. In writing about the sixteenth century, he admitted, he tried "to write about its intellectual atmosphere and conditions in a way that that some kind of parallels with the present would shine through . . . though nothing too stark or obvious".

In a scene from the third volume of *Between Three Plagues*, which, Kross later noted, was "merely a scene from the present cloaked in four-hundred-year-old costume", the Town Council debates the question of approving the ideological stance of Russow's *Chronicle* – and thus, whether to permit its distribution in Tallinn. Kross describes the scene:

> The attempt was made – perhaps devolving into caricature – to concentrate in one scene a fundamentally ignorant group of men lacking any interest in the matter at hand, but charged with the responsibility of passing judgement on something about which they know nothing. I also attempted to indicate, as clearly as possible, that today [in the 1970s], everything was just as it was in Russow's day. It was required, at that time, that the *Chronicle*

represent the doctrine of the Augsburg Confession, and, in our day, that works conform to the tenets of Marxism–Leninism. There is basically no difference: each is a confession of beliefs. In other words, the parallel between the council members and the comrades of the Central Committee was presented as comedy – at least that is what I attempted. By the way, the tragedy of the ignorant deciders is not represented in the novel. For that, the author was not yet mature enough at the time. And those with power still had too much power.

When Kross was asked by Soviet journalists why he wrote only about historical subjects instead of the current topics that readers would be most interested in, he would equivocate, invoking his love of history, his interest in the past, his regret that he had not studied history at university. And he dismissed suggestions that perhaps history was a "refuge" for him. After Estonia had become an independent republic again, he explained:

> In spite of my love of history, a parallel reason, and sometimes my main reason, was the attempt to withdraw from the present to the extent of becoming invisible – to elude the present and those who represented it. The more current the subject matter, the larger the cadre of advisers who would typically surround those writers . . . to ensure that the text corresponded in content and form and spirit to the standards and goals of the Party. The ranks of these advisers thinned considerably when one's topic was an historical one . . . it was liberating somehow.

* * * * *

Kross assumed the responsibility of reviving and preserving his country's historical and cultural memory. His description of Balthasar Russow's mission as a writer also defines his own: "to preserve the truth of the things that have happened here", to give his compatriots knowledge of their history and thus a sense of national identity. He "felt called to fill the gaps in Estonian literature in the historical-personage genre of fiction . . . to give life in literature to personages in the historical and cultural history of Estonia". His whole oeuvre, he said, is about how a people arrive at self-awareness. Jaan Kross wrote ten historical novels, as well as many novellas and stories, centring on figures from different historical periods, from the six-teenth century through the twentieth, who have managed by dint of effort and determination to overcome the constraints imposed by their background and accomplish remarkable things. "My gallery of characters consists primarily of those who have contributed to our cultural history." His hope was that his works would inspire and encourage other Estonian authors to undertake the writing of biographical–historical fiction.

An even broader goal for Jaan Kross was to bring Estonia to the awareness of the world as a nation with its own culture and character, "but always in the larger context of Europe and the rest of the world". And while he focused his writings on the history and literature of his own country, he was emphatic about the importance of all small nations and their cultures: "Literature is not defined only by the literary classics and bestsellers of the largest nations . . . The literature of smaller peoples plays a role, and often a more significant role than is generally recognised. And furthermore, the literatures of even very small nations are vital in the great whole, and indispensable."

Merike Lepasaar Beecher

BOOK ONE

CHAPTER ONE,

*in which a town witnesses a number of miraculous feats,
and a little scamp believes he has discovered the secret
behind them, in which conviction he is perhaps less
mistaken than people nowadays are prone to think.*

"Worthy craftsmen, upstart swells, yokels! Honoured lords and ladies of the nobility! Esteemed and gracious burghers! Hurry, hurry, hurry! You will see wonders you have never seen before, and will never, in your lifetime, see again!"

The crier, a fuzz of down on his chin and sweat on his nose, was a young fellow, no longer a child, not yet a man. Opening his pale eyes wide, he swooped the bright red, gold-banded hat from his head, and in that same motion his frayed sleeve brushed the beads of sweat off his nose, and the red-and-gold hat described a splendid arc across the blue sky.

"Honourable Council! Beautiful women! Modest maidens! Stone-cutters and shoemakers! Hurry! Hurry! Hurry!"

By now the crier's urgent summons and sky-sweeping gestures were no longer needed. For the throngs surging through the Great Coast Gate and streaming towards Köismäe Hill were already squinting up into the cloudless spring sky.

Hurrying through the gate came Councilman Vegesack, face red, dignity abandoned in his haste. Even his wife, exceedingly gaunt and usually pale, had colour in her cheeks on this day. There were other councilmen and their wives in the jostling crowd, along with merchants and shopkeepers, beer-bellied master craftsmen and freckled journey-men, prominent burgher matrons with their giddy daughters, underfed servant girls, militiamen in blue coats and the grey ranks of labourers. And they were all peering up-up-up and craning their necks towards St Olaf's steeple.

In the distance, to the right, droves of sailors from Lübeck came running, the pier rumbling under their pounding feet. Even they had never seen anything like the spectacle they were about to behold. To the left, groups of villagers from the hamlet of Kalamaja were hurrying up Lontmaaker Rise, raising clouds of dust in their wake.

When the townspeople had gone through the gate and across the drawbridge and were far enough to see the rooftops of the outermost houses above the town walls, they could make out round eyes peering at the sky from the open shutters of every attic storeroom. Three house-boys had climbed out through one merchant's roof hatch onto the pulley beam. They were sitting in a row, like village lads on horseback, staring up into thin air and swinging their legs over empty space, a sight that would have alarmed passers-by at any other time. Even on the Poxhouse walls surrounded by ditches and wooden barricades there were curious spectators – the inmates had climbed onto the walls and sat there gaping at the sky, their upturned faces disfigured by purple blotches and missing noses.

"Honoured knights and ladies! And villagers who happen to be in town with your ol' ladies! Hurry! Hurry! Hur—"

The crier felt someone tug at his coat-tail. Clapping his red hat back onto his head, he turned around on his seal-oil barrel and looked down behind him. A boy of about ten or twelve was pulling his coat.

"What is it, Bal?"

"I'm going to go see how they do it!"

"You can watch from right here."

"I can't work it out from here."

24

"Where're you going then?"

"Up the steeple."

"Oh, forget it! They'll never let you up there!"

But the little scamp had already disappeared into the crowd.

His progress to the gate against the flow of the crowd was slow. He was not particularly deft or nimble in making his way through. He did manage to duck to one side and slip past a few people – *Fie, you little devil . . .* – and make himself small enough to squeeze between others – *What's the rush? Blasted ruffian! . . .* – Even so, he was not slim or slight, nor especially agile; in fact, he was a rather sturdy boy and somewhat ungainly in his movements. His broad shoulders under a nondescript sparrow-grey coat were a little hunched; the ash-blond mop of hair on his round head stood on end in spite of frequent combing, like a clump of carelessly cut stalks of rye. His round eyes were the same grey as the town's stone walls on a day like this, with the sky lending them a touch of blue; and his gaze, though alert, was somewhat preoccupied.

"I'm going to find out about this thing," he muttered to himself, and pushed his way under the vaulted gate, where the sound of tramping feet was greatly magnified. "I'm going to find out . . ."

Here there was a bit more room – enough for an angry sentry to take a swipe at his backside with the long shaft of his halberd, directly under the gaze of the Crucified One suspended on the wall.

"Where ya' goin, *Sacrament*!"

Bal smiled absently, without resentment. He murmured, "I'm going to find out . . ." and ducked off Lai Street into the blind alley alongside the town walls.

Here he encountered only the occasional straggler. By rights he should have greeted them all, but this rule of etiquette was taken seriously only in the preparatory class of the Trivium School. Being a proper *quarta*-level pupil, on the street he was obliged to greet only councilmen and clergymen. Recovering his dignity after the sentry's

25

blow, he hurried cheerfully round the corner and raised his eyes two hundred and fifty cubits to the gilded cockerel atop the steeple of St Olaf's Church. There, like a silver strand of hair, stretching from the steeple to somewhere far beyond the town walls, sloped the magic rope of the aerialists, the never-before-seen wonder that the whole town was talking about.

Bal hurried on, head thrown back. But when he reached the half-open Hobuveski Gate he stopped to take a good look at the church steeple from a proper distance. He stood there a long moment, surveying its awful height. Then he looked down at the ground, marvelling at the smells that, all at once, flooded his senses. Along the uneven cobblestones from behind the gate of the nearby mill drifted the warm, mellow smell of fresh horse manure, just like the smell from his father's barn on the Kalamaja shore. And a bit higher in the air hung the scent of freshly milled wheat, strong as the smell of his grandfather's granary far away, beyond the River Kurgla.

When Bal raised his eyes again he was jolted back to the present. Striding briskly towards him, flanked on right and left by servants bent under the weight of the books they were carrying, was none other than Superintendent Bock! Bal instructed his neck to prepare itself for a bow and arranged the words of a Latin phrase in his mind: *Salve, pater reverendissime.* * But when he realised it was not a servant at all on the Superintendent's right, that it was Schoolmaster Frolink himself, fear froze his tongue. This Master Bartholomeus Frolink, nicknamed Panis Quotidianus,† was the very man who had just an hour earlier announced to all the classes: "Going to see the skywalkers is permitted only to the top levels, *secunda* and *prima*. Class monitors will ensure that no-one runs off! *Tertia* will memorise the Articles of Augsburg XVII to XIX. *Quarta* will decline *panis quotidianus*. To work!"

In spite of his shock, Bal was almost calm. A curious force prodded

* Greetings, most Reverend Father (Latin).   † Daily bread (Latin).

him straight towards the approaching masters. He felt an enormous temptation to test them – perhaps they would not even notice him! At the same time, another, wiser, force drew him to the right, towards the partly open mill gate. He felt glued to the spot, the way he sometimes did in dreams where he was standing on the street in the path of a heavy wagonload of wine barrels, or sitting in church under a crumbling vaulted ceiling. But then the second force overcame the first, and at the last possible moment he ducked behind the gate. He pressed his face hard against the rough pine boards – so hard that his nose got smudged with the grey mill dust lodged in the cracks, and he stood there listening as the three pairs of feet drew closer. They were just about to pass by when they suddenly came to a halt on the other side of the gate. Master Frolink said:

"I, for one, believe it. Athenaeus wrote that the rope dancers in Cyzicus made use of their towers the same way—"

The superintendent interrupted him:

"Our rope dancers are much less skilled than those of antiquity. But our towers are much higher. Do you think they had towers in Cyzicus as high as this one here? Of course not! I don't believe it for a moment. That would mean people can fly. And without wings, no less! Apparently, twenty years or so ago there was a tailor in Ulm who tried to fly down from a church steeple – he had actually constructed wings for himself – but he fell to his death nonetheless! There's even a verse about it:

> Let the bell toll!
> He died by his own lie.
> A man is not a bird –
> He will never fly."

Then the three pairs of feet moved on, and Bal came out from behind the gate.

A huge padlock weighing half a pood hung on the main door of St

Olaf's Church. A dozen people stood in the street, heads thrown back, staring at the sky. A rope stretched from the topmost window-slit in the steeple. Taut as a violin string at a dizzying height above the streets, it disappeared beyond the rooftops. Someone tried the gate in the court-yard wall to the left of the church. It was locked. Bal turned into the next street, slipped under grain merchant Hahnemann's vaulted passage into his courtyard, and then climbed up a pile of birch logs stacked against the wall. Halfway up he felt some of them slip and roll noisily under his weight as the entire heap began to give way. Caught by sur-prise, Bal flattened himself against the logs, feeling them ram into his ribs. He pulled himself warily up to the top of the woodpile and looked over the stone wall.

On the other side was a covered wagon with a large canvas top. Two horses stood nearby, unharnessed, their heads in their feedbags. Huddled together in the middle of the courtyard were four people, two elderly, moustachioed men, and two girls. They were dark-skinned, like gypsies, and appeared to be arguing. The men's agitated voices were by turns deep and high-pitched, and they flailed their arms as though their shirts were on fire. The girls responded in a curiously chirping language. They pointed in turn to the wagon and to the open church door. About ten paces away stood two dark-skinned yet remarkably pale boys, about the age of *prima* or *secunda* pupils, and so like each other that Bal squeezed his eyes shut and looked again to make sure there really were two of them. The boys were silent, holding hands, looking down at the ground. Then the covered wagon began to rock and a fat gypsy woman dropped down onto the cobblestones, a jumble of extraordinary white–red–gold items of shabby clothing heaped over her arm. She screeched at the others, something that sounded like *pork-a-mud-on-a-voy* . . .* tossed the clothes to one of the old men, slapped each girl across the face and went over to the boys, where she stood for an oddly silent

* What he heard was this Italian curse: "*Porca Madonna, voi*".

28

moment, made the sign of the cross on each boy's forehead, and then herding them all into the church pulled the door shut behind her.

Bal climbed quickly from the woodpile onto the wall, scraping the skin on his palms as he gripped the top of the wall. He let himself hang on the other side, legs dangling. Little by little he managed to stretch his legs, until his toes touched one of the hoops supporting the canvas top of the wagon. Just then his foot slipped and sank into the fabric. He fell heavily onto the hoop and slid down its entire length, feeling a streak of fire in his buttocks. Though he landed on the cobblestones, feet first, the impact left him dizzy for a moment. There was no reaction to his thudding fall from within the wagon. He instantly straightened himself up beside the large, mud-caked wheels and sprinted to the church door. *If the old woman's locked it from inside, there's nothing I can do . . .* But as he pressed down the latch, the door opened without a sound and he closed it hastily behind him.

He paused in the high, twilit antechamber at the base of the steeple and crossed himself, just in case, vaguely in the direction of the altar far away, beyond the columns where gilded angels touched by shafts of shimmering coloured light stood guard. Looking over his shoulder, he took a few steps to the right, towards the small door leading to the steeple stairs; it was too low even for him to get through without stooping. He had taken just three steps when he suddenly stopped, for instead of the stone floor he felt something soft underfoot. He turned his head and pressed a fist against his mouth so as not to cry out: his right foot was resting on the hem of the fat gypsy woman's skirt. She was kneeling between him and the door to the stairway, fortunately with her back to him. She was praying. Her neck, under long strands of black hair, moved in time to a half-whispered prayer, and she had turned her back – *blasted pope-worshipper* – to the altar. Bal held his breath for a long moment. Then he carefully picked his foot up from the woman's skirt and began to inch sideways towards the steeple entrance. It all went well. He kept one eye on the old woman and the other on the big iron key in the lock as he gripped it carefully and pulled. The door opened easily, but it emitted a frightful screech which reverberated in the empty antechamber like the cry of a seagull struck by a rock. The old woman jumped up with surprising agility and reached out to grab Bal by his shirt-tail. He lunged through the door into the near darkness and, feeling his way forward with his hands, raced up the narrow, circular stairs. For a short distance the woman's shrill cries followed him, but then they stopped. Bal continued running up a few more turns, pausing at a narrow window-slit to catch his breath. The old crone would scarcely try to follow him up stairs like these.

He looked out of the slit. The wind that blew against his face smelt of pigeon droppings, and he saw himself level with red roofs and white chimneys. Beyond them rose the grey neck and moss-covered stone "hat" – the conical spire – of Epping tower. But the magic rope that crossed the sky at the top corner of the window was no closer than it had been from below.

The spiral staircase came to an end. A series of rough limestone steps rose up steeply in front of him. He could hear no movement above him, but he knew that the others had to be up there, somewhere. He would have to keep a safe distance behind them. Then he reached the spiral staircase once more: it seemed endless. Instinctively, Bal pressed his back against the wall. From somewhere above, there grew a murmuring, clamorous roar – so loud that he involuntarily pulled his head down between his shoulders. It was odd that his body did not sense the slightest tremor in the wall, but the sound, swelling with a frightening intensity, passed over him like a great gust of wind. Ten steps below, flashing through the beam of light shining through the window-slit, a frightened dove continued its downward flight.

Somewhere even higher up, a side passage led into the shadowy recesses above the vaulted ceiling, where doves cooed and ruffled. He could just make out thick wooden beams crisscrossing overhead like a ship's cargo derrick – this had to be the belfry. Higher yet, the staircase opened out into a room with two somewhat larger windows. A mound of ashes and charred firewood lay in one corner, very likely the remains of some tower watchman's vigil. The view from here – the harbour and the crescent of town at its edge, the bay with its islands of Paljassaare, Nairisaare, Salmesaare – was no bigger than the palm of his hand. The scattering of tiny houses was now far below, but the magic rope still hung high in the blue sky, its position seemingly unchanged, still beyond reach.

Bal forged ahead up the spiral stairs, arriving at a spacious square room about the size of an assembly room. From all sides, light slanted in between boards nailed across windows that here were several fathoms high. Although the stone walls continued to rise for another two storeys, they now contained a wooden structure anchored to the outside walls, and the staircase too was made of wood. The air, which had been cool until then, became noticeably warmer. The sour smell of the sun-warmed lead spire penetrated the strange jumble of densely crisscrossing beams overhead in the dark, dusty interior. And then he reached the grey lower part of the spire itself. The landings were now a few fathoms apart. Gradually, they narrowed around a mighty, vertical axletree supporting an odd web of logs. It made him think of a tree trunk ten times as big as the giant fir in his grandfather's dooryard at Kurgla.

Bal began to count the nearly dark landings. On the fifth he came to the first open window-slit in the spire. By order of the Town Council the shutters were to be kept open that day – to allow a little light into the dim interior of the steeple, lest the aerealists start a fire, going up and down the stairs with candles and lanterns.

On the next landing, Bal was blinded all of a sudden by the blue brightness of a window as tall as a man. He let go of the railing and ran towards it. The dizzying sight of the vast emptiness beyond the opening forced him down on all fours. He held his nose close to the floor, shut his eyes, and thought it was a damned good thing Märten was not there to see him; a very good thing he was somewhere far down below, waving his red-and-gold hat for a shilling.

When he opened his eyes and dared look again, he saw a brownish smoke cloud hovering between the bright sky and the shimmering sea. His eyes took in the dark woods of Kopli, and above them the smoke rising from the brickworks (as it had for an entire year already). Then came the bright green marshland beyond the town, and beyond that, rundown village shacks like grey piles of rubble next to the black squares of garden plots. A good distance this side of the houses, the sandy slope of Lontmaaker Rise swarmed with people – like ants on a honeycomb. In the middle of the crowd, more than three hundred fathoms distant, he could see a light sandy circle marked off by a rope. From the circle's centre, attached to a low stake driven into the ground, the magic rope rose in a straight line, like a captured ray of sunlight stretching over hayfields and the moat and the town wall between the towers of Plate and Epping, where it was already higher than a hundred and fifty cubits. Above the streets next to the wall the rope was higher than Bal could see, and as it neared it seemed to shoot straight up into the blue of the sky. He gripped the edges of the opening with both hands and raised himself carefully up onto the ledge, then eased himself out as far as he dared, threw his head back, and looked up. In the sloping sides of the lead spire he saw six open window-slits. There were twenty-five landings between him and the top opening into which the rope disappeared: he could figure that out at a glance. But the moment he looked down, he felt the awful heavenward thrust of the spire above him and the yawning emptiness below become one dizzying torrent that coursed through his own hollow being – down, down, down – threatening to take him with it.

He collected himself, focused his eyes in front of his nose, directly on the black lead frame of the window-slit, and pulled himself back into the safety of the tower.

The sixth, seventh, eighth, ninth landings. Bal struggled with himself a bit, then continued up to the tenth, fifteenth and twentieth landings without looking out again. On the twenty-fourth he rested and listened. He imagined he heard the distant murmur of talk from above, but perhaps it was just the wind.

On the narrow twenty-fifth landing he clenched his teeth and moved carefully to the very edge of the window-slit. There he lay on his stomach and, firmly gripping the rim of the opening, let his eyes travel over its edge and down. When he turned onto his side he could look both above and below. A blue jet of emptiness threatened to course through him even here, but the rough boards under his stomach and side gave him some sense of security.

The sixth window-slit was now only thirty cubits above. And there, disappearing into it, was the pride of Tallinn's rope-makers, a yellow-grey hemp rope, thick as a man's thumb. Under the supervision of Lunt-Laos, three rope-makers of Kalamaja had twisted it so tightly that the moustachioed Sandro, the aerialists' headman, having run his palm over its entire length, could not find a single uneven spot the size of a baby chick's back. As Lunt-Laos told it, Sandro had clapped his hands and proclaimed something like *"merra vill'ya"*,* but no-one knew what he meant.

All at once Bal heard shouts from the crowd far, far below. He saw the ants on the street in front of the church wave their arms and throw their caps up into the air. The cries of the throngs on Lontmaaker Rise, and those behind the city walls, rose and merged gradually into one great distant roar. Suddenly understanding, he looked up.

Standing in the air, ten steps from the sixth window-slit, was one of the boys he had seen in the churchyard. He was wearing a skintight

* *Meraviglia:* a marvel (Italian).

outfit – its right torso and left leg gold; the opposite sides white – making him look like the Jack in a pack of cards Bal had once seen in a Dutch sailor's hands. A little white beret perched on his black hair. His hands were placed casually on his hips, and now, with calm and measured steps, he simply walked out into thin air. He was, of course, stepping his way along the rope, and Bal could clearly see how, turning his toes slightly outward, he placed his feet on it. Still, it seemed as though he were walking on air. In fact, the indisputable presence of the rope clarified nothing; on the contrary, the whole thing was more baffling than ever. Without the rope, it could all have been as a miracle or as witchcraft. But now there was no way to explain it except as as a feat of sheer skill.

With a glance he measured the distance between the boy and the street below: the two hundred fifty cubits raced up and down his own insides like a wet rope. His fingers clutched the edge of the window-opening, and though he pressed his stomach against the floor, he still felt queasy. At the same moment, the boy's outlines blurred for an instant – and then all of a sudden he was facing the steeple! Bal had not even managed to notice whether he had swivelled left or right. The boy looked even paler than he had earlier, down below. He smiled, somehow indifferently and stiffly, and for an instant Bal thought the smile was meant for him. Startled, he smiled back, then realised the boy had not noticed him at all. Without warning, the boy had again turned around. And now he spread his arms and broke into a run. With graceful, feather-light steps he bounded into the emptiness of the blue sky and continued downward towards the horizon; for a while he was dimly visible as he descended against the backdrop of the shimmering sea.

Bal pulled back from the edge of the opening, stood up a bit dizzy and listened, but could hear nothing in the tower – there was only the roar rising up from below. He mounted the stairs, creeping up another four flights. The twenty-ninth level was not much bigger around its cubit-wide centre beam than the outdoor kitchen in his grandmother's garden at Kurgla, where she cooked soup in the summertime. He could clearly hear, coming from up above, the whispering of two low voices in some foreign tongue. Then he heard someone knock hard on the ceiling and one old moustachio's voice say out loud: "*Va bene!*" It struck him with some astonishment that the gypsies spoke Latin well enough to be understood. It emboldened him. He swallowed, and, as quietly as he could, started his ascent towards the light visible in the landing above. The stairs opened out onto the next floor at a point where the huge vertical pillar was positioned exactly between them and the open window-slit. Bal's nose had not yet cleared the edge of the landing when he saw the magic rope. It was wrapped at least ten times around the pillar and tied into several strong knots. Between the pillar and the window, against the patch of bright sky, stood the twin of the golden page, dressed in a red-and-white outfit. The girls were busy buttoning his collar at the back. One of the moustachioed men stood at the boy's left, holding a willow pole about three cubits long, with a ball the size of an apple at each end. The other moustachio was not visible at first. But when Bal raised himself up a little he saw, to the right of the stairs, quite close to his face, the man's dark green trousers. At the edge of the landing was a small stool; the moustachio was sitting on it holding a silver beaker. Then the girls stepped back from the red-and-white page and one of them said: "*Pronto.*"*

The moustachio on the left stepped in front of the boy, turned the willow pole horizontal, and raised it to the level of the boy's chest. The boy stretched out his left index finger and the man removed his own hand from the pole, which now balanced, motionless, on the boy's finger. Throughout all this, the expression on the boy's pale face remained unchanged. He was wearing the same slightly stiff, absent smile with which his twin had walked off into space. But then the other moustachio

* Ready (Italian).

got up from his stool, handed his beaker to the boy and said in that almost comprehensible Latin-like language, in a memorably sonorous voice: "*Bevi – che non caschi.*"*

The boy raised his long-lashed eyelids, his dull brown eyes beginning to sparkle as they rested on the beaker; taking it carefully into his right hand he drank a measured draught, his face solemn, and handed it back to the old man. And it was then that Bal understood everything: *the magic was in the drink!* So overcome was he by this discovery that had the man returned to his stool just then he would not have had time to duck out of sight. But the old moustachio, reaching behind him, set the beaker back on the stool without turning, his sleeve passing so close to Bal's face that he felt the air fan his damp brow. The man went to help the boy step out of the window. And in the time that the girls and both moustachios crossed themselves, and the boy in the red beret turned his back to them, crossed himself, extended the pole out of the window, turned it at right angles to the rope, and stepped into empty space – for this entire time Bal stared at the beaker on the stool just a cubit's distance from his face. Then, when the old men and the girls went to the window to look out after the boy, blocking the opening and darkening the tower room, a wave of temptation surged and engulfed him. A jumble of vaguely defined impulses – the temptation to gamble, an eagerness to test himself, a craving for the thrill of a risk, the urge to tempt fate, alongside the desire to retain his dignity and, no doubt, a measure of ill-defined trepidation – all these forced him to proceed with caution. At last he moved, gingerly, slowly extending his arm, as though pushing aside a veil of angels and devils – the former stricken, the latter smirking – and lifted the beaker off the stool. He raised it to his lips and took a long swallow. Then he lost his nerve. He did not even put the beaker back on the stool but set it down as if it were red hot, and slipped noiselessly down the stairs.

* Drink – so you won't fall (Italian).

He had for some reason expected it to taste unlike anything he had ever tasted before – perhaps like peppermint, cold and tingling in his mouth and spreading out to the very tips of his fingers, but a hundred times stronger than the medicine that Apothecary Bastian had once given them to treat his father's lumbago. He had imagined it so vividly that when swallowing it he had no doubt as to its taste. He ran to his viewing post on the twenty-fifth level, stepped up close to the edge of the window-slit, and thought: *If I had a rope like that one here, right now . . .* Yet the very idea of a rope extending from under his feet into empty space, one he would have to step out on, made his knees go weak. And just then he realised that the peppermint taste of the magic potion had not been the least bit stronger than his father's medicine! It was weaker; in fact, much weaker. To tell the truth, it had hardly been detectable. It had actually tasted like cool, clear spring water. But then the airborne twins caught his attention again.

The red page had reached a spot above the houses at the edge of the town wall, while the golden one had turned around somewhere on the other side of the moat and was now coming towards his brother. They met at one hundred and fifty cubits above the town wall. The red one stretched out his balancing pole and the other boy grasped it. Holding on to it, they turned, and, keeping the pole parallel to the rope, arched their backs slightly, their legs and bodies forming an image of the cross-section of a boat – its keel defined by their toes, the top edge of the deck by their hands, and the deck railing by the profile of their heads and hats. Carefully shifting their toes, they accomplished four spine-chilling turns. And then, with the swelling roar of admiration rising up from below, the golden twin let go of the balancing pole, placed his hands on the rope, and threw his legs up into the air in a handstand. Six thousand mouths gasped – oohing like the sea rising and falling against the hollowed-out riverbank at Tiskre in a northeaster. As though supported on the crest of the admiring wave of sound, the golden page walked twenty steps on his hands in each direction, his white-gold legs bent slightly apart, like the blades of a pair of scissors.

Bal stared at the scene so fixedly, not looking away even for an instant, that his eyes began to smart. It seemed to him that he was seeing everything through the glass panes with which his father had replaced their pig's-bladder window the year before. The thick glass, composed of mysterious droplets, had made objects appear to be far away and their contours seem oddly fluid. And no matter how awe-inspiring the feats on the rope, Bal knew the magic was actually elsewhere.

He saw the red page stand calmly over empty space while his golden twin performed unheard of tricks – walking on his hands, making about-face turns so quick that one could barely follow them, and even – but this was probably a mirage brought on by eyestrain – throwing a cartwheel. But still, the magic was elsewhere.

Twenty paces from Bal, the golden page passed the red one, took the balancing pole from him, and walked through the opening, back into the steeple. The red page turned his back to the church. He raised his thin shoulders once, as though about to leap up from the rope, or perhaps it was simply to draw a deep breath. Then he spread his arms wide and broke into a run. But he did not run as his golden twin had, in a graceful, playful, calm rhythm; not at all. He flew with unimaginable speed along the three hundred fathoms of straight rope, down towards Lontmaaker Rise. Within moments the rope started to undulate slightly, and each wave under his feet seemed to lend his steps ever more speed. It looked as if his outspread arms would at any moment waft him upwards like a pair of wings. And there, far away, where the rope became invisible against the grey-green ground, he looked like a low-flying swallow before the rain. (But it was clear that the magic was elsewhere.) The boy reached the end of the rope, leapt over the stake that held it taut, and attempting to come to a stop was propelled to the very edge of the roped-off circle. At this point the surrounding crowds trampled over the rope barrier and with a roar of enthusiasm closed in around the red-and-white dot.

Cries of *bravissimo* and a burst of foreign-language babble now sounded from above. Bal imagined he heard the smack of kisses. And then there was a rumble of footsteps on the stairs. He sprinted ahead of the descending troupe. Nearly choking on the rising dust, he clambered down the ladder-like stairs, passing alternately through darkness and light. But he noticed nothing of all this. There was but one thought under his stiff mop of hair: *What was it that they, and he too, had drunk?* His skin felt strange, hot and cold and sweaty all at once with the knowledge that a drop of that drink was now in his body – within each finger and toe, under each nail.

He reached the low door leading to the church's antechamber. It was still slightly ajar – just as the large old crone had left it in her pursuit of him – so that Bal could cast a quick look into the antechamber without risking its creaking hinges. The old woman was no longer around. The door into the courtyard was open too, and with some effort Bal succeeded in getting across the courtyard and over the wall into Pikk Street.

Just before reaching the Great Coast Gate he encountered the crowds streaming back towards town. It was difficult to make his way against the returning throng of animated spectators busy discussing what they had just seen, waving their arms to demonstrate the red page's flying descent, or the golden boy's stunning turns, or just gesticulating in bewilderment, reluctant to believe, yet compelled to believe what they had witnessed.

He pushed his way somehow through the crowd and out of the gate, hurried across the drawbridge with its familar rumble, jumped over the low mud-and-cobblestone wall of the Rose Garden which served only to keep pigs out, ran as straight as he possibly could between bushes of elderberry and sweetbriar, landed with a thud on the other side of a higher wall on the sea side of the town, and in an instant disappeared among fishermen's boathouses on the shore.

A boat belonging to old Mündrik-Mats was in its usual spot on the beach. Rolls of oakum were lying about, weighted down by rocks to keep the wind from blowing them away. But neither old Mats nor his boy Juhan were anywhere to be seen. Nor did Märten seem to be back yet. The door to the boat shed was ajar and Bal stuck his head in.

"Märten?"

Inside the dusky shed smelling of tar, Bal caught sounds of contented chewing and swallowing. And he could just make out a pile of nets by the wall, and a pair of trousers torn at the knees, and Märten's sharp chin resting on them.

"Ah. Did you get into the steeple?"

"Yeah."

"Mmm! How was it?"

"Mm . . ."

"Here . . . It's good. Try it."

Bal bit into the sweet, chewy pod.

"What is it?"

"St John's bread. Bastian's old man has some too. But he charges a shilling for a dozen. This is holy stuff."

"Where'd you get it?"

"Off one of the mates from Lübeck . . . his leather hat fell into a cow-pat while he was watching the skywalkers. I washed it for him in a ditch – and he gave me the pod."

"And what makes it holy?"

"John the Baptist chewed on them!"

"When?"

"When he was in the desert, of course. And he washed them down with dew."

Bal chewed on his carob pod for a while.

"But what do these skywalkers drink? Before they go out on the rope? Couldn't we find that out?"

"There's nothing to find out. I know what it is."

"Don't blather!"

"But I know . . . They also drink dew."

"Hogwash."

"It's true! I was around them for a whole week, and the girls – they could manage a little German – told me the whole story: On three cloudless nights before the spectacle, they spread out two oiled calfskins in a hidden place, and when the dew collects they gather up the drops into a crystal bottle."

"But how does the dew come by this magic power?"

"Look, the sun takes dew up into the air in the morning, right? And if you have enough of it in your body . . ."

"I get it. But in that case, you could just collect all you wanted . . ."

"It wouldn't help. When they flew along the rope in Vilnius, it had to be dew from Lithuania; and in Cracow it had to be from Poland. And in Tallinn only dew collected here will work. It has to be dew from the country you're in, or you come hurtling down."

"I suppose they have to practise, too?"

"That's for sure. A whole lot. They practise seven hours a day. But without drinking the dew they couldn't do the half of it!"

"Of course . . . And no doubt they say some magic words over the drink."

"I would think so."

Bal was so deep in thought that only Märten heard the horns in the Town Hall tower far away, sounding two o'clock: toot-toot-toot, and toot-toot-toot.

"Aren't you going back to school today?"

Bal started. His sudden twinge of fear did not run too deep, but an uncomfortable unease spread up his neck and into his head. He shrank visibly, as though Rector Tegelmeister himself had placed his blue-veined hand with its two silver rings on his shoulder.

"N-noo . . . not today."

"So Panis will let you have it tomorrow, won't he?"

"I'll be lucky if it's only Panis. I'm going home now."

He nodded to Märten and started off towards home along the water's edge. He had no desire any more to stay around for the afternoon to watch Märten help old Mündrik-Mats caulk boats. Going home was somewhat risky, of course . . . What a curse, to have an older sister who would squeeze every last bit of information out of you. *Small fry weren't permitted to go and watch the acrobats, were they? Of course not. But no doubt you were there, on the spot! Don't keep staring at the soup pot! Your conscience is just as black as that pot. You were there, watching, weren't you? I can see it in your face. You always have to be part of everything – why do I expect anything else? . . . It's a wonder you didn't climb up into St Olaf's steeple . . . Oh . . . you . . . ! You'll break your bones one of these days . . . !* He did not have to worry that Annika would tell on him, but still . . .

Then he heard Märten's voice: "Bal, you coming fishing tonight?"

Bal came to a standstill and shut his eyes tight . . . *Märten has such a great fishing spot . . . and I'd be able to ask him a lot more about the sky-walkers. But, oh well – maybe another time . . .*

He turned around: "Noooo . . . I have to study Donatus."

He continued slowly along the water's edge towards Kalamaja, paused, picked up a smooth stone, skimmed it over the water. But the surface ripples were too strong and the stone skipped only twice. *I wonder what it would have done if I'd wet the stone with* that *dew before throwing it . . . ?* At the memory of the drink he felt a warm prickling of triumph and doubt spread through his body. It was so intense that he did not even turn down the stone path to the pier to watch the boats but crossed over it and continued walking, utterly engrossed in the sensation of the magic potion he had swallowed. On his left was a thicket of willows

42

that hid the first houses of Kalamaja from the shore. Between the willows and the sea were boathouses and fishing shacks.

I should try, actually, to see if I could . . . I should be able to . . . at least a little . . . After all, I did drink some of it. I have to *be able to . . .* There, in front of him, was a rack for drying nets – a crossbar, thirty paces long, resting on three gnarled posts about as tall as a man. There were no nets on the bar. It was about half a span thick and fairly straight. The houses were on the other side of the thicket, but not a soul was in sight.

Doubtful at one moment, confident the next, he hoisted himself onto one end of the crossbar, squatted for a moment at the top, then straightened up. Easy as could be. He spread his arms out wide and took the first step. Then a second and a third. He could feel a rush of confidence rising from his knees to his chest, and suddenly his breathing became oddly light, free. He was already halfway to the second support post. This did not take any special skill at all! The crossbar was rising and falling considerably with his every step, but that did not bother him a bit. Granted . . . if instead of being three cubits above ground he were as high as the steeple, it would be a different story. But still – he could do it, he could do it, he could do it! He reached the second support post, stepped over the rough joint between the crossbars, and proceeded unhurriedly to the wobbly centre of the next one. He stopped for an instant, steadied himself, and slowly lifted his left foot.

"What're you doing there – you witless goon!" shouted an angry voice.

"Why that there's Siimon Rissa's big lug!" cried another.

"You, hooligan, you'll break the rack!"

Bal looked to the left and saw the houses along the shore, and men and women gesticulating to him from their dooryards. He realised he could be clearly seen over the tops of the willows, performing his balancing act on the drying frame. Before he could set his left foot down in front of the right, his thin-soled, heel-less shoe slipped off the crossbar and he landed on all fours on the gravel plot beneath the drying rack.

He could still hear scolding voices from the other side of the thicket as he straightened up. Furious with himself for having fallen but elated by his discovery, he set off at a run, limping a little in his left foot.

CHAPTER TWO,

in which a rather unusual young man wants to teach a rather unusual
little scamp a lifelong lesson and subsequently finds himself encountering
vexations of lifelong duration; and although that which happens to him
is as common in his day as it is in ours, his attitude to it is probably
more common than people today might suppose.

Herr Bartholomeus Frolink, whose students, as we know, nicknamed him Panis Quotidianus, at times using the more familiar Panis (and sometimes resorting to the even more familiar "Crusty"), had been living here, in Mary's Land, less than two years. He had been orphaned during the plague at an age before memory and had lived the first twenty-five years of his life in various towns in northern Germany off the charity of relatives – struggling cobblers and merchants' clerks. He had helped sew boots and keep accounts, adding up on his abacus the sales transcribed on wax tablets. He had known his share of poverty but had worked his way through Latin school, and finally, exactly a year after Duke Philipp established a Protestant university in Greifswald, had hungrily bitten into the great loaf of theology. He had not been able to chew it to the end, however. And why not? Who can ever know exactly why a pale young man, apparently determined and resolute, especially cheerful of late – jolly enough to barely restrain himself from whistling snatches of soldiers' marching songs even during lectures – why such a one suddenly falls silent as a block of wood in his colloquium. And why he stops appearing at the university, ducking into side streets to avoid meeting his professor, and decides one day to withdraw officially; and then, with his Bible and three grammar books tied up in a bundle, sets out in his shabby boots, walking stick in hand, and heads for the highway, or for a ship to sail the-deuce-knows where. And why, as he leaves town, he summons all his willpower to avert his eyes from a high-gabled merchant house where guard dogs growl in the dooryard and a heavy curtain in an upper-storey window seems to move slightly at the touch of a gentle hand.

And it is just as difficult to explain why Herr Frolink happened to sail to Mary's Land. Perhaps in a pub in Greifswald or Rostock or Stettin – because in truth it cannot be denied that he did occasionally frequent such places – perhaps he had heard garrulous sailors humming a little song popular in those parts:

> Not in vain does one say,
> Livland is the place to stay
>> where especially just now
>> many are settling down

Perhaps he had heard that it was not difficult, even for one who had not finished his schooling, to find a good position there either as a pastor in a thriving parish or as a scribe for the Order. Or perhaps he had heard that meat and fish and all God's grains were cheaper and easier to come by there than anywhere else in the ever-hungry German realm of the Holy Roman Empire; and that the Germans already settled there, feeling they were still too few, enthusiastically welcomed every newcomer from Germany, even though there were already so many of their countrymen in the towns that one could get by speaking only German. Maybe he had noticed the steady stream of loud-mouthed fortune-hunters, rootless adventurers, and even outlaws who flowed northward from the harbours of northern Germany, with no-one trickling back from "up there". People seemed to have confidence in the stability of the peace and order which the unbending Master Plettenberg had established, and even the half-heathen Muscovite, having burned his fingers once, stayed within his own borders.

True, Herr Frolink had no friends or relatives in Mary's Land; nevertheless, things went remarkably well for him there. Before he quite knew how it happened, he had become a respected schoolmaster in the kind of trivium school of which both Lübeck and Bremen would have been proud.

Rector Tegelmeister, though a man of somewhat sour disposition, had with great effort managed to move the school, just that spring, from its previous rundown site to a new and quite impressive building. The refectory of the Dominican Monastery, burned down ten years earlier in the stormy aftermath of the Lutherans' arrival, had at last been renovated for the use of the school. And the Town Council had managed not to be too tight-fisted with funds for the repairs. As for his living quarters, only his undemanding nature made it possible for Herr Frolink to find the cell of a room he was allotted satisfactory – it was a space formerly inhabited by the gatekeeper. Every morning at six, when he stepped across the one-time monastery courtyard to go to school, the recollection of a certain soldiers' tune made him purse his lips, as if to whistle – at least at first.

At this early morning hour the doors to all the little shacks crammed between the burnt-out walls of the huge abbey began to creak open as the labourers – wagon drivers, porters, warehouse workers, slaughter-house butchers, lowly artisans and various others of inferior station who had sought shelter there – hurried across the courtyard, presently the schoolyard, on their way to their jobs. Towards Herr Frolink they were all remarkably, even somewhat comically, polite. From his second or third day there, Herr Frolink had been the recipient, every morning, of more eager smiles and deferential greetings than he had received in Greifswald over an entire month from folk equally lowly, and his hat and clothes and footwear were by no means of better quality here than they had been there. At first this courtesy and regard had surprised him, then it had amused him, and finally it began to embarrass him. And when, during his first week in Mary's Land, he noticed the same behaviour in the town as a whole, he raised the issue with Rector Tegelmeister.

"But they are the *Greys*!" exclaimed the rector, his face scrunched like a dried apple. As Frolink looked at him uncomprehendingly, he added by way of explanation: "You know, the non-Germans! Do you want them to become even more uppity than they already are?"

"These non-Germans – what people are they, actually?"

"They are the descendants of the Melanchlaeni. The ones Herodotus mentions – you remember. Quite a dimwitted people, I must say."

"And they're fit only for menial work?"

"That's pretty much it. Except those, of course, who have sense enough to become Germans."

"And some of those are in better positions?"

"Well . . . now . . ."

They had walked out of the schoolyard and reached the monastery gate on Munkade Street, where Rector Tegelmeister turned to look at his companion.

"Well, you can see from all these walls around our own present nest that the Dominicans had quite an impressive establishment here." They continued along the street towards town and Rector Tegelmeister pointed his willow walking stick at the impressive, if dilapidated, east wing of the former monastery.

"Their prior used to live in this palatial wing. In those days the prior was one of the most influential men in town. A hundred years ago it was Dominus Henricus Carwel, a man educated at Bologna and Montpellier. But do you know who he actually was? A country bumpkin, a non-German! Came from Luganuse, from the bailiwick of Rakvere. His real name was Karwepe, which means hairy head. Because, to keep it gleaming, as is proper for a true Christian, he had to have it shaved every day. So you see . . ."

With a smirk, brandishing his walking stick, the rector went on his way, presumably to take a little wine with the other elders of the Church Treasury.

Well then. There could not be too many non-Germans of higher standing if Rector Tegelmeister had to go back a hundred years to find an example of one. In any case, people here in Mary's Land were divided not only into rich and poor, as they were in Germany and everywhere else, they were also divided into Germans and non-Germans.

Herr Frolink was not even in nappies when the "greatest cleansing of the world" took place in October, 1517. His consciousness of the world had taken shape during the division of Europe into Catholics and Lutherans. So, one more small and entirely local crack in the visage of the world should not have created any special problem for him. But Herr Frolink had received a zealously Lutheran education, with its modern view of a world where Good and Evil were constantly at logger-heads, but in which Good was nonetheless so incomparably powerful that even its Chief Scribe could hurl an inkwell at Evil and be sure of hitting the mark. In other words, the craving for a kind of scholastic harmony was still so much a part of Herr Frolink's consciousness (or at least of his subconscious) that this division of humanity here, in Mary's Land, left an oddly unpleasant residue in the depths of his mind. But, most important, the ground where this residue settled was, as a result of injustices he had experienced in his own youth, still quite porous. And yet Herr Frolink, as his name implied, was of a relatively cheerful disposition; he did not have the tendency to brood over unpleasant things. And every morning at seven, as he passed under the imposing arched doorway into the new schoolhouse, he felt content with the world. At least at first.

He walked through the entry and opened the school door into a

49

room thirty cubits long and fifteen cubits wide, cheerful in the multi-coloured early morning light coming through the northern windows. The southern windows, shattered in a fire, their lead frames warped at points, had been repaired by the Town Council with plain grey glass. But in the four undamaged northern windows the old blue–green–red stained glass glowed in its original glory. As Herr Frolink soon learned, these windows had not only witnessed the daily meals of monks but had, on several occasions, looked upon the pomp and ceremony of knights' assemblies and rattled with the debates and drinking bouts of the lords of the land. Now their many-coloured patches of light glowed on the necks of Herr Frolink's pupils, even as they noisily rose to greet their teacher.

Herr Frolink strode across the freshly scrubbed, chequered stone floor, past rows of desks and the three thick columns that divided the hall into sections for the various grade levels. When he reached his low birch table, he turned to face the schoolroom.

One hundred and twenty boys stood between the rows of unpainted wooden desks and benches under the recently whitewashed vaulted ceiling. The young scholars were arranged by their grade level. In front the preparatory level, or *infima*, little ones with uncombed hair and sticky chins; in the middle *quarta*; then *tertia* and *secunda*; and at the back the young men of *prima*, many of whom were already experiment-ing with the shaving blade at home. Above them all, in the shimmering shafts of blue–green–red light, hung the perennial smells of youth: of milk and oatmeal porridge and boot polish, of well-scrubbed floors and not-very-well-washed bodies.

After a moment of silence the room exploded with the clatter of benches being pushed to one side, and when all the boys were kneeling at their desks the class monitor stepped up next to Herr Frolink. They both turned their backs to the classroom and knelt, Herr Frolink half a pace ahead of the monitor, who began the Lord's Prayer in an

exaggeratedly loud and nasal voice: *"Pater noster qui es in caelis"*. . .*
Then again the clatter of benches, allowing the work of ploughing the
fields of learning to start.

When he began, Herr Frolink had been directly responsible for the
lower levels, *infima* and *quarta*. He was to teach the first *infima* the
German alphabet, and to read by using the Lutheran catechism. To the
second *infima* he was to make clear the art of writing. He was also
responsible for teaching arithmetic to both, since Herr "Arithmeticus"
Monnink did not instruct anyone below *quarta*. And after all this it was
Herr Frolink's duty to use whatever time was left to cram the basics of
Latin into the heads of the *infima* boys. In *quarta* it was his task to drag
forward the boys' command of Latin with the doggedness of a pack
animal. And this was hardly sufficient to ensure that when they reached
tertia and the tutelage of Herr Balger, they would be able to recite from
memory the twenty-one Articles of Augsburg as required – meaning
day or night, backwards or forwards; or that they would be able to read
Latin, or know how to conjugate, decline, compare and write more or
less correctly. In addition to all this Frolink was to ensure that, by the
end of the term, *quarta* had learned by heart the entire *Symbolum
Athanasianum*, not to mention the whole of the catechism and selected
passages of Aesop's Fables. It happened, however, that already in the
second week of term the wiry Herr Vibalik had taken Herr Frolink
aside, and, tickling his ear with a chin stubble five days old, had lamented
that Rector Tegelmeister was so tight-fisted when it came to paying
salaries that he, Herr Vibalik, was compelled to spend time converting
several other assets into disposable income, and so he could not possibly teach his classes the next day or the day after that. Could his colleague, Frolink, not substitute for him upon occasion? At which point
Rector Tegelmeister announced that he would be spending every morning of the coming week with members of the Treasury, negotiating

* Our Father, who art in Heaven (Latin)

the schoolmasters' salaries (including Herr Frolink's). He instructed Herr Frolink to supervise the *prima* level until noon every day of the week to come. And so Herr Frolink did.

The division of labour thus established in the first weeks soon became standard practice, and Herr Frolink was not given to protesting against custom. At least not at first. It cannot even be said that these added burdens put him into a noticeably bad humour. For where could a 27-year-old threadbare young man go in a strange city? He could sleep off his fatigue on the bachelor pallet in his stone chamber, and then, staring up at the splotched, low-vaulted ceiling, simply think. For in his capacity as teacher Herr Frolink had learned certain things that he wanted to ponder over.

For instance, Herr Frolink had noticed that the line demarcating humankind in this country did not by any means extend only into the schoolyard which he crossed on his way to work, or to the market where he bought salt pork and beans, or to the shore where one could buy, straight off the boat and for a good price, the tiny silvery fish called *kilu*. No, it also extended through the cubit-and-a-half thick walls of the monastery and into the school itself.

In his *infima* classes a third of the pupils spoke that incomprehensible, bubbling, bland – like something in need of salt – native language among themselves. It was the only language he had heard of which seemed not to have a name of its own, being defined in terms of what it was not. In *quarta* and *tertia* about a quarter of the students seemed to be speakers of this language. But in the upper forms, *secunda* and *prima*, he had not noticed any. Had the non-Germans only recently begun to enrol their children in greater numbers? Or had their children already become German by the time they reached the upper forms, so as to be eligible for positions as priors?

In general Herr Frolink found the non-German boys quieter, slower, and more awkward than the Germans, often falling somewhat behind the Germans when it came to mastering Latin. But then again some of the brightest heads in his classes belonged to non-Germans. More than anyone else, Balthasar Russö, in his second *quarta* class, had caught his attention. He was a cheerful fellow, though taciturn – as was characteristic of most of the children of the Greys – but he was curious and thoughtful. He was the only one who, from time to time, asked Herr Frolink questions. Take for example the tale of Aesop in which a rich man is repelled by the stink of his neighbour, a tanner, until with the passage of time he stops noticing it.

"Herr Teacher, does this fable mean that the tanner's rich neighbour just got used to the smell?"

"Just so. But what did *you* make of it?"

Balthasar pushed his lower lip out over his upper, where in four years' time there would be an incipient moustache.

"I thought . . . maybe the tanner didn't actually smell bad at all."

Or take the example of the second of Doctor Luther's Catechism, where he speaks of Christianity, saying: "I believe that God has made me, along with all other creatures, and has given me body and soul, eyes, ears and all members, and mind and all senses and . . ."

"Herr Teacher, if someone were missing an eye or an ear or a leg, what would Luther have to say about that?"

As a result of such exchanges between instructor and pupil, Herr Frolink had developed a special interest in this round-headed, independent little lad. It was as though, on some indeterminate level, they had a special connection, in particular from the time when, three or four months after his arrival, Herr Frolink began using simple non-German sentences and, thanks to his extraordinary linguistic ability, could soon engage in brief exchanges using country tongue with a remarkably natural accent.

"*Tere hommikust*, Balthasar!"*

* Good morning (Estonian).

"*Te . . . tere hommikust . . .* Herr Fro . . . *õpetajahärra!*"* replied Balthasar quietly, staring at him in wide-eyed surprise. But by their next meeting – as Herr Frolink was shaking raindrops off his worn raincoat in the antechamber – he heard himself addressed quite freely and with an undertone of amusement: "*Tere hommikust, õpetajahärra!*"

"*Tere hommikust, Balthasar! Küll täna – vihmab!a.*† Wait, is that how you say it?"

"Noo, I've never heard anyone say that."

"How do you say it, then?"

"*Küll täna . . . küll täna kallab!*"‡

"Oh, yes. Thank you."

But there were problems with him, too, and not only when it came to answering his questions. Just recently he had taken a whole day off to watch the hanging of a horse thief. Instead of coming to school he had stopped at the gaol behind the Town Hall and tagged along behind the condemned man and the executioner and the guards and a small group of spectators as they proceeded up the Pärnu Highway and up Jerusalem Hill. Not only had he watched the execution, he had hidden behind some bushes to see the executioner's henchmen bury the corpse and get into a fight with each other over a tiny tin cross they had found in the dead man's fist. And just a few weeks earlier there had been more trouble with Balthasar. Three days after the Feast of the Ascension, a rumour caught hold that the town of Riga had burned to the ground. No-one knew how this news reached the school mid-morning. In any case, Balthasar abandoned, *causa uriendi,*§ the Athanasian Creed and did not return from the marketplace until the last lesson, sweaty and satisfied and, as it turned out, with fairly accurate information: the fire had apparently consumed a cathedral chapel, about a hundred

* Goo . . . Good morning, Herr Fro . . . Teacher Sir! (Estonian).   † Good morning, Balthasar. How today – it rains! (Estonian).   ‡ It's really pouring today! (Estonian).
§ For urgent reasons (Latin).

houses, and a dozen merchants' warehouses.

After this Herr Frolink took Balthasar aside and gave him a good scolding. He did not use the cane on him, nor did he box his ears. Herr Frolink recalled all too well being caned and thrashed over his own days in Latin school. Though, truth be told, he did shake Balthasar by the collar.

But yesterday! Yesterday, when Herr Frolink had emphatically announced to all grade levels – "Only *prima* and *secunda* are permitted to go and watch the acrobats" – at that very moment he had exchanged an absolutely unambiguous look with that young rogue.

"Understood?"

"Understood."

And yet the little devil had taken off and not returned to the school!

So Herr Frolink was indignant all next morning. Out of the corner of his eye he watched Balthasar industriously working at reading Donatus. The idea that he owed his teacher an explanation for taking off the previous day had obviously never entered that round head of his!

When Rector Tegelmeister, who was reading Hesiod with the *prima* pupils, had left, Herr Frolink said: "Balthasar, come and see me after class, please." And he added: "Monitor, if Balthasar should forget what I just told him, remind him."

His ears red, Balthasar sat in his seat until the end of classes, and when the last *infima* pupils had run off with whoops and shouts and the last of the *primaners* had prepared themselves for a dignified departure, he shuffled up to Herr Frolink's desk, his wheat-coloured hair incongruously upright, clutching the rope ties of a grey sailcloth bag. He kept his eyes on the mud-caked toes protruding from his boots.

"So, you went to watch the acrobats yesterday morning, after all?"

Bal looked down, not speaking, not moving. Then, barely perceptibly, he nodded.

"Do you understand that it was a swinish thing to do? And the third one, no less!" Without intending to, Herr Frolink had raised his voice.

Bal remained motionless, silent. He might have nodded again, but Herr Frolink continued. "Perhaps you haven't heard – some Arabian flame-swallowers are coming to town on Friday! Are you going to go watch them, too?!"

Two round grey eyes stared excitedly at Herr Frolink: "Flame-swallowers . . . ? In front of the Town Hall?"

"So!" Herr Frolink stood up and smacked the table so hard with his open palm that pain shot through his fingers:

"Let's go! Before the fires of Hell come and swallow you up! Take me to your home! I want to talk to your father."

Balthasar turned visibly pale. But he did not argue; he turned around silently and walked out into the dooryard ahead of Herr Frolink, and Herr Frolink could tell by the boy's dismay that this disciplinary threat had hit its mark.

They walked in silence until they had gone through the Great Coast Gate. When they crossed the drawbridge Herr Frolink stepped up to walk beside Balthasar and asked:

"What work does your father do?" He realised only after speaking that he had asked in country tongue.

"He's a wagoner," mumbled Bal. There was such gloom in his voice that it could have wiped out all the glow and sparkle of the world.

"Is he stern?"

Balthasar shrugged, suggesting he did not know. But his mouth – lips tightly compressed – seemed to express a pretty definite opinion on the matter.

"Does he thrash you?"

Balthasar was silent.

"Well, answer me!"

"He'll wallop me one. But then he won't talk for a week."

Herr Frolink spoke no more either, thinking over what he would say to this unknown wagoner. That his lad had a number of talents, but . . . but would the father follow what he meant by "talents" – that is to say, not the "talents" of the Parables but in the other sense of the word? And how to say this in country tongue . . . Herr Frolink could not remember. And if he were to ask Balthasar, it would create a sense of familiarity inappropriate in a teacher–pupil relationship . . . Yes . . . he did have quite a few talents, but they risked being squandered if they did not go with respect for the school, not to say respect for him as a teacher and superior. All these precious gifts of Our Lord would be wasted if the desire for learning were not accompanied by respect for authority! They would simply be wasted! And his own father's money would also be wasted. Precisely! For whereas several of the non-German children were attending school at the Town Council's expense, this wagoner was paying two silver marks a year for his son.

They had long since arrived at the small wooden cottages and the blubber sheds and garden plots of Kalamaja. They went on, Balthasar in front, Herr Frolink following, through the sparse maple grove of the graveyard, past the cheerless wooden church with its pine roof, past the old parish schoolmaster's house where school was held for the poorer non-German children, and then onto a lane leading towards the sea.

Aha . . . well now, the owner of this household could well afford to send his son to the Trivium School.

To the left, behind a dense slat fence, stood a stone stable big enough for at least half a dozen horses. At the end of the stable, facing the road, was an open-sided covered shelter for the wagons. Several neatly stacked sleighs were visible behind a slat wall. A partially hollowed-out log extended from a well in the middle of the yard to a long trough in front of the stable. To the right, on the other side of the small plantain-shaded dooryard and a few ripening blackcurrant bushes, was a long log house of rough-hewn timber with a hooded chimney. Visible under the eaves were twisted branches serving as racks for yokes, collars, halters and reins.

Balthasar went on ahead through the gate, quickly wiped his feet on a mat of old birch branches at the threshold, shot Herr Frolink a look – the look of someone drowning, and disappeared through the split-log door of the storm porch.

Herr Frolink wiped his feet as Balthasar had done, realising with a start of annoyance that he was following the little rogue's example. Stepping inside, he sensed, right away, something barely perceptible but most agreeable. He scarcely had time to think about what it might be when Balthasar came back and said:

"Father's not home."

It was clear the boy was not lying. And yet there was in his voice a note of hope, or perhaps of triumph, which irritated Herr Frolink. He was also annoyed by the boy's sudden appearance at the very moment when he was trying to figure out the source of the sense of well-being he had just experienced. Without further thought he said:

"Then I'll wait until he gets back." And together they stepped over the threshold.

It was much darker inside the house, and Herr Frolink shut his eyes for a moment to accustom them them to the dimness. An image of his Aunt Barbe's motherly hands flashed into his mind from beyond many miles and years. And then that strange feeling of contentment, of some-thing subtly enfolding him, returned – something that was not so much a feeling as something a lot more concrete. And all of a sudden Herr Frolink realised what it was – it was a *smell*.

He opened his eyes and saw a shaft of light filtering in through a small glass window. And in that beam of light, resting on a scrubbed wooden table with worn-down corners, he saw the source of the sweet smell: four hot, steaming loaves of bread. Like four warm and peace-able, blind, all-knowing beasts.

Resting on the table, next to the fourth and farthest loaf, he saw a hand. Herr Frolink's eyes travelled up the arm into the semi-darkness of the room, and there it encountered the flushed, freckled face of an eighteen-year-old girl looking at him quizzically.

"Ooh . . . !" he spluttered, noting the knife in the girl's right hand.

Herr Frolink was by nature serious, not used to joking, and knew this very well himself. But now he burst out laughing and said:

"Well, young lady – are you going to attack me?"

The girl looked at him in silence. She had curly, slightly reddish, wheat-coloured hair (just the same as that rascal Balthasar's), green eyes and a pretty button nose. "I'm not a burglar. I'm Balthasar's teacher—" He turned around to look at Balthasar but the boy had vanished.

"Oh . . . Is it Master Frolink?"

"Hmm . . . Master? . . . Uhuh."

"Well . . . then I know about you . . . all about you."

"Really . . . ?"

The girl picked up a hot loaf, its upper crust decorated with three indentations in the shape of a clover leaf. She held the loaf against her chest and cut off a good-sized endpiece. Apparently that had been her intent all along.

"Here. You're hungry."

Herr Frolink was aware of how, slowly and helplessly, he blushed to the roots of his hair. He saw the girl look at him and smile. He saw the innards of the hot bread steam ever so slightly. He felt the saliva collect in his mouth, forcing him to swallow, for he had eaten not a thing since his early morning meal of a slice of bacon and a piece of hard-tack.

"Well . . . thank you," he said as he bit into the soft, hot bread. He felt extraordinarily good, and at the same time embarrassed. To get over the embarrassment he added quickly, his mouth full:

"As a matter of fact, I came to make a complaint against Balthasar, to his father."

"Because he went to see the acrobats yesterday?"

"You already know about it . . . ? Such behaviour won't do!"

"I think you could have given all the classes permission to go."

Herr Frolink looked into the girl's green eyes – in the dim light of the room it was hard to tell whether they were quite innocently childlike or just a little impudent – and he breathed in the enticing aroma of the warm rye bread.

"You don't know what school rules mean."

"And what makes you think *I* don't know?"

"Because you've never been to school."

"And why are you so sure of that?"

"Girls don't go to school! Least of all non-German girls!"

"Some do, at least for a short time . . ."

"That's true!" Balthasar's voice sounded from behind Herr Frolink's back. "Annika went to school for two years, to the nuns at St Michael's."

"Be gone!" hissed Annika, turning red as a rowan berry. "This conversation is not about me, but about you, and you have no business listening in!"

The door slammed shut behind Balthasar. Herr Frolink again breathed in the aroma of the bread and said slowly:

"You, then, are a young lady educated in a real cloister . . . ? How did that come about?"

"My father sent me."

No doubt about it, an unusual wagon driver, thought Herr Frolink, letting his eyes wander about the room. It was fairly large and it looked like both a family room and a bedchamber. It had a long wooden table, scrubbed white, surrounded by six low chairs with woven seats, and a few chests and stools. Against the back wall stood a large cupboard which Herr Frolink thought could be the work of a German cabinetmaker. In the open fireplace, on an iron hook, hung a large, faintly steaming soup pot. Herr Frolink's glance wandered around and returned from the soup pot to the cook, who just then inclined her head towards the window as though listening to something. Her hair fell back slightly to reveal an earlobe, touched at that moment by a beam of sunlight. Herr Frolink recalled another earlobe, which had gleamed just like this one, but with a pearl earring instead of a sunbeam . . . gleaming exactly like this one, but not at all more brightly . . .

At that instant the big gate creaked outside and the sounds of men's voices and horses' hooves reached them. And Annika, startled, called out in a half whisper: "Father's home!"

"Good," said Herr Frolink, turning towards the door, "then I'll . . ."

"No! Please don't tell on Balthasar!"

"But that's why I . . ."

"Please!"

"Why not?"

"Father will thrash him! Talk about something else! Think of something . . ."

The girl ran to the hearth, set a big clay bowl onto the hearth stool, and with a large wooden spoon ladled into it the barley soup from the steaming kettle. The soup bowl had just been set on the table and four sturdy wooden spoons placed next to it when sounds were heard at the entrance and four men came into the room. The first appeared to be the father – a man of medium height, big-boned, about fifty years old. He removed a faded, no-longer-black felt hat from his light hair and said in a somewhat hoarse voice: "Greetings, God be with us." His face was browned by the sun, his forehead white under the brim of his hat. And when he turned to hang up his hat Herr Frolink was surprised to see how unexpectedly narrow he was in profile, given his breadth.

The men removed their short grey coats and went to the table in their rough linen shirts – the three hired hands, even though younger

61

than the master of the house, were remarkably similar to him. On his way to the table the father's small eyes, so pale that they were nearly white, fleetingly grazed Herr Frolink and, directing his question to the space between Annika and Frolink, he asked:

"What brings the young man here?"

Herr Frolink cleared his throat and said: "I am a schoolmaster from Munkade Street."

The father's light glance swept quizzically over him again: *I wonder if he's here because my boy's in trouble.*

"I came to ask whether you might be willing to deliver some wood to the school."

"What wood does the school need now, in springtime?"

"It was a rough winter and we burned up what we had." (This was God's truth.) "The walls are still exuding cold." (This also was entirely true.)

"Where is the wood now?"

What the devil was the name of the place where the wood was stacked? . . . Herr Tegelmeister had mentioned it in passing . . . something about how Herr Vegesack was to get it from some village that was indebted to him . . .

"Umm . . . it's at Kadakas."

"Why would they cut wood there? It's nearly barren as it is!"

"Herr Vegesack was supposed to . . ."

"How many loads?"

Herr Frolink had anticipated saying "ten". But by chance his glance met Annika's. She looked grateful and slyly satisfied, and he noticed the quiver of a fleeting, faintly smug smile on her upper lip. He surprised himself by his low-voiced answer:

"Forty."

"Hmmm. We'll get it delivered by next Friday evening. Let Balthasar bring me a note from the headmaster tomorrow so they'll know they must give me the wood. Annika, bring the schoolmaster a spoon –

I won't take money from the school, it's always in need. But in return the school will not ask me for a food donation next year. Agreed?"

He had in the meantime seated himself at the table and cut five thick slabs of bread.

"Ah...yes...agreed. Of course..." mumbled Herr Frolink, quickly calculating that if anyone ended up short in this deal it would not be the wagon driver.

"Come, share our humble meal then," said the master of the household, gesturing towards the table. The men pulled their chairs closer to the soup bowl and sat down. The father folded his large calloused hands on the edge of the worn table. The hired men folded their hands as he had done, and Herr Frolink followed suit. While the men bowed their heads and Annika, standing at the hearth, folded her hands as she looked into the fire (which, as Herr Frolink noted from the corner of his eye, cast a lovely warm glow on her face), her father said grace:

"And bless us and these your gifts which we receive from your bounty through Jesus Christ—"

Herr Frolink took in the mingled smells rising from the men – of horse stables and hemp ropes and pitch and sweat, noticing that the backs of their shirts were still dark and damp from their labour.

"Amen," said the father as each man noisily took up his spoon and started slurping down the soup. Herr Frolink sipped contentedly along with the others. And though it worried him a little that he was eating someone's portion, Annika's soup was splendid.

Meanwhile Balthasar was crouched in the stable loft. Here, on the side facing the sea, on the edge of the stone wall between the eaves and the hay, was his personal crow's nest, his pulpit and his gun turret complete with a "cannon". He had fashioned it by hollowing out the rotted core of a birch stump a foot long and a couple of spans thick. When he set a fist-sized stone – they were plentiful on the beach, just a hundred paces away – into the hollow of the stump and rammed it outwards with a long wooden pestle, the stone would fly through the opening – *kerplunk!* – onto the grassy area at the back of the stable, frightening into flight the seagulls on the manure heap and rolling on almost to the carrot beds. But the seagulls were actually horsemen from Moscow who had escaped from their Teutonic master and had now come to town as spies. Or else they were Danish ships planning to spit fire upon his hamlet of Kalamaja; or at other times Tartars in silver chainmail out for plunder. And also many other things. But today the cannon was only a birch stump and the seagulls were plain seagulls and Balthasar was lying on his stomach in the straw, his chin on the stump, waiting. Any minute now he would hear the door creak open and Annika's voice call: "Ba-a-al. Father wants you!" Balthasar thought guiltily of his games of war and killing, and of the sinful pleasure he had taken in those games. For a moment he even considered the possibility of jumping up and delivering a sermon on "victory over the devil of temptation" to the congregation of stone balls lined up on the wall. But actually he was afraid to move because he felt as if any movement would bring Annika's summons closer . . . Or should he just fold his hands on the stock of his cannon, and with a clear conscience pray, in the words of the confession of sin from the missal: Almighty God, Merciful Father! I, a poor sinner, confess to you all the sins which I have committed in thought, word, and deed (especially what I did yesterday . . .) by which I have earned your just wrath and punishment now and forever more. But I repent of them all deeply (especially of what I did yesterday). But when he reached this point in his prayer he felt that he was beginning, in spite of himself, to wriggle under the barrier separating truth from falsehood. And he gave up the idea of prayer. There was still nothing to be heard from the yard and, worn out with the tension of waiting, he decided to get into his crow's nest after all. So there he was now, on his fancy Lübeck schooner, stretched out on his stomach in its for'ard crow's nest, peering through the cracks between the boards at the sparkling afternoon horizon of the sea, squinting to determine whether the juniper-covered coast of the big island of Suur-Paljassaare was that of Rügen or England or Hiiumaa.

He had just decided it was the coast of England after all, and was about to direct his fire at London – because that awful Henry-with-Six-Wives had taken to taunting Hansa towns lately – when the door of the house opened and Father came out into the yard. The shock of seeing him approach made Balthasar bite his lip: if the old man was coming out in person to fetch him, things were really bad. The man walked across the yard towards the stable, Jaanus, Mikk and Peep following; Peep, as usual, was still chewing on a mouthful of bread. Bal could not understand what it meant. Was the old man really going to get his farm-hands to help ferret him, Bal, down from the loft? The men disappeared behind the wall. Bal heard someone clear his throat, heard the scrape of iron against stone. The men reappeared and went, single file as before, shovels on their shoulders, towards the ploughed fields on the sea side, where they set to work breaking up large clods. It was what they had been working at until dark the previous day.

That meant – what could it possibly mean? Had Annika really thought up some kind of magic spell – and had Herr Frolink held his tongue?

Bal stayed in his crow's nest, just in case. It felt secure there, up high. He turned back towards England's shore and directed a volley of cannon fire at London – though only from the lower guns and not from the cannon up in the crow's nest. And he commanded the gunners to be just careful enough not to hit the Steelyard. The volley took some time, of course. And just as a Danish pirate ship he had been pursuing near Ojamaa turned into the bay of Tallinn, the door opened. Herr Frolink, looking back over his shoulder all the while, stepped out onto the granite step, proceeded to its edge, and then stepped into empty air, nearly landing flat on the birch mat. Rector Tegelmeister, for example, would certainly have fallen, not to mention Herr Balger, and both would have invoked the Devil and cursed no end. But Herr Frolink regained his balance immediately and turned around to look back into the entrance for a moment and burst out laughing. Then Annika came out and they walked together, Herr Frolink leading, Annika behind him, as far as the nearer of the blackcurrant bushes. Herr Frolink stopped on the other side of the bush, and Annika stopped too, three paces away. Herr Frolink was saying something in a low voice and Annika was looking down, down at the ground. From Bal's vantage point she seemed to be staring fixedly at the newly opening bluish buds on the currant bush. And it seemed to him that Annika was smiling in an odd way, and at the same time not smiling. Then Herr Frolink moved closer to Annika, and Bal held his breath. Herr Frolink was taking Annika's hand, raising it up as high as his worn ruffled collar, and kissing her fingers! Annika snatched her hand away and ran back into the house. Herr Frolink stood there for a moment, looking after her, then turned and walked slowly out of the gate. A moment later the door opened tentatively, just a crack, and Annika looked out. Then she slipped out of the door and walked with hesitant steps, going as far as the bushes where she had just been standing, and looked for some time towards the church, in the direction where Herr Frolink had disappeared from view. Bal felt a great, almost irresistible temptation welling up inside. And when he then saw Annika raise her just-kissed hand and gaze at it, he opened his mouth, intending to call out: Hey Annika, what does a kiss smell like? But at the last moment he thought the better of it. He decided to keep his mouth shut, just as Annika was staying mum about his escapade, and as Herr Frolink was too. And in any case he suddenly felt he had just witnessed something of great and serious import.

CHAPTER THREE,

in which what ought to be described is the arrival of two ships in
a harbour, but because their arrival is known in advance, what is
described here instead is the scene along the fairway leading to the
harbour and the bustling activity on the docks, and much less is
said about what occurred on the ships themselves.

When Bal later thought back to the wedding of Annika and Meus, the whole affair converged for him around two great common denominators: first, the lengthy wedding preparations that preoccupied the household for weeks; and second, the visit to old Jakob Kimmelpenning.

The preparations had actually started long before the hustle and bustle at home, which did not begin until the chestnuts had ripened to a deep brown that autumn – the autumn of the year that Bal entered the *secunda* level at school. It was not until then that Father sent for Aunt Kati from Kurgla to come to town and take charge of the household, or began to think about fetching a licence from the brewers' alderman to make ale for the wedding. That was when it all really began.

Aunt Kati and their neighbour Traani-Krõõt, wife of Traani-Andres, busied themselves about the house, discussing and settling not only the young couple's affairs but also those of all the relatives and neighbours as far back as Adam himself. On several occasions Bal overheard his father mutter in irritation: "When your mother was alive, we managed with half the prattle." At times when Bal happened to be sweating over Horace in the back room and the door to the great-room had accidentally been left ajar or had been pushed open a crack by Bal himself, he heard things in Aunt Kati's and Traani-Krõõt's stories, some of which he understood right away and others which he did not understand at all. These he tried to figure out, even as he was working out the grammatical comparisons and combinations of lines of verse, such as *O navis, referent in mare te novi,** until the meaning of what they said suddenly flashed into his mind. In any case it became clear to Bal once again that the story of Annika and Meus began with that event three years earlier in which he himself had played a leading role. But once, when Aunt Kati sighed: "It surely was Our Lord Himself that guided little Annika – just think of it – to the German gentleman and straight to the altar, no less . . ." Bal heard Traani-Krõõt reply coolly:

"Nooo – at first old Siimon didn't want that German gent one whit, he didn't."

"What in the world did the crazy coot want, then?" asked Aunt Kati in amazement.

"That's just what folks in the village are wondering: what could he possibly have wanted," continued Krõõt. "But these days, it's not just any German upstart that's good enough for a townsman's daughter. It's not like it was when a townsman was so keen to save his daughter from the manor, it didn't much matter how well-to-do the prospective son-in-law might be – and especially if she could marry a German into the bargain! But now the townsman is master in his own right! Nowadays every haberdasher's shop clerk puts on a dog-skin coat and nods to a customer on his right and quotes a price to another on his left, all the while looking to open his own shop. So there's nothing to be surprised at in Siimon's case! He's hard as nails, that man! Shows no mercy either to himself or others. All summer long he's on the go between the town and the harbour, not that he's not making a heap in other ways as well. But as soon as the sea freezes over, he's off, hauling stuff on the Riga–Narva route, and piling up the silver so's you can hear it jingle. But

* O ship, new [storm winds] take you back out to sea . . . (Latin).

what did this Master Meus have when he started out? Nothing but a 'Thank ye' and empty pockets! So when Annika first brought it up with Siimon, he slammed his hand down on the table: 'Girl, you've been to school for two years with the nuns, at my expense, and you have a dowry of five hundred marks. And even though you're a non-German, you're not stupid. So there's no reason whatsoever that this particular young man has to get you for his wife!'"

"But then Our Lord Himself came to advise and support Master Meus and . . ."

"Well, yes, but there's no doubt that the way he got the wind under his wings, clever fellow, is how he managed to learn country tongue so well."

"That's how it goes – some folks, they get ahead by throwing a bit o' German about, but in this case it's the other way round!" added Aunt Kati.

"In town they've also been saying sermons in country tongue for years now, in every church. But you can count on the fingers of one hand those men of learning that can speak it. And when Our Lord's Scourge, the plague . . ." – here she paused to spit three times to ward off the scourge – ". . . carried off that there Herr Bock of St Olaf's, and all the other three churchmen moved up the ladder a step, that's how the position down below was freed up for Master Meus. 'Cause all the higher-ups in the Church Treasury agreed that even if he was a church mouse he was fit to be a churchman – based on his learning. No doubt old Siimon heard the good news in town himself, but did he go and talk to Annika, and say, 'Well, daughter, it's a different story now,' or something like that? Oh no, not him! He just sat back and had her come and plead with him again."

"But then, he did agree . . ."

"What else could he do . . . ? Then of course he said that a man with the entire peasant congregation of St Olaf's in the palm of his hand could indeed have Siimon Rissa's daughter for a wife."

Bal, on the other side of the slightly open door, continued to read from Horace's Odes by candlelight:

Quamvis Pontica pinus,
*Silvae filia nobilis . . . ***

In his view, his father had behaved the way a man ought to behave: he did not peddle his daughter, whom he considered too good for a mere novice schoolmaster, to that young man just because he had been elevated to pastor. Bal had reached the age, at the time of Annika's approaching wedding, when he was inclined to pass judgement on people more and more often – approving of some, disapproving of others. And Herr Frolink, that is to say Meus, was in the forefront of those who had won his approval. That was how it had been from the day when Herr Frolink – Meus, that is – had shown him how to make the round Gothic letter "a" from a hooked Gothic "i" on the dark grey slate at school. But above all Meus had won Bal's heart when, for some inexplicable reason, he had refrained from telling his father the story of the high-wire acrobats, and when, afterwards, the two of them, or rather the three of them (because Annika made several treks on this account between home and school), had settled the matter of the wood delivery. In the end Father had hauled twenty loads of wood from Kadakas to the school, of which not a single log was burned that spring. Because, after long grumbling, Rector Tegelmeister had categorically forbidden any more heating. Of course that was because he himself considered the morning cold healthful and invigorating. And as far as the boys were concerned, he said, a Spartan toughening could only be of benefit to them. In any case, the weather soon turned warm enough, sothat the cold exhaled by the stone walls no longer made noses run.

* Like the pine of Pontus, / The noble daughter of the forest . . . (Latin).

But now, in any case, things had proceeded so far that two Sundays earlier none other than the new superintendent himself had read the first
banns from the pulpit of St Olaf's for his young colleague-in-Christ –
that's exactly how he had put it – his "young colleague-in-Christ,
Bartholomeus Frolink, and Maid Anna Rüsso". Old Siimon had been
a member of the Holy Ghost congregation from the time he had
first arrived in town, dating back to the days of the blessed Koell; the
names of his dead wife Mallo and their children were transcribed in
the parish registry. Before the banns were read, Annika's husband-to-be
had registered her in the German parish. Siimon had gone to the
German service to hear the reading and had asked Bal to come along.
And Bal heard clearly how, after the reading of the banns, a slight
murmur passed through the rows of merchants and artisans. No
doubt his father heard it too, for despite his fifty-odd years his hearing
was sharp as a colt's. But he gave no sign. He sat there in his church-
going suit of black Göttingen wool, his round, gaunt, sunburnt face
immobile, his eyes focused on a mote of dust floating in a sunbeam
in front of his face. When Bal, at the sound of the murmuring, glanced
at his father, it seemed to him for a moment that he saw the corners
of his narrow lips twitch with just the hint of a smile. But he could not
be sure.

The following Monday something unexpected occurred to which at
first Bal did not pay much heed. After twelve o'clock on that beautiful
autumn morning, when they had concluded the first half of the school
day with a chorale, the boys were at recess in the monastery courtyard
– some playing a game of bat-the-ball-into-the-hole, others lingering
over their daily rations, still others bent over their lessons – Balzer
Vegesack walked over to Bal. The fellow had a greyish complexion, ash-
coloured hair, narrow grey eyes, and wore a suit of fine blue worsted.
He was a thick-headed, headstrong boy of a somewhat sour temperament. He had been in Bal's class since the *infima* level but was now

71

repeating *tertia* – even though he was the son of a councilman, someone the Germans called a *Ratsverwandter.* * Not only that, his father had recently held the position of Burgomaster. Over the entire course of their school career he and Bal had never wasted a single word in unnecessary conversation. This same fifteen-year-old *Ratsverwandter* now came up to Bal and said, with a chuckle:

"Listen, you, *Episkopatsverwandter*†– do you know that you're my milk-brother?"

Bal put down his bat and looked into the other's laughing eyes. But the councilman's son was grinning in an entirely friendly way. Still, it bothered Bal. He was in fact a bit jealous when he realised that this boorish stranger had once been so close to the mother he himself could barely remember. He also felt some dislike, perhaps even a touch of inferiority, because the fellow was of such high-class parentage – as though even as a nursing, kicking infant he had been wearing a fine blue worsted suit with a fur-trimmed collar.

"And what of it?" muttered Bal, nearly missing the rag ball whizzing towards him; at the last moment he managed to hit it after all. His sense of triumph after the successful swing tempered his indignation a little. Although the back of his neck sensed Balzer standing behind him, he ignored the feeling, waiting for him to say something more. Young Master Vegesack picked up the apparent challenge perhaps from the back of Bal's irritating, dishevelled head, for he asked:

"But do you also know you were named after me?"

Actually, this meant nothing. And even if it did, Balzer was not really to blame, so, though Bal would have enjoyed whacking him one with the club, it would have been pointless: he knew all that quite well. Just then he had a flash of inspiration and smirked at the councilman's son.

"Named after you, you say? And the third King from the Orient, he too was no doubt named after you: Kaspar, Melchior, Balthasar."

* Council-kin (German). † Bishop's kin (German).

72

Some of the *secunda* pupils snorted – this often happened in response to things Bal said. A freckle-faced, *prima*-level pupil chanced at this point to walk past the ball players, his nose buried in Cicero. Balzer Vegesack was standing squarely in his path and Bal's last utterance, *"Weise vom Morgenland"*,* echoed distractedly in his ears, his attention being partly elsewhere. The boy raised his eyes from his book and with the calm of his superior status said to Vegesack: *"Du, Scheisse vom Morgenland*† – get out of my way."

Afterwards, no-one could remember exactly what Bal had said to Vegesack. It was not even certain he had said anything at all. But "Dung of the Orient" stuck to the councilman's son like eczema. And on the next day the whole school was convinced it was Bal Rüsso who had called him that. An insightful witness to the event would have concluded that it all confirmed a singular truth: at the very moment that Our Lord touches a man's shoulder blade with His right hand to create an incipient thumbnail-sized wing-bone, He uses His left hand to add a little ball of lead to that wing.

But as for the brotherhood of milk and name between Bal and Balzer Vegesack, Bal had known about it all along, as was evident from his reply to the councilman's son. There had been talk about it at home more than once over the years.

The monks of Padise, who owned Raasiku estate at the time, had mortgaged it to the merchant Vegesack. And when Siimon Rissa of Kurgla decided, a quarter of a century earlier, to breathe the "free air of town", what might have been a difficult arrangement was made considerably easier by the fact that the town's transport station was just then looking for the kind of driver who would do the work of three men while eating for one. Herr Vegesack had appointed Siimon, a sturdy fellow from his home village, and thus "one of our own", for the job, and had put in a good word for him with the Town Council. And even though the

* Wiseman (King) from the Orient (German). † You, Dung of the Orient! (German).

merchant-councilman did not have much to do with the wagon driver, Herr Vegesack noticed, over the course of time, that Siimon Rissa not only had a strong back and neck but also an unusually sharp head. Five years later this one-time driver for the town had become an independent wagoner, and one Sunday after church he appeared at Herr Vegesack's house to ask permission to come courting the Vegesacks' laundry maid, Mallo. The merchant discussed it with his wife, who agreed with a sigh. Thereby Mallo got herself a most hardworking husband, but Frau Vegesack's household lost its most hardworking servant girl. At the birth of the young couple's first child, Frau Vegesack even sent baby Annika a pewter spoon. Some years later Our Lord sent a son to the merchant's wife but neglected to send milk to her breasts: this happened just a week or so after the birth of a son to Siimon and Mallo in Kalamaja village. And even though Tallinn was a big and populous town, news of the low-class birth reached the councilman's high-gabled house. Frau Vegesack sent a message – both a command and a plea – to Mallo, asking her to share that which she had in abundance, with her, Frau Vegesack, who was in need. She was not stingy with payment either. And perhaps as a reciprocal gesture the wagoner's son was given the same name as the merchant's – a somewhat grandiose name, Balthasar. His mother expressed some doubt over a name so exalted, for might it not seem as if they were prodding Our Lord to take notice of this child born to simple folk . . . ? But his father replied: "Every name is a kind of prod. And why would a name like Mikk or Mats be any better? Since it's a prod in any case, better that He raise our boy up a bit than push his nose down into the dirt."

And now Balthasar, that same wagoner's son, was indeed lifting his nose up out of the dirt, and even higher. For had not the other Balthasar teased him as "bishop's kin"? It did not stick as a term of abuse, yet it was true enough that in a week Balthasar would be Pastor Frolink's brother-in-law. He had already visited the pastor's, that is

Meus', new apartment, and driven the wagon Meus had rented from Siimon and helped him haul his things from the cubicle in the gatekeeper's quarters to the new apartment which was soon to be the young couple's home.

Incidentally, this taunt, *Episkopatsverwandter*, hit the mark in another, unexpected, way, as happens once in a while with turns of phrase. Not that there was any great likelihood of Meus rising to the position of Bishop of Tallinn. But it so happened that since the apartments set aside for the clergy of St Olaf's were inexplicably all occupied, the church treasurers had to intercede to find Meus an apartment within a private house. And it happened one day that when a gentlemen of the Treasury chanced to be sipping malmsey wine with certain merchant men, just as they were all feeling relaxed and generous someone mentioned the apartment problem. It turned out that in merchant Weselouwe's grand, recently purchased house, right on the Old Market, were some unoccupied rooms at a rent quite acceptable to the treasury members. This building had always been known in Tallinn as the Bishop's House, and not without reason, for such names are never conferred without reason. More than a hundred years earlier the house had indeed belonged to a bishop. So that, when they had carried Meus' two book boxes, three stools, a bundle of clothes and a chest up into the three rooms above the stables and courtyard, and sat down on the stools to catch their breath, Meus said, narrowing his eyes as he took in the freshly whitewashed stone walls:

"Well, Bal, it's all gone quite smoothly for us – from the monastery's gatekeeper to the bishop's coachman."

When Balthasar had fished out a copy of Livy from Meus's book chest and left, and when the empty wagon had rumbled out under the arched gate, Meus stood up, locked his fingers at the back of his neck and walked from one low-ceilinged room to another . . . *This is where the marriage bed will go, the one Siimon paid a woodworker to make for us. The* table, here, where we'll have our simple meals and evening talks. *The whole room smells marvellously of myrtle, just like Annika herself lately . . . 'And does your bride speak German?' . . . the superintendent had asked when he registered her at St Olaf's . . . And here, at this wall, I'll have them put my writing desk. This pig's-bladder window will let through a greyish light, like an everlasting winter morning . . . Though the wagon driver himself has glass windows . . . And here, at this desk, I'll begin to prepare my sermons . . . I am become as sounding brass, or a tinkling cymbal . . . Yes indeed . . .* He recalled Rector Tegelmeister's voice and in his right wrist felt the man's indifferent handshake. *"Let's hope you weren't in too much of a rush as you hurried past all of Tallinn's fair lilies . . . Yes indeed . . ."* And then, in a lower voice, *"You know, I don't plan to stay at the school much longer either. No I don't! As rector, I am of course better off than you were. But nonetheless – starvation wages! As soon as one of them at St Nicholas' bites the dust, I'll hop right up into the pulpit! Into the German pulpit, naturally".* . . . Meus walked through the row of low rooms, and for an instant it seemed to him as though he were walking along a bridge and keeping himself from looking over the railing . . . for the bridge posts rose from a river whose name he dared not utter . . . *But this is where the marriage bed will be. The head here. And the pillow will be here – the pillow Annika is making out of eiderdown. Her happy face will be on that pillow, and mine too . . ."Yes indeed"*. . . He heard Herr Balger's near whisper and started at the tickle of his beard in his ear: *"Don't worry! You're not the first! Nor the last! – heh-heh-heh. If you'd engaged in a caper like this as a schoolmaster, then maybe, of course . . . But a pastor can get away with such things! Yes, sir! And no doubt a young man educated in Greifswald knows full well what stone to turn over to find the feistiest fish. Heh-heh-heh! And did I hear right – five hundred marks! You are a crafty fellow!"* Meus brushed a dusty cobweb from the corner of a window with his sleeve . . . But there was that "don't worry". . . Why tell him not to worry? Why refer to his marriage as a caper? The fact that a pastor should marry a girl from among the very people he preached to three times a week, from among those he christened and married and buried – was it really considered some kind of *caper* in this country?

It was indeed. Annika could tell just by the looks that followed her as she passed the front gates of the houses in Kalamaja, skirting the autumn puddles on her way to town or returning home with a bundle of new sewing materials. And at home, as she sat in her own girlhood chamber, embroidering big ornate AF's in white silk onto the corners of alarmingly wide homespun sheets, she occasionally felt she was in a dream. Aunt Kati and Traani-Krõõt came one at a time or together to her door with advice or questions – Aunt Kati asked about every trivial detail, getting permission for every pot she was about to wash and stressing, somewhat tediously, Annika's new status as "mistress of a household" and "town-dweller". And Traani-Krõõt came to offer advice again on the various housekeeping tasks which needed doing here in the paternal household, and especially how such things ought to be done from now on in the young couple's home: "So that Master Meus won't get the impression that he's landed in some country yokel's household . . ."

Annika nodded and responded, often only at random and in a cursory way, because she was not actually able to follow the women's talk. And when they departed, smiling all-knowingly, she was left to stare into space with a catch in her throat, a curious mixture of joy and apprehension, as though she were floating on a cloud, happy because she was floating and fearful because she did not know where the cloud would set her down.

From time to time Bal stumbled into Annika's room, too. A year ago, when Annika had started to assemble her dowry, the boy's appearances had caused her acute embarrassment. For he could ask the most awful questions: "Yesterday at dusk, when you and Meus took a walk towards Paljassaare Island and then disappeared among the junipers, what were you doing?"

77

His round eyes stared at Annika intently all the while and his lips drew apart slightly in a faintly mocking, expectant smile. And Annika, silly child, turned red from her neck to the roots of her hair and lashed out darkly in a sharp voice: "Shut your mouth". . . even though they hadn't done anything like that, well . . . hardly anything. In the juniper grove Meus had only kissed her many, many, many times, that much was true . . .

But lately Bal had stopped teasing her. Juvenile though he still was, he had actually come to his sister's defence a few times, on a couple of occasions so pointedly and directly that she could only listen in wonder. For example, in response to Traani-Krõõt's curiosity, which was even more foolish than Bal's recent questions had been:

"Listen, Annika – tell me, what sort o' man is Meus anyway? Is he ambitious-like, or more of a slow type, maybe? And which o' these types would you say is more befitting a servant of the Lord?"

But before Annika could answer, Bal, who happened to be present, said:

"And just who do you think Annika is supposed to compare him with? Eh?"

And in his voice there was suddenly a sober, commanding ring, an unexpectedly authoritative tone that Annika had not noticed before and perhaps even now only partly heard. In any event, Traani-Krõõt dropped her usually imperturbable grey eyes to the floor and murmured: "Well I didn't mean . . ." and with a sniff went off to busy herself at the hearth. And this was something worth taking note of.

So that now Annika, her green eyes glowing, looked up from her sheet when Bal entered the room, grumbling like a full-grown man: "They won't let a man even read in peace . . ." He put Livy's *Ab urbe condita* under the lid of Annika's dowry chest and said:

"Let's go. Father's waiting."

"Where to?"

"To town. To Kimmelpenning's."

Annika folded up her sheet, threw her blue Sunday cloak around her shoulders, and was ready in no time, eager to go. Father put on his old work hat, handed Bal two rolled-up cloth sacks to carry under his arm, and the three of them set out along the village road.

Old Siimon walked ahead at a quick pace, the children following at his heels. They skirted the large puddles and jumped over the smaller ones, so that grey pants and blue skirt flashed over patches of reflected autumn sky. When the street below Köismäe Hill began slowly to rise and became a bit drier, Bal moved up next to his father.

"Father, who is this Kimmelpenning?"

"A haberdasher."

"And what else?"

"What do you mean, what else?"

"I think I've heard something about him . . ."

"What?"

"I don't remember. I think you yourself said something once . . . Have you known him a long time?"

"Kimmelpenning is the hardest rock of any of the Greys in Tallinn."

They walked on in silence for a while. Then Siimon said:

"Twenty-thirty years ago, things were different. At that time, when that man Wullenwever created a storm in Lübeck – you've heard about that, haven't you? – even we here could feel its winds. Just a few years before you came into the world . . . Well, the Town Council at that time sent Herr Plettenberg himself a letter to the effect that, with respect to the peasants, he should be informed that they had long ago all been made *free*, and that even during Danish rule they'd been free, and that they'd come from Danish rule to that of the Order as free men, and finally, that their slavery was not written into the law of either heaven or earth . . ."

"And was that the *truth*?"

"The truth, of course."

"But now?" asked Bal.

They had reached the stone road leading from the harbour to the Great Coast Gate and saw Herr Clodt, the syndic, coming towards them. He was headed for the harbour in the company of two guardsmen. Bal was no longer the lower-level pupil he had once been; and it was not Siimon's custom to greet strangers, no matter how grandly they were attired. On Herr Clodt's reddish hair was a floppy black velvet beret with a feather. His dark purple woollen cape was trimmed with gleaming brown beaver. The guardsmen had been ordered to walk five steps behind so as not to splatter mud on his deerskin boots.

"Nowadays," said Siimon when the syndic had passed them, "they're no longer the sort who'd be capable of writing that kind of letter to anyone."

"But Kimmelpenning? What about him?" asked Bal.

"Ah yes – Jakob. He went, at that same stormy time to challenge the Council on the rights of the dry-goods merchants. Already at that time most of them were country folk. And, to be sure, our Council had in fact written a nice letter to the Grand Master of the Order concerning them. But in Lübeck they cut Wullenwever's head off, and our gentry returned to the old ways. And then they started to squeeze the dry-goods merchants and raise their shop rents and demand that they also accept Germans into the trade. Jakob then brought suit on their behalf and delivered a speech at St Olaf's Guildhall. Apart from the dry-goods merchants there were a few hundred town Greys gathered there as well – and I was there myself when he hit the table – *karboom!* – with the haberdashers' official staff and cried: 'The Germans are all dogs! And there'll be no giving in!'"

"He said that? In St Olaf's Guildhall!? That . . . they're dogs? . . . And then what?"

"They summoned him before the Town Council and asked him

whether all Germans were really dogs. Jakob said maybe not in Germany, but here in Livonia, yes, they were. Because there were many who behaved like curs at the expense of the peasants, and those who were perhaps not actively hostile themselves but who watched from the sidelines and condoned it. So that, yes, they were all dogs. And then the councilmen told him to go home and get a hundred marks and return to pay the fine for slandering Germans. But right then and there Jakob raised the flap of his trouser pocket, took out a purse, and counted out a hundred Riga silver pieces onto the table. The councilmen told him to gather up his money and take it to the bursar. But Jakob buttoned up his pocket and told them it was all the same to him whether they took it to the money-house or to the outhouse – and the summoner could just as well do it himself! And he left.

Bal had once taken a peek into the big council hall when the *prima*-level students, under Rector Tegelmeister's direction, were performing Plautus. So he knew well what it looked like with a hundred and fifty wax candles glowing and all those strange figures – Solomon, and whoever they all were – gazing down from the tapestries, and the councilmen sitting high up in their chairs in a cloud of musk and lavender and muscat, looking down at you, and you were supposed to say something but felt as though you had no voice at all because your throat was full of sawdust . . . All the more clearly could he imagine Jakob Kimmelpenning standing at the council table, shamelessly fiddling with his money purse. He felt a shiver of admiration, and at the same time the urge to laugh.

When they had reached the marketplace by way of Saiakang Way, they went between the Town Hall and the market stalls and turned left. Here, directly opposite the corner house on Väike-Rataskaevu Street, stood a small shed made of half-logs about three of four fathoms long, with, for some odd reason, a slate roof. Its two wide lattice windows looked out over the square towards the Town Hall like two eyes, each conveying a message: the one with shutters open seemed to be innocently staring, the other with shutters closed slyly winking.

The market day had ended – the stalls had been cleared away, the peasants had left on the rattling, creaking, wooden axletrees of their farm wagons. Street cleaners were sweeping up straw, rubbish, and manure with big worn-down brooms, and even in the shops on the square the official hours of commerce had ended. There were those, however, who paid no heed to all this. Siimon knocked on the door of a shop and a friendly voice invited them in. The tall young man with close-cropped hair who came to meet them was apparently not the owner; he was one of old Jakob's three shophands and graciously invited them to look around and pick out what they wanted while they waited for the owner.

Kimmelpenning's store was considerably roomier inside than it had appeared from outside. From the floor, paved with the same cobblestones as the market square, poles rose up to the ceiling, supporting three wide shelves which extended around the entire store, laden with the most ordinary as well as extraordinary items. Siimon sat down on a roll of shoe leather and said to Annika:

"Well then, choose what you will, but within reason, mind you."

While Bal at first looked around timidly at the unfamiliar display of abundance, Annika was surprisingly businesslike in setting about the task at hand. Right away she found a shelf with birchbark containers full of dozens of bone buttons strung on a thread. She lifted some of the boxes closer to the window, took out then put back buttons, and asked the shop clerk the prices of the very smallest and mid-sized ones. It struck Bal that Annika was behaving very much like a pastor's young wife. The realisation buoyed him, but it also saddened him a little. There were in fact some marvellous things on the floor under the shelves. Annika picked out glass and silver beads, needles and needle boxes, buckles and little brass chains. She set aside some pillowcases, paused

82

in front of a stack of nappies for an instant, then realised what they were and, blushing, walked past them and began to weigh pieces of soap redolent of wax and mint. Bal had his eye on other shelves. There were dozens of pigskin mittens and dogskin gloves; there were hats of rabbit fur and lambswool and calfskin. There were bundles of yellow furs from Holland and reddish ones from Russia, some of them embroidered with flowers and birds; there were brass-studded belts with and without buckles; there were wonderful knives – with blades measuring one, two, and three thumb-joint lengths, and with hilts of bone or wood in embossed leather sheaths. There were kettles, pans, pots, axes, nails, candlesticks and plough blades; there were all sizes of pewter bowls, plates, trays and pitchers; there were locks – tiny ones for money chests and huge ones too for a small storehouse. On the floor stood barrels of herring, bundles of tanned leather, and bushels of onion seed and carrot seed.

To pass the time Bal tried to figure out what all the things in the shop might cost, and he had just decided it would take Herr Arithmeticus Mönnink at least a week to work it all out when the shopkeeper appeared.

Jakob Kimmelpenning was of average height, an old man with pepper-and-salt hair in a bowl cut, clinging to his head like the bristles of a bent and worn-out paintbrush. Red-rimmed blue eyes flashed above ruddy cheekbones and a rust-coloured beard, and his small, broad nose had an oddly sharp tip. He still had quite a nice little paunch, but his grey cloak hung from his shoulders as though he had recently shrunk in size.

"God Almighty – Siimon . . ." He held out his hand to Siimon, one finger bearing a gleaming, heavy gold ring. "And this then is the future bishop's wife" – he patted Annika on the back, drew her closer to the window, and looked at her, his lips moving silently. In the light of the window his small eyes were like two blue enamel buttons. "Ah, yes, this pastor-boy has good taste ... no doubt about it!" Even as he spoke he was already turning towards Bal. "And this then must be Siimon's little boy! Look at you ... a young man already! And he has a very learned name – wait, wait ..." He stuck out his lower lip, staring at the air in front of him and snapping his fingers, but could not remember the name.

"Balthasar," said Bal.

"Right!" cried Kimmelpenning. "And in school he's doing scandalously well, I've heard!"

Bal suppressed an embarrassed smile and shrugged his left shoulder.

"So far he hasn't given us cause for embarrassment," said Siimon, and then added, "Amazing – all the things that reach the ears of merchants ..."

"And why else would I be squatting here at the edge of the marketplace? It's my business to listen to what's going on – well, has the young lady Annika selected all her bric-à-brac? Let's take a look downstairs as well."

Kimmelpenning pushed open a little back door set in the stone wall between the shelves, and all four went down several steps to a half-cellar with a vaulted ceiling and barred window. The merchandise here was of a higher quality. Kimmelpenning winked at Annika, raised the lid of a large ironclad chest, and lifted out a burgundy bolt of fabric. He rested one end of it against Annika's shoulder and let it roll out, *swish!* to cover her from chest to toe. The fabric flowed over Annika's blue smock and skirt like a stream of shimmering, dark-red wine. She let out an "Oooh ..." and looked at her father; her eyes sparkling.

Bal noticed that his father was about to step closer, to touch the cloth, but then let his weight fall back upon his heels, saying only: "Hmm ..." He paused for a moment and added, almost offhandedly: "And what might it cost ... ?"

"This is taffeta from the Duchy of Brabant, and the good-for-nothings at the Town Hall don't want the haberdashers to sell it at all!

84

And if Weselouwe had it in stock – except that I know he doesn't – he would ask three marks a cubit. I'm selling it for two and a half. But to an old friend, for his daughter's wedding, I'll sell it for two."

"That's too much," said Siimon shaking his head.

"Well, as you like, but I don't see why Kuuse-Kreegor should be a better man than you . . ."

"You mean the tailor? . . . Why should he . . . ?"

"He had me measure off a ten-cubit length for his daughter Kärt's wedding."

"Hmm . . . you'll let me have it for a mark and a half," said Siimon, looking out of the cellar window into the backyard, and then asked with interest: "So those devils won't let you sell the better-quality fabrics?"

"A mark and three farthings," said Kimmelpenning offhandedly. "That's right, they won't."

Her ears burning with delight, Annika selected a pair of felt slippers with tassels, beads, and bells for Meus. Kimmelpenning sat down on the chest, the bolt of taffeta on his lap. Bal noticed that his wrinkled face around the flushed cheekbones was quite pale, and beads of sweat glistened on his wide forehead, near a shock of grey hair.

"And now they want to choke us for good," he said.

"Is that so?"

"Yes, indeed! The Council has decided to bring small-wares shop-keepers here from Germany. And once they're here, we won't be given trading permits anymore."

"Hmm . . . Listen, Jakob – what's wrong?"

Kimmelpenning gasped a bit, briefly kneaded his left side with his ring hand, and taking something black from a small wooden bowl on the same shelf put it in his mouth. "Every once in a while there's a kind of pang in my heart . . ."

"Hmm . . . thing to do for that is to drink some blood from a grey cat, along with lukewarm beer."

"That doesn't help. What helps me is dried frog's legs . . ."

"Yes, I've heard that's good too . . . But what's the actual reason that the Council swells and the haberdashers are like fire and water?"

The colour was returning to Kimmelpenning's slack face and his blue eyes flashed.

"Because a German or Frisian, or what have you, can travel through the villages of Harjumaa or Järva or Virumaa and, deal as he might, still return with an empty pouch. But when a haberdasher travels the same route with his shophands, he comes back with three times as much. Because the peasant will fleece the German shophands, or show them his arse, but his heart is open to the haberdasher."

"But does the haberdasher sell cheaper to the peasants?"

"Well . . . he will take what he's offered. Why should he be a saint?"

"Hmm . . . And what's the story now about the Germans coming?"

"The Council decided that Herr Clodt should write to Germany, to the town of Warburg – where he's from himself – to ask them to send us twenty shopkeepers. When they get here, the Council plans to set the dogs on us and drive us out of our shops."

"Uh huh . . . And you?"

Jakob's blue eyes narrowed. "We have our own little plan." All of a sudden his eyes rested on Bal and the blue slits grew round.

"Listen, Balthasar, do you know the dialect they speak in the south of Germany? The one that's been in the books since Luther – or do you know only that northern patter they use here?"

"Both."

"And where did you learn the southern dialect?"

Bal shrugged his left shoulder, but Siimon said:

"He just seems to pick these things up."

Kimmelpenning put aside the bolt of taffeta, pulled Siimon to the cellar window, and asked him in a low voice:

86

"Tell me, does he know how to hold his tongue?"

"He's safe alright . . . Why do you ask?"

But Kimmelpenning did not answer. He quickly measured out ten cubits of swishing taffeta, called the shophand in from the other room with the bill, and added up in his head the cost of Meus' slippers and some East India cotton Annika had picked out. It came to thirty and a half marks; he spat and rounded the bill off to thirty marks. Then he had everything packed into the sacks Bal was carrying under his arm, counted the money Siimon gave him, and said:

"Leave Balthasar here with me for a bit."

"So? You want to hire him to work in the shop?"

"No, no. For that he's a bit slow. But – we'll see."

When Siimon and Annika had left with one of the bags of things – Bal was to carry the other one home – Kimmelpenning closed the cellar door and asked Bal:

"Did you hear what I said about the shopkeepers of Warburg?"

"I did."

"Alright. I'll tell you more. Listen."

He sat down again on the fabric chest and continued, as he gently massaged his left side:

"There was a shoemaker here in Kuninga Street by the name of Schröder, a German, and – mark this – from the town of Warburg. He has a brother there, a dry-goods merchant. So. But he himself, shoemaker Schröder, that is, was ailing for almost a year. Once or twice he had a scribe write a letter to his brother, and the day before yesterday – like a gift from God – he gave up the ghost. But in the last letter before his departure – it is dated the day before yesterday – do you know what he had the scribe write?"

"What?"

"Well, something to the effect that, according to the latest news here, the town was planning to invite Warburg's dry-goods merchants

87

to Tallinn, and that our syndic, Clodt-Jodocus – you know who I mean, that beardless stripling Jobst, old Heinrich's grandson, the fellow who got rich dealing in wool – this same Jodocus was going to get twenty marks from the Council for every merchant he brought here from Warburg. 'But,' he wrote to his brother, 'you be smart and don't come here to fill the treasure chest of the wheeler-dealer's son, because he's a sorry fellow, and this is a sorry town and a sorry land. And I am glad I can sense in my illness that God will soon call me to Him and that my eyes won't have to see the ugly Muscovite trample this land to dust and ashes and send its people – with the Germans in the forefront – to Sarmatia in irons to be devoured by the cold and the wolves.'"

"Well then, if the brother of this Schröder is held in any regard there . . ."

"He is! I know he is!" cried Kimmelpenning.

". . . then no shopkeeper will come from Warburg!"

"Because of the letter?"

"Right, because of the letter."

"That's what I think, too," said Kimmelpenning, narrowing his eyes into slits.

"It's just that . . ."

"What?"

"There's no such letter, *yet* . . ."

"???"

"If there were such a letter, we'd have nothing to worry about. Because the dry-goods merchants of Warburg wouldn't come, as you yourself see so clearly. But the letter doesn't exist. Schröder didn't write any letter just before he died. But we need this letter."

"What do you mean . . . ? Schroder is dead, and—"

"And that's why someone else has to write the letter."

"Who, then?"

"We have no better man than you."

Bal was so taken aback by this that he recalled Kimmelpenning calling him a *man* only later . . .

"But I . . ."

"You know the southern German dialect, and the Schröders are from there. And even if you make a mistake, his brother will attribute it to the local scribe here."

"But – is something like this – permitted?"

"Aaah . . . That's a question you have to answer for yourself before you do anything. Well, think it over . . ."

Kimmelpenning started chewing on another frog's leg. "You know that the shopkeeper's job in Tallinn is the only more-or-less well paying position permitted to non-Germans now. Without all the stipulations – like the ones demanded of the old-book dealers and the guild merchants – that they deny their mother tongue and speak only German and bring false papers from the devil-knows-what drunken pastor – whom they have to bribe with a leg of mutton or a vat of ale to certify they were born of German parents. But now they want to take this occupation away from us too. You tell me, should *this* sort of thing be permitted?"

Bal muttered something, but did not know how to respond. Kimmelpenning was, of course, speaking the truth. But still . . . the Lord God before whom they knelt every schoolday morning, noisily pushing aside the benches and desks, and to whom he often forgot to pray at night when he sank down exhausted on his straw mattress, the Lord God whose face was hidden behind the smokescreen of pastors' and teachers' words – could He condone such a thing? This oddly off-putting yet appealing man – who now pushed the black frog's leg out of his mouth with his tongue and looked at Balthasar from the corner of his red-rimmed eyes – could it be that the Devil was using this old man to trap him, Bal?

Kimmelpenning sucked the frog's leg back into his mouth: "Alright.

Today they're doing it with the shopkeepers and you wash your hands of the affair. But as soon as they succeed in this, they'll come to your father and tear down his barn doors and take his horses and wagons and say: 'Siimon, from now on a wagon driver's job in this land is too good a position to be held by men of this land. We might permit you to own a pushcart, but from now on anyone who wants to keep horses and haul merchandise has to have been born in Germany, not in Harjumaa.' That's how it'll be. Balthasar, if we don't do something, they'll snatch everything from us and wedge their own Germans in everywhere."

They were both silent for a moment.

"Well," asked Kimmelpenning, "will you write the letter?"

"Yes, if I can," answered Balthasar quietly.

He wrote the letter right there, on the uneven, unsteady table, on a sheet of rough grey paper that Kimmelpenning gave him. And to tell the truth, when he had written *Mein Lieber Bruder** and was embarked on following the old man's dictation, he began to take pleasure in it. His enjoyment grew with every line. His ear caught the old man's words, his mind translated them, and his hand scribbled them onto the paper. In his mind's eye he could see the Warburg shopkeepers reading it with serious expressions and looking at each other in alarm and shaking their heads as they went home to unpack their assembled travel bags . . . When Bal had put down everything essential, Kimmelpenning asked:

"Well then, how should we end it?"

Bal felt he should wait until the old man himself came up with a closing. But an impish little hobgoblin took control of his hand, which began to write without waiting for the dictation: *As truly as I am soon to be* . . . and he was about to add, *standing before God*, but decided to leave God out of it and wrote instead, *your departed brother*.

"And what was his name?"

* My Dear Brother (German).

90

"Claus."

So Bal wrote *Claus*. "It's finished."

When Bal had read his letter to Kimmelpenning from beginning to end in country tongue, the old man chewed for a bit on his frog's leg and said:

"Ye-es . . . There are several parts much better worded than I could've put it. Well, how's school going? You'll be through in three or four years?"

"I should be."

"Have you . . . have you thought about going to Germany, to the university?"

"Indeed I have! . . . But Father says he can't afford it . . ."

"Ye-es," Kimmelpenning agreed. "It's expensive, of course. Costs more than you'd pay at the tollgate to Paradise . . ." Then he quickly stepped in front of Bal, put his hand on the boy's shoulder, and said, "Study hard. Go at your studies like a battering ram. And then, when it's time – bring Siimon to me. We'll talk it over, the three of us."

Bal felt as though he should say thank you. At the same time he felt it was all too vague and too big. So he just nodded and asked:

"May I tell Father . . . about the letter?"

"Aah . . . You want to tell him about it, do you?"

"It would be better . . ."

"Fine. You can tell him. But only him."

A few days later Bal was hauling home a load of hay with his father, and as they walked side by side behind the wagon along the road beside the woods of Telliskoppel, Bal made use of the occasion to tell Siimon what had happened. Siimon listened, chewing on a stalk of hay, and said only "Hmm." And when Bal asked about the Muscovite, and whether it was just Kimmelpenning's talk or if there really was a chance that the Muscovite would threaten Livonia, his father was silent for a long time. "It's hard to know about the Muscovite," he said slowly, "but it's true alright that the clouds do seem to be gathering in the east." And then Bal told him the rest too:

"And you know what? Kimmelpenning said he'd help out with sending me to Germany, to the university. I don't know – is there any sense in hoping he will?"

"I think there is," said Siimon. "He's that kind of man . . . Do you remember Susi-Hans? No matter! He died five years ago of the plague. He was the son of a bargeman and went to school in town, and he'd started to translate a songbook into country tongue for his congregation, and wrote a few songs himself too, I believe. So that he could have become the first songwriter in our tongue . . . if it hadn't been for the . . . Anyway, Old Jakob was supporting him too. I asked him once why he was giving the man money. Jakob thought for a moment and started to chuckle and said: 'It's like this . . . When that songbook is printed, there'll be many boys and girls who will be confirmed in country tongue, whereas otherwise, they would have gone to a German confirmation. And those confirmed in a German service will later buy things from the guild merchants, but the ones confirmed in country tongue will come and buy from Kimmelpenning.'"

CHAPTER FOUR,

*in which a youth, who is nearly a young man by now, discovers in the
most drab and ordinary places, wondrous things and wondrous lands
that he considers, by turns, to be Hell and Heaven, even as a second
youth, with whom we also concern ourselves as much as possible,
is happy to be doing a little business here on Earth.*

The two boys walking from the Old Market to Viru Street on that spring
morning of St Nicholas' Day encountered very few people as they strode
towards the main gate of the town. Indeed, they were young men now,
at least the more broad-shouldered and taller of the two was, especially
when seen from behind. His wheat-stalk shock of hair was as unruly as
it had been in his younger years. His wide, slightly sloping shoulders
threatened to split the seams of his grey jerkin, and his wrists, protruding from sleeves long outgrown, were no longer those of a child but
a real working man's wrists. Not to mention the hands themselves.
Some of the gentry's servant girls and Herr Kruwel's sauna maids
who encountered them at this early hour and glanced quickly into his
round grey eyes may have noticed a copper-coloured fuzz of beard,
shaved so close to his sunburnt chin that it was scarcely visible. From
the back the shorter fellow left the more boyish impression, but judging
by his face he was clearly the older of the two. Of slight build, with a
somewhat square head, light hair, and pointed chin, Märten was a little
over twenty already. The premature lines at the corners of his thin-
lipped mouth were characteristic of faces that seem at twenty to belong
to a man of forty, and remain nearly unchanged up to the age of sixty.

The youths had light pouches slung over their shoulders, and though they wore leather town shoes their steady, unhurried pace suggested they were setting out on a fairly long trek.

They passed a yawning town watchman growling at two servile, ragged street-sweepers, and continued on through the heavy, squat arch of the Viru Gate. Now they were between the town walls, in the slightly echoing, narrow passage reminiscent of a long stone casket, with the main gate behind them and the foregate up ahead. At each corner rose a tower and high up on the inside of the walls ran a defence gallery with tarred wooden railings. Several mercenary soldiers in striped pants and impressive moustaches were busying themselves on a gallery to their left. They had dragged a three-cubit-long bronze cannon out of the tower, and one of them was cleaning the barrel with a brush, pushing it back and forth, dispersing a cloud of acrid-smelling gunpowder into the slanting reddish rays of the early morning sun.

Midway between the gates Bal slowed down a bit and spat, continued a few paces, then turned around and spat again at the same spot on the cobblestones, as though he had missed his mark the first time.

"Why did you spit there like that?"

"Just because . . ."

"C'mon – tell me!"

"It's the bloodstone . . ."

"Whose blood?"

"The blood of Üksk’ll."

"Numbskull! That's at the Old Gate. The one that's been walled shut."

"I know. You can get into the space between the gates by way of the tower. I worked it out once. It's dark red. And there's a cross on it."

"So why are you spitting here, if it's actually there?"

"Just because . . . I willed it to be here . . ."

They went out of the foregate, between the high town walls and over the rumbling drawbridges, until they got to the other side of the moat, where they continued along the gravel path between gardens and ponds thick with bulrushes. Some decades earlier small houses with their dooryards and vegetable plots had squatted where now were gardens. The cottages had been torn down, in spite of protests and opposition, in anticipation of yet another war. At that point the town's merchants had appropriated the vacant plots for themselves, for their own gardens. Alongside the old twisted apple trees near the former house sites they had planted grand pear and cherry trees. The lilacs continued to bloom on their own, and when the war panic once again subsided the merchants started erecting summer cottages here and there on the old foundations. By now a good many were to be seen amidst the budding green gardens and no-one objected to their presence. For the builders of these cottages were the very people who gave orders and pronounced prohibitions concerning the defence of the town. But the Greys, with their once new and by this time old huts, had retreated to the neighbourhood of the Kivisild Bridge where the Karja Gate and Viru Gate roads joined and crossed the River Härjapea.

That was the direction Bal and Märten now took, because so early in spring no-one travelled the Narva road, which dipped to the left and in two hundred paces reached the sea. At this time of year even patching the road with bundles of brush did no good. When the north wind blew, the high water washed over the seaside road, flooding the marshland behind it, and then one could almost believe the old-timers' tales about a time long, long ago, when the dragon-bellied Hanseatic cogs rarely sailed to Tallinn, and the native vessels were light as seabirds, lighter even than boatmen's barges, and the harbour had been where now there was marshland. But slowly the land kept raising its broad back up out of the sea, and foreign ships needed deeper waters. And so the harbour gradually moved ever further from the town walls, at first to the Small Coast Gate where nowadays fishing boats came ashore, and later towards the steeper shore near the Rose Garden, where a proper breakwater and ships could now be seen.

The youths crossed Kivisild Bridge, the grey spring water beneath it nearly reaching the tops of its arched supports. They walked through a cluster of houses near the bridge and then through the Almshouse settlement, passing the Almshouse Church and several structures of wood and stone, and the walls and fences of the Almshouse itself. (There, in this building set slightly apart, its plank roof visible over a high fence, lived the town's last nineteen lepers.) The morning breeze carried with it the rank odours of the tannery from the river at the back of the settlement, and the soft thumping of the gunpowder mill and the shouts of Jürgen, the boss. He yelled at his workers morning and night, and it was said that when he held a handful of gunpowder near his mouth and shouted at it, it crackled into flame.

Beyond the Almshouse the trail suddenly worsened, and when the boys started the climb up Lasnamäe Hill the going was slow as they trudged laboriously through sand grooved and ridged by run-off from above.

Higher up, where the trail cut through a limestone bank, it became exceedingly steep. On both sides greenish water trickled from between layers of peat, exhaling cold. From behind, the flour and copper mill sounded the springtime roar of the millstream falls. Where the trail had been washed out, the boys hopped from one pile of brush to another. At the steepest spot horses' hooves had cut a zigzag groove across like the pattern on a viper's back, for here the horses could ascend and descend only by traversing the trail from bank to bank.

At the top of Lasnamäe Hill the two friends turned their backs to the sun and looked down at the town below. It looked pitifully small, no larger than a molehill, a sprinkling of reddish roofs inside its ring of grey walls. And the wide expanse of open countryside around them made the boys more than a little uneasy. All in all it was a reckless act, requiring a kind of foolish courage, to leave the town and set out into the country. Over all those rare times when he had left town and gone to Kurgla, Bal had always had the same feeling: the familiar surrounding walls would suddenly disappear, the shelter provided by the roofs and corners of houses against wind, sun and rain would vanish. Instead of the familiar smell of damp limestone, of refuse and horses' urine in the streets and of privies and blooming roses in the courtyards, the breezes would be redolent of juniper and heather, of the soil and the hot spring sun and cool waters . . . and a bleak, disquieting emptiness. This feeling arose, no doubt, from a conjunction of familiar lore and unfamiliar landscape. Somewhere deep inside the town-dwelling Greys, deep in their bodies and blood even after several generations of town life, nested a knowledge, or suspicion, or sense, or memory that leaving town and going into the country was hazardous. Bal, after all, was a second-generation town-dweller, for his father had lived there nearly a lifetime, and Bal himself had first seen the light of day at Kalamaja. But the stories of their forebears' fates had seeped into his consciousness. And more recent tales of what had befallen both relatives and strangers living in the country confirmed but one thing: terrible things happened there. In the country people were driven out of their homes and sold for money (this had gone on for several generations); in the country people were given away to strange masters in far-away places and used as prizes in gambling; in the country people were bartered for riding horses or setters or basset hounds. True, the nobles did not subject freeholders to such things, the freeholders being about on a level with the poorer nobles – but then, how many of them were there . . . ? For punishing the serfs and their descendants – people like Bal's and Siimon's relatives – there were whipping stools in front of, sometimes inside, all the barns of every estate in the land. And perhaps more than half the peasants had at some time or other been pushed onto one of those stools to chew their lips to shreds as the whips lashed their backs.

The small frothy waves of the blue-grey waters of Lake Ülemiste, swollen with springtime run-off, lapped at the edge of the road. The water reached halfway up the sides of Linda's Rock. There were three boats in the distance, with the fishermen of Mõigu hauling in nets full of bass and ruff. The windy expanse of the lake around the boats appeared even larger than it would have without them.

But there was nowhere a peasant could go. The manor lord would not give him permission to move elsewhere. Anyone who dared leave against orders was returned to his master by those who found him, beaten and locked into the stocks or into hand irons fixed to cellar walls.

Forcibly returned from wherever he might be. From anywhere – except from town.

"Märten . . ."

"Hmm?"

"Do you feel like I do – that you're more at home in town than country?"

Märten thought for a moment. "Nooo, no I don't."

"Really? You don't?"

"No. Look, the sparrow is grey in the country and it's also grey in town. And it finds grain in town and in the country, too."

The road turned away from the lake and they walked on in a bleak landscape of juniper bushes and thudding limestone and uneven turf yellow with marsh marigolds, heading in the direction of the great marshes and woodlands on the horizon.

"Märten, where was your father from?"

"Tallinn."

"He'd gone there from the country?"

"I don't know."

"What language did he speak?"

"Country tongue with mother, of course, as far as I can remember. But otherwise, I think he spoke Swedish."

"Hmm. He was a seaman?"

"Yes."

"And probably sailed all the seas?"

"I suppose so."

"Do you remember him?"

"I remember . . . his beard. And his open collar. And the blue seagull."

"What?"

"It showed when his collar was open and I couldn't prise it loose from his skin."

"Yes, seamen have those. On their chests and arms. I've seen them in the harbour . . . And where did he die?"

"Mother told me he was killed in a port tavern. In the town of Calais."

"Where's that?"

"I don't know. Mother didn't know, either."

"Hmm. And your mother died of the plague?"

Märten nodded.

"How old were you?"

"The women at the orphanage said I was seven."

On the desolate limestone expanse dotted with sky-blue puddles grew scrubby alder thickets, grey-brown now with catkins. Here and there among the thickets, behind high split-rail fences were wet fields, some bare and black, some greening with new growth. The moss-covered roofs of the occasional villages they passed rose like molehills on either side of the road. The boys walked through waves of warm manure smells wafting from the grey barns on the Town Council's estate and past its expansive fields. In the distance four sowers were striding side by side, downwind, bags of seed on their hips as they broadcast invisible oat seeds onto the gravelly soil.

They passed St George's Church with its squat steeple on a knoll to their left in a grove of oak and willow trees, and came to a river unexpectedly dark and swollen. A tumbledown footbridge without a railing extended across it. The crossing for horses was said to be about a quarter of a league downstream.

Bal stepped onto the footbridge and stopped. He could see, rising above the village of Vaskjala on the other side of the river, smoke from seven hearths dispersing over fields and brush and grazing land. The third structure from the left, the one closest to the river, was exactly like all the others: a very long, low building, its eaves almost touching the ground, with two such tiny windows under its thatched hip roof that the house appeared eyeless in spite of them. In the middle of the sagging roof ridge one could see the ends of rafters jutting out of the straw here and there. This was no manor but an ordinary ploughland peasant's farmhouse. From the roof of the dwelling, and visible between the rafters, rose the stout stump of a chimney, one that nothing could topple. This was the only chimney Bal had ever seen on a peasant farmhouse, and it was in fact the only one in existence, at least in the county of Northwest-Harju. Siimon had told Bal the story of the chimney over their travels a couple of times on their way to Kurgla. This marvel had started to take shape fifty years earlier and no doubt because Young Juhan, son of Vaskjala-Mats – a quite ordinary, lively lad like all the rest (or, who knows, perhaps a bit sharper than the rest) – had managed to get into St Olaf's school with the help of town relatives who worked as servants for a merchant. He had finished school and, supported by council money, managed to get himself admitted into higher institutions of learning in Germany. All this had happened in the dark ages of the popes. In Germany, the story went, he had heard the new, enlightened truth straight from the mouth of Luther himself. At any event, when he returned to his homeland he became the first pastor to preach that new truth in this very church of St George, and all of the eastern Harju County came to hear him. He had heated debates with nobles who supported the Pope. He had had this chimney built for his father so that the old man and his wife would no longer have to suffer the smoke that stung their eyes and made them water: they could now *choose* to cry tears of joy when they so wished. For twenty-five years Herr Kuun, as he came to be called, was in the pulpit, until the manor lords pried him loose and sent him off elsewhere. Old Juhan and his wife were by then long under the churchyard willow trees. And rumour had it that Herr Kuun too had been with his Lord for some years now. But the chimney on old Mats' house was still upright and smoking, the wispy strands sailing with the wind over the river and scrubby brush, towards the southeast.

"Well, are you scared to cross, or what?" Märten asked, waiting his turn.

"Who – me?" mumbled Bal. "Nonsense! Why I'm . . ." To keep himself steady he shifted his pouch further onto his back and stepped out onto the footbridge.

The river flowing beneath him was like a huge blue-grey herd of rushing sheep. The more closely Bal looked, the deeper it sank and the bigger it grew. Here and there he caught flashes of black and white sheep among the greys. The whites huddled around the bridge supports and seemed to lick the posts until scattered by a flood of grey sheep. Here and there in the flow of curly backs flashed a brown or greenish strip of turf. And where the sun touched the woollen backs they seemed, for an instant, to catch fire . . . Or was it all a flow of people? An endless grey mass . . . and among the greys the black coats of the gentry and the brown uniforms and green tassels of mercenaries and in the midst of the crowd the white robes of the Order, flapping as they rose up on the backs of rearing horses, the sunlight sparkling on their armour . . . ? And over this endless grey stream a magical way across, a magical wingless flight from one bank to the other . . . ?

Bal was so caught up in his fantasy that when he looked up and realised there were still ten fathoms of water to cross he almost lost his balance. A wave of apprehension rose in his chest and washed up against the iron cladding of his self-confidence. But he stretched out his arms, quickened his step, regained his balance, and reached the other side. Märten, who had followed him with small, calm, deliberate steps, took his thumbs nonchalantly out of his belt only as he stepped onto the shore.

When the boys had passed the two farmsteads of Jänese village they turned left off the main road onto a footpath which Bal remembered well. It passed first through a willow grove – partly reddish, then grey with pussy willows, and greenish with new young buds – and then crossed more barren, marshy ground where our travellers' soft-soled shoes, already wet, became thoroughly sodden; they removed them, along with their footcloths, and slung them over their shoulders. Soon the stunted birches and spindly firs became a dense thicket on an uneven, spongy forest floor, and the trail wound along the edge of the woods towards the northeast, while to the northwest lay low, brownish, moss-covered marshes.

They had walked a long way in silence when Bal suddenly stopped, pointed, and whispered, "Wolves!" Märten caught up with him and saw them too. Twenty paces ahead, directly in their path, stood two wolves, shaggy in their springtime coats. The male was big, his mate somewhat smaller. Their hindquarters were in the bushes, their tails between their legs, their fangs partly bared. Two pairs of unblinking green eyes were fixed on the youths. The cubs were no doubt somewhere nearby.

"Let's go back," whispered Märten. "Let's take the main road by the manor."

That would clearly have been the wisest course. For a half-starved wolf guarding a den in the spring is more dangerous than a starving one in winter. Yet for Bal the idea of backing away, turning around, and retreating went against the grain, and though his knees tightened with alarm and tension he could not really believe that these two mute grey shades, growling and baring their fangs, would leap at his throat. That kind of thing happened in stories long ago; they may even have happened yesterday or might tomorrow – but to strangers elsewhere, not to him, not here and now to him . . . With his left hand he motioned to Märten to remain silent, and with his right pulled out of his waistband a short, wide-bladed knife. Next to him, Märten did the same. Frozen beside him, his mind emptied of rational thought by sheer fright, Balthasar yet continued to think feverishly, and an absurdly defiant conviction gripped him against his own better judgement: *if you back away now, you'll back away all your life.*

"*Hur-yaaaahh!*" roared Bal, as loudly as he could. The grey shapes rose as though borne on the wind and landed, without turning around, a fathom further back. Bal took the blade of the knife between his teeth and clapped his hands, making them sound like two pieces of wood slammed against each other. The wolves did not move. "*Huryaaaahh-aaah!*" he yelled once more, and Märten echoed him at a slightly higher pitch. The wolves did not stir. Bal held the knife at chest level and took four steps in their direction. The beasts stayed where they were, motionless. Filling his lungs, Bal strode forward, roaring out the words of Doctor Luther and of Susi-Hans which they sang in church every other Sunday:

> Were the world of Devils full
> Wanting to devour us,
> We would not fear them all that much . . .

"All that much . . ." roared Märten belatedly, behind Bal. Silence. Bal did not know whether he dared cry out the next line:

> For God would keep them from us.

Maybe this was too brazen a challenge to God! Silent now, he stopped as well; he was five paces from the wolves, who had not moved. Their green eyes remained fixed, their snouts wrinkled, their fangs still visible . . . If only he could remember his grandfather's wolf spell . . . *how the devil did it go?* . . . Somewhere in an upper corner of his empty mind flashed odd words like the flaming tails of squirrels running in a cage: *gelingen – apostata – susi – gelingen – apostata – susi*. It seemed to him that the male's neck had bristled and that the animal was about to leap!

Just then Märten bellowed: "Go back wolfhound! Begone hellhound!" and Bal joined him, yelling in unison: "Begone evil one, back into the willow brush! You do not see me! I do not see you!" And brandishing their knives they walked towards the wolves. Confronting them now, it seemed to Bal he could feel the animals' warm breath on his face, but the creatures drew soundlessly back a few steps and the boys, walking backwards now, put some distance between them. After they had gone about twenty paces they stopped their bellowing. At thirty paces they swung back towards their destination, shaking themselves free: "Oooh, you hellhound!" And so they moved on, not talking, their skin damp from the tension, giddy at their miraculous escape. Only when they had gone some distance further did Bal speak.

"And you remembered my grandfather's wolf spell before I did!"

"You had it covered over with a layer of Latin," Märten said, and Bal was not sure whether he had said that admiringly or mockingly or perhaps both ways.

Despite that, he felt as though he had sprouted wings. Not that he really believed he would never need to back away, but still, if they were to encounter wolves again, he would . . . And, as though he had been reading Bal's mind, Marten said:

"If we were to come upon wolves now," and he spat three times over his shoulder, "you'd probably be itching to get your hands on them!"

"Don't be silly!" Bal shot back, astounded that he had seemed so transparent to his friend. Still, he could not entirely suppress a smile.

The sun was high in the southern sky when the top of the fir tree in front of the Kurgla farmhouse began to show above those lower in the forest, and the boys passed the split-rail fences surrounding freshly ploughed fields.

"What was named for what here?" Märten asked. "Was the farm named Kurgla for the village or the village for the farm?"

"Last summer I asked my grandfather the same thing – he was still alive then – and he told me the story. His grandfather escaped from the brutal Soie at the Maardu manor. He fled to this wild marshland owned by the monks, who made a kind of deal with Soie, and grandfather's grandfather built his farmhouse here. It was mainly storks that lived here then. At first the place was called Kureküla and later that was shortened to Kurgla. Where the others who live here now came from and how they got here, I don't know. And there are not that many – the two Pärtlis, Küti, Jaagu – five hearths in all."

The boys had scarcely been able to look around – Märten had taken in only the long barn-dwelling, the small shed, the summer kitchen, and the stone well – when a girl ran out from the black opening of the threshing room door under the shadow of the low, thatched eaves. Emerging from the dusky interior, she shielded her eyes against the outdoor glare with one hand while with the other she gripped a wooden milking pail. She was clearly hurrying to the well. Noticing the youths, she stopped in her tracks and cried out, "Lord! Some kind o' men from the manor!" and scurried back into the building. Bal had not been able to notice much more of the girl than her grey skirt, a pale braid of hair and a pair of firm, tanned legs.

A cow mooed plaintively in the barn, and then Aunt Kati came to the door. She was wearing old work clothes, sleeves rolled up, and looking a bit anxious. At the sight of the boys she brightened immediately.

"Aah, the gents from town've arrived! Halloo – welcome! Didn't know as you'd still be coming!" She called into the threshing barn: "Epp, you silly girl! This here's Bal from town, with his friend! Come now, hurry an' bring us some water!" And to the boys: "Epp from New-Pärtli farm's come to help us out a bit. Our Küüt's just calved, long since past her time – a nice black-'n-white calf – but at such a fool time! Not a single male soul at home . . . 'Cause the menfolk're all gone to Lammassaare to burn-beat a field . . ."

"If you need menfolk, what is it we can help with?" Bal asked. Just then Epp reappeared with her pail, and before she turned towards the well Bal saw light-grey shining eyes in a small suntanned face. He noted a nod intended as greeting, and the braid around her head, and the slender tan of her legs, and the skirt reaching only to where the calf started to narrow towards the knee. And he only half heard Aunt Kati's awkward response: "Oh, no . . . how could the likes o' you . . ." And only when Epp had lifted the full bucket with apparent ease from the well and returned to the barn without looking up did Bal ask:

"Is there anything Epp and you can't handle between the two of you?"

"Well . . . there *is* something," Aunt Kati said, hesitantly.

"Well, out with it!"

"I don't know . . . Maybe . . ."

"Well?"

"It's just that now that we've got a heifer . . ."

"Yes?"

"Next year we'd like to have a bull calf!"

"And just how can you make that happen?"

"I'll tell you how. If I boil old Küüt's beestings now, and then a boy-soul gets up on the stove and . . ."

"And what's he supposed to do there?"

106

Aunt Kati looked at Bal from under a grey lock of hair and then looked away and crossed herself.

"He's to bellow like a bull . . ."

"And that'll help?"

"It will."

"Is the milk boiling already?"

"No, but there's a fire in the hearth."

"Set the pan on the fire. I'll do the trick for you right now."

"You will – really?" Aunt Kati clapped her hands together.

"And why not? A cow's a good beast, but a farm needs a bull! Wait, Märten and I will both go – we'll bellow twin bulls for you!"

"No! No, don't do that! Or they'll both turn out sickly!"

The sheepskins had been taken down off the rough surface of the big masonry stove, for spring was so far along already that no-one would be sleeping up there for the time being. The skins had been spread out on wooden plank-beds. And the stovetop was as cool and hard against Bal's chest as a boulder – a boulder in a strange, twilit cave. Down below inside the rock a fire crackled, and from behind the sooty front edge of it a wisp of grey-blue smoke drifted up towards black racks used for drying grain. Through the acrid smell of burning alder twigs rose the sweet smell of the beestings cooking. The door of the room was open, as were the smoke vents. Two shafts of sunlight entered the dark room through them, a thick log of light came through the door, and the smoke swirled slowly through them as though suspended in upward-flowing water. Visible in the dim interior was a table about three spans high, one end of it against the wall, the other resting on legs set on the mud floor. And there were odd-looking three-legged stools of twisted wood, like fantastic lopsided animals that had risen part way and seemed to be moving in the flickering flame. Then Bal saw a sooty wad of rags disappear from the vent-opening above the door leading to the threshing barn. The mooing of the cow, or calf, or both, could now be clearly heard, and that was Bal's signal. He pressed his palms more firmly onto the rough stone surface of the stovetop, pushed his stomach hard against it, as though he himself were part of it, and raised his chin. So. He swallowed superstition and doubt and the shudder of sin along with the clay and ash of the stovetop, and bellowed loudly:

"Mooo-ooh! Mooo-ooh! Moo-hoo-ooh!"

His rational self smirked at all this, the witching made him anxious, and he worried about what Epp might think of his calving antics. And yet he also felt how the stove, made of stones dug out of the fields, was somehow humming along with him and with the cave-like house and the earth under the house. He would remember this moment all his life: of that he was certain even before the cow's plaintive lowing changed to a long clear *moo-oo-oo*. It seemed to be such a direct response to his bellow that it shocked him, for it appeared to prove that he had extended his hand over the gate and into the realm of witchcraft.

Bal was at the door, brushing the ash and dust of the stove from his coat, when Uncle Jakob rode into the dooryard with his son Jürgen. Wearing a tow-cloth work coat and shaggy slouch hat, and with the laces of his peasant moccasins wrapped round his trouser legs, he looked considerably older than his brother Siimon, even though he was the younger by ten years. In other respects he resembled his brother quite closely, though he was thinner and more agile and thus more wiry-looking. Nor were Jürgen and Bal very different, except that Bal had by this time acquired a certain town look. His cousin's face bore the effects of sun and wind. His voice was gruff whereas Bal's had been smoothened somewhat by choral singing. And compared with the coarse fabric of Jürgen's dress, Bal's and Märten's attire was as though from another world, even though it was merely threadbare woollen homespun. Bal noted all this quickly and only half consciously. And when he then offered his hand to Jürgen in greeting and noticed that their hands were quite similarly firm and strong, he was both embarrassed at the likeness and delighted by this evidence of kinship.

"How d'you get back home so fast?" Aunt Kati asked in surprise.

Uncle Jakob related how the four of them, he and Jürgen and two of the farmhands, had set out in the morning for Lammassaare, and on the way met Küti-Jaan, who told them that Brother Antonius had come from the monastery to the manor yesterday. Hearing this the Kurgla men had gone on to Lammassaare, gathered most of the brushwood into piles, rolled the smaller logs into the clearing, and Jakob had returned by midday to ride to the manor because he had to talk to Herr Antonius.

Aunt Kati was worried. "Better that you don't . . . No good'll come of it if the steward comes down even harder on you. He might even put you on the rack and give you a whipping. What's the use o' that?"

Aunt Kati had not actually said anything that Bal had not heard before. It was a familiar story: . . . *stretched on the rack, set onto the bench, tied to the post . . . beaten.* But now, with the unexpected shadow of such a possibility threatening this man, standing less than a fathom from him with his so-familiar face, Bal felt as though he had walked through the farmyard, past the sunburnt faces and the pig barn and grass and earth and smoke, to stand at the edge of an abyss, looking down . . . As he had done at the ledge of a window slit in the steeple of St Olaf's Church.

"I'll go and talk to him anyway!" Jakob said, almost angrily. And by way of explanation, he said to Bal and Märten:

"The new steward is insisting that we sell a quarter of our butter to him and buy our iron from him. But for generations we've been going to town to buy and sell these things!"

"Just how much . . . ?" Aunt Kati interrupted.

"We are in the right!" Jakob said, through clenched teeth.

"Well, in this, yes," agreed Aunt Kati and added softly. "But not in making the clearing in Lammassaare."

"Oh no?" cried Jakob in agitation, but then waved his hand dismissively and asked Jürgen to fetch the saddles.

"And why does it have to be you that goes to earn a whipping for himself on behalf o' the whole village?" Aunt Kati made one last try. "And why drag Jürgen along with you?"

"That's enough!" Jakob said, and to bring the discussion to a close he followed Jürgen into the barn.

Aunt Kati shrugged and went back to the barn. Bal and Märten looked at each other. Bal could tell from his friend's expression that they were thinking the same thing: . . . *feels a bit foolish to be standing here looking on and not understanding other people's troubles . . . pretty serious troubles, actually . . . we could just stroll on further . . . or whistle 'Ick bin ein lifflländisch bur, das Leben wird mir sur' . . . or maybe we could check where that girl Epp went . . . but perhaps we should go and see how it goes at the manor . . . 'cause it could be dangerous . . . of course, if we had any sense we wouldn't stick our noses into this business at all . . . wonder why Epp's cheeks were so flushed . . . does this Herr Antonius even know our language . . . or how will Uncle Jakob talk to him . . . ?* Jakob and Jürgen came back from the barn, Jakob carrying two saddles, Jürgen the saddlebags. For a moment Jakob looked at Bal as though he were on the verge of saying something, but instead he set the saddles on the ground and began laying the straw sacks onto the horses' backs. *The wisest course would clearly be to do nothing . . . What kind of man is this new steward anyway . . . unpleasant, no doubt . . . but maybe . . .*

"Uncle Jakob, would you have a nag for me?"

"What for?"

"I'd like to come along to the manor."

The corner of Jakob's bearded mouth twitched, and Bal realised his uncle had wanted to suggest this himself but not dared.

"You can wait for us here," Bal said to Märten. "Or . . . Uncle, would you have a fourth horse?"

"I do, but it's been at the manor since morning . . ."

"Let it be! You won't be gone that long," Marten said offhandedly. "I'll just stay here and enjoy our Lord's natural world."

Jürgen led a pretty, pale colt out of the paddock, and Jakob brought a third saddle from the barn. Bal noted that his uncle quickly untied the birch branch stirrups from the saddles and replaced them with the iron stirrups he had brought out with the third saddle. Jakob and Jürgen disappeared briefly into the farmhouse, and when they reappeared they had both put on, over their coarse linen trousers, their church-going coats of grey homespun smelling of smoke and candlewax. Jakob was even wearing his churchgoing hat.

As they trotted away, Bal looked back over his shoulder and saw, in the dark doorway under the thatched eaves of the threshing barn, Epp's red cheeks and light-blue eyes.

They rode between the fields and along the soft road surface pocked with hoof prints and over the grazing land, down towards the river. Bal pulled up alongside his uncle's dapple-grey mare and asked:

"Well, how is it going then – life here, and everything . . . ?"

The old man let his reins droop, so that they fell on either side of the saddle horn where Bal had branded a date the year before: 1556.

"Well now . . . can't much complain . . ."

"Really?"

"When we were in thrall to Herr Vegesack – he always wanted things to be going steadily uphill – that's when the ploughland peasant's lot really went downhill. But later the monks redeemed the mortgage – an astonishing thing that was – and the monastery took over the manor – that was more than ten years ago now, and since then things haven't been too bad . . ."

"How large are your obligations now, for example?"

"Well, for one thing, I have to send a farmhand and a wagon to the manor . . ."

"How many days a year?"

"Two hundred days."

"That many!"

"But you know, I do have two ploughlands of my own . . ."

"Well alright . . . if you don't have to provide anything more in addition to the two hundred work days, maybe you can manage it somehow . . ."

"Right . . . but of course there's more . . ."

"There's more? What?"

"Well, grain."

"How much?"

"Twenty bushels."

Bal whistled. "Leave off whistling," said Uncle Jakob. "The bishop at Kiviloo takes thirty from a two-ploughland farm. And in some of the nobles' manors they take forty."

"But – that's it then, the twenty bushels?"

"No . . . that's not all . . . there are still other obligations."

"What more do you have to hand over?"

"Well . . . let's see . . . for calves and foals – it's two shillings for a calf and three for each foal. And the sheep-tithe . . ."

"For every tenth sheep?"

"Every seventh."

"What do they mean by 'tithe' then, if it's every seventh?"

"Yes, well . . . at Anija and Vaase it's every sixth. So, if you compare . . ."

"That's it, then?"

"Sort of . . . but there're the foodstuffs twice a year: that's a portion of the meat, eggs, flour, and some chickens, and a payment of half a mark per ploughland and some shillings for mead . . . And then, every year, twelve cords of wood, which the lord sells in Tallinn, and four cords of wood for the manor, and three logs for construction and ten trees for boards. And three barrels of coal for the blacksmith . . . And then there's the hay, a wagonload per ploughland. And ten bundles of straw. And a pound of linen yarn, and two pounds of hops, a pound of honey, a bunch of hemp . . ."

Bal whistled again.

"You can't seem to stop whistling! But in the manors run by nobles, the obligations are a third again as stiff. And the payments are greater too . . ."

"You pay money too?"

"Well of course . . . There's the land tax and the hearth tax. And the name tax and the farmyard tax. And there's six shillings a year on each farmhand."

"Even on the ones you send to work for the manor?"

"Certainly . . ."

"And then there are the other fees: for gifts, for the chaplain and the marshal and the cook . . ."

"And the tithe for the Church," added Jürgen from behind them.

"What do all these payments add up to?"

"They come to twenty-five marks a year."

"That's about the price of five bulls . . . ?"

"That'd be right . . ."

Flattening their ears, the horses entered the river, the water at the fording point reaching their bellies. Bal was so deep in thought that his shoes and stockings got soaked through again by the icy-cold water before he remembered to pull up his knees.

The horses came out onto the bank, rippling their dripping hides, and as they rode on Bal asked: "But what if you didn't send your farmhand to the manor, what then?"

"I'd have to pay ten shillings for the first day, twenty for the second. On the third – I'd be hauled to the manor for a whipping."

"And in spite of all this, you say it's not bad?"

"Everywhere else around here . . . it's worse."

"But why, then, do you want to protest now?"

"It's because this Herr Hasse, who's been the steward here since the autumn of last year – he's pushing for everything getting worse. Treating us as if ours were a typical baronial estate when it comes to our obligations. He's been moving in that direction bit by bit since autumn, but this business of the buying and selling – that's the first really big blow . . . He's offering to pay us only half what we get for our goods in town! And he's demanding twenty shillings for a ploughshare. But Kimmel-penning, in town, charges twelve. And if we just swallow these wrongs, Herr Hasse will soon ruin our lives."

"And you think that this monastery brother, Antonius, will join with you peasants against the steward?"

"We'll see . . ."

The thatched roofs of both manor barns were damaged in several places, and the barn doors hung askew on their hinges. The men from Kurgla rode along the muddy bank of the carp pond – by summer it would be covered with a pale green slime – and passed an apple orchard of twenty trees with undersized buds, long overdue for pruning. At the gate to the steward's dwelling a big-boned youth came towards them, a bit stooped, his eyes darting here and there. "No . . . Herr Steward is out – overseeing the sowing of the oats. Yes . . . Herr Antonius is here at the manor. In the steward's house. In his writing room. Of course he'll see you. Why wouldn't he see you . . . ?"

The young fellow went off. The men from Kurgla tied their horses to the fence post and went towards the steward's house, a low building with a shingle roof and small, bullion-glass windows.

"Stay out here. Bal and I will go in," Uncle Jakob said to Jürgen. Bal noticed his uncle taking off his hat in the dooryard.

"Do you know this Herr Antonius?" Bal asked softly, as they passed through the dim entry.

"I went to talk to him once, five or six years ago," Jakob murmured.

Herr Hasse's study was a low-ceilinged room with a small window facing the garden. Next to the window stood a writing desk. On the bare log wall near the desk hung account books in soiled leather bindings and a few dozen striated tally sticks of various lengths. Under the open window was a sofa with a rough, hand-hewn fir frame, and in front of it a couple of stools and a small round table. Herr Antonius was lying on the sofa. His white Cistercian robe, not brand-new by any means, was open at the neck. Its wide sleeves had slipped back to his elbows, exposing the growth of reddish hair on his arms. In his hands was a small book bound in white parchment. He was about forty years old, neither too fat nor too thin. His smooth, hairless face with its even, ruddy hue and a reddish circle of hair surrounding a pink tonsure vaguely evoked a snake's head. He could have seemed threatening had it not been for his shining grey eyes, the eyes of a little urchin.

Bal and Jakob entered upon hearing the summons in response to their knock, and Herr Antonius sighed:

"*Schon wieder welche . . .*"* And he said to the pimply young man who stood under the window at the foot of the sofa: "*Frag die Kerle was sie wollen.*"† Then he set the little white book on the table in front of the sofa, upon which Bal noticed a large, square, green bottle – half empty – and a green drinking glass.

"What do you want?" the interpreter asked.

Bal was surprised at how succinctly and clearly Uncle Jakob replied, and the businesslike manner with which he concluded:

"The manor, that is to say, the monastery, will not get a crumb from this. But the coffers of the steward will echo with the jingling of coins! It will cause great harm to the peasants' livelihood and provoke their wrath as well. For generations we have had the right and the freedom to sell our goods in town and to buy what we need there."

* They keep coming (German). † Ask the fellows what they want (German).

When the interpreter had concluded a roundabout and fairly dis-jointed translation, Herr Antonius stretched his reddish, turtle-like neck out from his robe and asked, wearily, but with surprising interest, nonetheless:

"*Ja worum handelt es sich überhaupt.*"* Bal noted that he did not speak with the pronunciation of a native German or even of a would-be-German, so that he was probably a Latvian or a Pole or who-knows-what. The interpreter was about to start telling Uncle Jakob's story again, but it seemed to Bal that the time had come to interrupt.

"*Hochweiser Herr Pater*† – will you permit me to explain . . . ?"

Herr Antonius' eyes widened a bit, and he put one foot, clad in a woollen sock and leather sandal, onto the floor.

"Who are *you* . . . ?"

"I am this peasant's interpreter."

Herr Antonius sat up, set his other foot on the floor as well, looked sharply at his visitors from Kurgla, and asked, his upper lip laughing, so that his white teeth showed:

"And where is his page? And his stable boy? And his servant?"

For a tense moment Bal tried to comprehend the meaning that might underlie the man's words, but then he realised it was only a tipsy gentleman's joke. For a moment he considered playing along, but refrained – *Heaven knows how Herr Antonius might take it* – and said simply:

"At the moment, only his interpreter is with him. And the story that is to be translated for Your Reverence is this." And in a few direct, clear statements he laid out the story.

"Well, fine. I'll tell Hasse to leave things as they were in the villages of Raasiku," Antonius said, yawning. "Will that do?"

"Hmm-mm, I suppose so . . ." Bal murmured.

"And what more can I do?" asked Herr Antonius in a tone which

* And what is this actually about? (German). † Most Wise Father (German).

made it clear that there was not much more he could do, and he half smiled, as though finding his own helplessness amusing. "I could threaten to have him condemned by the Church if he disobeys me. Even if he believed I could do it, he would just laugh. As a Lutheran. Well, *bene*. But now tell me, who are you?"

He took the green bottle and poured Bal's glass half-full. "Drink!" Bal hesitated, and Herr Antonius added: "Courage! I don't have the Spanish disease. The one the Germans call the 'French disease'. Here we should actually call it the 'German disease', isn't that so? And in Moscow it would be called 'Polish', and in Kazan the 'Moscow malady', and so on. In accord with the law of loving one's neighbour." He turned to his pimply translator: "Tell the old man to wait outside."

Jakob having retreated from the room, Herr Antonius directed Bal to sit, and as Bal restively fingered the stem of the wine goblet, he said:

"You're not that man's son, are you? But his nephew, maybe – that's possible."

Bal nodded.

"Well then. *Primo*. You speak educated German. But you are too young to have learned it anywhere but at the town school. Am I right?"

Bal nodded.

"So. *Secundo*. But you do not have a position anywhere. Is that correct? Because a young man with a position would not come and play translator for his country bumpkin uncle. *Tertio*."

"I'm studying at the town school."

"Ah! A *primaner*?"

Bal nodded. He had removed his hand from the goblet, and Herr Antonius refilled it, taking small sips as he continued: "An educated Estonian is such a rarity that if he exists he must be confoundedly smart." With that he suddenly emptied the goblet, filled it to the brim, and set it in front of Bal again.

"You know that Moscow is planning to attack Livonia?"

"I've heard it said."

"And that the Master of the Order, Galen, is ill?"

"There's a rumour to that effect . . ."

"But who will take his place?"

"Who knows . . . In Tallinn they're saying, maybe Herr Fürstenberg."

"I see. But in that case Moscow is bound to put up a fight."

"Why?"

"Because Moscow considers Fürstenberg too partial to Denmark. But I'm interested in something else. Tell me, what will the Estonian peasant do in the event of war? Your uncle, for example?"

Bal was silent.

"Will he wring Hasse's neck?"

"Well . . . no . . ." Bal protested, startled.

"*Bene*," said Herr Antonius, laughing. "Let's say he won't, if Hasse lets him go freely to the market in Tallinn. He is, after all, one of the more well-to-do men in his village. Am I right? But what will the poorer peasants on the nobles' manors do?"

Bal could feel his left shoulder about to twitch, as it had each time when he was younger and struck by uncertainty, but he managed to be a man and stay motionless. Something in him – not simple distrust but a kind of stubbornness – began to seethe in resistance against Antonius' overbearing interrogation.

Antonius said: "Moscow has claimed Livonia as its age-old hereditary domain. Denmark makes the same claim – with somewhat greater justification. The Kaiser has promised us to the Swedes. The Finnish Johan wants to get us for himself. But there's a strong faction in the Order, convinced that our only true saviour is Sigismund of Poland. Tell me, which king would the Estonian peasant choose?"

Bal could see how Herr Antonius' questions were driving him into a corner. Why the devil did he have to answer this stranger's questions? Especially when he could not even answer them for himself? Why the devil should he put up with this? Something in him made him clench his jaw. The corners of his round eyes suddenly narrowed, but his tone was almost naïve as he asked:

"But which king would the esteemed monks of Padise choose as their ruler?"

Herr Antonius burst out laughing. "Oh . . . we are a dead house. There are only eleven of us monks left, including the abbot. So our preference is of no importance . . . Well, then. I won't waste any more of your time." He yawned lightly, set his legs back on the sofa, and picked up his little white book. Before he opened it he said, smiling:

"An educated Estonian is just as mistrustful as a yokel."

Jakob was waiting for Bal at the gate of the steward's cottage, and Bal was giving Jakob an account of what had happened, when Jürgen came up to them. He listened to Bal's tale and muttered: "The devil only knows what'll come of this muddle." And then he described what had happened: He had been waiting for Bal and his father in the dooryard, walking back and forth in front of the house, his hands behind his back. He had walked past one end of the house and stopped at the corner near the garden. The rear wall of the house was hidden behind a thicket of overgrown raspberry bushes, and through the open window he had heard his father's voice. He had ducked around the bushes and drawn closer to the window, and there he saw him, that same cursed Jürg, his namesake, that damn Ruunaboy, the one they had run into at the gate, who was working as a house boy here for Hasse. He was was squatting under the open window and of course heard every word Jakob spoke – the bloody spy! Later, when the talk continued in German, he crept away, straightening up once when he got to the bushes. 'Cause of course, he couldn't understand German – the tattling jaybird! But all the things Father said – he would no doubt take them straight to the steward as fast as his legs could carry him! He had smarts enough for that.

Jakob listened to his son with pursed lips, unhitched his horse from the fence post, and climbed into the saddle in silence. Bal had mounted already. Jürgen was still standing next to his horse when that same skinny boy came towards them from the garden. He seemed even more stooped than earlier, a smirk on his broad, freckled face.

"Well ... ah ... how did it go for the gentlemen ... ?"

Jakob turned his horse around without a word and galloped off. Bal met the boy's squinting glance and looked away stiffly, thinking uneasily: *why the dickens should I turn my eyes away?* Then he heard a thud: it was the wooden fence cracking. Jürgen was on his horse and Ruunaboy was half-lying against the fence, holding his chin with both hands, blood trickling down between his fingers.

"You ... damn devil ... you'll regret this!" he shouted at the departing riders.

The singing of larks sounded high above the morning fog which hovered over the fields, but it was lifting, promising a beautiful day. They walked single file over fresh, cool grass and budding dandelions – Jakob, Jürgen, both the farmhands, Küti-Jaan with his wife, Aunt Kati, Epp, Märten and Bal. They were all carrying axes and billhooks on their shoulders and food sacks on their backs, and their pace was hurried because the field they were to clear was apparently the size of six or seven bushel fields. By rights Bal and Märten should have been walking in front with the men, but Bal preferred to take up the rear. From there he had the best overview of the group. Märten stayed behind to keep him company. They could see the grey backs and square shoulders of the men, and the women's necks under their dotted bonnets, and Epp's light loose hair, and her legs glistening with the dew. In the course of half a mile she turned around twice and both times Bal felt something like a little stab in his stomach.

They walked over the sun-striped heath towards the shade of the woods. Bal forgot arithmetic and the Articles of Augsburg. He felt, half consciously, how the soles of his feet arched and how light they felt, and he tried to set his toes down soundlessly so that not a twig would crack ... It was impossible to say whether he was affected more by the memory of primitive forefathers hunting in the wilderness or the more recent war games of the village boys in Kalamaja.

The woods seemed to be turning into dense forest, but then shrank again to a marshy thicket until the path started rising to a ridge graced with alders and birches.

"This here is Lammassaar, then," said Epp over her shoulder to the town boys. Jakob had been walking at the head of the group until now. But as they started to ascend, the old man nodded to his son to take the lead and let the others pass him; he himself turned left into a stand of hazelnut trees. Even as Bal signalled to Märten with his chin and pulled on his sleeve to hold him back, he was unaware of what had aroused his curiosity.

Epp's fair head had disappeared into the bushes as she followed on the heels of the others. Bal gestured to Märten and they set off in the direction his uncle had taken. Moving quickly, they soon caught sight of Uncle Jakob's back through the trees. They followed him at a safe distance until they arrived, about a hundred paces later, at the southern end of the ridge. Over the tops of the low firs and sparse birches rose a spreading oak scarred by numerous lightning bolts. In the midst of the yellow-green springtime buds it looked all the blacker and more naked. Here and there on its twisted branches dangled clusters of the previous year's rust-brown leaves. When Uncle Jakob stopped at the tree, the boys hid in the hazel bushes. They had a clear view of the scene. Uncle Jakob took off his hat and put it on the ground. Then he opened his coat, untied his blue-striped woven belt, laid it out in front of him on the grass, and knelt on it. Bal could see dirt on the soles of his soft peasant shoes, toes touching, heels apart. They called to mind two timid animals stretching their snouts towards the ground and each other, ready at any instant to spring back and disappear . . . Then his uncle raised the rope of the little keg hanging over his shoulder, lifted it up over his head, and from the way his shoulders and hands moved it was clear that he was working the stopper – until he managed to pull it out. Bal heard the soft sound of liquid pouring onto the grass. After this, Uncle Jakob set the keg down beside him, tipped back his head, and raised his gnarled hands – their backs turned outward – up as high as his grey-streaked hair, so that one could see how he tried to straighten out his bent fingers and then let them fold down again. For a moment he stood there, unmoving, staring into the black crannies of the tree trunk, and only then did Bal hear the low sound of his murmuring. Try as he might, he could not make out the words. He could not even be certain that the murmuring consisted of words. Then the old man got up, tied the belt around his waist, slung the keg over his shoulder, picked up his hat, and backed a few steps away from the tree. When he reached the first hazel bushes he turned around, put on his hat, and started back down the trail the way he had come, passing fairly close by the bushes where the boys were lying on their stomachs, hiding. When he had disappeared into the hazel grove, they got up.

For some unfathomable reason Bal gestured to Märten to stay where he was. His astonishment at the strangeness of what he had witnessed gave way to excited curiosity and he drew closer to the oak, to where his uncle had knelt. He could see flecks of white foam on some blades of grass and the cool, sour scent of barley beer rose from the ground. Bal's glance travelled up the rough oak bark, into the thick web of branches at its crown. He would have liked to listen, to see whether he could hear last year's leaves rustling up above, but the early-morning birds in the surrounding bushes were chirping so noisily that he could hear neither leaves nor silence. But when his glance slipped back down the massive trunk – *it would take four men to circle the trunk* – and along the fissures and ridges and sooty lightning scars in the bark, he suddenly saw a face: a sharp vertical furrow and eyebrows and two black eyeholes and a deep line from the wide nose to the thin mouth. He saw it all in an instant, with indelible clarity. Incredulous, he crossed himself. Had he dared to look within himself he would have recognised the sign as a protective gesture, and also as an expression of reverence. It was his town self that shrank in alarm from meeting the Devil, and his slumbering country self that had been stunned by the existence of an earth-god. Just then the face dissolved back into the bark of the tree. No matter how hard he tried he could not find it again. Apparently the sign of the cross had frightened it back into the tree trunk.

As they hurried through the bushes after Uncle Jakob, Bal asked in a whisper – and he was not at all sure it was entirely on account of Uncle Jakob:

"Did you see . . . ?"

"Of course."

"Aah . . . what?"

"The pagan prayer."

"No . . . the earth-god's face . . . in the tree?"

"No, I didn't . . . did you?"

"Yes . . . but do you believe they exist?"

"Earth-gods? Of course!"

"Why?"

"Why else do you think they're always telling us, from all the pulpits, that there's no such thing! When there's so much talk about how earth-gods don't exist, it's a sure sign that they do. And you yourself just saw one!"

"Yes I did . . . but, I don't know . . . just because you see something, doesn't mean it exists."

Having walked a few hundred paces they reached the clearing in the middle of the hilltop where the others had already set to work.

The birch grove – some decades old, on a plot of ground a couple of hundred paces long and nearly as wide – had been cut down and the felled trees stripped of their branches soon after snowmelt. The boughs and brush had been heaped into long stacks a cubit or two high, covering over two-thirds of the field. Visible within the grey tangle of branches, brushwood and yellowish catkins were stumps with spreading black roots and the white trunks of birches, a span or two thick. The Kurgla folk were hard at work at the edge of the prepared field. They were dragging or carrying the hefty birches, setting them more or less in rows down the length of the clearing, and lugging the brush and branches and stumps into piles, with the base of each trunk lying in the jumble of scrub and twigs that would most readily ignite and fuel the fire.

Bal was somewhat embarrassed to have arrived after all the others, especially because he would not have wanted to reveal where he and Märten had been. He could not stop thinking about what they had seen . . . *The earth-gods do, then, really exist . . . ?! But what about the people who believe in them – are the gods their secret misfortune? Or also their secret good fortune . . . ?* He hoisted a good-sized birch onto his shoulder, gripping it near the roots, and looked around to see where Märten was, wanting to ask him about these gods. But the farmhand, Paavel, a husky youth with a flat face and light-brown hair, had called Märten away to help him. Bal hauled his heavy birch to the nearest pile of firewood. Its weight made his feet sink into the soil as he dragged it, swaying and bumping over the hummocks, its top branches causing the grass to crackle. When he rolled the trunk off his shoulder the dust flew, the ground thudded, the branches cracked, and he caught sight of Epp on the other side of the heap, laying down an armful of branches. Freed of his burden, Bal felt for a moment as though he were weightless, growing taller by virtue of some sweet inner force, as though his feet were rising off the ground on their own.

When Bal went off for a second birch he thought back to what had happened the night before – or rather about why nothing at all had happened. Returning from the manor he had looked for Epp, but she was nowhere to be seen. Märten had told him he had spoken a few words with her but then had gone to look around the village and not seen her again. Not until shortly before dark that evening, when the family sat down to a hurried supper at the low table – bread and barley soup and fresh beestings – had Epp come for a moment to sit at the table opposite Bal, and in the dim light she had cast a few quick glances his way. And when everyone rose from the table, she had thanked Aunt Kati and said it was time for her to go home. And then Bal – he was standing at the door looking out at a large fir silhouetted against the copper-red sunset, its every needle sharp and black – had let her pass by him, and when she was already out in the dooryard but he still felt on his face the air she had stirred in passing, he said:

"Don't leave yet."

"I must—" she had replied softly.

"Why?" Bal had asked.

"I'm afraid—" she had said, coming to a standstill five steps from him.

"What are you afraid of?" Bal had asked, noting all the while how strange his voice sounded.

"You . . ." she had answered, the copper-kettle sky behind her.

"Hmmh!" was all Bal had been able to say.

Epp had said, practically in a whisper: "After all, they say you're not afraid of wolves. Who knows what you really are."

Bal had sensed that somewhere, in this hurried half-whisper, there was an uncertain boundary – on the one side a fear of werewolves, which probably was no sin at all, and on the other a coquettishness, called *vanitas*, which was most definitely a sin because to see it was such sweet delight.

Now, when Bal arrived with his second and third trees, Epp was there as well, on the other side of the piled firewood, her arms laden with branches. Both times, as he heaved the tree off his shoulder, he had the same sensation of sudden lightness, of his feet rising free of the ground. And both times Epp and he had exchanged a singularly unnerving and yet somehow anticipated look through the heap of twisted root stumps with their clinging reddish soil and criss-crossed branches and catkins. The third time, Bal asked:

"Well, do I still frighten you?"

"I don't know . . ." Epp said, turning her small, flushed face towards him for an instant. "Not so much, by daylight . . ."

When Bal went for his fourth birch he noticed that the shoulder seam on his jacket had torn. He had, of course, intentionally selected the heaviest trees and hoisted them with calculated carelessness onto his shoulder, heaving them off just as casually. He hung the torn jacket on a birch at the edge of the woods and stretched himself with relish. His skin was hot. His muscles hummed under his coarse shirt. Somewhere behind him he could hear the Kurgla folk – the whack of the billhook and the murmur of conversation. Right there, near him, a clamorous hedge sparrow chirped excitedly and the birch grove with its first tiny buds gave off the fragrance of fresh, unfermented mead . . . *And the wolves backed away, and blood dripped from the chins of informers, and earth-gods did exist* . . . He was abruptly struck by the realisation – no longer merely alarming but thrilling – that what was happening here in the woods was strictly forbidden . . . and dangerous. Yes, indeed, if an informer were to notify the manor that Jakob of Kurgla had made a secret clearing at Lammassaare, the manor would confiscate all that had been cut in this patch of forest. Even before the barley they intended to plant there the next day had sprouted, Jakob would be ordered to appear at the manor. His back would be bloodied by whiplashes; he would be locked into a cellar for ten days on bread and water and mouldy flour

broth; and he would be fined and have to deliver a lamb to the manor
... But in fact none of what Bal envisaged was likely to happen, because
even if some tale-bearer got wind of their doings and went to report on
them at the manor, he would probably not go to Master Hasse but to the
overseer: just the previous week Jakob had paid a friendly visit to that
damn fellow to deliver a piglet as pay-off. Still, there was no escaping
the suppressed and increasing urgency in their work. From time to time
Bal looked towards the woods – *did human demons skulk there alongside
the earth-gods?* He stretched his body, feeling content with the morning's work, but also uneasy, a sensation that grew, almost imperceptibly,
along with the pace of their labours.

" So – you're not afraid of me any more ... ?" Bal asks, shifting scattered brushwood onto a fallen trunk.

"I don't know ..." says Epp, busying herself with the pile of branches
at her side. And when Bal remains silent she flashes him a look from
under her pale-blond shock of hair, her face rosy, a streak of dirt on her
left cheek, flakes of birch bark scattered in her hair: "I remembered
something about you ... and I felt afraid again ..."

"Well now, what was there to remember?"

"The way you were at your grandfather's funeral ..."

"And what way was that?"

"As though you don't know!"

Of his grandfather's funeral last August Bal does indeed know some
things, but there are others he really does not understand.

It happened that when his grandfather died – a most quiet and ordinary death on his plank-bed, under his sheepskin, so that the family
only became aware of it the following morning – Aunt Kati wanted him
to be properly buried in the churchyard. But the others thought: Why
do that? The churchyard was inconvenient and far away, the church
costly and unfamiliar, and the old man needed just to be taken quietly to
the old graveyard on the hill where the dead of the village had always

been buried (with the exception of Juhan of Uue-Pärtli farm and two or three younger souls who had over the past ten years been laid to rest by the church). Jakob, who had been running the farm for several years already and bore the combined responsibilities of head-of-household and son, and who in that capacity had to make the decision, found it was actually all the same to him. He feared that the pastor might object if the burial were carried out in the old way, and yet if done according to church custom the crops might fail, so either choice could prove unhappy. When Bal came in for the funeral from town – Siimon could not because he was en route to Riga with the year's first caravan – Jakob found a way to resolve the burial question which left both sides more or less satisfied: the old man would be put under in the old burial ground alongside his forefathers, but Bal, who was after all a learned boy, more so than some churchmen, would give him a Christian blessing. So Bal had intoned the blessing. Now he recalls the scene:

His grandfather is in the bedchamber, in a narrow fir coffin with a burial cap on his head. A wooden candlestick rests on a stool nearby and the candle is wildly flickering, for the smoke vent is open, and along with the cold moonlight of October, 'the month of strong spirits', wind and powdery snow are blowing into the room. Standing next to the coffin are Jakob with Aunt Kati, and Uncles Peep and Taavi, who live somewhere near Kodasoo Marsh, and their wives, and Jürgen with his cousins, and neighbours and farmhands, both men and maids, and little children – altogether about fifty souls, counting the relatives here in the chamber and others assembled at the door. And in the chamber there is the scent of fir branches, and in the main room the rising steam of the barley porridge prepared for the funeral guests. And then he, Bal, steps up next to the old man. He has seen this kind of thing enough times, many times – at school, when he was in *quarta* and *tertia* and went to sing at funerals with the choirmaster and ten other boys, the ones with the purer voices. But he has only sung on those occasions, he has never had to speak. Well, actually, he *has* spoken a few times – homilies and blessings and mild reproofs and yes, probably even words of farewell for the dead – but only to the seagulls or to rocks along the shore or to his stone cannon balls up on the ledge in the barn. But now he is standing next to his grandfather, looking at his eighty-year-old hands, which Aunt Kati has crossed over his chest today – hands heavy as stone and now eternally free – he is looking at them and cannot take his eyes off them. But he has to begin, because fifty people are waiting, and he speaks, almost in a whisper: *"What do I, child of man, know of life and death . . . ?"*

Bal cannot recall exactly what it was that he had said. But he remembers the feeling – his words like a shower of falling stars. Nor can Epp recall what it was. But she does remember that for the first time in her life she had understood everything that was said in church on such an occasion. And she remembers, that in the bluish winter light of the room, by faint yellow candlelight, she could see on the awakening faces around her the same wonder – they had all understood everything. She remembers the tremor in her soul. And from that time the same tremor returns whenever her thoughts turn to this boy.

She is not afraid of the tremor, of course, oh no – she cherishes it. The boy who spoke the magical words at the old man's funeral does not scare her but compels her to look at him, albeit secretly, as she did from the first, and is doing so now, even here, in this clearing. Nor is she afraid of the boy who yesterday bellowed like a bull on the stove at Kurgla farm – no, that just makes him all the more *one of them* . . . But what frightens her is that the boy with the magic words and the boy who bellowed like a bull – and the one who, as Märten put it, went right up to the jaws of wolves and put them to flight – is one and the same person. *This* truly frightens her . . . for even though she had miraculously understood the boy's words at his grandfather's funeral, she does not now understand where the captivating part of this boy begins and the frightening bit of him ends, nor where his saintliness ends and the witchery begins . . .

And Bal suddenly realises something . . . that his skin is hot not because of all the logs he has hauled since morning, and that he is anxious not because of the secret clearing they are preparing here, and that his heart is winged and triumphant not on account of the wolves he put to flight. He is feeling all these things because of this girl.

Their work is finished. Their stacks of wood lie fifty paces from the untouched forest. The strip of earth between forest and field has been carefully cleared of all brush and debris so that no passing wind can carry sparks from the fire to the surrounding trees. Those who have been working in the rear are also straightening up, for the clearing appears to be ready to be burned. They can hope, given the steady east wind, that from what they sow tomorrow they will reap at least a dozen good, clean grains (whereas a clearing burned during the north wind grows full of weeds). And the burning of the field should go well and pose no threat to the forest. Someone is shouting from the rear. When Epp and Bal look in that direction, they see Uncle Jakob, his hands cupped, calling to them.

"Hoo-hoo! Stop now and eat something!"

Bal takes his coat and food pouch from the birch branch, and Epp brings hers from a rowan bush. They sit next to each other on a log at the edge of the brush pile. Bal cuts a piece of his town bread for Epp to try, and Epp gives him a piece of country bread in exchange. When they unpack their herring the fish get mixed up, so that they cannot distinguish those from Jõelahtme River from those that came from Kalamaja. And since Bal has nothing to drink, they take turns drinking cool birch brew from Epp's little juniper-fragrant keg. It does not cool them down, however. Suddenly they both feel hot, as though they have passed the warmth of their lips from one to the other by drinking from the same keg, the warmth having flowed into the drink and into them, in the process growing a hundred times hotter. God knows how and where town boys – even those wearing simple sparrow-grey jackets (with a ripped shoulder seam, to boot) – learn those awful scholars' tricks! And it is not certain that even God knows just *how different* such fellows are – those who are part-bumpkin, part-town boy – compared to real scholars and young artisans . . . And a country girl from Kurgla and Uue-Pärtli could not know anything at all about this, of course. Still, when a gentleman-scholar or journeyman-artisan suddenly puts his arms around a country girl and showers her with kisses under God's own blue sky, and intends to do who-knows-what else, this does not necessarily mean all that much . . . But a half-homespun sparrow-grey boy who can stare down wolves could become desperately caught up in it, in all its sincerity and burning ardour, so that all his life, whenever he thinks back on it, he will feel hot – to say nothing of the country girl. In any event, Epp suddenly finds his arms around her and Bal's lips find her soft, burning cheek and then her mouth, tasting of juniper and birch brew.

"Yoo-hoo," calls out Uncle Jakob. "Let's light the fire." Bal takes flint, steel and a piece of tinder from his tinder pouch and a little bunch of straw from his food sack. His hands tremble slightly – no doubt because he has worked so hard all morning. He has almost returned to himself. And yet he notices that next to his acting self is another, strangely distant self, holding himself apart yet present all the same. This other self barely sees how the straw whooshes into flame, or how the bunched bark catches fire, how white lengths of bark in the midst of the flames curl up with a sigh. This other self barely notices how the dry mound of debris crackles as it begins to burn and how the flames lick at the greener brush and how the black smoke of the dry wood mixes with the grey and steamy smoke of the damp wood, and how the same kind of fires in six, seven, eight places spew smoke full of sparks until they all finally blend into one swirling milky riot.

This other self sees only Epp.

131

Nor does he later remember much more than her resistance and surrender. And the departure. Flakes of ash in the air. Fireworms on the ground. A tuft of grass, with a transparent yellow tongue licking at it, directly in front of their feet, until it trembles, turns white and disappears. And the red tails of flames leaping about in the smoke and on the piles of brushwood and turning somersaults on the bark of the birches. Fire devils. Fire angels. And he remembers that *earth-gods do exist and blood drips from the chins of informers and wolves flee*. And a blooming knoll of flowers known as "keys of heaven" ringed by young birches. And Epp's sooty, burning face in the midst of the flowers. And her light blue eyes, suddenly dark-blue and full of fire-squirrels. And Epp's body.

The early mornings in May this year are chill, and on the sprouting fields in Vaskjala lies a film of frost. But Bal's and Märten's backs are damp by the time they cross the footbridge and hurry towards town. The barley will be sown tomorrow, without their help, in the warm ashes at Lammassaare, because Bal is supposed to be back at school that very day, after the midday meal. He did not have permission for a longer visit from Herr Rector. Had it been up to sour Herr Tegelmeister, he would not even have had as much time as he did. That man would have wrinkled his nose, his watery eyes bulging, and said: "Young man, as *primaner* at the town school, it is not proper that you gad about with yokels. But if it should be your misfortune to have relatives among them, you should be mature enough by now to not encourage this – ahem! – situation. *Veto!*" But luckily Rector Tegelmeister's lifelong ambition had recently been realised: he was now pastor of St Nicholas' Church. The new rector was Master Sum, a much milder man who had preferred the opposite course, having exchanged his position as pastor for that of schoolmaster. With this friendly Herr Sum, Bal has been on good terms from the start, almost as good as those with Meus in the old days. So that on this day he will be back at school at twelve o'clock by all means – "like a copper shilling", as they say. Speaking of shillings, they are not exactly raining down on Märten's back either – the ones he will get from the foreman of merchant Krumhusen's warehouse when he returns today at noon to clean out the cellars of the storehouses. It has been rumoured that the merchant wants to bring his goods from Narva to Tallinn. And he is a member of the Narva Council, no less. But the Council there is apparently increasingly uneasy about rumours of war. That is something to take up with Bal, but the two friends do not talk much this morning. Not that there has been a falling-out between them. But Märten of course knows the whole story concerning Epp, the way friends do, without having to ask. Maybe there is, in his silence, the trace of a two-pronged jealousy: that of a friend and that of a rival. Märten is a true friend. And every boy is a bit of a rival. But all that is secondary because Märten understands he cannot talk about Epp. It would be unseemly to joke about her and futile to speak seriously. And to talk of anything else at this time would be pointless . . .

At the Lehmja oak grove they decide to sit down to rest and eat. Perched on the roots of the oak, Bal suddenly recalls something from that morning. As they were setting out in the early dawn he saw the farmhand, Paavel, stretched out on his stomach on the rail fence, watching them. They only noticed him late, and Bal called out: "Good morning! And farewell! Until next time!" But Paavel remained silent, continuing to look at them, his dark hat pulled down over his light eyebrows . . . Why was he staring at them like that? Bal cannot work it out. Suddenly he notices that Märten's food pouch, which on the way out of town was fairly flat, is bulging. He cannot understand this either. It is difficult enough just to regain his equilibrium. He is still riding a high wave – on its crest, the youthful joy of a world conqueror; in the trough, a poor sinner's fear of Hell; and overhead, in the sea fog and the smoke, Epp's happy, tear-streaked face – he gazes at it tenderly, fondly, remorsefully. Bal leans against the tree and squeezes his eyes shut. He sees two oval, dark-blue lakes of flaming-red squirrels swimming . . .

When he opens his eyes Märten is pulling something out of his sack – something that looks like a grey shadow-picture of the flames in the firewood.

"Märten! . . . what kind of sorcery . . . what are those . . . ?"

"Huh? These? Pelts – squirrel pelts! The bread got buried under them."

"Where'd you get them?"

"From Küti-Jaan. Kimmelpenning buys them."

"And what is your role in this business?"

"I'm working for myself – earning three pence a pelt."

CHAPTER FIVE,

in which a young man, in whose clothing the smell of woodsmoke can be detected even by someone with a stuffy nose, is astonished to find himself in the game room of grandees, where he begins to see entire provinces played as stakes in a card game and notices that, sitting behind the players, but soon joining them at the card tables, are – God forbid – crowned heads!

The great political card game did not, of course, take place in what was now Meus and Annika's apartment – the former dwelling of the bishop's coachman, or perhaps of his house steward. And the cubicle behind the kitchen, the former pantry, was an even less probable site for such an event. Though its whitewashed walls were unusually high, the room was barely four cubits long and scarcely the same in width. Its vaulted ceiling sloped unevenly for it was partitioned off from the kitchen by an insubstantial brick wall. Bal moved in with Meus and Annika in the autumn of 1557, when the new school year began. It was not Annika's idea to put him into this cubicle; she wanted him to settle himself in their great-room, but Bal insisted on taking over this former pantry, which was being used only for storage. And in the end he got his way.

There was no stove in his cubicle. In the cold weather the low wooden door with its huge iron hinges was kept open to the kitchen, and enough heat came in from the fire in the hearth below the hooded chimney to prevent Bal from having to warm his hands over the flame. And on his plank bed the old fur-lined coat that Siimon had worn on his winter trips was protection against all cold. There was room enough on a shelf affixed to the headboard for the ten or so books that Bal had borrowed from Meus and Herr Sum. And he managed to write out his *exercitia styli* in even rows despite the uneven surface of the narrow desktop that he and Meus had cobbled together with odds and ends of lumber and blacksmith's nails. On one occasion Herr Sum shook his head, smiling indulgently at Bal's excessively exuberant script, but still gave him a grade of *maxime*.

The main reason, of course, for Bal moving in with Annika and Meus was that from their place it was a mere three hundred paces to his school, whereas from his father's house in Kalamaja the distance was almost half a league. He had already been eating his dinners at Annika's for more than a year. And, everything else apart, life at his father's had lately become boring. He could of course have transported all his books there, but after Annika's departure the house had seemed empty. Old lady Truuta, the seventy-year-old determined penny-pincher whom Father had hired as housekeeper, did nothing to make the place more appealing. Father himself was seldom in town during winter. And aside from Märten there were not many young people left in Kalamaja who would drop in to the house anymore. Once in a while, true, a few schoolmates would wander in. Once, in fact, a group of six or seven of them had appeared at Bal's door and on the table set down little flasks of wine pulled out of their coat pockets. They were mostly *prima* students, merchants' sons, and a few younger ones as well, including Dung of the Orient Balzer Vegesack. Bal had been uncomfortably am- bivalent about what to do – whether to call out to his guests: Hello there . . . come in, sit down, sit down. And tell old Truuta, with the authority of the man of the house: I have guests! Bring out the best that we have! (The temptation was strong.) Or to say to the boys: Dear friends, you made the long trek here over snowdrifts for one reason only . . . this is such an out-of-the-way place that the story of your carousing won't reach the Rector's ears. I thank you for your trust, but . . . But just then

Siimon had unexpectedly arrived and, standing in the middle of the room in his sealskin boots with their turned-up toes, had brought Bal's dilemma to a quick end: "Boys! You are welcome, but there'll be no drinking here!" Bal still remembered glancing at his father and struggling with himself about whether to say: Wait . . . look . . . this fellow is Balzer Vegesack . . . But he had said nothing, even though his ego had suffered a bit, and the young scholars had left muttering. He had kept silent, actually, because of a fear that he himself did not quite understand, an apprehension, perhaps, that if his father learned who this Balzer Vegesack was he would snap his feet together politely and say, with a smile on his thin lips: Ah . . . well then . . . of course . . . And in that case, he, Bal, would have pitied the old man, and himself as well.

In general, a barely perceptible sense of pity had begun to plague him under the low, split-log ceilings of Kalamaja. A feeling that should perhaps have bound him more firmly to this particular low dwelling, but which in fact drew him towards the more exciting life in town. And in giving in to that urge he felt somehow guilty but yielded to it nonetheless.

The matter was settled with his father quite quickly:

"Ah, to Annika's . . . ? To be closer to school? Of course!" His father had looked hard at him, and then past him: "Well, in any case – sooner or later. Fine. I'll talk to Meus and find out how much he wants for room and board."

When Siimon approached him with his question, Meus cited the Gospel of Matthew: *And Jesus went . . . and cast out all them that sold and bought* . . . At this the corner of the old man's mouth began to twitch and he said to Meus: "Ah-ah-ah . . . That passage refers to God's house." And to Bal he said: "So you are going to live for free in God's house. Well then, what more is there to say?" And the old man made no further offers of payment – for Meus might, of course, have reconsidered – and with that the matter was settled.

Once the question of his lodging was sorted out, the matter of his room took no time. For the storeroom at the back of the kitchen had one marvellous feature: it had the only window opening directly onto the Old Market. The window was located in a splendid façade – with paintings of the Apostles dating back to the time of the popes – directly above the arched gateway to the courtyard. And even though scarcely a square cubit in size, and set in a wall so thick that to look out Bal had to stretch out on his stomach on the stone sill, the entire town lay before him as though in the palm of his hand – not in the sense of lying far below or at a great distance or as a whole. It was only visible in part, yet it appeared all very close and in wonderfully clear detail.

Looking to the right you can see almost everyone who is heading to the New Market in front of the Town Hall. Whether sellers coming to town through the Viru Gate or buyers from the eastern quarters of the town – they all cross the Old Market directly under your window: the country folk from the villages beyond Lasnamäe Hill and Lake Ülemiste, their soft-soled peasant shoes tapping, their creaking wagons laden with wooden vessels, bowls and sacks, with squealing pigs and bleating lambs and mooing heifers; the artisan journeymen and master craftsmen with their spouses from the neighbouring streets, and servant girls in grey skirts from Viru and Munkade and Karja Streets; and later in the day, the wives of merchants, holding up their silk skirts with bejewelled fingers as they pick their way in fashionable, dainty shoes, around straw and refuse and cowpats and horse manure. For the most part the crowds just flow by here and disappear around the corner of the Warehouse. Many do not, they go on circling about their business right here, in and out of shops under your very window.

Look to the left and the scene is even more exciting. Pulling up in front of the Warehouse are big-wheeled cargo wagons coming from the harbour, laden with all kinds of mysterious goods packed into hogsheads, barrels, casks, boxes and bundles, sometimes giving off unusual odours, sometimes still wet from the waves that washed over the sides of the barges. Carters, their faces sweaty, their backs bent, dash between the wagons with their incredibly wide carts and barrows loaded with merchandise. And the hirelings of the Warehouse haul bags and boxes on stretchers or on their backs or on handcarts through the vaulted doorways into the buildings. Barrels rumble down log ramps; carters and wagoners call and shout, laughing and cursing, and horses crunch their hay. From time to time councilmen and merchants step out in black velvet hats and short capes of fine brown wool to look over the merchandise with the Warehouse clerks, and their mouths move as they nod or shake their heads and wave their hands, and above the voices in the market one can guess at names and sums and quantities from the movement of their lips:

"Danzig."

"Bremen."

"Tiles."

"Malmsey."

"Amsterdam."

"Twelve hundred pieces . . ."

"Fifteen marks per cask . . ."

Sometimes a procession winds across the market square behind the corner of the Warehouse, heading towards Karja Gate. And then the buying–selling–dealing comes to a halt, and the din of the marketplace subsides. The Court's attendants, sullenly feigning indifference, accompany a poor sinner on his final walk. Executioner Brun follows, swaying sideways, hairy chest visible under his open red jacket, whistling quietly, casting defiant looks at the market crowd. On days like this he does not cast down his eyes, for on days like this he is indispensable to the town. And in a moment of silence – broken only by horses chewing their oats – one can hear women taunting the guilty man: "What a no-good!". . . or maybe young girls sighing, "Oh, what a handsome man . . ." And then the beggars in the crowd stretch out their hands more boldly and shake their hats more piteously, and pennies and shillings clink into them, for the grim example of the wages of sin strikes fear into the townspeople, making them open their purses even wider than usual.

In the afternoon the activity subsides. The farm wagons depart. Shutters are put up in shops. The beggars count the day's pickings in the shadows of the town gates and scatter, some to taverns, some to the Almshouse. And then bursts of grey October rain empty the square. Only a few hungry stray dogs are left to root around in the mud and garbage and to growl over especially large morsels. But when the rain stops and patches of blue again appear in the sky, the sounds of guns and drums and trumpets can be heard from the Great Guild. And even here, on the Old Market, gates clank open and curious servants rush into the street and run in the direction of the celebration. And the blare swells, for hired horn players from Haapsalu and drummers from Toompea Castle have come to help out Tallinn's own town band. The sound of horses' hooves grows louder, as though an entire company of horsemen were approaching at full gallop along Munkade Street, and the wedding procession of the Right Honourable Knight Diter Kruse and the Right Honourable Lady Elsbet Anprei trots into view from the direction of the cloister. First comes the groom's retinue. The groom himself is barely twenty, a slightly tipsy, fair-haired youth on a fine roan. Next to him ride his portly papa and proud mama (née Katharina von Tisenhusen), and in their wake a hundred nobles decked out in gold chains and feathered hats. And they are all sitting high on impressive stallions and lively steeds, their cavorting, gambolling horses similarly festooned with gold and feathers and all manner of other decoration. Each horse costs the equivalent of nine measures of rye, with no other function in life than to prance in this kind of procession. The groom of course looks happy, as a groom should. But his father too is merry, and that is something to give one pause. Yes indeed, Herr Kruse, Senior – he is in fact barely forty – laughs so hard that his white teeth flash in his wine-flushed face, and his grey eyes proudly survey the scene around him. His face betrays not the least sign of what is being bruited about town: to wit, that it is he who, in a few weeks, will bear the grave responsibility of heading Bishop Hermann's delegation to Moscow. He is charged with delivering the sixty thousand silver marks with which Livonia once again has to buy peace from the terrible Ivan. True, the sixty thousand has not yet been procured. But the Diet has decided to obtain it, for the destruction of Livonia cannot be averted in any other way. And it should not be too difficult to get the money. For if this wedding party – including the bride's retinue, which is approaching from the other side of Old Market, similarly richly attired and heading noisily towards the Great Guild – if this wedding party were to cast into the centre of the square all their gold chains, necklaces, rings, pearls and beads, their costly armour, helmets, feathers, spurs and medallions, and add to it the value of their horses, half the sixty thousand would already be in hand.

Lost in these musings, Bal suddenly heard the door creak open; it was Meus entering his room. He had paid his brother-in-law fairly frequent visits since Bal moved in, more often, in fact, than might have been expected from the Herr Pastor of St Olaf's Church. This peasant boy, his former pupil, had become his relative and was now becoming a friend. For Bal, Meus' friendship provided a new and different way of looking at the world – the perspective of one who had come from another place and belonged to another social class. He had at one point reluctantly arrived at the uncomfortable conclusion (which at times made him wince) – based on all that he had absorbed at home in Kurgla and at the Latin school and in town society – that everything the country people did, made and thought, though he might identify with it all on a sentimental level, was rather pitiful compared to the accomplishments of the Germans. Bal knew the plight of the rustic: the great cloud bank of society's injustice that hovered over a peasant's attempts to get an education, rarely letting through a ray of sunlight – the sense, in other words, that he was not master of his own life. From this cloud bank there came nothing but lightning bolts of insult and a steady drizzle of humiliation. Bal knew it all first-hand. But that this plight was not a creation of Our Lord and was rather an injustice wrought by men, this he heard now from Meus even more clearly than he had from old Siimon. And he found it more persuasive, coming from Meus. In the huts of Kalamaja one often heard people cursing into their cups of vodka and tankards of beer, fulminating against the stinginess and arrogance of the Germans. But at times it happened that someone would raise his nose above the rim of his cup and dare ask: "And who the devil needs these Germans in Mary's Land anyway?" Sometimes noses were lifted even higher and voices got louder, declaring the peasants' backs brawnier, their songs sweeter, their minds more supple than those of the stiff and stodgy Germans from Pomerania and Westphalia. Bal hailed from the outskirts, an area that was enough of a "bumpkinville" for its inhabitants to simultaneously envy and energetically mock the more successful would-be Germans who were becoming artisans and gaining acceptance into the ranks of true-born Germans. As a fifteen-year-old stripling he had fashioned for himself a myth of ethnic pride from the drink-fuelled, boastful tales he had overheard. But as a twenty-one-year-old graduating *primaner* from the Trivium School, having read not only Luther, Melanchthon and Livy but also the *Cosmographia universalis* of Sebastian Münster, he admittted that the consoling myth of his youth was but pitiful self-aggrandisement, and so he gave it up – feeling a little regretful and also a little superior. For what were our towns ten generations ago in comparison to the stone towns of Germany? What are the wailing folksongs of the old women of Harju compared to Ovid's hexameters? What is the flimsy *kannel* in the rooms of Kalamaja compared to the organ at St Olaf's Church?

And lo and behold – here is the German pastor of St Olaf's, walking through the creaking door into his chamber. And when Bal turns to his sister's husband and speaks in German: "*Du kommst zu spät die Krusesche Hochzeit zu schaun,*"* the pastor replies:

"Let's speak in country tongue."

"Fine," Balthasar says. "You want to practise it, don't you?"

"I do want to practise it," Meus replies, "but it is also a most beautiful language."

And in response to Balthasar's uncomprehending look he lifts his finger into the shaft of grey light from the window and says:

"Listen to this: *Kyll on se yx imeline ilos keel.†* Why, it sounds just like Pindar!"

By the way, Bal knows that Meus considers the peasants more hardworking than the Germans. And furthermore, Meus thinks that if they were treated honestly they would be more honest, on average, than the local Germans. And if they ate as well and had as easy a life, they would be healthier – even as it is, they have fewer cavities than do the Germans. And as for their bushy, coarse, wheat-coloured hair – which causes Bal some embarrassment in relation to his own head because among the Germans it is so noticeable – Meus considers it simply wonderful. Naturally, for Frau Annika Frolink has the same kind, and she exemplifies for him all the admirable qualities and dignity of country people. Which is why he comes to their defence. And in spite of his own youthful inclination towards a more critical stance, Bal drinks in Meus' words of regard.

It would be an exaggeration to say that Meus' "caper" of six years earlier has caused the pastor to suffer any overt social unpleasantness. Both the new head pastor, Herr von Geldern of St Olaf's, a rather proud gentleman, and Walther of St Nicholas', have treated him entirely

---

* You're too late to see the Kruses' wedding party (German).   † What a wondrously beautiful language this is (Estonian).

correctly. Yet from time to time he has sensed that they will never take that final step of granting him serious consideration, of regarding him as one of them, that is. Not to mention the fact that, at social events where the pastors' wives have also been present, he has detected a certain tone of voice that only someone of his even temperament would have described with a word as mild as "cool". Annika had her own way of reacting to this tone of voice. Once, when they were invited to the home of Pastor Walther of St Nicholas', where they met Frau von Geldern and her four daughters, Frau von Geldern wrinkled her nose at Annika's less-than-perfect German. Annika's green eyes flashed, and, when addressing one of the daughters, she referred to Frau von Geldern – in front of Frau von Geldern herself – as the girl's grandmother instead of as her mother. (Bad enough had she been talking to five-year-old Magdalena, but no, she chose seventeen-year-old Gertrude . . .)

"Oh, would Her Ladyship please pardon me . . . With my poor command of the language, I misunderstood . . . especially since . . . Well . . ."

From that day on Frau von Geldern was as stony as a fortress with Annika, but her cannons remained silent.

Annika managed to get over such things with admirable ease, and it was apparent that the ladies' snide references to her peasant origins had not succeeded in wounding her. She seemed not to notice them at all. Even after the death of her tiny baby, born in the third year of their marriage, Annika remained smiling and cheerful. When Bal chanced to look at her not as his older sister but as a stranger, he realised that she had become a remarkably beautiful and self-confident woman.

Meus clearly adored his wife. But he was not nearly as self-confident himself; gradually he began to worry more and more about the tensions created by Annika's proud bearing. His friendship with Bal provided him a refuge from the ongoing subtle battle he waged in defence of his wife's dignity.

True, no great social calamities resulted from this battle, but Meus noticed how his grey hairs had gradually spread. On his gaunt temples there was distressingly much more greyness, visible now as he stood in front of his wife's brother with raised finger, repeating in the tones of a sermon: "Just listen: *kyll onn se yx imeline ilos keel . . .*"

Then he lowered his hand and asked: "So, Herr Kruse rode by in his son's wedding procession? Well . . . They're holding a wedding and carousing and fondling their farthings and delaying so long that by the time they've finally collected the money they're planning to deliver to Moscow, Ivan's appetite will have doubled . . . Yes, Balthasar, I'm afraid war is inevitable."

"Why do you think that?"

"Herr Krumhusen wrote to me from Narva. He's from my region, from Treptow. He's done what he can to keep this war at bay. But now he's been to see the Grand Duke in Moscow, and he realises there's nothing more to be done. And Balthasar – this war will be the end of the Order's rule, because—" Meus stopped and they both listened. The steady cupping of a horse's hoofs broke the quiet of the afternoon, crossing the Town Hall Square to the Old Market, approaching the house, coming to a halt in front of it. And then someone was at the front door: *knock-knock-knock-knock!*

Herr Weselouwe had just last week moved into his other house on Rataskaevu Street, and there were no other inhabitants at the Bishop's House besides the Frolinks and Bal.

"Go and see who it is," Meus said.

Bal stretched as far as he could to look out of the window but saw only the backside of a well-fed dark horse and an empty saddle. Whoever was knocking was hidden from view. But he could tell by the gold embroidery on the black saddle blanket that it was most likely someone of distinction whom it would not do to hail from the window. He grabbed the keys from Meus and hurried downstairs. Opening a small rear door, he went down the corridor between two servants' rooms and arrived at the splendid great-room, nearly the size of a small church. Some of Weselouwe's magnificent cupboards from Holland still stood there, and the floor of white limestone from Padise seemed to reflect the rose-coloured log ceiling above. *Knock-knock-knock-knock!* The knocking was a command. Bal hurried to open the door.

Standing there was the town physician, *magister utriusque medicinae*, Doctor Matthias Friesner. That is who it was, of course – this man of medium height, slender, swarthy, slightly greying at the temples, with cool grey eyes, wearing a short black cloak. But for some reason Bal barely recognised him. He had never noticed that the Herr Physician was possessed of such impressive bearing and yet had such a kindly smile.

"But . . . Herr Doctor . . . there's no-one ill at this house," said Bal.

"God forbid that there be, my young friend! But I am the new owner of this house."

Stepping briskly, the Doctor walked past Bal, not stopping until he had reached the Dutch sandalwood table in the great-room. Here he turned on his left heel in a graceful chaconne step, black pointed beard making a three-quarter turn, and he smiled as he looked at Bal.

"Yes," he said, tapping on the table with the silver knob of his riding whip – *tap, tap, tap* – as if, even though already in the house, he were knocking to be invited even further in. "I've bought this house." He pointed with his whip to the cupboards and the table. "Along with whatever of Weselouwe's things are still here. And I see," he glanced casually around the room, "that things are in such good order here that I'll move in tomorrow. To get everything ready for my wife before she comes from the manor at Üksnurme."

"Oh . . ." Bal murmured, stunned. "Will we, in that case . . . I mean the Frolinks and I . . . will we have to look for a new apartment?"

"But no, not at all!" cried the Doctor in dismay. "I've heard only the best about the pastor. He's known to thousands of people here in town. And he knows thousands. That's no less important. And he has a lovely young wife. And you must be the young wife's brother. I know. In any case, let's go. I want to pay my respects to the pastor and his wife under my roof."

He walked ahead of Bal, across the courtyard and up the stairs, knocked on the Frolinks' door, went in without waiting for a response, kissed Annika's hand the way knights were said to at their celebrations before they got drunk, announced in passing that from then on the Church Treasury would be paying the Frolinks' rent to him as the new landlord, and then stopped in front of the bookshelf to survey with interest Meus' collection of religious books. But he did not take any down to leaf through. He drew his finger along the white-and-brown leather bindings and said, "Yes, deep wisdom . . . great learning . . . But whose ideas then does our Herr Pastor embrace – those of Flacius or Melanchthon?" But before Meus could answer, the Doctor looked at him with a smile and supplied his own: "Melanchthon's, of course. I conclude that from your kind eyes . . . Ah! these wars, these quarrels! . . . I know them. I'm from Kassel, after all. My childhood – that was the Peasant War. I know. My father was in Kassel, removing cataracts. He had a marvellously gifted hand. But he never became a doctor. You know how it is – the universities prefer the sons of merchants, or those with a strong Latin school education. Whereas his father was just a foreman in a coal mine. Still, in the end he became rich. For out of the hundred cataract patients he treated, ten got their sight back completely. And when the Count of Laurenburg happened to be among the lucky ones, he was so grateful that he showered Papa Friesner with gold, so that his son," here he pointed to himself, "could study at Marburg and Paris for seven years."

So, it's no wonder he managed to get two masters' degrees and learned how to tell the difference between the followers of Flacius and Melanchthon,

Bal thought, with a touch of resentment, even as he noticed the Doctor's black beard turn towards him.

"I don't recall who told me . . . wasn't it perhaps Herr Balder – a former patient of mine . . . came to me with the scabies – that this young man is planning to go abroad to study? Is that so? Theology, right? Like Pastor Frolink? Or perhaps he is going to follow in the footprints of Hippocrates?"

The stream of the Doctor's words was too rapid even for Meus, not to mention Bal, and they did not manage to respond before the Doctor said, with his penetrating glance and quick smile, even as he was turning away, "But we'll talk about all this more thoroughly when we are here together, under one roof . . . and when we have become friends."

Setting up housekeeping under one roof took very little time. The Doctor's servants came to clean and scrub the next day, a Sunday, just after services. And the furnishings were delivered on Monday morning, in five or six great wagonloads. The Doctor rode up alongside them on his shiny black mare, and under the sacred pictures on the façade of the Bishop's House he dispensed orders to the servants in great detail as to what to convey into which room. When Bal came home from school that afternoon the Doctor stopped him in front of the house, between the wagons.

"Good that you came, my young friend! Johann – that's my servant – is sick in bed with a fever since yesterday. I want to ask your help with something, alright?"

"Well . . . of course . . ."

"I have a couple of fragile boxes here . . . and especially one which I wouldn't want strangers to look into . . . It's this one here . . . I'm going to take this chest up myself right now, and then let's carry that one up together. Wait here!"

The Doctor picked up a two-foot-long brown chest painted with red flowers, tucked it under his arm and hurried into the house.

Bal stood with the packhorses and looked at the empty wagons and at the long box, this one without decoration, which he had been charged with guarding. What the devil could be in it? Curious market-goers milled around the wagons, gawping, and when a wide hay wagon and its shouting driver making his way to Kuninga Street passed too close by them, they jumped back, hurling curses at the driver. Loose hay rained down over Bal's back and neck. He stepped closer to the box, his curiosity over its contents growing. The movers had now taken the last chairs out of the wagons – eight ornately carved oak chairs. The men carried them upturned into the house, the seats on their heads to keep them from getting muddy. An onlooker whistled: "Cripes! Can you imagine what those cost! They look just like the ones in St Nicholas', the ones made by Master Andreas and his workmen. They cost one thousand six hundred and thirty thalers. I know that for a fact." Two movers emerged and took hold of the box Bal was guarding. When they raised it, a peg clattered into the empty wagon; it had apparently been pushed rather loosely into the hasp on the lid. "Wait! Wait," cried Bal. "The Doctor and I will carry that ourselves." Grumbling a bit, the workmen placed the box back onto the hay in the wagon. Bal laid one hand on the lid and with the other picked up the peg to push it through the hasp again. It was the right thing to do, but a sweet rush of curiosity got the better of him: *I'm going to take a look at what's in there* . . . Just to make sure, however, and without turning his head, he looked warily towards the house from the corner of his eye – and saw (oh, horrors!) the Doctor standing at an open window of the study, looking down. The certitude of instinct told Bal that the Doctor's gaze was fixed on his hand clutching the peg, the hand about to raise the lid specifically declared off-limits to strangers. With a deftness that would have surprised him had he stopped to think about it, he slipped the peg back into the hasp and brushed some chaff off the top of the box.

A moment later the Doctor was at his side and they carried it into the large study on the upper floor. Given its size, the box was not at all heavy, weighing only twenty or thirty pounds. The Doctor pulled a key from his trousers' pocket and opened an iron door in the corner of the room, revealing a vault in the thickness of the walls. The decorated chest was already there and the long box would not fit next to it, so they turned it on one end and wedged it in that way. When the Doctor had locked the iron-hinged door and put the key back into his pocket, Bal asked:

"But . . . what's in that box?"

"Ah," responded the Doctor. "Your curiosity won the day after all! But entirely legitimately. I saw how you managed to get the better of it down below, by the wagon."

Bal did not know whether he would ever need the good opinion of the Doctor. To tell the truth, he felt no particular desire to gain it. He had no reason to believe that he would gain his favour in this manner, nor did he take the trouble to think through his situation. He knew from his experience of school, if not of life, that he should now lower his eyes, twist his left foot in a bit, and say in a low voice: "But Jesus Sirach says – Chapter eleven, Verse nine – 'Do not involve yourself in another's business'." Yet he did not say this. Instead, he turned his round grey eyes to the Doctor's narrower and darker ones, and at the corners of his mouth, within a two-day stubble, flashed a quick self-conscious grin: "That's because I saw that you could see me."

The Doctor took a step backward and looked at him for a long moment. So long, that one could have counted to ten. Then he said quite audibly, "Hmm . . ."

Anyone who knows how to read behaviour would have been able to tell that the Doctor was thinking hard during the long moment in which he eyed Bal. Maybe Bal could sense it too. In any case he felt that the Doctor's tone was suddenly too light and easy; it was so clear that there was something else behind it.

"You want to know what's in the box? Well, why not?"

He took the key from his pocket again, clunked it around in the key-hole and opened wide the iron door in the wall.

"This will probably hardly surprise *you*. But please, not one word to *anyone else*. It would cause me unnecessary problems."

The Doctor pulled out the peg on the lid of the box and opened it, like a narrow door.

"Hmm . . ." Now it was Bal's turn to be left murmuring in surprise. Inside the long box, lined in black fabric, stood a greyish skeleton. It stared at him, its head slightly drooping, out of huge, empty eye s ockets.

"Livonia, of course, is fortunately a land of reason," said the Doctor with his irritatingly easy, self-satisfied smile. "That's clear. In my be-loved Germany they burn several hundred witches every year. But here, up to now, not a single soul has been sent to the pyre. Still, there's no point in provoking the dear Livonians. If it became bruited about town that I am in possession of such a fantastical thing, it would create an excessive stir among the otherwise reasonable citizens of Tallinn. So that, to repeat, just in case, do not talk about this to anyone."

"But what do you have it for?"

"Listen – not for purposes of witchcraft. First of all, it's an invest-ment. I paid three hundred thalers for it. Yes, I did. I had it delivered from Copenhagen. Second, I like having such an unusual item. Third, it might be useful to me some day: when a patient's health requires, for example, that the doctor make a deep impression on him." His self-congratulatory smile lit up for an instant and then faded. "Fourth, it pro-vides a clear picture of where a person's bones are located in relation to the others." He raised the skeleton's left hand and waved it up and down in front of Bal's face. "The ligaments are of silver wire, but all the bones are in tip-top condition, each in its proper place, all two hundred and forty-three of them!"

"Something like this . . . must be a very rare thing . . . as I've heard," Bal stammered.

"Very rare," said the Doctor with satisfaction, "as its price attests. The medical school in Paris has two of them, but the one in Marburg, for example, has none. Well, back to sleep, my friend," he said, turning to the skeleton. He closed the box and then the vault. "Oh yes – for you, for your trouble," he pressed a silver farthing into Bal's hand. "Go now, eat heartily. Frau Frolink is waiting with dinner. Afterwards, if you want to, come and help me a little more."

Well, why would Bal not want to? Of course he wanted to. As soon as he finished eating he was back at the Doctor's. He helped him set up his writing desk at the window. Together they unpacked a dozen books on medicine and placed them on a separate table in the study. These were all especially costly texts, the Doctor explained. He opened a few of them for Bal to see. Among them, for example, was the *Hortus sanitatis*, which had been published sixty years earlier, and the slightly more recent *Liber pestilentialis* and the even newer *Treating Wounds on the Battlefield*, dating from 1528 – all of them copiously illustrated with engravings. And there was the *Chessboard of Health* of Michael Hero, consisting almost entirely of woodcuts. The pictures, of which Bal managed to catch only brief glimpses, represented strange, at times repellent, but exciting things. In one, for example a man's leg was being sawn off with a small hacksaw. The patient was lying back with a curiously benign expression in an easy chair, a towel over his eyes, as two imposing-looking men worked on his leg, which was almost completely sawn through, though the tub under it had collected only about a thimbleful of blood. And above the happy-looking amputee was printed the word *Serratura*. Another picture depicted a man in a similar chair, in the middle of a field, against a background of soldiers battling in a thicket of spears. He looked like someone sitting in church, looking up at a preacher delivering an especially sweet sermon. And while the doctor's assistant rested his hands lightly on the patient's shoulders, the doctor himself was pulling a huge, barbed arrow out of the man's hairy chest. And so on, and so on.

That afternoon, when Märten came looking for Bal, Annika directed him to the Doctor's study. They had not seen each other in several days. While Bal arranged the huge pear-shaped urine flasks onto their designated shelves, they talked non-stop. But the Doctor did not let them go on for long.

"Ah – so this is your fine helper . . . Where do you work?" (With no hesitation, he addressed Märten with the informal "you".) "Ah, at Krumhusen's warehouse? Hmm. Well then, have his mink pelts from Novgorod arrived already? So, the first shipment reached early yesterday? Well, well. Listen, what's your name? Märten Bergkam? Aha. Hmm. Listen, Märten – you wouldn't mind earning a few extra farthings would you?"

Märten could not think of turning down such an offer. And in less than half an hour he was hard at work in the courtyard of the Bishop's House. He was supervising two villagers who had been summoned to town from Üksnurme manor. They were supposed to chop an enormous pile of logs into firewood and stack them in the shed, and to get the stable at the Bishop's House ready for the riding and carriage horses of the Doctor and his wife. Then and there the Doctor assigned Märten his tasks for the following afternoon, and for the day after that as well: tomorrow he was to clean all the rubbish and fallen leaves out of the courtyard – every nook and cranny! – and cover it with fine white sea sand. And the day after he was to straighten out the old prayer chapel built in the days of Herr Bishop – over there in the corner! – And most important of all, he was to scour, with the finest sand, the stone angel relief in the chapel – see, this one here – which had once been white but had turned grey with age.

In short, not only Bal but Märten too was earning a very good wage in his spare hours, working for the Doctor. The Doctor had a town-house servant as well: Paap, a villager from Üksnurme, who had been in his service for some years. He was a smart fellow, but mute. And then there was a grey-haired, yellow-complexioned servant, Johann, who had also moved to the new dwelling though still laid up with a fever and not of much help to the Doctor. And there was an ample maid-servant, Magdalena, who had her hands full with the kitchen and linen chests and bedclothes for the canopied double bed. Everything had to be in perfect order for the arrival of Frau Katharina. But on the fourth or fifth day the Doctor got a letter from his wife announcing she would not be coming to Tallinn. Bal was a little disappointed at this news, for he too was a participant in the great preparations for the mistress of the house. But the news did not seem to bother the Doctor at all: quite the contrary. Bal happened to be present when the Doctor broke the seal on his wife's letter and read it. Telling Bal that his wife was going off to Tartu first, he looked out of the window at the Old Market and his thin black moustache seemed to say calmly: Interesting, interesting, interesting . . .

That evening Bal and Märten were sitting in Bal's cubicle behind the kitchen. The October rain drummed against the window. Märten was gnawing on a pig's tail that Bal had fished out of Annika's soup pot.

"When it comes to money, the Doctor has more than enough," Märten observed. "If the warehouse foreman at Krumhusen's paid me for all my sweat and toil as much as the Doctor does for the little jobs I do for him . . . well . . ."

With a triumphant flourish of his quill, Bal put a full stop at the end of his essay on Marcus Claudius Marcellus. (He had argued that Marcellus had less good luck than bad. Marcellus had the good fortune to win the chain mail of Viridomarus, but of what importance was that when he had the misfortune to be sent into battle against so great a man as Archimedes? And although it was one of Marcellus' soldiers who killed Archimedes, the shame of this act clung to Marcellus' reputation as a general forever after.)

"And why wouldn't he have money?" Bal remarked, pursing his lips as he went over the last lines of his *exercitium*. "Just think of the patients he has!"

"Which ones?"

"Only the most distinguished. I've already seen a number of councilmen: Beelholt, Loop, Bade, Vegesack – who is apparently a relative. And Herr Clodt has been twice, and a Swedish ship's captain, dressed entirely in otter skins. And this morning he was urgently summoned to Toompea to see Bishop Mauritius himself."

"Wonder what ails these bigwigs all of a sudden?"

"It seems the bishop had water collecting in his stomach. And there are rumours that Clodt has the pox. I don't know about the others. At any rate, a doctor like that wouldn't move his little finger for less that three or four marks. So that . . ."

"He may be a doctor, but he's a bit odd just the same," Märten said evenly.

"In what way, odd?"

"Well . . . he does strange things . . . that don't make sense."

"Such as?"

"Yesterday, he has Magdalena fetch me from the yard. She tells me the Doctor wants to talk to me, and I should go to the study. I wipe my feet clean of lime dust and go upstairs to the study – the door is open. But the Doctor's not there. I wait a long time, thinking he's about to come. But he doesn't. Just as I'm about to go to ask Magdalena where he is, that iron door in the corner there, at the back of the new tile stove, starts to creak open with a horrible sound, very slowly . . . and the Doctor's standing there wearing some kind of smock with black-and-white stripes and great big, round, black-rimmed glasses."

"And then?"

"He stares at me with a look – as though he thinks I should find him really funny or some such. I'm wondering why he's bumbling about, and I say, 'I thought the Herr Doctor wanted to see me.' Then he starts to laugh out loud and asks whether I wasn't *frightened*. Frightened – why? Well, he asks, didn't I wonder who might be coming through that door? Well, you tell me why I'd imagine a burglar or someone coming through that door in broad daylight? Makes no sense . . ."

Just then Annika hailed Bal, wanting him to fetch some firewood for the hearth, and when Bal returned Märten had left. So Bal had good reason, in fact, for not revealing the point of the Doctor's joke to Märten, or the secret of the vault in the wall. Still, he did not sleep well that night, burdened with the guilt of keeping secrets from his friend. And in the morning, when he went to wash at the well, he realised he had forgotten to say his morning prayers. His face stinging from the cold water, he stepped into the old bishop's prayer chapel (he had never been there before to pray), knelt on the worn top step and asked pardon of the angel that Märten had scrubbed to his original whiteness the previous day. Of course he did not promise the angel that he would divulge the Doctor's secret to Märten at the first opportunity; he made that vow only to himself. Nor did he fulfil it as soon as he could. For every time, just as he was about to speak, the Doctor's voice came back to him – that menacing voice: *So, to repeat, just in case, do not tell anyone about this.* And he had not responded: No, Doctor! In that case I do not want to look into your secret box! Instead, he had looked at it eagerly and remained silent. *Qui tacet, consentit.** But he had, unbeknownst to himself, taken an important step towards gaining the Doctor's confidence.

A few days later the Doctor gave him four or five prescriptions and asked him to take them to Apothecary Dyck – an errand Bal ran each afternoon now. But this time, before Bal left the room, the Doctor said:

* Silence means consent (Latin).

"By the way . . . have you heard the details of the Treaty of Pozvol?"

"No I haven't . . . which ones?"

"Our dear Order Master and the King of Poland have joined in a defensive–offensive alliance."

"That I've heard. So now the Muscovite won't dare attack us . . ."

"But there's a clause in this treaty stating that it will not take effect until four years from now."

"Oh . . . So what does that mean?"

"It means that our own dear Order Master showed Moscow his backside, knowing that his chain mail trousers were being patched and that he wouldn't be able to wear them for another four years."

"So that now . . . ?"

"So that now there's not a fool anywhere who would bet against us when we declare that by Christmas we'll be at war."

"The Muscovite will attack?"

"Without a doubt."

"I'm not so sure he'd come at the coldest time of year . . ."

"Hmph! Have you ever been to Muscovy? No? I have. The winters there are so bitterly cold that the Muscovite would find winter in Livonia just right for warming his frozen fingers. As soon as the River Narva and the marshes of Lake Peipus freeze over, they'll be here."

"But what of the sixty thousand marks that were supposed to buy us peace?"

"Our miserly skinflints have still not managed to come up with that sum."

"What do you think will happen when war breaks out?"

"The Muscovite will conquer Livonia without too much trouble if we don't get a lot of help from somewhere. Loans, weapons and forces. And especially the will to resist. That's what we need more than anything else."

"And from whom could we get all this?"

"That depends partly on ourselves, doesn't it? It depends who we choose to gamble on. I'm a so-called stranger here. But you, as a born Livonian, where would you look for aid?"

"Livonia itself is so divided . . . there's the Order, and there are the bishops, the knights, the towns . . . And what kind of Livonian am I? Since when have Estonians been considered Livonians? But a Tallinner – that's another matter altogether."

"Well then, as a Tallinner, where would you turn?"

"Since we have the honour to be a backwater of the German empire, we could ask Kaiser Ferdinand."

"He's having difficulties with the Sultan, and even more with his own German princes. We can't even hope for crumbs from him."

"Well, then how about the Prussian duke – as successor to the German Order."

"Duke Albert is merely a vassal of the King of Poland. He doesn't make any decisions. If he's involved in politics at all it's to create intrigues and secret plots against Poland, that's all. And beyond that, he quarrels with his fractious theologians – men like Osiander and Funk, and whoever else there is."

"Then there's the Hansa . . ."

"The Hansa doesn't have anything against Livonia as a whole. But Tallinn has been a thorn for too long in the side of every Hansa town that deals with Russia for them to risk burning their fingers now on her behalf."

"Then there's Christian of Denmark. Fürstenberg was counting more on him than on Poland, in fact."

"Yes. But Christian has cancer – that I know. He's been kept alive for eight years by Bornholm's birch fungus. But he's as careful with politics as he is with his food. I'm certain he's not about to undertake anything. Well, that leaves Poland, yes? Or rather, Lithuania, which is closer. But Sigismund will not take a single step for the next four years.

That was our starting-point. And furthermore, according to the principle *praemissum semper verum,** we should consider the fact that we are now looking not only for a supporter of the Order but also for its successor. Would *you* want Catholic Poland to inherit Lutheran Livonia?"

"No-o . . . no, I wouldn't . . . I'd prefer Lutheran Denmark . . . or . . ."

"Or?"

"Sweden."

"Ah . . ."

"But this is just idle talk. 'Cause none of this depends on me in any way."

"Wrong! You could say this doesn't depend on you *to a great extent*. But *to some extent* everyone can help things move in a specific direction – once he's decided what that is. So. Go now. Or Herr Dyck won't have time to fill the prescriptions. Naturally, you won't mention at the Apothecary or elsewhere that you and Doctor Friesner are in search of a new ruler for Livonia. Of course not. This was just another little – skeleton-viewing talk."

In the meantime, the early snows of the year 1557 fell and then did their best to disappear as grey mud into the bottoms of puddles and under piles of refuse and into the spaces between cobblestones. But not before winter's icy hand had snatched it by its collar and frozen its grey-streaked back so smooth and hard that everywhere people with red noses and clenched fists slipped and slid and thudded on the sleek mounds of ice that had formed overnight. Doctor Freisner got a few new patients thanks to the condition of the city's streets, but fewer than might have been expected. For some reason, broken bones and torn ligaments seemed to occur with greater frequency among poor folk, who sought treatment mainly among quacks and sauna women and

* The premise is always true (Latin).

159

barbers. As for Doctor Friesner himself, he negotiated the icy streets with remarkable agility. When Bal went along as his assistant on a few afternoons, he had to work to keep up with the Doctor. And when a little later they got involved in the following conversation, it was no easier for Bal to keep pace with the Doctor's flights of thought:

"So, you've finished the 'Treatise on Bloodletting'? Good work! Very good! Now, you should tackle Vesalius. His *De humani corporis fabrica,** the basic text for medical knowledge. In spring you'll finish school, and you'll have a solid basis in anatomy as well. Then, a year of internship with me and a few good books – and one-two-three, you'll be off to Marburg to study medicine. With the kind of foundation you'll have, it won't take you longer than three years. I'll give you letters to take to Rector Phrygius. And we'll have you board at Professor Braunstein's. How? Oh – child's play! Ah . . . who'll pay? But who would pay if you went to study theology at Greifswald? In any case, by then you'll have had a chance to earn a little money for yourself. How? Oh, there are many different ways."

That was as far as the conversation went that day. And about a week later, on a Sunday morning after the church service, when Bal was alone with the Doctor in his study, their talk turned instead to politics again.

Behind the wavy green-glass windowpanes in their square lead frames, snow was falling in thick, lazy flakes. The Doctor, in red goat-skin slippers and a housecoat with a mink collar, stood by the window, raised the flasks with urine samples of his patients to the light, looked at them one by one, and wrote something into the book on his desk. Squinting at the snow through the urine of the town's gentry he said:

"Well my wife writes from Tartu that our envoys finally departed for Moscow the day before yesterday – Kruse and Hörner, and others."

"Thank God. They'll hold off war, after all."

"On the contrary. They'll be pouring oil on the flames!"

* The Fabric of the Human Body (Latin).

160

"How's that? They'll be delivering the sixty thousand marks that Ivan demanded . . ."

"That's just it – they're not delivering it! It is not generally known yet, but my wife tells me in confidence that Bishop Hermann dispatched them from Tartu without the money. They didn't manage to collect it. Ergo: the war's likely to start in a just a few days. It can erupt as soon as they arrive and it becomes clear that they've come with an empty purse, just to talk. The Muscovite will take the envoys hostage – if they're lucky. In the best case, the war will start after they return home."

He set another pear-shaped flask of yellow liquid onto the table and looked at Bal.

"Well then, who would you turn to? It'll have to be done soon."

Bal smiled, a bit naïvely. "Yes . . . I've been thinking it over. But what if it's the Lord's will that the Muscovite take over this country? In that case, should we be so opposed to His plan? . . . And would it in fact be so terrible?"

"Hmm." The Doctor coughed. "Of course, the Muscovite is betting on the hostility between the peasants and the German manor lords. So that if he's clever enough, he won't necessarily make himself unacceptable to you as an Estonian. But for you as a *Livonian*, as a citizen of Tallinn, as a Christian who has drunk at the springs of Augsburg," – the Doctor raised the glass flask with its golden fluid sloshing around in it, "as a medical student, *in spe*, of Marburg – it would be the destruction of the West! – So that . . . ?"

Bal had indeed been mulling over the question, and not for the first time either, though only after his talk with the Doctor had he tried to decide on the most acceptable ruler for Livonia. And it came to him, by chance, that he had actually known the answer for some time, without knowing it. Which was why, in his earlier response to the Doctor's question, he had circled around it, starting with the Kaiser and Prussia, naming Sweden only in the end. He had concluded that it was not the

Doctor's way to state things outright . . . But then, when he asked himself why he preferred Sweden, it was difficult for him to come out with a clear answer.

Bal had a vague sense of the German emperor and the Prussian duke as being somehow far away and yet unpleasantly near. Their names evoked in him an atmosphere of crippling contempt and mute cries of rage and the creak of rusty armour. He assumed a similarity, no doubt, between them and the local Germans whose rule over his land had been harsh and cruel. But the name "Poland" held a faint scent of things exotic and carefree, of pride and incense . . . What could that scent be but Poland's faith in the Pope? Denmark seemed to him the least likely of all future possibilities, who knows why. Somehow it was unappealing – perhaps because Master Fürstenberg and his Order were turning to Denmark for help. Or maybe because the Danish kings – and every child here knew this – had once sold this land for nineteen thousand silver marks to the Order. True, this had happened over two hundred years earlier and was now of no consequence. But still . . .

So – why should the Swedes be any better than the Germans? Perhaps because the Swedes were the only people, besides the Germans, that Bal had known personally. And a very different kind of experience it had been.

The Swedes in this town were artisans, above all shoemakers, carpenters, armour-smiths, and suchlike. In the best case, goldsmiths as well. Nevertheless, even in relation to these gentlemen-Swedes, the Order Master had some time ago sent a warning to the Town Council not to grant citizenship to too many . . . That was, of course, a more moderate injunction than efforts to keep down Estonians. Still, the suspicion and hostility of the merchants and the Order Masters fostered a sense of solidarity between the Estonians and the Swedes of Tallinn, all the more because the local Swedes worked for the most part as bargemen or wagoners or warehouse workers or in related occupations requiring a strong back. Most of them were quite a lot like the Greys – living on the outskirts of town, wearing grey work clothes, their hands work-roughened, their trousers tar-stained. Most managed country tongue fairly well, and the ones who did not concocted a kind of mishmash of their own language and country tongue, so that when you heard it the first time it was hard to keep yourself from laughing, but fairly soon you could work it out. Of course, all the Stures and Baners and others who were said to be near the top of the Swedish ruling hierarchy in faraway Stockholm were gentry – as is true of men at the top everywhere – and one could not detect even a whiff of the familiar, acrid smells of sweat or boat tar in their proximity. But the ones at Kalamaja and Pleekmäe – both the half-Swedes and the full-blooded – were still almost like one's own people. All those mischievous young whelps and slips of girls with their freckled, dirt-streaked faces and their reddish or linen-hued hair, with names like Jöns and Mats and Birgit, were a part of Bal's boyhood. At the *quarta* and even the *tertia* levels at the town school, the unwritten rule was that the Swedish boys would join the non-Germans against the Germans when fights broke out. Not until the *secunda* level were Swedish–German alliances formed against non-Germans. And only at the *prima* level did such alliances sometimes become commonplace, which happened if the non-German boys themselves still played any kind of role at that stage . . . So that was how it was. And then there was the fact that Märten's old man, who had been killed long ago in some pub in the faraway town of Calais, had been a Swede. All that Märten remembered of him was his curly reddish hair and a blue seagull tattoo that he had tried in vain to prise off his father's chest . . . And nevertheless, or maybe because of this, it would have seemed like a betrayal to prefer a Dane or Pole or someone else to a Swede . . . And of course the Finns of Kalamaja and Pleekmäe also had a part in making the Swedish king's rule seem more palatable. True, all those many Finns, named Hämäläinen or Nylander, who had in recent

years come from Finland in great numbers, were constantly complaining about Swedish rule – each with his own personal grievance about their harsh commanders in war as well as civil life, and the high taxes and inadequate farmland, and the unenlightened laws of town and trade. But there was one thing no-one could deny: no matter how bad particular manor lords
might be, peasants in all of Sweden and Finland were entirely free!

And the cursed rule of the Order had been despised for generations in Mary's Land. Besides, Bal's father had never taken a vow of allegiance to Plettenberg, Brüggen, or Fürstenberg, for he had always happened to be out on a trip whenever the Order Masters had come to Tallinn. As for Bal, that vow did not pertain to him one whit . . .

"So, I – well – I guess I'd turn to Sweden . . . ?"

"Good." The Doctor put the flask down and started to pace up and down the room. "Let's go over the plusses with regard to Sweden. First, the King. Not a mad halfwit like Ivan, but an old, reasonable and cautious man. Ivan denounces him as a tallow-merchant's son, but actually the Vasas are an old noble family in Sweden. And as for his caution – true, it can be as much of a drawback at times as Christian's, but for handling affairs in Livonia he actually has his younger son. Yes, Johan. He's been in Turku as Finnish duke since last year. He's young, smart, clear-headed, energetic. And, in the final analysis, Tallinn's closest neighbour. And in general the more of its own countrymen a ruling power has in a country, the greater its right to rule. Of course, by that logic we here should have our own Estonian kings," the Doctor smiled. "But seriously, the Germans have shown they can no longer handle governing here. So, who has the greatest rights here – based on numbers? There are five or six Russians in Tallinn, as many Poles, and about twenty Danes. But on every street corner you run into a Jöns Mattson or a Mats Jönsson. In the larger towns in Sweden there are so many Germans and Danes that Tallinn, by population, is the third largest Swedish town after Stockholm and Visby. And then there are the outlying Swedish areas – half of Hiiu and Läänemaa, and the lands of the old Lode family in Harju, and the islands. And if we include the Finns, who are also Duke Johan's subjects – and there are a few hundred of them in Kalamaja – almost a quarter of the people here are Johan's own people. Yes indeed. Balthasar, if you are interested in the future of the *peasantry* – in Finland the peasants are truly free . . ."

Bal listened closely to the Doctor's speech and, as often happened, he had trouble following his reasoning. When the Doctor paused, Bal asked casually, realising in advance that his question was unmistakably childish: "Do you know Duke Johan?"

The Doctor had stopped pacing a moment earlier, positioning himself at the stove with his back against its warm green tiles. Now he jutted out his black beard and said, "Yes I do. Very well." He took a moment to enjoy Bal's surprise before continuing: "I spent the entire month of July last year at his castle in Turku, with my wife, Katharina. Treating him. He had an imbalance of humours – yellow bile and phlegm. But now he's in perfect health. From time to time, to keep the yellow bile in balance, I send him a cask of Greek *vino santo* and butter-pears from Padise. And for his part – he pays for these . . . little services . . . ah . . . surprisingly well. But—" Here the Doctor extended his left hand and knocked on the iron door of the wall vault just beyond the corner of the tile stove: *knock-knock-knock-knock-knock*. He was looking at Bal with a smile like the one Bal's classmate Wenzel Pepermann had worn two days ago when Bal ran into him emerging from the Green Frog with a girl. Bal did not know how to react – neither to Pepermann two days earlier nor to the Doctor now. Just then, fortunately, Johann appeared at the door, his countenance still yellowish (though he had recovered from his fever sufficiently to resume some of his duties), and announced that the bishop had sent for the Doctor. The bishop was feeling worse. The Doctor dismissed Bal, saying, not without a touch of vanity: "See now, such is the life of a poor doctor – dukes here, bishops there . . . Well then, we'll have a chance to talk at length another time."

But they did not manage a more extended discussion for a long time. Christmas came, and bells rang for many days above the snowy rooftops – from St Olaf's, and St Nicholas's, from the Dome Church and Holy Ghost, from the churches of Almshouse and Kalamaja and half a dozen town chapels. And then all over the town the smoke rose towards the sky from Christmas roasts, and in the dark of the evening dancing townspeople, their faces aglow with wine and firelight, whirled around a crackling Christmas tree in front of the Town Hall, making the snowy cobblestones resound under their thumping feet. The New Year arrived and neighbours wished each other a happy 1558 as they met on the paths between banks of shovelled snow and the town's frosted walls. And Meus, with Annika and Bal, called on their landlord, the Doctor, with New Year's wishes, as good manners demanded. The Doctor served them *klarett*, and they heard from him about Jürgen Meissen. The Doctor's wife was, in fact, the first person to send news about him to Tallinn. She had left Tartu, as he explained, to visit relatives in Riga for a week or two. She had written to say that this barefoot prophet, with his ice-blue gaze and bright red beard, caused people everywhere to laugh when they first laid eyes on him. In the square of St John's Church in Riga, just as at Memel and Mitau, he had caused shivers of fear to run down the backs of his listeners as he prophesied, in a voice alternately thunderous and shrill, that Satan would soon afflict all the land of Livonia with the boils of Job, and the enemy would rain down upon it the horrors of war. Halfway through his speech some of his listeners had run into the church in terror, among them the Doctor's wife Katharina, so that she had not heard the conclusion of Jürgen's prophesies.

But what he had prophesied soon came to pass.

CHAPTER SIX,

in which it becomes evident that the dates recorded in the histories of states, marking their victories and defeats, their rise and fall, their birth and death – and in every case, the shedding of blood – that such dates could in the strictest sense also be fateful in the life of an ordinary person, someone still young, someone a bit frivolous or impetuous or curious, someone influenced by chance or by the will of another or by conviction or necessity, or what he imagines the one or the other to be – or perhaps, by all these things and the maxima summa *of many others as well, for which there was, in those days that have given rise to our reflections, no better word than "fate".*

On the Saturday afternoon of January 22 dusk settled slowly upon the town, which appeared to be steaming in the bitter cold. Because of the frigid weather the market hubbub under the windows of the Bishop's House had subsided early. By about five o'clock, when candles began to flicker behind panes of glass or pig's bladder or oil paper in the windows around the marketplace, only the occasional figure crossed the square, shoulders hunched against the cold, rubbing his cheeks or warming his nose in his mittens.

Bal, in a short sheepskin coat, with a dogskin cap in his hand, was standing in Doctor Friesner's study, waiting. The Doctor had gone to fetch something in the other room, and then they were to set off for the Vegesack house, where the councilman and his whole family were bedridden with a fever, Dung of the Orient included.

Bal heard the snow squeak under Paap's feet as the mute servant crossed the courtyard to the gate; he heard it open and creak shut. And then he suddenly heard the thud of approaching hooves. For some reason this vividly recalled in his mind the Doctor's arrival that autumn: the quiet of the afternoon and the crescendo of horses' hooves from the Town Hall, continuing right up to the suspenseful moment of the knock on the door. The horse's approach this time, through the silent, frozen town, was very different. It was coming from the direction of the Karja Gate, not the Town Hall, and not with hooves clattering over wet cobblestones, but thudding dully over hard-packed snow, and not at a steady, confident pace, but in a headlong gallop. There are times when one can anticipate what is about to happen . . . and, indeed, the rider stopped in front of the Bishop's House. Bal went to the window and saw in the half-light a pale horse, its haunches dark with sweat, and a grey shape in the saddle trying to say something to Paap at the gate. Then the rider turned in at the gate and Bal heard the horse snort and enter, *clip-clop-clip-clop*, under the vaulted passage and into the court-yard. After that he heard the housemaid call out and someone come up the stairs, and then the Doctor's voice. A few moments later the Doctor rushed into the writing room. He was holding a candle in one hand and a letter in the other. It seemed to Bal that his dark cheeks were flushed.

"It started this morning."

"What?"

"My wife is in Tartu again. She's sent word from there. At dawn this morning the Muscovite crossed the borders of Livonia from the direction of Petseri monastery, with an army of at least forty thousand men. And they pushed ahead towards Tartu, looting and burning throughout the diocese and leaving horrible devastation in a stretch of land two leagues wide. The leader seems to be the former Khan of Astrakhan, Shigali. You know, the one whom Ivan overthrew but who himself later went over to Ivan's side. There's no resistance in the diocese. Tartu was in a panic this morning, with fleeing refugees everywhere. Katharina tried to set out for Tallinn by way of Põltsamaa and Paide, around noon."

"How did it happen so quickly that . . . ?" Bal began, but the Doctor interrupted him.

"Quickly? I've been expecting this for two months!"

"No, I mean how did the news reach Tartu and then arrive here so quickly, if it's only at dawn today, that . . . ?"

"A well-paid rider can cover six leagues in an hour."

"But it's unlikely either the commander or the Council know a thing about it yet."

"The Council – probably not. And the commander—" The Doctor turned to look at Bal and said with smug disdain: "You know how things are with the Order: the couriers are drunk, the oats have been sold, the bridles are rotting. But that's their business. Ours is to—" Here the Doctor stopped, drummed his fingers on the table, and looked at Bal long and hard.

. . . The face young and round, the features not yet fully defined, a bit irritating at times – that mix of complaisance and potential defiance; an exasperating, wide-eyed stare, but a gaze obviously alert; the slightly ridiculous hair – a thick, dull-blond mass; exceptionally wide shoulders for one so young, and a well-built torso on long legs, strong, and planted wide apart like a peasant's. Hmm . . . the Doctor's eyebrows tensed, his nostrils quivered . . . it was as though he were trying to see and sniff out everything about this youth in that one moment of decision. It was unlikely, though, that through the scent of musk in the scarf around his own neck he detected the smell of wax from Kimmelpenning's soap, or the smell of the horse stable in the short winter coat made out of Siimon's old sheepskin, so his sniffing was purely instinctive. In fact he had already made his decision.

"Balthasar, would twenty marks suffice for your first few months at Marburg?"

"What do you mean?"

The Doctor repeated his question and added: "This would not be a loan, but your own money."

"Of course it would be enough." *What a foolish question, I could live on that for half a year.*

"Then earn the twenty marks."

"How?"

"By performing – for the sake of our joint venture – a quick service. And you'll swear, of course, on your own round head, that no-one other than our Lord God will learn about it."

"Namely?"

"Let's take off our coats. The Vegesacks will have to wait. Sit down."

They removed their coats, and the Doctor motioned to him to take a seat in Master Andreas' carved chair. He himself remained standing at his lectern and said, drumming his fingers rhythmically:

"You'll take the letter I am about to write. You'll take two horses and a sleigh. Paap will go with you as driver. He knows the way. You'll leave right now, tonight, cross the sea to Turku and take my letter directly to the duke."

The Doctor's proposal had arrived with a rapidity that left Bal no time to mull things over. What struck him were the highlights of the plan: the great adventure, the responsibility and trust invested in him, the exciting, heady prospect of meeting the duke, and of course the money for Marburg. Actually, that was perhaps more important than anything else.

"Fine," he said matter-of-factly, as though the proposal were something quite ordinary. "If you make sure there'll be no trouble from Herr Sum. And provide some explanation to the Frolinks. This'll take at least three or four days, after all."

"I will see to all that. And I won't ask you to take an oath of silence on the Bible. Anyone with any sense knows that God is everywhere."

Five minutes later Paap led two of the Doctor's horses to Master Lytke in Seppade Street, a silver farthing in his pocket to compensate the smith for the inconvenience of the late visit, and had the shoes on the horses' fore-hooves replaced with studded ice-shoes. Shortly before seven o'clock, when the Great Coast Gate would close for the evening, Bal and Paap rode across the rumbling, frozen drawbridge, one horse pulling the sleigh and a second following behind, with a few long boards and some boathooks and shovels stashed on board, just in case. They were wearing long travel furs from the Doctor over their short coats, and in Bal's pocket, under all those layers, was a letter with the Doctor's seal, addressed thus:

To the Most Honourable and Noble Highness, Prince Johan,
Crown Prince of the Kingdom of Sweden and Duke of Finland,
my Gracious Master.

In another pocket Bal had the twin of Doctor Friesner's signet ring. He would not get to see the duke himself right away, but Bal was enjoined to insist on seeing his proxy, Herr Henrik Horn, and show him the ring. After that, the Doctor assured Bal, the duke would receive him immediately.

The severe cold continued unabated. When the horses picked up speed on the road descending to the harbour, their new shoes sent blue sparks flying as they clattered over the bare cobblestones. The moon had not yet risen and the darkness was dense. Just before the harbour, Paap steered the horses left onto the Kalamaja road, and then soon right. Had a few snow-covered boulders not flown past in the dark, and the sleigh not bounced lightly as it slid over invisible mounds of ice on the shore, they would not have registered the moment of their gliding onto the frozen sea.

The town at their backs had disappeared into the darkness. The only

171

lights visible flickered from the watchtower behind the bulwark and from the shore of Kalamaja, like wolves' eyes in the gloom. A thin, greenish layer of icy mist hovered over the ice-bound sea, but the sky in the cold air above them must have been clear, for if you looked closely you could see the constellations. Bal wanted to know whether Paap was steering by the stars, and he turned towards him to ask, only then recalling that Paap could not be a partner in conversation. It was a comfort, nevertheless, to feel the man's shoulder next to his in this vast, unsettling emptiness. By making a little effort he could discern the shape of Paap's hat against the greyish background of snow, and even the horse's ears looked spectral against the black of the starless northern sky. There was something calming and reassuring in the horses' regular trotting rhythm and the steady forward glide of the sleigh, which mitigated the sense of lonely abandonment that had swept over Bal from the icy wasteland ahead of them. *Dear Lord*, he prayed, *grant that we succeed in this venture, and that it strengthen and protect our town at this grave time from the horrors at our door.* He was about to take off the big dogskin mittens and fold his hands under the coarse sleigh blanket, but then felt it would be pointless here, in the dark, under the faint though still visible stars.

The sky now seemed lighter, whether as a result of his talk with God or of the moon rising behind them into the cold fog on the southeastern horizon. Far away on the skyline he could see the sharp needle of St Olaf's spire rising into the moonlight from the misty cloak blanketing the town. The opaqueness ahead of them had lost some of its intensity. Quite unexpectedly, he could make out sleigh tracks, and debris here and there upon the snow. Naturally – for they were travelling along the transport route between town and the island of Nairisaare, along which two hundred loads of firewood had been hauled to town just a week earlier.

The full moon, shrunken with the cold, had risen high into the heavens inside its bluish halo. The current of cold haze over the ice glowed milky-white in the moonlight, and the ice itself was striped with shadows cast by the ridges on its surface. Paap reined in the horses and tapped his forehead – perhaps to indicate he had forgotten something? He took off his mittens and fumbled around in his bag, bringing out a small wooden container. He nudged Bal and then rubbed his palm over his face. He was asking Bal to smear his face with seal fat, to protect it against frostbite. As Bal rubbed the fat – which was hard because of the cold and smelling like whale blubber – over his face he worried about where he would wash it off tomorrow before his audience with the duke. At the same time he was watching Paap grease his own large, angular face, which looked faintly greenish in the moonlight until it assumed a silvery sheen. As Paap smeared his cheeks he moved his large square jaw left and right, and his small, deep-set eyes seemed to say: Well, now the cold will not be able to sink its teeth in our faces, no matter how fierce it gets. Then Paap pressed the reins into Bal's hands and gestured towards the north, where the silhouette of Nairisaare Island lay on the horizon. His hands drew arcs in the air, like the curves of bridges, and he lay down on his side in the sleigh and gestured again towards the horizon. Bal let him repeat the sequence once more, and then he understood: it was about a two- or three-hour journey to the island; Bal was to hold the reins for that stretch while Paap slept. From there to the Finnish coast would be another seven or eight hours. Paap would take the reins at that point and Bal could curl up under the blanket. Paap pulled the blanket up over his face, and before Bal could signal to the horses to move on, he heard the sound of snoring from under the blanket.

After a time his cheeks began to sting from the cold in spite of their layer of grease. He pulled the collar of his bulky sheepskin coat over his nose and breathed warmth into its thickness. The horses' hides seemed covered with fine white needles, and their hooves crunched and squeaked ever more loudly on the frozen snow and the glassy, wind-swept ice. Nairisaare's rim of woods was quite near now. Bal had never set foot on the island before, a mysterious place, like all islands. But from his boyhood play-space above the barn, he had always been able to locate its wooded strip. And he had heard all kinds of stories about it. The woods now rising up from the silent ice-locked sea were un-expectedly close. And somewhere in those woods was the Danish king's garden – he remembered that from stories his father had told him. The garden was long since gone, but his father had once been shown the foundation of the house, years ago, when he was still a wagoner at the town's transport yard, hauling lumber from the island. About two hundred years before, as the story went, a Danish king, a Knut or a Magnus – the deuce knows which one – had sent his own sister into exile there. The princess lived in those woods for years. Some people claimed that the name of Nairisaare was actually Naissaar at the time, meaning Woman's Island, and many continued calling it that. But there seemed no reason to suppose that it had been called Naissaar on account of the princess. For one thing, she did not live there very long. Apparently her brother-king did not think it secure enough as a place of exile and had her sent to the Kärkna Cloister, which the Germans call Falkenau, where she died and was buried. When Bal asked his father ten years back why the king had imprisoned his sister on the island, Siimon had mumbled something like: "Who can explain what kings do . . . ?" and changed the subject. Much later, when the *tertia* students had learned all there was to know about the world, Bal heard that the princess of Nairisaare had been a lover of women, and it was to subject her to a more severe punishment for this depravity that she had later been sent to the Kärkna Cloister. True, who can really understand the ways of kings? Their desires and actions can at times be so absurdly diffi-cult to comprehend that it is almost as though the Devil had a hand in making kings even more confused than ordinary people. Take, for example, this Muscovite, Ivan, who was now rampaging near Tartu. The entire world now called him a sodomite, as every merchant and artisan in Tallinn knew. Of course, there were right-minded kings and princes and dukes in the world as well. And the son of Siimon Rissa was at that very moment sweeping past the ice banks of Nairisaare Island's eastern shore, on his way towards one such ruler – a journey no-one could possibly have foreseen or predicted.

It was not likely that the duke would unreasonably assail him the next day. On the contrary, the noble duke would probably be most grateful for such speedy notification of the outbreak of a war that was of great interest to him. It was not out of the question – actually, it would be quite natural – for him to add something to the twenty marks the Doctor had promised. In which case, Bal's first year at Marburg would be all but free of care – he would not have to lighten his father's purse by much or ask Kimmelpenning for support. All the same, Bal felt somewhat apprehensive as he imagined getting out of this pleasantly gliding sleigh the next day and walking into strange rooms, under the eyes of strange men, and into unforeseeable circumstances. But now there was no going back.

He had turned right, near the south-east corner of the island, leaving behind the lumber-wagon tracks heading towards the shore, and a few hundred paces from there had travelled a good distance north, following the tracks of a single sleigh. The moon was starting to set and the dusky expanse of ice gradually opened up before him. At the same time, the air had become so clear that he could more or less see the tip of Viimsi Peninsula and the island of Salmesaare, and the strait between them, known as Wulff Strait, or Olaf's Strait, as the peasants called it. Bal did not stop the sleigh until the tracks made a sharp left to Nairisaare Island. Paap sat up for a moment, taking in the surroundings. He knew immediately where they were and pursed his lips in satisfaction. He let the horses lick the snow and crunch some oats, took out a little wooden drum-keg of vodka from under the straw, drank, and offered some to Bal too, as medicine against the cold, and in half an hour they were on their way north again, this time with Paap holding the reins.

Bal's thoughts kept him awake as he lay under the sleigh-blanket: *Wonder how I'll manage tomorrow, talking to the duke. In any event, I'll have to manage one way or another . . . We're reaching the open gulf now . . . wonder whether there'll be any cracks or open water out here . . . Probably not, not in this deep-freeze. And no doubt Paap knows what he's doing. And I should be able to make it over any cracks . . . after all I did once take a drink of that . . . I'll know what to do . . . Parr-purr – parr-purr – parr-purr . . . now that Paap has changed the horses around, the crunch of their hooves is even louder.*

Nairisaare had been swallowed up by the gathering gloom behind them. The moon had set and the sky was full of stars, like coldly glittering silver coins. Against the horizon ahead, the horse's ears formed an antique letter M with sharp black points. *Marr-purr – Marr-burrg – Marr-burrg . . .*

At about four o'clock in the morning they reached the rocky mounds of the southernmost islands. Bal did not wake up until the sleigh began to bump and thud along the promontory, up to the mainland. At first he thought, with surprise, that there were fishing boats everywhere, turned upside down and covered with snow, some as big as ships. But then he realised that only those closest to the frozen water's edge were fishing boats, and that higher up the road wound between snow-covered boulders. Somewhere, dogs took up a high-pitched yelping. In the starlight Bal could see two tiny wooden churches on the promontory ridge, and thirty or forty log houses, and the frames of about ten more with walls and no rafters or rafters and no roofs. Paap turned into a dooryard surrounded by a high wooden fence, in a stand of birches and firs, where the dogs were particularly clamorous. He pounded for a while on the door of the log house until, finally, it opened; the man on the threshold, with an angular face and coarse, thick white hair, had thrown an old soldier's uniform over his nightshirt. It was clear he recognised Paap for, wasting no words of greeting, he gestured silently to his early-morning visitors to enter. Inside the warm candlelit cabin they unpacked their provisions and ate. Meanwhile, the Finn led the exhausted horses, icicles dangling from their noses, into the barn and brought out two others. Bal asked Paap how far they had to go to get to Turku, and how much further east Helsinki was from where they were – for they must have come ashore somewhere between the two. But before he had interpreted Paap's hand signals, the Finn returned and Bal, using the Finnish he had picked up in the backyards of Kalamaja, asked him the same thing.

"To Turku – it's about thirty leagues. And to Helsinki, you ask? The gentleman from Tallinn speaks in jest. This is Helsinki."

So this middling village was the town that King Gustav had been building for eight years to eclipse Tallinn! No town houses, no stone churches, not to mention castles, towers, fortified walls . . . Judging by this, the Swedish king was not very mighty. But land – he had plenty of that, even if it was sparsely populated. Over the next ten hours all this became eminently clear to Bal. For, in the course of the thirty leagues they travelled that day, a trip lasting until three in the afternoon, their road took them through many villages, but only the two larger ones had churches, and even those were odd. In the first place, they had no steeples: their steeples had been lifted off their roofs and set down next to them. Even stranger was the fact that their walls were not of good, solid, dark-grey limestone slabs laid carefully flat, one on top of another, as the walls of churches ought to be, Bal thought. These looked as though they had been built of rocks randomly picked out of pastures and beaches and cemented with white mortar, making their grey–red–white walls resemble the mottled hides of the local cows. The churchgoers' sleighs and teams also looked different, somehow more colourful than those at home. But the horses at the tethering posts in front of the churches, and the people – as many of them as were out and about in the morning light during the sermon – were quite like the horses and people at home.

The bitter cold had let up; but now the west wind was whirling a powdery snow into their faces, which seemed even icier than before. The wind forced them to squint and the landscape became an ever-greater blur of snow-covered woods and jagged rock. Bal and Paap took turns holding the reins and Bal could not decide, during his off-time, whether it would be wiser to let himself drop off or fight the sleep. He wanted to stay alert enough to answer all the duke's questions clearly and to remember everything that was said, so that he could relay it all to the Doctor. A few hours after they had stopped off in Salo, where they were once again provided with fresh horses at a house known to Paap, they were flying westward on a well-travelled crown road. Reaching the top of a slope, Paap pointed straight ahead. Far in the distance Bal could see a cluster of snowy-roofed houses and, beyond them, visible against the light sky and strips of dark forest, two huge stone edifices – the castle and the church. Soon the wide wintry road led down the slope and turned onto the frozen river. Gliding between the riverbanks, they passed fishermen's huts and boats on either shore as they entered the town. Then on both banks, quiet on this peaceful Sunday morning, rows of log houses flashed by – presumably the dwellings of artisans – until the river abruptly turned to wind around a hillside topped by a cluster of stone buildings. From their midst rose an enormous church. To one from Tallinn the houses did not look particularly imposing or large, and to Bal the lack of surrounding walls or fortifications some-how made the town seem naked. And for a town in such a spacious set-ting, the narrowness of the streets made no sense at all. Yet, thanks to the church, Bal's estimation of the Swedish kingdom and the Finnish dukedom rose considerably. True, the church looked somewhat squat, and its steeple was not quite as high as St Olaf's, which Bal, because of Meus, in some ways considered his own personal church. But for sheer size and imposing presence this one seemed to outdo the one at home. To get to the castle they had to go past the church and under the bridge and a quarter of a league downriver, and actually a good distance beyond town. Comparing it to the castle on Toompea in Tallinn, it struck him as rather middling. It sat right on the edge of the ice and rose from the low river-mouth like an edifice of stone boxes spreading out in a slightly misshapen rectangle, with three high, narrow boxes side by side, and a few lower ones in a quadrangle in front of them; all the walls were splotchy like the hides of the cows, and all – seen up close – were awfully thick.

Before they rode on to the right bank Bal reined in the horses and, behind the bushes at the river's edge, carefully rubbed his face with snow, managing to clean off the grease fairly thoroughly. But instead of feeling refreshed, as he had hoped, he merely felt cold, especially since a large handful of snow had slipped down his collar.

He brought the horses to a halt at the castle gate facing the town, next to a pile of logs. He threw his sheepskin into the sleigh and, leaving Paap with the horses, asked an approaching soldier where to find the guardhouse. It was right there, off the echoing archway, so he just walked right in. The room was unexpectedly light, given its heavy vaulted ceiling. The walls were painted with sinuous flower patterns and strange-looking lords and ladies; in the corners of the room, halberds leaned against the painted walls, and around a table in the middle four or five guardsmen were playing cards. Bal greeted them and asked to speak to the captain. The guards looked at him as if to say: And who are you, anyway? He had inspired no respect in them. Bal felt he could either sound angry or seem intimidated; he had no courage for the the first and could not afford to indulge in the second, at least not at the outset. So he simply raised his voice a little:

"Is my Finnish perhaps not clear enough? In that case, I'll speak Swedish: I am asking that you please summon your captain. I've come from Tallinn and I don't have much time." It came out sounding more authoritative than he had planned, maybe because of those confounded cold rivulets still running down his chest. And he was surprised at the effect of his words. One of the guardsmen looked at him sharply, put his cards into the cuff of his voluminous sleeve, and sauntered across the room towards a door at the back.

"Hmm . . . I'll see . . ."

In a moment the soldier returned and motioned Bal into the back room. A florid-faced officer, weighing about ten poods, was sitting at a small table eating his midday meal. That is to say, he was chewing on a pork shoulder and using a wooden spoon to shovel barley porridge into the thickets of his red beard. These he washed down with draughts of ale from an earthenware jug. Having deposited a particularly large spoonful of barley into his mouth, he asked, unexpectedly loudly, in good German: "You've come from Tallinn? What do you want?"

"I wish to see Herr Horn."

"Aha. Who's sent you?"

The Doctor had told him: *remember, the less you mention me, here or there, the better* . . . So at this point Bal had to decide whether to name the Doctor or not . . . but before he could speak the captain asked, perhaps because he remembered the gentleman he had met in Tallinn the previous summer, or because he simply wanted to seem in the know:

"Was it . . . the Doctor?"

"Well . . . yes."

"Concerning what?"

"Well . . . I've got some medicines . . . for the duke."

"The driver's outside?"

"At the gate."

"Hey, Birger!" the captain shouted into the guardroom, and the

180

soldier who had hailed Bal earlier appeared, moving with noticeably greater alacrity than he had shown before.

"See to it that someone takes care of his driver and horse. And take him directly to Ensign Boije. Go!"

Bal followed the soldier across the large courtyard of the outer fortress. The approach to the main fortress was kept clear, but otherwise the forecourt was cluttered and strewn with brush. Some of the walls were covered with scaffolding, some were partly torn down, and in some places window openings had been hewn into the façade on the upper level. There were snow-covered stones and stacks of logs in the yard, and the wind swirled the snow and woodchips about. The winter had caught this ambitious building project by the throat.

From the high gate of the main fortress, Bal glimpsed further signs of half-finished construction in the rear courtyard – more scaffolding and surprisingly large windows framed by patterned borders painted onto the stucco walls. They passed through a dim corridor into a vaulted room similar to the one they had just left and stopped in front of a young ensign standing in the middle of the room. Bal eyed him while the soldier explained who Bal was. Even from a distance it was apparent that the young man was a member of the aristocracy. He was some three or four years younger than Bal, and without family connections could not have risen to be an ensign when so young. The black wool jacket and the spotless white pleated cuffs were somewhat off-putting in their immaculateness, but his thin, pale moustache seemed quite friendly. When Bal explained that he was from Tallinn and had a message from Doctor Friesner, to be delivered by Herr Horn to the duke himself, the young man nodded without curiosity, saying:

"Please wait. These gentlemen are ahead of you. You'll be next."

These "gentlemen" were five or six burghers or perhaps middle-level guild merchants, sitting on two long benches. These were the only ones in the room, and there was space on one of them. Bal hesitated for a moment, wondering whether it was proper, then sat at the very end of the bench. The gentleman next to him seemed to be of higher rank than the rest of the group. And what was immediately noteworthy: reading from a small notebook that looked like a breviary, apparently filled with his own notes, he was reading through seeing-glasses! Although some shopkeepers in Tallinn also used them, Bal had never seen a pair from such close range: two large, round, curved pieces of glass, about the size of silver thalers, set in two circles of black frame about as thick as – well, as a tiger-moth caterpillar – connected in the middle by wire, and with other wires that curved to secure them behind each ear. Bal was staring at this invention with such intensity that the man turned his pinkish face – curiously owl-like because of the seeing-glasses – towards him and asked in an oddly accented Finnish:

"If my ears do not deceive me – you're from Tallinn? Aha! Well now, and how are the merchants of Tallinn doing? The same as usual? Of course . . . They have all kinds of liberties there. And which of them do you know personally? Weselouwe, perhaps? Really! Well, isn't that something – how small our Lord's world has become in these modern times, thanks to trade! In that case, perhaps you can tell me – what's the outlook for the price of butter there next year? Eh?"

"Right now, it depends on how you buy it – whether with marks or by half-pood or by weight. And in what size casks. The price per pound can range from three to six shillings. But it's hard to predict what it'll be in spring . . ."

"Herr Horn will see elders of the guild now," the ensign announced from the door. Bal's neighbour sprang to his feet, took off his seeing-glasses, glanced at Bal with lively brown eyes, and said politely, "I'm summoned . . . You seem to be so well informed about trade that there's more I should have liked to ask you about affairs in Tallinn . . . Well, can't be helped . . . Please convey my greetings to Herr Weselouwe when you return. Tell him that Merchant Kyrö sends his regards."

The elders hurried off. For nearly an hour Bal fought drowsiness and nerves, until finally Ensign Boije returned:

"Let us go. Herr Horn is waiting."

They went up several flights of stairs and through a corridor, where artists in paint-spattered smocks were standing on scaffolding and, with long, thin brushes painting magical apple trees onto the stucco walls, and birds and lords and ladies into the branches of the trees. The partially completed gentlefolk were looking out of large windows – in surprise and some dismay, it seemed – at the whiteness of an approaching snowstorm.

The ensign led Bal to Herr Horn's study and closed the door behind him. The room was not what the Doctor had led Bal to expect. It did not look like one where the governance of all Finland took place. It was small, with a heavy, vaulted ceiling and bare, chalk-white walls. Even though Bal was focused on the man he had come to see, he took in and later, as always, remembered quite clearly all that fell within his peripheral vision. As for the man seated on the high-backed black chair at the table directly in front of him, he did not look like someone who had been close to the king for twenty years, someone who had recently been elevated to the position of principal counsellor to the King's favourite son, Duke Johan, the most powerful man in a province the size of a kingdom. Herr Henrik Claesson Horn was about forty-five years old and almost as sinewy as Bal's father, but with a notably narrower body, and he had a rather common face, somewhat like a peasant's, with calm, curious, grey eyes, light, very short hair, and a tawny skipper's beard. His black wool coat and narrow white pleated collar made him look almost like a preacher, but for the silver-studded sword belt around his waist. Bal stopped in front of the counsellor's chair and attempted a short, polite bow, which felt awkward, as always.

"Who sent you?" Herr Horn addressed him with the familiar "you".

"Doctor Friesner." Bal held out the Doctor's ring to Herr Horn, who took it and examined it carefully, holding it at a distance, as older people do.

"Good. Put it back in your pocket. You have a letter for the duke? Give it to me."

"The Doctor asked me to give it directly to the duke."

Only when the words were out of his mouth did it occur to Bal that they indicated a lack of trust in the counsellor, and he hastened to add: "It's a very urgent matter."

"Well, well. Do you know the contents of the letter?"

"In essence, I think I do."

"What does it say?"

"Yesterday at dawn, the Muscovite army invaded Livonia with a force of about forty thousand men."

Herr Horn stood up. "Did they come from the direction of Narva?"

"No, from the direction of Vastseliina and Tartu."

The news that the invasion had occurred in the south seemed to be something of a relief to Herr Horn. But he did not sit down.

"Give me the letter."

He spoke the words calmly, but with such a tone of authority that Bal could no longer insist on complying with the Doctor's directive to give it *only to the duke*. It would have been absurd.

Herr Horn took the letter and motioned to Bal to follow him out of the room, saying:

"Wait here. I'll deliver the letter straight to the duke. If he has any questions, he'll summon you." He left through a high oak-panelled door.

In the white light of the snowstorm outside Bal paced up and down the stone floor of the corridor, his restless shadow walking beside him along the whitewashed wall.

Of course, someday, at home, I'll be looked upon as "the man who visited the duke and talked with him". . . and I'll tell the grandchildren about it . . .

Hmm . . . it would be pleasant just to recall it myself, even if I never told anyone . . . Although it would be a relief if Horn returned and said, "You can go now, the duke has no further questions". . . But then again, to be here and not see what he is like . . . And if I answer his questions well, it's possible the duke will lay down twenty marks, which would go towards several more months of study in Marburg . . . Wonder if they've surrounded Tartu by now . . . they said the town has several cannons, but no-one had taken the trouble to position them on the walls . . . Strange – my shadow here on these white walls . . . And Tartu is possibly already cut off . . .

The oak door opened and a black-suited retainer crossed the threshold. "His Highness the Duke requests the gentleman to enter."

Bal was about to turn his head to look for the "gentleman" whose entry the duke requested, but stopped himself in time. Almost imperceptibly, he managed to change his startled smile into an expression of solemnity: the duke had summoned the "gentleman" – he had to look the part.

Dusk was falling, yet because of its high windows the anteroom they had entered was unexpectedly full of light. Bal wondered fleetingly whether the "gentleman's" face had been sufficiently cleansed of seal grease, but the retainer was already pushing open the next door.

The duke's study was the size of a small reception hall. Two huge square windows yawned in the whitewashed walls, framing the luminous snow on the other side of the glass. Oddly, it had no vaulted ceiling at all: it was flat and painted with a geometric pattern commonly seen on mittens. On the yellowish wooden floor between the windows lay a black bearskin. On that was a high-backed chair of intricately lathe-turned, light-coloured wood, and next to it a small square table. The duke, dressed in light and dark shades of brown velvet, was sitting in the chair, resting one elbow on the table, holding the Doctor's letter. Bal looked at him closely. He had the rosy complexion of a young man – what the devil – he looked as if he might even be a year or two younger than Bal! His round eyes, a bit brazen, were a mix of greys and browns, and he had the soft, reddish moustache of a mere stripling. Herr Horn was standing next to the table; on the wall between the windows at the back of the duke hung a large painting, several square cubits in size, in a carved frame of gilded laurel leaves. It showed an old man, his legs bent, his back curved with the years and rheumatism, dressed in black velvet finery, his high sloping forehead, beak-like nose, and long beard very similar to the way King Gustav appeared on Swedish silver thalers. Only after taking all this in did Bal remember to bow. It was a long salutation, for as he was bending forward and admiring the wide wooden floorboards it struck him that the old man in the large painting was not merely similar to the one on the thalers but was in fact the man himself.

"Approach," said Herr Horn. "The duke has a few questions to ask you."

Bal gave himself a little push – not that he needed an especially strong one – and walked across the floor, stopping four paces from the gentlemen. He realised he had lost all sleepiness and hunger. He glanced with interest at the large map lying on the duke's desk, but since it was upside down he could not tell what it depicted. Maybe he would not have known even if he had seen it right side up. *It'll be interesting to see what they want of me.* He raised his head and looked straight into the duke's importunate, round eyes, and had Herr Horn been one to draw such comparisons he would have remarked that in their exchange of glances there was a momentary resemblance between the two young men.

"This place where the Muscovite invaded Livonia – how far is it from Turku?" He asked the question in fairly good Low German, but Bal detected a note of suspicion in his voice. He made some rapid calculations: from the border to Tartu, ten leagues (that he remembered from his father's story of the trip to Pihkva); from Tartu to Tallinn, thirty

186

(everyone knew that). From Tallinn to Helsinki, thirteen (he had managed to get that out of Paap before they set out); and from Helsinki to Turku, thirty (as the Finn in Helsinki had told him).

"Eighty-three leagues."

The duke turned towards Horn, speaking in Swedish: "It says in this that the invasion took place yesterday at dawn. That means the message arrived here in barely thirty hours. I cannot believe that!"

"There is no doubt that the letter is authentic."

"That would be possible only if the Doctor had his own couriers and fresh horses available at each stop."

"There's no cause for doubt – the letter is authentic," repeated Horn.

"Anything can be forged!" said the duke darkly, with the voice of experience. Bal sensed that this was the time to interrupt. For the duke's doubts were not only foolish, they were possibly even dangerous.

"If I may speak – as far as the couriers and horses are concerned . . ." and he noticed mid-sentence that the duke was startled, looking at him and Horn with a faint blush rising into his face. It was, of course, because Bal had spoken in Swedish without even being aware of it, and the duke realised that his doubts had been revealed to the stranger. But there was no retreating now, and Bal continued: "As far as the couriers and horses are concerned, that's exactly how it was: the Doctor's wife was in Tartu and immediately sent us word by courier. It arrived in Tallinn at five yesterday. And before seven we were on our way from Tallinn. We rode all night. At four in the morning we were in Helsinki and by eleven in Salo. That's where we changed horses for the last time, and—"

Bal fell silent. A different expression had come over the duke's face, making further talk not only pointless but superfluous. Looking stunned, roguish, guilty and pleased at the same time, the duke asked, murmuring:

"Aha . . . So these tidings that the Doctor sent . . . so they're . . .

Well . . . then there's the other matter . . . Umm . . . How is Frau Katharina?"

"She has not been in Tallinn for many months. At first she was in Tartu, then in Riga, and now again in Tartu—" Bal paused for a moment, weighing the ratio of truth to untruth in what he was about to say, and continued emphatically: "Acting *in the interests of the duke!*" He added, after a pause: "Frau Katharina was to try to reach Tallinn yesterday by travelling over Põltsamaa and Paide."

"Well, I hope she succeeded. That far north, there shouldn't be any Muscovites skulking about yet, isn't that so? What do you think?"

Duke Johan looked at Bal, and his round eyes looked worried for a moment – whether about Katharina or Livonia or both was not clear.

"It would be a problem only if they'd already managed to surround Tartu before she got out . . ."

"Good. We will contact the Doctor and shall be expecting news."

The duke stood up, and Herr Horn was about to leave with Bal when the duke said: "One moment."

He strode to the painting of his royal father between the two windows and opened a small cupboard built into the wall behind it. After rummaging about in it, he closed it, came to Bal, and handed him a gold cross, two thumb-lengths long, on a slender chain. In its centre, held by five hooked gold clasps, was a sparkling red heart about the size of a hazelnut.

"Let the Doctor hang this around Katharina's neck for me."

At that the duke shot a glance at Horn and added, laughing: "*Intersit tamen crux mea inter eos.*"* Then he turned to Bal and asked: "*Intellexistine haec quoque?*"†

Bal looked down. He tried at lightning speed to weigh the conse-quences of a "yes" and the dangers of a false "no" that might later be discovered. And the more the threads of his calculations tied themselves

---

* Let my cross, at least, be between them (Latin). † Do you understand this, too? (Latin).

into a hopeless knot, the more clearly he recognised that modesty was not his strong suit. He raised his head and, eyes flashing with anger, replied in a voice so loud that he surprised himself: "*Verba quidem, sed non sentiam.*"*

When they were back in Horn's study, Horn waved Bal to a seat and asked: "You don't have anything else important to add?"

Bal shook his head.

Herr Horn opened a small iron-lined box on the bench behind him and counted out ten silver marks into his palm. Bal was looking at the table and noticed the merchant Kyrö's seeing-glasses, at the far corner, behind the pewter candlestick. The merchant had apparently left them behind.

"But what are you, yourself," asked Herr Horn, "German or Swede, or . . . ?"

"I'm a Tallinner . . ." Bal drew a breath and went through the little duel within himself that always took place when he was asked the question – the duel between honesty and the desire to elevate his status. "What I mean is . . . I'm an Estonian, from the town of Tallinn."

"And what do you do?"

"I'm a scholar in my final year at the Trivium School."

"So . . . aha! . . ." For some reason he sounded surprised. He looked Bal up and down and asked: "Are there many over there – like you?"

"There are eight. At the moment."

"Eight! So!" He burst out laughing. Just then there was a knock at the door.

Ensign Boije was on the threshold. "Pardon me, Herr Counsellor, Rodenborg says he left his spectacles here. There they are—" The ensign stepped to the table and picked up Mr Kyrö's seeing-glasses. Bal recognised them unmistakably: a piece of grey yarn had been wound

* I understand the words, but not the meaning (Latin).

189

around the left earpiece – a repair, probably.

"Herr Ensign, excuse me . . . I think those are Merchant Kyrö's spectacles."

The ensign looked at Bal from under his arched reddish brows: "Right . . . they're the ones, then." With sharp staccato steps he left the room, spectacles in hand.

"They're the ones, alright," said Herr Horn in reply to Bal's questioning look. "How do you know this Kyrö?"

"We talked a bit downstairs, while we were waiting to see you."

"Ah. That's it. His name is actually Rodenborg, a German from Germany. From Hamburg, or wherever it is . . . But he likes living under the rule of our duke so much that he's become a real Finn. Doesn't even want to hear the name Rodenborg any more . . . wants to be called Kyrö. There are others like him here."

Herr Horn pulled his hand, holding the ten marks, out of his pocket. When it came to money, he had adopted the penny-pinching ways of his king over the years, and had carried them out with a certain provincial thoroughness. From the corner of his eye he shot a quick glance at Bal and waited – the least sign of gratitude from Bal would have sufficed for him to save ten marks in the interests of the duke and the king. And even though Bal was burning with curiosity to know what he would be paid, he kept his eyes fixed on the edge of the table, where Kyrö's spectacles had lain. He was thinking: *Here, the Germans want to be Finnish, while in our land . . . and if even I . . . every time I am asked, first have to . . .* Herr Horn felt he could prevaricate no longer. With a mixture of regret and satisfaction he coughed and counted out ten more coins from the casket onto his left palm.

"Here you are. And I hope we meet again. In the interests of the duke." He glanced at the lead-framed windowpanes, now white with snow. "And I hope that the strong west wind has not blown cracks into the ice."

CHAPTER SEVEN,

*in which we briefly recount the travellers' travails on their homeward
journey across the perilous gulf, yet focus mainly on the greater dangers
that lie in wait in his own home for a youth just beginning to dry out
behind the ears, perils that are all the more menacing in that they
are so curiously interwoven with the apocalyptic events about to
roll across the land, and so enticingly redolent of the fruit of the
tree of knowledge, the fruit that brings both bliss and woe.*

To a much greater extent than is generally recognised, a person's character is determined by the way the winnowing basket of his memory is woven. Or, conversely, the weave of the basket may itself constitute the person's character. For in the process of separating what is worth remembering from what should be forgotten, the winnowing memory can magically transform chaff into grain, and vice versa.

In retrospect, Bal might have viewed his encounter with the duke as the brief and sudden emergence of a mote of dust into a circle of candle-light, and its retreat back into darkness. Or as an ennobling moment of participation in the politics of the wider world. But in neither the one case nor the other would he have been himself. He had no sense, after his encounter with the duke, of being a puppet master in the fate of states. And even less did he have a sense of being a mere mote of dust momentarily illuminated by the glow of the duke. He knew they were from different worlds, but he actually felt he was on a par with him, even half a head taller, as he had ascertained in the large Venetian mirror at the moment when the duke handed him the golden cross for Katharina.

But it was clear that by his journey he had accomplished nothing of note, for the duke played no part at all in the events that followed.

As for his travel homeward, he could have recalled that too in various ways. It could have lodged in his memory as a desperate struggle in a blizzard, with sea water rising onto the ice from the widening cracks on its surface. North of the island of Nairisaare, the western storm winds had blown rifts into the ice and sent the floes moving east. Fortunately, Paap had ascertained this eastward movement and pulled the horse's muzzle towards the west so as not to end up on the island of Salmesaare, or who-knows-where. But afterwards, as they lurched onward, sodden and half frozen in the whirling snowstorm, over cracking rifts and through sloshing pools of surface water, only to be overtaken by twilight, it was their chestnut gelding that delivered them from the darkening tumult to Nairisaare's northern headland. They landed exactly at the spot where a juniper cross, blackened by many storms, rose from between snow-covered rocks. Hanging from it was a box, called a *fattigbyssa* by the Swedish inhabitants of the island, placed there for the offerings of those who had escaped the perils of the sea.

To Paap it was immediately clear what God expected. Though his knees were still weak and trembling from the strain – he had been walking in front of the horse, wielding the boathook – he went straight to the offering box, and, even as his wet linen trousers froze hard in the bitter wind, he mumbled a prayer of thanks and dropped a whole silver farthing through the slit in the lid. Bal stayed where he was by the sleigh and calculated that, in addition to the twenty marks he had just earned, the only money he had were two silver mark pieces that the Doctor had given him. He had used up the smaller coins for a good meal and beers for himself and Paap at an inn next to the Turku bridge, and now had only a few shillings in change. He balked at the idea of putting a whole mark into this box – how could one know who would empty it, and when or even whether the offerings would ever reach the poor box at St Olaf's, which was where they were supposed to go . . . ? No, a whole mark, whether it came from the Doctor's two or his own twenty, would simply be much too much to leave out here in the open. He took the feedbag from the sleigh, went close to the gelding, and pressed his face, hot from effort and sleeplessness, against the horse's twitching snowy ear for a moment. Something seemed to rise from his body into his head, more a feeling than a thought, something he could find no better word for than *gratitude:* expansive, warm, triumphant. In his mind he pictured this gratitude thumbing its nose at the darkness behind them – and realised that it was directed primarily towards the gelding, and only in a kind of ceremonial and perfunctory shiver towards God. Then he took half a loaf of bread from inside his coat, broke it in four, dropped the pieces into the feedbag with the oats, and hung it around the horse's head.

After some days and nights with a Swedish fisherman on Nairisaare Island in the village of Lõunaküla, they were finally, on the morning of January 28, able to cross the cracked and refrozen gulf, and by midday were heading up from the coast towards the Great Coast Gate, its blue–red–gold coat of arms partially hidden under a layer of sticky snow. They kept a watchful eye on their surroundings, but could see nothing between the coast and harbour and Gate to indicate that the news of imminent war had reached town. Ten cogs, belonging to gentlemen of Tallinn, Vibourg and Danzig, along with a few barges and single-masted boats, rested calmly in the ice by the bulwark, their masts bare, and snowdrifts several cubits high on their decks. Smoke was rising in the most ordinary, unremarkable way from the chimney of the Pox House; and in the Rose Garden, in bushes nearly buried by white, Bal could hear sparrows scrabbling in hollow spaces beneath the crusted snow. To the left of the Coast Gate, below the bank with its flattened top where Gertrude Chapel had stood before its destruction, four men were busy on the frozen moat. They were chipping at the ice, unhurriedly, each on his own grey space cleared of snow, and the sound of their clinking picks was as measured and steady as if they were engaged in the most important activity in the world.

As the sleigh passed the workers at a distance of about fifty paces, one of the men straightened up and, waving his ice pick, ran shouting towards the sleigh: "Hey! Baa-aall!"

Bal reined in the horse and the man reached the sleigh. "Märten!? What are you hacking at here?"

"Hah. The Council had the moat stocked with pike just recently. Now we have to make air holes for them. At a shilling a crack. Other-wise, two hundred fish dinners will be done for. An unacceptable loss. But what are you doing riding into town by this gate – on your way back from Üksnurme?"

The Doctor and Bal had agreed that they would tell everyone – the Frolinks and the school and everyone else – that Bal had gone to Üksnurme to deliver medicines to the steward, purportedly suffering from swollen glands. And that Bal might have to stay a few days to mon-itor the man's health. Märten had apparently gone looking for him and had heard the story either from Annika or Meus or the Doctor . . . So . . . Now Bal had to stick to the yarn.

"I stopped by at Father's place in Kalamaja on the way back."

"Did the steward bite the dust, then?"

"No. What makes you think that?"

"Or maybe it's on account of the war that you're looking so glum?"

"Yup. I heard about the war."

"Where'd you hear about it?"

"They were talking about it in Keila, at the Black Angel tavern."

"When?"

"Well . . . sometime this morning."

"Yes? I hear they're plundering the area south of Tartu pretty badly. And it looks like they came over at Narva, too."

"At Narva too? I hadn't heard about that. Is there any other news?"

"Not really."

Bal was quiet for a moment. "Märten—"

Märten looked sharply at Bal from under the edge of his flap-eared, mangy dogskin hat: "Well?"

"I'll come over to your place tonight. I'm in a hurry right now. See you later."

Bal pulled on the reins and the sleigh swept under the coat of arms on the arched gate. The familiar, protective town walls suddenly seemed oppressive.

The only thing that had noticeably changed in town – and at the Bishop's House it was a considerable change – was that Frau Katharina had arrived. The servant Johann, who had been charged with clearing the yard of snow during Paap's absence, announced the news as soon as the sleigh pulled up at the stable. Bal gave his travel coat to Paap, and when he pulled open the door of the house he noticed a faint but decidedly new scent. As he proceeded through the great-room, up the stairs, on to the second-floor landing and along the hallway between the rooms, the fragrance became more pronounced and puzzling. Bal knocked and sniffed again, waiting at the door of the Doctor's study for his "yes". When Bal stepped in the Doctor was standing with his back to the snowy window, and his wife, in a shimmering amber gown of silk, was sitting on a three-legged stool near the lectern, one leg crossed over the other, her hands, with many rings on her fingers, on her knees. She was smiling a satisfied smile. From under the edge of her skirt, like a pert nose, peered the light-red tip of a shoe – it was the first thing Bal noticed about Katharina. After that he took in the rest: She was very pretty and clearly much younger than the Doctor, definitely under thirty. Her shiny auburn hair was swept smoothly off her forehead and gathered abundantly at the nape of her neck. Her eyes were long ovals of such a dark grey that even facing the light they seemed nearly black, and above them, as though painted on, arched a pair of dark brows. Unlike most brunettes with reddish tints in their hair – those who had pink cheeks, white skin and freckles – her narrow face was smooth and evenly rosy. Her laughing mouth looked as if it could tease and lie with ease. And Bal saw, in both the Doctor's face and hers, an expression he did not quite understand – as if they had just been either embracing or quarrelling.

"Aha – you're back! Well?" the Doctor called out, and then explained to his wife: "This is young Master Balthasar. He's just returned from the duke."

His wife turned her oval-eyed gaze on Bal. Suddenly her eyes rounded with delight and she became animated.

"He's just as I imagined him!" Her voice was marvellously mellow.

"Well?" repeated the Doctor, turning to Bal, who recounted the story of his trip in a few sentences.

"Aha," said the Doctor. "And the duke seemed well disposed towards us? Is that right? He was courteous, amiable towards you?"

Frau Katharina laughed, a low, deep laugh.

"And he paid you?"

"Not directly. Herr Horn was the one who paid me."

"How much? Ten marks?"

"Ah . . . No. Twenty."

"Well! That is unusual for Herr Horn. But you were no doubt most capable. And I certainly don't want to be tight-fisted by comparison."

"Just think, Matthias, what a storm they had to come through," said Frau Katharina.

The Doctor opened the hobnailed door to the vault and went in. Bal looked at Frau Katharina and, unfathomably, felt himself blush, perhaps because he was trying in vain to find a way to respond to her friendly comment. After some effort he said: "The trip from Tartu could not have been easy for you either . . ."

She laughed. "There were a dozen of us women together – all as timid as I. And gentlemen too, of course. It was amusing at times . . ."

She said all this in a surprisingly casual, friendly, girlish manner, as though she were not a high-born lady conversing with Bal for the very first time but some girl from Kalamaja he had known for years. Then she turned to him, her eyes now dark, and in a completely different tone of voice, in a half-whisper full of alarm, said:

"But you must have been face to face with death, out there on the sea . . . ?"

Bal gestured nonchalantly. Just then the Doctor came out of the vault. Though he had partly shut the door behind him when he went in, Bal had noticed through the crack that he had taken money out of the casket with the painted red flowers, next to the box with the skeleton. Now he counted out twenty-five marks onto the corner of the lectern. Bal swept the silver coins carefully into his left hand. Frau Katharina's shoe caught his eye just then, and he thought of the satisfaction it would give him not to take the money at all. But he quickly calculated the sum of his capital for Marburg and dropped the coins into his pocket, taking pleasure in the sound of their jingling.

"And I have something for you from the duke."

It had occurred to Bal that it might be better to give the cross to the Doctor later, when they were alone. Let him decide for himself when or if to hang it around his wife's neck, and even whether or not to mention it to her . . . in either case it would hang between them, whether on a chain or on a word. But he would have to come up with a convincing reason for the delay. He could not very well wait till the next day and say to the Doctor, *I didn't want to give this to you yesterday in your wife's presence* . . . No, the only thing he could say then was that he had forgotten about the cross. Yet a cross of this kind was worth a small fortune in gold alone. If a quarter-weight of gold cost six marks, the cross was worth at least fifty, not counting the red stone. The Doctor would never credit his excuse; he would have worked out that his wife's presence had inhibited Bal, and infer that Bal knew something he had no business knowing. Moreover . . . Bal looked at Frau Katharina, at the graceful tilt of her head, at her red lips – like a child's – at her eyes like smoky glass as she gazed at the frost patterns on the window, and he knew he wanted her to know that he knew something. It seemed a desire not pleasing to God, to be sure, yet not terribly sinful either. Because he *did* know: he had heard the duke say it in Latin, had seen his look and his smile.

"The duke asks the Doctor to hang *this* around the neck of his beautiful wife."

Bal stopped in confusion, distressed that he had dared call the lady "beautiful" in the name of the duke. But in spite of his momentary qualm he noticed that perhaps he had been mistaken: not in that the lady was beautiful, but in his supposition that there had been something between her and the duke. On the contrary, there was not a trace of displeasure in the Doctor's expression. His eyes gleamed as he snatched the necklace from Bal's hand, and he called out in great delight: "Kati, look, he's sending you a gold cross, and in the cross, his heart – a ruby! A gallant knight, wouldn't you say? The heart alone is worth a hundred marks!"

The lady blushed as she hurried to the Doctor with an *Ooh!* of delight, her eyes a lustrous grey, her lips parted in surprise. She held up the cross, dangling it in front of her, examining it from all angles. But the blush on her cheeks appeared to be one of pleasure, not at all of guilt.

"Well then," she said coquettishly, "do as the duke commanded!" With a laugh, she leant her slender, tight-fitting bodice and shapely neck towards the Doctor, who unfastened the clasp, hung the necklace around her neck, and fastened it at the back. The cross gleamed between the rounded curves of her breasts, just above the low neckline. And then – the Devil take these gentlemen with their German and French customs: they allow themselves such liberties that a man does not know where to turn his eyes! – the Doctor clasped the lady around the waist – he did not need to lift her up, since she was only slightly shorter than he – and kissed her long and hard on the mouth. As though there were not even the shadow of another person in the room! In his first moment of astonishment Bal cast his eyes down towards the floor. But after the fourth or fifth heartbeat he looked up again. The Doctor had turned slightly and now had his back to Bal. He was pressing his face against Frau Katharina's, and Bal could see her left eye over the Doctor's back. It was closed at first, but then its long lashes slowly rose and she looked directly into Bal's eyes. Her look was suddenly so desperately dark that for a moment Bal's breath stopped short.

When the Doctor released her – it could not have been more than a moment later – she said in the most ordinary way, that is, with an extraordinary ease of manner: "But Matthias – let's invite Herr Balthasar to dinner. Just think of the present he's brought us! And Magdalena's roast goose is almost done."

"Of course," said the Doctor with the greatest kindness. "Go and wash the dust off your travels and do come, definitely."

Bal mumbled a thank-you. He did not usually feel at ease among strangers, but was eager to accept the invitation. For where else but here, he asked himself, could he learn the latest, most accurate news of the course of the war?

They had the midday dinner in the great-room, sitting on the famous chairs carved by Master Andreas, around a small round table that their predecessor Weselouwe had brought from Holland. The fourth person at the table was Councilman Beelholt – grey-haired, portly, ruddy-cheeked – wearing a short grey-green cape edged in mink over a black coat, and several heavy gold rings on his fingers. As far as Bal knew, the man had been cautioned by the Doctor to abstain from meat because of a kidney ailment and consulted him regularly every week. Apparently the Doctor also paid the councilman the occasional visit. But here he was, chewing on a hunk of goose right under the Doctor's eyes, a serving the Doctor himself had carved for him.

Bal had scrubbed himself thoroughly with Annika's resin soap and put on his black suit of Göttingen wool, his father's suit, altered for him last Christmas and intended for his graduation ceremony in spring. Yet he felt confoundedly ill at ease – not on account of the grandeur of the white linen tablecloth (which resembled the Kalamaja table covering at Annnika's wedding feast, and the one they ate off even on less festive occasions at Meus' house); nor on account of the silver dishes (even his father had some of those on his shelves – not as finely wrought, perhaps, but no less solid) – no, the problem was that the entire process of eating was somehow refined in a way new to him, and he felt conspicuous among the other diners. The main difficulty was that the goose was being eaten with those cursed utensils that looked like Neptune's trident or miniature silver pitchforks, called *gaffel* in German, and for which there was no word in country tongue. Bal relaxed only when he saw Councilman Beelholt, his face damp from effort, put down his pronged silver utensil and, in keeping with local custom, pick up the goose leg with both hands.

As soon as Bal had taken his seat the Doctor had related to the councilman, with some pride, the story of Bal's trip to Turku. The councilman was evidently in the Doctor's confidence on these matters, though he seemed more detached and cautious than the Doctor. His watery blue eyes appraised Bal with a look at once evaluative and appreciative, and taking a bite of goose off his *gaffel* he said: "Hmm. That's not bad. The sooner the duke knows he needs to grant a loan quickly to Fürstenberg, the better."

Later, when the councilman had drunk two large goblets of Rhine wine and a third of malmsey – Frau Katharina kept smilingly refilling his vessel – and had begun to tackle the roast goose in the homely manner described, he clarified a number of things. The enemy had left Ivangorod the night before and crossed the frozen river just south of Narva. They had burned countless villages and manors in the parish of Jõhvi. But the forces that had invaded the bishopric from the south had not, as far as was known, cut off Tartu. They were busy laying waste to the landscape, including areas north of Tartu. And when Councilman Beelholt had quaffed his fourth goblet – the other diners were at that point just finishing their first – he stuck out his lower lip contemptuously and said:

"Just imagine this – the Bishop of Tartu, just two weeks ago, sent a letter to the Master of the Order, warning him not to rush *needlessly* into preparations for war. You tell me, how the devil are we supposed to defend this country with leaders *like that*? The Master of the Order has, in any case, neglected all preparations in the most *inexcusable* manner . . . right now, by the way, he's on his way from Võnnu to Viljandi, where the forces of the Order have been commanded to assemble in all haste. But we know what their idea of haste is . . ."

After this Herr Beelholt asked Bal to relate to him once more how Herr Horn had received the news of war: "How did he react?"

"Well . . . he didn't, actually . . . He just . . . stood up."

"See now!" said the Doctor triumphantly.

"Oh yes!" cried Herr Beelholt. "At that, all of them will stand up over there – Horn, the duke and old Gustav himself . . . Well, may God grant! But how did the duke seem?"

"He seemed to be seriously worried . . . about Livonia—" said Bal, looking towards Frau Katharina and meeting her soft dark eyes, their enigmatic glance both intimate and distant. He did not add: *and worried about Frau Katharina, as well.*

The servant Johann appeared at the door, coughed and announced in a whisper that filled the room: "Herr Town Syndic is pleased to . . ."

Bal glanced at Herr Beelholt and saw him compress his fleshy lips into a narrow line, drooping at the corners. The man was ill at ease. The Doctor raised his right eyebrow for a moment, just for a moment, and then called out: "Oh – but of course—" and smiling broadly went to greet the official. Herr Beelholt gazed darkly into his empty goblet. Bal felt something like a little dog's nose sniffing at his left leg under the table. He had just about realised that the Doctor had no dog when he felt a gentle but definite pressure on his foot; and as he stared in confusion at the goose bones on his silver plate he felt the pressure go up against his leg. It was not strong, nor was it hot. It started at his ankle and extended only to his knee, but somehow he felt it all the way through his thigh and groin and to his heart, and it made him start in bewilderment. He looked at Frau Katharina. She caught his look – her eyes teasing, anxious – and signalled with them, not moving her head, towards the door where Syndic Clodt and the Doctor were approaching. Her index finger with its apple-tree sealing ring rose to her red lips, pursed as though in alarm: "Shhhh . . ."

Bal moved his lips slightly to show that he understood – and then Syndic Clodt was there. On his way to the table he had handed his dark-purple fur-lined cape to Johann and now, baring his long teeth in a smile, came towards Frau Katharina to kiss her hand. He was, after all, the sole expert on the art of statecraft in Tallinn and its most highly educated burgher . . . Just how he had gained such a reputation was not clear, for he was not especially well liked. The Greys had long known, as had Bal, that he was so arrogant and treated the lower classes with such contempt that even among the real patricians it was hard to find his like. There were some master-artisans and herring-sellers who considered him very clever. But among the more prominent merchants he was looked upon as an educated upstart and a tiresome windbag – Bal had long ago learned the fathers' opinions from the merchants' sons at school. And as for women finding him attractive, the possibility could not exist: he was tall and scraggy, with a large nose and freckles; his limp reddish hair had been turning grey over the past few years and was especially noticeable close up. Even though his reindeer boots were immaculate, and his brown wool coat and collar and cuffs brand-new, he gave off an impression of shabbiness. But perhaps Bal saw him in a worse light than he deserved, for he had found out, by chance and from acquaintances, that Herr Clodt was three months in debt to Kuuse-Kreegor, alderman of the tailors' guild, who had made the very coat Clodt was wearing. Apparently Clodt did not even intend to start repaying the debt. On the other hand, one had to admit that the rumours spread about his syphilis were false. The rash on his forehead some months ago was not a *corona veneris* but ordinary eczema, and the Doctor's salt treatment had rendered it barely visible. If it had been the nasty malady itself, the Doctor would not have failed to use strips of guaiacum wood in treating the honourable syndic. So, indeed, this story did the man injustice. Still, next to him the Doctor was the embodiment of refinement, with his unwavering smile, his black beard directed towards each of them in turn, and his splendid coat of green Lombardy velvet.

They drew their chairs closer together around the small table – and suddenly Frau Katharina was next to Bal. Herr Clodt sat on the Doctor's right. Frau Katharina was about to have the goose brought back when Herr Clodt declined, with thanks, and Magdalena brought the marzipan to the table instead. The Doctor was not reticent about explaining that it was made to order, by Apothecary Dyck, of the finest white flour and sugar, and of sweet and bitter almonds and rosewater. The pleasantly dense mixture had been poured into precious antique, silver-plated moulds in the shape of blossoming bouquets and wreaths of flowers, crafted by the late renowned Michel Sittow himself.

Partaking liberally of the malmsey wine to wash down the marzipan, Herr Clodt began to hold forth on the affairs of the world, weaving in both pertinent and pointless questions. In the oddly casual and super-ficial manner of a detached observer, he related the story of the arrival of Jürgen Meissen bearing the message of Job to the town of Pärnu. Then he asked the Doctor what manner of man Bal was – but he did not seem to register the information that this was an assistant to the Doctor and soon-to-be disciple of Hippocrates in Marburg. He did, however, tell a few somewhat coarse student jokes by way of response. Without pause, he next asked the Doctor what he thought of the current war sit-uation, but before the Doctor could answer he went off on a new tack – wondering whether the Doctor thought Duke Johan already knew about the outbreak of war.

It was not so much alarm as a kind of immobilising suspense that Bal felt for a moment. And, just then, fire coursed up his entire left side in a strange, sweet-hot glow, as Frau Katharina pressed her leg hard against his. The Doctor was filling the syndic's beaker from the silver pitcher, but he glanced up in response to the question and, looking the syndic straight in the eye and continuing to pour, replied with the utmost calm: "That's hardly possible. How could he . . . so soon . . ." He did not pour a drop too much and not a drop missed its mark, and with the beaker full to the brim, still holding the pitcher, he continued: "Does the syndic think the duke should be informed? I send him medicines from time to time." He placed the pitcher carefully on the table. "I could, for example, send him a message – let us say, on the recommen-dation of Herr Syndic of our Town Council?"

"Just a moment," said Herr Clodt with a faint half-smile, "what does Herr Beelholt think?"

Herr Beeltholt had thought of nothing new to say in response to such a question and repeated what he had said earlier, before Herr Clodt's arrival: "The sooner the duke finds out that he'll have to provide a loan to Fürstenberg, the better." He ran his tongue over his lips, as though tasting something sweet: *that's what I think.* He was pleased with himself for having stated the Order's perspective in a nice round response for Clodt to chew on. Then his blue eyes opened wide in astonishment, for Herr Clodt was saying, in his superficial, evasive manner, swallowing another mouthful of malmsey: "Of course, Fürstenberg will ask the duke for a loan. But there's no chance he'll get it. It'll take some time to amass two hundred thousand – two hundred thousand is what they're asking. So it's not certain that Herr Fürstenberg will continue to be our Master."

The Doctor burst out laughing: "Herr Syndic is speaking in jest! . . . I think the duke—"

The syndic swallowed his marzipan: "You think the duke will pocket Livonia himself rather than provide a loan?"

"Ha-ha-ha-hah," the Doctor laughed. "No, that I do not believe."

"Ha-ha-ha-hah," the syndic laughed. "Nor do I. What I mean is, Herr Fürstenberg is an able, competent man. Without a doubt. But the Order needs someone even abler."

"And who would that be?" Frau Katharina asked, fingering the duke's cross.

"W-e-ell . . ." Herr Clodt drawled, and his wine-reddened eyes rolled towards Katharina. "If the Frau Katharina herself wants to know . . ." He reached across the table for her hand and, lurching over the goblets, kissed her fingers, ". . . if the lady wants to know, I must tell all. Have you heard of Herr Kettler?"

"Not really . . . no," Frau Katharina said.

"Wait a minute!" cried the Doctor. "Isn't that the Westphalian who, a few years ago, was appointed as – what was he appointed as?" He snapped his fingers and tried to recall, but the wine had affected his usually superior memory.

"Never heard of him," Herr Beelholt growled.

"The commander of Dünamünde, in fifty-four," Bal said. The devil knows how that popped into his head.

"Look at that," said Herr Clodt, turning towards Bal for an instant, "*out of the mouths of babes*, and so on . . . As the Evangelist Matthew says, and Doctor Matthias will soon say. Herr Kettler will, in the immediate future, become the commander of Viljandi and shrewd men will put their money on him. And by the way I've been planning to introduce you to his secretary. I invited him here tonight. A man called Henning, from Weimar, a wagoner's son to be sure, but he's studied at three universities, an intelligent lad. His first name's Salomon. Once in a while you find someone . . . even among the rabble."

The wine had run out. Frau Katharina hailed Johann, but he did not hear her. And then she called for Magdalena, forgetting that earlier, when the girl had brought the candles to the tables, she herself had sent her to the pastor's wife with a small pitcher of wine.

"Then I'll have to ask you to come and help me fetch more wine," the Doctor's wife said to Bal.

She took the empty silver decanter from the table, and, since another guest was expected, got a second one from the cupboard, handing both to Bal. Holding a candle from the pewter candelabra, she preceded Bal to the kitchen and through a low side door and down the cellar stairs. And Bal, suddenly recognising the scent he had caught earlier, followed at her heels in a cloud of carnations and roses. Katharina, with graceful step, went down the stairs, the candle in one hand, raising her skirt with the other so as not to trip on the steep flagstone steps, the shadow of her hair moving like a huge bundle of witch's broom across the low, rough, vaulted ceiling. On two levels of shelves ranged along the walls lay at least ten barrels of wine. Katharina pointed to a barrel on the second shelf. Bal pulled out the plug and let a light, slightly sour, sun-fragrant Rhenish wine run into the silver pitcher.

"We'll fill the other with malmsey. It's over here."

The cask of malmsey was on a lower shelf, actually at floor level, and the tall pitcher would not fit under its spout. But Frau Katharina possessed ingenuity.

"Turn the cask a bit, so that the spout is higher."

This presented no obvious difficulty, though it would have been even easier to tilt the rim of the pitcher to push it under the spout. But for some reason Bal decided on another course. He put the jug on the floor, took hold of the two handles of the heavy oaken cask, and heaved it up onto an empty space on the upper shelf. Just like that. He heard the shoulder seam in his graduation suit rip. Frau Katharina exclaimed, "Oooh . . ." The spicy, seductive aroma of the wine mingled with the lady's scent of roses and carnations, and with the remembered fragrance of fresh sap in a distant birch grove. Frau Katharina walked ahead of him again, Bal following with a brimful pitcher in each hand. Again the shadow of the lady's coiffure moved over the vaulted ceiling; a red shoe flashed from time to time from under the hem of her amber gown. Halfway up the stairs she suddenly stopped and turned to face him. She was two steps above him, holding the candle at chest level. Her eyes were completely black, in each one a reflection of the flame flutter-ing with Bal's every breath. She took a step down, closer to him – she was now half a head shorter than he – and blew out the candle. He felt some of the wine slosh out onto the steps and tried to hold the pitchers steady. The sudden current that coursed through him – of shock, dis-belief, guilt, delight and bewilderment – made his hands shake. Then, as he held his breath, he felt Frau Katharina's fingers on his face, in his hair, felt the hot candle sweep past his left ear and her burning lips brush his. And then she ran up the steps in the dark and disappeared into the light-filled rectangle of the kitchen door. When Bal reached the kitchen the lady was already in the living room, greeting the new guest.

Herr Salomon Henning had arrived.

Bal went in and set the wine pitchers on the table. He did not dare look at Katharina. He sat down next to her and stared at the rings on her fingers – *Oh God . . . the same hands that had just . . .* Here they were, fluttering over the table, arranging a goblet for the new guest. He heard her voice, but only her voice, not the words. And it took a while before he could bring the visitor into focus.

Herr Henning was about thirty, and for a German his blond hair was quite dark. His face was soft and round, his grey eyes meek and obliging, his mouth petulant and selfish. He was wearing a plain, dark-blue woollen suit which, with respect to quality of attire, put him somewhere between Bal and the other assembled guests, but closer to Bal. And the middle finger of his right hand, on the thumb side, was ink-stained. But the way he repeatedly moved his right hand close to his hip, even mid-sentence, and then rested it awkwardly on his hip, made it clear that he was accustomed to carrying a sword.

Herr Henning sat directly across from Bal and was already deep in conversation with the Doctor. Even though Bal now dared once more glance at Katharina, and even though her shining red-brown hair was less than five spans away from him, the conversation between the Doctor and Henning gradually began to interest him. From time to time the whiff of warm roses and carnations reached his nostrils, making his heart pound so desperately that he would not have been surprised to hear pitchers and goblets chiming with his heartbeats. Between the heady aromas he became aware of Herr Henning's placidly droning voice:

"My master told the Order Master as far back as the sixth of December, 1554, that in his opinion it would be necessary to find an accommodation with Poland . . . My master thinks that Herr Radziwill is the most influential man in the kingdom. He's not only the Grand Marshall of Lithuania and the King's Chancellor, but also – don't forget – the Queen's brother . . . When my master was in Lübeck at the Klingenberg Inn on the seventh of June, of the year '53 . . . When my master returned from Dünamünde on the eighth of April last year, in disguise—"

"How is it you remember these dates so precisely?" the Doctor asked.

"I always write them down."

"Oh . . . and why?"

"I'm writing a chronicle of my master's accomplishments."

"I'm aware that there are chronicles about the Order Masters," Herr Clodt said. "Yours, then, would be the first such chronicle of a commander, correct?"

Herr Henning put a flower-shaped marzipan confection into his mouth and narrowed his grey eyes: "Well . . . hardly . . . My master is only forty years old."

"So, as mercenary soldiers are wont to say," Herr Beelholt drawled, with evident irony, "at eight o'clock a soldier-boy, by twelve o'clock a captain . . . ?"

Bal did not hear Herr Henning's reply. The reference to the time made him look at the Doctor's wall clock, and he saw that the hour hand had moved from the thick Roman six a good way towards the seven, and at seven o'clock the town gates would close. And now that the enemy was abroad in the land, the gates for pedestrians would also shut. And suddenly it seemed of the utmost importance for Bal to keep his word to Märten. He murmured an apology to the gathered company. The Doctor nodded, smiling: "Until tomorrow, after school—" His voice was most kind, but then became unmistakably insistent: "And the steward at Üksnurme is still afflicted with swollen glands." Frau Katharina caught Bal's eyes with her own, in which ten candles flickered, and held them for a long moment before turning away to pour some more wine for Herr Beelholt.

Meus was bent over his lectern cluttered with books. Annika was sitting on a three-legged stool, knitting. Both were working by the light of a single candle. It quivered in the draught, which also made the dog-skin curtain at the pig's-bladder window move slightly. They looked at

Bal as he entered and it seemed to him that there was the trace of a taunt in Annika's question:

"Well, and just how does it come about that all of a sudden you get invited to dinner?"

"Well . . . you know . . . he asked me to go . . ." murmured Bal, putting on his coat, "to Üksnurme and . . ."

"Is the estate manager seriously ill?"

"Well . . . his neck is badly swollen . . ."

"Is it a big estate they have there?" Meus asked.

"Well, yes, fairly big . . ." Bal murmured. "It's hard to tell with all this snow . . . But I have to go and see Märten. I ran into him earlier and promised."

"Hmm—" Meus remarked and was about to go back to his books, but said instead: "You're doing well in school. I know that. Herr Balder was praising you just recently. But you have less than half a year before you finish. Don't you think . . . even you need to do some studying? *Tu quoque,** as Herr Sum said to you!"

"I'll manage . . ." Bal mumbled, and was just about to leave when Annika called him back: "If you're going to Kalamaja in any case – and you'll have to stay the night – maybe you could go by the house and see if there's any news of Father . . . He was supposed to be on his way home from Narva, but now . . ."

"Father . . . ? Yes. Of course."

Bal navigated his way through town by the occasional glow of windows in black walls and the silhouettes of roof lines against starlit clouds, but mostly by the memory in both his feet and his mind. Even in the pitch dark he could not have turned a single wrong corner in the heart of the town he knew so well. To get out before the gates closed he took a shortcut across the New Market, where the Town Hall's drainage

* You too (Latin).

pipes, choked with snow, creaked in the wind, and then went along Väike-Rataskaevu Street with its snowdrifts stained by horse urine, arriving at the Nunnavärav Gate just as the gatekeeper was struggling to place the crossbar across the main gate. But the side gate was still open.

Proceeding along the footpath on the other side, despite the cold and the wind and even without the glowing windows on Toompea Hill, he could have surmised its location, for from the left, a wintry gust carried the stench of the excrement that at the base of the hill trickled into mud in summer and into snow in winter. Then the wind shifted to the northwest and blew in a clean, broad sweep from Köismäe Hill, straight at Bal, and he breathed deeply of the fresh air. The dark did not impede his progress here either, for the road over Köismäe Hill to Kopli, used for hauling logs and hay, and the sleigh road that turned right to Kalamaja, and the winding footpath were all firm and secure under his feet. Only the improbable, fantastic events of the past few days seemed unreal, especially here in the gloom. And he had drunk more wine today than ever before. (Where would he have had the occasion, earlier?) At his father's they drank only ale, and only on special occasions, never wine. And if perchance Meus had a tiny carafe of plum wine on some corner shelf they would sip a little of it from a tin cup, but only on Christmas Day or New Year's morn. But it was not the full silver goblets he had quaffed from today that were propelling him onward. He could, of course, have gone and confessed to Meus – it would not have mattered whether to Meus as his former schoolteacher, or current relative, or pastor. Did the Doctor's injunction to keep his mouth shut include confession to a pastor? Oddly, the simultaneous existence of all three roles seemed to him to cancel each other out. For all three versions of Meus would, each in its own way, have begun to instruct, guide, scold, preach, wish well . . . no doubt about it. In some ways Bal felt that he and Meus, with his prematurely greying temples and anxious look, had been growing closer, not only in terms of their social standing but also because of the familial relationship. At the same time, his authority with Bal had been waning . . . Why the devil did the world for Bal consist of only two categories of people? There were those whom he *envied* – whether the envy was strong or vague, there was no denying it. And there were those whom he *pitied* – whether the pity was deep or superficial, there was no denying that, either. And why, in Bal's mind, were Annika and Meus now slipping from the first group into the second? Was it because of Meus' reticence, his cautiousness? Or was it because of the birch candlestick in the Frolinks' apartment, as against the pewter candelabra downstairs? Or because the spirits upstairs were served in a little tin cup whereas the great-room's silver goblets had been overflowing and still seemed to chime with his heartbeat? Yes – all the strange and improbable situations into which Bal seemed to have been plunged over the past few days seemed utterly bizarre in relation to the brazenness of Katharina's behaviour. *What did that kiss mean?*

Bal strode on, the earlaps of his dog-skin hat flapping. He pursed his lips in the dark and blew his hot, youthful vanity out into the wind that carried the smell of cooled wine back to his face . . . Who was this woman? An angel? A devil? Or just an accursed female, a strumpet whose kind has existed from the time of Plautus to this day, the woman who pays no heed to the sacrament of marriage and the concept of honour?

The lights from the cottages in Kalamaja bobbed above the snow-drifts like the eyes of wolves rapidly approaching, and Bal was thinking: *But some people say that some women, sometimes, listen to their hearts . . .* Take, for example, the story of that same Apothecary Dyck whom Bal had visited every other day on the Doctor's errands. Everyone knew that this meagre, blond-moustachioed marzipan confectioner and cough-medicine maker had had to forsake his job in Tartu a few years earlier because his wife had left him for the arms of his own journeyman, Oldekop. And some people had put it out that even after her public humiliation in church the lady announced she would be true to the promptings of her heart. Others had sneered, saying the fount of the whole problem was her penchant for wine. And Oldekop, in a town now lacking an apothecary, had earned a bad name, to be sure, but also a profitable business. Even in that cold wind Bal felt his cheeks burn as he imagined himself in the journeyman's position. For whatever the Doctor might be, there was not a soul he had ever harmed, and with Bal he had not only been consistently kind but was planning to help him further. So. Bal forced down the shameful thought of what might have happened had his hands not been clutching those cursed wine pitchers there, on the cellar steps. Deep down in his heart he knew that the question was not only shameless, it was false, because of course nothing more would have happened on those stairs even without the pitchers – my God . . . on someone else's stairs, the doors open, the visitors and husband above . . . *He* at least would not have taken matters further. No-no-no. He was no journeyman Oldekop . . . But could he really be sure . . . Perhaps, had they been free, he would have dared to put his arms around Katherina, and then . . . No-no! . . . But how sweet to think of a lady as beautiful and important and fragrant *as that* having done things to him *like that* . . . and it was heady and mad to think what might come of it all in the future . . . ? But no-no-no . . . Still, *why* did she do it? In any case, Bal would tell Märten all about it.

Old Mündrik-Mats' mongrel started to bark, but then recognised Bal's scent and pushed its snout into his mitten. Bal did not go into the boatman's hut but walked across the wood chips and shavings in the yard, towards the snow banks at the corner of the fence, and banged on the sauna door.

"Hello . . ."

Bending over, Bal let himself in, past the creaking door. He went on through the dressing room with its sheep-stall smell and the sound

213

of Mats' lambs bleating in the dark, and ducked through the next low door into the smoke-blackened sauna lit by a flickering splint-flame.

Märten scrambled to his feet from a stool next to a pile of wood chips. He was wearing an old rag of a sheepskin coat over his homespun shirt, his feet in mangy dog-skin slippers. The burning pine-splint was clamped in a stand on the windowsill, and, on a bench under the window, as though on display, were brand new hollowed-out wooden bowls, smooth white spoons of juniper, scraping tools with rough handles, curved blades to shape spoons with, and various knives. On the dirt floor lay partly carved wooden blocks of various sizes.

"Busy carving?"

"Chopping holes in ice and hauling wood – that's all mindless work, doesn't exactly wear a fellow out . . . Evenings I like to tinker . . ."

"And does Kimmelpenning buy your things?"

"He certainly does."

It suddenly came back to Bal: his first foray into things political four years earlier at Kimmelpenning's little table, and his question: *May I tell Father about it?* And he realised that this time he had not even thought of his father as one who could help him understand the situation . . . Partly, of course, because the old man was presumably not even in town. But was it not also because even his father – with his tarred boots and his worn coat smelling of horse sweat, and with his ever-older fading eyes peering out from under the edge of his ever-older and fading hat – his father too, in the context of the two big categories in Bal's mental world – of those he envied and those he pitied – was, God forbid, slipping into the company of the pitiable? And what of Märten, sitting again on his stool and looking searchingly at Bal from under his pale brows? He belonged, as to a point he always had, among those for whom Bal felt sorry . . . Definitely. And yet not entirely, thanks to Märten's elusive air of self-possession, which could be annoying but at the same time was liberating. But now Bal started talking so as to keep his thoughts from returning to his father:

"Do you remember the time when the Doctor appeared in costume at the door of his vault and asked whether he'd frightened you?"

"Of course I remember."

This was the way into his story. Bal relayed the entire episode of the skeleton to Märten. And of the way the mutual trust and confidence between him and the Doctor had grown since then. Then he spoke of the subsequent "skeleton-viewing" episodes and the Treaty of Pozvol and the future rulers of Livonia. As he had anticipated, Märten listened mostly in silence, interjecting the occasional "Aha", or a "Hmm", or a "Well, well". Before Bal began the tale of his trip to Finland, he paused to stretch his leg, which was on the verge of going to sleep, and bumped the toe of his felt boot against a block of wood. He picked it up, saying: "So, it looks as if spoons aren't the only things you make!" The triangular piece, with its pointed lower tip, looked like an animal with a narrow snout and fangs. "Holy hell!" said Bal, a little taken aback. "It's a wolf – clear as daylight! Where've you had the chance to get a good enough look at one to—?"

"Same as when you did."

"You old devil . . . Anyway . . ." And then Bal described his trip to Finland, sketching in a few words some of the people he had met and even the rooms he had seen. As he was describing the wall mirror in the duke's study, his eye caught a broken piece of mirror, the size of his palm, propped up on the edge of a sooty log by the wall next to the window, its jagged edge reflecting the flame of the burning splint.

"Where'd you get that?"

"Found it in the rubbish in Krumhusen's cellar."

"Aha!" And then Bal told the rest of his Finland story. "And this morning we returned. And before we'd managed to turn in at the Coast Gate, there you were."

"Wait a minute," Märten said, fastening his coat and going out.

Bal extended his legs and stretched, relieved, for he no longer had to bear the burden of keeping to himself the singular and clandestine matters that had so weighed him down. He could anticipate just how it would be when Märten returned. His friend would sit in silence awhile, then clear his throat three or four times as though to dislodge a hayseed, and his flat stomach would rise a little each time as if he were trying to shake off a flea. And then he would say something – brief, curt, funny – not necessarily pleasant but usually containing a kernel of truth. He might cast a glance at Bal's woollen coat, and widening his nostrils and remark: "I say, you're starting to smell like a duke yourself." Or, "So this Doctor is busy peering up arses and dealing in affairs of state as well!' Or – well, no doubt he would say something about Frau Katharina if he knew about her. Bal had neglected to mention the duke's cross so that he could include it as a link in the chain of his story later, once Märten returned . . . Anyway, it was cold in the sauna. He would make a decent fire in the stove. There was firewood piled on the floor, and at his feet lay a heap of dry shavings. A northwest wind was blowing – he would have to open the door to let the smoke out . . . Bal bent over and scooped up half the pile of wood shavings, scraping his knuckles on something. "Damn!" He dropped the shavings and pulled out the block of wood from under the heap.

It was a shaping of birch, the carving of a head, clearly a man's, apparently unfinished yet readily recognised: narrow, sharp-chinned, oddly similar to the carving of the wolf lying on the dirt floor – it was clearly Märten, definitely Märten. His abrupt brows, his cheekbones, his narrow, slightly bitter, mocking mouth. The likeness was stunning, even in its wooden form, and even in the dim light.

Looking over the pile of wood shavings, Bal caught sight of his own astonished, ruddy face in Märten's little mirror. Märten had sat right here, had looked into the mirror from this same spot, and had fashioned his face – carving it out of the wood, or perhaps into the wood . . . Bal recalled how hastily Märten had scrambled to his feet when he, Bal, had come in . . . He had come to unburden himself to Märten, even as Märten had hidden the carving of his face under the wood shavings, hidden it from *him*.

He heard Märten grope around in the sauna's dressing room, then reappear in the sauna through the creaking door, leaving behind the bleating sheep. He was holding a big wooden tankard of beer and wore an expression unusually mellow for Märten.

"I know you're full of high-class wine today, but have some of this anyway. It's left over from the christening at Mündrik-Mats' place."

He handed Bal the tankard, sat down, and gave three or four little coughs, as though to expel a hayseed, not seeming to notice that Bal was merely holding the tankard but not drinking.

"Well, seems this duke isn't so clever after all."

"Really! How do you know that?"

"If he were clever, he'd have said something clever . . . Go on, drink up!"

Bal took a polite sip and then four or five long thirsty draughts. The bitter beer tasted good after the Doctor's sweet wine.

"Well, go on," Märten said.

"That's all."

"Really? I thought . . . alright. Did you see the Doctor's wife too?"

"Yes, I did."

"Quite a high-class wagtail, isn't she?"

"Haven't taken her measure. Listen, I've got to go." Bal put the tankard on the bench.

"Really? Was there something in Mats' beer to make you rush off now? What's the hurry?"

"I want to see if the old man's come home. He was supposed to be on his way back from Narva. But at the Doctor's today I heard that the Muscovite has pushed into Alutaguse, too."

"Yes, so it seems . . . Well, in that case . . . It appears, though, that around Tartu he's attacking the Germans more fiercely than the peasants. But of course no-one would want to get in his way."

Bal nodded a goodbye and made his way out of the sauna into the yard, a little knot of disappointment in his chest over how easy it had been to explain away his hasty departure. Emerging from the boatman's yard onto the road, and guided by a few dimly glowing windows, he made his way between the dark drifts towards the sea and the northern edge of the village. Anxiety about his father gripped him: given recent events, a lot could have happened on the roads around Narva. It was reasonable to surmise that Siimon's trip out to Narva had passed without incident. As far as Bal knew, his father had left with five hired hands and eight horses, and very likely other wagoners had joined their caravan. They were transporting mostly wheat left behind in the warehouses of some of the merchants in Tallinn from the previous year's foreign cargoes, grain that the prominent merchants in Narva were eager to buy and store in their own warehouses. For, at the very moment that fear of the war was making Herr Krumhusen and his guild brothers send off their finest furs and other expensive belongings to Tallinn, they were buying all kinds of everyday necessities and imperishable foodstuffs as fast as they could. It was clear why: in the event of war, a blockade was quite likely. And the price of all staple items, such as grain, for one, would double or triple or even quadruple. At the last moment, an urgent government shipment had been loaded onto Siimon's sleigh: the Commander in Tallinn, Herr Franz von Segenhagen, nicknamed Goldbeak because of his expertise as a whistler, was sending a barrel of gunpowder to Herr Schnellenberg, the Advocate of Narva. This kind of shipment should by rights have been sent in a government conveyance. But for some reason Goldbeak's comrades had at the last moment put it on a private sleigh.

Bal had no evidence, of course, that Siimon had safely reached Narva, but there was no reason to doubt it either. It was well known that the journey from Tallinn through Valkla, Rakvere and Jõhvi took four days. He would have arrived on Friday, the twenty-first. And he had not planned to come back with an empty sleigh, especially as the Narva gentry were eager to send their treasures to Tallinn for safekeeping. The merchants all had a good nose, and not many among them were like the Bishop of Tartu who felt it was premature to make preparations against war. Actually, it was not as though clergymen were not known for their keen noses, so it was strange, what Herr Beelholt had said today about the Bishop in Tartu . . . Oh, well. But given the more valuable goods that he would be transporting on his journey home, Siimon would seem a sweet morsel to highway robbers. And the twenty-fourth would be the earliest and most likely day that he would pass through Jõhvi on his way back to Tallinn. It was his habit to load up all in one day and not countenance long periods of rest and relaxation, not for his horses or for his workers or for himself. Not even now, when he was already – Bal had to calculate it – in his fifty-eighth year.

Bal could tell from a distance that the wagoners had just arrived. Madis, the hired hand, was moving about the yard with a torch and Juhan and Taavet were unhitching the horses. Käsper, Mikk and Siimon were all pushing the loaded sleighs into the shed. Evidently they had been so late getting back that they had not been able to get through the town gates, and therefore had had to return home for the night with full loads.

Bal had hardly reached the fence and was about to call out to the men in the yard when he saw old Truuta come out of the farmhouse, carrying a lantern. She unlocked the grain shed at one end of the dwelling and pushed the door wide open. Juhan appeared with a stretcher under his arm and stopped at the last sleigh, putting the stretcher down on the snow. Together with his father they lifted a long bundle from the sleigh onto the stretcher and carried it into the grain shed. Madis walked behind them with the torch, extinguishing it in the snow before going in. And as Siimon and Juhan passed Truuta at the doorway, the old woman made the sign of the cross.

"What are you hiding here?" Bal asked in a mock-threatening voice as he stepped into the circle of light cast by Truuta's lantern.

"Holy Jesus . . . you just 'bout scared me to death," gasped Truuta, "as if it's not enough that . . . How did *you* get here?"

"I walked. What's going on here?"

"Your father just got back from his trip. Peep was killed along the way."

Truuta had heated the sauna, and a warm flour broth and chunk of pork with fresh bread were laid out on the table. The old stingy sourpuss must have been doing a good job of keeping house for Siimon, else she would not have lasted four years with him. Her sauna grew red-hot and gradually it loosened the men's tongues. Bit by bit, to the smack of birch bundles, and later at the table amidst the clatter of spoons, Siimon told Bal what had happened on the way home, his hired hands adding the odd word now and then.

The trip to Narva had gone smoothly. The only problem had been the bitter cold, but then that had also smoothened the movement of the sleighs. Their troubles had begun in Narva. Late at night, after he had made his deliveries and the sleighs were in the sheds, laden with new merchandise and ready for departure the next day, Siimon had been shouted out of sleep and ordered to appear, of all places, at the castle. There, upon the wagoner's arrival, a drunken Lord Schnellenberg had had him clapped in irons. It so happened that they were celebrating the feast day of St Paul's conversion at the castle, and in order to prepare fireworks for the festivities they needed to get the gunpowder in the barrel that Siimon had brought from Tallinn – it was still in the passageway leading to the courtyard, though the rest of the merchandise had been put into the cellar of the Hermann Tower. Upon opening the barrel they had discovered that what Siimon had brought them was a hundred pounds of soot mixed with a little dirt. So it was sheer luck that Siimon was not shackled or given a taste of much worse. Sheer luck, for Herr Krumhusen was among the guests and happened to be present at the scene when Siimon, whom he had known for years, was being taken at swordpoint to a side chamber off the great hall, and the esteemed Advocate was hurling accusations at him at the top of his lungs, saying Siimon had sold the gunpowder to the Muscovites of Ivangorod and substituted for it a barrelful of sheep manure for the Order's Advocate.

It took some doing on Herr Krumhausen's part to calm the fury of His inebriated Excellency. He affirmed that he had known Siimon for twenty years and that he had always delivered, down to the last crumb, everything he had been commissioned to deliver. At that, Schnellenberg's masculine moustache started to twitch and he let fly a truly lordly gob of spittle onto the hexagonal floor tiles, then said, "Yes . . . well . . . this swinish stunt was probably the work of that damned Goldbeak as retaliation . . . for an old feud over girls . . ." And saying this he winked at Krumhusen. "But I'll make him whistle a tune for this caper of his!"

He released Siimon then, who started out for Tallinn on the following morning with his crew. It was slow going against a snowstorm, and it was nearly evening before they reached the Jõhvi transport station, a quarter of a league from the church, towards Tallinn.

Night had fallen; all was quiet. Thirty or forty freight sleighs stood under cover of the sheds in the yard, and the horses, unharnessed, were crunching their hay. The drivers had had their evening meal of soup and bread (though Peep was probably still chewing his last piece). All of a sudden there began a loud pounding of the gate, and shouts in a foreign tongue. Forty or fifty Tatars on horseback were stamping and shouting and hacking at the gate with their axes and sabres. They would soon have succeeded in their intent had it not been for the dozen mercenaries sent by Herr Huini, in Rakvere, to Herr Schnellenberg, in Narva, to make the border between Livonia and Muscovy more secure . . . Roused by the commotion, they performed fairly well from behind the protection of the high log fence. Four or five Tatars, daggers between their teeth and sabres in hand, climbed over the fence to open the gate from inside and landed on the soldiers' halberds before they reached the crossbar. And when two gunners from among the mercenaries, in the loft of the headquarters, finally got their guns loaded and stuck them out from under the rafters and let loose two volleys directly into the band of horsemen at the gate, they could hear cursing and groaning and howling, and the bandits' horses vanished into the darkness as quickly as they had appeared. Not until then did those in the compound notice that around them, in the distant blackness, four or five estates or villages were in flames. And only then did they realise that, among the bodies of the Tatars lying on the blood-stained snow in front of the gate, two were theirs. One of them was a driver from Narva. His neck had been cut halfway through by a Tatar's sabre, his soul already with our Lord. The other was one of Siimon's hands, Peep. He was still holding a bloody axe – some of them now recalled how several of the transport crew had run to the gate to assist the mercenaries – but from Peep's chest protruded the shaft of an arrow about a foot and a half long. One of the Tatars who had climbed onto the roof had evidently shot the arrow down into the courtyard.

Siimon's men carried Peep inside and laid him down on the straw. By the dim light of the splint-flame they cut open his coat. A slice of half-eaten bread was visible; the arrow had gone through it, right into the left edge of his heart. He still had the breath of life in him. Siimon removed the blood-soaked bread from around the arrow as carefully as his large hands would permit. Then he cut open the shirt, hardened his heart, squeezed his small light eyes almost shut, and pulled the arrow out of the wound. With that the blood spurted out of the cut and nothing could stop its flow. In an hour Peep was dead.

In the morning, before they set out, they tied him on the sleigh and kept their axes and picks ready in case of bandits. Siimon's men also took the blades of three sickles from the yard and fastened them to three stakes. None of this would have helped much if the bandits had fallen upon them along the way. But word reached the transport station that the Tatars had retreated towards the east during the night, and the caravans from both Rakvere and Tallinn, made up of about twenty drivers and loads, dared to set out. By evening they had reached Rakvere. And now Peep was stretched out on a plank in the grain shed.

Bal lit a lantern and went in.

He had memories of Peep as far back as he could remember. Odd songs, without beginning or end, that Peep would hum when, on the rare occasion, he had had a larger than usual draught of holiday beer. The mottled cattle with their wide-angled legs that Peep had fashioned for Bal out of sticks, bigger than anyone else had ever taken the trouble to make. And the awkward letters he tried to shape onto birch bark with a piece of coal, under the guidance of Bal's hands, from angular A's to rectangular O's. A and O. Alpha and Omega. Beginning and End.

Bal put the lantern down on the bier and went close to the dead man, stooping a little because of the low ceiling. Truuta had already washed him and dressed him in a clean linen shirt. His faded, usually upright shock of hair was oddly limp on his scalp. Under the sharp cheekbones were deep black shadows. Bal folded his hands, but while his lips were murmuring "Our Father . . ." his mind turned unaccountably to the wolves he had encountered on the road to Kurgla – and that odd childish feeling that here, now, it could never be that they would leap for *his* throat . . . And yet, right now, the wolf of war was howling in the heart of Livonia, and although it was skulking out in the fields and snowdrifts, its teeth had bitten into his father's home.

Alpha and Omega. Beginning and End . . . The beginning is at hand. And for some the Beginning is already the End . . . Is it not also the end for many others? As that man, Jürgen of Meissen, has prophesied . . . ?

He stepped out of the grain shed into the farmyard and looked around without fear, but with clear-eyed, chilling apprehension at the barely visible little outbuildings and fences hidden by the drifts in the windy darkness . . . A week ago the enemy was in Tartu, the day before yesterday, in Jõhvi . . . When will the Muscovite be at Tallinn's walls? When will the Tatars ride howling through the burning villages of Kalamaja and Pleekmäe and Seegiküla?

When Bal returned to the house the farmhands had finished eating and left, and his father had turned his chair to face the dying fire; he was staring at the dwindling flames. They were silent for a while. Then the old man spoke:

"Well – I suppose it's the end of transport trips for a while. Riga's probably the only place left . . ." And after another silence: "They say you've become a great chum of that Doctor's. And what do you clever fellows have to say about the war?"

Bal sensed in the phrase "clever fellows" both tenderness and estrangement. The mixture of pride and affection he detected made him want to tell his father everything he knew. But the way his father acknowledged him and yet distanced himself – not in a way that was at all unfriendly, but a bit sad – made him flinch. He looked at his father's bare feet, unbelievably large, knobby and reddish by the light of the glowing coals, and at the calves, a bit bowed in their grey leggings. At his slightly stooped frame and round head, barely visible in the dark, and his face, of which he could see only its iron-grey swatch of beard. It made a kind of anguish settle on his heart like a great load, like the weight of the entire town wall, a fathom thick. Outside the town wall, the grey dwellers of the outskirts: the hired hands of the wagon drivers, the dead Peep, and his father – living in fear of fires and plunder and the wolves of war. And inside the walls, he, Bal, eating marzipan and drinking malmsey wine with councilmen and settling the affairs of kings and dukes . . .

He said in a low voice: "They don't know that much . . . They're saying that Tartu is not yet under siege, that so far it's just been plundered . . . we'll see."

CHAPTER EIGHT,

*in which we gallop through a crumbling peace and through the
momentous events of a war flaring up once more, in order to take
note, beforehand, during, and also afterwards, of lesser events
overlooked by Clio's owl-eyes, some of which turn out to be decisive
in the life of a young man in stubborn pursuit of knowledge and
wisdom – in ways both entirely foreseeable and wholly unexpected.*

On Sunday morning, May 14, St Nicholas' Church was full to overflowing. Even the councilmen's seats and those of the Great Guild and the Blackheads were taken, especially the benches towards the rear, where people sat tightly packed. And many were standing, crammed into the area near the door where there were no benches. It was the last day of the school year. Most of the schoolboys were standing behind the guilds' benches, but the *primaners* were seated in front, in the choir, to the right of the altar, and directly behind the councilmen's seats along the wall. They had been ranged close together on two benches; in the front row sat the eight boys who had completed their second *prima* year and were thus bidding farewell to the highest-level school in Tallinn. The little organ completed the processional. Shuffling and scraping, the congregation rose for prayer and sat down again. Bal let the organ music wash over him as he examined the interior of the church and the people around him.

Red and blue patches of light from the high stained-glass windows flared on the vaulted ceiling and the cream-coloured walls when the sun came out and faded when it went back behind the clouds. Likewise,

flakes of light gleamed and dimmed on the huge brass candelabra standing six cubits high next to the pulpit, like a seven-branched horsetail
spruce that had burst miraculously into bloom, by turns shedding its
sparkling blossoms of sunlight and then flowering once again. And so
too the hanging silver chandeliers glowed bright and grew dull, along
with the chalices on the altar and the two-cubit-high monstrance of
Ryssenberch in a niche in the wall next to the altar, behind a padlocked
iron grate. And, along with these, all fifty or sixty carved wooden saints
withdrew in turn into soft shadows and emerged again into red-gold
brightness, with their flowing robes, crowns, emblems and canopies –
their beards modelled after the captains of merchant vessels, their
snub noses after the washerwomen of Lübeck. All this problematic
grandeur dating from the time of the popes had survived only because,
on the historic day that the great cleansing of churches took place in
Tallinn – in some quarters already referred to as the "destruction of
images" – on that great Christian day of the axe-and-the-broom the
terrified deacon of St Nicholas' had drunk so much communion wine
that the devil of a fellow actually summoned the courage to pour molten
lead into the keyholes of the church. So that the broom-wielding
"sweepers", who were to rid the church of its objects of idolatry, when
given the keys they demanded, could not get in. In the meantime their
pious ardour cooled somewhat and now all these grand and suspect
items were in service here, in this temple to the spirit of Augsburg, even
if Ryssenberch's monstrance was kept behind a padlocked grate. But a
dozen years earlier – and even Bal remembered this – the monstrance
had been kept in the sacristy, hidden from the congregation . . . And,
after all, what was *right* in the end? The way things were *now*, of course
. . . Or perhaps, some other way, after all? . . . Monstrances in all the
churches . . . the receptacles for the Host . . . the holiest of holy receptacles . . . Many of them thrown into the trash, crushed to pieces, melted
down for their metal . . . And the one *here* had miraculously been spared,

227

hidden in a pile of rubbish in the corner of the sacristy, later placed into its niche once more, but kept behind an iron grate . . . *What* is good and *what* is evil? What is true and what is false? And what is the will of the Lord? How does He view all these battles over the receptacles for His body? Bal turned his eyes to the backs of the councilmen's necks and thought: *no, there's no point asking them.*

He recognised, from behind, Herren Hoye and Beelholt and Luhr and Vegesack, and both Boissmanns, father and son, the son having come to visit his home town while wearing the uniform of another country. In the women's section the councilmen's wives sat in silk and velvet, most of them a bit overfed and yet faded, and behind them the guild wives – looking just like them. Towards the back Katharina bloomed in their midst, a cherry blossom in a thorn bush. Frau von Geldern was sitting there like a cannon tower, flanked by her four daughters. Even seven-year-old Magdalena had been given a little song-book so that everyone could see what a clever child she was. She knew how to read already, but not how to hold a book. Three times it fell to the floor when she stood up for prayers.

The main reason Frau von Geldern was sitting there so properly and prominently that day was that the preacher was not the wrinkled, croaking Pastor Walther from St Nicholas' but one of the alternative pastors, the proud, slightly stiff Herr Geldern from St Olaf's. He was tall, big-boned, with light-grey eyes, reportedly from somewhere around Holland, and, as Bal had learned from Meus, with a jug of fine wine he could become quite spirited and merry in good company. And although here there was no wine goblet on the edge of the pulpit, it was clear he could speak with ease and pleasure even without it. The cornerstone of his sermon was quite appropriately 1 Samuel 25:8: "Ask your young men, and they will tell you. Therefore let the young men find favour in your eyes: for we come in a good day . . ."

From the "young men" Herr Geldern went on to speak of those

who were graduating, for they too had been examined the day before by the councilmen and the pastors of St Nicholas', and they too had demonstrated their learning. Bal and young Luhr had together declaimed from memory the entire first act of Terence's *Andria*. And earlier Bal had even recited the prologue:

> *Poeta quam primum animum ad scribendum adpulit,*
> *Id sibi negoti credidit solum dari,*
> *Populo ut placerent quas fecisset fabulas . . .**

And that the young men might find favour before God – an apposite blessing for those graduating, especially as they had all gathered there before Him on a "good day". . . . It was easy to declare this a good day, for it was a day of celebration, and moreover, the winds of war had more or less subsided over Livonia, the Muscovite having withdrawn across the borders at the end of February. (Though lately there had been rumblings near Narva again.)

And then Herr Geldern spoke about a bad man, Nabal, who was very rich. He had three thousand sheep and a thousand goats but would not fulfil his obligations to David. And as Bal listened – his ears sharpened by following conversations at the Doctor's house – it seemed to him that this wicked Nabal could stand for all bad rulers, such as those who had so inordinately delayed the decision taken by the provincial diet of Volmar, long back in March, to buy a lasting peace from Moscow for the sum of sixty thousand marks – they had only just sent off the money. And Herr Geldern also spoke of Nabal's beautiful and intelligent wife Abigail, who "took two hundred loaves and two bottles of wine, and five sheep ready dressed, and five measures of parched corn and a hundred clusters of raisins and two hundred cakes of figs and laid them on asses, and went to meet David – but she told not her husband Nabal."

---

* When he first applied his mind to writing, the poet thought that his only duty was to write plays that would please the public (Latin).

Bal tried to picture the churlish Nabal, but he did not, after all, appear as a dark-complexioned man with narrow grey eyes and a black wedge of beard. He had an indeterminate face and a broad yellowish forehead. But Abigail, with her hundred clusters of raisins, was none other than Katharina.

Herr Geldern continued from his post above them to tell them that God Almighty then punished Nabal, who died. And David wooed the beautiful Abigail for his wife even before he became king . . . When Bal tried to picture David's face, it too appeared but vaguely defined, with a broad yellowish forehead – maybe a sign of the crown to come – but the image suddenly changed to a boyish face with round grey eyes and a wheat-stalk clump of hair . . . and recognising it Bal lowered his eyes and stared fixedly at the tombstones on the floor of the choir and felt his face grow hot, and he prayed: "Lord, prevent such thoughts from entering my mind – at least here, in Your holy dwelling place . . ."

No, he did not like this church. Not only because it was the church primarily of the German merchants, whereas the Holy Ghost Church was the church of the Estonian Greys, and St Olaf's belonged to the German–Swedish–Estonian artisans. He did not really know why, but as he had sat listening to sermons as a child, his recurrent nightmare had been of the vaulted ceilings of the church of St Nicholas coming crashing down upon him. But he did know that the right panel of the altar triptych, depicting the martyrdom of Saint Victor, had long transfixed and troubled him.

The right-hand panels were open just enough for Bal, from where he sat, to gain a clear view of the scene. In the middle of the painting, in the foreground, a river flows calmly into a distant moat, in which ducks are swimming in front of the town walls and church steeples. In the foreground, on the left bank of the river, two odd puppet-like executioners are holding onto Victor's headless body, caught in the act of tossing it into the river, and on the grass in front lies the saint's head, smiling. Ten steps downriver, on the right bank, are three angels, two of them supporting the headless body which is about to topple over, the third holding the head at chest height, apparently with the intention of placing it back on the neck. But the head is still in the angel's hands and the body is still headless. Bal has known this painting for as long as he can remember – for three-quarters of his life – and the saint's bloody neck is still waiting for its head. The artist has employed a devilish trick in depicting two sequential events such as these, the one happening ten steps downriver from the other – there is something equivocal and elusive in it, something more than there should have been. As though all one had to do was look round the corner, and suddenly everything that had occurred and was about to occur would be visible at once: the executioners heaving the headless body into the river, the body floating on it, the angels rescuing it . . . *but there's no plank across the river, it seems . . . nor is there a rope for wingless aerialists to walk on . . .*" Schoolboys, graduates, you who are about to step into life. You who are about to step into life!" repeats Herr Geldern up in the pulpit. And waves of organ music swell in the church, and the congregation tentatively sings "A Mighty Fortress". The sparkle of sunlight is gone from the windows, and when the little organ starts the recessional, the last red-and-blue flakes of light have faded from the vaulted ceiling; the candelabras hang in grey shadows above the heads of the departing congregation and the clustering groups at the doors; and a white rain splatters down upon the stone slabs in the churchyard.

Having waited in vain by the door for a while, a few intrepid parish-ioners rush out, followed by others in growing numbers. Herr Geldern emerges from the sacristy, the crowd parting respectfully to let him pass, and the bell-ringer at his heels is already opening a black rain canopy fastened to two willow sticks. Herr Geldern hails his sour-faced colleague Tegelmeister and the kindly Herr Sum, to accompany him, one on either side. They manage to crowd under the canopy. Herr

Geldern jokes: "Well then, Doctor Luther is said to have declared: 'And even if it should rain knives . . .'" The expressionless bell-ringer raises his collar – and they all step bravely out into the downpour. The remaining schoolmasters hitch up the skirts of their coats a little and pull their berets down closer to their brows and follow them out, and a hundred and fifty boys stream out after them as well. What does it matter to boys if their backs or even their trousers get soaked? The procession crosses the churchyard to emerge onto St Nicholas' Street and turns to begin its descent along the uneven cobblestones. Groups of people, crowded together in doorways and under archways, stand watching the passing procession, from time to time tossing greetings and comments towards the boys through the curtain of rain. The boys would like to be walking faster. There is still quite a distance to the school. Herr Balder and the others would also like things to move more quickly, for a table has been laid at the school for the masters. But the gentlemen under the canopy are setting the pace and the backs of those behind them turn black and then shiny with rainwater, which is soon running down in rivulets. Then Herr Sum turns around to face the procession and, walking backwards, calls out: "Let's sing!" He begins, and the others join in as well as they can, singing one of Herr Sum's own compositions, which they have spent a long time rehearsing: "*Erhalt uns, Gott, bei deinem Wort . . .*"* When they arrive at the New Market and the head of the procession has already passed between the Town Hall and the pillory, and is proceeding, singing, towards the Apothecary, Herr Dyck's assistant runs out, pulling his coat up over his head, and hurries towards Herr Geldern to tell him something. The black canopy comes to an abrupt halt, billowing and flapping. The latter half of the procession merges with the forward half, the song falls apart, and a hundred and seventy people stand in the rain, confused. Herr Geldern calls out: "The Burgomaster has asked us to wait here!"

* Keep us, God, by your word (German).

Herr Tegelmeister is looking up into the rain, squint-eyed and scowling as always. He draws his head lower down into his wet ruffled collar and maintains silence. Herr Balder mutters: "What's going on here . . . ?" Someone remarks: "Something must've happened!" The boys hunch their shoulders, some giggling, and Herr Sum says: "Let's at least take shelter under the arcade!"

The procession flows under the arcade, and they stand there shaking the water from their coats. Three horsemen appear from the direction of Toompea, galloping down Väike-Rataskaevu Street. Rainwater streams down their armour. The head horseman wears the white cape of the Order, flapping wetly over his protective chain mail, as though, in spite of the rain, he were riding to a ceremonial tournament. His gloomy young face is instantly recognisable: it is Goldbeak himself. The men leap off their horses in front of the Town Hall; a sentinel has come out and tethers their horses to a post. As the men separate from the crowd of schoolboys and go to meet the horsemen, Bal hears one of the riders say: "See – a right good squadron here at hand!"

The other replies: "Nine out of ten are snot-nosed pups!"

Between clenched teeth Herr Segenhagen mutters: "No worse than Schnellenberg's men!"

Herr Sum follows them into the Town Hall to find out what it is all about. He comes back surprisingly quickly, and the expression on his face is such that the entire gathering falls instantly silent. And then Herr Sum says, in an unnaturally high voice over the sound of the driving rain:

"The Town Council asks us to have our end-of-school meal quietly and disperse as quickly as possible. The day before yesterday, the Muscovite set fire to the town of Narva and occupied it."

The unforgettable downpour of that day came to an end, of course. The summer sun of the year 1558 burned hot and dry, but to everyone it seemed to be shining through ever-darker clouds. The head and hilt of the old sword of the Order was Tallinn; its blades were the fortified castles of Kiiu, Toolse and Kalvi in the north, and Paide, Porkuni, Kiltsi and Vasknarva in the south. And now the fall of Narva suddenly broke the tip of this rusty but still powerful sword. If it had at least been broken in honest battle . . . But it turned out that Herr Schnellenberg of the mighty moustache had fled Narva a week before its fall. And it also became clear that there were those among the Narva merchants who did not consider the Grand Duke such an unacceptable ruler after all. And, furthermore, the Ivan who was known in countless stories as "Ivan the terror of all the world" and was reputed to be the scourge of inherited property and a sodomite to boot – that very Ivan had immediately reinstated the old privileges of trade and commerce and even added a whole lot of new ones! But everyone knew this was just bait – and that no honest soul in Livonia would bite. But the merchants in Narva who did bite were also all honest Livonians . . . at least they were yesterday, or the day before, or a week or month ago . . . And what of the brave warriors, the commanders and advocates and knights of Virumaa, who, on June 7, on the shores of the River Purtse, retreated in a flurry of flight from the overwhelming force and headed back to Rakvere, instead of following the command of the Master of the Order to pursue the enemy into Russia? Why, all of them were even more honourable Livonians . . .

What a moving letter they wrote to Fürstenberg in their distress:

> . . . but we were compelled to retreat from the enemy's vastly superior might, for at the first light of dawn the enemy came upon our sentinels and killed one and took the other prisoner, and since their cries reached our camp we prepared ourselves immediately for battle, assuming our agreed-upon standby battle positions, and Christopher von Monninkhusen and Hinrich

Yxküll crossed the river with fifty horsemen to the enemy's side to see what they might undertake against them, and they saw such great numbers of gunners and flags and so many reinforcements arriving in three barges that it was clear to them that there was no way of resisting or driving back this army even with all our strength, but that we were perhaps a little better placed with regard to standby positions and we held these for a time and waited to see whether the enemy would attack us with its great forces, but at the same time we received a message that a large contingent of the enemy had just left Vasknarva, which they had earlier taken from Herr Steinkul, and that they had invaded our old Sembruiken camp, intending in that way to set upon us simultaneously from two directions, and after some consideration we thought it best, as far as was humanly possible, to retreat to Rakvere to await Your Merciful Princely Highness' new orders, for the enemy would not be flaunting its great army and its strength on just one day but rather on a regular basis every day, and furthermore, as we have heard tell, the enemy has continued transporting large numbers of peasants over to its side from the River Purtse area, taking some by force but luring others with favours, but as for us, of whom there are left barely five hundred horsemen and two hundred mercenaries – we are too weak to resist such a large army, much less drive it back . . .

Three days later the Doctor learned that these milksops at the Purtse encampment, under the command of Segenhagen, Monninkhusen and Schmerten, numbered six hundred cavalrymen and four hundred infantrymen, most of them members of the nobility of Virumaa, with well-outfitted supply wagons and sixteen cannons, and two thousand more-or-less armed peasants as well. One of the scribes of the Order, who had taken part in the retreat at Purtse and been trampled by the retreating horses, called upon Doctor Friesner with his bruises and recounted all the details. Bal talked with the somewhat dull but serious man and learned that he, Johann Renner by name, came from Bremen and was the scribe for Herr Schmerten in Paide.

True enough, the size of the Order's forces at the River Purtse, God knows, was not exceedingly large. But on the other bank the Russians numbered neither more nor less than four hundred men. And yet the army of the Order retreated without firing even one of its sixteen cannons!

And all this was just the beginning of a shattering chain of events. More incomprehensible things happened in Livonia over the next thirty days than had occurred in the previous thirty years. On June 15, Herr von Segenhagen and Christoph von Monninkhusen precipitously departed from Rakvere and hastened to Tallinn. It was not known where Monninkhusen went, but young Herr von Segenhagen appeared on a horse all in a lather at Doctor Friesner's door and requested, in private, that the Doctor testify, if it should be necessary, that he, Segenhagen, had been suffering great gallstone pain before and during the retreat from Purtse. Doctor Friesner did not tell Bal what his reply to this request had been, and Bal had not dared ask. But it seemed to Bal that after this private audience the Doctor's chest with the painted red roses was slammed shut with a vehemence greater than before.

On June 17, the provincial diet of Tartu met and, at the urging of Fürstenberg, sent a plea for help to Christian of Denmark. Upon hearing this Doctor Friesner stroked his black wedge of beard and observed: "No matter. That was to be expected. We can wait a bit longer." But they did not have to wait even a week. On June 23, the Master of the Order sent a plea for help to Duke Johan in Turku. Doctor Friesner had the supper table set with silver, toasted Katharina and Bal with his carafe of Rhenish wine, kissed his wife in Bal's presence, and said: "Things are progressing. But just between us, I'm still not sure how quickly it will all come to pass." In the same week fortified positions in Viru fell, one after the other, to the Russians. And in the same week Herr von Yxküll, after a perfunctory battle, surrendered the mighty castle of Vastseliina to the Russians, following an attempt, with Bishop Hermann's knowledge, to hand over the castle to the Russians with no battle at all. Also over the same week Fürstenberg retreated from the well-situated Kirumpää encampment without a fight, and the sixty thousand troops of Prince Shuiski marched towards Tartu from the south and southeast, encountering no resistance . . .

"What is the meaning of this?" the Doctor asked at lunch on July 13, as he tapped his *gaffel* against his pewter plate (which had displaced the silver dishes reserved for special occasions). "Is it stupidity? Or paralysis? Or treachery?"

And since he was staring intently at Bal for no particular reason, Bal said: "There's only one thing it can be . . . it's *old age.*"

"What do you mean? Segenhagen isn't even thirty yet!"

"I don't mean him. Some of the others. The Order, as a whole."

"Really . . . Hmm . . . What do you mean by that?"

"Well . . . a thing like the Order – or a kingdom – is somewhat like a horse. Or a dog. Or . . . wolf. It gets old and can't get up again. It'll drag its hind legs, or just lie on the ground, with neither dignity nor purpose. But it'll go on eating ravenously as long as it has breath . . ."

"Ha-ha-ha-ha . . . Hm. You know, that sounds like something you got from Aesop. But I think we need to look closely at what happened on the River Purtse. In my opinion, what paralysed the Order Masters was simply *fear*—"

"Ah! – fear of four hundred Russians!"

"No, that's not all. The crux of the matter is that it was fear of four hundred Russians *and* of two thousand peasants. We read that letter together. Remember, the Muscovites are winning the peasants to their side with *favours*. And we've heard the same from other sources as well. They don't have to give the peasants a lot to win them over, am I right? But imagine, if Segenhagen had engaged in battle with the Muscovites – true, he's a weakling, but still, not a fool, and he might have had information that we don't know about and which he did not dare include in the letter – just think: what if he'd joined battle and the two thousand peasants had, in the course of it, turned their weapons on him . . . ! What then? There are peasant units in all the Order's forces."

Bal was silent. To tell the truth, he had little enough faith in the battle readiness of peasant units, and none in a battle that pitched them against enemies of the Order. Yet against the Order's army itself – *that* might, in fact, be another story . . .

"Balthasar, you know them better than any of us. Be honest with me: the Estonian peasant would side even with the Russians if that liberated him from the knights, wouldn't he?"

"Hmm . . . About a year ago a monk asked me more or less the same question. So it's something I've been thinking about. Yes: he would. And why not? After all, half the merchants at Narva are in collusion with Moscow!"

"I can understand the peasants, they're half pagan anyway," Frau Katharina said, inhaling the roses wrapped in a damp cloth sent that morning by the estate manager at Üksnurme. "But as for the Narva merchants – that's inexcusable."

The Doctor smiled, throwing Bal a look that seemed to say: Don't mind her – childish nonsense . . . and then he asked Katharina: "You permit the peasants to act to their own advantage, isn't that so? Then why won't you allow the merchants to do the same?"

"Matthias . . . what's *advantageous* – is not always . . ." The lady's oval grey eyes, which looked slightly greenish on this day in July, grazed past Bal and foundered in the faintly mocking amusement she saw in the Doctor's glittering dark ones.

"Our Kati is pretending she has the wings of an angel! Ha-ha-hah! The merchants want whatever is most profitable, and women want whatever is most delectable. And that's all there is to it."

Katharina, taken aback, lowered her eyes to the table. It seemed to Bal that a gradual flush spread over her graceful neck, and he felt himself blushing along with her.

"Kati," the Doctor said, "remember – you are twenty-six years old. But you talk like a sixteen-year-old."

Oh yes, truth be told, Katharina not only talked like a sixteen-year-old, at times she acted like one. Or perhaps the way she acted *was* in fact the way twenty-six-year-olds act . . .

Take, for example, what she did at the end of February . . . School was over for the day and the boys were walking in groups along Munkade Street, up to the Old Market, from where they went their separate ways. But six or seven *quarta*-level boys started a snowball fight in front of the Bishop's House. After long days of freezing cold the weather was milder, the snow softer, and when Bal walked past them and towards the gate of the Bishop's House, a good-sized snowball flew down his collar. He turned around with the full dignity of a *prima*-level scholar and would have grabbed one of the rascals by the neck if he had been closer, when he suddenly caught sight of Frau Katharina's face – about to burst into silent laughter. She was walking across the Old Market and past the group of boys, slapping her fine glove against her fur coat to shake off the snow. Maybe it was the early spring thaw and the end of the bears' long winter sleep that made Bal brazen. He waited until Katharina reached him, then addressed her almost sternly:

"And what if I'd boxed the ears of one of those little fellows?"

"In that case I would have offered you my ears too!"

Well, what can one say to a retort like that? Or take what happened just the day before yesterday, when the Doctor was invited to Herr

Clodt's to examine his ailing daughter – she was afflicted with a liver parasite – and to share a beaker of *klarett* with the syndic and his wife, in honour of Gotthart Kettler's success. For on June 9, the Diet had assembled in Valga and Kettler's supporters had laid all the Order's defeats at Fürstenberg's door, and thus, by fair means and foul, had elected Kettler coadjutor – meaning regent and field commander to boot. In effect, however, given the current state of war, he had been elected the new Master of the Order, or, to put it more accurately, had been manoeuvred into that position, as the Doctor explained to Bal, adding: "Balthasar, I've been gathering information about Kettler. He's nothing but an opportunist. And at this time, it's a fair certainty he's collaborating with the Poles. So his rise to power is such a threat to our Swedish interests that it should spur our duke to action. Except that . . . oh well."

On the whole Doctor Friesner was in a fairly dark mood about all this. Bal could tell because, outwardly, he seemed especially jovial and high-spirited. He accepted the syndic's invitation with a sparkling smile. He had Katharina put on her green silk dress with the golden lilies, handed his medical chest to Bal, and asked him to keep his eyes and ears open at Clodt's house. Among the dozen or so guests at Herr Clodt's grand house on Lai Street, Herr Christoph von Monninkhusen was perhaps the most notable. He was dressed in a brown velvet suit, trim and sun-tanned, with the quick movements of a man of about forty. But his nose was so long, thin and crooked that Bal's imagination went to work: as God was shaping Herr Monninkhusen from clay, He must have bumped into him by mistake, and to keep him from falling and being flattened He must have grabbed hold of whatever His hand chanced to touch – hence the nose. But Herr Monninkhusen had tumbled neither then nor on later occasions – no matter how much beer or Rhine wine or *klarett* he had in him. And somehow he grew no belly from it all either. The education he had acquired seemed to aggravate his tendency to pomposity instead of rendering him more mellow and affable – which was the effect of education on most people – and he maintained his air of snobbish learning in his caustic utterances and Latinate aphorisms even when his nose was quite red from drink. Perhaps both the learned air and the flushed visage were only reflections of his boozing bishop-brother in Kuressaare. Bal was just wondering, in astonishment, why Herr Monninkhusen, as the strongest pillar of the Danish army, was here, at the home of the inscrutable Herr Clodt, celebrating the victory of the Polish-backed Kettler, when he recalled that the Doctor was around as well . . . And anyway, when the councilmen and guild members and their wives had departed, flushed and jovial, Herr Clodt and Monninkhusen insisted on playing a game of tarot with the Doctor. (Or maybe it was the other way around.) But Monninkhusen's wife was not present, Clodt's was busy attending to her sick daughter, and Katharina said she was bored and sleepy. At that the Doctor, engaged in his card game, proposed that Bal escort Frau Katharina home.

When Bal and Katharina emerged onto the street from the coolness of the stone house, the July night around them felt unexpectedly dark and sultry. There had been signs of an end to the drought for several weeks already, and now purple-grey clouds hung heavy in the sky. The houses with their peaked roofs were dark in the stifling night air, and the black tracery of linden branches hanging over low stone walls exuded a fragrance almost feverish.

They had walked twenty or so steps along the uneven cobblestones, side by side – the streets were empty at this hour past midnight – when a flash of greenish lightning lit up the leaden underbelly of the clouds in the west, and Katharina, startled, grabbed Bal's arm. She was not play-acting. Bal felt a real tremor of fear in her grip even before the unexpectedly loud thunderclap rolled over the rooftops.

"Don't be afraid, Frau Katharina . . ."

"I am not afraid."

She let go of his arm, leaving Bal both relieved and disappointed. The thunder had rolled on and subsided. The echo of their footfalls bounced back from the black walls and faded in the electrified air, as though in water.

"But you are afraid of me," said Katharina.

Bal was silent, feeling a lump in his throat – of fear and joy simultaneously, for he knew that Katharina was leading the talk to the forbidden and unknown thicket of the knowledge of good and evil. He swallowed the lump and asked, in a surprisingly matter-of-fact voice:

"I . . . ? Of you? But why?"

"Because I am afraid of myself, too."

"But why . . . ?"

She paused. "Balthasar, how much wine did you drink tonight?"

"Half a beaker."

"That's not much . . . Me too . . ."

Now! Now! Now! – I should say something to her. I should help her out, even a little – no, she doesn't really need it – still, I should encourage her, somehow – But no, oh no, oh no, I should start, quickly, talking about something trivial, something nonsensical. – Too late (good!).

"Balthasar . . . I wish I had drunk more."

"Why?"

"So I could tell . . . you . . ."

Now! Now! Now! – say to her, "It's unfortunate neither of us drank more." – Say to her, "Speech is silver, but silence is golden" – but no, not like this, in a voice husky with strained curiosity . . . "Tell me – what?"

They have walked past the high, dark windows of the Great Guild and emerge from a long vaulted passageway onto the small square in front of the the building.

"Balthasar, *you've* never had a spell cast on you, have you?"

"Ha-ha-ha-ha! Me? No, never."

"I know, Balthasar. But don't say it that way, as though there were no such thing as witchcraft!"

"Of course, people can be put under a spell . . . It's just that . . ."

It's just that, right now, here, with us, that is not what has happened. Even if there were witches around here somewhere . . . Even if wolves happened to cross our path, they wouldn't necessarily be at our throats . . . Even if this war . . . But I can't explain all this to Katharina right now.

"Yes, Balthasar. There are terrible cases of witchcraft." At the steps of the Great Guild House Katharina pauses and turns to face him. In the near darkness her eyes are black as coals and something in her usually mellow voice crackles like a branch burning to ashes: "Balthasar, there is a spell on me."

"*You?* Oh . . ."

Bal sees Katharina's eyes in the gloom, big and black with alarm, and her lips, moist and dark, although he knows well how red they actually are. And he just barely makes out the lilies of her silk dress over the roundness of her breasts, which are undoubtedly more ample than he can imagine, and their fullness agitates the country boy. But as an admirer of Ovid, Bal feels a little sorry for Katharina (or is he clutching at straws by fabricating this sympathy?), a little sorry that everything is becoming so – one might say – crass: a poor woman under a curse and the big bad sorcerer Balthasar . . . Ugh!

"Are you saying that . . . that I . . . ?"

"Heavens above! No!"

Katharina is standing in front of him. Her hot hands are gliding over his face as he looks down in embarrassed confusion – it is an exploration, a caress, a plea: "Heaven forbid – no! Not you! You are good, so good!"

"Who, then . . . ? How, then . . . ?"

"Oh God in Heaven – I cannot tell you. If at least the wine were giving me courage . . . but it's not you, not you . . ."

Katharina is sitting next to Bal at the top of the Guild House steps and crying. The old limestone bench is still warm from the heat of the day and Katharina is burning hot – it is not clear whether on account of the temperature or the curse she is under, and her hair lies on Bal's shoulder in disarray, exhaling the intoxicating fragrance of a bed of carnations. Shafts of phosphorescent lightning crackle along the flat, leaden undersides of the clouds, and Katharina startles and draws closer to Bal. Great barrels of thunder roll over the roof of Holy Ghost Church. Katherina is close, close to Bal, and she is trembling. After the thunder there is a suffocating silence and Bal hears how his hand, roughened by the shovel and axe and sickle at Kalamaja, catches and crackles over the silk skirt as he draws Katharina's knees against his. Katharina lifts her tear-stained face, opens her tear-filled eyes, and Bal kisses her and she kisses him, and the leaden-purple clouds start to whirl and spin around the church steeple, and Bal thinks: *If God's lightning does not strike us now, then this woman is truly an angel under a spell!* And he feels the last plank in his little boat of virtue slip out from under his feet – the wood on which are burned the words Bal overheard the Doctor say to the syndic just as they were leaving Clodt's place: "That is an irreproachable young man." But God has compassion for these two sinners, after all – saving them from the fires of Hell into which they are about to hurl themselves – and with His elbow He pushes aside the cloud cover above the Guild House steps, and through the humid air a cool rain falls down upon them.

Bal returned from these recollections of the night before last, back to the present. He looked up from his silver plate, past Katharina, at the Doctor: "I have to go now."

"Yes," the Doctor agreed without hesitation, "of course. Look over our fleet of privateers and let me know what it's like. I could find out for myself. But it'll attract less attention if you do. And this fleet will be of utmost interest to the duke."

"But it's odd, in any case," Bal said, "that the ships of Tallinn are now attacking those of Lübeck . . . the fleet of a daughter-city going after that of a mother-city . . . instead of . . . Hmm."

"You know how it is with such historical family relationships – there's always confusion. I've been told here that Tallinn is in no way 'daughter' to Lübeck or Bremen – and that it was not even founded by the Danes – but that it is an old town of non-Germans. The devil alone knows. Or maybe you know the story. But let's suppose it is Lübeck's daughter-city; what should the daughter do if the mother keeps sending ships to the Muscovites in Narva and sells them iron and lead and gunpowder for good money that the Muscovite will use to come courting the daughter? Now that Toolse is in Ivan's grip, it won't be long. Yes, what is a daughter to do with such a mother? I understand of course: business is business. But privateering is also business. And a double business: first, to deprive Ivan of the cream, and second, to lick the cream oneself. It wasn't for nothing that our Schmedemanns and Bolemanns and Hochgreves solicited their letters of marque from Fürstenberg. And they wouldn't be pouring their money into those ships otherwise!"

"But why is this of such great interest to the duke?"

"Because Bartholt Buschmann's seamen have been blabbing – saying that if, out of fear of them and in order to avoid them the ships of Lübeck start taking detours in the coastal waters of Finland on their way to Narva – what of it? – they'll go after their vessels and seize them right in front of the guns of Vibourg. And old Gustav fears that if such things start happening it will turn Moscow fiercely against Sweden."

And in the end – what in fact would all that amount to? Bal thought, as he marched towards the harbour. *A new war between Sweden and Russia (the last one ended just last year) – it would be just the normal course of events, definitely more so than battles between the vessels of Tallinn and Lübeck – if anything can be called normal in a world of such disorder as this.*

The purplish sea glittered in the blazing sun, and over Viimsi and Salmesaare hovered a greyish heat, like gunpowder smoke. Not until he had already gone through the Rose Garden and was about to climb over its low seaside stone wall did he realise that he was taking the same shortcut to the harbour that he had as a schoolboy. He stopped on a low knoll, rising like a bastion in the midst of fragrant honeysuckle, rested his elbows on the wall and let his eyes range over the harbour.

It was a hundred paces from where he stood to the water's edge. And right there, stretching out from the gravelly shore into the bay, in the direction of the red roof of Pirita Convent, lay the pride of Tallinn's shipowners – their bulwark, a hundred and fifty fathoms long, constructed of cobblestones and logs. Ten wooden shacks, resembling boat sheds, had lately been erected equidistant from each other along the high outer wall, and Bal knew that each sheltered a cannon, resting on an iron-clad block and aimed at the sea. On the inland side of the bulwark was an unimaginably long wharf on thick pilings that had turned green in low water. In the middle of the harbour, protected from the gulf by the bulwark, the walls of a four-storey watchtower, with a serrated rooftop balustrade, rose straight up out of the sea.

There were ten ships at the wharf, and judging by their number it would have seemed the profitable days of Tallinn's sea trade were not over. But Bal knew that the vessels lying at the far end of the bulwark had nothing to do with trade, at least not at the moment. Privateering was more piracy than business – piracy sanctioned by the sovereign, to be sure, but even so . . . Fine, but what does it mean to say "even so"? If one constructed a syllogism on the "even so", it would turn out that Master Brun, in carrying out the sentences of the bailiff's court, had, in the course of his service, sent at least a hundred people to God by means of the sword or the rope. Even so, Master Brun would be, yes, a murderer a hundred times over . . . And the commanders-in-chief, the field marshals, dukes and kings, not to mention the mercenaries – all of them would, even so, also be murderers . . . From Moses to the Gospels, even so . . . the "even so" only gets worse: after all, Moses merely said, "You shall not kill"; but Jesus said, "Whosoever smites you on your right cheek, turn to him the other also." Yes. But all the battles ordained by God in the Old Testament and all the blessed and damned massacres of our day – what are they? An abyss between words and deeds, an abyss within words and deeds . . . Or is there, somewhere in the depths of the abyss, in the clashing of swords and pounding of feet, in the smell of sweat and stench of blood and, gasping for breath – is there, even so, a voice within our inmost self that can tell us the difference between truth and falsehood, between good and evil . . . the singular voice that Melanchthon reputedly wrote about, the voice that everyone who listens carefully is supposed to hear . . . ? Fine. One can philosophise. But to philosophise to the end is pointless. Logical reasoning is to the human brain what swordfighting is to the body. (Bal had recently tried it out with some of the young Blackheads in the cellar of their guild house.) And it seemed to be a useful exercise – to practise up to a certain point. But not to the end. That would mean to kill or be killed.

Bal leapt over the wall and onto the stone road leading to the bulwark, where he walked past three or four discharged vessels from Rostock or Wismar. Continuing a few hundred paces along the pier's rumbling planks, he could see the brownish water between them rising and falling, and he breathed in the exciting smells – saltwater, fish leavings, tar and hemp. He jumped over the ropes securing the privateers' low-riding, single-masted ships to the bollards and arrived at the high stern of Captain Bartholt Buschmann's two-masted *Minerva*. But the chequerboard windows here were too high for him to see inside. And it is doubtful that he would have found what he was looking for behind them anyway. He continued alongside the ship, spotted a dangling rope ladder, and was up on deck in an instant.

They had not lately been keeping a specially vigilant watch on the privateers, at least not while they were in their home harbour. It took a while for the watchman on the high ship's bridge to notice him and call out: "Avast there! What do ye want?"

"Is the lookout on board?"

"Yes . . . so?"

"A friend to see him."

A deckhand went off to find the man and Bal looked the vessel over. The *Minerva* was a typical two-masted merchant ship, about fifteen fathoms long and at least fifty years old, but built with boards laid edge to edge, and smooth-sided like the more modern caravels. Four squares had recently been cut into both sides of the lower deck, and at each crouched a sizeable falconet ready to spring with action. In some way or other, without directly involving the Town Council, Herr Blasius Hochgreve had managed to wheedle these old bronze beasts from the town armoury for his own ship.

"Well if it isn't – in God's name – hello!"

The lookout, Märten Bergkam, came towards Bal barefoot, in blue canvas sailors' trousers and his own tan skin. His light hair stuck upwards – the more so for the light red bandana, with a dark red stain at the left temple, tied across his forehead. "Well, so where has the future scholar been keeping himself?"

"Where have you been, yourself?"

"We've been going out 'for a little action', as Papa Buschmann puts it."

"You were out at sea, reconnoitering?"

"No, we were actually pirating!"

"Shhh! Careful, one of your superiors might hear you referring to his trade as piracy—"

"They won't hear a thing. Come, let's go to my post – it's just the right height for spitting."

Märten jumped remarkably lightly up onto the high railing, and from there scrambled up the rope ladder of the foremast. Bal was still on the lower rungs of the ladder when Märten went up through the opening in the floor of the crow's nest and out of sight. When Bal had worked out how, he was up the ladder in a flash as well, but it took him a bit longer to climb into the crow's nest. Then they sat up there side by side, high in a basket woven of rushes and fine slats, leaning against a topmast flying a pennant, their feet – one pair in peasant moccasins, the other bare – resting on the crosstrees white with gull droppings, as they looked down and then at each other.

Bal's conscience with regard to Märten was not entirely clear. First of all, because of the business in winter with the birch carving – they had never cleared up the bad feelings that incident had given rise to. And second, because of the reason for Bal's present visit. No, he had not come just to make Märten talk at random about what it was like on a privateer – where they went and where they were planning to go next, and so on. He had to let Märten know why he was interested in the topic. On his way to the harbour he had thought all he would do was get Märten started. But now, looking at Märten's bare, tar-stained toes, he decided he would confess the reason for his interest. But even before he could open his mouth Märten asked:

"So – the Doctor wants to know what our fleet is doing, isn't that so?"

After a moment of astonished silence Bal had no choice but to respond calmly:

"Yes he does."

"In that case I'll tell you. As much as I know. But not him – I would not tell him a thing."

"Why would you not?"

"I don't like his face."

And then Märten related the privateering business to Bal better than any merchant could have described it to the Doctor. He talked about the one-masted ship with the four cannons that belonged to Benedictus Bock, and a similar one to so-and-so, and a barque to someone else. And he disclosed the number of cannons they had on board. And that they had exchanged fire near Prangli yesterday with a ship from Lübeck (a piece of the mast had hit Marten in the temple, where it was still bleeding). And for tomorrow the plan was for all seven vessels to sail out and take up watch north of Suursaare because that was the route the ships from Lübeck were reportedly travelling these days. And those of the Muscovites as well. (Imagine that – even they have a few vessels under sail!)

"And so, what's it like, living on board . . . ?"

"The way it usually is. All the rules were laid out clearly before we were signed up: obey your superiors or be hanged; don't complain about the food or you'll be hanged; keep your watch when it's your turn or be hanged. And do not touch a crumb of the booty – which, may God grant us in abundance – or you'll be hanged."

"That's most generous . . ."

"It's the custom aboard ship. And whoever loses a hand or leg, Herr Hochgreve will have a new hand or leg attached. But if the new one won't take, the Herr will provide him with all the bread and sardines of his heart's desire up to the blessed day of his death."

As far as the privateers' future plans were concerned, Märten did not know much, of course.

"But listen, didn't Papa Buschmann set up his son Kaspar as steward on his ship? And Kaspar was a classmate of yours, wasn't he? Go and talk to him. He's on board. And he'll offer you an ale as well."

As they were talking they heard shouts from below and orders barked from the pier, and at the end of the bulwark the harbour patrol boat set out with a clanking of oars. Bal and Märten watched over the edge of the crow's nest as a caravel in full sail, with its long blue Swedish banners flapping, came into view from behind the island of Suur-Paljassaare, approaching the harbour at great speed. And later, when Bal was sitting downstairs on Kaspar Buschmann's bunk in a cubicle between the pantry and the galley, and Kaspar was standing behind a partition filling a second mug of ale, his young moustache twitching as he regaled Bal with tales of his two weeks of adventures at sea, Bal looked out at the scene behind the square window with its torn pig's-bladder pane: a large boat had been let down into the water from the caravel, on the seaward side of the bulwark, and eight rowers guided it close alongside the *Minerva*. In the bow stood three men, two of them lackeys, but the one in the middle apparently a merchant of some importance, judging by his velvet beret, his light, well-groomed beard, and the short cape thrown over his velvet suit. This impression was confirmed by the appearance of a second boat carrying eight oarsmen and three horses, their bridles tied one to another. Two were bays with simple saddles; the third, a chestnut, wearing a grand saddle decorated with embossed metal, stood out from the other two even more noticeably than its owner did from his attendants in the first boat. The gentleman raised his eyes as though sensing he was being observed. He could not, of course, spot Bal's face behind the torn pane. But Bal recognised him, and in his surprise almost called out. It was none other than Herr Henrik Claesson Horn from Turku, counsellor to Duke Johan and de facto the ruler of Finland.

The boats passed close by the pier, all the way to the gravel strip of shoreline. A wooden plank was lowered and the horses led ashore. Herr Horn was already there with his two companions. The three men mounted and galloped off towards town.

Bal's immediate impulse was to leave his classmate and race to town. For between the unannounced arrival of Herr Horn and the Doctor's house there had to be connecting threads of some sort that were worth knowing about. But then he remembered that his businesslike discussion with Kaspar had to be brought to a businesslike conclusion, and he sat back down on the bunk. He was troubled by no sense of obligation to be open with Kaspar. Enjoying a feeling of superiority – perhaps not entirely free of envy – he again prodded the captain's son to relate the story of the last weeks' events, and from there it was not difficult to proceed to the adventures still to come. Herr Sum had had good reason to send Kaspar straight back to *tertia* level, for Kaspar never did work out *who* came first, the Greeks or the Romans, and Herr Sum was convinced that a *primaner* at the Trivium School had to know things like that. No-one made such demands of the steward of the *Minerva*, and that is how Kaspar had become the dispenser of rations on his papa's ship.

"This is some job, I tell you! You can soak your moustache in a mug of ale all day long. Though even I'm not allowed t'spill more ale than I can cover with the sole of my foot. Or else – it's a farthing for the poor, clink! But once we actually go on a raid, that's when the *booty* will start to flow . . . No doubt about it—"

"So, you want to seal the sea routes completely?"

"Absolutely"

"But on the Finland side it'll still be open, won't it . . . ?"

"Look, don't go ringing out this information from the Town Hall tower: the day before yesterday, all the captains came together in the evening on Schmedemann's *Scylla*. My old man is – well, he's their, well 'admiral'. And they decided to do as he proposed: any ship headed for Narva that they can get close to will be seized. No matter what waters they're in. Even if they're on wheels, riding along the Finnish coast – as the guv'nor said!"

The red glow of sunset was still high in the sky above the Kakumäe peninsula when Bal set out from the harbour towards town. When he had paid his half-farthing to get in through the Great Coast Gate and was hurrying towards the Bishop's House, the dwellings in the brownish dusk of the streets were like great grey birds stretching the glowing red beaks of their gabled rooftops into the red-streaked sky. The windows of the Bishop's House were lit, and stunning news greeted Bal at the threshold to the Frolinks' apartment. Meus, a man of calm, deliberative temperament most of the time, called out over his bowl of pea soup even before Bal had closed the door behind him.

"You've heard?"

"Heard what?"

"That Shuiski has surrounded Tartu and is bombing the town."

"But we have a much larger bomb in this very house!" said Annika, ladling soup out of the pot with a short-handled tin spoon, even as Meus' spoon stayed anxiously suspended above his bowl.

Meus' announcement was not unexpected, in fact. Shuiski's huge army – there was talk now of eighty thousand men – had moved a week earlier in the direction of the defenceless and damaged bishopric. Still, the fact that Tartu was being besieged struck Bal dumb for the moment. He swallowed hard: it was as though, once again, the ground had been cut from under his feet. As though he had been sucked into quicksand, or been told that a relative, whose worsening illness had plagued him with a daily worry that he had tried to ignore, was now in *agon* – by which the ancient Greeks meant "struggle", but by which the doctors who knew such words meant "death throes". For, according to the Doctor's information, Bishop Hermann and his counsellors were of the opinion that the more easily Tartu fell into the Muscovite's hands, the better the chances were that they and their canons would survive with their purses and skins intact.

"And just what do we have in our house?" Bal asked.

"Well, the notable regent or ruler of Finland is sitting at the Doctor's supper table. But they say he's very sick with some kind of intestinal ailment. And since our Doctor is so famous in many lands, he came here to be treated by him."

"Ah . . . that I know."

"You know already! Humph. You know everything. But what you don't know is that the Doctor had Johann bring a basketload of medicines from the Apothecary and asked that you be summoned as soon as you got home."

The supper table in the great-room was still abundantly set, but the meal was over, and Herr Horn was sitting in the Doctor's study. Judging by his energetic manner, the man was in the pink of health. One of his servants was standing by the Doctor's lectern, writing, but the other, apparently his valet, was pulling off his master's boots.

" I remember this young man," said Herr Horn, pleased with his memory, as Bal entered in response to the Doctor's summons and bowed. It would have been appropriate, of course, for Bal to remain politely silent. But Herr Horn's "Aha" and the man's comical posture, one boot on, one off, animated the imp in him, and the tanned, robustly healthy face framed in its light-brown skipper's beard gave rise to a gleefully brazen thought: *My dear old chap, I've got you in the palm of my hand, as one might say* . . . He said: "So, what you last told me in Turku has indeed come to pass."

"What was it I told you?"

"That we would meet again, God willing," he paused briefly, "in the interests of the duke."

"Just so, just so, just so," the Doctor interjected quickly. "Balthasar, please go to Dyck's and bring us, say, a half-cup of Mithridates' potion and tell them that this, too, is for Herr Horn, who has come to me from Turku for treatment. What I mean is, you needn't spread it about, but we're not making a secret of it either. For why should we deny our fame? Isn't it so: we are not holding a candle in front of our face, but neither are we hiding it under a bushel?"

When Bal went out of the study, bowing, the Doctor followed him and asked:

"What did you learn about the privateers?" And right there on the stairs, Bal told him Kaspar Buschmann's latest news, and right there he got from the Doctor another two weeks in Marburg (for he had calculated that he could get by on about a mark a week). But when he came back from the Apothecary with the medicine, the Doctor placed the clay bowl containing Dyck's costly potion offhandedly onto the lectern behind him and said, as he stared out of the window into the darkness:

"And now, Balthasar, put *your* candle under a bushel, as far back as possible. Understand? And deliver these two letters. The more discreetly, the better. This is for Herr Beelholt, and this one is for Herr Hans Holstein." Inclining his head in the direction of Herr Horn, who was now wearing fine black furry slippers with upturned toes, he added: "Beelholt is a true servant of the duke – you know him. He's our contact with Tallinn's Town Council. And Holstein is the head of our Great Guild."

Bal set out with the letters through the sleeping town. The green eyes of nocturnal cats glinted on piles of rubbish, and the watchmen in the gate towers snored less and rattled their halberds more often than had been their wont, for the town's mounted mercenaries had special orders to be on the alert. One might say that, against the background of the fateful events that had cast their shadow upon the land, the strangest weeks of Bal's life began with the delivery of these letters. What had been feared in winter and had not, with the help of God, come to pass earlier, was now at hand: the fragile, red-and-grey, brick-and-iron walls of Tartu lay smouldering in the fires ignited by Shuiski's guns. Eighty thousand men surrounded the town. There were just two

hundred defending it, but there could easily have been two thousand –
had they been summoned in time. On exhausted horses, refugees and
messengers with bandaged heads and dusty armour arrived in town
from the estates around Tartu. And Tallinn's anxiety grew oppressive.
Officials of the town treasury went from house to house collecting con-
tributions for fortification projects, and groups of labourers had been
hired to work day and night to build a rondel at the Viru Gate. And in
the midst of this feverish activity Herr Horn was sitting in the Bishop's
House, treating his spleen. Apothecary Dyck sold the Doctor one bunch
of ivy and mandrake leaves after another, and ever more of Mithridates'
miracle potion, and in the evenings Bal delivered new letters to the
councilmen and to the heads of the Great Guild and of the Kanuts' and
St Olaf's guilds. Many of these gentlemen visited the Doctor late at
night, seeking treatment for varieties of ailments. And wafting above all
this fever was the scent of the bewitched Katharina's carnation garden.

When the news came, on July 20, that Tartu had fallen, the Doctor
said with relief: "Well now, that should soften even the toughest hides!"

Yet even now neither the Town Council nor the guilds took action.
They were still resistant to asking Duke Johan (by way of Herr Horn) to
be so kind as to take them under his rule and protection (in the interests
of the Order, of course!).

"This is the work of our dear friend Monninkhusen," the Doctor
said. "And our even dearer friend Clodt has inexplicably joined forces
with him. It would be interesting to know how much Christian is paying
them for this scheme. By the way, there's talk of sending them to
Christian as emissaries of the town, and Clodt will probably be authorised to offer the town, if need be, to Denmark. So you understand: we
must absolutely achieve a definite advantage *before then* . . ."

But instead of gaining a definite advantage, the Doctor's strategy
nearly led to a decisive defeat. On the morning of July 25, an odd rumour
began circulating in town, to the effect that, at dawn of that same day,

Commander of the Order Franz von Segenhagen, nicknamed Goldbeak, had opened the Toompea Castle gates, and Christoph von Monninkhusen, advocate of the bishopric of Saaremaa and brother of the bishop, had marched in at the head of his mercenary company. But by noon the entire town knew that, immediately upon taking over the castle, Monninkhusen's heralds had ridden down from Toompea, blowing their trumpets, and delivered Monninkhusen's letter to the Town Council. The council members, still drowsy at that early-morning hour, read the letter and were momentarily jolted into wakefulness, but could not quite understand whether what had apparently taken place was dream or reality or feverish delusion: that is, that Herr Monninkhusen had declared himself the Danish king's vicegerent in the province of Estonia.

And above this fever . . . the maddening scent of the bewitched Katharina's carnation garden . . . Katharina, with her unfathomable eyes – intimate, merry, imploring – Katharina, walking with the maid Magdalena across the market square to buy the required victuals for the ailing Herr Horn (carrots and fresh cabbage, but God forbid, no turnips! All the vegetable vendors knew that Herr Horn could eat no turnips). Katharina at the house door – Katharina on the stairs Katharina at the dinner table, pouring apple cider for Herr Horn, for he did not drink wine, and Bal never did manage to discover whether this too was in jest.

On the evening of August 6 – *Ha-ha-hah: as though I were planning to write my own chronicle!* – Bal stepped out into the courtyard of the Bishop's House. He had just been upstairs relaying the news circulating among the peasants at the market: that is, that Muscovite forces would soon be at the walls of Tallinn. He had caught sight of Katharina at the Friesners' bedroom door, where she had gone to see whether Magdalena had made up the canopy bed to be sufficiently soft. For that was where Herr Horn slept off the fatigue of his diplomatic efforts.

The evening was dark, the air close. And all at once Bal felt – and it was this feeling that had driven him out of the house – that there was nowhere he could go. The Frolinks were not at home. Meus had been called to a deathbed and Annika had gone to visit a newborn. His father was on the road, transporting Herr Krumhusen's possessions to Riga (he had fled from Narva to Tallinn in the spring) – *God grant that Father gets home safe.* And Märten had vanished like a twig in water. People were saying the duke had captured the *Minerva* and another corsair off the coast of Finland and gaoled the crew. . . *It's curious how little, at this bewildering time, I have thought of God.*

Bal went out, feeling his way along the stony path to the remote corner of the courtyard. He opened the door of the prayer chapel, stretched out his hands, touched the cold limestone folds of the angel's robes, and sat down in the pitch-black corner between the angel and the wall. Somewhere in the vicinity of the monastery a dog started howling and then suddenly stopped. And somewhere beyond the Almshouse settlement, or Ülemiste, he heard distant thunder.

Lord God, what do you have in mind for this land and its people? Are you holding out your hand in blessing over this scheme of Monninkhusen's, which apparently even the Danish king does not yet know about . . . ? Or do you really mean to give us to the Muscovites? And nullify any claim of Sweden's here . . . even though it would seem like the most reasonable alternative for the peasants, and that's why I've been working for it . . . God, I cannot argue with you: Not only because . . . but mainly because . . . alright, alright – also because you are right . . . and because it would protect the holy teachings of Augsburg in the best way in this land . . . because all the men who formulated this teaching under your guidance have said that this is the right way . . . even though I don't know whether it is right in its revised or unrevised form . . . God, I feel there is something wrong in my thinking . . . I feel there is a kind of scorn in it . . . but I cannot put my finger on it . . . I've been worn down by these turbulent days and this oppressive evening . . . perhaps it is not my place

to ask to know your plan for this land . . . perhaps I should humbly ask
only: What have you in store for me . . . ? Why have you set this woman in
my path . . . ? In my heart, I have committed adultery with her ten thousand
times . . . you know that . . . and I fear that soon her husband's kindness
towards me will no longer restrain me . . . Lord, must I leave this house and
seek a new path in order to become good . . . ? You see how arrogant I am . . .
as though those who had not studied at Marburg were not good people . . .
Must I . . . ? I thank you, I thank you, that you have said so clearly: "Listen
to my voice within you, but do not be a fool." *Yes, I will listen to your*
voice . . . yes . . . for it will help me know good from evil . . . yes. Odd: for a
moment, God's face was that of his eighty-year-old grandfather at
Kurgla, and then it became the face of the earth-god who vanished into
the tree trunk, and now God's face too disappeared into the darkness.

Bal paused to listen – not to God's words but to the light, hurried
steps approaching along the gravel path. The door creaked open; someone entered the chapel, breathing heavily, on the other side of the limestone angel. The scent of carnations suddenly filled the night. Bal drew
a deep breath – either to take in the fragrance or to call out to Katharina.
In any case, he swallowed his words, for he heard other steps approaching along the path, and then they were in the chapel, and the Doctor was
asking in a low voice:

"Is it you, here?"

"I told you, I cannot do it," Katharina said in a whisper.

"Dear one, you *must*. You have to keep him here until the fate of the
town is decided. If he leaves, they won't come to any decision."

"I cannot do it."

"My dear – how then could you, with the duke?"

"It's because of the duke that I cannot!"

"Really . . . ?"

"He'll tell the duke!"

"My dear . . . am I to think that you don't know men?! We men boast to each other about our whores. But when it comes to our ladies, we are silent as a tomb. A man's behaviour depends on what he considers you to be."

"And what am I to you?"

"To me you are my little Kati. My little Katt. My little Kratt. As you've always been. Come, let's go. It's too cold here."

They rose and moved in the dark, towards the door. The Doctor said:

"You say I've cast a spell on you. Alright. But you've done the same to me. I have lived in thirteen lands, but nowhere have I found a woman with skin as stunningly smooth as yours . . ."

CHAPTER NINE,

in which we resume our horse ride alongside events in the affairs of states and individual lives, continuing the tale that could not be contained in the previous chapter because of its many twists and turns, but here, in strict accordance with all the rules of drama, it is brought to a near conclusion; history itself, however, or let us say life itself, would trample these rules like a herd of wild horses breaking down their corral – if we observed events as they were actually unfolding.

The November sky was as cold and grey as a stone wall. Up on the barren slopes of Lasnamäe Hill, the low clouds just about touched the hats of the two men on horseback, Uncle Jakob in front on a dapple-grey mare, and Bal following on a borrowed ash gelding. All that needed to be said had been said the previous night in Annika and Meus' kitchen, and now each was lost in his own thoughts. Bal twisted his fingers absent-mindedly in the horse's thick mane, thinking back to everything that had happened.

On the tenth day after he overheard the conversation in the chapel, Herr Horn gave orders for his fur slippers to be tucked into his travel bags and pulled on his boots. Whether and how much he paid the Doctor for his treatment remained a secret. He gave Bal a mark "for the sake of our old acquaintance, and in the hope that perhaps we'll meet again." And, given that he was a man known for his decisiveness, he spent a long time turning the coin over in his hands before relinquishing it. That same morning Herr Holstein (suffering from a bad headache and flatulence) came to the Doctor to tell him, confidentially, on behalf of the Town Council and the guilds, that the Council and the guilds humbly thanked them for so graciously and willingly taking upon himself the defence of their ancient rights at this dangerous time, *however* . . . And that same morning Herr Horn and his companions mounted their horses in the courtyard of the Bishop's House. The Doctor and Katharina were standing in the withered rose garden to bid him farewell. Before bounding into his saddle Herr Horn kissed Katharina's hand and Bal, looking down from the Frolinks' window, could not tell, in spite of his best efforts, whether Katharina had behaved like a *lady,* or *otherwise,* with Horn. We must confess, Bal had been struggling mightily with this question for ten days. At one point he was fiercely determined to find out for certain – whether by hiding in Herr Horn's bedroom during the day, for example, or by stealing down the corridor late at night and listening behind the door, or by climbing out of the Frolinks' window onto the white stone roof and making his way to Herr Horn's candlelit window. But then he had simply sat himself down hard on his stool, so firmly in fact that he had heard its tenons crack, and sitting there in his cubicle, at his rickety table, he had said to himself through clenched teeth: "What does this strumpet of Duke Johan's and his counsellors have to do with me?" And he had picked up that cursed book of Vesalius, *De humani corporis,* and felt as though he were running head first into a wall: he had read and read and felt that all of Vesalius' wisdom flowed over him like water over stone. He had jumped up in a rush of pity and tenderness: *Who will save the unfortunate Katharina from this terrible doctor, this witch doctor, this man of razor-sharp intelligence . . . from this man – my benefactor?!* And then he had sat down again at his little table and said to himself: *But the Doctor told her to behave like a* lady. And with a dark smile on his young, badly shaven face, he had asked the world: *But what does that word mean? What does that word mean in today's foul world?* And again he sat and gripped

262

the edge of the table, his hands not much smaller than his father's, and vowed to listen to God's voice within himself and, above all, *not be a fool* . . . And without being aware of it he had become engrossed in Vesalius again and noticed all of a sudden that as he settled his own human body on the stool and instructed his human heart to beat in rhythm with God's word – the way the sluice gate of a gunpowder mill regulates the pounding of the pestle – the truths of Vesalius began to take root once more in the eager furrows of his mind.

Herr Horn departed. For an entire evening the Doctor paced up and down in his study, summoning his full concentration to the writing of a letter to the duke on how best to persuade Tallinn's gentry to act. For two or three weeks he waited for a reply. In the meantime, life at the Bishop's House followed its usual pattern. Katharina walked about in the market square outside the front door, and on the stairs leading to the Doctor's living quarters, and try as he might Bal could not say that her smile was more forced or her glance more uncertain or her voice affected when she said, in her customary, disarming, playful tone:

"Balthasar, hello. I'm glad you chanced to be in the courtyard. Would you please open the stable door for me? It's too hard for me to turn the key, and I want to go riding."

Bal took a deep breath, unlocked the door, and went away in silence. To repeat, life went on in the Bishop's House as before. As before, there were alternating moments of relief and dread as the events in this summer of war unfolded. There was relief when the duke, to gain favour with the townspeople, ordered the captured ships belonging to Tallinners released, and they arrived in the harbour laden with rich booty – actually, it was after the town had rebuffed the duke via Herr Horn. And there was dread when it was reported that Muscovite forces, though only small reconnaissance units, had reached the Almshouse settlement on the outskirts of Tallinn. And uncertain relief when the enemy quickly retreated, as a few hundred town soldiers and some twenty or so Blackheads descended upon them to the sonorous pealing of church bells.

On the morning of August 28, Katharina came face to face with Bal under the vaulted gate of the Bishop's House. He greeted her, and Katharina said lightly:

"Matthias is leaving today at noon for Turku. He has to go and see the duke." She paused and looked at Bal, her oblong eyes slowly rounding, and Bal felt with breathless certainty that during the Doctor's absence things would have to be resolved with Katharina, one way or another. He said, his voice hoarse:

"For how long?"

"I don't know," Katharina said, "for two weeks or a month. And he's taking me with him."

Bal's guilty surge of excitement plummeted with such force into a well of disappointment that his momentary "Thank God" feeling plunged down with it and disappeared. He could not utter a word. Katharina looked up at Bal. Her eyes were suddenly coal-black. She said, with utmost casualness, in a tone one would use to say, "It's raining after all", or, "It's already evening":

"Think about me while I'm gone. It would please me."

It is not the case, however, that Bal did nothing but think about Katharina until mid November. Nor is it at all the case that it would have done him good to think about her.

"You know, you've become somewhat distant lately," Meus said, stopping at Bal's door after dinner on a day in early October. "Or perhaps it seems that way because I myself have had more to do now, at this time of war, than usual," he added, as though to lessen the effect of the disappointment in his remark.

Bal felt that his brother-in-law had touched a wound inside him, too, and he remained silent. Meus stooped to step through the low door and sat down on Bal's pallet.

"I haven't even had time to have a real talk with you. Tell me what plans for the future you've been discussing with your doctor friend. It's too late this year, of course, for you to go to Germany."

Bal was grateful to Meus for bringing up his future plans and pursued the topic with enthusiasm – hoping to make amends, somehow:

"This year, true. The Doctor wants me to work under his tutelage for another year. And study his books. And then it'll be off to Marburg, he's promised."

"To study medicine?" Meus asked, not exactly with disapproval, but with just a trace of disappointment.

"I suppose so."

"Hmm. You know, I'd planned to send you to Stettin to study theology at the Pedagogical Institute there, with Master Wolff. He was a friend to me. What does your father think of this doctor business?"

"Father?" He says: 'You have to know yourself what you have to do.'"

"But who will pay?"

"Well, Father will help. And I've saved some money, too. From the Doctor."

"How much?"

"Well . . . I've got fifty marks . . ."

"Fifty marks . . . ? Hmm. The pastor at Oleviste earns three hundred marks a year and works so hard he's turning grey, as you've seen . . . and the Doctor has paid you fifty in one year – for the few things you've done for him . . . He doesn't know how to handle money!"

"Who?"

"The Doctor. And how much are you hoping to get from your father?"

"We'll see. I'll go abroad next autumn with my own money. By then I should have about a hundred. And I've calculated that I should be able to live on that for two years."

"I was able to do it. But it seems you're developing . . . rather expensive tastes."

"What do you mean? In any case, Father will send something too. And I can do all kinds of work while I'm living at this fellow Phrygius' place that the Doctor has recommended. I can do copying work or proofreading, or chop wood or make hay. No doubt the Rector has horses. And maybe an estate somewhere. We might agree, for example, that I plough the bushel fields in the spring and in winter attend a week's worth of lectures, or at least earn by the day for each field. I'll manage, one way or another."

Meus had planned to give Bal a little lecture on themes in Aristotle's *Ethics* – in particular, the theme of trust. But when he shifted position to make room for Bal on his plank bed and turned to look at him, ready to launch into his topic, he suddenly stopped himself and smiled involuntarily, not visibly, but somewhere inside: *What strange folk these peasants are, after all . . . even this one here . . . this big-boned, rough-hewn titan with his round head . . . When it comes to learning, he's second in Tallinn only to the academicians, and he can get the better of some of them in matters of concrete knowledge . . . a philosopher, in some ways, but still a stripling in others . . . the way he looks at you with those wide-open blue eyes, naïve and all-knowing all at the same time . . . and he exudes something – the devil-knows-what – something like the hot steam from the sauna stoves in this region, and he's prepared to work as a coachman for the rector in Marburg or as a proofreader or a ploughman . . .*

"Well, set about it then . . . Let us trust in God . . ." Meus said – now it took some effort for him to conceal his smile – and he left without lecturing Bal.

And so, life at the Bishop's House went on as before. The master and mistress of the house remained absent. They never even wrote. Various gentlemen and ladies came by from time to time, looking for the Doctor, and of the few who chanced to enquire at Annika and Meus' door some had need of the Doctor and some were just curious. Herr Geldern, the voluble and somewhat stentorian head pastor of St Olaf's, had with his wife honoured his young colleague with a visit in October – evidently fear of war, which brought people closer, had enabled Frau Geldern to forget Annika's past impertinence. Herr Geldern said his lower back had begun to ache again with the fogs of autumn, and it was too bad the Doctor had not returned. Thereupon he emptied the Frolinks' only large silver goblet of plum wine and related the story of Fresemann, pastor at Harju-Jaani: "Just think, we had to dismiss him last week at the joint meeting of the ministry! Can you imagine – he went mad – from reading too much of some nonsensical book full of untruths. A Dutch preacher named Menno Simons published it the year before last with the shameless title, *The Foundations of Christianity*. It's nothing but benighted foolishness: for example, that children should not be baptised before the age of fourteen. Fresemann said at the meeting that the same Simons had visited Livonia a few years ago, and that he'd gone to hear him in Lihula, and from that time on had had doubts about the baptising of infants, for it is written that 'he who believes and is baptised will be saved', but a newborn cannot be a believer . . . Whether he himself had failed to baptise children brought to him for baptism, he did not say. So that now – dreadful thought – no-one knows whether the children he baptised are actually baptised!" With a shudder of disapproval, Herr Geldern refilled his goblet and went on to expound upon the events of the war: that the Muscovite had gone back home for the most part, leaving behind only a few garrisons in the towns, and that the war would no doubt break out again in spring, and that – just imagine! – some of the merchant gentry in Tartu were apparently boasting about how well they were living under the Grand Duke and calling the Tallinners fools for their resistance. And that the coadjutor, namely Kettler, was quite aggressively ingratiating himself with the Muscovites living in the bishopric. And then suddenly, he asked:

"But it seems that the lovely Frau Katharina, together with her doctor husband, has disappeared, like a pearl in a haystack, hmm?"

Bal could not remember how Annika and Meus had answered. And he would not even have remembered the question, of course not, had he not noticed *how* Frau Geldern had started at her husband's question. But, oh well, God be with them . . .

Uncle Jakob had arrived in town with his problem the day before yesterday. No, no, their few buildings had gone untouched until now and the herds were healthy and this year's grain was in the hopper, as much as they could keep for themselves. But the problem was that the last monks at Padise, the ones still living at the monastery, had offered the Raasiku estate, and Uncle Jakob along with it, to the bishop of Saaremaa as security – who knows what debts they needed to secure. The owner was new, living somewhere beyond land and sea, but the steward of the estate was that same wretched scoundrel, Hasse. And since his hands were no longer tied by last year's regulations, those defined by Herr Antonius, Hasse was at it again, aggressively laying down the law: any grain, produce, and so on, remaining to a peasant after payments had been made to the estates and elsewhere had to be sold to him, Hasse. Whatever a peasant bought had to be bought from him alone. And no-one had better try to make a trip to town without his permission. In the villages of Raasiku it was known that Jakob had settled this very question only a year or year-and-a-half earlier, and the men of Raasiku had asked Jakob to go to Hasse again, or elsewhere if necessary, to get these new demands revoked. And so now Uncle Jakob was in town to ask his nephew to come to his aid and his neighbours'. They had no-one else suitable – and could he not come and try to clarify the situation for

Hasse? The villagers had tried, Jakob himself had tried, but to no avail: Hasse had said that if they bothered him again they would learn that his patience was short and his whip long . . .

When Uncle Jakob recounted his tale of troubles, Bal muttered at length to himself – at considerably greater length than usual, but then pulled on his shoes and went to Kimmelpenning's. It was a long time since he had last been there. The old man was sick, lying in the cellar of his store, on a pallet wedged between the shelves of goods. But he recognised Bal instantly:

"Look who's here – hello, Balthasar! So, tell me, where've you been this long time . . . ?"

Bal spelt out the problem to Kimmelpenning, and his approximate plan as well. For, partly as a result of the letter he had once written for Kimmelpenning in this very place, and partly from snatches of an old Roman comedy, and God knows from what else, he had devised a plan. And it was the only course of action he could think of.

Kimmelpenning listened, his colourless lips pursed in a half-smile, and the corners of his feverish-looking eyes, below his shock of salt-and-pepper hair, narrowed:

"Well . . . let's give it a try . . ."

He directed his lanky shophand to bring Bal a pair of boots of the best black leather, got up from his bed, found in a chest a ruffled collar only very slightly dusty, and in another a black beret with a green feather. He had Bal put on the boots, collar and hat, stepped back a bit to look him over, then sat again on his bed and pulled off his heavy gold ring. He slipped it onto Bal's finger.

"So. Do you have a sword?"

"No, I don't."

"Hmm. I don't either. How about your father?"

"He might have some kind of sword somewhere . . ."

"*Some kind* won't do. Wait. You know about writing letters from dictation . . . Here." He pushed a little piece of paper towards Bal: "Write, but in German: 'Greetings from Kimmelpenning, and may God protect you. Send me for a few days that handsome two-edged sword that young Bolemann ordered but has not picked up. I have need of it for a brief while.'" Bal wrote it out and Kimmelpenning made three crosses at the bottom, and the shophand ran to deliver it to Master Lytke on Seppade Street.

And now here was Bal, riding towards Raasiku Manor through the swampy woods of Kurgla on Kimmelpenning's pretty pale-grey gelding, a pair of silver medallions gleaming on the borrowed saddle as he rode, decked out in borrowed finery and with a brand new short sword – its bronze handle visible under his graduation suit. But when the horse suddenly jerked back its head as they were riding through the thicket, Bal grew alert and looked around for wolves lurking nearby, belatedly aware that he had been thinking again of Katharina and the Doctor and the duke and Horn and himself, and in the process of unravelling this knot had wound his angry hands so tightly in the horse's mane that the animal had reared up in pain.

"Well then," Uncle Jakob said, reining in his dapple-grey, "I'll turn off towards home now. I don't know what advice to give you. Do what you can and what you think best . . ."

Bal stopped next to Jakob, whose worried expression made him want to say something reassuring, but he could not find the right words. He patted Jakob's dapple-grey on the neck and rode on.

Yes, now he had to think through how he would carry out this thing . . . But what was there to think about? Actually, it would be a matter of luck, more or less, and all he could do was act, as Herr Sum was wont to say, *ex improviso*. And of course he had to hope that he would not run into that wretched Jürg at the steward's house, or, if he did, that the fellow would not recognise him . . . In general, as he rode along on the half-muddy, half-frozen road, in that undisguised, naked world of grey and rust, Bal felt strange and ill at ease in his costume. But let us admit, part of him enjoyed the situation he was in. And not just because he imagined that his antics might help the peasant farmers of Raasiku, but because – if we really look closely – he hoped he might not exactly discredit himself with Thalia, either . . .

As he approached the barns, where startled farmhands pitching hay into the hayloft stopped to stare at him warily for a moment, it became clear to him that he could delay no longer. He spurred on his horse and galloped to the steps of the steward's house, where he tied the animal to the picket fence and strode through the low entry, straight to Herr Hasse's study, his showy leather boots thudding on the uneven floorboards a bit louder than intended. Ruunaboy was nowhere to be seen.

"Estate manager Hasse, I presume?" His tone was somewhat more curt than necessary.

"Uh-huh. That's me . . ."

Bal's entrance was apparently impressive enough, for this quick-eyed small man, with his thin neck and the face of a well-fed field mouse, had risen hastily. He had been sitting on the same fir sofa, picking his teeth, where Herr Antonius had sat reading his parchment book and sipping wine. Recovering his dignity, Hasse now asked:

"And whom do I have the honour . . . ?"

Bal did not deign to respond. For the sort of the person he was pretending to be would not, in his opinion, have responded. It could be, of course, that he was burdened by a certain reluctance to lie. He sat down quickly but deliberately on the three-legged stool and noted with amusement that Hasse, nonplussed, remained standing. Adopting an exceedingly official tone, Bal asked:

"Is it known on this estate that in Tallinn, living at Toompea Castle, is the Danish king's vicegerent for the Province of Estonia?"

Before Hasse could reply, it flashed through Bal's mind just how complaisantly he had stood here before Herr Antonius, less than two years ago. In that instant he grasped with particular clarity the differ-ence between that previous role and his present one, and the change in himself that those different roles exemplified.

Hasse replied carefully: "Of course. Vicegerent Monninkhusen. He's the brother of our esteemed mortgage master. I'm referring to the Bishop of Saaremaa."

"But what you do not know is that the peasants of Raasiku have written a letter of complaint to Herr Vicegerent, asserting that in viol-ation of their long-standing rights you are harassing them." Only now did he glance at Hasse, and he saw how the man's wheels were turning: *A letter of complaint? To Monninkhusen? No way of telling what might come of this . . . Not likely that anything will . . . the times are so uncertain . . . But at whose instigation? . . . Aha – it's that . . . that . . . that . . . that damnable Jakob of Kurgla, with his town relatives . . . there's supposed to be someone or other in town . . . But, in fact, what the devil . . .* His shifty brown eyes landed on Bal:

"And . . . who might you be . . . ?!"

It was not likely that Hasse would identify Bal as one of Jakob's town relatives. Still, Bal had to reply now in a way that would elimin-ate any possibility of being seen as the son of Jakob's wagon-driver brother. And besides, he felt something rise soundlessly up within him. The same silent surge of protest that had only made him stubborn when facing Antonius now made him aggressive. Yes, he knew he had to be shameless. It was not only the price of success, it was also the best self-defence. Perhaps he also sensed that it was his arrogance alone that stood in the way of the ten thousand humiliations his people suf-fered every day. Maybe somewhere in the depths of his peasant self he took dark satisfaction in knowing his aggression was a façade on behalf of tens of thousands of others.

He slammed the flat of his hand down so hard on the table that it resounded from the impact of Kimmelpenning's gold ring:

"I am asking the questions here and you are to answer them! Not the other way around!"

"Sir, you are giving too much weight to peasant talk," Hasse said, with greater composure than Bal liked . . . True, Bal, as a member of the gentry, should not give too much weight to the gossip of peasants. He sensed this was the right moment to conclude with a more powerful mortar round – if only he could find the right argument, one that did not focus on defending the peasants . . . ooh, if only he had taken the trouble to think through his position properly beforehand . . . Aha! The spirit of God had not abandoned him after all – or perhaps it was the schooling in worldly thought and language he had received at the Doctor's house . . . So, now he trampled cold-bloodedly, and true to his role, over his opponent's briefly won equanimity, thundering:

"You, with your petty personal greed, are driving these loyal peasants straight into the arms of the Muscovite! Are you not aware of what is happening around you? Do you not understand what is *expected* of stewards in these times?!" And now, purely for the pleasure of crushing him, Bal rounded off his attack on the steward in a low voice full of contempt: "*Idiot!*" He was a little embarrassed at having used the word because he saw how Herr Hasse changed under its impact, not turning pale with indignation nor blue with wounded pride, no, for it was the word of a high official of the Vicegerent's government and, *ergo*, without moral implications, though clearly carrying great force. And thus Hasse merely shrank, becoming a smaller target. Bal was embarrassed nonetheless. He stood up, concluding precipitously:

"The peasants are not to be provoked in any way whatsoever! Every such act benefits the Muscovite! If the King's estate manager aids the Muscovite out of stupidity, he'll be given a warning. If he doesn't heed the warning . . ." *Well, what then, in fact?* he wondered, but, having to finish the sentence, he placed his hand on the brass knob of his sword handle, pulled the blade a third of the way out of its sheath, and said ominously, ". . . he will lose his head!"

Bal's performance must have been more effective than he had dared hope. For Hasse whispered, sputtering: "Of course, Herr Counsellor . . . I had no way of knowing, Herr Counsellor . . . Understood, Herr Counsellor . . ." Then he summoned a bit more voice and spoke more audibly: "If it please Herr Counsellor to stay to dinner . . . roast pig on a spit and pear wine and . . ." But Herr Counsellor let the sword drop back into its sheath with a clunk and marched out of the room. Only when Hasse saw him trot past the windows on his pretty horse did he remember that he should have seen him off – a damnably high-placed fellow like that . . . But there was nothing to be done about it now. He spat upon the muddy boot-prints left by the Counsellor and said, audibly only to himself:

"If that's what Danish rule is going to be like, it's not worth a pup's penis!"

They were having neither roast pig on a spit nor pear wine at Kurgla that evening, but the barley broth, with fresh griddle-bread and butter, was delicious, and Bal's appetite was not in the least diminished on account of his somewhat dubious triumph. It was just the family at table, sitting by the light of the splint-flame – Uncle Jakob, Aunt Kati, Jürgen and Paavel, the farmhand who had been working at Kurgla for seven or eight years and had long since become part of the family. The story of Bal's visit to the manor that day was not one for strangers' ears, but in this gathering he recounted it in detail. When he came to the end, that is, to the part where he threatened the steward with the loss of his head, a soundless smile flashed inside Uncle Jakob's beard, Jürgen choked on a spoonful of broth, and then, coughing and laughing, gasped for air. Paavel stopped chewing his bread but remained silent, and Aunt Kati said softly, her voice hollow with astonishment and admiration:

"Oh my, you're a brazen devil alright . . . hit 'im that hard, did you . . . ?"

Uncle Jakob thought Hasse would stop his harassment now – a high official from Tallinn having pounced on him so furiously . . . To make the case that squeezing the peasants was aiding the Muscovite – that was the work of a man with a head on his shoulders, especially at a time like this when there was no rhyme or reason to anything.

When Bal had finished the story of his visit to the manor, Paavel opened his mouth for the first time to ask:

"Listen . . . could I, maybe, ask my little woman to come out 'ere now, or . . . ?"

"For heaven's sake," said Aunt Kati, "why not? . . . *Her* lips'll be locked tighter'n anyone's . . ."

"Yo-hoo! C'mon out and join us, my wife!" Paavel called.

From the low door of the back chamber a woman's form emerged into the half-dark of the main room, paused for a moment, and then walked briskly to the table. "Hello."

She stepped into the light of the splint-flame as she spoke, and Bal's eyes widened with surprise.

"Epp—? You—?! Did Paavel take . . . you . . . to be his wife . . . ?"

Between his ribs he felt a sharp pain, as though a thin barbed arrow, caught there and nearly forgotten, had been suddenly yanked out.

Epp sat, took a spoon from her apron, and was about to fold her hands in prayer, but first she cast a quick look at Bal:

"And why shouldn't he have—?"

Then she set the spoon on the table, folded her hands briefly, and after that began to eat her broth.

"A long time ago?" Bal asked after a few moments.

"Not a long time. Last summer," Epp said.

Bal was deeply sorry and deeply relieved. It was no doubt his lesser self that was sorry – the way we all regret the marriage of a girl from our past – and his better self that was relieved – the way we feel easier when one of our debts is cancelled. With all the activities of his life in town, he had thought shamefully little about Epp, though perhaps less infrequently recently, since plunging into the fever of war and politics and Katharina's oppressively fragrant shadow. Yes, a girl like Epp should have had a man of more mettle, at least a landlord's son, if not a village craftsman or even a freeholder. Uue-Pärtli farm was known to be a rather shabby place. On the other hand, though Paavel was as poor a hired hand as could be, and, like most of them probably somewhat thick-headed as well, still – he was honest and hard-working and a rather strong, husky sort of fellow, and were he and Bal to wrestle it was far from clear who the victor would be . . . But in spite of these generous concessions with regard to Paavel, a feeling of guilt, of having wronged Epp, returned, a sadness and sense of injustice that at times weighed heavy on his heart, like the town wall that split the world in two. His awareness of the world divided was especially acute now – pity and sorrow for this wife of a farmhand and her limited world in this backwater of swamp forests, and for everything that would remain dormant, never to be be realised in her – and deep unease about the falsity of the borrowed ring on his own hand, gleaming dully in the low light of the splint-flame, and about all the undeserved, unearned, foreign and borrowed things within him. Had he had leisure to observe himself carefully, he would have noticed that, fairly close upon his feelings of pity, the memory of their fall into sin glowed like a blazing sunset . . .

After some casual talk of this and that, the conversation turned of itself in the direction that his thoughts often took in these troubled times. Uncle Jakob said, sighing:

"True, the future's never looked so dark as now . . . No way of even knowin' who your master's goin' to be tomorrow . . ."

Bal said, looking each of the others in the eye, in turn:

"Let's keep this story to ourselves too. I threatened Hasse with the arrival of the Danes, but I doubt that the Danes will take over – even though the Order is coming apart."

"Do you think the Muscovite'll lay his paw on us?" Jürgen asked.

"There're others with their paws poised," Bal said, and it came out sounding a bit more knowing and mysterious than he had wanted it to at this low, scrubbed table.

"Who're you thinking of?" Jakob asked, putting his piece of bread on the table.

"I'm telling you. Herr Duke of Finland will sink his claws in . . ."

"Is that so . . . ? Haven't heard that story before . . ." Jakob said. "And for folks like us – is this s'pposed to be bad or good . . . ?" His left hand slid palm-down along the table towards Bal and turned onto its side, stopping between them like a boundary. "I'm thinking of us country folk, of course . . ."

"And why would that not be a good thing?" Bal said. "After all, the peasant is much freer under the Finnish nobles."

"That I've heard tell," Jakob said quietly, "but can't say's I believe it. A jot better, per'aps, if the nobles are more reasonable, but . . ."

The talk turned elsewhere and after a while petered out. The sound of Epp's spoon scraping the bottom of the bowl filled the silence. She put the spoon down and said:

"Bal, listen, I want to talk to you about something."

Bal was grateful that Epp took it upon herself to address him, and astonished at her new self-assurance.

"Tell me then."

"Have you heard about our pastor?"

"You mean the story about Fresemann of Harju-Jaani? They say he's become a Mennonite. It's a kind of sect somewhere around Holland. They believe children shouldn't be christened, only adults.

And apparently this Fresemann of yours has also stopped christening children. And now he's been relieved of his duties . . ."

"See – you already know the whole story. But . . . but now I don't know . . . is my child christened or not?"

"Ah . . . so you have a child too . . . ?"

"Yes. But I've been wondering, did that preacher really christen him?"

"Why, weren't you there yourself?"

"'Course I was. Went through a big March snowstorm, we did. But I don't remember his sprinkling water on him. Not that I noticed at the time. But afterwards, when people started to talk about him, it seemed to me like he didn't . . ."

"But you heard him say the words, didn't you?"

"That's just it, I didn't hear them. 'Cause he didn't know our country tongue very well, and whatever he was mumbling there was in a foreign tongue."

"Really? But Paavel was there too, wasn't he? And the godparents?"

"All of them're no cleverer than I am about this. That's why I want . . . ?"

"Well?"

"I want to be sure that the child's a Christian."

"And what would make you sure?"

"If you'd christen him again."

"Good Lord, why *me*? Take the child to Jõelähtme, or Jüri, that's the closest, and let the preacher there christen him. Or – ask the pastor first if he even thinks it's necessary."

"Why should we drag him all that way? Such a lot of fuss. And the expense."

"That's true enough. Luther in fact said any member of a Christian congregation can do it. But why does it have to be me . . . ?"

"'Cause, the way you buried your grandfather, no-one'll ever forget it . . ."

If Bal had not felt the need to do something to make amends to Epp, or to at least soothe his own conscience, he would scarcely have agreed to her request, even though it was sweet to hear the note of naïve reverence in her voice as she spoke of his grandfather's burial service.

"Well, if it will make you rest easier . . . and if Paavel has no objections."

"No, not at all," Paavel murmured, "else there'll be no knowin' if we have a little pagan in the house . . ."

Epp returned from the chamber allotted to the farmhands, carrying a child wrapped in a clean sheet. He was a little boy already, with soft, light hair and grey eyes, with the wide-eyed look that children have. He looked, Bal thought, just like Paavel. From a big wooden bucket Aunt Kati filled a small bowl with water for the christening. She and Uncle Jakob and Jürgen were the godparents, and the boy's name was Tiidrik, and Tiidrik it would remain. Bal was about to remark on what a genteel name they'd thought up for him, but then he recalled how embarrassed he had felt when teased about his own name, so he held his tongue. He did not quite know how to begin, because he had never christened anyone. Just in case, he said softly, though clearly: "Our Father, which art in heaven . . ." Then he took the little boy into his arms and the child did not cry but looked up at him, his eyes dark and serious under his light, slightly puckered, eyebrows. And Bal cleared his throat, about to say, as was proper on such occasions: "And if you have not yet been christened, then I christen you now . . ." But at that point he remembered Kimmelpenning's borrowed ring on the hand that would sprinkle the christening water. For a moment he considered taking it off, but then decided that he had been given it by an honest man, to use in an honest deception, and he left it on and intoned, more solemnly than he had anticipated:

"Then I christen you now in the Name of the Father, and of the Son, and of the Holy Spirit."

He dipped his fingers into the cool water and sprinkled it on the boy's wispy hair, and the child started to cry, as they usually do when, along with the hope of salvation, the fear of hell and damnation enters their hearts.

Paavel looked at the ground, expressionless, but Epp stood there with her lips compressed, staring at the burning candle that Aunt Kati had placed on the table, and her chin seemed to tremble. But perhaps it was because their breaths made the candle flame flicker as they followed Bal in singing, their voices quavering a little, but full of feeling:

"Now I have been christened and become my Father's own . . ."

When Bal arrived in Tallinn the next morning, the Doctor and his wife had finally returned. Bal did not see Katharina, but it was clear from the Doctor's animated expression that his visit with the duke had gone well.

"Yes," the Doctor said as soon as he had summoned Bal into his study, "it did take some time. The obstinacy of the Tallinners had so affected the gracious lord's innards that it took me several weeks to purge him of all the bile swilling inside him. But now everything has been put right. The duke will write patient and thorough letters to the Town Council and each of the three guilds. That is – he authorised me to write them in his name and discuss matters with the town fathers in the manner I deem best. And we will be a little more flexible than Herr Horn. So that anything they do not grasp immediately can gradually work its way into their brains. As it is said, *gutta cavat lapidem.* *
In any event, the duke was quite satisfied with us in the end. And I've never been able to accuse him of greed. But I haven't yet told you our most surprising news . . ."

He glanced at Bal and then out of the window as if weighing up whether to tell Bal his news and decided, yes he would, but then got

* A drop of water wears away stone (Latin).

caught up in his own thoughts and looked out of the window again as he said:

"Balthasar . . . opportunities are opening up for us that will triple the duke's generosity. If you can commit yourself to helping me now, your studies will be fully paid for." He turned to look at Bal with a secretive, knowing smile.

"What is your news, then?" Bal asked.

"I got a letter this morning. Our coadjutor has been in a battle with the Muscovite. Apparently he fell from his horse near the Elva Bridge – that's somewhere in a southern bishopric – and was injured. He's had to end his autumn campaign – and is coming here."

"To Tallinn?"

"*Here*. To my house. To be treated."

"Ohhh . . ."

"His major-domo, who brought me the letter, has already gone off to make arrangements. He wants to rent the Busch house next door for the coadjutor's advisers and bodyguards and cooks. The coadjutor himself and his secretary will be living *here*. Katharina and I will move into the three back rooms on the top floor. We must have stoves built into them immediately. I've already sent Johann to fetch Master-Potter Traube. In short, it'll be getting confoundedly lively here soon. You understand: the whole administration of the Order – no matter how shaky and slipshod its rule and how near collapse – its entire administration will be moving into this house. For Fürstenberg is in effect in retirement, as you know. Kettler makes all the decisions."

And of course the Doctor was right: things immediately got "confoundedly lively" at the Bishop's House. The unfinished rooms on the top floor were hastily completed. Potter Traube's assistants hauled up wooden buckets of clay, brick hods and straw-lined crates full of Dutch tiles. With Bal's help the Doctor's instruments and books were carried into the half-finished attic rooms. Long wooden seats with carved backs were transported from the homes of many burghers into the Doctor's great-room: here the lordships of the Order would soon be conducting their deliberations. Apothecary Dyck made several hurried visits to the Doctor to consult him about brewing the necessary medicines for the coadjutor. The Doctor dispatched his own horses to the Vegesacks, thus freeing his stables for those of the coadjutor. And Katharina helped the housemaid Magdalena shake out the pillows and feather beds from the open bedroom window. The general hubbub was such that Bal had, in truth, no chance to ponder the surge of doubt, pain, shock, and – God forgive him! – hope that shot through him when he saw Katharina bending over those bedclothes . . .

News of the coadjutor's imminent arrival spread quickly, of course, and all kinds of merchants, offering their wares and services to the Doctor's prominent patient, began to appear at his door. He received the more important of these himself – those offering ivory chess pieces or velvet Flemish slippers or Polish honey-wine. The ones selling armour or canvas cloth or shoe leather were sent next door to the fat and noisy Breitkopf, the black-moustachioed major-domo. In any case it seemed that, in spite of the sorry state of the Order, its coadjutor was a surprising magnet – after all, his "brother superior", Fürstenberg, demanded that he himself be addressed as "His Serene Highness and Master of the Teutonic Order in Livonia, by the Grace of God." The merchants of Tallinn, ever quick when it came to searching out new customers for their stores of wheat and seal-oil, seemed as conservative as insects when it came to any *matter of state* or of tradition, especially anything that involved the swearing of oaths. So, in their view, the glow of His Serene Highness and God's Grace unquestionably emanated from the coadjutor as well.

At noon on November 22, five or six councilmen and twenty or so Blackheads rode out in parade regalia into the sandy hills alongside the Pärnu highway to greet the coadjutor. With the first snow clouds of the year had come a bitter east wind that whistled across the uneven, frozen ground and blew stinging, icy snow into the gentlemen's faces. And although no fanfare sounded from the Town Hall tower, and only half the councilmen and a third of the Blackheads were present, the arrival of the coadjutor was such that one might have thought the Order Master himself had deigned to come to town.

Ahead of and behind the coadjutor's coach rode ten knights in heavy armour, bearing swords and halberds and wearing the white cloaks of the Order, decorated with large black crosses. Six matching grey steeds drew the coach, the coach itself being a small black cubicle constructed of thin wooden boards, with two windows and two doors, swaying from braided straps between four high, clumsy wheels. Behind the armed escort came half a dozen wagons bearing the coadjutor's personal belongings; after that four companies of mounted mercenaries, and then a dozen rustic vehicles bearing their baggage. The mercenaries, numbering four or five hundred men, had been tried and toughened in battles the world over. Most of them were from the company that Commander Ebert Schlagtodt had hired for the Master from the Duke of Braunschweig. They far outdid the town soldiers, both in the variety of their motley attire and the evidence of combat etched on their battle-scarred faces: there were men in armour and doublets, helmets and hats, with scarred faces and bearded faces, bare heads and bandaged brows; there were mere striplings and feeble old men. But they did not appear at first glance to be noticeably shabby, forthe coadjutor had recently paid them fifteen marks "commission" per horse and a Dutch guilder per man as "marching money". But their slings and bandages were evidence of the heavy price they had paid to recapture Rõngu from the Muscovite. And from the way their drooping moustaches turned up at the sight of the town walls, it was clear that they intended to make the most of their free time here.

As soon as they entered the town through the Karja Gate the quartermaster of each company led his men to the homes of designated burghers, who received them with only minor grumbling, for it had been bruited about town that the coadjutor's purse was not empty this time, after all. The Lords of the Order accompanied Kettler's coach to the Old Market and dispersed to the homes of Busch or Asse, or to those of relatives or friends in town. The coadjutor's attendants lifted a litter from the supply wagon and set it down next to the coach, and the coadjutor hopped out, supporting himself on his valet's shoulder.

Herr Gotthart Kettler, dressed in a short, black sable-trimmed cape, was a man of above-average height, fairly long-legged and somewhat stooped. He had a large, round head, straight brown hair, and his eyes, of an oily yellow hue, were remarkably observant and imperious. From between a thin brown moustache and a thick full beard flashed a red-lipped, white-toothed smile. His bandaged left leg was wrapped in green silk and he held it straight out in front of him. He waved casually to the onlookers, patted the Doctor jocularly on the back, rested his left arm around his valet's neck and, with a little hop-step for balance, managed to plant a gallant kiss on Katharina's hand. At the same time, he said something to her – Bal, at his window, could not make out what – at which the gentlemen standing nearby burst out laughing. Kettler then sat down on the litter and let his four servants carry him into the house, ahead of the Doctor and Katharina.

The Order's servicemen, armed with swords, followed with several riveted chests of the coadjutor's belongings. Two men wearing helmets and light armour emerged from the crowd of onlookers; the one bringing up the rear was gripping the handles of a coffer and had rolls of papers clasped under one arm. They walked past the guards stationed at the entry and in through the door. Bal recognised the first man: he was unmistakably Herr Kettler's secretary, the chronicler Salomon Henning. Of the second man, who appeared to be Henning's assistant,

Bal could see only a ruddy cheekbone under the rim of his helmet, yet somehow he seemed oddly familiar.

The Doctor had assumed that, on this first day after his long journey, the coadjutor would want to rest after dinner, and that his treatments would begin the next day, but the coadjutor insisted that they commence immediately. Thus, the esteemed guest took only a light meal with his host and hostess – smoked venison with Danish beer from the coadjutor's stores, and Magdalena's plum compote, with a few beakers of Tallinn's famous *klarett*. After that, Herr Kettler commanded the Doctor to look him over right away and explain his injury. So the coadjutor's leg was freed of its dressings, and on his hairy thigh the Doctor found a wide, partially healed contusion that reached almost to the groin. He carefully kneaded the whole injured leg – Herr Gotthart Kettler squeezed his eyes shut a few times and once shouted: "Hellfire and damnation! Get me some wine!" Which he was instantly given. The Doctor sent Johann and Bal upstairs to bring down the familiar chest, which they set upright in front of the coadjutor. From the ceremonial and nonchalant manner in which the Doctor opened it, Bal knew at once that this was an occasion on which he had decided to make a strong impression on his patient. The Doctor lifted out the skeleton and had the box moved to one side – and the Lord of the terrifying Dance-of-Death mural in St Nicholas' Church stood there, in the middle of the room, oddly frail but real, and looked with his slightly drooping head straight at the coadjutor. Bal saw most vividly the shock that leapt into the coadjutor's widening eyes, and the effort he made to suppress the jolt to his system. The Doctor pretended not to have noticed a thing, but when he stepped up to Death to begin his lecture on the coadjutor's injury Bal could not help but feel that under his serious expression there lurked a triumphant smirk that seemed to say: *Even were you His Royal Highness by the grace of God, it is I who am master of the situation here.* Then the Doctor began, using the skeleton at his side, *exempli causa*, occasionally tapping its left thigh bone or manipulating its kneecap. His explanation, even though full of Latin terms, was clear and simple: there were no broken bones, but there was a tear in the thigh muscle, and improper treatment had caused an infection to set in which would take time to heal. The first thing to do was reset the slipped kneecap, and he had decided to do this immediately and painlessly.

Herr Dyck, ready and waiting, was now called in with his medicine chest. The Doctor asked him to take out the necessary medicaments: opium, henbane seeds, mandrake leaves, unripe mulberries, lily-of-the-valley, hemlock, ivy and mezereon seeds. The apothecary mixed all these in a small bronze mortar, pounding the pestle with such energy that his moustache quivered. Then he strained the thick brew through fine silk. The Doctor put a pillow under the coadjutor's head – he was lying on a bench – and placed a sponge steeped in the brew over his nose.

"Now, Your Highness – breathe in deeply and slowly. Deeply and slowly. In ten minutes Morpheus will take you into his arms, and when you awake your knee will be back in place."

With a glance he signalled to Johann to quit the room and asked both Herr Dyck and secretary Henning to leave as well. As Bal moved to follow them, the Doctor said:

"Stay here. Someone has to hold his . . . His Highness' leg." He himself sat down on the three-legged stool at the coadjutor's head, out of sight of the patient. The coadjutor stared at the black eye sockets of Death looking down at him and closed his eyes to escape their gaze. The Doctor said slowly:

"Soon now, very soon, His Highness can again devote all his energies to the good of our dear Livonia. As he has for the past twenty years . . . twenty years, isn't that right?"

"Twenty-two," the coadjutor said, correcting him; he opened his eyes and closed them again.

"Twenty-two years . . ." the Doctor resumed, slightly lowering his voice, "twenty-two years . . . since the organ of the castle church in Riga . . . sounded at the ceremony . . . twenty-two years of the white robes of the Order and the consecrated sword . . . years of carrying out commands . . . of issuing commands . . . twenty-two years of *advancement* . . . At first you were . . . ?"

"Bailiff of Doblen—" Herr Gotthart said, already somewhat mechanically.

"And after that you advanced to the position of . . . ?"

"Steward of the Order," Herr Gotthart said in a murmur.

"Guarding all the Master's treasures, isn't that right?"

"All his treasures . . ." Herr Gotthart repeated, his voice even lower, his eyes closed, a contented smile on his lips.

"And after that, you became . . . ?"

"Commander of Dünaburg . . ."

"And as such, the Order's most important liaison officer between the ruling powers of Europe, isn't that right?"

". . . That's quite right . . ." Herr Gotthart said after a pause, ever more softly.

"And the year before last you rose to the position of Commander of Viljandi . . ." the Doctor continued, "and that means the Order's third in command . . ."

". . . I rose . . ." said Herr Gotthart in a near-whisper.

"And now you are feeling good, light, isn't that so? You're floating, rising . . ."

"Mmm . . . yes . . . true . . ."

"And then you rose to the position of coadjutor . . ." the Doctor continued, as softly as before, "and next year, you'll be elevated to the position of Master – it won't take much more . . . ?"

"No . . . not much more . . ." Herr Gotthart whispered.

"But *what* is it that you want to attain . . . ?" the Doctor whispered.

The coadjutor's eyes had shut. His face had turned pale, making his brazen black eyebrows especially prominent. Fine beads of sweat shone on his wide brow, and the lurid November sun, setting between snow clouds, cast a yellow patch of light on it. It seemed to Bal that he had seen the face before. Then he remembered: this was how he had imagined David, as he, Bal, had listened on his graduation day to the sermon about the beautiful Abigail. David, who wooed beautiful Abigail before he became king; David, on whose broad forehead sat the imagined yellow crown. And, as though a witch doctor were pulling the strings of both Bal and the coadjutor's thoughts, or the way the Italian performers on Saint Gertrude's Square had the previous year manipulated their puppets, the Doctor's ministrations made Herr Gotthart Kettler say in a laboured, broken whisper:

"What . . . I want . . . to attain . . . is the crown . . . of King of Livonia . . ."

The Doctor stood up with a victorious smile and gestured to Bal to step closer. In two minutes he had pulled the coadjutor's kneecap back into place – the man groaned just once in his sleep. The Doctor rubbed balsam salve above the bruised femur and asked Bal to summon the servants, who laid the sleeping lord on the canopy bed to recuperate.

The next morning Herr Gotthart was fit and eager to work but stayed in bed, in compliance with the Doctor's orders. He jokingly complained that his damned injury had for all of two weeks prevented him even being able to hold a girl on his lap, and the Doctor reassured him: "Your Highness, by the day after tomorrow, thanks to my balsam salve, your injury will no longer hinder you . . ."

For two days people trooped into the coadjutor's sickroom: to deliver food, receive orders, and then report they had been carried out. On the evening of November 24 the Doctor said to Bal:

"Tomorrow at noon, on Jerusalem Hill, Herr Brun will draw and quarter two peasants. A large crowd will gather to watch. I would like you to go and observe how the people react to the event."

"And what have these peasants done?"

"Gathered information for the Russians. That was all. But now I am going to go and write to Duke Johan about the arrival of the coadjutor."

The Doctor went up to his attic room and wrote a letter to the duke:

Most Esteemed Right Honourable Prince, Most Gracious Lord:
My most humble and loyal actions are always performed in your service and I most humbly convey to you the following news which I cannot conceal from you: on the ninth day after the castle of Rõngu had been recaptured, the Herr Coadjutor attacked the Muscovites in their large encampment where they had over twelve thousand troops. He expelled them and pursued them for a distance of three leagues, killing more than three hundred as they fled, and taking two boyars prisoner. The Coadjutor himself shot one of them and took him hostage. This one, incidentally, knows well French, Italian and Latin. In the course of combat the esteemed Coadjutor fell with his gelding, injuring himself in the left thigh *circa pudenda*, which is greatly to be regretted. Upon the advice of his knights and soldiers he came to my home on November 22, where he is at this moment content to abide, in order to receive treatment and recuperate, which, with the help of God, can be hoped for in three weeks' time. On November 23 the Coadjutor demanded of all hired men and knights, both nobles and non-nobles, whosoever were born Livonians, under threat of losing their honour, life, and worldly goods, that they declare themselves no longer bound to the self-proclaimed lord of the castle of Tallinn, Monninkhusen. On the selfsame day more than one hundred and five of them obediently appeared. He also sent word to all the nobles, estate managers and peasants in the jurisdiction of the Tallinn castle that none of them was bound

to serve it or provide supplies to it, but should transport everything to his castle in Viljandi until further notice, which happened as he prescribed. I shall humbly inform Your Serene Highness most expeditiously of whatsoever next transpires.

Your Serene Highness's Humble Servant,

Matthias Friesner

The Doctor then added a note to the letter that was not intended to be preserved even in the archives of the duke:

In addition, I do not wish to keep secret from Your Highness that Herr Coadjutor confessed to me the day before yesterday, *in somno factitio*,* that his ultimate goal is nothing less than the royal crown of Livonia.

The first snowstorm of the year streaked the frozen black ground with white and lashed at faces with icy cruelty. Had the weather not been so forbidding there would no doubt have been more people on Jerusalem Hill at noon that day. Even now there were several hundred at a guess. But grey coats, jerkins and worn dogskin caps outnumbered considerably the velvet berets and mink collars and fur coats that usually predominated at such spectacles.

Bal arrived a little late. At Katharina's request he had carried firewood to the upper storey before departing, for there were more tasks in the household now than servants, and Johann was busy with other chores, as were the coadjutor's servants. And they had exchanged what were perhaps the first words since Katharina's trip to Finland. When Bal straightened up after dropping the wood noisily onto the floor of the small, chilly attic room, Katharina spoke, standing on the other side of the woodpile. She was pressing her cheek against the stove and

* In a troubled dream (Latin).

sliding her hands over its green tiles, as though she could warm the cold stove by her caress, and said, using the formal "you":

"I was thinking of you all the time I was with the duke."

Bal was silent.

"But you probably did not think of me . . ."

"Ohh . . . and how . . ."

". . . But it did not protect me . . ."

"From what?"

"From the cursed spell . . . But thoughts cannot protect me anyway." Suddenly she turned bright red and ran from the room. And Bal went to his room behind the Frolinks' kitchen, pushed open the window – because of the heat – and stared out at the snow whirling and whistling through the Old Market, and at people heading towards the Karja Gate. Trying to puzzle it out, he noticed neither the wind blowing into the room nor the people in the square – *What confounded spell is she talking about?* And then he was plagued by a shameless, painful, indecent, naked thought – *What does she mean by saying she thought of me all the while she was* with *the duke . . . ?*

And now here he was, trudging through driving snow and a grey throng of people, up the slope of Jerusalem Hill, panting with the effort. And he began to hear, through his own shameless, painful, indecent, naked thoughts, the words tossed about in the crowd: "Just like they do with murdering robbers," someone said, and it was not clear whether the speaker considered the "just like" right or wrong.

"Worse," said another. "With murderers they chop the head off first – as an act of mercy."

"Traitors to the Fatherland!" a contemptuous voice added.

"What 'Fatherland' are you talking about . . . under Master Fürstenberg . . ." someone muttered from under a hat with earflaps. "You think there's more of a 'Fatherland' under the Grand Duke . . . ?" another muttered.

"Shut your mouth!" someone yelled. From the front of the crowd came sounds of strange, hoarse, unintelligible speech. When Bal straightened himself up to peer over the heads of the throng, he saw that the administering of the punishment had begun. Of the two condemned men, the younger had for some reason been marked the greater culprit, and so was forced to wait his turn and watch, while bound, the manner of the older peasant's death. The elder was a man of slight build, with a full grey beard, bareheaded, with knotted reddish hair. Herr Brun had not let him change into the tow-cloth smock usually worn by condemned prisoners, for the fellow's shabby clothes – which would normally be possessed by Herr Brun – were in such tatters after weeks of torture in numerous gaol cells that he had decided against the trouble of salvaging them from the tearing and blood and excrement of the execution. The old man stood in the muddy snow, surrounded by militiamen, his torso strapped to a low post. Five or six paces distant stood four well-fed horses in black harness, their rumps to the post, facing the four corners of the earth, each with one end of a long strap fastened to a horse collar, and the other to one of the condemned man's extremities. Waiting next to each horse was an executioner's henchman with a barbed lash. Five paces away stood Herr Brun, legs apart, his red jacket unbuttoned on his hairy chest. Sword in hand, he was all prepared to participate in the process of quartering, if necessary, when the man's body was torn apart. At the back of the executioner, shifting uneasily in his official black robes, was Pastor Härder, nick-named Mündrik, of the Almshouse Church. He had served communion to the condemned men and now shut his eyes tight, to block out what was imminent. The strange, unintelligible, rattling speech that Pal heard was coming from the grey, bushy beard of the doomed man. The wind scattered his words and the voices of the crowd drowned them out, even though everyone was trying to hear what he was saying. Straining hard, Bal finally understood that the old man was repeating something over and over – and at last his ears caught the words:

"They ordered me to . . . they ordered me . . ." rasped the old man, ". . . and promised me . . . bread . . . They ordered me to . . . and promised . . . bread."

Master Brun raised his sword as signal. The executioner's hench-men leaned back a bit and four whips cracked in a simultaneous whistling explosion. The horses lunged forward, snorting. The old man groaned – exactly the way Herr Coadjutor had groaned when his knee was pulled into place. His bent arms were drawn out straight, his shoulder seams ripped, and his right leg appeared to come out of its socket. His yellowish face turned grey, and though he did not scream his hoarse stammering continued. Through the rising waves of calls and cries it was no longer clear what he was saying. Then the whips began to crack without pause and the horses sprang apart again. The old man's coat and trousers were ripped apart. His horribly stretched-out bluish shoulders came into view from beneath his rags, his legs drawn to an inhuman length. But the old ploughman's tough tendons did not give. And still God did not grant him the merciful dark of unconsciousness. His gaping mouth with its broken teeth taut with pain, his body torn, the blood trickling from his rags into the mud at the base of the post – he rasped on frantically, his voice apparently gone. Then there was a hollow crack as his left arm detached from his shoulder and the horse, no longer restrained, charged into the nearest militiamen. Blood spurted in a wide arc from the enormous wound and – something no-one had expected any more – the old man began to shriek, as though only now, his body sundered, had he grasped the finality of what was happening.

Bal tasted blood in his mouth, not the imagined blood of the exe-cuted man risen from the muddy earth, but his own: he had bitten his lips so hard that they were bleeding. He felt as though something inside him had turned to stone. He wanted suddenly to be someone else, to be somewhere else, to mobilise the full force of a scream and his immobilised strength to escape from this moment, this place which had turned into himself. And the incredible cold – his eyeballs were burning with it and he whispered: "Lord Jesus Christ, why do you will it that the two thieves be crucified over and over again in an ever more ghastly manner, when you have already forgiven them their sins – at Golgotha and here . . . ?"

He started to push his way through the crowd, back towards the open space. The mud, snow, blood, the grey glances of the spectators, and the condemned man's dying screams mingled in his consciousness and he felt he was about to vomit. As he emerged from the last rows of onlookers, someone behind him put a hand on his shoulder and called out:

"*Salve*, Herr Primaner!"

Bal turned around to confront a flushed face and the smell of wine. Then he recognised the man; actually he recognised two people in him simultaneously. One was Herr Henning's ruddy-cheeked assistant, whom he had seen the night before last on the front steps of the Doctor's house. The other – and this was a surprise which drifted over his present raw and disoriented state of mind like a cloud over the ground – the other man was Herr Antonius, from the study of the steward's house at Raasiku Manor.

Herr Antonius was wearing neither the Cistercian robe of the previous year nor the helmet and armour of two days earlier, but instead the black woollen beret and winter doublet of a soldier of the Order. His face was evenly flushed from cap to collar, and he was clearly considerably more inebriated than he had been that time at Raasiku.

"Ah yes, my friend, they're treating your dear kinsman badly. For God's sake: he's been the Order's horse, Moscow's horse, Poland's horse and Sweden's horse! What in hell's name? – He no longer has an arm or a leg left to serve as horse for Denmark or Lithuania or Finland or Prussia!"

Bal remained silent, and Herr Antonius put his hand on his shoulder as he walked along beside him:

"But we will keep quiet. Ooh yes. As I told you last time already: man is nothing but a *rat*."

"Wait – you never told me that!"

"Really . . . ? Maybe not. But I've known it twenty years. Listen, I'm damnably cold – what about you? Yes. And speaking of rats, right here, at the base of Tõnismäe Hill is the Grey Rat inn. Come on, let's go and warm our noses."

When they had each drunk a small tin cup of rye vodka that immediately warmed their bodies and were chewing on a handful of salted beans at a low, dirty table in the gloomy tavern, Herr Antonius returned to his theme:

"Of course, man is nothing but a rat. Do you know the story of the rat-catcher of Hamelin? You know it, yes? Well, then, that means it's all clear to you. Whether they blow a fanfare or pound a drum, what difference does it make? The rats follow the piper into the river, or wherever. And if a rat thinks he'll gain by it, he'll chew up another rat. Would a dog do something like that? Never! But a rat would. And so on. All the same traits as humans. But the most important thing: rats know when a ship is about to sink. It's true. I've seen it in Danzig with my own eyes – the way they all stream down the cables to the quay and escape before a ship casts off and sets sail for the sea and sinks. Man's the only other creature that can sometimes sense disasters in the offing. Not as well as rats, but to an extent – 'cause men don't *really* sense things, they *see*. Listen, shall we have another round? Not for you? I'll have another."

The innkeeper sent a boy around to the table with another cup, and Herr Antonius continued:

"Take me, for example. I foresaw long ago that the Cistercians' last song had been sung. At Padise, there are seven monks left. But this is a ship that has nearly sunk. And I jumped ship. And now I serve the Order."

"Do you think that that ship will not sink?"

"All ships sink. If not earlier, then at the Last Judgement. And the Order will sink much earlier than that. I am now quite in touch with things through Herr Henning. But we are rats and will escape to the quay in good time. And I'm telling you, with a nice pile o' booty into the bargain."

"Is that so . . . ?" Bal said "I thought the Order had fallen on hard times . . ."

"The Order – maybe. But not the coadjutor."

"Really . . . ?"

"The money that our estates sent to Moscow last May remained in Fürstenberg's hands because Moscow would no longer accept it. Otherwise, it could not have attacked us. But the coadjutor forced Fürstenberg to turn it over to him. In order to recruit and supply troops. So, to the coadjutor's health!"

He emptied his third cup.

"How much money does the coadjutor now have . . . ?"

"Ha-ha-ha . . . He has let it be known that he has *some* money, but not *much*. In fact, in the four ironclad chests that he had delivered to the Doctor's house, he has – well, how much would you guess?" Here his voice dropped to a whisper: "A hundred thousand marks in each."

In the meantime the tavern had filled up with shivering spectators returning from the execution, and the buzz of voices and smell of ale and clouds of steamy breath were so thick that Bal began to feel queasy again. He left Herr Antonius sitting with his fourth cup, departing without having revealed that he was living in the same house as the coadjutor. He hurried, as twilight deepened, through the icy whirling snowstorm back to town. In his imagination he saw, hovering against the darkening sky, the bulging eyes of the dying man and the executioner's horses and Herr Brun's red jacket, all merging, and he felt a

296

vague and boundless sense of shared guilt settle on his conscience: something of vital importance was awry – and everyone was guilty, everyone was guilty of an enormous, boundless, worldwide sin. And he, as one of the few who understood it, was guiltier than the rest. And this culpability was all the more damning in that it was so distant and vague and insubstantial; and it crumbled, eluding his grasp entirely when he was once again within the town walls and his thoughts returned to Katharina . . .

In the evening, in his temporary little study, the Doctor said to Bal:

"By the way, the duke is exceedingly angry with us. No, no, not with you or me – with the town of Tallinn, of course. And justifiably so. He returned the corsairs, thinking that that would bring the councilmen to reason. But they sent Herr Horn packing. Now the duke is demanding that the ships be returned to him – Buschmann's *Minerva* and Herr Bock's *Dolphin*. If the duke repeats his demands, our merchants plan to send the ships away from Tallinn, regardless of the time of year."

"Where to?" Bal asked, for Märten was still aboard the *Minerva*.

"The *Minerva*, probably to Riga. But Bock was planning to dispatch his *Dolphin* to Stettin. It's a risky route for so small a ship at the end of November. He's transporting stone steps. Two hundred thousand steps of that Vasalemma limestone, you know, the same as was used for our great-room floor. By the way, there were forty more of Monninkhusen's men yesterday in our great-room, swearing allegiance to the coadjutor . . ." He tapped his finger on the table in a nervous staccato. "If things continue on this track, the coadjutor will repossess the Danish king's Toompea in two weeks, without firing a shot."

"So it seems . . ." Bal said.

"But we would be doing the duke a disservice," the Doctor said, "if we did not attempt to hinder this somehow."

"And how could we . . . ?"

"We have to think of something! Because this Monninkhusen poses a lesser threat to the duke's interests than Kettler, in other words, Poland."

The Doctor's finger tapped the tabletop again. "It's strange," he continued, "that this Kettler can attract so many, in spite of his meagre funds."

"Meagre funds—?"

"Of course. That's common knowledge."

"That's exactly why it's false."

"Oho! You are a real philosopher of the art of politics! What are you saying?"

"I'm saying that I have it from a direct source: the coadjutor has, in this very house, four hundred thousand marks in pure silver."

The Doctor remained silent for a moment. "Hmm . . ." he said in a most nonchalant tone of voice, "we'll have to look into this . . ."

It was not until much later that Bal recalled how suddenly the Doctor had risen to his feet upon hearing of the four hundred thousand marks – as had Herr Horn, once, when receiving news from Bal that war had broken out in Livonia.

CHAPTER TEN,

in which the horse ride not yet completed in the previous chapter finally comes to an end, and in complete accordance, moreover, with all the rules of drama, although life itself would trample these rules like a foolish young bull breaking down its pen (were we to look at things from the perspective of this same young man whose tracks we have primarily been attempting to follow).

On the evening of St Andrew's Day, November 30, the Doctor organised a little gathering at his house in honour of Coadjutor Kettler.

On that same morning he had summoned Bal upstairs and said:

"Balthasar, living in my house right now is practically His Serene Highness himself. His retinue goes in and out, and his bodyguards are stationed at my door. In my position as master of this household, I need a few more people in my service. Herr Dyck promised to send me Franz, his medicine-mixer, to help out. But I am in urgent need of a secretary as well. You'll earn fifteen marks a month until your departure for Marburg. Agreed? You see, in a town like Tallinn I just don't have recourse to a man with an academic education. That's the first point. And second – you're an accomplished young man. So, put on your best suit this evening and come and sit at the foot of our table."

At the head of the table that evening sat the coadjutor in black velvet, between the host wearing a green velvet jacket and the hostess in a gown of wine-red silk. On either side of these three sat members of the Town Council and the Order. Several of the former had brought their wives – the red-headed Herr Clodt, for example, and the stout Herr

Vegesack, who was apparently a distant relative of the Doctor's. Herr Clodt had returned from Denmark some time ago: the only thing he had brought back from Christian was a promise to send a delegation to Moscow, which would attempt to wrangle from the Grand Duke a peace agreement for Livonia. Also seated near the head of the table was Herr Henning, attired for the occasion in dignified raiment with a white collar. He had just been promoted from position of secretary to that of counsellor to the coadjutor, and in that capacity was to set out soon on a diplomatic mission to see Kaiser Ferdinand in Vienna to request support – not for peace but for war.

At the foot of the table were lesser officials of the Order and town government, among them Johann Topff, the cat-like council scribe whom Herr Clodt had brought, and next to Bal a slightly tipsy Herr Antonius, whose tonsure, encircled by a reddish wreath of hair, quite readily visible at close range, looked like a round plot of rust-red grass. Bal felt it odd to sit next to him on the same bench as an equal, but it pleased him nonetheless. Herr Antonius himself had looked somewhat per-plexed and embarrassed on first recognising his bench-mate, but a gen-erous swig of Rhenish wine helped him overcome the initial discom-fiture. Burgomaster Packebusch delivered a fitting speech in honour of the coadjutor's recovery and the Doctor's skill – indeed, he had improved so considerably in just a week that, with the aid of his ivory-topped cane, he could move about quite briskly. The burgomaster's speech was more respectful than could have been expected, given the town's recent display of recalcitrance. Generously refilled goblets accompanied the apple-stuffed, spit-roasted duckling, followed by silver trays of spiced sugar cubes and cinnamon-coated ginger con-fections. And the Doctor's silver utensils gleamed and clinked along with the coadjutor's. Above them, on the balcony of the great-room, four foreign musicians from Toompea Castle were playing. They, along with the soldiers, had come into the service of the coadjutor from

Monninkhusen's forces, but were neither blowing trumpets nor beating drums. They were making wonderfully sweet and spirited melodies ripple and flow from their unidentifiable stringed instruments that hailed from Italy – or who knows where.

Bal let his eyes wander over the goblets and candles to the wine-flushed faces here and there, taking in the Vegesacks, the stout husband and the gaunt wife, and suddenly the peasant in him felt, with a rush of unabashed delight, the sensation of the hard oak bench under his rump: *he* was here – at the lower end of the table, to be sure, but here all the same; and Dung of the Orient was *not*. He most definitely was *not*. Somewhere deep within him a sense of the great sinfulness of the world surged; and then, quietly, the unease ebbed once more from the gravelly shore of his mind, for written on it in angular letters werethe words God had spoken to him in the chapel: *Be not a fool!*

No, no! Bal did not want to be a fool . . . But Coadjutor Kettler was in a most jovial mood and kept putting his left arm over the back of Katharina's chair, and then around her shoulders as well. Evidently Herr Antonius noticed the expression that crossed Bal's face at the sight, for he leaned over to Bal's ear and said:

"Hee-hee-hee . . . there's nothing to be surprised at. Our esteemed lord is more enterprising with the women than he is with the Muscovite! Haven't you heard that pretty song they sing about him—?"

The musicians on the balcony had paused to rest, and against the growing clamour of talk and the clink of goblets Herr Antonius, his breath redolent of wine, sang into Bal's ear:

> Coadjutor in Livonia am I,
> My name is known in places far and nigh.
> I'm known in the towns, I'm known in the country:
> Pretty women I value exceedingly highly.

They can always light a fire in my heart,
And I give them golden guilders, for my part.

And certainly, the coadjutor seemed to grow lustier by the minute. He emptied his goblet in a gulp and brought his ivory-topped cane crashing down on the table with such force between the serving trays that Bal thought: *It's clear why these madmen have to observe the custom of leaving their swords behind the door when they go to a gala*...

The coadjutor turned to Katharina again and, inclining his brown beard rather too close to her face, said something to her. Katharina smiled at the table and seemed to glow with high spirits. In the meantime the Doctor, sitting on the other side of the coadjutor, sipped wine from a slender silver goblet. His right eyebrow was just a tiny bit higher than the left. His dark eyes twinkled merrily and his thin moustache brushed the goblet like a blackbird rising to fly.

I can understand his asking her to be nice to Herr Horn, for the fate of the town hung in the balance, thought Bal, *but why the devil, this, now*...? An awful premonition, a sensation almost physical, rose towards his heart from the base of his spine, where, just a short while before he had felt pleasure in the solidity of the oak bench ... At the other end of the table the coadjutor put his arm around Katharina once again and, in full view of the guests at the table, kissed her. And the Doctor's dark eyes twinkled with laughter.

It was a good thing that Bal had planted both his thumbs on the table and clenched his fingers around its edge, for Herr Antonius was whispering in his ear:

"The lady of the house has been the coadjutor's mistress for three days now ... And my lord took advantage not only of her but also of the master of the house, who had apparently found out that the coadjutor was sitting on a pile of silver ... and so offered his services ..."

302

Bal gripped the edge of the table so tightly that his thumbnails turned white.

"Rubbish!" he said hoarsely.

"My dear young man . . . yesterday Herr Henning, in the name of the coadjutor, had him take an oath – as an informant. And paid him three thousand marks. For his loyalty and for his wife. But I don't know what share of the sum was intended for which service."

Bal was silent. "And why are you telling me this?" he asked dully.

"No particular reason . . . Your – how should I put it – your non-German equanimity gets on my nerves. Or maybe we should say I envy it. I want you to know what kind of master your master is, and what kind of mistress is your mistress."

The instruments on the balcony rippled on. Doctor Geilsheim, an energetic man and friend of the Order, whose greedy eyes seemed to survey the company on one side of the hall even as his twitching nose sniffed the scene on the other, stood up and delivered a speech that no-one heard above the trilling music and hum of conversation. For a brief instant it seemed to Bal that the look Katharina gave him was a plea for help. He squeezed his eyes shut and the hubbub of the party swelled two-, three-, fourfold, and seemed as though it would continue without end. Then he opened his eyes, turned to face Herr Antonius directly and said in a low voice:

"Come with me. I want to talk to you."

He stood up and Herr Antonius did likewise, though he was hesitant, uncertain whether to resist or comply. Bal guided him from behind, just short of pushing him into the hallway that led from the great-room into the courtyard. When they stepped out into the court-yard and the door closed behind them, Herr Antonius said: "Where are we going?"

Bal said nothing. He strode ahead, Herr Antonius following, pushed open the door of the prayer chapel and went in. The windows facing the courtyard were lit and the ground was covered with snow, providing a transparent glow to the darkness of the chapel. In a low voice Bal demanded:

"Here – in front of this angel – swear – that what you told me – is either true or false."

"Listen, boy – what do you mean," Herr Antonius said, a bit shrill. "Why the devil should I swear anything to *you*?"

Bal took hold of the front of Herr Antonius' doublet and shook him – he was powerless to compel him any other way. Herr Antonius seemed made of straw. Bal heard the man's doublet rip at the seams.

"Swear! True or false!"

" I . . . I can . . . of course swear. . . *hic* . . ." Herr Antonius swallowed.

"Well?"

"I – swear – it is – true."

Antonius was holding his hand up, and, though quite visible, Bal had to make sure it had been properly raised for an oath. Keeping a grip on Antonius' doublet, his free hand travelled up Antonius' right wrist and felt, in turn, each of the two raised fingers. Then, leaning his shoulders against the stone knees of the angel, he turned away without a word.

"Wait," Antonius called out in a hoarse voice, "if you're thinking of telling anyone—"

"What then?"

"Then – either Herr Henning will have you dispatched behind some corner, or the Doctor will poison you!"

For a moment Bal remained standing at the chapel door. Antonius looked at his large, dark shape against the lighter background of the courtyard, and it must have crossed his mind that this big clown, this foolish clod of a peasant, might plan to grab him again. But the clown, the foolish peasant clod, did not move. Only, after a moment, he uttered a word which, given his education and status as a *primaner*, was entirely

unexpected – at least to one unaware that he had already been bold enough to use it recently. Bal said, accentuating each syllable clearly:
"*I-di-ot!*"

For two hours, late that night, he trudged across bleak, empty, gusty streets through the frozen town, feeling at every moment that he had been stabbed in the ribs. Incredible: the town walls were still in place, the towers stood as they always had, the gates were securely shut (*though they could be opened for half a farthing – ha-ha-ha-ha . . .*). The impassive countenances of the houses did not register the gusting wind whip fine grains of dirty snow around corners where dogs had raised a leg. Their stony mouths uttered not a word against the rubbish, the dirt lying about in – oh, so many – courtyards. (*Oh, how few of the courtyards are as clean and kempt as that of the Friesners' – ho-ho-ho-ho . . .*)

Along Kuninga Street – a choppy river with its uneven, snow-streaked cobblestones – came the bell-ringer, his lantern showing the way to a pastor in a long, black, fur-lined coat. Ah, it was Pastor Härder – whose nickname, Mündrik, meaning Boatman, recalled his all-but-forgotten peasant origins – on his way to read the last rites to someone or the other: condemned man or executioner, master or servant . . . *Oooh* . . . In the alleyway behind the Nuns' cloister, candles flickered in pig's-bladder windows, and shouting, squealing shadows cavorted about inside – the coadjutor's mercenaries with their strumpets. And in the Doctor's house the coadjutor was carousing with his . . . *Hmm* . . .

Two hours . . . But a young man could not wander about town for two hours in the middle of the night merely because his world had collapsed. Not, at least, when he had had a conversation with his Lord God recently, and when the Lord God had clearly said: *Listen to my voice within you, and be not a fool . . .*

The huge and splendid window of the great-room was bright. Bal could hear the voices of the revellers inside. The musicians were at it still. As he started to go through the gate a mercenary guarding the entrance jumped down from the stoop, looked closely into his face, and nodded, saying to the other guard on the watch, who was swinging his halberd to keep warm:

"The Doctor's secretary."

Bal clanged the gate shut and went through the courtyard door and quietly up the Frolinks' stairs. But the first thing he sensed, as he stepped on the stairway, was what he had encountered the first time – and since then, many more times – upon his return from the trip to the Duke: Katharina's carnation fragrance. A fragrance like a hand closing around his heart. A hand exceedingly soft, and yet capable of inflicting intense pain . . .

But be not a fool . . . Bal crept up the stairs like a mouse and opened the door into the little front room that served as Meus' study. It was dark and empty. Light from the second-storey windows of the coadjutor's apartment across the courtyard shone upon Meus' bookcases and desk. Bal could hear his brother-in-law's short, quick breaths, like little sighs, behind the door of the back chamber where he was sleeping. Bal opened the door to the Frolinks' small, dark great-room, and closed it behind him. Then he opened the kitchen door and closed that as well. He pulled off his boots and put them quietly down next to the door. Then he stood in his stockinged feet on the smooth, cool, limestone floor of the kitchen, smelling the ashes in the hearth – in the dark the smell was especially strong – and the knife in his ribs did not seem quite as sharp as before . . . *Now, I'll go into my cubicle, sit down, and think about what should happen next.* Carefully, he opened the low, heavy, creaking plank door and closed it behind him. He extended his leg, located the stool with his toes, and sat. *I must think about what happens next . . . The whole world is brimful of that cursed woman's scent . . .*

And then, quite close to him, a voice whispered:

"Balthasar."

"Annika . . . ! What is it? What are you doing here?"

"Shhh. It's not Annika. It's me . . ."

"*Katharina* . . ." Bal whispered – if there is such a thing as a whispered cry.

The wind sounded hollow behind the window. From down below came the voices of the dinner guests and strains of music.

"You have to leave, Frau Katharina. They'll be looking for you," he said after a long pause. His voice, muted, sounded as though it were coming from the bottom of a stone chest.

"No-one is looking for me," she said in a hurried tone. "Matthias thinks—" She stopped and then dragged the words out of herself: "You'll find out anyway – Matthias thinks I am with the coadjutor." She paused, and one could hear her listening, with every cell in her body, to Bal's every movement. He allowed not even the tiniest muscle in his body to twitch, and she continued: "But the coadjutor is asleep. I took some of Matthias' sleeping powder and sprinkled it into his wine."

"And what is it you want of me?"

Katharina must have had the answer ready for some time. With the certitude of a sleepwalker she said, her voice hushed to a murmur:

"I want you to release me from the wicked spell that is upon me and keeps me in Matthias' power so that I continue to sleep with him and with all the lords he serves and tells me to . . ."

She got up from Bal's bed, where she had been sitting, and came to him in the dark. She stroked his face with her cool, fragrant, trembling fingers. Yet it was not desire that made them tremble. And then the Devil entered Bal – oddly pitying and furious, a grinning and lecherous Devil that took him over completely. Shrouded by the dark, Bal picked Katharina up in his arms and nearly threw her onto the bed. He tore off her silken clothing with awkward, secretly smug, furious peasant hands. *Here you are* – gloated the pitiless Devil as he took her – *a lady and a harlot* – on his father's ragged old sheepskin. And his aggression was a world full of all his feelings – a sense of his own inferiority, jealousy, betrayal, rage, a thirst for vengeance. And the Devil, grinning at his bedside, cited Apuleius – the most comically vulgar sections of the *Metamorphoses, or, the Golden Ass*:

Woe is me, who would be thrown to wild beasts if I open up a virtuous woman . . .

But oh, how inconsistent, after all, are the poor demons of a human heart! . . . Bal's rough, angry, caressing hands glided over Katharina's maddeningly smooth limbs and breasts . . . ("*In thirteen lands I have not found a woman with skin as smooth . . .*") His lips tasted her tears and he sensed that she felt his, and then he felt her hot wave of passion rise and crest. The darkness turned dark purple, full of falling green showers, and he whispered: "Oh you child, you harlot, you hapless-marvellous creature, beloved, blessed, you sister of the Virgin Mary . . ." And then he whispered, groaning: "My God, we are what you have made us . . ." Only with great effort – and perhaps not even then – could one have made out the Devil waiting in the dark corner, chin in hand, elbow resting on the cover of the *Metamorphoses, or, the Golden Ass*, and the scribbled words along one edge: *But be not a fool . . .*

When Katharina could finally bear to loosen her arms from around Bal and put them behind her head, and when her mouth was freed from his kisses, she whispered, using the informal "you" with him for the first time: "I found out about you in Matthias' letter. He'd written 'a nice peasant lad and, it seems, one with a spark' . . . The following night, I saw you in a dream. And it was you, even though I had never seen you. And I was told: 'If he can love you, you will be freed from your curse, but he has to do it on his own . . .' And now I do not know whether it will help or not, since I had to ask you to free me . . ."

"But you did not tell me how. . ." Bal murmured.

"True, that I did not . . ."

When Bal awoke, the scent of carnations still lingered in the hollow of his father's old coat and a grey dawn filled the square of window. Bal could now see clearly: the little Devil was sitting in the darkest corner of the room, waiting, chin in hand, elbow on the cover of the *Meta-morphoses*, and the message along its edge: *But be not a fool . . .*

He put his feet down on the floor, pulled on his shirt, and sat on the edge of his pallet. *I must think – what to do now . . .*

He glanced at the table. He could see the pale rectangles of two or three sheets of paper, one on top of another – oh yes, a week ago he had started keeping notes about events at the Doctor's house, that is to say, events in his own life. Notes for his own chronicle. Not for his masters. Why write a chronicle for his masters when they were Judases! He had put a horseshoe on top of the papers, one he had found in the Old Market, to prevent drafts blowing them away. He picked it up now and sat motionless. Then he drew in his breath and hunched his shoulders: they bulged up under his shirt, and his wrists and elbows cracked – he had bent the horseshoe. And he said out loud:

"I'm leaving this place."

In a few hours all was settled.

He dressed. He packed some papers and underwear and a few items of clothing into a wooden box, rolled up his father's old coat on top of it and secured it with a strap. He heaved the box onto his shoulder. At daybreak he went to Kimmelpenning, who gave him his blessing and a hundred marks:

"I might not be here much longer. If you need more money later, ask the Town Council. I'm leaving them a thousand marks for the schooling of poor Estonian boys. You understand . . . I would like to help more of them. Well, off with you. God willing, perhaps we'll meet again."

Next he went to the sacristy at St Olaf's – Meus was there already. Bal put his chest down and said: "Write that letter to Wolff now. I am going to him in Stettin."

Meus sat down, looking stunned: "When?"

"Tomorrow, at dawn."

"It's as though . . . as though you were running away! – Have you committed a crime?"

"I don't know. Maybe . . ."

"Hmm. And what should I say to him?"

Bal dictated a short missive: "The bearer of this letter is my wife's brother. He has studied under my tutelage in Tallinn. I am asking you to continue his instruction. I believe he will not betray my confidence."

"Do you believe that?" he asked, looking Meus in the eye.

"Yes, I do," Meus answered, thinking to himself: *I cannot be completely certain of that, of course. Maybe not even very certain . . . but apparently the boy has need of my confidence right now.*

"And you can tell Annika about my departure yourself."

"What can I tell her about it?"

"Just explain it somehow . . . Maybe I'll write . . ."

"And what should I tell the Friesners?"

"Anything you want!"

At the door of the sacristy it was more painful for Bal than he had anticipated – to tear himself away from the worried and dispiritingly benevolent look in Meus' eyes.

From St Olaf's Church he went down to the harbour and located Märten's *Minerva*, which was due to set sail at noon the following day. The *Dolphin*, however, was to depart at dawn already, for new demands and threats had arrived from Duke Johan.

Märten took Bal's box for safekeeping until morning. He wanted to make arrangements with the boatswain of the *Dolphin* and to take Bal there that evening, but Bal said he had things to attend to in town.

310

That last night, he slept at Kalamaja. There was no-one at home besides old Truuta, for Siimon and his hands were in Haapsalu with a caravan. Bal got Truuta to pack up some food for him and asked her to explain to his father that he had left for the university in Germany because an unexpected opportunity had presented itself. Then he took a walk around the place, around the house and along the snow-streaked, ice-crusted shore, towards Kopli and back, and climbed into the loft of the barn, where he found his old stone cannon balls lined up on the edge of the wall.

He slept a short, dreamless sleep under the low, split-log ceiling of his father's house, and before dawn he was at the harbour with Truuta's bag of provisions.

He could think of nothing sensible to say to Märten as he bade him farewell. On the dark wharf Märten helped Bal wedge his bundle under one arm, and the large bread bag he had brought for Bal under the other, and the boatswain of the *Dolphin* led Bal to the ship.

This same boatswain, who for five marks was letting him travel as a stowaway, explained that the straits between the shore and the outlying islands were already frozen, so they would have to sail further west, into the open sea and around the islands of Hiiumaa and Saaremaa. And Bal was not to emerge from the hold until they had passed the lighthouse at Kõpu – at the earliest, on the day after tomorrow.

Bal curled up on his side in the low, dark hold, and was about to put Märten's food pouch under his head when he felt something: one of the loaves of bread in it seemed to be as hard as a chunk of wood. He took it out, exploring it with his hands, and then started as he felt the sharp cheekbones and narrow face and mocking mouth. It was the birch carving of Märten's face that he had once hidden under a pile of wood shavings.

And then he lay in the dark hold on his father's old sheepskin coat; beneath him, slabs of native limestone destined for a high staircase somewhere far away; in his nostrils, the scent of carnations from a daydream. He heard the shouts to cast off, heard the roar of the open sea grow ever louder, and everything about him began to rise and fall and sway as though there were nothing stable in this world and no way to hold on either to scents or to stone.

BOOK TWO

CHAPTER ONE,

in which a sturdy young scholar, sporting a new growth of light-brown beard, overcomes all manner of obstacles, some of which are entirely apparent, but others barely evident, and thereby acquires a certain status among his fellow scholars, so that those who seek his favour – though there are unfortunately not many of them – begin to address him from time to time as "Herr Studiosus".

The tattered storm clouds above the sand dunes at the mouth of the River Swina were edged with the iron-grey of dawn as the *Dolphin*, with its broken mast and torn emergency sail, left the sea behind and began tacking against the current towards Stettin.

The single-masted ship had been en route from Tallinn for two weeks. From Hiiumaa on, it had been buffeted by winter storms. It had nearly been dashed onto the limestone reefs of South Gotland and had barely managed to evade the chalk cliffs of Bornholm. It had been stripped bare and scoured grey by winds and waves, yet its cargo of two hundred stone slabs, cut from the white rock of Vasalemma, was intact in its hold. And on board was a youth who had been elevated from stowaway to sailor, replacing three deckhands washed overboard in the storm, and the palms of whose hands, unaccustomed to hauling ropes and cables, were cracked and raw.

Sailing into the broad, calm river after two weeks of brutal pitching and tossing was dreamlike: gliding past the Swinemünde fortress at the river mouth, seeing men atop the fortress waving to them from beside the falconets – these were the gunners of the Duke of Pomerania, surprised by the arrival of a ship during the season of winter storms; entering the quiet cove, wide as the open sea, seeing green riverbanks streaked with snow draw closer on this suddenly sunny December midday; and then catching sight, on the high right bank of the River Oder, of a town about the size of Tallinn, its proud red-tiled towers rising above the river with its sprinkling of green islands. All this, after the miserable weeks on the raging sea, was like plunging from a nightmare into a beautiful dream.

Among the sailors on board the *Dolphin* were a few who had visited the town before:

"See that building – the one with the golden weathervanes, that's Oderburg, where their duke holds court. And that's his town palace – that fancy gabled one that looks like a gingerbread house." – "And behind it is St Mary's Church and then St Nicholas's and St Jacob's."– "And now we're going under their Great Wooden Bridge, and over there you can see all ten riverside gates in a row in the brick wall. On the shore in front of the wall – that's the market where we'll go and buy some mossberries right away – over there, see . . . where people are milling around the tents and market stalls." – "Look, that's where the boat docks are. That's where we'll be going." – "And that low-lying area across the river – the alder groves and houses and St Gertrude's Church – all that is Lastadie. It's mostly non-Germans who live there."

"In *these parts?* Who are the non-Germans living here . . . ?"

"Oh they're Pomeranians or Kashubians or Wends – whatever they're called . . ."

But the question of the Pomeranian non-Germans faded away, along with the dreamlike Sunday feeling of their arrival, when they reached the harbour with its palpable smells and sounds. The odor of tar from the shipbuilders' lots, the stench of fish oil and fishy salt water from the herring houses along the riverbank and the startlingly fresh whiffs of milk and meat and sauerkraut from the markets on the shore intermingled with the sounds – the shouts of the skipper, the clamour of the people in the market, the calls of curious onlookers jostling onto the wharf at the Jahuvärav Gate.

Afterwards, Balthasar could not recall the exact moment that he stepped onto land. He had already walked a stretch with the boatswain, Hans, at the edge of the market on the bank of the Oder when he was suddenly surprised to feel solid ground underfoot, and it struck him that this was truly a foreign and faraway country. Even so, the pedlars selling milk and bacon and herring looked like the most ordinary inhabitants of Tallinn, and the wind blowing from the river, softer than an October wind in Tallinn, was tossing about snippets of conversation in comprehensible Low German under the grey market awnings.

Balthasar remembered the acknowledgement in the boatswain's handshake. They had been standing in front of a snub-nosed peasant woman's market stall heaped with root vegetables and berries. Then Hans' round-shouldered back disappeared into the crowd, and Bal was left with an unusual little willow basket – Hans' going-away present – full of dark red mossberries, just like the ones that grew in the bogs of Kurgla. He remembered how their acrid taste reached deep below the roots of his teeth, and how the strange craving for that sour-bitter taste made him wolf down a second and third and fourth handful as he walked along, and how it invigorated his senses as he passed under the echoing brick archway of the Kolmapäeva Gate, with its griffin-head coat-of-arms, and continued into town.

Balthasar remembered: he walked past brown and reddish half-timbered houses along streets which seemed, compared with the slate-and-cobblestone streets of Tallinn, lighter and more cheerful, but not actually finer in the least. For even in the centre of town a good third of the buildings were, by Tallinn's standards, "lodgings" rather than "residences". And he saw hardly any burghers' homes that were two hundred years old, or with three or four storeys, and none with façades decorated by paintings and sculptures and with gables as high as church steeples – such as Doctor Friesner's house at the edge of the Old Market in Tallinn.

Balthasar remembered: he walked past the undeniably grand duke's castle. And, in spite of himself, he also recalled the sharp stab he had felt there, on Nunnade Street in Stettin, as he thought of the Doctor's house. The castle was indeed grand, but he could not get a close view of its grandeur because of all the walls, fences and moats surrounding it. And then he walked past an imposing burgher's house, far more imposing than any in Tallinn. It had a driveway leading right up to its front steps, something he had never seen before. He stopped a passerby and learned that this was the main residence of the Loitz family of merchants and bankers.

Balthasar remembered: he continued in the direction of the steeple of St Mary's Church, passing rundown one-storey houses, until he came out into a large square courtyard. Behind him were the back walls of the same low houses; in front of him, the high wall of the church tower, and at its base the huddled chapels and dwellings of the *köster* and bell ringer. On either side stretched a long, two-storeyed building with high windows and faded plaster walls and a yellowish stone roof in the process of turning green.

Balthasar threw his head back to look up at the sectioned steeple of St Mary's Church, at the flock of cawing jackdaws flapping around it against a sky of mottled grey clouds. It reminded him of another church courtyard from long ago, and of another steeple, maybe even higher than this one, and of the nearly forgotten magic drink he had swallowed, high in that distant tower; and he recalled the wonder of its promise, the wonder of his hopefulness, and he still did not know whether he could believe in it or simply smile at it all. Then the corners of his mouth in his light-brown beard did in fact turn up into a smile –

of embarrassment, but also of confidence and conviction: *Well . . . since I did once have a sip of* that, *there's no question but that even now it'll . . .*

He shifted the chest and the rolled-up winter coat into a better position on his shoulder and walked across the courtyard.

"Ah, *Master* Wolff?" repeated the pimply-faced student whom Balthasar encountered by the puddles in the courtyard. Balthasar noted how the student's impertinent blue eyes looked him over, reaching a verdict before he replied:

"Well, you see, *Kister Behr* ate *Magister Wolff* for dinner last night – don't be shocked – and shat him out again this morning. What remains of him is sitting there, to the left of that door, in the *rectum's* study."

The student had disappeared into the street before Balthasar could fully take in the cheerful insolence of his words. By the time he had walked the length of the long, grimy stone floor of the corridor and was knocking on the rector's door, Balthasar realised that the pranksters and big-mouths he could expect to meet among the students at this place were much worse than anyone at the town school in Tallinn. But it would be interesting to see what the teachers here were like . . .

And Balthasar recalled the scene: he is standing in front of the rector's round table, looking at an ink-spotted tray with inkpots and quills and a small bronze bell for summoning servants. The bell bears an image of the owl of Minerva. Also on the table are a lead candlestick with a congealed bit of paraffin and a blackened wick, a few scattered books, and a huge leather-bound registry of matriculated students. A bronze clasp secures it. Hovering above the book, the rector's extended hand, in a slightly ink-stained lace sleeve, holds Meus' letter of introduction between thick reddish fingers. Then Master–Professor–Rector Mattheus Wolff lifts his eyes to look at Balthasar and thinks to himself: *Curious, he looks just as I would have imagined him, had I known of his existence, but he has a fairer head of hair than we Germans generally have.* For his friend Frolink had written some time ago that he had married a

319

non-German girl up there in Livonia, and according to the letter this would be her brother. *He's just as I would have imagined him – a little like a bear, his hackles up a bit, clothes streaked with sea salt, and smelling of tar . . .*

He thinks it "curious", but actually there is nothing odd or curious about it. For Rector Wolff has seen so many faces like this and so many other kinds of young oafish visages that he can classify and categorise them with his eyes half shut . . . Oh yes, gentlemen-students with velvet collars and beggar-students with bare feet; the carefree, swaggering, shameless, self-important young louts from privileged noble families, generations of whom were being educated here with the duke's letters and money: the Putbuses and Putkammers, the Manduvels and Zitzewitzes. And then there were the more or less hard-working German burghers' sons from Pomerania, a somewhat phlegmatic breed – seven guilders a year for each youth – and the high-spirited clowns, the easy-going Polish scamps from Stargard or the great forests of Gorzow; and the angular, meek, mostly industrious sons of the Kashubians or Wendish artisans or fishermen – five guilders a year, their circumstances being straitened. . .

Rector Wolff examines Balthasar from head to toe and concludes that the only thing he could not have anticipated is the lad's footgear, made of some kind of dubious animal hide, with outlandishly upturned toes. (In fact, they are made from the paws of otters, after a Finnish boot pattern.) He has never seen their like. But then, he supposes, even these Livonian non-Germans have to be uniquely themselves in some respect.

And, in fact, Rector Wolff too is a man uniquely himself. If there were anything curious in this meeting, it is only in that Balthasar is also thinking: *Curious – he's just as I imagined him –* even though Wolff is the first rector of a pedagogical institute he has ever seen. *The only difference is that in my imagination he was more hazy, more indistinct, as though he were standing behind the thick, uneven window glass of the living room at Kalamaja.*

Mattheus Wolff is about forty-five years old, with a tawny complexion, wide cheekbones, and a forehead that narrows at the hairline. His features are coarse, like Luther's, but his nose is a surprise: thin, hooked, with clearly delineated flaring nostrils. His small, well-defined mouth looks severe, his lips tightly compressed. His dark eyebrows meet above his nose, accentuating the intent and probing gaze of his slightly intimidating, dark-grey eyes.

Then the rector is opening his severe mouth and saying in a surprisingly friendly tone of voice:

"*A teraz ty přzideš wučić se kolo nas?*"*

Balthasar stares at him blankly or a moment and then says:

"If Herr Rector would pardon me – I do not know this language."

"How is it that you do not know it? Are you saying you're German?"

"No . . . I'm not . . ."

"But you no longer speak a word of Slavic?"

"I've never spoken it."

"Humph . . ."

Balthasar does not understand what is happening, but in the ensuing silence he senses something like the invisible iron grill of a portcullis slowly descending between them. Then the rector is addressing him in Latin. The Latin has an oddly cold sheen and dull ring compared with other languages, even the ones unfamiliar to him. It makes him think of the well-scrubbed, imported clay platters in the Doctor's cupboards.

The rector asks his name and land of origin and his father's occupation, and mutters a bit condescendingly at the mention of "wagoner". For Balthasar does not know how to say "wagoner" in Cicero's language, and he says, *furman*. But, as if out of spite, the rector continues

* And now you've come here to study? (Sorbian).

321

in Latin and asks now about Balthasar's studies. And he proceeds, ever more quickly and aggressively, barely giving Balthasar a chance to answer before posing the next question. And Balthasar is concentrating feverishly on constructing answers with his inadequate vocabulary, and when he realises, in the middle of one answer, the grammatical errors he has made in the previous one, he feels as though he were drowning, swallowing mouthfuls of water. But the rector arrives, in spite of himself, at a clear conclusion: *This lad is so obviously ready for the second level of the pedagogical course that there's no point in sending him to the superintendent or to the deacons of St Mary's Church to be tested – as is prescribed in the statute.*

"*Bene . . .*" the rector says, opening the matriculation register with a brusque gesture of irritation. "Seven guilders a year. Three and a half payable to me now. And *on no account* are you to pursue your studies the way the young noblemen here do! Fully three-quarters of them do not study at all! If the son of a *wagon driver* has come this far, he must *study* – so that he will amount to something! *Humph.*" His tone changes; he stops lecturing and elaborates: "And whom are we preparing here for our duke? Schoolmasters and clerics. But I have to tell you this: in the fifteen years that we have been in operation, there have been only *a few* cases where someone who completed the pedagogical course was considered ready for the pulpit, without first spending a year or two at the university in Greifswald. But for a bumpkin from a *trivium school* – *humph* – your Latin could be a lot worse. And it is our duty to help promote the Christian Church, wherever it may be. But educating schoolmasters or clerics for Livonia is really not the task of the Duke of Pomerania. However, since it is Bartholomeus Frolink who has sent you here – *humph* – I will admit you into the second course-level and prepare you in theology."

The rector drummed his fingers on the table, nervously for some reason, saying: "*Cubiculum* nine. There's an available pallet there."

322

Balthasar had in fact been weighing studies in one of two possible fields: one was theology, which, under Meus' aegis, he had long thought of as the summit of his aspirations; and the other was medicine, which idea Doctor Friesner had planted among the possibilities for his future. But he had rooted out that profession from his mind as furiously as he had slammed the Doctor's gate shut behind him two weeks earlier. And now Rector Wolff settled the question of his life and vocation with utter simplicity, as if no-one had ever considered any other. Balthasar did not protest. Perhaps it was godly fear that lay behind his unquestioning acceptance of the rector's decision, and behind everything else that had spurred him to his precipitous flight from home: he had fled in anguish and anger – wounded, fearful of being smothered, suffering the pangs of love and the pains of jealousy, and longing to be free of it all. He had fled, spurred by the godly fear that had suddenly gripped him in the mad whirl of the wide world's actors and their antics. From there the concept of good and evil, as embodied in the mores of daily life at Kalamaja and invoked in hollow catchphrases at the town school, had suddenly appeared paltry and pitiful, like the herd of black-and-white wooden cows that the departed Peep had carved for him, and which Bal had one day accidentally left by the seaside, where the waves had blindly scattered them and buried them in the mire . . .

That same afternoon Balthasar took his chest and coat and moved into the east wing dormitory. He was allotted a wooden pallet and straw mattress in a room with narrow windows, a grey vaulted ceiling, cold walls and five roommates. It was a bit bigger than the pantry room he had had with Annika and Meus, but otherwise remarkably similar. Even the narrow window in this scholars' cubicle reminded him of the one in his former room. But *there* he had looked out on Tallinn's Old Market, part of the heart of the town, nestled as though in the palm of his hand; from *here* he had a view over the low roofs of houses straight into the duke's courtyard beyond the moat, with its guardhouses and old castle church, its apothecary and prison tower. And in the square between them was a bear, shackled to a stake, swaying back and forth at the end of its iron chain, on a patch of muddy, trampled snow.

Balthasar's roommates were five Pomeranian burghers' sons – Weger, Bagmiel, Zastrow, Kümmel and Gluck. The first was just fourteen and the last, who was also the *praefectus cubiculi*, the room monitor, was twenty-five. The Pedagogical Institute, like the universities, accepted students from the age of thirteen on, but it did not keep them longer than eight years.

The initial encounter with his roommates remained etched in Balthasar's memory. Only much later did he realise the many ways in which that encounter determined later events.

"Greetings!"

The roommates were all there for the midday study hour, and five pairs of eyes looked him over: three of them were raised from books spread out on the table – Weger's and Bagmiel's grey eyes and Kümmel's brown ones. The fourth pair looked at him from a straw mattress, through a haze of sleep – these were the stocky Zastrow's eyes. The fifth pair, bored and half-closed, belonged to *praefectus* Gluck, leaning lazily against the wall beside the window.

"I was sent to this room. Which one is the free pallet?"

"Really? So you were sent here, were you? To plaster the ceiling maybe?" Gluck asked, and his roommates noticed how his dull glance livened in anticipation of some fun.

Balthasar glanced at the ceiling with its dirty cracks, then again at Gluck, and noticed the smirk at the corners of his mouth.

"No. I was sent to live and study here."

"Ohooo . . ."

The heavy Zastrow, his face redder than usual from sleep, rose slowly to a sitting position on his straw mattress.

"Which one is the free pallet?"

No-one answered.

"This one?" Balthasar pointed to the left of the door, to the only empty pallet.

"No," Gluck said. "That's the wedding pallet. That's for whoever brings a girl into the room. We draw lots for it."

"Well, as there's no girl here for the moment," Balthasar said, and put his chest down on the pallet. He took off his short sheepskin coat and sat down.

"Here the new man sleeps on the floor," Gluck said, taking a pork rind from a tin plate and popping it into his mouth. Zastrow was completely awake now, and Weger, Bagmiel and Kümmel had abandoned their books.

"And how long does he sleep on the floor?" Balthasar asked casually, as he calmly pulled off his otter-paw boots.

"However long it suits us," Gluck said, chewing on his pork rind. "The higher class the man, the shorter the time. A privy councillor type like you . . ." Gluck bowed towards Balthasar, "can get off the floor in a couple of years."

Balthasar sat on the edge of his pallet, moving his toes inside his knee-high stockings, and looked mildly at Gluck: "Enough now. Save the nonsense for the greenhorns."

"*Primum*," Gluck said, "it is ascertained that the privy councillor does not know the customs of the duke's pedagogical institute. *Secundum*, all kinds of things can accidentally happen on the wedding pallet at night. Zastrow, put the privy councillor's chest on the floor. And him, as well." He turned to Balthasar once more: "I trust the privy councillor is not someone who is looking for trouble . . . ?"

Zastrow stood up and walked slowly up to Balthasar. He was a big and brawny twenty-year-old, somewhat corpulent for his age. His face was flushed; in itself it was not especially arrogant, though at the moment it was impudent enough. His mouth twitched with a kind of condescending enjoyment. He picked up Balthasar's chest.

"Put it back," Balthasar said.

Zastrow put it down on the floor at the head of the pallet and turned towards Bagmiel:

"Go and get a straw mattress from the housemaster for the privy councillor. But don't bring the cleanest one. It's for the floor here."

Bagmiel stood up from his place at the table but stayed where he was, for Balthasar said to Zastrow: "Put my chest back on the pallet."

"Herr Privy Councillor is accustomed to giving orders," Gluck jeered, "but here with us—"

"Here the rector gives the orders," Balthasar said, "and the rector said that . . ."

"Ah – you intend to live here," Gluck called, "but now you fart in our faces with the *rectum*!"

Being unfamiliar with the situation, Balthasar had not realised that invoking the rector was not wise, but these "gentlemen" were hardly in a position of superiority to the rector. He said:

"I am quite capable of farting without the rector. Aren't you?"

"First of all, move! Get up! " said Zastrow, grabbing Balthasar under both arms to pull him up.

Balthasar struggled to free himself and felt his anger slowly rising. *The devil take them! – Why all this nonsense? I was just about to ask them to tell me who they were and what it was like here . . . Idiots . . . But of course they're just trying to make a fool of the new man. And this one with the broad face pulling at me, he could easily pick me up . . . Why you, confound it – so you're going to use force on me, are you . . . ? Well if that's what you want, you leave me no choice, you swine . . .* Balthasar jumped to his feet and Zastrow, taken by surprise, fell back against the wall, his shoulder tearing in half the sheet of beautifully penned house rules posted there. In the next instant they were at each other, lurching between the pallets, and Balthasar discovered with some alarm that his opponent was an unusually strong fellow, half a head taller and proportionally much heavier. But the main problem was that Zastrow's moves to grab hold of and bring down his adversary were unexpectedly quick for one so heavy. Above the thumping and thrashing of their struggle Balthasar heard the others shouting:

"Ooh – the privy councillor is straining!" – "Give it to 'im! Let 'im 'ave it!" – "Where'd this bull come from that he's ready to butt heads with the Pomeranian bear?!" – "Well, well, look at that: he's not even down on his arse yet!" – "Zastrow! How long will you just fool around with him?"

They kept staggering from side to side, each trying to trip the other up, or grab him by the belt, or get behind him to lift him off ground. Balthasar could tell that Zastrow's face was dripping with sweat. His own skin was damp as well. The blood was rushing in his ears, and through the huffing and thrashing and puffing he grasped one thing with awful clarity: to lose would be irredeemable humiliation. With a different part of his brain he was thinking feverishly: *if I could just get behind the bastard's back!* He was not exactly sure what he hoped to achieve by this, but suddenly he managed it. And when Zastrow attempted to dislodge him from there with his right hand – Balthasar's coat ripped, but he did not even notice – Balthasar thrust his own right hand under the other's arm and onto his flushed neck and forced his head down. Zastrow stumbled and fell. Under the combined weight of the two fighters, the nearest pallet crashed and splintered. While falling Zastrow had to put his left hand down for support, at which point Balthasar managed to hook his arm under Zastrow's left arm as well. He locked his fingers behind Zastrow's neck and thought: *Bless you, Peep, for teaching me the neck hold.* Zastrow thrashed around and tried to shake him off. Another section of the pallet splintered. Balthasar shut his eyes: all he had to do now was hold tight and press unrelentingly. He heard the blood rushing in his ears. With God's help he still had strength in his arms. *Blessed be the long hot days of making hay in the soggy fens of Telliskoppel, and the days of carrying bags and crates in the harbour, and of tying down Father's cargo, and hauling manure and wrestling with the farmhands . . . Blessed be the soil of Kalamaja and its grass and stones and birch stumps . . .* Suddenly his opponent's shoulders sagged, as though something had drained out of them. Balthasar opened his eyes. He saw his own red, blue-veined, white-splotched hands, and the other's torn collar and broad purplish nape. He loosened his stiff fingers and sat down on the edge of his pallet. His knees felt weak.

"What a grip – he's a regular iron-paw – he brought down Zastrow!" Kümmel said admiringly.

They poured cold water on Zastrow's head and hoisted him onto his pallet. He came to immediately and, propping himself up on his elbows, said in a subdued voice, but in a tone which revealed that he took pleasure in the correctness of his behaviour:

"Bagmiel, put his confounded chest back on his pallet."

"A brute of a bear!" Weger said in his pre-adolescent voice.

Bagmiel did as Zastrow ordered. But Gluck spoke scornfully:

"Well, by that measure, the fellow out there would be the best student of all . . ." – and with his chin he indicated the square outside the window, where the duke's bear was swaying at the end of its chain. "But in this house, you need to show you also have a brain before you settle in on a pallet. Know what I mean?" And he said something long-winded in a language unfamiliar to Balthasar – it was so unexpected that Balthasar missed the beginning of it entirely. Then he began to hear the words and, just as he was thinking to himself, *What the devil is it today with these unfamiliar languages raining down?*, all of a sudden he recognised the words: it was the First Book of Moses, and the only section that, with Meus' help, he had learned by heart in Hebrew, just for the fun of it.

"Well – tell me what it is!" Gluck said.

Elated, Balthasar was about to answer and reveal his triumph, but the little demon that occasionally tempted him made a sudden appearance, raising a finger to his lips. Instead of answering, he recited in his native tongue: "*Ja Jumal ütles: saagu valgus, ja valgus sai. Ja Jumal vaatas valguse sisse, et ta hea oli, ja Jumal tegi vahe valguse ja pimeduse vahele. Ja Jumal nimetas valguse päevaks, aga pimeduse nimetas tema ööks...*"*

"And what was that?" Gluck asked.

"The Book of Moses. I continued from where you left off."

"In what language?"

"Chaldean."

The price of their test of strength – twenty shillings for the pallet and twenty for the housemaster, to seal his lips – were paid jointly by Balthasar and Zastrow, and Balthasar's life as a student began.

They were roused each morning at five. The way it was supposed to work was that the *praefectus* would get up in time to awaken the others with a song: *Veni sancte spiritus.*† As it turned out, it fell to little Bagmiel, the squirrel-like son of a Wendish bargeman, from the town of Gartz, newly arrived that autumn, to awaken the others each morning with his annoyingly loud, clear voice, because the slug-a-bed Gluck, spoilt son of a court organist, had let his *cubiculum* oversleep every day for an entire week.

In the corridor, snuffling sleepily and out of sorts, the boys splashed cold water on their faces. The water was carried in at night from the well in front of the institute, and on mornings when the north wind blew the pitcher was crusted with ice. Gradually, the one hundred and fifty students, their faces scrubbed and dried, more-or-less awake, having

---

* And God said, Let there be light: and there was light. And God saw the light, that it was good: and God divided the light from the darkness. And God called the light day and the darkness He called night (Estonian). † Come Holy Spirit (Latin).

managed to wriggle into their coats, trickled down the three corridors and out into the courtyard. With their footsteps thudding or sloshing or resounding hollowly – depending on the weather and the condition of the ground – they proceeded, the *praefectus* at the head of each *cubiculum*, through chill morning winds, through snowstorm or rain, in the pitch dark or by the light of the cold moon – gleaming on towers and gables that rose above them like bluish swords – and, emerging from the courtyard of the institute, they continued along the street, rounded the corner and entered St Mary's Church.

In the dusky interior of the huge church, only very slightly warmer than the outdoors, half of them nodded off again into a half-sleep as they stumbled along, guided by a few sputtering candles, bumping into each other and tripping against empty benches, until they finally made it into the chapel in the west aisle. Here Andreas Gluck Junior briefly awakened the dozers with a short organ chorale, and thereafter lulled them into an even deeper upright sleep. Bagmiel was the only one from Balthasar's *cubiculum* who sang along. After the chorale an older student, one considered sufficiently mature, recited a short prayer, but usually in a voice so low that the growling of empty stomachs was clearly audible every morning, drowned out only by young Master Gluck's closing chorale.

Half-asleep, they made the sign of the cross as they turned around and slowly filed out of the chapel, the *praefecti* poking those who had dozed off in the pews. And a hundred students clomped through the church, wending their way unsteadily across the pitch-black street and streaming into four auditoriums. Breakfast, also counted as lunch, would not be served until ten o'clock. So that the wealthier students chewed on buns they had half-secretly bought from the cook, Buttel, or crunched on pork rinds, and those who did not have the money swallowed their own saliva.

By the time the ten o'clock bell rang it could barely be heard above the rumbling of stomachs, but no-one ever failed to hear it, and leaving the professor's utterances suspended mid-sentence the students surged towards the smells of barley or turnip or bean soup wafting in from the refectory.

In the centre of this dining room, in the midst of steam rising to the vaulted ceiling, stood the professor of church history, Master Martin Rühl. Stout, brown-eyed and bald, he monitored the students' daily lives and habits, and in return for his troubles received an apartment at the institute. With disapproving gestures he curtailed the impatient haste of rushing students. For he himself had already eaten his fill twice that day in the kitchen of the institute, where the cook, ever solicitous of the masters, had cut a thick slab of roast pork onto his slice of bread and filled his soup bowl three times, adding a chunk of butter to it each time, so that it glowed, golden and cheerful. As a result, Professor Ruhl had the irritating habit of delivering long mealtime prayers in his trumpet voice. To make matters worse, the kitchen maids and the students on meal duty had already set on the four long tables a hundred soup bowls, fragrant and steaming.

The mealtime was too brief for hungry, growing boys. And the reading of psalms from the Bible by the kitchen assistant did not markedly lengthen it. It was the same at supper, which was served at five. By that time they were so hungry again that the oat porridge with peas and herring, usually over-salted, disappeared along with the accompanying three-quarters of a cup of beer, as though it were nothing at all. And the readings, which fellow students took turns at delivering during mealtimes – from historical works, from the chronicles of Charrio, from Livy or Justinian – did nothing to warm the stomach. The meagre ration of beer did, though, and on occasion, when Ruhl left before the students had emptied their cups, a song might be struck up at one of the tables:

Pour and drink and pour some more.
Our mouths we'll open wide
To let the wine go to our heads,
This *bonum vinum latinum.**

Vinum, of course, was in the song purely for the rhyme, the students not having been given anything other than weak beer. But *latinum* was to be taken seriously, for the students were expected to speak the language amongst themselves, and this rule was observed, at least within earshot of the professors and beadles, of course, because there would have been fines to pay for using German or Polish or Wendish.

And then there were the lectures, starting from six o'clock in the morning, in Greek and Hebrew, read by Master Petrus Becker, former preacher at St Mary's, sixty years old, with salt-and-pepper hair and ant-like movements, a restless early riser. He loved Greek with such intensity, following the example of Erasmus of Rotterdam and all other great men, that he would always assign a better grade to students who addressed him as Master Artopöus over those who used Master Becker.

Kümmel usually sat on Balthasar's right at these lectures. He was tall and lanky, with close-cropped hair and lively weasel eyes; his father was a scribe in the chancellery of the duke in Oderburg. On Balthasar's left sat Andreas Gluck Junior – when he was not absent, that is, because of a "headache", his excuse for laziness, or, as it on occasion turned out, a hangover. He was a somewhat indolent fellow, with black curly hair and an air of self-importance. Both Balthasar's bench mates were already in their fourth or fifth year at the Pedagogical Institute and well acquainted with the scene and the characters in it. Kümmel's father went around in the threadbare ink-spattered grey coat of a chancellery rat and knew the duke only from a distance. Gluck's father, on the other

* This good Latin wine (Latin).

332

hand, wore the proud robes of the court organist, glittering with metallic trim, and just the week before, Duke Barnim XI had patted him on the shoulder and presented him with a necklace for his inventive *ricercar*.* This disparity between the fathers gave rise to many disagreements between the sons on the accuracy of all kinds of facts. Sometimes they even started arguing during Master Artopöus' lectures, not necessarily about Greek, and engaged in such vociferous exchanges, talking past Balthasar's face or behind the back of his head, that he could not hear the lecture and had to intervene to restore peace. Since it seldom worked if he simply asked them to be quiet, he tried poking each of them in the ribs. This was sometimes effective, but not always, and finally, when they all knew one another better, he would simply bark: "Shut up!" And when he then banged his fist on the desk – so that the ink splashed out of its clay pot and the candlestick jumped, causing their three shadows to quiver on the ceiling – it always worked: Kümmel would pull his head down between his shoulders and fall silent. Gluck would grow quiet as well, muttering: "If the bear in the castle courtyard should die, I'll suggest they chain you there in its stead . . ." True, the boys stopped talking when Balthasar barked at them, but Master Artopöus heard him too, which was something Balthasar tried to avoid. Because what he really wanted was to understand how to form the cursed dual number in Greek grammar . . . Of course, more often than not, many other things interested him as well. For although the difference in status of their fathers meant Kümmel and Gluck had very dissimilar notions of what constituted "facts", they actually had a surprisingly large store of all kinds of them – again, thanks to their fathers. For example, they knew that this same Petrus Becker – "Artopöus" in Greek, or "Baker" in country tongue – was practically a sorcerer! Four years ago he had been removed from the pulpit of St Mary's, and just last year was sent to Wittenberg so that Melanchthon himself could

* A late Renaissance instrumental composition (Italian).

examine him. Shaking his head, the *Praeceptus Germaniae* had sent the old man back to Stettin without employment, and only Rector Wolff's politics of feeding the wolves and guarding the sheep had succeeded in gaining for him the position here as teacher of ancient languages – on condition that he keep his mouth shut, for God's sake, on questions of theology. The early hour of his morning lecture was apparently not a whim of the old man himself, but engineered by principled Melanchthonians out of spite for their disgraced colleague.

After he heard this story Balthasar looked upon Master Becker with greater interest, even though he realised it would be politic to keep his distance. Sorcery was no longer the issue it had been when the popes ruled, not in these enlightened times of Augsburg: sorcerers, for example, were no longer burned alongside witches. But still, a man who chose to embrace heresy was as intriguing as a voluntary leper and possessed the power of attraction of a man marked by fate. Balthasar had not yet worked out whether the story of Becker's sorcery was true or fabricated when he happened to hear something even more astounding. Something he had in fact known for a long time. Something that now, suddenly uttered by another, was so obvious that it was shattering in its clarity.

Paulus von Rhoda himself was the one who told them.

Rhoda was a seventy-year-old patriarch, a man Luther himself had sent to Pomerania so that he might cultivate the seeds of religious reform planted by his friend Bugenhagen. Fifteen years earlier he had founded this pedagogium and was now, in his dotage, lecturing on the exegeses of the Gospels. He was fond of spinning out memories of encounters with Luther and his friends, and fond too of discussing world affairs with an old man's incisiveness and a child's frankness – in a way that the other teachers never did.

On one of the mornings when his "brain matter moved", as Doctor Friesner – *May he be damned!* – would have said, Rhoda sat in silence at the lectern for some time, eyes closed, the flickering candle flame casting its yellowish hue on one cheek, and the sun just then rising above the dormitory roof, lending its rosy glow to the other. He had just finished a long tirade about the rending of the veil in the temple. Then, raising his sparse apostle's beard, he said calmly, keeping his eyes closed:

"Rent asunder. To reveal that which is most holy."

After a moment's pause, he continued with a singular, quiet intensity: "But it is not only the veil of the temple that is rent. *The Reformation is also rent asunder. And terrible things have been revealed.* Flacius reviles Melanchthon from his own town of Magdeburg more fiercely than Luther ever inveighed against anyone – and there was a time when he revelled in the rankest of utterances. Amsdorf is spitting fire and tar from Jena to Wittenberg, and has university professors imprisoned if they incline towards Melanchthon's ideas. But at one time they all sat together at Luther's feet and were equally dear to him. And Melanchthon, once the brightest young star ever seen in Germany, is old and stooped and has turned grey from the accusations hurled at him . . . And if we examine the issue closely, we see that the accusations are in fact true, in the sense that Melanchthon preaches about *synergism*, which Luther rejected. Luther said that the Son of man is saved by God's mercy but is incapable of participating in his own salvation. But Melanchthon says that man's *will* can turn him either towards God's mercy or away from it. The followers of Flacius are shouting that there's nothing more monstrous than human will, or a more monstrous person than one who coddles his own will, for he is weaving a nest for the Devil in his own bosom . . . And perhaps that is so . . . And yet . . ."

He fell silent. Most of his twenty or so listeners dozed, sniffled, stared out of the window. A few goose-quills scratched mechanically, attempting to write something down. But some of the students were inexplicably moved by his peculiar monologue. Balthasar, apparently forgetting that this was not the Munkade Street school in Tallinn, and

335

that the teacher was not Master Sum, to whom he had addressed questions as to an equal, called out from his seat, to prompt the old man to continue his thought: "And yet . . . ?" He waited a moment. When the old man remained silent he asked: "What is the truth, then?"

"Pilate," said Paulus von Rhoda, opening his watery, old-man's eyes, "Do not ask . . ." He closed his eyes again and said in a whisper, as if to himself: "The only truth I know in these wretched times is the striving for truth . . . *the striving for truth* . . ." and he continued, even more softly, "*and hope* . . ." His cheek on the candle side turned reddish. Maybe he had turned his face towards the sunrise, or perhaps he was embarrassed that he had no more to say in response to the question from Pilate, or that he had revealed too much to his students . . . He opened his eyes suddenly, looking at them with an incredulous but absent expression, and said, surprisingly clearly and loudly:

"Boys, I don't feel well. Help me down from here."

Two of the more nimble boys hurried to the professor and helped him down. That same day they heard that Rector Wolff had summoned a barber-surgeon and, after a major bloodletting, Rhoda was carried home, alive but paralysed. Zastrow, who was one of those to carry him, said that the paralysis had affected the old man's speech as well. The only words he had intelligibly uttered on the ride home, words he murmured over and over, were "striving" and "hope".

CHAPTER TWO,

in which a young man learns that the human soul, unlike a traveller who takes shelter from the rain and dries off by the hearth, cannot be cleansed of sin by a little remorse, but that sin, like his own shadow, accompanies him wherever he goes; nevertheless, the young man evidently does not acknowledge this simple truth, for he seems to find, in events quite possibly arranged by Satan himself, ever greater confirmation of his shallow, blind self-confidence, as he plunges deeper into the thickets of vanities.

There were the lectures: Rector Wolff's lectures on practical theology, Professor Rühl's on church history, Master Becker's on Greek and Hebrew. And again and again, Latin – Cicero, Plautus, Terence, Horace. And the various public lecturers, with their lectures on mathematics – yes, that too – and on cosmography, because Melanchthon had declared the subject, provided it was properly taught, the most effective means of imbuing young souls with reverence for Our Lord.

And there were the students: grouped as children, milk-moustaches, and "old men", that is, the older students, or pedagogues, who lived in burghers' houses in town, earning their bed and board as private tutors. And there were the actual children, the ten- to twelve-year-olds taught by the pedagogues. These were the burghers' offspring, who were permitted by the rector to accompany their pedagogues to some of the lectures.

There were midday dinners and evening suppers in the warm, steamy, chattering refectory, and the hours spent there cramming when the weather was cold – for the *cubicula* had no heating. And the services at St Mary's Church, with the boys' choir of the orphans' school. And evenings up in the *cubiculum*, with the swaying bear outside the windows. And the writing of poems on assigned topics in pentameters and hexameters. And listening to debates on Saturday afternoons in the big auditorium, with the rector presiding and the older, more articulate, students participating as respondents and opponents, as announced in advance.

Suddenly, already in March – with water gurgling in the gutters and the entire town seemingly afloat in the fog rising from the river and drifting over the marshes – it was time for Balthasar's own debate, on the topic "The Universal Love of God", with that blue-eyed chap, Bade, as his opponent, the same pimply-faced rude fellow who had been the first student Balthasar had spoken to at the Pedagogical Institute.

It was only with great effort that Balthasar managed to back this glib windbag, this sophist, into a corner; it occurred at the point in the debate when, with a cunning smirk, Bade began to draw inferences from Balthasar's arguments which he, Balthasar, had never even entertained: to wit that, in return for God's great love, man is obliged to love not only God but also His whips, diseases, tyrannies and calamities, His Attilas and His plagues – to love them all as the means by which the loving God leads man out of the thicket of his sins and back to Himself. With great effort Balthasar trapped Bade within his arguments, pressing him – as Kümmel later described it – against the wall like a frog. Yet Rector Wolff assigned both Bade and Balthasar the *sufficit* grade, bestowing "adequate" on both, not because Professor Ruhl and other sympathisers of Flacius – as against Melanchthon – considered theological topics in debates to be a bad thing. No. Balthasar had the strong feeling that he had received the same mark as Bade – whom the rector did not like – because the rector did not like him, Balthasar,

338

either. The man acknowledged him but seemed to harbour no great liking for him. Why?

He stood at the window of his *cubiculum*, looking out. Gluck and Kümmell were snuffling on their pallets, exhausted from listening to the cursed debates, which could wear down even the most stalwart of men on a Saturday afternoon. Bagmiel was pacing between the pallets, cramming Caesar.

Balthasar's knees were throbbing and sore – a familiar post-examination sensation. His head still buzzed with a jumble of debate rules, though diffuse and distant now; his ears caught the sound of water running in the gutters, and his eyes fixed on the duke's bear, who had climbed to the top of its post, clawed white from repeated ascents, and was sniffing the early spring air as he strained at his chain. Instead of rejoicing at having put the debate behind him, Balthasar was disappointed. Because of the poor grade, because of the inexplicable injustice that, clearly in his view, lay behind it, because of an urge to get away, to escape, a desire that seemed to rise vaguely from his throbbing knees towards his heart – and because of something which, in a kinder place than this forbidding and austere institute – and maybe at a gentler time than this childish, quarrelsome, coarse century, would have been called the feeling of homelessness.

"Ah – so this is where you're hiding out!"

It was Bade, his opponent of the day, who had suddenly pushed open the door and marched in. He narrowed his hard blue eyes, happened to glance at the "house rules" written in Latin calligraphy which had been repositioned on the wall, and exclaimed:

"Oh, you little lambs! You've got this shit nicely displayed on the wall!? . . . *Pedereque praesumptuose porcorum more precaveant . . .** He who breaks this rule, has to pay a penny fine right away. Ha-ha-ha-ha-ha!" He let loose an impressive fart and put a new copper penny

* Prevent yourself from farting like a pig (Latin).

into Bagmiel's hand: "Here, put it in the money box." Then he turned towards Balthasar:

"Listen, if we don't do some serious drinking today we can't call ourselves real students – we'd be nothing but milquetoasts!" He started to shake Gluck. "He's coming too. And we'll get Zastrow off kitchen duty." Then he turned to Bagmiel: "We'll stay out tonight – ah – until a bit past nine. But if Lupus" – meaning Rector Wolf – "finds out about this tomorrow or any time after that, someone's arse will land on the grill the next time he has kitchen duty, and he won't be able to get off until his balls turn black. Right?"

"Right!" cried Bagmiel cheerfully.

"Good," Bade said, turning back to Balthasar, "put on your philosopher's shoes and let's get going. It's something of a hike to the best dens."

So as not to attract the attention of the watchman, they left the dormitory one at a time, each with a different story. Balthasar, for example, was taking his boots to be repaired. In the foggy, slippery street, redolent of spring, he pulled his head down, hunched his shoulders and, jumping over puddles, hurried to reach the shadows of the slimy wooden fences and wet stone walls surrounding the castle. In a few moments he was at the White Tower and went by way of the Valtavärav Gate to the riverbank. They had arranged to meet at the wooden bridge.

The others had not yet arrived. Balthasar sat down on a piling and looked out over the desolate grey water, which flowed harmlessly, sluggishly, past the boat docks, but swirled and foamed dangerously close to the tops of the pilings under the bridge.

He poked at the mud with the toe of his boot, a question flaring up in his mind with ever greater insistence: *why* had he actually gone along with Bade's questionable invitation – damn the fellow! He closed his right eye and with his left stared at the ships, where men were mending rigging and caulking hulls, readying the ships for sea, their voices sounding across the surface of the water in the misty, windless air over a distance of several hundred cubits. But with his closed right eye, he took a look inside himself. He was sitting here at least in part because it was customary for debaters to go out drinking after a debate. But the custom was in fact not *really* binding, and Balthasar felt he was even less obliged to observe it than most. True, over these four months at school he had lived such a monk's life that he could indeed be called a milquetoast rather than a student. God knows. Especially considering how often the rector and the beadles had to punish the students – with the lock-up or a whipping or a scolding – for all manner of stunts: for breaking down fences, for creating a ruckus in the streets, for throwing stones through professors' windows or at Jews or gypsies, for drinking and doing forbidden things with the tavern girls, for playing cards and dice. In some situations, such as where students lived in private apartments, their wrangling with landlords at times escalated to dumping slop pails on each others' heads . . . Besides, though Bade had set traps for him in the course of the debate which clearly violated the rules of the game, he had done it with such an obvious inner chuckle – *You understand, don't you, you bumpkin, I'm doing it for the pure fun of it, and if you're a reasonable man . . .* – that it would have seemed petty to take offence and not join him for a drink. And furthermore, Bade himself – though he hailed from a line of wealthy Lübeck merchants – seemed not at all upset by his inglorious capitulation to the son of a wagoner. To be sure, his reputation at the institute was pretty poor. "A scoffer without convictions" is how Professor Rühl was reported to have described him. And Rector Wolff had apparently nodded in agreement. Incidentally, the rector was himself in large part to blame for the fact that Balthasar was on his way to the drinking dens of Lastadie.

He had had only a few encounters with the rector. But on each occasion he had sensed with his skin the man's controlled but deep displeasure, an inexplicable, unspoken reproach: "Young man, you are not what I had hoped you would be." People of different temperaments react in different ways in such circumstances. Balthasar's response was to be closed and terse, which Rector Wolff appeared not even to notice. For how often did a student at the institute have the opportunity to choose whether to be stonily taciturn or unreservedly loquacious at his meetings with the rector, so that the rector would take notice or ponder over the reason for his behaviour? In any event, it would be an exaggeration to say that the rector's attitude towards him kept Balthasar awake at night. His sleep was more often disturbed by fatigue or restlessness, when, for example, he read late into the night the werewolf tales of Olaus Magnus in the recently published work, *On the True Customs of Northern Peoples*, which made him think of the werewolf stories of Kurgla and Kalamaja. Or when he hovered on the boundary between sleep and wakefulness, and his imagination set in motion the wheel at the well in front of the institute, whereupon grey and black and blue bob-tailed creatures began leaping out of all the pails and raced into town in every direction, swarming over streets, walls and rooftops. Or when he lay thrashing on his bunk, eyes closed, tormented by an intractable flow of images, yet was at the same time standing at the *cubiculum* window, watching shooting stars streak across the night sky and packs of wolves race across the castle courtyard, and sensing again his long-standing certitude – *But me they will not touch, not here, not now* – grow weaker and weaker and weaker. At other times, and more often than by dreams of werewolves or sorcerers or witchcraft or comets, his sleep was disturbed simply by restlessness, by an urge to flee. But the rector himself – that is, his inexplicably disapproving attitude towards him – did not disturb Balthasar's sleep one whit. No, not his sleep. It did, to some extent, disturb his waking hours. At least, so much so that if, here and now, as he sat on the piling, he had looked into himself with the same attention he bestowed on the ships and the river and the girls loudly laughing as they walked over the Puusilla Bridge into the fog which blanketed the bank on the Lastadie side – yes, if he had indeed examined his inner self with equal attention, he would have realised that to some extent this trek to the taverns and to what would surely happen after the drinking was happening simply in order that *that which has been written might come to pass*, as it is said. *If I am to be accused of something, damn it, I might as well do something to warrant the accusation! At least in my own mind.*

Bade, Gluck and Zastrow came hurrying from the direction of the marketplace, their knuckles blue from the cold and their cheeks flushed with exertion. They crossed the three-hundred-cubit-long bridge, its wooden planks echoing underfoot. The fog was so thick that from the middle of the bridge the banks on either side were barely visible, and over the black water a dense fog foamed like milk rising into the air. On the other bank the boys, with Bade and Gluck leading the way, turned left and soon arrived at the alder thicket at the edge of the River Dunsch, opposite Bleekholm, where footpaths alongside ditches full of water branched off into the thicket, towards the dark shapes of hovels and huts. "I don't want to say too much in advance," Bade explained, "but the hostess is very generous at the place we're going to. I'll tell you that much. Not that we get to see her up close. But the girls she's got are . . . well, here we are."

It was a little tavern for the bargemen of the Oder, and for seamen from further away as well, in summer. Because of the fog and the brushwood, which reached the tiny windows of the tavern, the candles were already lit. Sailing on the dancing shadows under the sooty log ceiling hung a cubit-long model cog, one that would not have been out of place in a classier tavern. A few bearded men were seated at single tables, hunched over their beer mugs, and at the bar stood the hostess of the tavern, a stout woman in whose turnip-like face flashed a pair of tiny, cheerful, ruthless eyes.

The boys started with a few mugs of Gartzer beer and salted beans. After the first few swigs the boys' talk began to flow, and the shadows on the dark ceiling, to sway, and the sailing ship under the eaves, to appear as if it were rocking in a stiff wind. Gluck and Zastrow were arguing about something – oh yes, over whether to believe the story told by the people on the island of Rügen about the model ship that hung in their church. It was said to be a gift from the skipper who had flown his magic ship over the island at the time of their grandfathers. Gluck said the story was true, Zastrow said it was nonsense and Bade sat and smirked, egging the others on in turn to more heated argument. A bearded fellow was plucking a zither; someone else was droning a song. Balthasar listened but was at the same time pursuing different thoughts within separate areas of his mind. One part recognised that Bade, the impossible windbag, had really tried to play him for a fool today at the debate, but he forgave the windbag. The other part decided it would be foolish to fear God's punishment for something as natural as what they were about to do. And a third concluded that the story of the magical provenance of the model ship might actually be true – it would be vastly more interesting than if the airborne journey proved to be merely a silly fairytale. Unfortunately, the fairy-tale theory was the most likely one.

Then Bade ordered plum wine for the table, and soon girls appeared as well. There were four of them, one for each of the boys. They were wearing ordinary, brightly coloured dresses, their cheeks rouged with beet juice. With a big "Hello" Bade and Gluck pulled two girls, apparently old acquaintances, onto their laps. The other two were about to sit next to Balthasar and Zastrow, but Zastrow, having emptied a beaker of wine already and thus full of courage, pulled the brunette near Balthasar over to his side and pushed the girl who was near him onto Balthasar's lap.

"You, go with him – he's a fellow student. I'm afraid of redheads.

He's almost a redhead himself and he always pays redheads five farthings extra."

The girl was an eighteen-year-old Wendish girl, still respectable-
looking, with rust-red hair and a voluptuous white body.

"What's your name?"

"Lada."

Her German was so faltering and odd and soft that Balthasar
had trouble understanding her. But her easy familiarity – whether stem-
ming from her nature or her profession – helped the awkward young
student overcome his initial embarrassment. And the student very
much wanted to overcome it. Soon they were drinking wine and sharing
a chewy greyish bun and Balthasar pressed her against him, enjoying,
with a sense of sinful pleasure, both the pressure of her body and the
knowledge that the town was far away, on the other side of a very wide
and deep and foggy river. And that his home was at the other end of
the earth. The wine went to his head. He played with Lada's red hair
and laughed gruffly, and at the same time stood behind his own back,
smiling weakly in embarrassment, looking through himself. Somewhere
far behind his real self and his other self stood – he was not exactly sure
whether it was Rector Wolff or the Lord God Himself (in any case, the
one looked exactly like the other), and the look on his face condemned
him: *Well, well, isn't this just what I have been expecting of you the whole
time . . . ?!* Balthasar started and winced, or at least that second or
third self looking over his shoulder started a bit when he suddenly
saw, in the rector's or perhaps Jehovah's disapproving glance the glint
of old Siimon's pale, tired eyes, and Siimon's hunched back as he raised
his whip to his horse and turned his face away, careering between the
rector and Jehovah, on his empty transport wagon . . .

Balthasar later remembered: he had called for a farthing's-worth
more wine and vowed he would keep one farthing for the girl – he
would not spend any more – thus attempting to buy Siimon off with his

345

thrift. And then he had felt ashamed of this calculation. They had finished the wine in great gulps and gone off somewhere to the side and up some kind of ladder . . . A candle was flickering; the dusty oat-chaff smelt pleasant and the sheepskin smelt – oh how utterly different from his father's old sleigh coat *that time*. The pain of the memory made him perhaps a bit rough with Lada, but afterwards Lada said in her strange chirping speech: "All the students are not as polite as you, and you are so strong . . ." Balthasar had blushed in the darkness on account of both his politeness and his strength. And then Lada had asked:

"Tell me, where are you from? You talk differently from the way they talk here." And Balthasar had answered: "From far away. Reval is the name of my town."

At that Lada had raised herself up on her elbows and whispered in the dark:

"Reval?! . . . I've been trying to find someone from Reval for two years already. There used to be a lot of them here, they say, but I haven't come across anyone . . ."

"Why someone from there?"

"Well, I'd have asked . . ."

"Asked what?"

"Whether he knew anything about my brother. Maybe *you* know . . . ?"

"You have a brother there?"

"An older brother."

Balthasar wondered for a moment: who in Tallinn could be the brother of this little playgirl? There were plenty of ignominious occupations – the sauna men or latrine cleaners or gravediggers or executioner's underlings.

"And what does he do there?"

"He . . . he's the abbot in a monastery."

"Abbot?"

346

"Uh-huh."

"Oh, well. I thought maybe he was Master of the Order."

"No, he's an abbot."

"He wrote to you to say he was an abbot?"

"No! How would he write to *me*? Don't be silly. A fellow from here was on board a ship that went to Reval, and he saw him. He told me when he came back."

"Well, he certainly pulled your leg."

"No, no. He knew for sure. I even sent a message to my brother when the man went to Reval again. I was already here at this house at the time. And I also know that the ship arrived and that he went to see my brother. But he didn't make it back. The sea got him."

"But he was a liar, in any case. An abbot? Little fool! For your information, there is no monastery in Reval."

"No, he wasn't in Reval. A few miles out of town. With the White Monks."

And now Balthasar was speechless with surprise.

"Is he . . . a redhead like yourself?"

"Just like me."

"And his name is – Antonius?"

"Anton, yes. So you do know him?!"

"I do."

"Really? God, what a miracle!"

"I'm amazed, too. But listen, he isn't an abbot any longer."

"What is he now, then?"

"Now – he actually is Master of the Order. Or rather, the Master's right hand."

"Really? But are you planning to go home to Reval?"

"Not for three years."

"Well, in that case, you're no help. Otherwise I would have asked you to look up Anton and tell him . . ."

"What?"

"What happened to our mother here."

"What happened?"

"He does know part of it already . . . From that sailor. They started to accuse her, saying that in the tavern where she worked as proprietress, the Green Angel near the Passow Gate, the clients were robbed. And then they locked her up in the duke's prison tower and they took away all the little we had. And Kasimir, that's our younger brother, had just managed to get into the paupers' school. But then they started to spread witchcraft stories about my mother and they threw Kasimir out of school. They didn't care that Anton had been the best pupil there. And now Kasimir is God-only-knows where. And I ended up here . . . Anyway, that part Anton knows. But last St Martin's Day eve, mother hanged herself in the tower. And Anton does not know about that yet."

Bade roused them from their beds of straw at about half past three in the morning. On the way home Gluck hummed a chorale that he was to play in church in two hours. Zastrow stepped off the path in the dark and sank mid-thigh into ice-cold water. All the way to the city gate he repeated, eight times, that his knees would be swollen all of next week.

"Maybe your mouth will swell up and shut right now!" Balthasar said.

For four pennies they were let in at the gate. At the fish market square Gluck broke off a willow branch overhanging the wall and they drew lots with the twigs. Bade got the short end and said, grinning:

"You dogs! It's me again!"

At the south wall of the dormitory, he stayed behind in the dark street. The others went quietly to the door, crept onto the step, pulled off their boots, and waited behind the door, holding their breath. Gluck was on the verge of starting on his chorale again, but Zastrow jabbed him in the ribs just in time. Then they heard a thud

348

and the breaking of glass at the other end of the building: Bade had thrown a rock through the small pane of the window at the end of the corridor. Through the door they heard the watchman's stool clatter to the floor as he jumped up and ran thumping down the hall towards the sound. The boys opened the door soundlessly with Gluck's spare key and in a flash were on the stairs leading to the upper storey. They were only halfway to their *cubiculum* when Bade caught up with them: "The old man stood bellowing at the broken pane for so long, I got in with no problem." He looked at Balthasar in the light of a candle that had been left burning in the corridor, so that those going to the urinal would not run into the wall: "Well? *Omne animal . . . triste?** But it does feel damned good to let oneself go like that, doesn't it?"

When Balthasar was herded into church at six o'clock, after a brief and feverish sleep – on Sundays they were awakened an hour later – he was certain that God's punishment would not fail to descend upon him for all his abominable deeds. God had already shown His wrath through a remarkable coincidence: by permitting the Devil to lead him to Lada. And He would display it again for another abomination: when Balthasar raised his dishevelled head and his flushed, boorish face to the altarpiece depicting Mary, he saw, in the flickering candlelight – even as he prayed fervently that the curse be lifted from his eyes – Lada's white thighs under Mary's blue skirt.

Balthasar thanked God that on Sundays they had onion soup for breakfast, which would wipe out the smell of drink on his breath. But he would be punished – of that he was just about certain.

After breakfast Zastrow and Gluck launched into a discussion of their most recent conquests, and previous ones as well, at which sixteen-year-old Kümmel, flushed with excited curiosity, delighted

---

* After coitus all creatures are melancholy (Latin). The complete phrase is: *Post coitum omne animal triste.*

them with his detailed questions. Balthasar left them there to go for a walk along the town walls. Settling into a brisk pace, he decided to circle the entire town.

The fog on this windless day still wrapped itself around the houses like white lamb's wool, extending halfway up their peaked roofs. And church bells sent waves of booming sound, solemn and disturbing, over the rooftops. But in the sky the fleecy clouds were starting to thin, and here and there the sun lit up the weathervanes atop the city towers. From above, next to the White Tower where the city wall was the highest, one could catch glimpses of the black river beneath the fog blanket, winding northward all the way to the marshes of Oderburg. The chattering jackdaws around the red-tiled towers were heralds of spring. And the towers were perspiring, like Balthasar. Perhaps the thought of God's punishment was nothing more than the chagrin of a *melancholy creature* contemplating his empty beaker.

But no! When Balthasar returned from his tour around the walls, he heard someone behind him call out on Väike-Toom Street:

"Hey! Young man! Look here!"

He turned around and was astonished to find that he knew the modish older gentleman who had hailed him. It was a magistrate of the Narva Town Council, Joachim Krumhusen, the man who had once saved Siimon from serious trouble in Narva and had been suspected in Tallinn of traitorous collaboration with the Grand Duke of Moscow, but who in fact was one of the first to flee from Narva to Tallinn, and thence to Germany – the fellow whose goods his father had recently transported from Tallinn to Riga.

It turned out that Herr Krumhusen was living here in Pomerania, in the city of his birth, Treptow, and was beginning an undertaking to build a salt works under the auspices of the duke and the merchants of the Loitz family. And at that very moment he was on his way – where? To pay a Sunday visit to the home of his young friend, Rector Wolff . . .

Balthasar stepped back from Herr Krumhusen in alarm, for he could readily imagine what the latter would be saying in a quarter of an hour: "By the way, I was just talking with one of your students, that Rissaw from Tallinn. Ha-ha-ha-ha – he didn't just have onion soup on his breath, no sir, it was beer and wine! Stank like a goat!" And then Rector Wolff would say, with the utmost calm, not revealing just how angry he was: "So. Thank you for telling me." And as soon as Krumhusen left, the rector would send the beadle to fetch Balthasar. Not that he would get a word out of Balthasar – who would be silent as a tomb. But then the rector would start putting pressure on Zastrow and Gluck, and he would have them all put into separate rooms to write an account of the previous night. And if that did not work – since they would all put down that they were each on their pallets all night and dreaming of Our Saviour rescuing the lost sheep – he would summon little Bagmiel. Bagmiel would think: *You never know with that crazy Bade,* and though he would not go to the rector of his own accord to tell on the others, if he were summoned to stand before the rector and Lupus looked at him with those damned owl eyes and asked him what he knew of this business, that is, *what* he knew and not *if* he knew, Bagmiel would no doubt be afflicted with a kind of verbal diarrhoea and would let loose the whole story, earning for the night wanderers three days of confinement in the lock-up and ten whacks with the knout.

Balthasar bade Herr Krumhusen a hasty farewell, and at three o'clock he was summoned.

The beadle accompanied Balthasar to the rector's apartment in a house where Balthasar had never been. Of course: why should the rector come to his office on a Sunday afternoon because of a drunken student?

There's no point lying, and even less telling the truth, Balthasar thought as he stepped into the house, *ergo, mouth clamped shut and see what happens.* Just how he would stand in front of the rector with his mouth clamped shut he had not quite worked out, but he had made a rock-solid decision to do so.

The rector's great-room, with its dark panelling and light walls and a painted log ceiling, was grander than he had expected.

"Aha. One moment. Master Rector will see you soon," said the smiling, rat-faced servant Hans when Balthasar entered. "Well, well, and just what pranks have we been up to . . . ?"

Balthasar grunted and remained silent. Hans turned away, offended, and went to announce him to the rector. Usually the sinners summoned to the rector tried to get on the good side of his servant; they did not behave like this lout.

"Yes. Show him in," said the rector from his study. "Hello. Take a seat."

Hypocrite. He would not normally put on this kind of comedy – asking somebody whose backside he was about to warm with a whipping to take a seat.

"You're from Tallinn?"

Keep mouth shut. But it should be alright to nod.

"Hm. And you don't know any Slavic at all?"

Lord, does he know already that it was Lada who . . . ? Keep mouth shut. And shake head about the Slavic language.

"Hm."

Now he's looking for an especially scathing remark. Clear. Something that will let him dump all his contempt on the sinner's head at once. Wait. What was it he said to that fellow Wede, who'd been caught visiting girls last month . . . ? "Oh, so the farmer-boy had to go and sow some oats, did he? You might have taken your assignments along and put some effort into cultivating them as well."

"Balthasar – I have treated you unfairly."

Let him prattle on. I will humble myself before God. What he says is water off a duck's back to me.

"I wouldn't have thought it would make you quite so contrary towards me. But it is a contrariness I deserve, unfortunately."

Let him go on . . . But . . . wait, what is it he's saying? He's *wronged* me?

"Yes. I was under the impression that everyone living to the east of the Germans were Slavs: the Wends and Kashubians of Pomerania, and you Estonians in Livonia, as well. And when you told me you'd never known a word of a Slavic language, I thought you were just another one of those types that we've got more than enough of here – the ones who befoul their own nests. I'm thinking of the Sorbs of Pomerania – instead of patching their Wendish rags and remaining who they are, they're so eager to get their Slavic behinds into German trousers that in two hundred years even their ears won't be showing above the belt. That's how it is. But today, along comes my old friend Krumhusen and says: 'I was just talking to one of your students on the street, that Rissaw from Tallinn . . .', and then we start talking about Livonia, and suddenly I realise that the non-Germans there are an entirely different people . . ."

Rector Wolff asked Balthasar to tell him in detail about Tallinn and about Meus' life there, and at the end he said:

"Then things have gone very well for him. Something that doesn't often happen with such honest young men. Unfortunately. And he has a wife as well . . ." He leaned back in his chair and looked Balthasar over once more from head to toe, ". . . a wife as well – and to judge by you – quite a hale and hearty one at that."

Balthasar left the rector's home at half past four that afternoon, in his hand the old worn dogskin hat that the servant Hans, bowing, had handed to him; in his mouth the strong taste of the housekeeper's ginger confections; on his shoulder the sensation of the rector's farewell pat; in his mind total confusion as to the utterly incomprehensible workings of Divine Justice.

There was half an hour left before supper and he used the time to circle the Wendish sector of the old town. A whistling east wind had blown the fog away from the city. The weathervanes creaked and icy early-springtime stars glittered in wind-rippled puddles. But along with the fear that a punishment much more severe than ten blows of the knout was in the Lord's right hand, in readiness for him – along with this fear, and already poking out its round, whiskered, squirrel head was hope – the hope that to those born under a lucky star God Himself would, with His left hand, extend a footbridge, a pole, a magic rope, over the abyss of Original Sin. And when Balthasar had nourished his body and spirit with two large bowls of bean soup in the refectory, he was fairly certain that God would help him – in spite of Himself.

In any event, from that March evening on Rector Wolff no longer treated Balthasar as though he might perhaps be a decent enough fellow from a dishonourable family; he treated him as his young friend.

Later, it sometimes happened that when Herr Krumhusen again came to Stettin, to confer with the masters Loitz about the salt works and chanced to visit the rector, the rector invited Balthasar to his place as well. From Herr Krumhusen Balthasar learned that in the latter part of New Year's Month, January, the Muscovite had severely plundered southern Livonia and Courland, and that the citizens of Riga had burned down their outlying towns for fear of being surrounded. Furthermore, he heard that the esteemed Coadjutor Kettler – at the mention of his name Balthasar felt for a moment like someone reminded of an unpleasant disease from which he had long ago recovered – had been in Cracow during Lent, discussing aid to Livonia with the Polish king. Whether these discussions yielded anything useful was not yet known. But the meetings with Herr Krumhusen were without doubt of use to Balthasar. First of all, Krumhusen offered him the opportunity to send a letter with more or less guaranteed security to his homeland, for the Loitzes' warehouse still just about managed to maintain its contacts with Tallinn. And Krumhusen assured him that, even should these break off, the ones with Riga would remain, for there was no mountain range between Riga and Tallinn.

When autumn came Balthasar wrote his first detailed letter to his father and to Meus about his life in Stettin. He spoke not of what lay behind his departure – that was old news – but described his life in the dormitory with the broad strokes of a pen-and-ink artist, taking pleasure in his own word pictures. In the letter to his father he also casually asked for money. He had no real need for it at the moment, but he felt he had the right to ask. Towards his studies he had received not a shilling from his father, and the need for it was on the horizon because war threatened Livonia again, which would jeopardise all communication. And besides, on more than one occasion during the summer Balthasar had allowed himself to be tempted by Bade, that cursed fellow, onto the "wide road", the devil knows why. And in the Green Angel, and elsewhere too, he had not wanted to look like some impecunious nobody next to the offspring of wealthy merchants, so he had spent about twenty marks to uphold the honour of the sons of Tallinn's wagon drivers. And when, in September, he had gone to the Loitzes' bank to exchange his Livonian currency for Pomeranian money – there had of late been problems using Livonian money in everyday purchases – he was given about 15 per cent less than he had been getting. "The silver content of my coins is the same as before. Or are you of the opinion that I've melted them down?" he had started to argue. "Oh no, but these days, the coins minted in Livonia have a much lower silver content," an infuriatingly soft-spoken official had explained, "and the bank cannot ascertain, in each case, whether some of your coins are freshly minted." It could be true, of course, that Herr Kettler, newly elevated to the position of Master of the Order, was minting inferior coins. But there was no doubt that the masters Loitz were making a profit here, and at Balthasar's expense.

The year 1559 went its way with the slush and nasty winds of winter, and 1560 entered with a crackling frost. But winter disappeared again into slush and rain and the fogs of the Oder wetlands. In the second half of April church bells rang out for days on end, as though a royal personage had been called to his Lord, and the entire institute attended services several times a day, for days in a row, in mourning and commemoration. And there was no shortage of words of praise for the departed: Melanchthon, having long been widely derided and scorned, had died on April 14, in the town of Wittenberg. And for some time Balthasar had the feeling that he had unavoidably missed – because of Melanchthon's death – seeing and experiencing something of true significance . . . And then it was spring.

In the middle of June, when renovation work was started in the dormitories, the students were given a special four-month summer holiday. The sons of Stettin's burghers went to their homes; the offspring of the landed gentry went to their estates; the sons of Wendish craftsmen and artisans disappeared into the narrow streets of the old town, between the river and the Haymarket, or to Lastadie, or to the nearby villages along the Oder. Staying behind at the institute were about twenty students whose homes were either too distant or nonexistent. And they too sought some kind of activity for the summer. Some were encouraged to sing in the choirs of St Mary's or St Jacob's churches; some were aided by their professors in procuring tutorial positions with families in town. Some went off travelling to nearby university towns to live and experience summertime student life there. Often that did not involve much more than wandering idly from one church estate or schoolmaster's home to another, sometimes begging – in the strictest sense of the word, though an ennobling, sanctioned form of it – in the name of serving the muses. Still, it was not something especially pleasing to the Lord.

Bade, of course, needed to do nothing of the sort. He was in no kind of occupation at all, he said, chortling, for his uncle in Lübeck supplied him with more than enough money. Early in the spring he was planning to go to Lübeck for the summer, but later decided he would rather go to one of his other seven or eight merchant uncles in the harbour towns on the Baltic Sea – yes, he had them in Barth and Rostock as well, and Wismar and Königsberg, and one – it was true – even in Tallinn. This time, he finally decided, he would go to Wismar:

"Actually I'd like to go to Tallinn," Bade said to Balthasar, "because I've never been there and, according to you, it's the world's most pleasant town, and my uncle in Wismar is the world's most boring old man. But up there, in your Livonia, there's a war going on, and in wartime you always have to take sides. And – confound it – that goes against my grain."

Balthasar stayed on. One day, at the Green Angel, he met a boatman who worked on the Oder. He had noticed Balthasar's muscular arms and patched pants and mentioned, in passing, that when the professors all went away during the summer maybe he, Balthasar, could work with him as an oarsman for two marks a week.

And so, from mid June to the beginning of October, Balthasar rowed in a wide four-man boat, ferrying crates and barrels from the Wendish trading towns and the ships of Lübeck and Denmark to the docks of the Oder, and Stettin's merchandise from the docks to the ships.

He got sunburnt on the river, turned a copper-red, and itched until his skin peeled, but then he darkened to a deep reddish-brown, like a devil. At first his shoulders and ribs were terribly sore in the evenings, and his palms were blistered from the oars, but after two weeks he stopped noticing such things. He got to see the ships fore and aft, their anchors and figureheads, their cargo and crew. He tucked away phrases in Danish and Wendish and soon could entertain his boat mates with them. He and his three Wendish rowing mates – professional rowers – usually ate lunch somewhere in the willow groves of Pleekholm. Balthasar ate whatever Herr Butte had directed his maid Liisel to pack,

357

for a set fee, into Balthasar's lunch bag. For dessert he had the morsels that Liisel had slipped in of her own accord, and afterwards he did something improper – in which the Sorb boys joined him only for a few hesitant steps. He stripped and went into the cool water up to his neck and swam upstream, keeping close to the bulrushes, and then back downstream, awkwardly, like a large dog holding up his big hairy head. It was marvellously refreshing, as though St Veronica herself had wiped away his fatigue with her miraculous handkerchief.

With the rector's permission he lived and slept in his empty *cubiculum*. But in his free time he often wandered about town. From the town wall next to the Veskivärav Gate he examined the unfamiliar trees and mysterious half-hidden pathways of the duke's pleasure garden. Or he walked to Oderburg and talked with the townsmen and villagers, or circled the castle and stared at the white marble figures of former dukes and duchesses looking down from their niches in the wall. Or he eyed the thriving, red-bearded Duke Barnim and his coiffured Duchess Anna when they went out riding. Or, and this was even more intriguing: with a golden word and a silver coin handed to the guard at the gate he bought his way into the duke's zoo. There he stared at a huge moose with wide, shovel-shaped antlers, and red-brown aurochs, and wolves half-mad with restless discontent, and yellow-eyed lynxes in their iron cages. But he could not find the door to the cave where the Pomeranian dukes of the Greif dynasty kept their eponymous beast. The wondrous creature, with its eagle's head and lion's paws, could reportedly fly to its nest gripping twenty lions in its claws, as though they were but a single ram. When he mentioned the griffin to the guard, the man said that for three Pomeranian marks he would show it to him, but Balthasar noticed the hint of a smirk hiding in the man's matted beard and managed to avoid being played for a fool.

Sometimes, before sunset in the long summer evenings, which were much shorter here than at home, he climbed up to the attic of the institute. From the packed dirt floor rose waves of warmth; the rafters gave off an acrid smell of tar, and the shafts of sunlight entering through cracks between the roof tiles climbed imperceptibly up the dusty cobwebs and rough chimney sides. Down below, the town hummed its fading evening hum. The prison tower cast its shadow over the chained bear in the courtyard, and the flies swarming at his raw neck were buzzing their final buzz of the day. The last freight wagons made their way, wheels creaking, towards the salt depots of Pikksild Bridge. And then the rungs of the ladder creaked close by. It was Liisel, bringing Balthasar a fresh cottage-cheese cake. She put her hands, soft and damp from the daily dishwashing, around Balthasar's neck. Her black hair flowed over his dark-blond mop, and from her breasts rose a warm cottage-cheese-cake scent. Through each other's hair they looked up in alarm at the two thousand glowing tiles above them, arranged, two-by-two, in a "nun-and-monk" pattern.

Later, with the sky still reddish, but with enough light at the *cubiculum* window to manage without a candle, Balthasar took from his trunk a hardcover notebook, something like those he used for his lessons, smoothed out a page, hooked his thumbs into his waistband, and, having stacked the five empty pallets on top of each other to make room, paced up and down on the stone floor of the room, whistling. Then he stepped up to the window, dipped his goose quill into the inkwell, and wrote:

> Pomerania is divided into nine sovereign jurisdictions: Wenden, Kaszuby, Stettin, Pomerania Proper, Usedom, Gotzgau, Wolgast, Rügen, and Barth. Its old borders follow waterways for the most part: the Rivers Weiksel, Warte, and Penuse and the sea. The land is rich in field crops and game and fish. It is a flat land, and notable mountains are not to be found here. The more important towns are all situated near

the sea, which the Germans call the East Sea and the Livonians the West Sea, according to where it is located with respect to themselves. And the sea here deposits on the shore the very same kind of golden stones that it does in Prussia and Courland, and reportedly even at the tip of Saaremaa. But the most important capital city of this realm, the duke's city, will be described in the next chapter.

CHAPTER THREE,

in which it becomes apparent that there is no chance in this chapter, after all, to speak of the most important capital in the realm, the duke's city, for upon the mountaintops of history great events once again leave their deep footprints, and the sand rills trickling down into the valleys of ordinary life alter the routes of the ants below in unforeseeable ways, at least of those who have the good fortune not to be buried by the sand, and of the ones who, though trapped, manage to thrash their way out again.

The three-masted caravel visible far out on the open sea was sailing towards the northeast, in a stiff southwester. It was not, of course, the low-slung, single-masted *Dolphin* belonging to Herr Bock of Tallinn: that was evident even at a distance. And upon closer examination the green copper letters on the bow ploughing the waves were readily legible: *Seejunkfer*. Which name, as the foul mouths among the seamen insisted, did not in this case mean "maiden of the sea", but rather "old whore of the sea".

This boat had seen many days but was still more or less sound; it belonged to the famous merchant and banking house of the Loitz family of Stettin. Herr Hans, the youngest of four brothers, was the director of the massive enterprise. He was known as the "Fugger of the North" by those eager to find favour with the brothers – and, God knows, such men were legion. He was a most enterprising man with respect to all kinds of risky ventures and was now dispatching this ship to – what should one say – Livonia, or, in fact, to Muscovy? For it was not clear just *where* the town of Narva was situated these days.

The trip to Narva was risky, of course. But businessmen in Lübeck, as well as merchants and shipowners of many towns in Holland, were now engaged in a flourishing trade with the Grand Duke of Muscovy, via Narva. And naturally, the more successful a business the greater the risks. This law of trade, acknowledged everywhere on land and sea, was perhaps better known to Herr Hans Loitz than to his older brothers. One heard ominous tales about the privateers of Denmark, Sweden and Tallinn, and rumours – who knows their source – of the Grand Duke's henchmen gaoling the seamen and merchants of western countries in their prison tower and subjecting them to gruesome tortures. In addition to these stories against their undertaking, Herr Loitz collected all kinds of pertinent facts from as many sources as possible. Based on these he determined that now, in the autumn of 1560, the prices for iron, copper and lead were especially favourable on the Narva market.

The *Seejunkfer*'s cargo of these so weighed her down that the bow of the ship was at times chest-deep in the dark waves, and the stern at times as low as its shoulder blades. The weight also caused the mainmast to sway so violently that the lookout up in the crow's nest kept a firm grip on its railing. Thanks to a few fortunate events, which will be recounted forthwith, it was a certain student, sporting the beginnings of a light-brown beard, who was the lookout on the ship sailing towards Mary's Land. As he stared at the dark wall of cloud rising on the eastern horizon, his round grey eyes in his nicely tanned face squinting from time to time like a regular seaman's, he made an astonishing discovery: when he turned his face towards the wind he could not remember a thing, nor could he think about anything at all. The wind simply stopped his breathing. It forced all words and images that rose up in him back down inside. All he could do was sway with the mast, feeling both elated and miserable, both intrepid and weak, gasping for breath as the wind pressed its cold, suffocating palm against his mouth. But when he turned away from the wind and it blew his wheat-coloured mass of hair flat against the back of his head, the events of his life rose to mind as if of themselves, and the happenings of the last twenty months lined up in his imagination like a hundred students at morning prayers, or after prayers, with Rector Wolff hurling the thunderbolts of his rhetoric over their heads . . . All twenty months. And the past few weeks. And the last days before their departure three weeks earlier, when Rector Wolff had summoned Balthasar one afternoon, with Herr Krumhusen also waiting for him at the rector's apartment, and, over a beaker of wine, addressed him thus:

"Balthasar, your father there in Tallinn is a very proper man and has done me several favours. And he has never had cause to regret them. You know that, don't you?"

"I do."

"Good. And I believe that the son of a man like that might do me a favour as well. And he would have no cause for regret either, not one whit."

"Namely?"

"Perhaps you know that my son, Melchior, stayed behind in Narva when I fled the Muscovites the spring before last. He stayed behind because I could not manage to liquidate all my holdings there. And, in addition, we wanted to know for certain whether it would be possible for us to continue doing honest business under the Grand Duke . . . Well . . . According to my son's messages – those that have reached me at this chaotic time – it would, indeed, be possible. By the way, this is something I can say here, in Stettin. In Tallinn I would probably have to protest staunchly that doing business there is no more possible than the prospect of the Devil gaining salvation . . . But the Grand Duke wants to have his salt works built quickly. And for that I need both the help of my son and additional capital. In short, I want Melchior to leave

Narva and come here. And I need to send him instructions about what holdings we have there and how to sell them and to whom. But I do not dare put all this information in a letter, the times being what they are."

"And I am to deliver these instructions to him?"

"That's what I have in mind."

And now Balthasar, with the wind in his fair hair, was sitting up in the crow's nest on the mainmast of the *Seejunkfer*, trying to pull his thoughts together, like a man tightening his belt as he sets out on a mission. For the journey was drawing towards its close, which meant his assignment was imminent.

Two nights ago, when the autumn clouds scudding across the sky towards the northwest occasionally parted, they had seen by the brief glimmer of moonlight the massive dark cliffs of Suursaare Island on their left. Only at this point, so far to the east, did the ships sailing to Narva dare turn south. And now, in the greyish light of midday, after hours en route, the *Seejunkfer* was heading straight towards the low, wooded, sandy shore. And just when it seemed to Balthasar that Grand Master Kettler must have bribed the captain to run them aground, the sandbanks suddenly fell away on either side and they entered the mouth of a wide river.

For several hours they battled a stiff crosswind and rapid current up a river the width of the Oder until at last, as the high riverbanks drew closer to each other and rose ever higher, they caught a glimpse of German Narva to their right and Russian Narva to their left. On the right stood a small town with rough stone walls and two wrecked church towers. Low roofs of tile and wooden shingles, visible above the low walls, revealed fire-blackened rafters here and there. And directly next to the town, on the steepest cliff, the inaccessible and haughty Hermann Castle, rising straight up against the leaden sky. On the left the massive, fabled walls of mighty Ivangorod stretched out along the ridge of

Neitsimäe Hill. Between the two flowed the dark, foam-flecked river, for several hundred years the boundary between two worlds, and now an artery to the mysterious east. And indeed, trade appeared to be quite lively here. For in the middle of the dark-grey river, over a dozen foreign cargo ships with noisily flapping pennants lay at anchor, and at the quays of both Hermanstad and Ivangorod could be seen many more. When the ships and the quays drew closer, Balthasar could see clean-shaven Netherlanders, Englishmen with trimmed moustaches, and Russian merchants with full beards of reddish-brown. Big-wheeled freight wagons lumbered across the high bridge that connected the riverbanks between the fortresses; boatmen rowed their small, low-bottomed boats across the current between the quays and the ships. Above the threatening dark river and the singular rugged walls and the toy-like ships and people and wagons – all somewhat insubstantial and fanciful – arched the grey autumn sky of Mary's Land. And under this leaden sky, a strangely muted roar, distant yet powerful, filled the air.

The sound entered the open window of Herr Melchior Krumhusen's great-room as well.

The merchant's house on the corner of Kiriku and Rüütli Streets, almost opposite the Väike Rannavärav Gate, had escaped the great fire at the time of the fall of Narva, though the smoke and flames had come fairly close. Later, he had had his outer walls thoroughly white-washed to eliminate all traces of soot. The interior of the house was in impeccable order as well. The great-room was perhaps a bit small compared to the finest of such rooms in Tallinn and Stettin, but it was richly appointed with costly chests and pewter dishes from Holland and England; on the wall above the broad dining table hung a portrait of an older gentleman with a seaman's greying beard and bright-blue eyes. Bal recalled that only once before, in the study of the Finnish duke, had he seen something similar. There, of course, it had been a portrait of King Gustav – who was said to be seriously ill now – but the one here was quite recognisable as Papa Krumhusen. Melchior resembled his father closely, especially now, with his probing blue eyes under reddish eyebrows, fixed on Balthasar as he talked. And Balthasar explained: First of all, this house and everything in it, as well as everything in the warehouses, was to be sold to Alderman Heinrich Rönne alone, and to no-one else, with the proviso that the real estate could be bought back upon demand. The elder Krumhusen had made an agreement with Herr Rönne to this effect long ago, etc., etc., etc. After Balthasar had spelt out everything in detail, not forgetting a thing – even while helping himself to copious portions of succulent roast pork and the strange, snake-like local fish called lamprey – it was time for him to pose the father's questions to the son. But first he asked:

"Herr Melchior, what is that odd sound that seems to fill the air and the entire town?"

He learned – and was surprised that he had not remembered it himself – that it was the sound of the great Narva Falls, located about a quarter of a league above the city, at the island of Varessaare, dully roaring day and night, to the extent that the townspeople would have been jolted out of their sleep had it ceased for an instant some night, but strangers to the town were sometimes sleepless for several weeks until they grew accustomed to it.

Balthasar thought that this low, lulling roar would scarcely disturb his slumbers, but in fact he was fated to get not a wink of sleep that October night. But it was not because of the falls of Varessaare Island.

Balthasar repeated to the master of the house all the questions raised by his father, Joachim, and carefully committed every answer to memory: that it was entirely possible in the town of the Grand Duke to engage in honest business; that twice a week the *voevoda* invited the gentlemen factory owners of Lübeck to the castle for a carouse, where he fed them as though they were the ultimate gluttons and plied them with drink as though they were the greatest drunkards and pampered them like royal children; but that the business was more profitable for the Grand Duke than for the merchants, who would soon begin to suffer from it, and that in fact they were in some instances suffering already because there were so many of them from all over the world crowded together here. Yes indeed. A cubit's length of beautiful damask fabric costs just one thaler here, but try to get it in Germany for less than two! And good English cambric was often available for a fifth less than what one paid in any western port, where there were far too many vendors. So even a pound of gold nuggets, which had never cost less in Germany than fifteen thalers, as is well known, had occasionally fallen in price here to ten. But of course for copper and tin and iron and gunpowder the Muscovite still had to pay a price that cancelled out any losses a trader might incur on luxury items; and in the matter of war supplies the Muscovite was prepared to swallow up everything that was offered him, and in such quantities that it was like flinging drops of water from a birch bundle onto red-hot sauna stones. And so he, Melchior, had put aside three thousand thalers of pure profit over the past two years . . . In other words, shrewd sellers could do well here, whether they were natives or foreigners. And how did the nobles fare? Well, it seemed the duke was not exactly planning to do them all in. In '58, when the war was on, many were killed, of course, especially those who got in the way of his campaign to take over castles and estates. But now some of the Taubes and Hastferds had returned to their estates in Viru and Alugtagune, and they had even been seen in the company of the *voevoda*, coming and going, looking self-important.

"And what does he have in mind for the peasants?"

It was not a question to which old Krumhusen had requested an answer, but Herr Melchior provided a quite thorough reply:

"The Muscovite has coddled the peasants more than anyone else. The manor lords – and there were quite a few of them – who were captured by the peasants and hauled before the *voevoda* to hear the

367

peasants' grievances were all sent off to Moscow. And the peasants whose houses burned down during the war were often permitted to cut new lumber at the estates that were left without their lords. And just last spring the *voevoda* distributed seed to them from the Grand Duke's stores near Narva. So that the peasants in a number of places have sworn absolute fealty to the Grand Duke."

"And finally: what weight does the name Krumhusen carry with the Muscovite?"

"We-e-e-ll," Master Melchior said, taking a sip of wine. "It seems in this respect father Joachim has managed to perform a miracle. Since he was declared innocent in Livonia last year of being a traitor to his fatherland, the Grand Duke's letters of pardon to him and to me have been preserved here. So – the Krumhusens are still held in such high esteem by the *voevoda*, that . . ." he paused, looked around, and continued . . . "that at times it becomes worrying."

Just then they heard the clatter of hoofs from the direction of Market Square and Lossi Street, and as the sound quickly drew closer along Rüütli Street Herr Melchoir rose from the table and hurried to the window.

"Well, well, here they are then. Hmm. I thought the *voevoda* would send his servants to summon me to the castle, but he's come himself . . ."

Apparently Balthasar looked quite astonished, for Herr Melchior hastened to add:

"This isn't the first time. By the way, don't say you're from Tallinn. These days, better not to mention it. You're from Stettin and are bringing me greetings from my father. That's all. Not that I'm afraid of the *voevoda* . . . I'm more apprehensive with regard to . . . the other one."

Herr Melchior Krumhusen went out to instruct the servants in their tasks and welcome his distinguished guests – they were already leaping from their saddles, their spurs jingling, their well-fed horses snorting as they thudded onto the flagstones in front of the house. And then the *voevoda* of Narva, Aleksei Danilovich Basmanov, along with his son Fedor and another man and an interpreter strode into the great-room, accompanied by the scurrying, bowing Herr Melchior. From the window one could see four or five guardsmen at their posts by the entrance.

The *voevoda*, dressed in a black woollen caftan from Flanders, was a portly man of about forty. He had angular cheekbones in a pale face, his brow hidden under black hair, his chin concealed under a reddish beard – hair and beard like two grassy hummocks of entirely different origin, with the red and the black mixing, improbably, near the ears. His eyes were piercing black slits. At first glance they seemed the sort that took in everything, but once you looked straight into them you realised they did not see anything at all. And Balthasar recalled that the name Basmanov could mean one of two things in the Tatar language – someone at Doctor Friesner's house had told him that two years earlier, when the name of the conqueror of Narva struck fear in the inhabitants of Tallinn. But the teller of the tale himself was not sure whether the name meant "portrait of the sovereign, displayed for his underlings to bow before", or "underling who regularly bows before his sovereign's portrait". Young Fedor Alekseivich Basmanov resembled his father so closely that, by comparison, Melchior did not look like *his* father at all. Young Basmanov was the image of what his father must have looked like twenty years earlier, and the age difference notwithstanding therewas something sinister, even uncanny, about the likeness.

It cannot be denied that Balthasar felt some unease as well as surprise at finding himself less than five paces from these men. Just then Herr Melchior said:

"This is a young man from Pomerania, from Stettin – our Emperor's renown in trading and commerce has *also* reached there, of course. He brings greetings from my father."

"And how is his health?" the *voevoda* asked in fairly intelligible German, but added, before anyone could answer:

"You know, Melchior, if my Emperor did not think so well of him, I would be angry at your father. Very angry – that he was attracted more by the favour of that minor duke than by the generosity of the mightiest of emperors!"

As the guests were noisily taking their seats at the table, Herr Melchior said:

"My Lord, my father holds our Emperor's affection in the very highest regard, but he is an old man and desires to be nearer the soil of his birthplace."

The *voevoda* asked that the comment be translated for him. He raised his black right eyebrow a bit and asked the interpreter to respond:

"It may be that merchants get sentimental in old age. I haven't noticed it with those of middle age. As a soldier, I desire to be wherever I can best serve my Emperor."

Herr Melchior had ordered that the table be quickly cleared, for Muscovites apparently ate neither pork nor lamprey. A large pewter tray of smoked venison was immediately brought to the table, and the host filled the silver goblets with cool Rhenish wine brought up from the cellars. And so, gnawing on the somewhat tough venison – in quite a casual manner, without the help of those annoying *gaffels* – Balthasar was nonetheless a little perturbed at just how easily the unsavoury "Grand Duke" had become "our Emperor" in Melchior's mouth. After all, only the Grand Duke himself and his officials and the most ambitious of his subordinates called him "Tsar", which meant "Emperor" and was the equivalent of the German "Kaiser"! *Oh well – here – now – of course* . . . Balthasar was just about to pour some wine of understanding and forgiveness over his sense of disaffection when he was prevented from violating the protocol of the dining table, for someone else raised his goblet first. It was the gentleman who had arrived with the *voevoda* and his son. Although the man had taken a seat next to Balthasar, there was a window behind it, so Balthasar had seen only a broad, energetically moving silhouette against the violet-grey of the evening sky. The gentleman raised his goblet and called out in the purest German:

"To the health of our Gracious Emperor!"

Raising his goblet out of politeness and taking a sip along with the others, Balthasar stole a look at his neighbour over the rim of his goblet and nearly choked. He was certain he had seen the man before – this large fellow with a protruding chin and sparse, ash-grey hair. And those small, quickly darting, distant eyes and the broad, confident, sensuous mouth. His first shock of confused recognition was quickly superseded by the faintly intoxicating pleasure of recall, as the honeybee of memory took flight faster than a bullet, past all the faces he had known in Tallinn, Harju, Finland, Pomerania, past a thousand faces, until it came back full circle and lit upon that one face in those thousands: a face which Balthasar had chanced to see only once, in the Old Marketplace in Tallinn, from his window in Meus' apartment.

Balthasar put his goblet on the table and was about to ask where, then, the gracious Frau Katharina, née Tisehhusen, might be staying, and the young Master Diter, with his beautiful wife Elsbet, née Anrep, and how the dickens did Herr Kruse himself happen to be here, raising his goblet to the health of *our Gracious Emperor* whom he had called a brute, a tyrant, and a cannibal the year before last?! But, just in time, Balthasar remembered that he was merely a young Pomeranian from Stettin, ignorant of all the doings of this land – yet was it not true, in that case, that he was all the freer to ask his honourable neighbour whatever he wished? But before he had a chance to formulate his question, Herr Kruse addressed him:

"So, you're from Pomerania? From Stettin, I gather? And what are people there saying about our Gracious Emperor? No, no, speak frankly! Frankly and openly! You can be completely open *with me!*

Yes indeed. Have those old farts from Nuremberg not sent their foul muck to Stettin? Oh, so they have! Have you read any of their pieces? Ha-ha-ha-ha! *"Gar erschröckliche newe Zeytungen von dem grausamen Feynd dem Moscowiter!"** And so on. There were dozens like that! Do the Pomeranians believe them? You don't know? And what about that vile pen-pusher, Grawingell – bought off, he was – do they sing his sordid songs in Stettin? Oh, you don't know that, either? Ha-ha-ha-hah!"

But – who are you? Balthasar wanted to ask, but then Herr Kruse said:

"I am the first Livonian nobleman with a head on his shoulders. When everyone else was looking for help from the west against the Muscovite – from everywhere – from the Prussian prince to the Pope, and from the German Kaiser to the Turkish sultan – and without getting a crumb, as we know – back then, already, I was telling everyone in the council hall of the Tartu bishops and the beer hall of the Livonian Diet: 'Gentlemen, brothers in destiny! Open your eyes and see that our future is in Muscovy! And if we don't want it to be lying in wait for us somewhere in the overgrown muddy marshes of Vjatkamaa or Pskov – half the rebels of Tartu have now been sent out there by our Gracious Emperor – but rather here, in Livonia, on our beautiful estates, we need do no more than *accommodate ourselves* to our Gracious Emperor.'"

Herr Kruse had become greatly overheated in his harangue against invisible opponents. He emptied his goblet noisily and continued:

"And those Livonian leaders, the noblemen who would not listen to me, where have they led Livonia? Narva and Rakvere are in the hands of our Gracious Emperor. Tartu and Viljandi are in the hands of our Gracious Emperor." *Oh, so Viljandi as well?* Balthasar had not heard that before. But he assumed a disinterested expression, as though it did not mean a thing to him, a young man from Stettin. And Herr Kruse continued: "A few months ago, our Gracious Emperor reduced to a

* The latest most shocking news about our vicious Muscovite enemy! (Low German).

pitiful state the last forces of the Order in Härgmäe. But in northern Livonia, Tallinn, Pärnu and Paide still defy him in the most stubborn and stupid manner. And our Gracious Emperor is thus forced to raze the land between them and burn it to the ground. And for what? So that Kettler, that whore-hunter and lapdog of Sigismund, can be Grand Master of the Order at the thirteenth hour and move the Polish forces into our castles! And so that Magnus, that one-eyed Danish puppy, can make himself lord of Saare and Lääne! Tell me, what would a true Livonian, whether nobleman or burgher or peasant, gain by that?"

"But . . . did you . . . benefit . . . from your foresight . . . ?" Balthasar asked, so quickly and quietly that Herr Kruse, flushed with wine, answered without the slightest indignation:

"Did I?! And do you think that our Gracious Emperor does not understand *to whom* it is worth showing royal favour?" He now turned to the entire table, but most directly towards the *voevoda*, which indicated that Balthasar was not the only one hearing the details of this story for the first time.

"After the fall of Tartu, two summers ago, I was a pitiful refugee in the path of the fires of war, with my wife and children and wagonloads of possessions. The whole country was full of people like us. And in my blindness I kept fleeing west, to escape. Just as all the Germans were doing. Our Gracious Emperor's plundering forces were galloping through the countryside. At night, keeping to wooded areas, guided by light from fires, we moved towards Pärnu in a roundabout way. But when we reached the sea it became clear that it would be too dangerous to go to Riga along the coast. In a seaside farm south of Pärnu, in a shabby home of non-Germans, we were given shelter for a week in exchange for pure gold. But we could not find a boat or an oarsman to take us to Riga, not even for gold. And then a plundering gang of our Gracious Emperor's men came upon us. Yes, well . . . There's no need to mention what they did to my two-year-old Gertrud."

Herr Kruse had, in the meantime, refilled his goblet. He took a long draught and went on:

"I was separated from my family, and it's a miracle I wasn't executed near Paide. As the soldiers tore off my clothing to keep it from getting bloodied, they found three thick gold chains under my shirt, and in my underwear, a linen pouch with two hundred guilders sewn into it. At that they threw me, still fettered, onto a cart loaded with war booty and sent me on to Pskov. And, I must say, God abased and degraded me, but He saved me. For in that load of booty there was not only pewter and silver, there were calf hides. So I did not freeze to death along the way. From Pskov I was sent on to Moscow, where I was thrown into the prison tower. There I mouldered eight months. Eight months! And I starved!"

The *voevoda*, about to bite into his hunk of roast elk, said with an odd smile, "Serves you right, such a one as you then were!"

Meanwhile Herr Kruse sank his white teeth into his own slab of elk, whether from the memory of hunger or the wish to avoid responding to the *voevoda*. He talked on with his mouth full:

"Then, on the twenty-second of July, the feast day of the penitent Mary Magdalene, I was abruptly dragged out of prison and led to the sauna by bowing servants and given a red silk caftan to wear. And some variety of scribes or functionaries from some kind of government agency conveyed me in great haste to Chancellor Adashev. A commission was in session at the time, called to settle the border between the spheres of influence of Denmark and Moscow here in Livonia. Our Gracious Emperor wanted to get whatever he could from the Danes, without angering them excessively. But there was no-one in Moscow with sufficient knowledge of the land they were about to divide up. However, there happened to be a German, by the name of Oberfelder, from Germany, serving on this commission, a humble servant of our Gracious Emperor, and all of a sudden he recalled that I was rotting away somewhere. And from that time on . . ." Herr Kruse held the goblet in a hand glinting with gold rings and greasy with venison, and turned his white teeth and elusive grey eyes triumphantly from side to side. "From that time on, I have known the benevolence of our Gracious Emperor. He had my family brought to Moscow. He gave me a stone house right next to the Kremlin. He took care to see that my table was set from the stores in his own kitchen. And he returned to me my old estate, Kalleste, near Tartu. And in addition to everything else, he granted me the rights to sell vodka to half of the kingdom of Muscovy . . . and that is as good as if he had presented me with three gold mines."

Then Herr Kruse turned to face Balthasar:

"You know that fellow Krumhusen. That old man had the best head of all the merchants in Livonia. Tell him what I just related to you. Explain to him what our Gracious Emperor's benevolence looks like." Herr Kruse pulled out a goatskin purse, untied its silk cord, and poured a clinking pile of various gold coins on the table. There were the German Kaiser's gold thalers and Plettenberg's *Portugalöser* and Ivan the Third's sun-yellow *ugors*. "This Krumhusen of yours goes in and out at will at the Pomeranian duke's – here, take this." Herr Kruse pushed the prodigious sum of a dozen gold thalers towards Balthasar. "Here, take them, and see that he tells his duke how the Emperor in Moscow rewards the loyalty of his subordinates." Balthasar hesitated to pick up the thalers, for how could he . . . ? But Herr Kruse pressed the coins into his hand:

"Just let the Pomeranian duke talk about it to all the German princes, up to Kaiser Ferdinand himself! Let it be an example of how a Livonian nobleman in Moscow is thriving under the hand of Moscow's Gracious Emperor. That's what most of the fuss is about now in Germany. But Herr Melchior will tell you how Christian merchants fare here, how they get fat on their fat purses. Spread the news! And you will see for yourself if you keep a sharp eye out. And as for the peasants – the *voevoda* has begun to so mollycoddle those non-German fleabags that I have to keep telling him, 'Enough! Don't be taken for a fool, Aleksei Danilovich! I don't know what the Russian peasant is like, but I do know ours. He will not remember today that yesterday your seed grain saved him from starvation!'"

"Don't you worry, I'll see to it that they remember," the *voevoda* said, slurping some Rhenish wine to wash down his venison. "Not a single grain of rye have I distributed simply on account of their blue eyes. The only thing that matters to me is what benefits our Gracious Emperor."

"By now they have been encouraged by your generosity," Herr Kruse said, "and are murdering their manor lords in the counties of Harjumaa and Läänemaa. How does that benefit our Gracious Emperor?"

"But those are the manor lords of the Order. Let them kill the dogs," the *voevoda* said calmly.

"But when our Gracious Emperor has taken possession of these lands – and it won't take him long to do that," cried Herr Kruse, "you won't be able to manage there without the manor lords!"

"I'm sure there'll be enough clever fellows like you who'll survive," the *voevoda* said, his black eyes fixed on Herr Kruse – whether looking through him or past him was not clear. "Besides," he said, continuing to chew, "our Gracious Emperor will soon completely reorganise the business of the manor lords in the entire realm. It'll be settled in the next few years."

"How will he do that?" Herr Kruse asked. Balthasar noted the surprise and unease in his voice. He seemed to be saying: Wait just a minute. Even though what you're saying is just blather that you've thought up to mock me – still, I know you and I know our Gracious Emperor and one can never be sure about either one of you . . .

"How will he do it? Very simple: he will take half the realm away from the boyars. He will drive the boyars away – let them live somewhere else. And he will claim as his patrimony the land he has cleared. We even have a name for this new land: *Oprichnina*. And he will appoint his loyal military commanders as rulers of this land. Tried and tested men who are willing to go through fire and water for him."

"And as for the boyars, he'll shake his fist at them. And especially at the Livonian boyars. Ha-ha-ha-hah!" Fedor Alekseivich echoed his father.

"With the exception of those who honourably enter his service here, isn't that so?" Herr Melchior asked, and Herr Kruse mumbled:

"Naturally. But in order that the Livonian noblemen be able to come to their senses and begin to serve him, it is above all necessary that those cursed peasant boors not kill the noblemen!"

"Is it a big uprising?" Balthasar asked.

"Seems to be the biggest since the St George's Night Uprising in the year 6852, when they killed their German masters."

"But that was in . . ." Balthasar began, and then realised the Russian's calculation was according to his country's calendar, which started not from the birth of Christ, as did the rest of the Christian world, but from the time of Creation. And as it would have been improbable for a youth from Stettin to know anything about Estonian peasants and St George's Night, he asked:

"Are any details known about these recent uprisings?"

"Three or four of the Estonian counties are in rebellion," Herr Kruse said. "Especially in the region around Tallinn. 'Cause it's in the towns that resistance starts fomenting, and it spreads from them. And above all from Tallinn. At least in Livonia. This Lutheran nonsense and every-thing else, too. We even have a saying: 'Whatever the townsman throws over the wall sprouts into thorn bushes in the countryside.' And now the fracas has erupted. In any event, thousands of peasants are rioting all over the countryside. They say they've elected their own king."

"*Their own king?*" Balthasar cried, with greater undisguised astonishment than a young man born in Stettin would probably have shown. "How? And who would that be?"

"Oh, just some yokel chieftain."

"Come, come . . . ?"

"And why not?" Herr Kruse said, smirking. "It would be just like them – a Grand Master, two dukes – Johan and Magnus, yes? – three kings and two emperors, including our Gracious Emperor, are all ready to rule them. But with the stupidity of oxen they start a rebellion and choose some kind of Hayseed Harry as their king! I'm telling you, that by itself reveals exactly what these Livonian peasants are!"

Herr Melchior's servants began to clear the table of bones and bring out spit-grilled goose, cabbage turnovers fried in oil, Russian style, and fresh German beer in Bohemian clay pitchers. The *voevoda* noisily quaffed one whole pitcher and put a stop to their bustling.

"That's enough. Now it's to the castle."

It was past midnight and black as pitch outside. Herr Melchior ordered horses from the stable for himself and Balthasar. The *voevoda*'s guardsmen rode on ahead, clattering through the distant roar of the falls, through the dense darkness of the night, bearing torches to light the way. Balthasar saw slim façades and pointed gables emerge from the darkness and disappear again into the night and the smoke from the torches. The archways echoed as they galloped through them into the large outer court of the castle and then the narrow inner courtyard. By the light of the flaring torches, the hulking walls rising towards the night sky appeared especially rugged and massive. Balthasar recalled Herr Melchior explaining that to affirm the eternal alliance of Russian and German Narva and their respective hinterlands, the *voevoda* resided by turns in Ivangorod and here.

The stable hands rushed out, swallowing their yawns, to take the gentlemen's horses. Discipline and order, reputedly wanting among the

Muscovite forces, seemed under the *voevoda* to be beyond reproach.

With their shadows dancing alongside them in the stairwell and upon the ceiling arches, they ascended by torchlight to a vaulted hall bright with glowing candles, divided in half by two pillars. There appeared to be a carouse in progress – as Herr Melchior had described it – for the distinguished merchants. It was surely a special gesture of respect on the *voevoda's* part for him to have gone in person to invite Herr Melchior, and to have spent several hours at his place, even as all these Dutchmen, Englishmen and Flemings, not to mention Germans from Lübeck – a couple of dozen gentlemen, in effect – had been sitting around without their host, eating roast duck and goose and quaffing a variety of German, and even French, wines.

At Herr Melchior's house Balthasar had, along with the others, raised his goblet several times, and even though he had drunk very moderately he felt that he had benefited from those sips of wine – in that adapting to yet another new, unfamiliar, dreamlike place had been easier that night. Apparently he had attracted attention by arriving at the same time as the *voevoda*. In any case, when the clamour of voices had swollen and then ebbed somewhat, and the playing of the four or five German musicians on the balcony had permitted, his table mates were eager to converse with him, though they themselves were gentlemen of rank, attired in ermine-trimmed cloaks and silver chains and velvet berets. "We're from Lübeck. That's right. Trading linen and lead. Mainly. And where does the young gentleman come from? Ah, from Stettin! Ah, on business for the Loitzes – right, right. Well, my greetings to Herr Hans! From whom? From Bade. What was that? B-a-d-e – yes, yes."

And from the other side, at the same time: "So you come from the Loitzes? Well, well, well! So they're out for their share!? Well, why not. There's enough here for everyone. And what was it you brought to the Grand Duke? Copper. Aha. A most profitable commodity. And you

379

know Herr Krumhusen as well? He's in special favour with the *voevoda*. Just a minute – come here, try it – I'm from Schiedam, you've heard of it? We always keep a supply of Schiedam gin in stock. Here you are – give it a try."

Balthasar took a sip of the intoxicatingly fragrant, fiery, juniper-berry spirits, and suddenly a strangely strong, painful memory came to mind, of a juniper-wood beer mug at Kalamaja. And the taste of a juniper-wood spoon carved by Märten, and the crinkled needle-leaves of the junipers, a deep green from the moist air on the grey, gravelly shore of Paljassaare Island – on a muggy, windless day, when the berries are ripe and they look at you with their ripe, dark eyes . . . The gentleman from Schiedam was talking, at the same time, about how difficult it was for them to get here from the North Sea to do business – because of the tolls at the Sound, which King Friedrich had raised so high that . . . Balthasar was holding the vessel under his nose and looking casually around at the inebriated merchants and at Herr Kruse, who was explaining something in a resounding voice to all present, and at the *voevoda*, who had removed his black caftan and was laughing at something in a frozen kind of way, and at his son, who was singing and accompanying himself on the three-stringed rebec he had snatched from its owner. Balthasar's nostrils widened, and behind Schiedam's words he heard Annika's quiet voice telling a story she had heard from their mother about junipers: that the juniper was a holy tree, its berries sacred, for Jesus Christ himself had marked each berry with a cross, and thus the juniper berry guarded against plague and war and lightning . . .

"Whatever the case with the tolls," Herr Schiedam continued, "there are plenty of other problems this side of the Sound. How did you manage to get past Tallinn?"

Balthasar nearly jumped at the question.

"How did I get past Tallinn?"

He was about to answer: Up in the crow's nest on the mainmast, straining to see if I could catch a glimpse of the tip of St Olaf's steeple across the barren sea . . . in vain, of course, for we sailed so far to the north that one could not even make out Prangli Island . . . But all he said was:

"Easily."

"No privateers chasing you?"

"No."

"That's how it is – some are lucky, some aren't. Those gentlemen from Lübeck, look there, the ones on the left, at the end of the table, they've lost two ships already on the Narva route and a lot of seamen and deckhands as well . . ."

On the Narva route . . . Balthasar might have said that his father, too, had met misfortune on the Narva route – losing not a ship but a farmhand, one who had been like an older brother to him, Balthasar. But he said nothing, merely inhaling the juniper-berry fragrance of his gin. And when the Englishman to the right of Schiedam started up a conversation in a barely comprehensible language, Balthasar thought to himself: *this is the hall where Bailiff Schnellenberg held his ceremonial gathering at the end of last January.* He stood up – with all the activity and changing of seats going on he attracted no attention – and glanced into a couple of small side rooms that opened onto the great hall. In one hung the image that someone had been talking about a short while earlier. It was apparently the copy that the *voevoda* had commissioned of the icon of St Nicholas, reputed to be endowed with miraculous powers, the very one that had withstood the flames in the great fire of Narva and had later been transported in a ceremonial procession from Narva to Moscow. Balthasar recognised the room because of the image. For he remembered from his father's story that an icon had been hanging here then, as well. Of course, not a Russian but a Catholic icon. But the room was definitely the same, of that Balthasar was certain: here, on these hexagonal limestone floor tiles, old Siimon Rissa had once stood. And Herr Schnellenberg had stood here, shouting at his father and threatening to clap him in irons – maybe right here, where Balthasar was now standing. The small lamp in front of the icon left the room in semi-darkness; only the saint's dark silhouette against the full-moonlike halo of gold leaf was clearly visible, and the shadows of the three chains of the hanging lamp divided the floor into four sections. Balthasar stared intently at the grey hexagonal tiles. Of course, even by daylight the prints of his father's sealskin boots would no longer have been visible. Yet they had been here. Without a doubt. Large. Snowy. Only slightly wider at the toes than at the heels. The old man's tracks – he would always put each foot down as though he were carrying a five-pood weight on his shoulders . . . Behind him Balthasar heard the flow of the revellers' talk, which, after the *voevoda*'s son had finished his song, was newly animated:

"For hauling a pood of cargo from Narva to Novgorod – you get three kopecks in winter, five in summer . . ."

"But from Novgorod to Moscow – nine in winter, and a good thirty in summer."

"And you know: there'll be no merrymaking without Fedor Basmanov."

And then a clear male voice rose above the flow of talk and left a name suspended in air: "Katharina . . ."

Of course, of course, it was Herr Kruse's pulpit baritone, dissolving immediately into his own laughter, and the person he was referring to was his honourable wife, née Tisenhusen, at that very moment no doubt asleep in the stone house – the gift from the Gracious Emperor – next to the Kremlin. Nevertheless, the sound of that name added a feather's weight to the burden which had imperceptibly been accumulating on the lever of Balthasar's decision-making apparatus. A feather's weight . . .

It was still dark when he and Herr Melchior, led by a guard sent to guide them by torchlight, trotted back to Rüütli Street early next morning. Herr Melchior lit the candles in the great-room.

"You see," he said – all at once adopting the familiar "you" – "I have to take part in this kind of merrymaking camaraderie several times a week . . ." Balthasar noticed that he looked tired and bored, and that he was a bit drunk in spite of himself. Balthasar, however, came right to the point.

"Herr Melchior, a few words before you go to bed."

"I – ?" He yawned. "Aren't you going to bed too . . . ?"

"I would like to request your help with something."

"Certainly, certainly, of course . . . anything at all . . . But at dinner-time."

"No. I'm requesting it now."

"Well? What is it you want?"

"I will not go back to Stettin on the *Seejunkfer*. I want to go to Tallinn first."

Herr Melchior was planning to say: My dear boy, that is a rash and foolish idea. In times like these! It's not much safer this side of Rakvere than it is on the other side. But on that side – you've heard, haven't you – it's all turmoil, and chaos! But he only looked at Balthasar in surprise, his weariness dispelled by the boy's words, and noticed Balthasar's compressed lips and the line on his forehead between his two wheat-coloured eyebrows, before he spoke:

"So that's how it is? I'll get you a permit from the *voevoda* as far as Rakvere. If you watch what you say – on the road, and in general, and also with regard to my name. Unless you change your mind by morning. Which I would advise you to do. Let's go to bed now."

"I've thought over all the possibilities," Balthasar said. "Given the present situation, it would be simplest to go on foot, close to the main road, but keeping out of sight and dressed as a peasant."

"Every soldier of the *voevoda* or Grand Master could spear you if he wished. And beyond Rakvere, any of the rabble, as well."

"I'll need a little luck. And I must have peasant clothes. That's what I'm asking you for."

"Me? For peasant clothes?"

"I don't dare go looking for them in town. It would attract too much attention. They'd wonder what a fellow from Stettin was doing west of Narva, wandering about in peasant clothes."

"Hmm . . ." Herr Melchior said, "and where am I supposed to get these clothes for you?"

"You could ask your servants to get them. Maybe you can even find some in your house. I think that the journey I undertook to get to you has earned me an old rag of a coat and a hat and a pair of stinking bast shoes!"

Herr Melchior did not attempt to dispute this – that can be said for him. And the sun had not quite risen, having barely burnished the pale October sky above the Joala forest, when a broad-shouldered young peasant walked out through the Karja Gate, wearing an old coat, linen trousers, a faded slouch hat on his dishevelled hair, and bast shoes on his feet. Twice he stopped, turned around, and looked back. The first time was in front of the gate, when he had passed three or four wagons on their way to market and had just emerged onto the muddy open road. He looked at the stone shield with its carved coat of arms above the gate. It was evident from the inscription that it had been positioned there some time ago, when he was just an eleven-year-old boy. He looked at the fish on the town's coat of arms and the roses, and the helmet with its cross and visor, and then at the bearded wood-carver pushing his cart full of wooden mugs and bowls and spoons from the ruins of the settlement outside the walls to the wide road leading through the gates. And he saw that, for some reason, the wood-carver crossed himself as he passed between the gate towers. The young peasant turned around a second time when he had passed the weedy, overgrown ruins and the new shacks that had sprung up between them, and the garden plots with their wet, bluish heads of blossoming cabbage, and had reached the place where the road he had been following through a many-hued alder grove curved and entered a dark forest of firs.

When he now turned and looked back he could see the whole town against the grey dawn. The round towers at the southwest and northeast corners of the wall, where the ground sloped down to the river below, rose up like two giant, cone-shaped, dark-grey stone heads, with the arrow-slits like sleepy eyes in their flat faces. From one round tower to the next snaked a crenellated wall – with cone-shaped towers at each corner and to either side of the town gate – encircling like a stone belt the jumble of houses and roofs within. To the right of two church steeples, and towering above the gabled roofs, rose the dark west wall of the castle and the Hermann Tower above it, looking like a strong-man's square, headless neck on top of a strongman's square shoulders, set against a lustrous silvery sky, shimmering like a sheet of hammered steel.

The peasant's light-grey, probing eyes studied the town and he listened for a while to the persistent yet scarcely audible roar floating over the level ground from the invisible river to these woods, as though it were the sound of the grey sky itself. Then he turned and set out towards the northwest and disappeared into the yellow birch grove and red-brown alder thicket, as though he had never been there.

CHAPTER FOUR,

in which a young man, whose comings and goings and the reasons behind them we are attempting to pursue and explain to the best of our ability, concludes that, here and now, he is about to land amidst a greater fury of devastation than anything else life will ever devise for him; in which conviction he errs, in one respect, even more than the young usually err in such rash predictions (for although they have barely tasted of life, they are ready to draw conclusions, make deductions, and pronounce judgements, instead of taking the trouble to find out, patiently, exactly what God has in reserve for us at the bottom of our cup); in another respect, however, this young man is perhaps right after all, for he will not, in fact, ever again participate in events as astonishing or remarkable as these.

Arriving at a destination at the right time could just as well, from a different standpoint, mean arriving at the wrong time. To arrive at the right time presupposes dozens of timely departures beforehand – or, on the contrary, untimely departures, should the arrival turn out to be inopportune.

And yet when, on the fifth day of his journey, Balthasar abruptly turned left off the big Tallinn road and continued along a barely visible footpath through a brown-mottled coppice of autumn alders, as it wound towards the south on the other side of the Jägala Bridge, it was not clear to anyone, except perhaps to God, whether taking that turn would ultimately be judged right or wrong in His eyes.

Even for Balthasar himself, his journey to Tallinn was in fact an unplanned detour, one he had decided to make at a moment when a clamour of inner voices had overpowered the voice of ratio, and he could no longer determine which of the blowing horns was sounding loudest – the megaphone of curiosity, or the dark, hollow horn of home-sickness, or the red penny whistle of sinful lust played by the devil of desire and vanity . . . Indeed, perhaps it was not our merciful Lord God, but the squint-eyed, foul-mouthed Evil One who had guarded and watched over Balthasar like a father all these four days of his journey to Tallinn. He had no trouble along the way at all, walking at times along the road, at times in the brush alongside it, with copper-striped, pale-grey sunrises at his back, and red-streaked, dark-grey sunsets before his face.

He had travelled over the open lands of Laagna, passing not only ruins but also occasional new cabins in the middle of small plots of autumnal farmland. He had been lying on his stomach near the Blue Hills of Vaivara, in a thicket of firs by the side of the road, when a regi-ment of a hundred bearded soldiers of the Grand Duke galloped by, spraying mud left and right as they thundered towards the west. They had onion-shaped steel helmets on their heads and stubby, knobbed crossbows across their shoulders. Their commander was even wearing chain mail. Balthasar had made a detour, just in case, through the brush and around the recently burnt-out village of Türsamäe. He had crossed the empty bridge over the Pühajõgi at dusk on his first day of travel. Its curved stone arches destroyed, the bridge had been patched by fresh pine logs and could only just be traversed. He had found an abandoned, partly charred house a short way into the woods, and the gurgling sound of water led him to a nearby spring. He had drunk with hands cupped and gnawed the unleavened barley bread and venison thigh that Melchior had packed for him. He had given thanks to God for his trouble-free journey and spent the night in the charred farmhouse, sleeping fairly comfortably, for inside the threshing barn was relatively dry straw that had escaped the fire. Before dawn he had washed his face in the spring, said his morning prayer, eaten a little, and set out again. He had considered the northern coastal road not only shorter but safer than the main road leading to Jõhvi, and at first break of day had come out on the limestone cliffs high above the sea, where he stopped to look at the view and had felt, with deep pleasure and a touch of fear, a chill in his stomach at the great height and the vast distances before him, and maybe also at the memory of something he vaguely recalled as significant. For this vertical limestone cliff – he had dared to venture to its very edge – was truly three times as high as the steep banks along the River Oder, and perhaps even a little higher than the stone section of St Olaf's steeple below its metal spire, and the impression of height from the cliff was incalculably more powerful. For directly below was the sea, spreading out from the pebbled shoreline and beyond its foamy rim; and the sea under the iron-grey dawn sky was not only awfully far below him but extended all the way to the horizon, and was itself, between the wisps of early morning fog, nearly black. Balthasar had paused there, on the northern edge of Livonia, and in his breast, growing alternately cold and warm, half sensed an odd feeling of having arrived at a brink and needing to plunge in again. He had looked towards the west, his eyes following the coast to where it turned north for a bit, and where, five or six miles away, the harbour of Kaupsaare Island would be. And he had thought: Five or six more leagues to the west of Kaupsaare Island lies the castle of Toolse, which the Order considers its northernmost stronghold, and Toolse, too, is said to be in the hands of the Grand Duke . . .

He had journeyed all morning along the road, at times right along the edge of the cliff, and here had exchanged the first words of his trip with some peasants, four men from the village of Saka who had crossed the road ahead of him, oars on their shoulders and bundled nets on their backs, starting their descent along a barely visible stepped trail down the steep bank to the shore. Balthasar had looked at them and decided that these scraggy, anxious-looking villagers would do him no harm. And he called out: "Halloo! God be with you!" The men started as they turned towards him, apparently prepared to bolt down the cliff path like goats, but remained where they were when they saw that the stranger was alone and had no weapon other than his bundle on a stick over his shoulder. He went closer to the men and addressed them from the edge of the cliff above them, and then carefully made the treacherous descent to where they waited, and talked with them for a while. After a time they climbed down ten more fathoms and sat on a promontory which was still ten fathoms above the tops of the fir trees that rose from the shore. One word had led to another, replies had followed upon questions, and he got the men to tell him, albeit laconically, of events over the past year: of the way the war had twice swept over them, of the burning of estates and villages and churches, of manor lords fleeing and peasants scattering into the woods and then returning to their villages. And of some landlords who had stayed put and were held in great esteem by the Russians. Like Herr Rens at Edise, who, under the new master, had started to persecute the peasants much more cruelly than before, and had been killed by his own peasants, for which the entire parish had had to pay the Narva *voevoda* a fine of three shillings per soul. There, high above the sea, under a grey midday sky, and just a step away from dizzying emptiness, the Saka men related to Balthasar how last year privateers from Tallinn had plundered the northern villages as far out as Narva. Even here, on the coast of Saka, seamen from the privateers had come ashore, shooting off their hackbuts and burning down farmhouses and emptying out storage sheds. The men of Saka told him: "We're now paying the *voevoda* of Narva a tithe on fish and grain and, on top of that the Tallinners are plundering us . . ." Balthasar asked if they had actually come in their big ships, and the men of Saka replied: "Oh no . . . they came in those clumsy open barges that the folks at

Kaupsaare call 'lighters'." And Balthasar had thought: If Märten was with the privateers at that time, then, in any case, he did not come here . . .

But these villagers did not know much about the big uprisings and rebellions said to be taking place towards the west, in Harju and Haapsalu. All they had heard was a rumour a few days earlier about an interpreter from Rakvere, working for Russian commanders, who had apparently told the men of Purtse, on his way to Narva, that the peasants of the Order had risen and elected their own king, and then had asked if the men around here did not want to go and help them out . . . The Saka men also told Balthasar about a group of Russian soldiers in Purtse, quartered in an unfinished manor owned by the Masters Taube. And so Balthasar had avoided the village, making a wide detour to the north through the woods, and fairly close to the mouth of the river he had found a canoe and with the help of a pole had managed to punt across. Then he had walked through the partly razed village of Kestla and moved towards St Nicholas' Church. But meanwhile darkness had fallen, and near the village of Raudna he had spent the night in a haystack, not arriving at the church until mid-morning the next day. And already from a distance he had seen with dismay that after the recent war there was nothing left of the church but smoke-blackened walls. Again he took the northern fork in the road so as to pass far to the north of the town of Rakvere – or actually, as he had heard tell, the castle and the ruins of the town. And since the men of Pada village had advised him to avoid even this route, he had travelled entirely on side trails through great swamps and barren wilderness, and slightly north of Kohala crossed the River Sämi. In Haljala the *köster* of the scorched church of Saint Mauritius offered him lodging for the night, but not a crumb of news. The pastor himself had escaped to Tallinn a few weeks earlier, in fear of Russians and manor men and peasants, and the *köster*, looking like a starved badger, had stayed at his post from both a sense

390

of duty and the fear of hellfire. Labouring as he was under the awful burden of his many-layered fear, he remained silent when confronted with the suspicious questions of this stranger. After Haljala, Balthasar had plunged into the boundless fir forests of the Viru plains, which, from the perspective of Narva, were the beginning of the no-man's-land beyond Rakvere. He had lingered there, in hazelnut groves along the road, filling his hungry belly and empty sack with delicious, ripe nuts. And here, near the Loobu Mill, he had suddenly come upon the first signs of violent battle: in front of the mill stood a dozen horses, some with leather saddles, others with wooden ones, but there were no wagons or wagonloads of grain, only a dozen peasants moving around, armed with most curious weapons. For, in the course of the past fifty years, during which peasants had been forbidden to bear arms, their weapons had not disappeared from the corners of their storehouses and haylofts. Furthermore, at the outbreak of the present war, and in contradiction of the old prohibition, Herr Fürstenberg had, in order to swell the Order's forces, arranged for peasant units to be formed and supplied with weapons which, though few and shabby, were better than nothing. And now the long, colourful history of these arms was on display in the hands or on the hips of the band of peasants, or propped against the wall of the mill: two halberds, only slightly rusted, three swords made by the village blacksmith at the time of their forefathers, a sickle fastened to the top of a stake, wood-chopping axes and a time-blackened club with iron spikes dug up from somewhere or the other. Balthasar had hesitated for a moment in the bushes, for the peasants were sufficiently threatening, armed as they were. But then a great gust of curiosity filled the sail of his confidence, and emerging from the shrubbery he approached the men. They were not particularly alarmed at his appearance – what harm could an unarmed youth do them? Might he be a spy for the Order? Hardly – not after what had happened right here, in Viru, when the peasants who had brought news to the Order's forces about the activities of the Muscovites were later hanged by command of the Order Masters themselves, fearful that they might be leading the Order's army into a trap. Could he be a Muscovite spy? . . . So what . . . what harm could he do? A chance wanderer? Not a problem . . . they were everywhere these days. Let him come along . . . The boy posed no danger to them. And consequently neither did they to him. The sheer urge to kill, so rampant now, and which was driving mercenaries to violence, was simply absent in the peasants. So Balthasar had walked up to the men and surveyed their sun-browned, unshaven faces, their angry or weary or childishly brash eyes, their jerkins, their shapeless floppy hats, their heelless peasant footwear. He noted that one man had his head bandaged and was wearing mercenary soldier's fine boots – the kind no-one would have surrendered voluntarily. Greeting them, Balthasar struck up a conversation and learned that some hailed from right here in Haljala, others from the villages of Ilumäe, and that they were on their way to . . .

"Where?"

"Over there, to the southwest . . ."

"Aha . . . And what for?"

"Well, to war, of course! Can't you see for yourself? What cloud have you just dropped down from? Didn't you come to join us?"

And the young man with the bandaged head, who seemed to be the leader – they had called him Vatku Vilbo – said: "I thought you were from somewhere near Tõrma. Day before yesterday word reached there, too, that . . ." Balthasar answered: "No. I'm from the village of Kurgla, near the Harju-Jaani church, if you've heard of the place." One of the men remarked: "Then you're a man from the middle o' Order country – wouldn't be no-one that'd want to fight 'gainst the masters more'n you." Another said: "Well, that settles it. We just happen t' have an extra horse." Perhaps Balthasar even closed his eyes for an instant to digest this unexpected suggestion, and heard the water fall over the mill dam and the horses crunch their feed and stamp in the dry alder leaves and one of the peasants sharpen the blade of his spear on a grindstone. It is possible that he thought: That would mean . . . not being home by dinner tomorrow, not seeing the farmhouses of Kalamaja and the walls of Tallinn, or Father, Annika, Meus, Kimmelpenning – none of them. It would mean no possibility – even indirectly – of getting near Katharina . . . Balthasar opened his eyes to shake his head: "No . . . I have to be in Kurgla by dinnertime tomorrow afternoon . . . I'm joining up with our villagers there . . ." The men said: "Well then, God go with you!" And Balthasar answered: "And with you."

He had continued on through the village of Vahastu, and the men there related how the Muscovites had passed through a few months earlier, on their way from Rakvere, laying waste to the Kolga estate, which the Danish king somehow considered his property. Afterwards Balthasar had continued walking until evening, and, with darkness falling, had spent the night in a ramshackle boathouse near the Kahala lake – fortunately the threat of rain had dissipated after a mere peppering of the rotten bulrush roof. In the morning he filled his growling stomach with nuts, thanked God for everything thus far, and prayed for one more day of easy travel. He hurried on towards Tallinn in a bitterly cold and thick fog, passing a church razed to the ground at Kuusalu, the castle of Kiiu in ruins, the half-abandoned villages of Valkla and Kaberla. And then he had suddenly decided . . .

Perhaps someone more insightful than Balthasar, or capable of looking with greater objectivity into human hearts, would have smiled a knowing smile and said: By no means did he turn off the road to Tallinn and head towards Kurgla merely because at the Loobu Mill he had claimed – casually and in passing and constrained by the circumstances – that that's where he was heading. No, he went to Kurgla because he so very much wanted to get to Tallinn. And his eagerness to reach the town was intense not only because of the obstacles he might encounter as a

393

traveller at this time of uncertainty and confusion, but even more perhaps, because of those he had to overcome in himself . . . Heavens: Katharina's name not only set off fireworks of passion and desire and tenderness and sympathy in Balthasar's ardent mind, it also summoned up many unpleasant sensations, even a rush of deep contempt – though perhaps one born of jealousy. And perhaps someone capable of seeing truly deeply into Balthasar would have recognised something else too behind his oddly sudden reluctance to continue on to Tallinn. This insightful soul might have ventured to say that, in this grey October fog, behind the wet junipers and the lobed brown leaves of alders, between the paw-like clusters of pine needles, Bal saw Epp's shining eyes: dead-earnest, glowing with the candlelight of last year's christening ceremony. In any event, it seemed to Balthasar suddenly worse than unacceptable that, having come over thirty leagues from Narva, he should simply forge ahead past Kurgla, a mere league distant . . .

When he arrived at the fields of Kurgla he became aware of the secret apprehension that had been smouldering beneath the surface of his thoughts, acknowledging it only when he was freed of it: Thank God the farmhouses here are still standing and their roofs are still intact! But when he walked into Jakob's farmyard, he had to rub his eyes. It seemed that the group of men he had met at Loobu Mill had somehow passed him, who knows when or where, and, having doubled in number, arrived here ahead of him, at Jakob's door . . . Uncle Jakob, standing at the well, stared incredulously at him for a long moment and finally called out, hoarsely: "In the name of God! Bal! Is it your ghost or is it really you?" Only then did Balthasar manage to shake himself free of the illusion, realising that the entire village of Kurgla had gathered here, in Uncle Jakob's farmyard and in his house. Just like the ones at Loobu, the men here were armed for battle – Jakob himself and Jürgen and Paavel. There were Küti-Jaan with his farmhand, and the two farmers of Pärtli with their sons and farmhands, and some men he did not know, probably from Antla and even further away, and women of all ages, and young wives – among them Epp with her two-year-old – and several others, with little ones trailing behind them, altogether an assembly of more than twenty-five. A dozen horses stood saddled. Four were hitched to loaded wagons in front of the storage shed.

"What's happening here?" Balthasar asked.

"See for yourself – we're going off to war," Jakob said darkly.

"Going to war? . . . The entire village? With all the women?"

"What choice do we have?" Jakob said, agitated. "The women and children are going into hiding, and the men into the peasant force. We killed Herr Hasse and his brother this morning at Raasiku."

"You?! Who?!"

"Just who and how many were involved in the attack – no-one will look into that. But their souls have departed. His nephew got away, along with a friend of his, a monk from Padise who happened to be visiting the manor. They took off for Tallinn and promised to return immediately with the mercenaries from Toompea and level the murderers' villages – starting with Kurgla."

Balthasar tried to explain that there was no need to fear revenge or interference from the town authorities in such a matter, and especially not at a chaotic time like this. But it seemed that the men of Kurgla were better informed. True enough, the town authorities would not lift a finger. But the head of the Order's forces in Toompea, Herr Plaate, or "Coat-of-mail-Joachim" as he was called, had lately been a frequent drinking companion of Herr Hasse's and had often come to Raasiku to carouse with the overseers and the magistrate. And Herr Hasse's brother was in fact one of his overseers. Consequently . . . The men had, in effect, already decided what to do: the women and children would be taken directly into the great Soesoo Marsh, to the island of Hongasaare, a league and a half south of Kurgla, where they had sheltered on previous similar occasions. The herders had already left mid-morning with the farm animals, which moved slower than cargo horses and people on foot. And the men? They would ride towards Kangla and Limu and Nabala. They would send scouts ahead and keep moving towards the southwest. That was where the forces of the peasant king were gathering.

"Listen," Balthasar said, when he had followed Uncle Jakob into the house and looked around, taken aback at the barren room stripped of the little it had held in the way of utensils and clothing. Uncle Jakob gathered up the last sheepskins from the top of the stove, to take them out to the wagon. "Listen, Uncle Jakob, how has this come about . . . this king of the peasants? I heard about him in Narva . . . Is there really such a person?"

"And why not?" Jakob muttered. "He was elected and he exists. It's not the first time. Never mind that six or seven generations have passed since the last one." He stopped in the entryway and turned towards Balthasar:

"So you've really come from Narva . . . ?"

"That's right."

"From Germany to Narva and . . ."

"Uh-huh."

"And from here you're going on to Tallinn?"

"That's where I'm headed."

"Right . . ." Jakob turned again and stepped out, carrying the sheepskins under his arm. He walked across the yard, its chamomile and ribgrass trampled to mud by many feet, and Balthasar followed him. Halfway to the wagons, near the limestone well, he stopped and turned again towards Balthasar. Looking him straight in the eye – and Balthasar saw this was not the look of that other time, years ago, when Jakob had not dared tell him just how happy he would be if Balthasar were to accompany him to the manor – he said:

"But I was so glad to think that you'd arrived in Tallinn and then come here, to the country, and would now be joining us." And the stubble of beard that, three years earlier, had brightened when Balthasar offered to accompany him to the manor, remained dull and iron-grey. He said, looking past Balthasar:

"But of course. The peasant uprising is not your concern." Balthasar was startled by Jakob's abrupt verdict. He had become accustomed to viewing his peasant uncle as mild and circumspect, as someone with a quietly growing respect for a nephew who was becoming more of a town boy with each passing year – perhaps even an excessive respect for a callow stripling like him. But was there not now a hostile tone to his words, of someone angry with himself because of how small, how limited, his rights were compared with those of the larger world, of someone furiously insisting upon those small, limited rights . . . Of course here, now, something unforeseeable was afoot, and Jakob must feel that events had pushed him into a critical position . . . It was no doubt the immediate crisis that made his eyes hard and his words curt . . . But the words themselves – were they true, or not? The peasant uprising is not your concern . . .

At this point Balthasar reached a decision.

Had anyone later wanted to analyse Bal's motives and lay out a sequence behind his decision, and had he himself not taken such pains to forget how the matter had proceeded, his deliberations might have gone something like this:

Primo. It would have been easier for him to say no, had Jakob simply asked him to go with them, instead of declaring: "You, won't becoming with us, of course."

Secundo. To an extent, whether because of the emergency at hand or his sense of shame or sheer foolishness, the peasants' uprising did concern him – if for no other reason than that it concerned all his kin at Kurgla. And what then, after all, was he doing in this farmyard at Kurgla, at this moment – why had God sent him here – or was it actually the Devil?! – if none of this concerned him?

Tertio. It would be truly interesting to be part of it, to get to know, to understand what was actually happening here. What did they want? What did they hope for? And who and where was this chimerical king of theirs?

"But Jakob, do you know anything about Father and our people in town?"

"I went to Siimon's last week."

Quarto. What if he were to get into the saddle and ride along with Jakob, just for a league or two? His uncle might then be able quickly to tell him what he had heard at Kalamaja.

Balthasar's eyes swept close over the farmyard, registering everything, imprinting his mind with an unforgettable scene: the way the master of Vana-Pärtli farm, a man with a broad, strong back, tightened the harness on his horse; the way a young mother tried to calm a crying infant at her breast; the way Küti-Jaan looked askance at him and then recognised him, his face brightening as he recalled, no doubt, the last day they had been together at Lammassaare, making the clearing . . . Balthasar remembered it too. And then his glance glided over Paavel's flat face, and . . .

Quinto . . . He was looking straight at Epp. And Epp was looking at him, even as she was restraining – what was his name – that tubby little fellow, Tiidrik, from the stomping hoofs of the sorrel. At that very moment Jakob said – Lord, why did you make him say it just at that moment – or was it the Devil again? – "Paavel, take a horse and ride over to Pening and tell them we're setting off now. And bring the men along, to join us in Kangla."

Balthasar turned his eyes from Epp's to Jakob's and asked:

"Do you have a nag for me?"

They were the very words he had uttered three years ago, when they had set off together to seek help from Herr Antonius against Hasse.

"I do," Jakob said, his voice nearly booming – even though he did not really know to whom they could turn for help this time round. Even though he understood even less clearly than Balthasar could imagine just how great was the power of the forces that they, in their incomprehension, had decided to confront.

The women sat atop the loads in the wagons or on the rumps of the horses, behind their husbands. The girls walked alongside and the men rode a little ahead of the wagon train. One here, another there, looked quickly, silently over their shoulders, until the dark-brown alder leaves and young fir woods hid from view the farmhouses perplexed by their own emptiness.

Balthasar pulled up his grey mare alongside Uncle Jakob so that he could learn right away the news from Tallinn. Yes, Siimon's health was getting worse all the time, but he himself had merely said: "It's the right time for it to be going downhill . . . it's two years already that the cargo-hauling business has been in a slump in town, and the long transport trips have become impossible – on account of all the robbing and rioting in general . . ." Otherwise things in Kalamaja had been same as usual just a week ago. Ah, Annika? And Meus? . . . Good Lord, had Balthasar not heard, then? Meus . . . Meus had been under the sod since the autumn of last year! Yes – at the beginning of November, with the first frosts, the plague had returned once more to bare its teeth at Tallinn . . . though not too fiercely this time. It had only taken twenty or thirty souls. No, it had not touched Annika, thank God, and she was still living in the apartment at the edge of the Old Market, with the housemaid, Piret, the same one who had been there last . . .

Balthasar felt his throat constrict with grief. The fateful words sounded only half-real, sliding over his consciousness like the brown and yellow autumn branches overhead, wet with fog, touching his face . . . My God, Meus, beneath the sod . . . A third, if not more, of his initial eagerness to go to Tallinn, deflected now though still present, fell aground into the mud, like the wet leaves that the treetops tossed down with the misty rain onto the travellers and their horses. Meus beneath the sod . . . and his debt of gratitude to go unpaid . . . never to be repaid . . . Meus' kindness never to be repaid! His debt had secretly weighed on him every time he closed his eyes, and in the brown twilight behind his closed lids saw Meus, his eyes full of benevolence and worry, wishing him well . . . All in all: debts, trespasses – unpaid, unredeemed . . . And now, this sudden, strange journey to the Soesoo Marsh and into unimaginable dangers . . . these fleeing women, their wagonloads of belongings, the men of Kurgla and Antla, some with hog-butchering knives stuck into their belts, three of the twelve with swords from their great-grandfathers' time wrapped in strips of bast and secured at their hips by a piece of rope . . . Debts . . . Whose debts do they plan to pay with these swords, and before whom . . . ? And who would become the new debtors – with debts so large that they could never be repaid, or so small – worth mere shillings – that human hearts would not even be aware of them amidst the detritus of daily life, but which would be noted, all the same, in God's great account book?

Balthasar held back his grey mare, letting Uncle Jakob ride on ahead, and waited for Aunt Kati's wagon, where Epp was sitting with Tiidrik. The sight of Epp gladdened him, warmed him: even as everything in this land seemed to be changing, its people becoming more worn down, its buildings more shabby, its woods more spare and grey despite the autumn, Epp was exactly as she had been three years ago. As though this fearful time of troubles had simply passed over her small rosy face and shining grey eyes and left them untouched. He looked at her and tried to find words that would not add to his burden of debt, but sensing there were no such words he remained silent. Epp turned and looked him in the eye and asked:

"How – precisely at a moment like this – did you happen to . . . ?"

Balthasar felt that the only way he could perhaps repay a shilling's worth of his debt was to maintain, at this hour when nothing was ordinary, a calm, encouraging, confident mien – even if it was largely pretence. He said:

"Right. Exactly at the right moment – can't even imagine a more timely moment. I get to meet all my people – and see you and your little boy too. Who knows when there'll be another chance."

Epp seemed to smile at him, but maybe it was not a smile – it seemed to tell him that, in some unaccountable way, his words had simply increased his debt. "Well, we'll talk more later," he said, although he did not know about what. Waving to her and Aunt Kati and serious little Tiidrik, he dug his heels into the horse's flanks.

"Tell me what actually happened with Herr Hasse. And what is going on here in Mary's Land in general," he said to his uncle when his grey mare had caught up with Jakob's dapple-grey. Over the time it took to travel the remaining league to the marshland, Balthasar heard the whole story. Briefly but clearly. Everything that Jakob knew. And in fact Jakob knew exactly what had happened with Hasse. Early that morning, Hasse had commanded the men of Kurgla and Antla to assemble at the manor, where he had issued his orders: on the day following, every farm was to deliver to the manor two sacks of oats per ploughland – for war horses! And every peasant was to bring him, in the course of the week to come, payment in the form of money or provisions, to be delivered to Tallinn. And he would specify by name the peasants who were to pay a mark, or a mark and a half, or two marks – for protection! The men had been standing there, some with their farmhands, so that they comprised a group of fifteen or sixteen in front of the steward's house, and Hasse was on the steps, holding, for some reason, a whip. And then, all of a sudden, Jakob had opened his mouth. Opened it he had, yes, and who knows why . . . Probably because, a few days earlier at Siimon's, he had heard of rumours simmering amongst travelling pedlars . . . Strange tales of runaway serfs and other landless folk banding together in a various places. And about peasants near Pääsküla village who had apparently robbed and killed a group of high-born travellers from Riga. And about manor lords who had already returned to their estates after the departure of the last plundering bands of Muscovites, and had now mostly fled back to Tallinn from West and South Harju – in fear of the peasants. For in those regions the villages were in ferment, and the rumblings were growing louder: It's time to kill the masters, once and for all . . . That was probably why, yes, and also because these stories had been heard before in the village, and because Jakob had discussed them in the last couple of days over beers at the Michaelmas lamb-roast, with many of the men standing beside him this very morning, at the steward's door. Yet he had certainly had no intention there, at Hasse's entrance, of stirring up talk of killing anyone! He had simply asked what kind of warhorses they were supposed to be providing oats for, since he had not seen a single warhorse belonging to the Order from the time the war had begun . . . And what kind of protection fee was it when the only protectors they had seen in the villages were the Order's mercenaries out to rob the peasants of their sheep . . . At this a general muttering had started up among the men, and they had begun yelling and jeering louder and louder – it was like nothing ever heard before. They had started shouting: "Yeah – what kind o' protection fee is it anyway? Ha-ha-ha-hah! It's whorin' money for the Order Masters! We're not about to pay for that!" And so on . . . And then Master Hasse had lashed one of the farmers standing near him – from Antla, he was – across the face with his whip. But the man, grabbing hold of the whip handle, had tried to pull it out of Hasse's hands. Watching them both struggling to get hold of the whip, some of the men had burst out laughing. But then someone had thrown a rock at Hasse, who had let go of his whip, taken a step back, and from under his coat had pulled out – you know, one of those pistols with short muzzles, like the ones mercenaries in town sometimes wear in their belts. He had fumbled with it a bit and finally managed to shoot it, the lead piercing Kurgla-Jaak's farmhand in his left shoulder. Strangely, Herr Hasse was the only one unnerved by his shot – maybe because that pistol, or whatever you call it, cannot deliver a second round. By now the men were fired up and emboldened and full of rage. The farmhand was standing in their midst, groaning, his shoulder bleeding, when someone grabbed the pitchfork he had dropped – some of the farmhands had come with pitchforks and God willed that this one be iron-tined – and plunged it with such furious force into Hasse's stomach that the man was pinned right into the doorpost of his house. Had Hasse's brother – the foreman who had come for a visit to Raasiku from Tallinn – arrived even just a little later, there would have been time for the shock of their act to sink in and sober the men up, and the whole fracas might have ended with just one killing. But this brother, hearing voices and the shot and the blows and Hasse's screams, had rushed out just then, and someone had swung a muddy axe at his bald head . . . And only when the windows of the steward's house had been broken and Hasse finally killed at his doorpost and the straw roof of the house set on fire – all this had happened as if in a dream – had Hasse's nephew and a monk from Padise jumped out of a back window and into the garden. Sprinting to their horses, they had fled to Tallinn. The peasants had emptied the burning house of its best items. They had picked up Herr Hasse's pistol from the steps and taken it with them. Of the men in charge of running the manor, neither the taskmaster nor the foreman had shown so much as his shadow. The peasants had pulled open the barn doors and let the herd out; they had taken six horses from the stable and proclaimed to the four or five farmhands just arriving with several loads of hay at the barn that the will of the peasants now ruled in the countryside; and then they had hastened from the manor . . .

Now they were at the edge of Soesoo Marsh, a league-wide expanse of scrubby pines and scattered pools. Küti-Jaan rode ahead of the band of refugees, and for a quarter of a league they moved along an ever more uneven and barren bog that gave way under each step as they travelled over its dips and depressions; and then they stopped and crowded together between marsh plants and pine stumps at the edge of wide brown water. Küti-Jaan urged his horse into the rusty bog up to its chest and they proceeded cautiously, now a little to the left, now to the right. Then the horse found the submerged old log road and Küti-Jaan let him move forward, testing the road a step at a time. At first the water reached the horse's knees but then came up to his chest once more. He was jittery, moving slowly between the islands of peat with their floating clumps of broken roots, making unexpected turns in a diagonal path across the lake. Some of the men had jumped into the water before and behind the wagons, to steady them as they swayed and rocked along the sunken road of upright stumps hundreds of years old, keeping close behind Küti-Jaan's horse. A couple of men walking behind the wagons were leading horses tied head to tail – skittish and snorting, sensing the men's nervousness – on the precarious path through the rust-brown water. About a quarter of a league on the road turned towards a rocky rise, dense with young firs and pines, and the wagon train rolled onto the firm ground of Hongasaare Island. Behind the cover of young firs they found the walls of a former marsh fortress built of limestone slabs. The men, wet to their thighs, set immediately to work helping the women. Firs and pines of a suitable size growing within the enclosure were cut; slabs of limestone were prised out of the old wall; in a matter of a few hours they had built four huts from branches and rock. They tried to make them as tight as possible, for no-one knew how long those hiding on the island would have to live in them, and snow could fall any day now. Something else as well may have spurred them on to finish the huts so quickly: there were rocky remains of other structures in the grassy hollow between the walls, and it was not clear how long they had been awaiting new builders to complete the job.

Like a goose-herd wielding a long pole, Küti-Jaan's mother, as old as the earth, was watching over seven or eight toddlers in the middle of the old walled enclosure, keeping them together lest they wander off and get lost in the thicket or toddle off to drown in the swamp. Everyone whose hands and legs could function at all was busy building shelters. Balthasar, of course, was working alongside Jakob, Jürgen, Aunt Kati, and Epp. Jakob and Jürgen spoke only when it was absolutely necessary to the job at hand. But Aunt Kati talked of other things as well. When Balthasar prised a large moss-covered stone slab off the wall and hauled it across the wet grass, Aunt Kati said, pressing sod between the slabs: "I said to myself when you stepped into the yard today: He may've put on peasant clothes, but there's no way he'll be riding out with our folk to this war . . . But see now, all those books and the air of Germany haven't got into your bones at all . . ."

Balthasar, to tell the truth, was a little disconcerted that his newly acquired education was so easily dismissed as being, at its core, of no consequence. But on some deeper level he was glad – even if he did feel like a heretic of sorts – that their inmost bond was still strong and that this village woman, with her childlike acuity, accepted him as one of them, audibly moreover, and within earshot of Epp. He carried a new slab of limestone across the grass and thought: A good thing it is that there are still earth-gods . . . After all, no-one could take away from him his trivium schooling or German and Latin languages, or his distinction as a student. But that pale-eyed old woman could have excluded him from this world of straw-roofed shacks of mud and branches, cut him off from this world of earth-gods; she could have refused to accept him as one of them. In spite of his sloshing bast shoes and soggy hose he felt such a surge of good feeling that he did not stop to consider any longer how his words might add to his burden of debt. He looked at Epp through the fir branches they were piling onto the stripped branches that served as rafters – he looked at her and asked:

"Epp, do you still remember the day we prepared the field at Lammassaare?"

She looked at him through the dark fingers of fir, her face flushed with the exertion of the day's work, her eyes dark in the falling dusk. She shook her head slowly. She looked straight at him. The way she shook her head said clearly: Do I remember? Oh no, oh no, oh no. But her darkened eyes were astonished: Can you really be asking such a thing? . . . Or was that but the sudden fancy of a vain young cock?

By the time their shelter was nearly finished, the grey October evening was upon them. Those on their way to battle had to stay on the island for the night. A bonfire was built in the deep hollow of their enclosure, that they might warm their cold hands and wet clothes and wash down their bit of dried meat and bread with a little hot water before settling down for the night in the damp fir branches. All this hurriedly, that they might put out the fire before the darkness grew deeper, when its glow would be visible from a distance.

And then they were lying there, side by side in the pitch-dark night, like herring in a barrel, mute with apprehension, with weariness, with this upheaval of their lives, which they had vaguely anticipated, and yet which had come to pass precipitously and without warning. On his right, Balthasar heard Jürgen taking long, deep breaths. On his left, Jakob and Aunt Kati were wheezing uneasily in the restless, wakeful sleep of people their age. Between Kati and the fir branches lining the walls lay Epp with her little boy. Balthasar simply knew that she was *there*. Outside, the horses snorted. The cows that had arrived on the island just before dark lowed in the rain. Balthasar smelt the fresh-cut fir under them and the fresh-cut fir in the roof above them – it smelt strongly of sap, as it did at funerals and church festivals. He breathed deeply, in a restless half-sleep, too wound up to sleep, taking in the smells of fir, sodden clothing, wet hides, sweat and weariness, and under all these earthy smells a whiff of something singular, both earthy and dreamlike: the springtime smell of young birches, as in the grove at Lammassaare.

Not even Aunt Kati ever knew, not to mention anyone else, that on a young birch behind the fortress wall, in the softly falling rain, were branches that had just been stripped of their few handfuls of green leaves. And that Epp had crushed and crumbled the leaves and rubbed her face, her neck, her shoulders, her breasts with them, until her skin tingled.

When at mid-morning the devil's dozen, the thirteen men of Kurgla and Antla, arrived at Kangla manor, neither Paavel nor Pening's men were anywhere to be seen. The manor had been looted and set on fire, and it was not clear whether the flames had been extinguished by men or permitted by God to die out. Be that as it may, the log walls of the main house were standing, but the window openings were black with soot. The village was empty. Except for one feeble old blind woman, the Kurgla men found not a soul. They told her to tell anyone who asked – provided the ones asking were Pening men – that the men of Kurgla had continued on to Nabala. At about noon they rode through the Nabala estate; it had been raided and ransacked. From here there was no road south through the great forests, so they turned west and were joined near Tõdva village by eight men on three horses and two manure wagons. They had weapons equal to the number of men – pitchforks and axes, and a sword with a broken tip sharpened to a fine edge. These men said it would be a sin to turn south before they rode on west for half a league to the Saku estate, to see what they could get there to add to their small stock of weapons. Uncle Jakob thought for a moment. Balthasar observed, with admiration, as he had been doing now for two days, how naturally he assumed the role of leader; he was acknowledged not only by his own people but by complete strangers, and displayed qualities that had become evident only as a result of their perilous circumstances, aspects that God had long ago hidden under Jakob's homespun shirt. Jakob thought for a moment and looked at his troops:

"We could do that . . ."

The Saku estate had not been pillaged, but it was devoid of provisions and goods of any kind, as well as of its owners, as the riders had known, of course. The only one there was a servant, an old man with a wooden leg. He showed the house to the group at Uncle Jakob's request. They walked through the rooms and the shabby little chambers of the log structure, with its stone steps, straw roof, and chimney. There was nothing to be found, except for a tile stove – a surprisingly showy one for a country manor – and on the flagstones in front of it an iron poker that Jürgen shouldered as a possible weapon. The vacant storehouses and barns echoed with emptiness. The animals had been herded to Tallinn, the food had been hauled there as well. All that remained of the horses was last week's manure in the mud in front of the stable.

"Well then, don't we want to set fire to the roof?" the Tõdva men asked of one another and of Jakob as they rode out of the gate in the low log fence.

"Not much point . . . It was peasant hands that built it . . ." Jakob said, and with that the matter was settled.

"No problem at all," one of the Tõdva youths said, as they turned south towards Hageri. He was an odd one, with lively blue-grey eyes, a drooping lip, a stubborn chin, and a reddish-brown beard so sparse that each hair had to shout to its neighbour to be heard. He was a type whom Balthasar had no problem classifying as a brawler and a braggart; yes, but after a while he had to admit that, though a brawler and a braggart, the fellow was of the incorrigible sort whose sins are for the most part forgiven, even when weighed in the heavenly scales. For he was not the type that puts up a row only where he has something to gain, but one that fights everywhere, without ceasing, all the way to the pyre or the gallows or the rack.

"No problem at all," the youth said, his voice hoarse and cheerful. "Before we reach Hageri, we'll have a chance to loot another place for what we need. It's right on our way – let's go and take a look at Üksnurme!"

Since that morning a greyish glass of indifference seemed to have settled over Balthasar's faculties, no doubt because of the bloody acts of outlawry that he was about to plunge into with these peasants, something he had not anticipated. Since morning, after deciding to go along with the Kurgla men – no, actually after his last look at Epp waving from under the young pines on the small rise at the edge of the swamp, when the warriors riding to battle were already up to their chests in the dawn-streaked lake – Balthasar had felt himself outside and separate from everything that was happening. Riding along on this muggy autumn day, he had let the woods and thickets, the abandoned and mostly abandoned villages, and the entire gloomy, desolate, autumn country-side, feverish and anxious, flow over and past him. In the morning they had met two scantily armed bands of men moving on foot towards the southwest. They were fugitives who had emerged from the brush – ploughland peasants who had been stripped of all they owned, half-pood peasants, and day labourers. From them he had learned that groups of men from many villages were travelling southwest, and that several Germans had in recent days again been killed and robbed on highways and in pubs. And that the manor lords of Harjumaa had fled to Tallinn, and those of Läänemaa to Haapsalu and Kolovere, and that the Muscovite force of ten thousand, as of the day before yesterday, was still laying siege to the Paide castle in Järvamaa. Apparently a stripling of a knight, by the name of Oldenbokkum, had been sent there by the Order Master as castellan and had been fighting tenaciously in defence of the castle for a month already. And still, around the town the deafening roar of cannon fire was audible day and night for many leagues. It seemed that the peasant revolt was widespread in Harju and Lääne and growing by the hour. All this Balthasar had heard in the course of the morning. Even so, his faculties had been overlaid by that grey glass of

409

indifference. It was as though all these events were taking place in a dream, and of themselves, on the other side. Suddenly, a name uttered by a ladle-lipped youth from Tõdva had hurled a stone through that glass!

Let's go and take a look at Üksnurme!

God Almighty! This was where it would be: Doctor Friesner's Üksnurme manor! Whose manager was supposed to have been suffering from swollen glands, the one to whom Balthasar was "delivering medicine" when he was actually, at the behest of the Doctor, travelling to see the Finnish duke. It was the place where Katharina loved spending her summers, from where the steward sent her roses wrapped in damp cloth . . .

"Why should we take a look at it?" Balthasar asked, feigning indifference.

"We'll search it!" Kulpsuu said, grinning: "There's sure to be all kinds of fancy stuff . . ."

"Who's the lord of that estate?" one of the Kurgla men asked.

"Friesner. He's from Tallinn – expert in looking up arses," Kulpsuu said.

Jakob shot a surprised, knowing look at Balthasar – he recognised the name "Friesner" in connection with his nephew but did not say a word.

God Almighty, what to do? What to do? What to do? Or – is there nothing to be done? Balthasar feels as though he were inside a round tower encircled by a great arcade, its vaulted ceiling rumbling ever more loudly as it ruptures. He could run towards any point of the compass – every arch of the arcade a possible escape route, a hope at least . . . but he cannot decide. And the ceiling is collapsing. *God, I could run in any direction, gallop to the head of the group and shout: Men! Let's give it up! Why waste time at Üksnurme! What weapons would that fool doctor have anyway! Urine flasks, that's all, and probably not even those! They'd hardly serve as weapons anyway . . . Or gallop to the head of the group and shout: Right, men! Let's go! Let's strip it bare! Burn it down! Reduce it to ashes . . . this nest of Judases! . . . Or ride along calmly with the rest? Just say: Of course. If it's been decided to burn down the manor houses in Mary's Land – and this Üksnurme is right in our path – why should we leave it standing?*

He rode along with the group. He was, in fact, near the head of the group. He was silent. He saw with crystal clarity the tracks left by the rolling wheels of peasant wagons – grey strips of muddy water in the black earth; the wet leaves, yellow, red, brown; the ragged, ashen clouds low overhead; and every grey and white hair on his horse's withers. Every footfall of the horse on the soft mud, every step felt to him like the blow of an axe, chopping off pieces of the distance between himself and the dreadful inevitability ahead. He prayed fervently, imploringly: *Lord Jesus! Let them not be there! Neither of them! You can see into my heart, and I beseech you: neither of them. But if it is truly your will, let it be the Doctor. For if it must be, let him be killed. Why should he escape, if everyone is being killed. And if it is truly your inscrutable will that I be among his killers – let it be . . . I cannot change that . . . even though I would . . . But I beseech you: let not Katharina be there! Jesus Christ, do not let her be there!*

She was not there. Neither of them was. But the traces of them were still warm! The men rode through the open gate in the log fence surrounding the estate buildings and dismounted, and when they broke open the lock on the fairly modest main house, with its straw roof, and entered the low-ceilinged rooms, Balthasar could smell the lingering bitter-sweet fragrance of carnations, unmistakable even within the log walls. Yes, the trail was still warm. In the limestone hearth of the main room smoke seeped thinly from the remnants of a fire. On a round table under a small lead-framed window stood four pewter cups and a green bottle, a third full. Kulpsuu was emptying the bottle, gulping the drink down fast, his Adam's apple rising and falling as he swallowed. Balthasar found the sight somewhat distasteful – or perhaps just pitiable. He turned aside, stepped into a passage at the back of the main room, and found the open door to the bedchamber. A down quilt of wine-red silk had been hastily thrown across the bed. There was a visible hollow in the linen pillowcase – made by two heads . . . Confound it . . . Balthasar walked down the hall to the back door. He heard the doors of storage sheds being broken open and saw the Kurgla men, heeding orders from the zealous Kulpsuu, carrying smoked sides of mutton to the steps of the manor house and piling them up there. Five or six hands from the estate had appeared from somewhere and immediately set to work helping them. Balthasar lifted the latch on the hall door and stepped out into the back garden. Under the brown leaves of apple trees lay muddy garden plots, black under thorny rose bushes, no doubt the very same bushes that those roses had come from which . . . but just then he heard quiet footsteps behind him. Before he could turn, someone's arms encircled his shoulders and a hand covered his eyes and he felt voiceless laughter on the back of his neck. Alarmed, he wrenched himself free – to look into the face of Paap, the mute, glowing with delight at recognising him.

"You – here!?"

Paap nodded quickly and kept nodding, closing his small eyes for emphasis. Balthasar had noticed, already at the Doctor's house and during their journey to Finland, that this mute man of Üksnurme, with his bony face and jutting chin, had two modes of being: an uncommunicative stoniness that revealed as little as the hard grey ground when he decided not to know or understand a thing, and the exaggerated, insistent gesticulation characteristic of mutes, when he urgently wanted to communicate something. Now he opened his small iron-grey eyes wide, patted himself on the chest, patted Balthasar on the chest, and gestured towards the men in the house and the dark fir woods beyond the apple trees. Balthasar had had enough practice communicating with him to understand his message: *I am coming with you.*

"Were the Doctor . . . and his wife . . . just here?"

Paap nodded excitedly and stretched his right arm out towards the east, raised three fingers of the left hand, and with his right gestured towards the north. So that was it: just today – at noon – they had fled on horseback to Tallinn. After they had received a message from a servant who had raced here from Saku.

"The steward as well?"

"Uh-huh."

"Are there any weapons on the estate? For our men?"

Paap scratched the back of his head and turned his palms up at first, but then his large hands began to gesticulate in front of Balthasar's face, and when Balthasar understood, he and Paap and Jürgen went to the attic of the main house to look around. Under the straw up there they found two beautiful old knights' swords and a real lance with a handle worn smooth, God knows in what wars. That was all there was, but they could not complain. And in the storage sheds they found so much food – fresh rye flour, apple-ginger preserves, smoked lamb and wild boar – that they had to choose what to take and what to leave behind. In any case, when they left, the wagons of the Tõdva men were considerably heavier than when they had arrived at the estate. Even more so because five or six of the hired hands from Üksnurme who had helped in the looting of the manor were also now on the wagons. From the grove of fir trees beyond the garden Paap brought three horses he had freed from their fetters. He had taken one for himself but handed over the other two to Jakob and his men. Balthasar let the cohort pass him at the gate and held back to wait for Paap. The men had already disappeared into the alder grove and even the creaking of the wagon wheels had died out, but Paap had still not appeared in the yard where his grey horse stood waiting. Balthasar rode back towards the manor house. Paap, with two large iron pans of smouldering coals, was hurrying out of the damaged front door hanging askew on its hinges.

For a moment Balthasar did not grasp what Paap was intending, but suddenly he knew. He knew even before Paap had put one of the pans down on the step, and with the other climbed the ladder to the loft hatch in the master wing of the house. Balthasar dug his heels into the horse's flanks to race to stop him – but then reined the horse in, causing it to rear and snort. Paap had already shoved the pan into the dry straw, which was not tightly packed near the opening and would easily catch fire. Balthasar could not yet see the smoke, but the flames were now visible inside the loft. Paap had already carried his ladder across the yard to the barn, to the triangular hatch in the hip roof. He drove five red-and-grey cows, with stumpy horns and bony flanks, out of the barn, waving his pan of hot coals at them. They stopped in the middle of the farmyard, lowing in fear, their haunches pressed against each other. And then the straw in the barn and the hay in the loft burst into flame.

Something of the wild flare, irreversibly unleashed now, glittered in Paap's small eyes when he pulled up alongside Bal, and they rode side by side out of the gate. But his flat, greyish face was as expressionless as a slab of limestone. Especially when Balthasar attempted, several times, to ask him why he had taken it upon himself to set the estate ablaze. Perhaps Paap really did not understand the question, for they were galloping away just then. And perhaps, being mute – or maybe, even if he were not so impaired – he would not have been able to answer Balthasar.

They spent the night in the half-empty village of Hariküla near the Hager church. They were welcomed, as brothers, into five or six homes by complete strangers caught up in the feverish excitement of the great insurrection, people who offered them lodging and freedom ale, half-brewed and just beginning to ferment. As they drank, the men of Harila bellowed a strange new song:

> The masters will be ravens' rations,
> manors will be burned to ashes
> field and forest will be ours . . .

After his third draught Balthasar joined in the loud singing, next to the others on the straw-strewn floor, by the dim light of the splint-flame, propped up on his elbow, stubble-chinned, tired, his thoughts scattered, his mind a muddled ferment of ardent battle-readiness and sluggish indifference.

The next morning, when they set out for Adila, they were fifty men. Arriving there after midday, they found the widespread flames already dying down. The walls of the manor house had collapsed into a jumble of criss-crossed logs still glowing upon smouldering mounds of ashes in the blackened foundation. Nothing remained of the steward's house or the barns but great charred piles. About fifty peasants who had found a keg of beer in the granary, half of them drunk and reeling, were busying themselves with this and that, or staggering about, or simply standing and staring among the smoking ruins, their faces reddened by the fires. There were about a dozen women, too, the younger and angrier among them carrying off things from the house, the older and more fearful attempting to drag the men away from the riot scene. For the uprising here had been especially fierce, and before the torching of the manor there had been a real battle. After the plundering Muscovite troops had withdrawn from Läänemaa two weeks earlier, bypassing the area, some of the braver manor lords had dared to come back from Tallinn or Kolovere to see what remained of their estates. One of the first to return had been Lord Risebitter of Adila. Shortly thereafter when, after considerable ferment, the peasant revolt had erupted, he had decided, in his lordly pride, to remain on his estate, proclaiming: "It's not the first time this herd of cattle has bellowed. And even though they've been encouraged by the swinish deeds of the Muscovite, the whip will silence them, as always." Except this time it did not. They arrived at the manor in the morning and asked that Herr Risebetter step outside, and when he did not they broke down the door and forced their way in and struck him down at his kitchen hearth with an axe. The steward, who rushed to his master's bedchamber, perhaps to grab a sword in self-defence, was run through on the threshold of the chamber with that very sword. The taskmaster, Joosep, had also fallen into their hands. Some wanted to club him to death on the spot, others thought that for a dog like him, a traitor to his own people, it would be too easy an end. So they dragged the scraggy taskmaster, incoherent with terror, to the whipping stool at the barn door and whipped him so long that, when they finally threw him on the bloodied straw and manure next to it, he did not get up again. Afterwards some of the older men wanted to carry the three corpses into the empty doghouse, the only structure that had not been razed, so that they could readily be moved should someone wish to lay them in holy ground later. But in the meantime taskmaster Joosep had regained consciousness and, judging by the bloody trail he left behind, managed to drag himself away from the burning barn. So Balthasar found only Herr Risebitter and his steward on the doghouse floor. Herr Risebitter was wearing a short linen shirt and his head had been bludgeoned at the left temple – his hair, beard, and shoulder covered with dried blood. One could not tell by looking at the steward that he had been run through with a sword, for a blue wrap was pulled over his chest and a handful of straw had been strewn over the pool of blood next to him. Both their faces had frozen into strange, astonished expressions, and both were barefoot. Not only their clothes and high hunting boots, but also their stockings – the steward's, no doubt stitched of linen fabric and Herr Risebitter's, knitted of woollen yarn, of course – had gone as booty to the peasants. To Balthasar the dead men's bare toes, or at least those of a high-ranking personage like Jürgen Risebitter, seemed alien, ghastly in their lifeless nakedness. Their helplessness and simultaneous air of superiority made them more gruesome than the gaping wound in the man's forehead. With a slight shiver of dread and elation, Balthasar recalled the apparently contradictory truth of the apostle's words, as the blessed Koell had translated them from Doctor Luther's text:

> And God has chosen what is weak in the world, that it might shame what is mighty. And that which in the eyes of the world is lowly and despised, and that which is nothing, these has God chosen, in order to make nothing of that which is something: that no flesh might glory in His presence . . .

But is not the flesh glorying in His presence every time someone grabs a sword? This thought flashed through Bal's mind later, that same afternoon, and it was as if someone had lightly tapped his chest above his heart with the shaft of a sword – that very afternoon, as he stood, sword in hand, three leagues southwest of Adila, within the log walls of the great-room of Limandu manor, among the men of Kurgla and Antla and Tõdva and Üksnurme, with the men of this estate itself and of many others as well. They were crowded into the dusky room, where the light from the small, greenish, windowpanes was the colour of fish bile; around him the sounds of laboured breathing, sporadic hoarse oaths, intermittent shouting, and the surprisingly occasional clanking of swords . . . The flesh glorying in His presence – But no! For though there were fifty men packed into this room, shoulder to shoulder, men who were base and despised and were nothing, and the one who was something, Herr Jacob Üxkyll, lord of the manor of Limandu in his high boots and brown wool coat, tall, pale, looking panic-stricken and furious, his face blotched red, a bleeding cut on his left cheekbone from a sword thrust he had failed to parry – in spite of the fact that this gentleman was alone against fifty peasants, what was happening here was not the flesh boasting in the presence of the Lord! For this was, after all, the weak rising up against the mighty. Herr Üxkyll was pressed against the wall – he had been driven into a dark corner of the log walls. But the imprisoning nook also protected him from his attackers on three sides. And since he had no hope of escape, the corner at least gave him a few additional moments. He had tried to fight his way out of the main door and through the crowd blocking it. He had killed five or six men and wounded at least as many more – he was sure of that. But he had not managed to get out. (Odd. What in the world could have come over this muttering herd? Normally the threat of fifty, no – fifteen, or sometimes just five – lashes of the whip would have made them grovel in the mud, on all fours.) He might possibly have succeeded in breaking through the throng, for the surrounding pack had few weapons and did not really know how to handle those they did have; but his wife, Hedvig, had been standing behind him. And they both knew that, even if they managed to get out, they would scarcely find horses. It had all happened so quickly, like an incomprehensible nightmare. And now Hedvig had been struck in the head – to make her stop screaming – and been dragged unconscious into their stinking grey mass. Of course, he should have killed his wife himself. But his hand would not rise at the right moment, and then it was too late. And now it was all too late. He still had a minute or two left in this game of cat and ratpack . . . he could sense it from their persistence and the weakness in his wrist. To conserve his strength he struck out only occasionally, holding them at a distance of three or four paces. It was all he could do. A man attacking from the left inadvertently stepped too close. Herr Üxkyll's sword pierced his shoulder and those behind the wounded man pulled him back to stop him being trampled. At the same time, Herr Üxkyll noticed the mob pushing forward a replacement, whom he did not see clearly, for sweat stung his eyes and fatigue was beginning to make the faces in front blur. The fellow looked pretty much like all the others; a broad-shouldered young man with rye-stalk hair and angry eyes, wide open, though perhaps not quite as livid as those of some of the others. He came after Herr Üxkyll with a heavy sword forged by a village blacksmith, but the cornered man parried his first thrust, managing it with ease, in fact – bear in mind four hundred years of generation upon generation practised in fencing; but he felt the bull-like strength of the young peasant in his deliberate, unhurried thrusts, wielded without rage or fury. And there was something – confound it – in the way he forced Herr Üxkyll to draw out his parrying, to tire him out, that indicated he was not handling a sword for the first time. And that he knew how to size up the situation. Their swords crossed again and Balthasar thought: *Damn that confounded curiosity of mine!* For it was sheer curiosity that had brought him to this. Out of curiosity he had joined the group surrounding the manor. A childish curiosity had propelled him through the throng to where he heard swords clanking in the dusky room, so that he might see the extraordinary sight of a manor lord about to be killed by peasants . . . And now he was in the front line of Herr Üxkyll's killers, next to three jostling peasants, trying to keep from falling on his opponent's swift sword. He looked at his adversary, which is what he had actually wanted to do, and exchanged a few blows with him. Then he realised with a shock the unspoken death sentence imposed upon Herr Üxkyll, this grotesque and terrible thing that filled the charged half-darkness, which had somehow become his lot to carry out. *Damnable curiosity* . . . He noted that underlying Herr Üxkyll's narrowed eyes and rapid breathing, kept in check behind his clenched teeth, was a mixture of desperation and defiance, irritating and offensive. An infuriatingly arrogant defiance and an infuriatingly resilient four-hundred-year-old arrogance, with which he was still scornfully fending off the yokels' swords. Balthasar felt two opposing waves wash over him and carry him onward: rage at this man's sense of superiority, his complacence, his insolent presumption of people as dumb beasts; and at the same time an impulse towards mercy (to finish it, to finish it faster!) – and he felt how fear of the flesh glorying was holding him back. In the space of a second he reflected: *As for me, I am neither fish nor fowl – neither soldier nor man of God* . . . And then he felt the jostling and shoving behind his back grow more agitated, felt someone being held back and someone else pushing his way forward. He heard someone shout: "Men! What the hell are you doing . . . you're just nibbling at this bloody bastard?! Die – you filthy swine!" Balthasar caught a glimpse of Kulpsuu's bulging eyes and bared teeth behind him – his own sword was just then crossed with Herr Üxkyll's – and then something swished past his right shoulder, so close to his cheek that it left a bloody scratch, and the rusty tip of a halberd plunged so deep into Herr Üxkyll's neck, just above the sternum, that its tip scraped his left clavicle. Herr Üxkyll gurgled and lurched forward, for Kulpsuu pulled the halberd out of his neck, and the stream of blood that shot out of the severed artery missed Balthasar only because he threw himself to one side. Herr Üxkyll crumpled to the ground, and peasant feet in peasant footwear walked over him . . .

Balthasar later remembered the hubbub, the shouting, the thudding footfalls, the breaking glass, the cries of "Fire! Fire! Fire!" He recalled standing in the yard, surrounded by burning buildings. Only the steward's house, located slightly off to one side, had not been set ablaze, and several dozen peasants lingered near the main door, some standing around, others busying themselves here and there. But in the middle of the farmyard, directly in front of Balthasar and the men around him, crackled a burning woodpile, three cubits high, made of firewood and household goods hauled into a heap. The flames from the burning buildings rose up in the windless, heavy air like red hair standing on end in fright. And up from the bonfire rose black-and-white smoke, billowing and frothing towards the low clouds. As though God had accepted Herr Üxkyll, whose corpse was burning on the pyre, as a satisfactory offering.

Standing there Balthasar barely registered the two riders who stopped in front of the steward's house, dismounted, and went in, nor did he pay any heed to the men pacing back and forth in front of the steps. He was thinking, as he turned towards the bonfire again: *But for me, Üxkyll would not have died. At least not at that precise moment. For if his sword had not been crossed with mine, he could have defended himself against Kulpsuu's halberd. So . . . it means that . . .*

He saw Uncle Jakob come out of the steward's house and walk across the wide farmyard towards the bonfire. From the glow of the flames on his uncle's gaunt face it was evident that the twilight of the autumn evening had begun.

"Here you are! Come with me," Uncle Jakob said. Balthasar marvelled again at how self-assured and authoritative, even with him, his uncle's calm voice had become, in the course of three days.

"Where to?"

"There." His uncle gestured towards the steward's house.

"Why?"

"The king is there. He wants to talk to you."

"The king?! . . . He's there? . . . And he wants – me . . . ?"

"That's right."

"And how did he come to be here, all of a sudden? . . . And what does he want?"

"He'll tell you himself."

Balthasar started for the steward's house ahead of Uncle Jakob. And had his uncle not been an old peasant but a noble, he would have concluded from Balthasar's energetically quickening step: This boy will be a gentleman-in-waiting in no time. But Jakob was an old peasant who had known his nephew from the time he was in the cradle, and so he looked with narrowed eyes at his broad shoulders and mass of hair that was a bit long, like a peasant's, and thought: *He's still just a colt . . . eyes popping, making a beeline for wherever there might be something interesting to see . . . He-he-he-he.*

Balthasar asked him as they walked: "And how should I behave with him?" He realised the oddness of the question because, coming from him, who had had an audience with the Finnish duke and studied at the university with the sons of Pomeranian noblemen, it was especially odd when addressed to Uncle Jakob, who had spent his life ploughing the fields of Kurgla and Raasiku . . . But Uncle Jakob would have known this. Even the word "king" sounded strange! It could not possibly mean what it said! And yet that is what he was . . .

"Hmm. How to behave with him. As you would with any other human being. He used to be the blacksmith at Alaküla village. A "one-foot" man. What do you mean – how should you behave?"

When Balthasar attempted to go up the three stone steps of the steward's house, two peasants in their typical shoes, but armed with swords, stepped out to block his way,

"Where are you going, man?"

"The king has summoned me," Balthasar said – and thought: *Oho – this is just as it was with the coadjutor's bodyguards on the Doctor's front step*. But in fact it was not exactly the same, for in response to his author-itative, peremptory answer the swordsmen stepped awkwardly aside and one of them muttered:

"Let 'im go on in then."

Balthasar and his uncle entered the great-room of the steward's house and looked around. On the hearth burned a few logs and the ends of roof trusses brought in from the razed buildings. Two villagers busied themselves around a large iron kettle. But it seemed that the water in the kettle was still quite cool, for when one of the men started to pour flour from a wide wooden vessel into the water, the other one yelled: "Stop, you blockhead! You can't make broth with cold water!" The first fellow stopped pouring the flour and muttered: "Ah! At this rate, we're never goin' get no bite to eat!"

Sitting on two long benches, around a low table under a small pig's-bladder window, were five or six villagers, their swords tied to their belts with leather strips cut from reins. Oddly, there were four or five shepherds' horns and a bagpipe lying in a heap on the table. The door into a large back chamber was ajar. Some villagers emerged and crossed the great-room on their way out, others entered, and a voice sounded from within:

"Take the horses! Ride through all the villages within a distance of three leagues and ask all the men to gather here, in Limandu, at dawn the day after tomorrow!"

Just then Kulpsuu of Tõdva entered the great-room and, with a flurry, holding his head high, made his way to the king's chamber. As Balthasar stepped to one side for the departing messengers, he heard the same clear, energetic voice in the room addressing Kulpsuu:

"Aha! You're the man who killed the lord of Üksküla manor? What's your name? Fine. I will call you Kulpsuu. And you can be my chief of bodyguards. It used to be Jaanus of Odalemme, but he was done in by Lord Üksküll's sword. Agreed?"

Balthasar and Jakob entered the chamber without knocking on the door frame – for Balthasar had seen others enter without knocking. Balthasar's curiosity was again at as high a pitch as it had ever been – vacillating between a readiness to take this new king seriously and an inclination to be amused by him.

"Of course I agree! Why wouldn't I?" Kulpsuu quickly responded. "When it's the king himself that gives the command. Ha-ha-ha-ha! But what am I to do with the bodyguards?"

"Keep them together. There are twelve of them. They have good swords and a bagpipe and shepherds' horns. You will pass on my orders to them. And lead them when it comes to battle. You do know how to handle a weapon, don't you?"

"Hell! I'm the one who . . . Spear – sword – crossbow – makes no difference to me. You know, I'm . . ."

423

"Good, good. Go now and see to getting your men fed." Kulpsuu went out without a word, beaming with self-importance.

In the meantime Balthasar had had a chance to look around. On a long bench against the blackened log wall in the half-dark room sat four silent, serious, expressionless villagers, swords fastened to their belts with rope, shaggy hats on their knees. He noted with surprise that six holes had been punched in a circle around the crown of each hat, and green oak branches, the length of a handspan, stuck into them. The blacksmith of Alaküla, a one-foot peasant, now king of the peasants, was standing in the middle of the chamber, a man of about forty, considerably shorter than average. He was facing a small window with a torn pig's-bladder pane. The fires cast a reddish glow on his round face with its full, square beard, just as the blaze in his sooty forge, wherever it was, had no doubt done every day. He was wearing the high boots of a nobleman – war booty. But above the footwear his peasant hose sagged, disappearing under a short grey jerkin of homespun wool. He turned now towards Balthasar, with his lively, jovial blue eyes reflecting the fires outside, and as he stepped closer, so that his outline emerged in the dim light of the room, Balthasar saw that this small man was exceptionally broad-shouldered and sturdy.

"You're back already with him." This was addressed to Uncle Jakob.

Now he looked at Balthasar.

"So you're the man o' learning who's taking an interest in the affairs of peasants? Well, well. So, this kind of thing does indeed happen. Let's sit down."

The only piece of furniture remaining in the room, aside from the stripped bed frame and the round table, was a narrow bench a fathom long. The king straddled the bench at one end and gestured to Balthasar to follow suit at the other. Balthasar sat – but still could not work out what he thought of this king: should he be grouped with those he pitied or with those he envied . . . ? Indeed, there was no doubt that he himself had the advantage over this little man, in many things . . . The king even seemed a bit comical to him – squat and burly, with his wiry, reddish beard almost as long as it was wide. Yet with his quick, childlike blue eyes, his terse utterances and brisk movements, he seemed to be, in spite of his thoroughly peasant mien and huge, freckled peasant hands, a figure of galvanising shrewdness. After all, there had to be some reason that it was he who had been chosen to head this unimaginably consequential undertaking.

"Listen, this is why we need you," the king said. "We are sending our spokesmen to Tallinn. First, they must explain our cause to the town Greys. They need to tell them that we have decided to sweep the manor lords from our land, and that there are now – well, around five thousand of us, and that whoever wishes to join us is welcome. Second, and this is actually the main thing: they have to go before the Town Council to request cannons and cannon balls and powder from the town's artillery yard, to use against walled fortresses. And that they supply us with half a regiment of mounted mercenaries – to be sent out to the various peasant units, to teach them how to fight a war. We're sending a delegation of three of the sharpest men that we have at hand here, your uncle Jakob among them. You are the fourth, and we need you for both missions. I heard you're from Kalamaja. I imagine the men there would have vastly more trust in you than in the dirt-grubbing hirelings of the manor. But at the Council your assignment is this: to back up and provide support for those presenting our case, but mainly to listen, and take note of exactly what the councilmen say about it amongst themselves. For you will ask them to respond right away, and they will talk it over in your presence. It will not occur to them that any of you can understand what they're saying. But we need to know. That's it. You will return as soon as you can. You will come here, to Limandu. If I'm not here, there'll be a message directing you to me. Be here tomorrow at dawn, you and

Jakob. The other spokesmen will be here too. Four of my bodyguards will go with you. I'll see that you get good horses."

The king stood up. Balthasar did the same. "And if they really do give us cannons, what then?"

"Try to find men and horses in town who will deliver them to us. And one more thing. We can expect some serious battles ahead, and it is absurd for me to go into battle wearing this . . ." The king gestured towards the round table and Balthasar stepped closer to it, to look at the odd-shaped thing that had caught his attention earlier. It was not just a coarse, felt, peasant hat, with those oak branches weirdly stuck into it, like the ones resting on the knees of the men along the wall. Only now did Balthasar realise that it was the same kind of hat, but a double hat: a larger hat, inserted with oak twigs, had been set upon a smaller, similar one, and the branches in the inner hat extended down between the two brims.

"I can, of course, wear this thing, since the elders . . ." – he indicated the men sitting at the wall – "have so determined. But for a real war," he turned to Balthasar, "buy me a proper helmet in town. Not one of those with a visor, but a simple, iron helmet with a deep crown. I don't have time to make one. Well, it could have a little stud on the crown, to fasten a rooster tail to. So's I can be seen from a distance if need be. Tomorrow, I'll give you the money."

He picked up his comical hat-crown – it looked like a small, stunted oak – and set it on Balthasar's head:

"Does it fit?"

"It fits."

"Go to the armour-master and pick one out that fits you. Our heads are the same size."

CHAPTER FIVE,

in which the young man, whom we should now perhaps call a young rebel, notes that, as the rising torrent of events pulls him along into its turbulent current, and as he nears the great falls where everything roars into the abyss (only to subside into the languid, grey flow of time once again), the events themselves become ever more dreamlike, even against the temporary backdrop of familiar walls and towers and the curve of the bay; and even when familiar faces flash into view in the multi-hued maelstrom of iron and limestone, blood and ash, earth and sea, the faces are more frightened, more helpless, more stony, more secretive than usual, as is always the case when flood waters rise.

Riding along with the Kurgla folk to aid them in their flight, galloping in the company of the rebel forces, witnessing manors plundered and set aflame, observing the thoughts and words and looks of the peasants, singing their boisterous songs of rebellion with them, crossing swords with a manor lord doomed to die – all this must have seemed improbable, even hallucinatory, to a young man of calm temperament, by now a townsman through and through, one who had even acquired an education abroad. But so long as he was his own man, free to come and go at will, it was one thing. It was entirely another to be riding, as he was now, bearing on his shoulders and conscience the burden of the mission assigned him by mandate of this strange woodland king who wore oak branches in his hat. Around him and in front, to the left and to the right, the king's spokesmen splashed through mud puddles, thudded along dirt roads, galloped across limestone surfaces, their rough grey doublets black from the autumn rain, their sodden shaggy hats pulled down over tense faces wet with raindrops. To his right rode Jakob. His presence lent a sense of reality to the situation and bolstered Balthasar's self-confidence, but it also increased his burden of responsibility. (Jakob was, after all, an ordinary peasant, whose life experience made it even more difficult for him than for Balthasar to assess the feasibility or infeasibility of their unprecedented mission.) To his left rode a fifty-year-old peasant, a man of few words with shrewd yellowish eyes who had been addressed as Leemet of Ohulepa in that brief dawn at the king's house when the spokesmen were given their final orders. Jakob had told Balthasar about Leemet: he had lived for many years in Tallinn, in the service of a councilman. When the man died, Leemet somehow landed back with his former master, where he was given the opportunity to experience all the whippings and stocks available at Ohulepa manor. He had been selected to serve as a delegate as much because of the whippings he had received from the manor lord as because of the familiarity with town life that he had acquired in Tallinn. Galloping at the head of the group was none other than Kulpsuu of Tõdva, sword on hip, a hat with a green oak branch stuck in it at the back of his head – as though he were the leader, when in fact the leader was supposed to be Leemet. Kulpsuu's eyes were bulging, his teeth, bared; it was not clear whether he was grinning or overly excited. He had not been among the first spokesmen chosen, but at the daybreak rush at the king's house it became apparent that the peasant selected as the third delegate had either taken ill during the night, as some claimed, or had simply vanished, as others asserted, probably daunted by the burden of responsibility . . . but who can know for certain? At the last moment Kulpsuu had jumped up and offered to go in his stead. And the king had said: "Well, alright then." And for some reason Balthasar had thought of Rector Wolff – how like a dream beyond distant hills were Rector Wolff and the institute and Stettin and Germany and the entire real world! – who had once said, speaking of Roman history and the more recent history of the emperors, that when the prefects of the Praetorian Guard began to voice their views in matters of rule, the end of Rome was at hand. The prefects of the Praetorian Guard and Kulpsuu . . . *Ha-ha-ha-ha!* The comparison would make any reasonable man laugh, even here, in this morass of rain, mud, haste and fatigue. And in general the entire present situation was so muddled and bizarre and topsy-turvy that, if you thought about it clearly, it was laughable and at the same time frightening: the sheer impossibility of what was in fact happening – this feverish march to somewhere, to carry out something, the big picture so ominously blurred and the details so remarkably sharp . . . The two wet jackdaws flapping into flight from the ruins of the inn at the village of Pääsküla . . . The streaks of iron ore in the limestone balustrade of the Pääsküla bridge, flowing into long, red-brown bands as their horses thudded across it . . . And the hopelessness of their mission – or was there, perhaps, a glimmer of hope? . . . For there seemed to be some kind of connection – Balthasar surmised as much from a chance remark he had overheard in the dimly flickering splint-flame of the king's house – *some kind* of connection between the peasants and at least one of the councilmen, Herr Schmedemann.

As evening fell, the grey northeastern sky grew darker above the town's distant grey towers and St Olaf's Church, the sight of its needle spire sweetly pricking Balthasar's heart as the glow of the sun setting below the fog and the rain clouds cast the nearing steeples into bright relief against the overcast sky. It seemed that the weather would clear at last. To the sounds of baying dogs and splattering mud they rode through Tõnismäe, on the outskirts of town, and turned onto a road heading towards the harbour. It was surfaced in part with logs, but sank under them wherever it crossed a spring, as though lacking all support beneath. They ascended the sandy Lontmaaker Rise, trotted between the wet, empty worksheds of the ropemakers, and continued on. Balthasar would have wanted to stop and greet these dear, familiar walls – strong, impregnable, enduring – that he was now leaving behind. He would have wanted to breathe in the purple-grey expanse of the sea that opened out before him from this height, now disappearing into the misty twilight. They rode down the northern slope of Lontmaaker Rise, and the sea sank behind the leafless tops of a dark alder thicket and sparse maples. In a few minutes dogs ahead started barking again, and the riders arrived at the wet rail fences of Kalamaja and its houses with their waterlogged thatch roofs. Here once again, close behind the houses, was the somewhat disquieting, softly murmuring expanse of open sea. And for a moment Balthasar felt as if it were rising to his mouth and eyes, smothering and soothing him, as though it had never, in any other place, been as close to him as it was here.

Eight horses thundered through Kalamaja, dogs growled in the dooryards, house doors and workshop windows were fearfully opened on their left and right – God Almighty, at these times one could never be sure when and from where plunderers and arsonists might descend to attack a village on the outskirts of town. It was a wonder that the Tallinners had had such nerves of steel till now that the Council itself had not ordered all of Kalamaja burned to the ground . . . For as soon as the Muscovite took Paide castle, he could be expected at the edge of Tallinn. And, fearing a siege, the town would be quick to lay waste to everything outside its walls where the enemy might take shelter or find material for barricades and blockhouses and such. "Ashes outside the walls will put the besieger to flight." That was a saying in fortified towns. Kalamaja had been reduced to ashes three or four times in the last three hundred years, as Balthasar had heard long ago from his father. And it had risen again.

They turned in at Siimon's farmyard, and in place of – or along with – the reassuring closeness of the sea, Balthasar felt for a moment the comforting presence of all the small, insignificant, dear things he had left behind: here were the roofs and the walls and the grass; here, the yokes and halters hanging on spreading branch-prongs against the wall, as usual. And, as always, the bundle of birch branches from last week's sauna bath, lying on the large black stone step, serving as a doormat, like a humble and constant reminder of the warmth from the family sauna.

Two farmhands, Käsper and Laar, came out and took their horses. It was so dark already that neither recognised Balthasar. In fact, because of the dimness of the room, his peasant attire and his unshaven face, even his father did not recognise him. And, of course, Siimon could not possibly have expected Balthasar to be among such men. With a quick glance of his small, nearly white eyes, old Siimon looked the eight men over as they entered his family room. Yes, his eyes were as sharp as ever. But even in the gloom and the uncertain, flickering light from the hearth, it was evident just how much, in the course of two years, he had faded and aged. He was tight-lipped, wary and disapproving as he interrupted Kulpsuu's loud, boastful talk, and after listening to Jakob's account asked:

"And did you have to get involved in such a messy affair?"

Of course, Father did not know the story of Hasse's murder . . . So his disapproving words were clearly beside the point. But in essence he was right . . . he was right . . . And yet . . .

Had Balthasar taken the time to think his situation over carefully and weigh the words he planned to utter, he might well have asked himself with some amazement: *What kind of person would get involved – no matter how, but willingly, in any event – in something he holds to be of importance, and then, when he encounters obstacles and sees a thunder-cloud of trouble and danger rising, says suddenly: "I wash my hands of the whole affair? Thanks, brothers for making clear to me just how bad this thing is that I've got stuck in . . ."* What kind of person would do that?

And Balthasar would have said to himself: *I for one could not do that, because I am – I'm not really sure how to put it – either too stubborn or maybe just too weak . . . Because once I get involved in something, I start to think of it as right and just. Even if I've been dragged into it against my will – provided it is not actually a work of Judas . . . I begin to consider it right and worthy. When I look into the depths of my heart, I realise that my way of doing things is perhaps not pleasing to God. Because I probably do it when pride nudges me – pride, which is from the Devil. If I were to decry my present situation, I would be admitting either that I am a pitiful creature, incapable of conducting my affairs the way someone more competent would, or that God considers me deserving of punishment – which is not easy to admit, either . . . Yes, it does appear that I am one of those who think – taking their self-love to an utterly absurd level – that, whatever army they have decided to join has to be fighting for what is right and true, simply because they themselves are marching along with it!*

But Balthasar did not take the time to think it all over. He thrust his stubbled chin out of the shadows, into the flickering light, and called out:

"Father – Jakob had no choice! None of them did . . ." (At least he did not say *none of us.*)

"Bal . . ?" The old man gripped the back of the chair he was standing behind and stared at Balthasar, fixing him with his pale little eyes.

"Where on earth did you come from?"

"From Narva. Krumhusen sent me from Germany to Narva. To go and see his son." And to win the old man over he said: "For good money. I'll tell you about it later. But right now, what we need is . . ."

"Take a seat then . . . in your father's house," the old man said, and sat down as well. And when he noticed that Kulpsuu pulled out a chair with a back for himself, but that the others were still standing, he added: "And the rest of you, too – Jakob and all of you, take a seat under my roof. Truuta! Bring out something for them to eat. They've travelled a long way. And now, tell me what you have in mind."

Truuta put the soup kettle on the coals and sliced some bread and clasped her hands: *Jesus, if it isn't Bal . . . thasar . . . ! Now, how in the world did he get here?!* In the meantime the men explained their plan to Siimon. Leemet talked in a low sing-song, as though he were afraid of eavesdroppers, and Kulpsuu loudly confirmed one tale and objected vociferously to another and interrupted someone else's story. Jakob and Balthasar talked too. Sometimes they took turns and sometimes they all talked at once, and Balthasar noticed how his father's round gaunt face remained impassive, but how the expression in his eyes changed as he listened to the men's tale, alternately turning to his son and the others, including Jakob. And Balthasar sensed how the old man resisted the story told by Kulpsuu, Leemet and even Jakob, about the great rebellion ("We know, we know, we know!"), and of the freedom of the peasants ("Well now, well now . . ."), and of the killing of the manor lords ("What are they bragging about? Better if they kept their mouths shut . . .") – out of caution, of course; but he was stunned, in spite of himself, as he listened to Balthasar, and began to soften, and, even though he resisted, began to believe them. Had he opened his tightly compressed lips he might have muttered: So, you little whippersnapper, you rapscallion, you student . . . ho-ho-ho . . . you educated stripling – are you mixed up in all this too? You are also of the opinion, and not just these ignorant peasants, that this . . . village-blacksmith-become-king . . . hm . . . could possibly set the affairs of country folk to rights? Indeed . . .

In any event, when the pea soup had been eaten and Siimon had wiped his mouth with the back of his hand and briefly thanked God, he asked Truuta to bring in straw for the men and make up Balthasar's pallet in his boyhood chamber. He asked Käsper to saddle a horse for him and rode into town.

He returned after midnight and shook Balthasar awake. The others rose from their straw bedding and came to Balthasar's door to listen.

433

Siimon used flint and steel to light the pine splint. His news was this: he had gone to Kimmelpenning and won him over. For, whatever the quarrel between the dry-goods merchants and the Town Council, Kimmelpenning's purse always carried weight with the councilmen, and for the moment he had even more influence because the Council knew through his purchasers that he was on good terms with the peasants of Harju and Läänemaa. Despite the late hour the two men had gone to see Herr Vegesack and had persuaded him, too. Fortunately the time was such that the councilmen were anxious and agitated and, in their state of bewildered distress, more grateful than angry to be getting news, however late the hour. Kimmelpenning and Vegesack had gone to the bailiff right then and negotiated safe conduct for the peasants. Of course, word of the agreement was taken to Burgomaster Packebusch. The assistant to the council scribe had by chance dropped in at Herr Vegesack's, at around eleven o'clock, to sip a little beaker of wine, and, incidentally, to offer the opinion that the Council could perhaps receive these rabble-rousers and disturbers-of-the-peace the next morning, at seven.

That made Balthasar smile to himself – a brief, wry smile, in spite of his drowsiness and agitation and fatigue. For *seven o'clock* indicated clearly just how eager they were to know what the peasant spokesmen had to tell them. Had the enemy surrounded the town at five, they would have assembled at five-thirty. And had they the chance to gain ten thousand marks, it would have been at six. But in any other case it would not have been until eight or even ten o'clock . . . And given the gravity and uncertainty of the moment, Balthasar was thinking, with surprising relish as he dozed off: what an extraordinary, ancient creature was this town – his town . . . It could remain unmoved, not giving a sign of life for years on end – for example, when confronted with a written petition – just like that creature in the Pomeranian duke's zoo, with the grey stone bowl on its back, called a "turtle", who could purportedly

434

stand immobile all winter long on a lettuce leaf. This town could nod off like that, in its stone shell, on the murmuring shore of *Historia*, God knows, without poking out its nose or extending a foot out of its shell, exactly like this strange creature of God's, but then it could suddenly awake and unexpectedly stretch out its sinewy neck – whether because of anger or hunger or curiosity or who knows why – and *bite* with its hard, grey, surprisingly muscular jaws.

In the early morning darkness, when the four spokesmen were about to set off for town, leaving behind at Kalamaja the four peasants who had come along for security, Balthasar's father took him aside and asked:

"Hmm. Don't you think it would be wiser for you not to go with them?"

"Why?"

"You might be recognised in town."

"And so?"

"So . . . For today, you have safe conduct. And for tomorrow, too. But no-one can know, a month or a year from now, how the Council will look upon the men who approached them in connection with their uprising."

"If the town joins with the peasants . . . ?"

"In case it doesn't."

"But you dared join the peasants yourself. And so did Jakob . . ."

"Jakob is an old man who lives in the countryside. And he'll stay in the countryside. You are young and want to live in town. And you want to rise to a position of distinction, God willing."

"But nobody will recognise me in town! No-one there has seen me dressed like this. Or with such a hairy chin. And aside from you, not a soul even knows I'm in this country."

"Not at the moment. But once you're in town . . . Are you planning to see Annika?"

435

"Well, certainly. But she'll keep quiet. If I ask her to."

"Of course she will. But who knows, who . . . Well, go on then. You won't give in anyway . . ."

Balthasar smiled at the old man, a little embarrassed, but forgiving, and went off after the others.

Siimon followed Balthasar through the entryway into the farmyard. He stepped off the cold black step onto the wet birch-branch mat and walked behind him slowly, as far as the gate. His bare feet found the walkway of stone slabs sunk into the mud. He stopped at the gate, arms folded on his chest, and watched his son, who had emerged so unexpectedly from the darkness of evening, disappear into the darkness of early morning, behind the pole fence of his neighbour, Traani-Andres. He stood there, deep in thought, scratching his left arm with his right index finger. Had someone been standing on the other side of the gate, looking at him carefully, he would have noticed his bent finger rise a thumb's length from the rough sleeve of his jacket and hang in the air and move, as though silently beckoning, "Come back." And had the onlooker possessed particularly sharp cats' eyes and a quick imagination, he would perhaps have understood that the old man's finger was tracing the sign of the cross in the darkness.

The faces of the councilmen revealed no particular eagerness to hear what the peasants' spokesmen had to tell them. If there was anything to indicate a measure of curiosity on their part, it was the fact that the gentlemen, *consules et proconsules,* were nearly all present at this early hour. Of the four burgomasters, three were there, including the chairman, Burgomaster Packebusch. Also in attendance were ten of the fourteen councilmen, making thirteen men in all, and the Syndic, Clodt, looking exactly as he had two years ago, as though he had been preserved in vinegar all this time; and his assistant, the small and always slightly shabby Herr Loop, whose face was that of an aged child. So that

Balthasar was not quite sure whether the composition of the Council could be considered a devil's dozen or not. That no-one would recognise him in the wan candlelight, kept so for reasons of thrift, he was certain. Recognition depended too much on expectation, or the lack of it. Of the very few in the hall who knew of Balthasar's existence on God's earth – and, even then, only if they had regularly been reminded of him– not one would have expected to find him among these shaggy rebels. He, of course, recognised half the councilmen right away, in spite of the fact that they were all wearing the flat black velvet berets of their office, identical dark-blue woollen robes with ermine trim at the collars and cuffs, and – hanging on chains around their necks – official medallions half a span in diameter. The councilmen were sitting on long benches with carved backs, set against the walls of the small council hall, while the burgomasters, with Herr Packebusch in the middle, sat at the end of the hall, facing three tall windows that looked out upon the high peaked gables of the buildings around Town Hall Square and the steeple of Holy Ghost Church, looming black against the streaked dawn sky. The first councilman on the left bench was the fat and ever-glum Herr Vegesack, blinking at the peasants as he moved his prematurely toothless mouth. He was the only one who was not, for some reason, wearing the official silver medallion around his neck. Next came the sour-looking Herr Beelholt, our old acquaintance from the Doctor's house, and Herr Boissmann and Herr Dehn, and several unfamiliar, worldly-wise old men with shrewd and stubborn faces, and then the broomstick-thin Herr Pepersack; next, a slight old man with fine wrinkles and yellowish skin who seemed to be made of straw. The Council did not, of course, offer the peasants seats, but left them standing between the door and the burgomasters' table, and there they remained, close together in a group, shoulder to shoulder, four broad, bearded faces, four pairs of peasant feet planted solidly upon the oak floor. And Herr Clodt, who was sitting at one end of the burgomasters' table, with his side to the peasants, was so close to Balthasar that had he not been not known for his nearsightedness, Balthasar would have had cause to worry about being recognised. Then Herr Packebusch opened his wide frog-mouth and said to Herr Loop, who was acting as interpreter (although it was unlikely that any of the councilmen needed one):

"Tell them: before they inform the Honourable Town Council of Tallinn of the matter they are bringing before it, the Honourable Council wants to know, *primum*: in whose name they are speaking, and *secundum*: what the goal and purpose of that cursedly large *tumultum* is that they have started – if, that is, anyone thinks it actually has a purpose."

They were standing so close together that Balthasar felt the entire group shift uneasily. He also heard Leemet of Ohulepa swallow twice before he responded in his quiet, husky voice, but smoothly and fluently: that they were speaking in the name of the king elected by the peasant army, but that was the same as speaking in the name of all the rebelling peasants; and, as for their goal, the Honourable Council should recall, first of all, how long and how much the peasants had suffered under the injustices of the manor lords. After all, they were all free men in the Danish era, and were free men still when they came under the rule of the Order, which fact this very Honourable Council itself confirmed just twenty or thirty years ago, in a letter to the Master of the Order. *Just listen to him*, Balthasar thought, *the things Father told me many years ago are known to Leemet and the others, too*. Leemet went on, stating that the Council should recall, furthermore, for how long a time and in what dire circumstances the town of Tallinn had given shelter and refuge and its free air to breathe to those fleeing the countryside. And this same Honourable Council had even ordered that some nobles lose their heads as punishment for the injustices they had inflicted on the peasants . . . Here it appeared to Balthasar that the magistrates listening to Leemet were not all delighted at the mention of their valiant deeds and that, upon being reminded of them, began to shift uncomfortably in their seats. Then Leemet talked on about the whipping stools and the leg stocks, and Balthasar raised his eyes from the councilmen's wooden but attentive faces to the tapestries on the walls behind them. The candle flames in the high chandeliers quivered noticeably in the warm air rising from furnaces beneath the floor, the flickering light creating the illusion of movement on the faces of the councilmen, as well as on the scenes high on the tapestries: the knights and horsemen in armour and turbans, the vassals with swords, the women playing harps, people walking, running, kneeling; and wise Solomon journeying to Gihon and being anointed king and waiting for his bride and sitting on his throne as judge. The dim, trembling candlelight brought it all to life, especially Solomon sitting on the judge's throne with his overly bright red knees and sagging blue stockings. And with his sceptre and crown. Not a crown of oak branches stuck into a coarse felt hat, but a crown of real gold more than two thousand years old. Though up there it was merely woven of gold yarn . . . Balthasar heard Leemet quietly continuing: And these burdens and sufferings had not been getting the least bit lighter, they had worsened, and it could not be expected that the lords of the manors would ever take it upon themselves to lighten the burden on the peasants . . . Balthasar did not have time to finish his thought – the thought that Leemet of Ohulepa simply did not dare reveal the rebels' plan – when he heard, next to him, the shrill, grating voice of Kulpsuu of Tõdva. It was even more jarring than usual. For on their way that morning from the Nunnavärav Gate to the Town Hall, along cobblestones still wet with dew, he had taken them past the Green Frog tavern. The padlock on the cellar door was just being removed, and Kulpsuu had proposed that they go in to slake their thirst. The others had thought it was not in fact the right moment, but Kulpsuu had thundered: why should he, confound it, have to suffer from thirst for half a day, or the deuce knows how long, on account of those dirty

439

swine in the Town Council!? And he had gone in alone, slapped his shillings down on the counter, and drunk two tankards of ale. Which was why his voice, in this vaulted hall with its unnerving echoes, sounded more gratingly strident than usual.

"Leemet! What are you doing – you're like a cat circling a bowl of hot porridge! The porridge is hot! Yes! And it's getting hotter! Wring their necks – the necks of all the nobles! *That's* our aim! And that's what we'll do, with or without the help of the town! 'Cause the Germans have already fouled their trousers in fear of the Muscovite!"

"But ask them," Herr Clodt said to Herr Loop, pushing his lower lip forward so that his long lower teeth were bared almost to the gums, as though he had just put something indescribably sour into his mouth, "Ask them: if they succeed in killing the nobles – with or without help from the town – under what king would they then want to serve?"

"Yes, that's something we'd like to know!" Herr Beelholt cried, raising high his reddish, grey-flecked eyebrows.

"Of course, under whom?" A councilman unfamiliar to Balthasar leaned forward eagerly. And now Balthasar recognised his veined face, as well. It was Herr Ivo Hoye, who, two years ago, had gone to the Danish king to seek help for the town.

Oh yes: behind Herr Clodt's question Balthasar detected Herr Kettler and the issue of the Polish king. For by now Herr Clodt was known to be more an adviser to Kettler than he was Syndic of Tallinn. And Herr Beelholt voiced his question, of course, on behalf of Duke Johan and old Gustav who, as Balthasar had heard in Narva, was just then on his sickbed (or maybe his deathbed). So that, perhaps Beelholt's question was actually raised, with God's will, on behalf of King Erik. And Herr Hoye, a supporter of the Danish king, pricked up his ears as he waited to hear the peasants' response . . . It brought to Balthasar's mind Aesop's fable of the crayfish, the swan and the pike, and he had such difficulty suppressing the laughter welling up in him that he had to avert his eyes, unable to look at the councilmen. And while Leemet was answering Clodt's question, Balthasar gazed at the huge mural covering the entire right wall of the hall. What he saw stunned him. He was looking at it for the first time, and he saw that it depicted the town of Tallinn – he had no doubt about that – but it was a scene of Tallinn engulfed in a terrible fire.

The artist had represented the town viewed from somewhere near the harbour. The houses clustered outside the town walls were in the foreground, and the apple and cherry trees in the gardens were ablaze. Black clouds of smoke and bright fringes of flames shot up from the burning houses in a dozen places above the town walls, as though huge vats of tar had caught fire. And more awful than all else, against the black field of smoke church steeples rose out of forked flames like the red, upright ears of frightened squirrels, tipped with bright tufts of fire . . . Balthasar had recently seen something very similar somewhere . . . And along the base of St Olaf's Church, on the near side of the town wall – just as at the Last Judgement – ran gleaming streams of molten lead. Leemet was talking: ". . . In the matter of what king we would submit to . . ." and Kulpsuu called out, interrupting him: "And why the devil should we *submit* to *any* king at all, eh? Is a man of this land an old woman, or what, that he must always *submit* to someone?" Leemet continued: "To whom and how – that is something we want to consider carefully and, of course, discuss with the Honourable Council, as the Honourable Council itself has discussed these matters with many kings and is at this very moment discussing with the Swedish king, Gustav." Under the fresco of the fire Balthasar read the barbed, white Gothic letters on the black plaque:

> *In the year fourteen hundred and thirty-three,*
> *On the eleventh day of May,*
> *All Tallinn burned, from Toompea down,*

Houses and sheds, gardens and courtyards,
Churches and cloisters, all burned down,
Organs, bells and folk beyond number.
Let us pray to God all the days of our lives
To spare us another such calamity.

Just then Herr Packebusch spoke through the interpreter, Herr Loop:

"As much as we have seen so far, your compatriots have been more than ready to submit to our main enemy, the Muscovite, and why, in that case, should we support your efforts?"

To which Jakob replied:

"Our greatest enemy is the German manor lord. And the Muscovite is our greatest enemy's greatest enemy. But our greatest enemy is no friend to Tallinn either, as everyone has known for some time. For thirty years now, ever since the time of the Great Cleansing of the Faith, people have heard the nobles singing in town – boosting their swaggering self-importance with a few swigs of ale – about how they want to bash in the heads of all the louts in town and see the gutters run red with their blood!"

"And what is it that you now want from us?" Herr Packebusch asked.

Leemet of Ohulepa continued, explaining that they requested half a company of mounted mercenaries, with all the necessary gear and equipment, to be sent out among the peasants, to teach them how to fight a war.

The councilmen began to discuss the matter amongst themselves, in German, of course:

"Why, something like that would be worse than sending half a company directly into the arms of the Muscovite!" Herr Clodt cried.

"Perhaps not quite as bad as that," a broad-shouldered gentleman said, smiling. "It might in fact be a clever move: it means the town would have all those thousands of men on a leash as well . . . at least to some extent!"

"Ah Schmedemann, you have let yourself be led down the wrong path by your nephew, Franz!"

Herr Schmedemann replied: "I am not the one saying that our town Greys will rise up if we say no to the peasants. All I am saying is that *if* the Greys stage a rebellion, and it is possible they will any day now, things will get bloody for us. And as for Franz – he's a hothead, and blatherer to boot. No-one will take him seriously."

Herr Beelholt remarked: "If Lord Erik ascends to the throne in Sweden, there's likely to be a regime quite friendly to the peasants there, judging by rumours . . ."

Herr Boissmann rubbed his broad jaw with gold-ringed hands. "So the thing is – to make friends with the peasant . . . hmm . . . yes . . . To put a knife in his hands, so he can take off one of the knight's balls . . . Well, it's worth thinking about . . ."

One of the councilmen said: "But he'll take them both! And cut his throat as well! We cannot allow that!"

Someone began: "In my day, in Germany . . ."

But Herr Clodt interrupted him: "It was an entirely different story in your day, in Germany. There, it was German peasants who were rebelling and German towns that supported them. But look at who's rebelling here!"

"And just what *more* would you want?" Burgomaster Packebusch asked, talking over Herr Loop.

"Guns from the town arsenal. To use against the fortified castles," said Leemet, as they had decided at the king's quarters.

"Ha-ha-ha-ha!" Herr Clodt laughed.

"Well-well-well-well!" Herr Packebusch added. "But you don't know how to fire cannons!"

"You don't even know what to *ask* for," Herr Dehn continued: he was in charge of the town arsenal. "You wouldn't know what to ask for if we wanted to know what kinds of cannons you needed, now would you?"

The spokesmen were silent. The only one of their group who knew about cannons was unfortunately the man who had fallen ill, or perhaps had fled in fear, the evening before. There were of course a few peasants among them who had learned how to load and fire cannons in the coadjutor's war. But at dawn yesterday time had been short and, anyway, no-one had thought of looking for them.

And now the imp of vanity made a sudden appearance here, in the Town Hall, standing beside Balthasar, egging him on. It was the same wicked little devil, goading him to take a chance, the way it did on that day, many years ago, on the big day of the skywalkers' stunts, when it had dared him to jump out of the shelter of the Hobuveski Gate and run towards Herr Bock and the now-departed Meus – which he had not, in fact, done at the time. But instead of retreating with his childish pranks, that imp had become more brazen. Or at least cleverer, or more adept at self-justification: Balthasar, you cannot let your compatriots be humiliated like this! Look at the arrogance in that chestnut beard of Herr Dehn's ... see how relieved he looks ... And look at the sour expression on Herr Schmedemann's face, as though he were really prepared to give you the cannons ... and the same for Herr Beelholt – of whom I would not have expected it. And how triumphant are Herr Clodt's grinning teeth! But you know something about cannons! Why, you have explored most of this town's citadels and strongholds and round towers, and in Stettin and Oderburg you saw the weapons arsenal – of Herr Barnim ... Ergo. And Balthasar heard himself say, calmly, as though it had been carefully considered and decided long ago:

"Translate for the gentlemen: We would like four good field culverins, and it would be desirable if they were on those Burgundian, um ... bases" (for there was no word for *Lafetten* in country tongue,

444

and he could not very well utter the German word). "And eight falconets and two hundred lead balls and a hundred iron balls for each cannon."

At this point Balthasar noticed that Herr Vegesack had raised himself up from his carved seat, the one with the armrest depicting the figure of a man without a tongue, which, as he had heard, was supposed to represent the Silent One. Herr Vegesack seemed to be looking at him, Balthasar, and gesturing to him, as though waving him away. But then Balthasar realised that the councilman's gesticulations were intended for someone who had just appeared at the door of the hall. Balthasar turned to look, managing to catch a glimpse of a figure in the shadow of the closing door. He continued: "We think that if Tallinn gives us these twelve cannons from its arsenal of at least two hundred and fifteen, it will not be weaker in the least, and we will be much stronger." When he realised that he had said "we will be stronger", he felt annoyed, irritated with himself; at the same time he also felt, with some satisfaction, that he would certainly be forgiven. But there was no time to dwell on it, because the door of the council hall opened again in a way that made all the councilmen turn towards it. It was the same white-haired council clerk who had directed the peasants into the hall. He hurried to Herr Packebusch and whispered something in his ear and handed him a sealed letter. Herr Packebusch opened it and read. It was apparent from his expression that it contained important news. The clerk departed, closing the door behind him. Herr Packebusch looked up from the letter, speaking in German:

"Gentlemen, Brothers: A ship has arrived in our harbour from the town of Turku, with a message from our ambassador in Sweden: King Gustav was summoned to his Lord God on the twenty-ninth day of last month, in the city of Stockholm."

Balthasar looked at the faces of the silent councilmen. They were impenetrable, at least to his eyes.

445

Herr Beelholt said: "Then we should ring the church bells."

Herr Clodt cried: "Why? Where is it written that we should do such a thing upon a foreign monarch's death? With all due respect to the departed king, let us not forget: the sound of ringing bells would not be at all pleasing to the ears of our Grand Master."

Herr Schmedemann added: "And even less so to the ears of Herr Sigismund . . . isn't that right . . . But for that *very reason* . . ."

It seemed that a rather lively argument was about to ensue. Herr Packebusch raised both hands: "Gentlemen . . . Not now! We must discuss this right away, of course . . . Herr Loop, tell these peasants that unexpected developments compel us to consider other matters at present. We are advised of their request. Have them come tomorrow morning at eight o'clock . . . seven o'clock. We shall give them our answer then."

When the peasants walked out of the Town Hall and into the market-place, it was broad daylight. The remains of ragged rain clouds streaked the blue-grey October sky. The shutters of over half the market stalls along the edges of the square were closed, and padlocks hung at most of the doors of the cellar shops. About a dozen farmers' wagons had never-theless arrived with their meagre produce. Considering the insecurity and confusion that reigned outside the town walls, it was surprising to see even this many, and yet, considering the frightful rise in food prices, it was not many at all. As a result there was a crush of shoppers around the wagons. Balthasar tried not to be too obvious as he stared at them, for he really did not want to be recognised by one of the jostling women or maidens or servant girls. But as he tried to pass by them he felt something he struggled to define – a mixture of admiration, pity, tenderness, something vague and fleeting, but something nonethe-less – towards these old women, these matrons and maidens and young girls, buying peas and onions and cabbages for their masters and husbands, fathers and children, as they crowded around the wagons with their empty baskets, and left, balancing full baskets on their hips. If Balthasar had had the chance to articulate it for himself, he might have voiced something both admiring and pitying about the *aeterna mulier** who, whether towns blazed and battles raged or the fates of thrones and kingdoms hung in the balance, would persist in making a fire in the hearth and hanging a soup pot on the hob and coming to market to get peas and onions and cabbages. And the peas and onions and cabbages would become a sacred offering, and the soup pot a hallowed vessel, and the fire a sacrificial fire, forever and ever. But Balthasar had no chance to ponder all this. Not because the peasants at the wagons were craning their necks to look at the spokesmen, nor because many of the women shoppers turned to stare at them. Not because the town's weigh-master, standing at the door of the weigh-house, nudged his hired hand, muttering audibly: "Look at them. The spokesmen of the rebels. Your blood brothers . . ." Not because of any of this. It was because a familiar voice, though he could not yet identify it, called out suddenly from somewhere behind him:

"Hey! *Balthasarius perditus!*† Look at the company you've taken up with!"

Even before he could turn around and look the speaker in the face, Balthasar recognised him by the odd timbre of his voice – at once vulgar and mocking and confidential – and regardless of the fact that he, Balthasar, was now, because of his attire, being addressed with the familiar instead of the formal "you".

"Hmm . . . Greetings, Herr Antonius . . ."

He turned to Jakob and said in a low voice: "Go to Kimmelpenning's shop. I'll follow you shortly."

The peasants withdrew and Herr Antonius said: "What a surprise! At the Doctor's they said you'd gone to the university. To Marburg, or

* The eternal woman (Latin). † The long-lost Balthasar (Latin).

447

wherever it was. So – a "master" already, are you? Ha-ha-ha-ha. And now you're a member of the council of state of this yokel king, eh? He-he-he-heh!"

"And how does Herr Antonius himself fare? And Herr Henning and the rest?"

"Splendidly! Just splendidly! But still: this yokel rebellion is a mirage, not a ship! How can an intelligent rat board it?"

"Is Herr Henning in Tallinn, too?"

"No he's not. He's in Dünamünde with the Order Master. But let's talk about you . . ."

Balthasar sensed malice in Herr Antonious' desire to talk about *him*. His face, flushed red, his small mocking mouth, his bulging yellow eyes, the play of his wanton fingers on the sword handle – everything about him exuded ill will, suggesting he had not forgotten the humiliating oath he had once been forced to swear in the Doctor's chapel. He shut his left eye and with his right peered at Balthasar from under the rim of his black beret. He sneered, showing gleeful white teeth:

"Well, I suppose the Doctor was too malleable a master for one with your plough-ox temperament. And besides, his wife interested you much more than the well-being of his duke. Ha-ha-ha-hah! And now then – back from Marburg? But how did you get mixed up with *them* from *there*?" He jerked his chin in the direction the peasants had taken. "Or perhaps you were in Pskov in the meantime, instead of in Marburg? Maybe at the school of the Muscovite spies? I know they have such a school there. There are plenty of yokels hanging about who've had their training there. The ones we helped to draw and quarter on Jerusalem Hill were from there, too. Remember?"

"I remember."

"It was so pleasant afterwards, sitting in the Grey Rat together, dissecting human nature. Ha-ha-ha-ha. Come, let's go to the Wolf Den behind the Holy Ghost. That's an even more pleasant spot."

448

"I'm not coming."

"You're coming, my little dove. It's like this: from *me*, our friend the Order Master can immediately learn what your rabble-rousers' plans are."

"You will learn nothing from me."

"Really? But the Doctor learned all kinds of things from you, for his duke."

Balthasar was silent.

"See? And now every hair on your head belongs to that muck-and-mire king of yours. *Vox sanguinis.** Ha-ha-ha-ha-hah! But when I want your help in the name of our *rightful* sovereign, you resist?? Well, once a yokel always a yokel, no matter how much Terence he's crammed. I'm telling you, as a friend: come, let's sit down with a drink. And you'll answer my questions."

"I won't."

"Fine. If that's the way you want it, I'll do the talking. Ha-ha-ha-hah! These blood brothers of yours, they've burned down so many manors and killed so many nobles, they'll be crushed like bedbugs. Of course they'll be crushed! As I said, all this is not a ship but a mirage. And then they'll draw and quarter this king of yours. And his advisers as well. Just like those on Jerusalem Hill, whom you recall. Be clear about one thing: if you refuse to answer me, the bailiff of the Order will be informed that among the peasant-spokesmen there were some who were not just anonymous yokels, but . . ."

"We have safe conduct."

"Fool! Not now! But when it's all over with them, when they're through – tomorrow, in a week, in two weeks. I'm telling you, even if you manage to get out of this stew without being drawn and quartered, it will be *impossible* for you, in any case, to live in this town! So – come on!"

Balthasar heard horses snorting behind him. He heard the voices of

* The voice of (your brother's) blood (Latin: Genesis 4.10).

449

the market goers in the damp morning air, and their footfalls on the cobblestones, and the curses of the town guardsmen shambling across the square for a changing of the guard. He smelt sauerkraut and hay and horses. And in the middle of this fantastically real square, in the midst of these real voices and smells, he felt Herr Antonius' unreal and inescapable threat around him and in front of him and above his head . . . Should he . . . should he . . . strike a lightning blow to the temple, near that red hair? No . . . Terrible complications . . . Should he grab Herr Hasse's short fire iron from under his coat? No . . . Even more terrible complications . . . And then he recalled something that had been hovering this entire time in the vaulted cellar of his mind. No, he did not want to go down that road. He certainly did not. But in a matter of a few brief moments, the necessity of doing so had become absolute. And the temptation to play the game was irresistible . . .

Balthasar looked genially into Herr Antonius' yellow eyes, all the while anxious, apprehensive about the effect of his words – his only usable weapon – on this false monk, this false knight, this marketplace Satan. The foreseeable effect of the words he was rehearsing caused him some little embarrassment. For there were things he knew that now, unexpectedly, had thrust the dagger of self-defence into his hands. He spoke in a voice almost nonchalant:

"Herr Antonius, do you think your mother is still sitting in Duke Barnim's prison tower?"

"*What?!* What are you talking about?" Herr Antonius asked, clearly unnerved, which response he was attempting to disguise as incomprehension.

"You're hoping she'll succeed in talking her way out of the accusation of witchcraft . . . ?"

"What on earth are you talking about?" cried Herr Antonius hoarsely.

"And that she'll have to stand trial only in the matter of the gang of thieves? Vain hope. She has confessed to witchcraft. Confessed *by means of an act*."

"How?"

Herr Antonius stared at Balthasar, his yellow eyes bulging and giving out an odd uncertainty.

"On last St Martin's Eve, the Lord called her soul to Him. By means of the noose that He Himself helped put around her neck."

"What? What are you saying? Are you the Devil himself?!"

"It doesn't matter. What I'm saying is this: if you breathe *one single word* about having seen me here among the peasants, in three days' time it will be known in Dünamünde that you are the son of a thief and a witch."

He almost added "and the brother of a harlot", but left that unsaid, not only because it would have undermined the climax of his blows, but because of that red-headed Lada, who had given him a taste of the pitiable sweetness of sin.

Herr Antonius' face, frozen into a smirk, changed colour twice under Balthasar's gaze. First the red drained away, revealing the thin purple mesh of veins on his cheeks, even as his face was turning darker. And then the even-red flush returned, rising from his collar, up his neck and into his face. An observer of the two men's expressions might have said that Herr Antonius collected himself more quickly in the changing situation than Balthasar managed to do. At the same time, Herr Antonius' expression was more transparent, as he reloaded and repositioned his cannons, than Balthasar's wooden countenance during similar manoeuvres, even on days when he was clean-shaven. Herr Antonius said, suddenly adopting the formal "you": "Humph. Do you know how to play that Indian board game? Chess, I mean."

"Not very well," Balthasar grunted. (This was less an assertion about his skill than an expression of contempt for the question, and thereby for the questioner.)

But Herr Antonius proceeded pleasantly: "Well, then you know what they say of a situation where the pieces are so placed that each player is completely protected. Assuming, of course, that neither does anything stupid."

"No I don't."

"Ah. But there's no word for it in German. What they say is *remissum*. Ha-ha-ha-ha. *Ergo: remissum*. Hence, it's a draw. Convey my greetings to your king. And don't worry about me any more than I am going to worry about you."

With a casual wave of his hand he turned and walked through the market-goers in the direction of the Old Market. Balthasar took a deep breath, a mixture of triumph and doubt mingled with the smells of the market, which now reached him again, and hurried off after his fellow spokesmen to Kimmelpenning's shop.

The door was bolted from the inside. Only after he had knocked twice did Kimmelpenning's tall, slender shop assistant open it and direct Balthasar to the cellar room. And then Balthasar was once again standing under the low, dark, arched ceiling where he had first become involved in affairs of town and state. He recalled writing the letter from the shoemaker Schröder to his brother in Warburg. And now here he was again, on behalf of country and state, except this time it was not a matter of using of a goose quill, but a matter of cannons and of life and death.

In the light coming through the mud-spattered windows, the cellar seemed to have become smaller and more faded and emptier – several of the shelves were bare – in the two years since Balthasar had last been there, and old Kimmelpenning himself seemed to have shrunk, looking markedly more shrivelled than he remembered him. His sparse hair now recalled a paint brush with mingled streaks of white and grey. But his red-rimmed eyes in his tired face were as alert as they had been before and still resembled blue enamelled buttons. The way he greeted

Balthasar – with a gesture of welcome and a pat on the back – was so businesslike and familiar and quick, it was as though Balthasar had left the store just two hours, not two years, ago.

Kimmelpenning was saying to the peasants: "You yourselves were saying the same thing – that it seemed to you, too, that some of the councilmen were considering giving you the cannons and mercenaries. Right. As far as I know the council, such men cannot be the majority. But there are a number of them: Schmedemann and Beelholt and maybe Boissmann. I'll say this: if, without the cannons, the peasants were to undertake something that would make the town take notice and rouse our own Greys, those *know-nothings,* then we could get the town to join with the peasants, that's certain . . ." He turned towards Balthasar: "So, what news from our own Master *Studiosus?*"

Balthasar had not yet had a chance to tell even the spokesmen his big news. Now he said:

"The councilmen got a letter – while we were standing there, in front of them: King Gustav died in Stockholm on the twenty-ninth of last month."

The peasants, Leemet sitting on a barrel, Jakob on a roll of leather, and Kulpsuu on an empty shelf, received the news impassively.

Kulpsuu said: "Hope he has a pleasant journey!" And spat.

Leemet muttered: "Well, well . . . then there'll be a new one . . . Erik, or whoever . . ."

Jakob asked, with apparent indifference: "And just what will that mean for us?"

Balthasar replied: "Herr Schmedemann said that when Erik assumes the throne, Sweden will have a ruler well disposed towards the peasants."

Kimmelpenning raised his top lip oddly, as though something were causing him pain, and said: "That will be in Sweden, and it will be in the future, maybe . . . But *for us,* at this moment, the death of their king is bad news."

"Why is it bad?!" Kulpsuu asked querulously.

"Because the Council in Tallinn is indecisive and split and confused as it is. And every such change, with its uncertain consequences, paralyses them the more. It will just increase their inclination not to decide anything, to shrug their shoulders and hide their heads in their ermine collars. You are trying to get culverins and falconets from them to use against the walls of Kolovere . . . What I'm saying is that if you could capture Kolovere without them, *then* the Council might open the gates of its armoury to you . . . But like this . . . and now, with Sweden's Gustav having just bitten the dust . . . well . . ."

Kimmelpenning's younger shophand, Niglas, a lad with a pale shock of hair and blue marten-eyes, returned from his errand into town with an ample supply of bread and stewed beef. At Kimmelpenning's behest he had also slung a good-sized keg over his shoulder and had stopped in at the Green Frog, or maybe the Wolf Den, to have it filled up. When the men had eaten and were passing the keg around to wash down their salted beans with the ale, and when they had explained to Kimmelpenning, as best they could, where and how the peasant forces were gathering, and Kulpsuu was beginning to rant in bursts of drunken anger – "Why should we bow down to this crowd of scoundrels? . . . In a week we'll have ten thousand men!" – Kimmelpenning sent Niglas out to summon some of the other shop owners – Jaan-of-Vanakulli and Andres of Saxapette. The lanky, older shop assistant was sent on a speedy mission to some members of the directorate of St Olaf's Guild. Kimmelpenning himself reached into a familiar wooden box on the shelf and popped a dried frog's leg into his mouth – Balthasar wondered how many thousand of those he had eaten the past few years – and asked Balthasar to follow him. In the back wall, between the shelves and hidden by a blanket, was a low door that Balthasar had not noticed. He went through it on Kimmelpenning's heels, up a few steps to a vaulted half-cellar which seemed to be the old man's living quarters. A simple rumpled bed with a catskin spread, some partially burnt logs on the cold hearth, a few medium-sized ironclad chests, a couple of stools, a little table with a pewter plate holding a half-eaten piece of bread, a simple pewter candlestick, and next to it a slightly dulled heavy silver goblet a good hand-span in height, which, in the middle of the simple room, under the stained vaulted ceiling, unexpectedly and impressively brought to mind the measure of the man who inhabited this room.

Kimmelpenning removed the plate to a corner of the hearth, cleaned off the breadcrumbs with his sleeve, and took a sheaf of octavo pages out of the smallest chest, setting them on the table, along with quill and ink. He filled the goblet from a wine keg in the corner of the room and said:

"Take a seat."

Balthasar remarked, sitting down on a stool: "I feel as if Clawes Schröder has risen from the dead and I have to write another letter to his brother . . . What's the story?"

Kimmelpenning pushed the goblet towards Balthasar: "Drink. No, no, I won't have any. God grant that your work today bear the same fruit as the letter to Schröder. Not a soul came here from Warburg that time."

"And what is it I am to do today?"

The old man took four or five larger sheets of paper out of the chest and put them down in front of Balthasar. They were covered with writing – a fine, barbed script – clearly the work of a practised hand. "You've heard, no doubt, of the Twelve Articles that the peasants in Germany distributed at the time of their great revolt, more than thirty years ago?"

"To tell the truth, I haven't read them. But I've heard of them . . . if you're thinking of the most famous of them . . . Someone by the name of Hipler is supposed to have written them down, a man in league with the peasants, former secretary to a count he'd run away from."

"I don't know who wrote them down first. But now I would like someone who is in league with the peasants here, a former secretary to a doctor he ran away from – heh-heh-heh-heh – I would like him to translate them into country tongue."

Balthasar had sipped a little of the wine. It was a good white Rheingauer, though a bit sour in his opinion, causing his mouth to pucker the way bird cherries did, but a wine valued by connoisseurs and said to make one particularly clear-headed when consumed in moderation. He pushed the goblet towards Kimmelpenning and picked up the papers.

"Articles of the Peasant Rebellion, anno 1525." But from there the fine script continued in Low German: "To the Christian Reader, Peace and the Grace of God through Christ. There are many Antichrists at this Time who on account of the Assembling of the peasants are finding Cause to blaspheme against the Gospels, saying . . . etc."

"Where did you get this?"

"I had it copied from the old documents at the Town Hall."

"Secretly?"

"Well . . . of course."

"And . . . who copied it for you?"

"Alright, I'll tell you. Maybe it'll be useful at some time for you to know. But you have to keep your mouth shut even if they put you on the rack: it was Topff, the scribe of the lower court."

Balthasar recalled the cunning, mild-mannered man with the grey-cat face, from Doctor Friesner's fateful dinner party. He asked:

"And what do you need them for?"

"Well . . . since they were so famous in Germany, I thought they might also be of use here, in Mary's Land, to say some things that haven't been said before. No matter that several decades have passed. At that time in Germany, many towns joined with the peasants. The lower classes first, and then half the town councillors after them. I reckon the articles sort of set things in motion. And maybe it'll happen here, too . . . It's up to you to identify the things that speak to *our situation* and those that don't."

Dusk had fallen by the time Balthasar could draw a scratchy line under his day's work. He had been hard at work right through the middle of the day and had scarcely raised his eyes to look out of the low, grey glass panes of the mud-spattered window, at the hustle and bustle of the market: the market folk and well-dressed burghers and beautiful women of the town, walking about. Translating from German into country tongue was a strange and laborious task. And three times as strenuous to put it down in writing, as he had been charged to do. It was like stripping someone of his clothes in order to dress him in those of a stranger, and in the process seeing that person – for clothes do change the wearer – become different from the person he had been . . . The sleek German doublet of the smooth German account had to be removed, to be replaced by coarse peasant leggings, homespun shirt, and ragged coat, in order that the core and essence of the statement not end up with a bare backside, but so that its rump be wholly covered. But this did not make the statement any more comprehensible. Not that it required any kind of special genius to write in country tongue. True, for many German words there were no real equivalents, and for some of the sounds of country tongue there were no corresponding letters in the German alphabet. And then again, for some sounds there seemed to be more letters than necessary, first one, then another and then a third, all presenting themselves for the same sound, so that whichever came first to the pen was the one that ended up on paper. But still, there was no special art to it: all the pastors did this kind of work when they wrote their sermons in country tongue, and if not all, then at least the more conscientious among them – in this town, for example, Harder and Huhn and Mönnick. And the departed Meus was one who had taken special care with this task: making outlines of his sermons, and

457

sometimes even writing them out in full. It was over Meus' shoulder that Balthasar had seen, for the first time, the letters of country tongue appearing on paper from a writer's pen. But somehow the letters only became that which they were meant to be when they were read out loud, so that they changed from the strange and unfamiliar *written* words to the living, spoken words of country tongue. As it happened now, when Balthasar softly read out his own straight, bold lines of script. Furthermore, these articles of the German peasants were quite curious. Things were stated in an unusually direct, outspoken manner, so it was clear that behind such a masterful, forceful statement there had to be a thousand solid supporters. But then, nearly everything was immediately retracted again, as if out of fear. True enough, from time to time the iron tip of a spear appeared among the words, but it was not thrust into the body of the one for whom it was intended; instead, its tip was bent back by the very same hands holding it, and then hidden again, with a humble plea for forgiveness.

"There are many Antichrists at this Time who on account of the Assembling of the peasants are finding Cause to blaspheme against the Gospels, saying: Is this the fruit of the new Gospel? That no-one obeys, that there is revolt and rebellion everywhere, that people band together in great throngs to" – *reformern* – how the dickens should that be translated?! – "to overturn, root out, and perhaps even to kill the temporal and spiritual authorities". . . Indeed. But then it said: "To all these villains issuing such condemnations, the following articles provide an answer in that they will, first of all, bring to an end the blasphemies against the Word of God, and, second, will extend Christian forgiveness for all the acts of disobedience and even the rebellion of the peasants." Article Three stated: "Hitherto we have commonly been considered the property of our lords, which is a wretched thing since Christ has sprinkled us all with His own precious blood and redeemed us and bought our freedom, that of the lowly shepherd boy as well as the highest authority, without exception, and therefore according to Scripture, we too are free and want to be free . . ."

True enough. But immediately after there was this: "Not that we want to be absolutely free and under no authority, for God does teach us that we should live by the Commandments, which is testimony to the fact that we must obey those in authority and be humble not only before our superiors but before all, and that we need to carry out with a willing spirit the commands of those superiors chosen and determined (determined by God, that is), in all matters proper and Christian . . ."

So it went. Whatever seemed to be stated forcefully and clearly was immediately rendered confusing and murky, as if on purpose . . . As in Article Seven: "We shall not hereafter allow ourselves to be further oppressed by our masters, but wherever a lord has given the peasant his proper share, the peasant is to have the right to use it according to the agreement between them. And a lord is not to compel or force or demand work or aught else in excess of that" . . . Fine and good. But then there was this: "If, however, a lord have urgent need of the peasant's labour, the peasant must obey and comply" . . . No-no, whatever the situation in Swabia or Thuringia thirty years ago, we here in Livonia have no use for these articles. We could write our own articles, stating that we have decided from this time forward to perform no more tasks, to bear no more burdens. That we have decided to sweep away the master race from this land – let them return, voluntarily, to the land where their fathers, or they themselves, came from. Or, let those who resist or fight back and refuse to be killed or trampled underfoot, as Herr Üxkyll was trampled yesterday . . . Or maybe our articles could . . . Ha-ha-ha-ha – now I'm arguing as though there were no longer any difference between me and my words, as though these old peasant clothes brought by Krumhusen's houseboy had cast a spell on me – or maybe our articles could be the same kind of two-pronged statements as these. For, as I've

459

heard, villages and towns and provinces were burned in their time as a result of these words, and a long and terrible bloody war was fought. And once again, the written word and its fulfilment are as far apart as Heaven is from earth – what kind of confounded curse is this . . . ? "To the Christian Reader Peace and the Grace of God through Christ . . ." And thousands of chopped-off heads and thousands of cut-off noses. And gallows along the roadsides for miles on end . . . Balthasar had heard this in Stettin from a carter working in the salt mines – a man who had fled from Mühlhausen. But he did not get the chance to think more deeply about the strange and apparently inevitable contradiction between word and deed, text and life. Not only because the present moment was not amenable to such reflection, neither in history nor in his own personal life, but because Kimmelpenning came in just then, chewing on his frog's leg. He picked up the completed translation with a nod of acknowledgement, saying: "Niglas will take this to St Olaf's Guildhall. Guild officers and a large number of common people have been summoned. It'll be read out loud there. And you – what are your plans?"

"I want to see Annika. Since Meus' death, I haven't had the chance to . . . And Meus was, after all, my – how should I put it . . . ?"

"Right. By the way . . ." Kimmelpenning filled the goblet with plum wine, took a large draught, and pushed it towards Balthasar. "You said you considered it your task to *explain* the peasant uprising to the towns-people, wherever possible. And to ask them to join you, whoever so wished?"

"And so?"

"Don't you want to come to the Guildhall tonight, fairly late? After they've discussed these articles and the present state of the town amongst themselves. So that you can deliver a real sermon or give a speech or however you want to put it. About what the town Greys should do now or whom they should support."

"You think that is necessary?" Balthasar asked, sipping his plum wine.

"I do."

"And what should they be told?"

Kimmelpenning thrust out his yellowish-grey beard. As he talked, he straightened up. He was clearly saying something he had been thinking through for some time:

"If the town Greys want to keep their lives and livelihoods from completely falling apart, if they want to keep the few shops and the few decent jobs they have and resist being coerced into accepting wretched menial jobs, if they do not want to be driven out of the guilds for refusing to declare themselves German – in a word, if they want to hold on at least to some of their rights and perhaps gain a few more, *then let them support the peasant uprising in every way they can!*"

"Hmm." Balthasar sipped his wine. "And you don't want to explain this to them yourself?"

"I'll be telling them anyway. But it's another thing coming from a man like you. Of course, if you lay it all out in front of a hundred or a hundred and fifty men and stir them up to rebel against the Germans, and this peasant war comes to naught, you know that your future in this town will be . . ."

"I know."

"And so – what do you think?"

"I think . . . that I'd better come. But first I want to see Annika."

"Uhuh."

"You know, I don't want to appear at her door in these rags. It would be a shock to her: her brother, the university student, suddenly returned from Germany . . . and afterwards, at the Guildhall too . . . Can you find me something more suitable to wear?"

"Hmm. But of course."

461

CHAPTER SIX,

*in which the young man whom we are obviously determined to portray
as a hero (because we know not how to manage without a hero), makes it
difficult for us to fulfil our good intentions, at the same time as a wanton
woman carries out what is perhaps her most remarkable act. Yet none
of this actually matters, for everything takes place on a boat caught
in a whirlpool, where it spins, suspended for a few heartbeats, yet is
carried irrevocably towards precipitous falls, as their roar draws
closer moment by moment.*

Twilight had fallen when Balthasar set out to see his sister. He was
wearing the black woollen suit of Kimmelpenning's son, who had died
over a year earlier. Though not visible in the dark, a narrow strip of
white shirt collar showed above the neckline of his suit coat. His high
leather boots had once been worn by a Danish royal counsellor. And he
had trimmed the edges of his nine-day-old beard. It was to his advantage (unless it should turn out to be to his disadvantage?!) that he did
not go straight across the Old Market to the Doctor's gate, for dusk was
not yet so deep that he would have escaped notice had someone chanced
to look out of the windows. Instead he circled around by way of Harju
and Müürivahe and Karja streets and arrived at the Doctor's gate
without having to pass by his windows. The gate was open. He slipped
under the archway and in a moment was on the back stairs. A faint carnation scent made him catch his breath. And although no-one would
have seen him pause to draw breath, he did not pause, not for one
moment. He bounded up the Frolinks' stairs, taking the steps three at

a time, dashed through the great-room, and burst into the kitchen. A fair-haired woman, a stranger, rose from the hearth and looked at him in alarm.

"Ah," Balthasar said. "Hello. You must be Piret, am I right?"

"I am . . . But, who might the young gentleman be?"

"Where is Frau Frolink? In the bedchamber, maybe?"

"No. She's not here."

"What do you mean?"

"She's not at home."

"She's not?! Where is she then?"

"How would I know her comings and goings . . . ?"

Balthasar looked at the girl's eyes, gleaming in the firelight from the hearth, and he thought: *She knows. But she's not telling. Why won't she tell me?* He had been absent from this house too long to be able to guess what was going on. And yet a shadow of jealousy briefly darkened his spirits: He had travelled great distances over land and sea, and made time, amidst his urgent obligations, at this dangerous moment – and his sister was not even at home! By God, where was she? (But his disappointment was perhaps a preparation and justification for whatever else might happen in this house.) Anyway, why *should* this girl tell a total stranger about her mistress' comings and goings when he had pretended not even to hear her ask his name!

"And when will she return?"

"I don't know."

"Really? So . . . she could be away overnight?"

"Could be . . ."

"Where does she usually go?"

"How could I know that? "

"You *must* know!"

"The parishioners say . . . she visits the sick . . . and . . ."

Balthasar stood in the middle of the kitchen and looked at the low pine-plank door, at the grain of the wood repeatedly scrubbed clean of its ever-recurring coating of soot, now brightening, now darkening as the flames flared and subsided in the hearth, seemingly trying to conceal, solemnly and then playfully, what lay behind the door: the humble little cubicle where he had lived his last years as a schoolboy. Below its window pulsed the heartbeat of the town; at the little table he had struggled with God and the Devil, and himself; on the plank bed he had dreamt many strange dreams, and that final, mad dream that was not a dream . . . At the age of twenty-four one does not yet indulge in nostalgia about the past. Especially when that past is a mere two years distant. And yet he shifted his weight from his toes back onto his heels and did not approach the door of his old chamber. Annika's looms were no doubt once again behind its sooty boards, where they had been before Balthasar moved in. As far as the house was concerned, it was as though he had never been in it . . . As though he alone knew that he had lived and dreamt his strange dreams here . . . including that one mad dream . . . No, no, no! He would leave immediately, the house had become too alien. He would go back to Kimmelpenning's shop and lie down on the hard rolls of leather and listen to the sounds of the town as its evening bustle sank into night behind the muddy cellar window: the burghers' footfalls heading home; the troops of town guardsmen humming on their way to or from their night watch in towers and bastions; the horn in the Town Hall tower sounding the ninth hour . . . And he, Balthasar, staring up at the low, dark, invisible vaulted ceiling, rehearsing what he would soon be saying to the restive group assembled in the Guildhall . . . *If you want to hold on even to some of your rights – and if you want to gain further rights, then support the peasant uprising in every way you can!* . . . He could feel it: he would not be at a loss for words or passion! Nor for conviction! No, not for conviction either! . . . *Men of Tallinn, listen to me! I am one of you! You are all my fathers and brothers and kin. We have known each other long. We know each other well. And they who are out there, in the villages whence we ourselves or our fathers have come, they who have now risen up to shake off the arrogant might of the manor lords – they are, like us . . .*

"Hmm. Does the Doctor happen to be at home?"

"No . . ."

"How do you know?"

"The housemaid, Magdalena, told me. Someone from the Pirita Convent just came to fetch him."

"From Pirita? Alright. Perhaps I'll come by to see Frau Frolink in the morning."

Balthasar started down the stairs, stepping hurriedly and softly, for he wanted to get out of the house undetected – he truly did. But even before he was halfway down the steep, narrow stone stairway, he knew he would not manage to depart in secret. He knew it with the same kind of mysterious premonition that animals in seaside wetlands apparently have, hours beforehand, of the approach of flood waters. It is said, for example, that moose calves begin heading inland, lowing as they go, and that young pike, having kept close to the bottoms of shrunken rivers, start swimming towards the rising water well ahead of time. Balthasar reached the bottom of the stairs, opened the door leading to the vaulted passage, and came face to face with Katharina.

He took a step back to let her pass. Then he closed the door, pressed his back against it, and looked straight at her.

His mind came to a standstill as a strange, swelling rush of feeling coursed through him, swallowing everything with it. Had he managed to think about it, he would have realised, not without astonishment, that it was a wave of jubilant gratitude mixed with suppressed misgivings: gratitude to God for guiding Katharina to this encounter, and for thus granting His approval for everything that would now ensue. And deep down, underneath it, a shiver of doubt: *But maybe it's the Devil toying with me?*

465

Balthasar did not say a word.

"*You* . . ." Katharina said. It sounded like a thin, high-pitched cry muffled in a silky whisper. "You were supposed to be in Germany . . ."

She was half-backing towards the great-room and Balthasar followed. Afterwards he did not know by *what* light he had seen Katharina's eyes under the passageway – grey-black, round with agitation and surprise . . . Then Katharina was in the great-room, next to the round Dutch table where three candles flickered in a candelabrum. And she turned to face Balthasar. Her eyes, even darker than just moments before, were now narrowed, their lower lids nearly a straight line. She said:

"Matthias is not at home . . ."

"I know, I know," Balthsasar murmured. *I know, I know,* he was thinking, and this incomparable woman, this outrageous woman, this angel and harlot who, two years ago had lain down upon his father's old sleigh-coat, so that Balthasar could free her from the spell once cast upon her, was here, right now, to free him from the spell he was under . . . What's that?! What spell are we talking about with regard to Balthasar? Ho-ho-ho-ho! No spell of any kind, of course . . . But then why the sudden spasm, why the twinge of pain in Narva when Herr Kruse had happened to say "Katharina", making him twitch as though his heart, a locked box, was being forced open by someone who knew where to find the secret button. But never mind, never mind. Now he was here. And this woman was here. Balthasar stepped towards her, his Russian-leather boots thudding, advanced into the cloud of her carnation fragrance, and said hoarsely:

"Katharina."

"Matthias is not at home, and I cannot permit *you* . . ." she whispered, and slipped away to the other side of the table. It was the same Weselouwe Dutch table at which the touch of Katharina's leg had once sent a streak of fire shooting from his groin to his chest.

Matthias is not at home – in the first moment, Balthasar had taken that to be an invitation. Naturally. And especially because of the way her grey eyes had sparkled in surprise, as he had noted at the gate, under the archway. *Matthias is not at home* – now the words suddenly seemed intended to hold him off. He tried for an instant to discern their real meaning but could not: perhaps there was none. He tried to catch her glance but could not do that either, for her eyes were downcast in the light of the quivering candle flame. Why should she be pushing him away? *What right* did she have to reject him? He stepped closer to Katharina. He laughed at her attempted claim to virtue, a low, coarse, awkward laugh. But in his heart he did not sneer at the possibility that Katharina had, by some miracle, remained true to him, to him who had freed her from her spell . . . He murmured: "And *just why* can you not *permit* me . . . ?"

He pulled her forcibly towards himself:

"Have you already freed yourself so completely from Matthias' spell, that . . . ?"

Katharina pulled her arm out of his grasp and rushed to the stairs: "No! No! No!"

"Katharina . . . What game are you playing with me?"

Balthasar charged after her. He picked her up in his arms. He saw her long narrow eyes flash. He saw the small red shoes kicking under the hem of her brown skirt. He overwhelmed her firm, silent, resilient resistance with his hands – a wagon-driver's, an oarsman's, a swordman's hands. But as soon as he loosened his grip a bit, she resumed her struggle

– genuine, unrelenting, making clear her willingness to inflict pain.

"Katharina – what is this? After everything that you . . ."

With his right hand he held down her thrashing arms, and with his left he pressed her knees against his heart. A misunderstanding? Mean-spiritedness? A joke? A game? Thank God, Katharina did not cry out. Even though the servant Johann had gone along with the Doctor, and Paap was with the rebels at Limandu, Magdalena was in the house. A cry could have been heard in the neighbouring houses and on the marketplace. Balthasar pushed open the door of the Friesners' bedroom with his shoulder. He later remembered that it was, indeed, with his shoulder. For the duration of a heartbeat he had considered kicking it open. And yet he had decided on using his shoulder. And he knew that he wanted to bribe *somebody* with that decision. But he did not know whom.

He threw Katharina down on the canopy bed, onto the pillows of Babylon where the Doctor and Herr Horn and the Grand Master and the devil knows how many others had lain. He overpowered her there, still resisting, still mute, in the carnation-coriander fragrance that filled the darkness. Only later did he recall how different her resistance had been to the furious rigidity he had encountered a few times with girls who had had reason not to want him. Only later did he recall that Katharina had so suddenly yielded to him – and he blushed *post factum* at the comparison, and then blushed even more deeply at his pretended, or genuine, prudishness – that he had felt like the conqueror of a city who uses a battering ram to break down a gate that is in fact open, and finds the forces defending the town greeting him with cheers and laying down their flags at his feet.

"You came back to me . . ." Katharina whispered when Balthasar's lips gave her the chance to whisper. For Balthasar, on his part, made use of all the conquering arts he knew, spurred on by his youthful lust and his enthusiasm for these arts. Spurred on by the vanity of a young troop commander. And what he had not formerly tried out on the field of battle for himself, he had gained some intimation of from Ovid's wise book, when Gluck Junior brought it for his roommates to read. (He had taken it behind the back of the senior Gluck, who had borrowed it from Duke Barnim's library.) He had not understood everything,

468

in spite of his quite respectable knowledge of Latin. But enough. And certainly the most important parts:

> If you have a voice, sing, if your arms are supple, dance,
> And however you know how to please, do please . . .

"Why did you come back from Germany?" Katharina whispered.

There was no need to explain. No, no, not to Katharina . . . But Balthasar still held her in his embrace. And her hands, circling his neck, played with the hair at the back of his head. Not a single item of clothing came between them under the blankets, and their legs had entwined in the dark – two rough strands of hemp with two smooth linen ropes . . . Merely to establish his manly independence Balthasar said:

"I didn't just come from Germany."

"From where, then?"

"From the rebel peasants."

Katharina was silent for a moment. "Strange . . ." she whispered, "they are, of course, your blood brothers, but still . . . And where are you planning to go now?"

There's no need to say anything. What for? Tomorrow the Doctor will learn about it, too. But no, not the Doctor. At least not from Katharina. And if he does, this meeting tonight in the Guildhall is not a secret meeting. But still, to what end? And then he told her anyway:

"From here – I'm going to St Olaf's Guildhall."

"And what are you going to do there?"

"The leaders of the town Greys will be there." He fell silent. He felt that if he said out loud to Katharina and to himself, I want to urge them to join with the peasants, it would be saying more than he could declare with a clear conscience in the Guildhall . . . A union of the town Greys with the rebellious peasants, a joint rebellion of the town Greys and the peasants – why, this would be demeaning something that was

469

obviously higher by something unfortunately much lower. Yes . . . But was not that just what Balthasar had been doing, in recent days, with respect to himself? And why? That was what he had not yet managed to work out. To be sure, looking upon the town Greys and the country Greys as equals demeaned the townsmen, but simultaneously it elevated the country Greys and the peasantry as a whole . . . and thereby his own kin, who were part of himself. And, Lord God, was there not, smouldering in this violent, desperate, impossible thought – but in these chaotic times perhaps not impossible, after all – another spark, another burning passion: the sweet desire and blinding temptation to use violence to bring about justice, to use violence to realise the equality proclaimed in the Gospels . . . ?! In one hour in the Guildhall . . . ho-ho-ho-ho – to startle the leaders of the town Greys, men of petty municipal pride and self-interest and timidity, with the call to arms of thousands of peasants . . . And at this moment here, in Doctor Friesner's bedroom – to spite and vex Katharina, and thus all those like her, and their unsparing, intolerable arrogance – to set himself, his base-born peasant brawn against their genteel airs. To set against their arrogance the united strength of the Greys of town and country – that grey, dark-grey, black, bubbling, murmuring ferment that would cause the knees of the high born and haughty to quake . . . He said:

"The leaders of the town Greys are gathered there. I want to urge them to join the peasants."

He felt Katharina pull away from him for an instant and then move up so that her mouth was right above his. In a hot, fragrant whisper she said:

"You're mad! You cannot do that! This uprising will be crushed, as all such uprisings always are. And then you will have to flee this town forever . . ."

"Stop it!"

". . . Unless you want to be drawn and quartered!"

"Stop your silly yammering!"

His outburst was loud and vehement because he knew very well just *how right* she might be.

Katharina was silent for a moment. "Fine. I'm sorry. When are you going?"

"Shortly after they sound the hour of ten."

"That means we still have a little time. Wait, I'll get some sweet Mosel wine."

She rose from the bed, naked, found something in the darkness to put on, went out, and in a little while returned. Groping in the dark, Balthasar located the large pewter beaker in her hands. They took turns drinking from it. And then the horn in the Town Hall tower sounded ten o'clock. Balthasar put the beaker on the floor in the dark.

"Now I have to go."

Katharina was silent. Balthasar groped around for his clothes.

"Katharina, what's the meaning of this?! . . . Oh no! . . . Bring back my clothes! *This instant!*"

"*I will not!* As God is my witness, I am not Potiphar's wife – that's not why I'm doing it. But I realised I would not be able to make you listen to reason."

"Listen to me, I gave them my *word!*" Even though he had not, in fact, in the strictest sense, done so. But still . . .

Katharina remained silent. Balthasar could not, after all, get down on his knees in front of her to beg – which is what the grinning imp in the corner of the room was waiting for, so that he might sneer his silent sneer. And since it seemed to Balthasar that he had no weapon to use against this woman but his own brute strength, he grabbed her pliant, naked, remarkably smooth arms with his hard hands:

"Bring me my clothes or I'll squeeze you so hard you'll have marks like two blue gloves around your arms tomorrow. And Matthias will see them . . ."

Still she stayed silent. Balthasar squeezed her arms with genuine rage at being treated like this, pressed so hard, his hands like pliers, that Katharina should actually have cried out, and even though he was ashamed of the empty bravura of his words, he growled:

"You don't know me yet!"

"No," whispered Katharina, "and you know me even less." When the pressure of his hands grew worse, Katharina whispered: "You want me to cry out, but I can't, you see. Magdalena would come running into the room—"

"Bring me my clothes!" Balthasar said.

She said nothing, but Balthasar felt her shoulders move as she shook her head vehemently.   And then – God only knows what it was, but two hundred years earlier, at the outbreak of the Black Death, half of Europe is said to have indulged in an orgy of self-flagellation in atonement for its sins, and maybe there was, in Katharina's behaviour, a trace of the same kind of ardour for atonement – Balthasar felt her press against him. Her nipples brushed his bare chest, moving upward as she stretched up on tiptoe, and her hot lips glided over his chest, towards the base of his throat. Stories of the knight Tannhäuser in Venusberg and the witchcraft of Walpurgis Night and Bagmiel's tales of beautiful dead women rising out of their graves in Slavic villages to suck the blood of the living – all these flashed through Balthasar's mind, but still he yielded, and the inebriating rush of pleasure, at surrendering and becoming one again, throbbed in his neck and down his spine and knees . . .

In the pale grey dawn the Lynx was already stretching itself above the roof ridge when Balthasar was awakened by Katharina's kisses on his face and the occasional pain they caused on his right cheek. He had forgotten the wound from Kulpsuu's sword, but now he flinched – apparently the wound was beginning to fester.

Balthasar got dressed – Katharina had hurried this time to bring him his clothes – those of Kimmelpenning's dead son. Her searching fingers caressed his face, as though she were trying, in the grey darkness, to commit to memory his stubborn chin and uncertain mouth.

"I want you to hurry. And I don't want you to leave at all . . . You know, I don't even know where you're going now."

"Hardly anyone these days knows where he's going . . ."

Balthasar took Katharina's hot face between his hard hands. He kissed her goodbye. It was a cursory kiss, conscious as he was of his sin and wanting to forget. He had to hurry. Because of the Doctor, and because he had to arrive at Kimmelpenning's shop before seven o'clock and get back into the rags he had borrowed from Krumhusen. He freed himself from Katharina's encircling arms: "Yes, yes, yes. Stay well. May God have mercy upon us. Until we meet again? I don't know. No-one knows . . ." He bounded out through the archway gate into the bustling early-morning market. Oh yes, he was already there with his whole body and spirit, already with his band of peasants, on the rounded cobblestones, under the forbidding October sky, between the rough walls, already in the Town Hall, in front of the mural of the conflagration, awaiting the decision of the burgomasters . . . He walked through the liberating morning sounds: doors creaking, wooden wheels clattering, town shoes tapping, soft leather slippers shuffling on the slate walks, the thud-thud-thud of the town guards' heavy boots, horses snorting, dogs barking, occasional foreign words, foreign and familiar words . . . And gradually his strange, hallucinatory vision, born of fatigue and agitation, dispersed into the sounds of the town: the vision of an un-familiar dark room where one of the two – he could not tell whether it was the infatuated country bumpkin or the jeering, smirking imp himself – had stayed behind at the shameful bedside of a strange, wanton woman and was, even now – though Balthasar was already far away – embracing the hot knees of this benighted woman, this harlot and angel.

473

And now punishment would surely follow upon his fall into sin. Or maybe not? Maybe not, after all? When he recalled that misty morning, damp with guilt, when old Krumhusen had hailed him on Väike-Toomi Street in Stettin – and, by the inscrutable will of God, he had not suffered the humiliation and beating he had expected after the encounter: it had paved the way, instead, to the rector's growing regard for him and all the events leading up to his present stay, here – yes, when he thought of that morning, he could actually dare to hope that this day would bring a succession of achievements, one on the heels of another . . . But the ways of God are mysterious, and it could happen that just when your heart arrogantly dares hope for the best, knowing full well how undeserving you are, He decides to flog you for your pitiful, cavorting grasshopper pride.

The day began in a way that made Balthasar's sinful heart leap with relief – even though, had he taken things more seriously, he might have been disheartened or even frightened. As Leemet and Jakob and Kulpsuu waited at the shop, ready to leave, with Balthasar still in Kimmelpenning's cellar, hurriedly changing his clothes by candlelight, Kimmel penning appeared at the door, and Balthasar said, with a feigned calm designed to conceal his shabby sense of himself:

"As you know – I never made it to the Guildhall, unfortunately . . ."

"Just as well you didn't . . ." Kimmelpenning said, dully. "The prophet Ezekiel himself would not have been able to talk them into action."

Today the councilmen had not troubled themselves to interrupt either their early-morning sleep or their breakfast. Only Herr Packebusch and Herr Loop, of course, were in the council hall. And this is what Herr Loop had to say under its high vaulted ceiling, to the peasants standing there, smelling of smoke, of earth, of grain, of sweat, sullen and stubborn, awkwardly crowded together, numb and stony-faced, as they sensed the imminent failure of their cause:

474

"The Honourable Council has this to say: You are blind fools! Are you not aware that all the masters, kings, dukes, princes and your manor lords *inclusive* are ordained by God Himself?! And that, *ergo*, whoever rebels against these rulers is rebelling against his Lord God?"

Aha! Is that all? There's no need to say more. This was entirely predictable, of course. It's hard to imagine that they'd thought any other response possible . . . Wonder whether the Doctor has returned from the Cloister yet . . . Is Katharina serving him breakfast? . . . And kissing him . . . ?

"But if your understanding of God's commands is so pitifully wanting, which would be no surprise, of course, in those of your kind, who have not the slightest inkling of higher things, but worship bushes and trees and shameful idols and pitted hunks of rock – yes, even if you do not understand a thing about God's commands, have you really been struck *so* blind that you do not ask yourselves: what could you possibly accomplish here, surrounded by the forces of five anointed rulers, given your meagre force, your ignorance of the arts of war, and your bare hands?!"

True, Herr Antonius said exactly this. Too bad it is true and that Antonius was right. Why did it have to be he, of all people, who was right? . . . But people like him are the ones who are often right . . . Yet what if God's will were something else, after all? . . . Even though God did not permit it to be realised in Germany years ago, can He not, in another time and place – here, in Livonia, now, where injustice cries out to the heavens even louder, can He really not permit it to be fulfilled here: *that the pride of the nobles might be trampled into the dust? . . . (Right now the Doctor, looking like a servant of Hell, is probably drawing Katharina onto his lap, but he doesn't suspect a thing . . .) True: these men here cannot decide this. All they can do is refuse to hand over the cannons to the peasants. But that was to be expected. Even the king said the day before yesterday: "We don't want to pin too great hopes on this. But we cannot fail to try." Now it has been tried. They don't consider us worthy enough even to discuss the cannons with us. It's as though they'd never*

even heard us ask for them! But the rebellion continues. There are said to be
five thousand of us. Kulpsuu said, in a week we'll be ten thousand. And Kim-
melpenning said that if we could capture Kolovere without the cannons . . .

"In light of that, be reasonable and halt your wicked actions! God
will punish those who have treated you unjustly! Behave not so that you
incur His punishment as well! And even though now, in this time of
confusion and disarray, it is difficult for you to persuade your lawful
sovereign to bring the manor lords to justice – the honourable Town
Council of Tallinn wants you to know this: if you help restore peace
throughout the land, then our lord and master, appointed by God, will
listen to and look into your just grievances!"

Hmm. "Our lord and master appointed by God.". . . But you yourselves
are negotiating with three kings to see which of them it would be most advan-
tageous to serve . . . Your Tallinn? . . . My Tallinn!? . . . Your Tallinn is full of
betrayal . . . My Tallinn is pursuing its affairs with admirable energy and
skill . . .What kind of disagreement is this? Where's the truth in all this?
This smell of smoke, this stink of sweat, this whiff of sheaves of grain around
me and on my own self . . . You – they – I . . .

At this point Herr Packebusch spoke:

"Don't forget the Master's letter."

And in a louder voice, Herr Loop said:

"In this matter, a letter from the Master himself reached us from
Riga last night . . ."

Herr Loop took a roll of parchment from the painted chest on the
floor, waved its wax seal under the peasants' noses, and said:

"Touch it yourselves! It is the Master's own seal."

To Balthasar's chagrin, Leemet of Ohulepa held it with two fingers
for a moment, sliding his thumb across the seal. But he was relieved that
Kulpsuu did not spit on it. Herr Loop rolled open the letter and held it
out to the peasants:

"And here, in our Master's own clear words, it is written:

'But the peasants are to disperse, to return home. They are not to kill their masters or beat their overseers; they are to thresh the grain that they have not yet threshed, that the land and its defenders might have food to eat. And then I shall take care that all their grievances against oppressive manor lords be investigated and that justice pleasing to God be understood by them and their masters, and it shall remain unto them and unto their children and their children's children . . .'"

Balthasar stared at the broad surface of the parchment covered with script. He strained to swallow, in one glance, everything on it, but managed to make out only the first and last lines and a few words in between:

To the Town Council of Tallinn from Dünamünde.
Dear Loyal Subjects, the letters which you did send us have we received from your messenger . . . and their contents . . . The freeing of Paide castle from those besieging it . . . that we have considered no effort too great . . . from His Imperial Majesty . . . the Imperial Diet of Speier . . . the Presidium of H.M. the King of Poland for the town of Tallinn . . . to our especial pleasure . . . On the above indicated date . . .

But then, when he felt he could not take in another word, Balthasar caught a clear reference to the peasants at the beginning of the final paragraph – and saw that there was nothing there but these lines: *"We also humbly insist that you undertake, forcefully, to warn the peasants to abandon their rebellion and return to their work . . ."* It was clear as could be: not a single word about justice for children or children's children.

Herr Loop lowered the letter, rolled it up, and put it back into the chest.

"That is all the response that the honourable Town Council considers necessary."

No written response. No protocol at all to speak of. Even though it seemed to Balthasar that Herr Loop had scribbled something, from time to time. But in principle no discussions whatsoever with the rebels about the cannons – God forbid! And Balthasar felt in astonishment that the unwillingness of *his* beloved old stone-turtle town to join this uncertain cause was probably a worldly-wise, predictable trait of the town's wise, turtle-like stubbornness. And God knows, as long as he could consider it a characteristic of *his* town, he was even pleased by this cool, superior demeanour. But to think that this town of merchants and councilmen, of Great Guild members and their affluent daughters, this wretched stronghold of their arrogance had stooped to such shameful deception in turning away his peasants and himself – this caused the bitter dregs of mortification to rise up from the depths of his heart. He shut his eyes and saw clearly the miraculous instrument he had once seen, with open eyes, in a bronze chest on the deck of the *Sea Maiden*: the surveyor's compass, with its all-knowing needle quivering irresolutely when Klaus, the artillery master, teased it with a small iron anvil from one side, and with a hammer from the other . . .

One way or another, their work was done. They walked out of the dim council hall, where the glow of candles had mingled with the wan light of dawn, out into the harsh light of early morning. The cobblestones between the town walls were wet and shiny from the damp air, but it was so cold that the hummocks out in the open fields would no doubt be rimed over. The north wind whipped the ragged, sooty shreds of clouds across the cold bronze sky, and Old Toomas, in his thirtieth year atop the Town Hall, held out his spear with its tin-plate pennant and pointed to the southwest this time, the direction the peasants had to travel, and in haste. Not only because they suddenly felt unsafe among the cold looks of the townspeople and the ill-tempered militiamen, as if now that their mission had failed the safe passage accorded them had been imperiously revoked. And not only because they were no longer negotiators with the town, discussing the fate of the land, they were criminals and rebels. But above all because this was what the king had commanded . . . And confound it! – in some way and *to a certain extent* it pertained to Balthasar too. *To him too!* Even though in this matter of the peasants he . . . Oh well. He was not one to obey commands with alacrity – if we recall how many times he had disobeyed Master Frolink and Rector Wolff and, God have mercy, God's own commandments . . . Nevertheless, when it came to this large-headed, pale-eyed village blacksmith, this sturdy king with his oak-branch crown, it was different somehow. This matter concerned them all: level-headed Leemet with his unfortunate rasping voice, Kulpsuu, noisy and pitifully brash, tired old Jakob with his craggy face, who looked so much like Balthasar's father Siimon. And all those grey thousands. And one able to see into the depths of his heart might have observed, in explaining Balthasar's sense of belonging, that it concerned Epp as well. Under his ice-cold skin that morning Balthasar vaguely sensed that if he had any chance of staving off God's punishment it could only be by remaining faithful to this cause. And that same perceptive observer would have seen equally clearly that this cause was drawing him, with the irresistible force of duty, contrary to reason, towards itself – and that the more hopeless it became, the stronger was its pull.

They walked across Town Hall Square. Kulpsuu, who had already managed to quaff a morning mug of ale somewhere, shook his fist at the high windows of the Town Hall:

"I'm telling you, they'll be crawling to us to offer us their cannons, the old farts! Break 'em on the wheel!"

"Quiet down!" Leemet tried to calm him. "When we get to Kalamaja you can sound off to your heart's content."

479

They had already reached the Great Guild when Balthasar suddenly remembered something important – he was not certain he could accomplish it, nor even that he should in the present circumstances try. Nevertheless, he said: "Men, wait for me at my father's place. I'm going to stay in town a bit longer." He sent his companions off towards the Great Coast Gate and went back across Town Hall Square.

The king had asked Balthasar to buy him a helmet, a proper one, suited to a king. For there were serious battles to be fought. But in the rush of the departure the day before, the king had forgotten to give him the money for it.

Balthasar continued on, deep in thought and calculations, past the weigh house, coming to a stop in the midst of the market goers, right under the pillory. He was about to turn towards Kimmelpenning's store, for the old man would no doubt have lent him the two or three, or perhaps in these times of devalued money even four or five, thalers. Or he might have given it to him outright. With Kimmelpenning, in such matters, you never knew. But then the corners of his mouth inside his beard turned up to reveal a flash of teeth, and he lengthened his stride as he continued on into Seppade Street. He tramped past St Nicholas' Church and Nõelasilm Passage, straight to the vicinity of the Old Gate and some wooden houses that had risen there during the hard times of the past decade. At the arched gateway of a once wealthy but now noticeably rundown stone house he came to a halt. He tried the pedestrian gate and, finding it unlocked, went in.

The smithy of Leinhard Platensleger Junior was a spacious limestone building with two vaults and an imposing hooded chimney over the forge, located at the back of a courtyard that widened on the side abutting Rataskaevu Street. It was, in any case, a most stately structure for a smithy. By rights it did not really belong to the junior Leinhard, who was known as something of a popinjay, and who had been operating it for a mere two or three years; it was actually his father's, the elder Leinhard's, ironworks – his forge and anvil. Old Leinhard had worked here, under the sooty, vaulted ceiling, for several decades with his journeymen, pounding out suits of armour that had brought fame to Tallinn from many lands and beyond many seas. For not only had he been the armour smith for Tallinn's town militia, he had also provided armour for the Toompea soldiers and their officers. And thus his name became known all the way to Narva and Riga and beyond. On one of his visits to town the now-departed Order Master, Plettenberg himself, had ordered a suit of armour from the aged Leinhard, and Leinhard's fame then spread so far and wide that it was very nearly his undoing. For, shortly thereafter, Grand Duke Vassili Ivanovits of Moscow had sent a messenger to Leinhard, inviting him to Moscow to work for him, offering him a dazzling salary to be paid out in pure gold. With the help of God, Leinhard had managed to overcome this terrible temptation. But Old Nick had tried to lead him astray, nonetheless, inducing him to make four exquisitely wrought, engraved and polished suits of armour and sell them secretly to the Grand Duke. To be sure the sale was officially made to certain high-ranking gentlemen – some had even suggested they were canons – in the town of Tartu, and from there they were shipped off, hidden in Russian merchant barges, to Muscovy, by way of Pskov. But who knows . . . perhaps all this was but the gossip of colleagues vigilant in defence of the honour and advantage of Tallinn, or perhaps the hearsay of others merely beset by envy. At the court hearing in the Council, the accusations against old Leinhard had run aground. For how could an armour smith in Tallinn be held responsible for where his armour ended up *after* it had arrived at its destination in Tartu?

In the opinion of the town – and Balthasar had learned this at the time the son took over the forge from the father – the younger Leinhard was more vigilant and adhered more strictly to principle than his generous father. But, according to the old smiths, his stubby hands were considerably less skilful than his father's. As occurs in many crafts and with many men, a man who clearly recognises, or perhaps simply senses, that his talents do not lie in the trade he has acquired will often embrace the task of organising the members of his own craft, and even those of all the others, taking upon himself, as a personal mission, the defence – especially the verbal defence – of their rights, honour and reputation. And he will hoist himself up, scolding and quarrelling, right up to the leadership of the crafts and even of the guilds . . . and everyone else had better look out!

It seemed that Leinhard Platensleger Junior, lacked the prerequisites for such success. On the other hand, although his armour was apparently too heavy and too stiff at the elbows and knees, his helmets were said to be very good. And so this Leinhard Junior, now strode forward, hands on hips, self-important and querulous, to meet the young country bumpkin in his bark shoes. Leinhard Junior, was a red-moustachioed man of about forty, with a veined and discontented face, wearing a leather apron singed by sparks and spattered with beer stains. He fixed his lustreless grey eyes on Balthasar: "What do you want?"

Balthasar smelt the blazing fire in the forge and stared at the great vaulted, sooty cave in which it burned. He looked at the whooshing bellows and at the boy, his naked torso glistening with sweat, pumping the bellows steadily with his foot, and at the journeymen, one of whom was turning the red-hot breastplate of a suit of armour with long tongs, as the other tapped at it with a slender hammer. And although the scene made him think of the activities of witches or masters of *homunculi*, Balthasar replied, in a businesslike, calm voice, over the clanking of hammers and the wheezing of bellows:

"I want to try on some of your helmets and buy the best one you have."

"Wha-a-a-t?" *Ooh yes, these local yokels and the town Greys just like 'em have become impossible of late! Where does such a fellow even get an idea like that – that he's going to buy a helmet? He walks into Leinhard Platensleger's smithy and wants to try on helmets!? To try on helmets on his louse-infested head!*

"If you could find one of the proper size, with a high crown, one that your father made, that is what I would prefer above all."

"What the deuce?! Who's instructed you to play me for a fool?!"

"Play you for a fool? No-one. God forbid. All I want is to try on some helmets and buy your best one."

"And with what, you filthy crow, are you going to buy a helmet?"

"With good money, of course."

"Hah! If you didn't know it before, you know it now: Leinhard Platensleger does not sell his work to yokels."

"But he'll sell them to German traitors?"

"Watch your mouth, you brazen bumpkin! *Who* are you thinking of?"

"It's a problem isn't it? There are so many, it's hard to know . . . For example, Herr Monninkhusen, when he was here in the role of the Danish vicegerent."

"Humph. Herr Monninkhusen was at least a *gentleman*."

"And he owes you three hundred silver marks for his armour. But I will pay you on the spot. In gold."

"Oh? And where did you get this gold?"

"Does it matter . . . in times like these?"

"But it does, you shameless lout! I'll have my journeymen seize you! I'll have you hauled before the bailiff! For robbery!"

"The bailiff would fine you a lot of silver marks. For the bailiff granted me safe passage last morning."

"Ah . . . then you're one of the spokesmen of the yokel king! Well, if that's the story, then my answer is even more decidedly no!"

Balthasar fished the money pouch containing Herr Kruse's gold out of his coarse linen trousers. If there was any right place for this gold, it was here, in this shop. He let the gleaming Emperor Maximilian thalers fall onto his left palm in time with the hammer striking the anvil. The journeymen and the bellows-boy looked greedily over their shoulder sat him. Clink-clink-clink – two, three, four, five . . .

"Well? You won't sell?"

Leinhard Platensleger's pursed lips protruded even further out of his red moustache. He sucked in his cheeks, making of them two bluish indentations:

"No!"

Fine. It was not as though there were no other armour smiths in Tallinn . . . But somehow, getting the better of Leinhard had, by this time, become a challenge for Balthasar. Perhaps even a matter of superstition. Somewhere in the dark back chamber of his thinking, victory or defeat in the matter had assumed the significance of a good or evil omen, quite vague, to be sure, but all the more broad and deep. And so he decided to change the game. Good Lord, whether it was an *honest or dishonest game* – of what consequence was that in these times? No-no, that was not it! *In spite of everything*, that was not it. *Of what consequence was it if the course of* such critical events as these *depended on it?* . . . That was it.

Balthasar took hold of Leinhard Platensleger's apron straps. Lord knows how he thought of such things just at the right moment. Or perhaps one should ask the question of God's Great Adversary . . . Balthasar took hold of Leinhard's apron straps and pulled him a little towards him and to one side – exactly the way a high-born gentleman who wants to whisper something into the ear of a craftsman holds him off, so as not to soil his clothes with the soot on the man's apron. And one must admit, as long as he had been playing an honest game with Leinhard, Balthasar had felt completely confident: his experience abroad and at the university, all his short but intense life experience,

484

was secretly stored in his arsenal. Now he said quickly:

*"Leinhard! Mot ick iedem Schapkopp van hantwerker alle klar maken?! Man ys by den upprorischen tho ervaren, wat se driven. Unde man brukt enen helm!"** That was his mortar round, fired into Leinhard's ear in a whisper. That was all the ammunition he had, nor did he feel particularly confident any longer. He watched apprehensively as Leinhard's mouth dropped open, but, thank God, he had shot a hole through the man's defences. And for five of Maximilian's gold thalers (*ha-ha-ha-ha*) Leinhard brought out, silently nodding and bowing, a beautiful, high-crowned helmet with a leather lining and chinstrap. It fitted Balthasar's head comfortably, and thus would be just right for the king.

Balthasar hid the helmet under his coat, which did not sufficiently conceal it, so he decided to stop in at Kimmelpenning's to ask for a bag or a length of cloth to wrap it in. For he would arouse curiosity and suspicion walking around with such a magnificent and warlike thing. Old Jakob was not around, but Niglas brought Balthasar a suitable piece of cloth, along with something that Kimmelpenning had asked him to give Balthasar should he chance to stop in at the store. It was a saddle-bag, old, worn, but entirely usable. Balthasar would not have been himself had he not immediately looked inside to determine why it bulged so. Inside were a pair of boots, a shirt, and the black wool breeches and jacket of Jakob Kimmelpenning's son – the clothes he had worn the previous night. And with a start he detected, mingled with the smells of the tanned leather saddlebag and the mugwort in the clothing, the unmistakable scent of carnations.

They did not manage to get away from Kalamaja until late morning the next day, for Balthasar did not want to leave town – God knows how long his absence would be – without going by Mündrik-Mats' hut to ask about Märten. But he did not need to ask – Märten himself met him

* Leinhard, do I really have to lay it all out for every muttonhead of a craftsman? I'm in with the rebels, to find out what their plans are, and we need a helmet! (Low German).

at the door, still wearing his ragged old sheepskin coat and worn-down sealskin slippers. He recognised Balthasar immediately, in spite of his peasant dress, but showed scant surprise, which was just as Balthasar had expected.

"Aha. So you return from time to time. Well, come in."

They went into the sauna and sat on a bench behind a pile of wood shavings.

"No, the privateers have all gone their way. The master did not give out any new permits this year. Didn't want to anger the Swedes too much. No, I was not on a boat last year either. What am I doing here? . . . Making spoons and . . . What else? Oh, not much. Well, you can always find a crust of bread. But *you*? That's a much more exciting story . . . *Where* is it you want me to go with you? Here, stick it in your cheek." He handed Balthasar a carob pod, which he was ever fond of chewing in spite of his meagre means – it had long seemed to Balthasar that it was his only vice. "Tell me about yourself . . ."

"There's not much to tell. Come with me. Join the peasant forces."

"You're in the peasant forces now?"

"I am . . . so to speak. But you come too. What's the point of just sitting around here? Getting a shilling for a spoon! I have plenty of money. We'll borrow a horse for you from Father."

"And what will I do there?"

"There? But I ask you: what are you doing here? A butter churn is the biggest thing you can make. But there – well. You'll get a pitchfork or sword in hand and help with the cause: maybe life in this land will change . . ."

"Nothing will change. Or if it does, it'll just get worse," Märten said with unshakeable wisdom, spitting into the shavings. "But to go along with you . . . Hmm."

"I'll take you directly to the peasant king!"

"So you and he are chums, are you?"

"Indeed."

"Humph."

"Well?"

"Well . . . I could come and take a look at him. If you tell me about your time in Germany along the way."

Nine horses galloped towards the southwest, over brown fields of mown hay, through black woods and rust-coloured brush, the gravel crunching and the limestone thundering under their hooves. Leemet was shrunken and silent, Jakob was upright and silent. Kulpsuu, who had hung a keg from his saddle and drank from it as he rode, was more aggressively talkative with every mile.

"Oh Satan! With our bare hands, I say, with our bare hands we'll take that damn Kolovere! And I'm telling you: we don't even need to do it with our bare hands! The king told me – when the Order's forces took to their heels at Härgmäe – however many of 'em could – they lost two field culverins, wheels an' all, in a marsh somewhere between Härg-mäe and Pärnu. The king said he knows the exact spot, and he's already sent men and horses to get 'em, a week ago. So let's set up our cannons and blast away at the walls of Kolovere! Let's break into the fortress! Damnation!! Let's trample 'em . . . Down with Satan's spawn! The whole lot of 'em! There're hundreds of 'em hiding there. And I'm telling you – they've got so much stuff that whoever gets there in time will never be hungry again . . ." Kulpsuu's narrow, bearded face was splotched with rage and ardour, his small grey eyes glowered, and his hoarse voice grew shrill at times.

The night was at its darkest when they arrived, their horses drenched in sweat, at the estate manager's house. The entire army had gone on to Kolovere three days earlier, and the king had followed a day later, but two of the king's bodyguards were there. Since one of them had just returned to Limandu from Kolovere to await the arrival of the delegation from Tallinn, he had much to tell.

The guns dragged out of the marsh were now in the possession of the besieging forces. They had been cleaned of muck and rust and greased by men who knew about such things. And then, from behind a barricade of earth and thick brush, they had started bombarding the fortress. The first gun had exploded with its first shot and reduced three of the peasants to bloody shreds. In spite of that, those remaining had shot seven or eight iron-bound stone balls from the second gun, on the first day. True, they had not hit the wall, or even the large square gate tower. But some of the cannonballs had fallen through the roof of the living quarters in the northern wing and, judging by the screams, had caused their share of damage. The bodyguards could not say how many besiegers there were. But in the alder groves, in the inlets of the River Vaikna, they had assembled a great many piles of twigs and branches and, during the second night, had managed to move them to the moat northeast of the town. They had even talked with the king about digging a tunnel for mines in the inner bank of the moat. And they had found, among them, a mine expert, no less, a man from Lihula, who had been sent to war by the coadjutor and claimed to know about mines. But since they had no explosives, they decided to postpone the digging of the tunnel until the delegation returned from Tallinn.

Upon their return the spokesmen sank, exhausted, onto the straw in the steward's house. Balthasar nearly fell asleep chewing on smoked pork shoulder, even though the pork, which he was sharing with Märten, had been sent by Truuta and was as tasty as could be. Balthasar had planned to tell Märten about his German adventures that night – there had been no chance to talk during their headlong gallop – but now Märten too was so tired that he could not even grunt in response. Through the sweet smell of the hunk of bread in his fist and the sounds of rustling straw, Balthasar only dimly heard Märten's wheezy breathing and the fading tale the king's bodyguard was telling. He was describing the difficulty of managing the peasants besieging the town, since most of them seemed to think that all they had to do was form patrols and wait outside the walls until the town ran out of provisions and opened its gates. Apparently, when cannons were fired at them two days earlier from the round west tower, and the balls flew over the moat and landed among them, a good number fled into the brush, which was not in itself surprising, but what was most lamentable was that the fugitives did not later return to the company.

All night long the hiss of flying cannonballs sounded in Balthasar's dreams, in which he was roaming aimlessly on a bleak and barren landscape in search of a clump of brush, driven by a fear that he tried with all his might to deny – a fear that he might not have been able to overcome had there been any brush at all in sight. But the grey peat landscape of his dream was an utter wasteland, and there was nowhere to hide from either hissing cannonballs or fear.

Waking at dawn, Balthasar thought it was probably the wind he had been hearing in his dreams. But when they mounted their horses to go on to Kolovere, a little over two leagues distant, he noted that the day was unusually quiet. In the still morning light the grey fields with their sodden, flattened grain and the rust-coloured thickets and woods and leafless treetops were oddly mute and motionless. Although the sky was clouded, a dusting of early snow on the frosted grass sparkled here and there like powdered glass in the grey light. As the men of the king's delegation rode through a dense birch wood, the sod thudding and leaves rustling, Balthasar, riding in the rear, saw that there was not a breath of wind in the air: occasional yellow birch leaves floated down in silent spirals to land on the grey riders. Then he remembered that it was October 14, the morning of Leaf-fall Day. But he forgot it again immediately and began, there in the saddle, to rehearse the speech he had not delivered two nights earlier at the Guildhall, and which he had been reciting to himself throughout the previous day, riding through the autumn woods and rain showers and red-brown landscape: *Men of Tallinn! Listen to me! I am one of you! You are all my fathers and brothers and kinsmen. We've known each long and well* . . . It was the speech he had been rehearsing alternately with a new one, yesterday – the one he might deliver to the king's army at Kolovere: . . . *If you want to retain a fraction of your rights. If you want your descendants to flourish – men of the land, brothers* . . . True, he was a townsman. He was different from them. By virtue of his education he was one of the gentry. Of course. But by virtue of blood, of roots and of *language*, the language in which he formed his thoughts to this day (and in which he would continue to think to his dying day) – provided they were not thoughts on overly learned and complex topics – and by virtue of the soil on the soles of his people's shoes, and the earth-gods (in whom he did not believe, of course – God forbid that he should, but then whose face was it that he had seen that time in the bark of an oak, with his own eyes – who knows . . . ?) – by virtue of all this, because of all this, he could in fact say:

Men of the land, brothers! For the first time in over two hundred years, it has happened again that several thousand armed *men, no matter how meagrely outfitted, are assembled in battalions! And they are learning to follow their own landsmen as leaders. And they know – perhaps only vaguely, but nonetheless – they know what they want. Or, more accurately, they know what they do not want. And they even have one bronze siege-culverin – which they have set up to spit at the German walls. And these walls are in front of them – the clearest goal of all their goals! . . . Brothers! Fire at these walls – from the mouth of that single pitiful cannon and our dozen arquebuses! Fire with full force! Fill the moats with brush! Plait rope ladders as you crouch in trenches, as you hide in reeds and in brush, as you lie on your bellies in the dirt!! Climb up onto the walls! Ignore the wind blowing and the arquebuses exploding, the shiver of fear and the cries of triumph . . . Brothers, if we can prise open the gates of Kolovere, the gates of Tallinn will open for us of their own accord! (Lord knows, is that actually true?) And from this time on, it won't only be the masters of the Great Guild in their velvet hats who decide the affairs of the town, but we too – the Greys, too! Oh Brothers: how wondrous strange to think what life will look like here in this land . . .*

And then he thought:

Yes, but if the manor lords have been killed or have fled to Germany, and power in Tallinn is in the hands of the Greys and the burghers friendly to the peasants – who, then, will become the ruler of this land? . . . Or will we look high and low amongst ourselves to find men fit for the position? . . . The way our present masters are doing, with such foolish zeal? Will we then again send some emissaries to Denmark, others to Sweden, and yet others to Finland, to Poland and to Muscovy? . . . And thus bring about our own "peasant wars" between the various groups, each supporting a particular emissary, since each faction will suspect that all the others have been bought off for thirty pieces of silver? . . . Or should this one-foot peasant from Alaküla, this "king" – a title which in our tongue doesn't mean much more than "chieftain" – should he become the "king" of this country, in the sense of the word as used in the Bible and in foreign kingdoms? . . . And if we raise him up to be the ruler of this land, and if he goes to live – well, let's imagine it (what's to prevent us from imagining it?) – up to Toompea in Tallinn and takes off his helmet up there (the very one I've got here, wrapped in linen cloth, hanging from my saddle), and puts a crown on his head . . . Ha-ha-ha-hah! . . . But I can think about all that afterwards. *For now, the main thing is to scale the walls!*

"Right high, those damn devils . . ."

Märten had stopped and let the others ride on ahead. Balthasar pulled up next to him on the hilltop, and they raised themselves up in their saddles to look to the southwest. Less than half a league away, on a low-lying island of grassland formed by a loop of the meandering river, rose Kolovere's yellow-grey walls and bulky towers with their heavy old brick turrets.

491

They surveyed the forbidding, self-enclosed stone structure in silence. The men lower down on the slope were also silent. Even Kulpsuu did no more than spit.

The fortress was delineated by the square shape of its moat. Several hundred paces of surrounding hayfield, dotted with hummocks and hazelnut bushes, sloped down on every side to the river below. In the windless, misty air, smoke from the campfires of the besieging forces was rising from the scrub brush and the woods at the edge of the hayfield, and at a height of a few fathoms it spread out, forming motionless, grey mushrooms. There was no sign of the peasant army or of its activities. But just as Balthasar turned in his saddle towards Märten – to mumble something of an apology for having dragged his friend along into such a questionable venture – just how questionable became evident to him at the sight of those unmoving smoke clouds and the limestone expanse before them. Just then they saw the peasant army appear in the west, from the woods behind the fortress.

"The men of Lihula are coming to our aid!" cried the king's body-guard, who had been riding at the head of the group. At the same time, the brush at the eastern edge of the fortress came to life. Even though grey tufts of smoke appeared from the arrow slits in its walls, and the hollow booming of the cannons and arquebuses resounded clearly through the still morning fog (fairly infrequent booming, to be sure), units of the besieging force could be seen moving on the near side of the scrub brush, and shouts of joy muffled the sound of the shots.

The spokesmen spurred on their horses and rode down the gentle slope, descending into the shimmering yellow birch-and-aspen woods, flecked with red here and there. The thudding of hooves and the calls of encouragement to the horses drowned out the sounds from the fortress. After six or seven minutes the trail opened out onto the hayfield surrounding the fortress, and the scene lay before them.

A grey column of men from Lihula – there could have been as many as four hundred – approached slowly from the southwest – odd that they were marching in such a long, strung-out column over the open fields just below the fortress, and not in the shelter of the brush. The northwestern end of the column was bravely, dangerously, close to the fortress. From among the besiegers at the edge of the woods where the spokesmen were headed, a detachment of a hundred to a hundred and fifty men separated themselves from the others, with ten riders at the head, and galloped parallel to the moat southeast of the town, just two hundred paces from the town wall, across the meadow towards the Lihula men. The king was in that detachment. His rust-brown horse and oak-branch crown were clearly visible. The spokesmen turned off the gravel road leading towards Kolovere's gates and started across the meadow; they pressed their spurs into the horses' flanks, riding the length of the open field between the approaching Lihula force and the besiegers keeping to the shelter of the thicket, and headed towards the king and his men moving diagonally across the narrowing expanse between them.

The horses' hooves thudded dully on the soft sod near the river. From time to time the approaching Lihula front line disappeared behind the hazelnut bushes. Kulpsuu raised his sword up high and called out to them. Balthasar was surprised to see that, to his right, some of the besiegers were standing in groups at the edge of the thicket and shouting greetings to the men of Lihula (though he could not make out just what they were saying), but that the latter remained oddly mute. Their swords and pitchforks and scythes tied to poles were all clearly visible, but it seemed as if their sharp tips were inclined every which way, and as if the men were moving over the bumpy terrain with a heavy, awkward, tread, as though their feet were sinking into the uneven turf. Balthasar did not see a single hat raised in greeting to the waiting peasant army, even though the Lihula men had come to join them.

493

The king's troops had travelled over half the distance from the hazelnut bushes towards the approaching force. The king snatched his oak-festooned hat from his head and waved it, hailing the Lihula men. Four riders accompanying him simultaneously raised their curved herdsmen's horns to their lips, the deep, hollow sound resounding as though in a dream over the foggy field:

"Too-too-loo-too-Too-too-loo-too-Too-too-loo-too-Too-too-loo-too . . ."

Had he been paying attention, Balthasar would have been even more astonished that the Lihula army kept approaching without making any response whatever. He noticed a slight disturbance on the left wing of the Lihula force, on the fortress side. Wait a minute – there were more horses there, at the back of the front row – but Good Lord, what did that mean? . . . The herders' horns fell abruptly silent, the besiegers' shouts died down, not a shot was fired from the fortress. Now, from the shelter of the left flank of the Lihula army, which had been pushed to one side, emerged a gleaming black-and-white centipede that thundered out onto the field, an iron monster with four hundred legs, with a crest of horses' manes and feathered helmets, bristling with swords and spears . . .

For an instant Balthasar gaped in amazement, wondering how and where the peasants had managed to get such a well-equipped army of knights to come to their aid. Had things really advanced to such a point that Livonia's knights were joining the peasants? Something utterly inconceivable before now . . . But something quite conceivable in Germany, thirty years earlier: Balthasar recalled stories he had heard in Stettin, about Götz of the Iron Hand and his forces. For just one foolish instant . . . And then the reality of what was happening *here* crashed down upon his head – as though Kolovere's square gate tower had risen into the foggy dawn and, right over his head, was raining down grey blocks of stone onto the grassland, in an avalanche a fathom wide . . .

(A sheer miracle that one could stay in one's saddle, untouched, and watch it all happening, feel it happening.) *Lord Jesus Christ, why do you permit things such as this to happen?!* This Lihula army was nothing but an army of slaves, forced to march by the knights themselves, forced under threat of death, rape, the burning of whole villages! *Lord Jesus Christ, why do you once again permit such things to happen?* A herd of wretched slaves, whose slave bodies provided a shield for the knights – and is this display of contempt not itself an outrage?! – the devil knows where they came from – the knights who thus managed to get face to face with the besiegers, within reach of the king, a mere spear's throw away.

The army of knights, armour-clad, shining and sharp-pointed and of a piece, like the iron glove of a giant, curved with dreamlike speed around the king's forces, cut off the besiegers at the edge of the clearing, and bore down upon the king's men.

*"Ehre der heiligen Jungfrau!"**

The iron wedge bit into the grey foot soldiers like an axe into wood. Some knights were dragged from their saddles, but the blade of the axe still reached the men on horseback surrounding the king. Shouting. Screaming. Horses neighing. Gurgling. The sounds of swords plunging into human bodies, horses' bodies. The desperate clank of blows against steel armour. From the group at the edge of the field, half a dozen men raced on foot, another half dozen on horseback, to the aid of the king's group. The king slashed with his sword and shouted something to the men of Lihula, immobile, rooted to the field. The spokesmen, spread out among the hazelnut bushes, galloped towards the king . . . *Thud-thud-thud*, Balthasar's heart thudded in his temples like a warning bell about to crack. In one visionary moment he saw with unwavering clarity what *should* happen: *the Lihula forces should rush out roaring, from the left. The besiegers should leap out in concentric*

* Glory to the Blessed Virgin! (Low German).

formation from the brush (at least three–four–five hundred men) and from two directions (with a thousand men), fall upon the knights attacking the king and, heedless of death, run purposely onto the knights' spears and swords, grab hold of the horses' tails, stirrups, bridles, hack at the horses' legs (in the shelter of bodies about to be hacked to death), converge upon those threatening the king, like a river defying death, to stand for five fateful minutes above death, on the shoulders of the dying – and the army of knights would be buried under the grey bodies, and the gates of Kolovere would open in a day or a week and the king . . . Just then the king received a sword-blow to his hat and sank across the saddle of his rust-coloured horse . . . *Lord God, if only he'd had the helmet!* The knights swarmed over the trampled bodies of the king's defenders and turned towards the spokes-men. Forty paces from the blades of the knights' lances they managed to rein in their horses and veer off in whichever direction they could. Balthasar saw Uncle Jakob's bony back, saw Märten's light head pressed down low against his horse's ears . . . Kulpsuu alone refused to change course. This mad youth – Balthasar saw it all, looking over his shoulder as he galloped off to take cover in thicker brush – this wild, mad youth, spurring on his horse, raising his sword above his head, and racing, bellowing, straight towards the knights. His grey eyes were bulging, the corners of his grinning mouth inside his beard were white with froth, and his cries rose, roaring above the knights' hoarse shouts and the horses' thudding hooves.

"You sons of whores . . . *Life or death! . . .*"

He reached the knights, dodged the first lance with a sharp turn, lifted his sword with both hands to deliver a blow to the knight's neck, threw the latter from his horse, and then was himself lifted into the air, impaled on three spears.

"Oo-oo-oooh . . ."

Balthasar pulled his horse into the cover of brush and turned around to look for Märten. Just then the knights' army raced by on the other side of the hazelnut thicket, passing so close to him that the rust-spotted leaves in front of his face quivered. He could see, behind the first ranks of knights, a dozen or so wounded prisoners piled on horses – their heads bloodied, their bodies limp. He saw that some of them had already been tied to their horses, others were having their hands tied behind their backs even as the horses sped past. And he also saw the king, draped over the back of an unfamiliar grey horse. A narrow hemp rope had been wrapped many times around his chest and stomach and hands, which were twisted behind his back. Another hemp rope formed a noose around his neck, its end gripped in the iron glove of the knight riding in the middle of the front line. The rope was taut and pulled the king's large, wheat-coloured head of hair to one side, so that Balthasar could not see his face. The oak-branch crown had, of course, fallen under the horses' hooves. Among the prisoners there were at least two men whom Balthasar recognised as elders who had been present at the king's house. Among the lords he recognised no-one: only a few of them had raised their visors to reveal their faces. One of those was the horseman in the front line, the one dragging the king behind him with the noose. When he arrived at the spot where Balthasar was hiding, Balthasar recognised him through the fluttering, rust-speckled hazelnut leaves: he knew that narrow gull's beak of a nose, so shaped by God's fingers; it was unmistakable there, in the middle of that official, arrogant face flushed with wine and victory. It was the protector of the bishopric of Saaremaa, Christopher von Monninkhusen, whom Balthasar had met two years earlier at Herr Clodt's house, and who had later designated himself vicegerent of the Danish king in Estonia. Now he was apparently serving Duke Magnus – known in Narva as the "one-eyed Danish puppy" – who had arrived in Kuressaare in St George's month. Herr Christopher von Monninkhusen, the man whose counsellor Balthasar had pretended to be when he had gone to Raasiku to give Hasse a good scare about his treatment of the peasants . . .

The false vicegerent rode past him with the knights and the prisoners, at a distance of just ten paces. The false counsellor in the bushes flattened himself against the neck of his horse, and the intelligent animal stood there, utterly still, as though someone's strong hand were holding him, whether the hand of Jehovah in Heaven, or that of the earth-god of the local marsh.

And then, twenty paces away, Herr Monninkhusen called to his knights to fall in. They turned towards the dense thicket where the besiegers were hiding. At a signal from Herr Monninkhusen, a young man, wearing a light suit of armour, raised himself up in his stirrups and, facing the thicket, barked out in a slightly hoarse voice – but in fluent country tongue:

"Peasants! Your king is dead! Your elders are dead! Many of those in your forces are lying here, on the marshland, in their own blood! Those of you who disperse and go home today before noon will be pardoned for your foolish uprising. But whoever is found in these woods after that will be drawn and quartered at Kolovere!"

The advance guard from Lihula stood in a grey huddle, a hundred paces distant. Herr Monninkhusen's horse pawed the ground impatiently, and the herald of pardon and punishment stood, straddle-legged, in the midst of the silence that fell upon his words, broken only by the groans of a prisoner here and there. Then from somewhere in the woods came the dull explosion of an arquebus, and the young herald, grabbing at his chest – metal gloves clinking against metal breastplate – sank with a shriek onto his horse's rump and slid down, to remain hanging from the stirrups.

"*Ack, dat ist der Rebellen Antwort!?*"* Monninkhusen cried. He had an astonishingly booming voice for one so slight.

"*Landfahne links – vorwärts! Ehre der heiligen Jungfrau!*"†

* So that is the rebels' answer?! (Low German).   † Company left – forward! Glory to the Blessed Virgin! (Low German).

Balthasar pressed himself against his horse's neck and held his breath. For an instant he considered pulling out Herr Hasse's short pistol – he would be able to use it alright – and firing at Herr Monninkhusen . . . Not much point in that. For even if he hit his mark, even if the bullet went through Monninkhusen's armour – of which there was practically no hope – even then the cause was lost. Even with Monninkhusen dead, the knights would not end up leaderless and dispersed, as the peasants now were.

The army of knights turned to the left in an arc as swift and seamless as the swing of a giant axe, and cut, to a distance of a hundred paces, into the sparse brake at the edge of the thicket. The sounds of branches breaking, of screams, of the clank of swords, of horses snorting, and of curses in both German and country tongue resounded from the thicket. The manoeuvre lasted less than five minutes, during which time Balthasar dared not move, for the last line of the knights' forces had not delved into the brushwood, but had stopped at its edge, directly across from him. And then they emerged from the thicket. A few of the knights in the front wing were clutching swords with bloodied blades. One soldier's horse collapsed at the edge of the brush and remained there to die, its breath rattling, its innards spilling out. The others dragged half a dozen prisoners out of the brush.

Again the false vicegerent galloped past Balthasar, so close that he felt the air stir. And again the false counsellor in the brush held his breath, his eyes searching for the king, but he did not spot any of the prisoners he had seen earlier. Evidently they were at the left flank of the troop formation, but it was the right flank passing by him now.

Balthasar turned his horse around and galloped off into the thicket.

False vicegerent . . . False declaration of peace . . . False counsellor . . . False freedom fighter . . . False! False! False! Jesus Christ, tell me: is everything truly destruction and humiliation and falsehood?! And was the only honest act that of Kulpsuu, with his piercing cry, running headlong, purposely, onto the enemy's lances?!

Balthasar galloped over trampled campfires and past lifeless bodies lying next to them. The helmet in its linen wrapping, still hanging from his saddle, banged against his right knee. Wet, bare branches brushed against his face. He felt chills up and down his spine, as though the branches were spattering blood onto his face. But in the midst of the merciless thunder of a descent into the abyss, the creature of reason in him struggled to its feet. He saw a dozen mute, bent peasants running across his path into the woods, towards the east. He wanted to call out to them, but remained silent. He weighed whether to search out the scattered peasant forces in the woods. And decided: for what? What could he say to them? He weighed whether to track down the spokesmen, track down Märten. And decided: the spokesmen were fleeing wherever they could, and Märten was surely making his way back to Tallinn. But all that *he*, Balthasar, could expect to find in Tallinn was the gallows. He decided to ride under cover of the woods to the northwest of the town and head towards Haapsalu. His knees were shaking, he was ravenously hungry. He felt that from the moment the knights emerged from behind the supposedly friendly forces, everything was foreseeable with such shattering clarity that what then transpired could no longer crush him completely . . .

Balthasar galloped into the woods and the wet branches dripping blood closed behind him.

As though he had never been there.

CHAPTER SEVEN,

in which the adventures of a young man are strung on the string
of our tale – very nearly in the order of his own thoughts and
recollections – like tiny, multicoloured seashells, each of which,
singly, is too small to contain the roar of the ocean, but taken
all together – who can say? Our main hope, in fact,
in stringing them (even though we have not ventured into
the sea itself to collect them) is that it will thus be
easier to continue our tale or, more
accurately, to return to it.

The spire rising from the green-speckled "helmet" of the church steeple rested on sixteen slender pillars. Visible between the pillars, the grey-green landscape, brightened by sun and darkened by cloud shadows, stretched all the way to the misty horizon; at the foot of the steeple clustered a red-roofed town. It was evident from the pillars alone that the town was not Tallinn and the church not St Olaf's. That was also evident from the height of the steeple. For although it was one of this country's most imposing towers, the steeple of St Ansgarius' Church in Bremen was at least twenty fathoms lower than St Olaf's. Still, it was more than high enough to cause a prickling sensation just below the heart within someone taking in the view from there.

The broad, summer-blue River Weser, bustling with boats and seeming even wider than the Oder in Stettin, divided the landscape into two sections, from southeast to northwest. And the curving moat cut off a narrow strip of land below the town, separating it from the outlying settlements and fields, like an oval tray of strawberries or rowan berries. Rowan berries, rather, considering the bitter taste of the urgent circumstance that had driven Balthasar to climb up here, to deliberate with himself. And considering, too, the shudder that seemed to course through his stomach when he let his eyes wander towards the northwest, along the gleaming ribbon of the winding Weser, and when he recalled the names of the villages on its banks: Rabbings-hausen, Gröpelingen, Mittelsburen and – far away on the foggy horizon – *Vegesack*...

Balthasar sat down at one end of a beam, next to the bells. There were two bells. The smaller was probably the one Puttemann, the churchwarden, had called the "bell of St Vitus" when the three of them – Puttemann, Herr Sum and Balthasar – had come to the church two Sundays ago, and the bells had begun to boom: *bim-bam-bim-bam*. The larger bell had to be the one Herr Puttemann had called "Big Boomer", three cubits across at the bottom and higher than Balthasar was tall.

As he gazed out over the array of steeples – those of the cathedral and of St Mary's and St Jacob's and St Stephen's churches – Balthasar took Annika's letter out of his pocket to read it once more. The wind blowing over the bells caused them to emit a nearly soundless peal and rustled the greyish sheet of paper, as if urging him to read it through quickly. Annika had written:

Dear Brother, Balthasar!
God willing, this letter will reach you, for even though you have not taken the trouble to write to us, it has been His will that twice I have received news of you ...

The letter was written in German, in a practised hand, which meant that Annika herself had not written it, but someone who had been asked to set it down, someone trustworthy.

. . . The first time, it was news that brought us great alarm and sadness, but the next time, it was such news as brought great joy to our life, lately so overfull of unhappy events, even though, along with the joy, it also brought us sorrow. The first news I received about you was what Herr Wolff in Stettin wrote to our father: that he had taken you on as his student, on the recommendation of my departed Meus, and taught and advised you for several years and considered you superior to the other students, and that he had even lent you money when you could not get any from home during those troubled times, but he says that, in January of this year, 1562, you fled the town of Stettin in a shameful manner for an unknown destination, without giving a thought to your debt to him of eleven thalers – which he requests be paid on your behalf and sent to Treptow, to Herr Krumhusen . . .

Eleven thalers in debt to Herr Wolff . . . It is not as though I tried to deny it or hide it from anyone or even from God! But where on earth would I have found the money at that time? . . . And where could I get it even now? . . . Eleven thalers in debt to Herr Wolff . . . Not only a debt of eleven thalers, dear Annika, because it is God's honest truth when he says that he taught and advised me for many years, and even considered me better than other students . . . But tell me, what could I have done? On that day, Leaf-fall day, when I had to get away from a certain situation about which you, dear sister, do not know a thing, I did not get to keep those cursed and yet blessed thalers of Herr Kruse's – not a single one! That is to say, with their help – and the shoes and clothes that Kimmelpenning gave me – I managed to escape, by way of Haapsalu and Kuressaare to Riga, and from there back to Stettin. I had hoped to be well rewarded for my successfully completed mission to Narva, for Herr Krumhusen had very definitely promised: "You will have cause for no regrets whatsoever!" But those hopes came to naught. Herr Krumhusen was neither in Stettin nor in Treptow. He had left for Lippe or Salzburg, or the devil knows where, to broaden his practical knowledge of saltworks, and then it was rumoured that he had taken ill somewhere, and he did not return. But I had used up my money, as much of it as I had left after two and a half years at the institute – including for some escapades with Bade and a few nights on the town. Yes, I had used up what I still had left, for preparations for the trip to Narva – for a pair of better breeches, a new coat jacket, a volume of Marcus Aurelius – the former scarcely worn, the latter barely read – all of which I left at the home of Krumhusen Junior. So that by Christmas of 1560, when I finally got back to Stettin, I was penniless. But I can tell you that I did not go to Herr Wolff to ask for money. No, it was he who asked me whether I needed money. He said he had noticed that I had added a few holes to my belt – and not in order to extend it. It was then that I revealed my straitened circumstances to him. And he, generous as he had been towards me for some time, offered me a loan: a thaler a month for as many months as I needed, to be repaid in January of 1562. I rashly accepted his generosity. It was rash because I still hoped to repay him with money from Krumhusen, or from home, and knew very well that the other means of repayment I had considered were just not possible: that is, he had no land that I might have ploughed, no writings that I might have edited, and his servant Hans was both stableboy and coachman and tended both his horse and his coach.

I simply could not make ends meet on a mark a week – which is what I had calculated earlier. Strange to say, life in Stettin had rapidly become so much more expensive, it was as though the war in Livonia had reached it too. But somehow or the other I lived on this money for nearly two semesters, always in the hope that Herr Krumhusen would soon return. Without my adding any more holes to my belt – and without making use of the old ones. But when Herr Krumhusen did not appear, and no money at all came from Tallinn – my letters home had apparently gone missing – and my debt to Herr Wolff had increased to ten thalers, I had to do something. Especially since the approaching year of 1562 brought a deadline for the payment of tuition, which had been reduced from five to four thalers for me, and for that very reason could not be postponed. And I had other debts, here and there, of a mark or two, for example, to Herr Butte, for pork rinds and extra broth. True, I could have asked Bade for a loan. It would not have been hard at all for him to toss me five or six thalers. But for some reason I could not bring myself to do it. Even though my penniless state was largely a result of all the carousing Bade had instigated – I could not be seen as a poor wretch at the dancing and drinking parties that this merchant's son organised. I could not. Even though Bade was, more or less, a friend . . . But then, at the start of winter in November, when my pride had worn rather thin, and I knew not how I could face the coming year or look Rector Wolff in the eye, God sent us a new *lector publicus* to teach the wisdom of Euclid. He hailed from the town of Wittenberg and asked each of us from where we came, and when I mentioned Tallinn he said that, although he himself had not been in that town, he had recently met a man from there: a week before his departure, a kind master of theology from Tallinn had arrived in Wittenberg and taken up residence in the vacant rental room below that of our lecturer on Fisher Lane. In order to earn a doctorate at the university. And when I then enquired as to this man's name, he said it was Herr Johann Sum, formerly rector of the Trivium School in Tallinn.

That same evening I made my decision. For Herr Sum had always thought well of me – one can just sense such things – which had spurred me on to do my best for him. From him I could hope for both advice and help. I had to expect it of him, for God had chosen this unmistakable and unusual way of letting me know that Herr Sum was here now . . . Actually, that means "there". . . . For it was close to fifty leagues from

Stettin to Wittenberg, as I managed to learn from the new lector, without arousing his curiosity too much.

I set out the next afternoon. A light bag and a walking stick were all my baggage. And although it wavered at times, my faith in God's help, and even more in my own good luck, was sturdy and carried me along.

And that is the tale, my dear sister, of my shameful flight. And I dare to think that it was not all that shameful, simply because it involved such bitter risk: if the rector's letters sent in pursuit of me – or some other wretched luck – had dragged me back to Stettin, my bare posterior should have received twenty lashes before the entire institute. Or I could have been put in the lock-up for a month on bread and water and charged a fine to boot. For fleeing because of my debts! Yes, there are things in God's world that are the height of foolishness . . .

But that letter from Rector Wolff – written, as I said, to your school address in Stettin, despite your flight, for to where else could I have written it – that letter from Rector Wolff fortunately reached not our father. So that I can tell you, as consolation: it could not cause him grief during his brief illness nor reduce the days of his life, which would, alas, have happened had his ears heard the news. Because – I know not whether a daughter ought to say or think thus of her father, whether it be before or after his death, but seeing as you are so far away and there is not another to whom I can talk about this, I shall tell you – our father was more proud of his honesty and that of his people than is perhaps appropriate in a purely Christian sense, and such news would have been as a blow from God's own scourge. But by good fortune we did not receive your letter until a week after our father was called to his Father – on the fourth day of April, which fell on Good Friday this year, at three o'clock in the afternoon, at the very hour that our Saviour gave up the ghost on the cross . . .

Father is dead.

I have known since this morning, when Herr Sum's servant brought me this letter from the vestry. Odd . . . it did not hit me terribly hard at first. Even though it was as unexpected as the death of a man his age could be. But my heart contracted as I read it. As though there were a knife in my breast that I did not even know was there until its handle bumped into something. No more than that. Yet, I have not been able to accept it till now . . . That his pale, bright, appraising eyes are no more. That his voice – hoarse, and a little weak from calling out to his horses – is no more. Nor his solicitous, fatherly queries – aiming at humour, a little silly, a bit helpless; nor his attempts to bridge the divide between us, which went against my grain, yet now that they are no more I am as though forsaken . . . Father . . . forgive me . . . I cannot . . . right now. Look, I am up here, yes, so incredibly high, up here, where all the world's winds can blow at me . . . When I have the chance – someday, when I have set my feet upon the ground, when I have peace and quiet to examine my thoughts and my heart, I will come to you, assuredly. But not now, not here . . . There, on the gravel at the back of the old church at Kalamaja, between the nameless hillocks, there . . . I will have a beautiful headstone carved in beautiful lettering, to be set on your grave:

IN HOC LOCO REQUIESCET IN PACE DEI
SIMON RISSA . . .*

. . . *vectuarius* or *heniochus* . . . which would it be? – I still do not know how to say "wagoner" in Latin . . . *Revaliensis* . . . No, no, old man, don't worry, no headstone . . . Because I hear your retort: "Better to see that you pay your debts". . . Alright, alright . . . Annika's letter continues:

> The next news I had of you came a week ago from your former schoolmaster, Herr Balder, according to whom great and

* In this place rests, in the peace of God, Simon Rissa of Tallinn (Latin).

positive changes have occurred in your life, but by what magical
route you got there is something I cannot begin to understand—

"By what magical route?". . . Dearest sister, I travelled that route
eleven days straight, without stopping . . . For my footwear, patched
seven times in Stettin, was wretched, and there was already snow on the
ground as far as Eberswald. So that after each mile I had to sit by the side
of the road to rub my toes, warm them, and look for dry straw to stuff
into my footcloths. Southward from Eberswald there was the autumn
mud, not as deep as it might have been, because the roads there are
mostly sandy, but an annoyance just the same. And I was hungry all
the time. I could only afford one middling meal a day at the roadside
inns. Fortunately I found unusually big, light-green spotted pears still
hanging on trees that were nearly bare of leaves. And mounds of the
year's last turnips lay in the fields and provided something more sub-
stantial to chew on alongside the sweetness of the pears. A few times I
had the good fortune to get a meal at a tavern at someone else's expense
– if I happened, for example, to get into conversation with people who
had heard of Livonia and were eager for news of what had been going
on there. In a tavern in the town of Bernau some merchants in leather
breeches said they were on their way to Danzig, and after drinking a
few mugs of ale they even ordered me a whole leg of pork. That was
how much they enjoyed my talk, and especially when I told them about
the customs and prices of doing business in Narva. But I never got to eat
the pork. Because before it had been delivered from the spit to the table
we were interrupted by three mercenary soldiers sitting at a neighbouring table, and their spokesman said they were honest soldiers in the
service of the Prince-Elector of Brandenburg and that my story was full
of base, false flattery of the sodomite, the Grand Duke of Muscovy, who
was the curse of the whole world, and whosoever took pleasure in telling or listening to such tales was himself no better than a dirty dog!

I tried to explain that I was only describing what I had seen a year ago with my own eyes, limited though that was – and at this point the merchants on their way to Danzig patted me on the shoulder, and one called out to the cook to get my leg of pork to the table a little faster – but I said that I could of course also talk about what I had heard, and that I had heard much more than I had seen: that the Muscovite forces in Livonia set fire to churches full of refugees – this had happened in '58 even in Jõhvi – and how half the people had suffocated from the smoke and those who still had life left in them were impaled on stakes. But at the same time that the mercenaries were beginning to express their solidarity with me and to swear at the merchants, the most agitated of the latter gestured towards me with his empty mug and swung it into the red face of the nearest soldier. And what happened after that was the only thing that could happen after such an act: the merchants and mercenaries went at each other, and the table at which I was waiting for my meal, all the while swallowing my saliva, was splintered before my leg of pork could arrive. Because it seemed to me that there was some reason why I might receive my share of blows in this argument, and maybe even be asked to pay the owner for the damage – which I could not have paid in any case – I hastily eased my way out from among the brawlers, and in the falling twilight made tracks away from the town of Bernau, with an empty stomach but, thanks be to God, with my *skin intact*.

The little towns of Brandenburg are in many ways similar to small towns in Livonia, but they are built mainly of brick. And the villages of Brandenburg, too, can be compared with the lesser towns of Livonia: in both you find, next to stone houses and stone roofs, mostly wooden buildings and straw roofs. Anyway, I left Bernau in a hurry and slept in the open, in a haystack, as I usually did on that journey. The next morning I went through the only large city of the trip, named Berlin, almost as big as Tallinn, and soon was again among the grey stubble fields and sandy turnip fields of Brandenburg, and continued on into great, brown pine forests. In the south, near the border of the lands belonging to the Prince-Elector of Saxony, the pine forests retreated ever more, yielding to beech woods, and these autumn woods of beeches are a wondrous sight for one who has never seen them before: the trunks are smooth, streaked grey and white, as though they had been coloured thus by flowing waters over a long stretch of time, and as you walk through the woods you hear the thud of your footfalls and the rustling of the blood-red leaves that blanket the ground.

By what magical route? To tell you the truth, it is a mystery to me, too. And I do not know how else to explain it, but that it must have been God's own hand that guided me. On the morning of the eleventh day, a few miles south of Treuenbritzen, we all – I and five or six students and journeymen travelling to Wittenberg – left the high road so as not to be stopped at the toll gates by the border guards. Why the others should have feared the border guards, I do not know. No doubt each had a reason of his own. My fear was that the warrant for me from the Pedagogical Institute in Stettin might have arrived there. In any case, we were all so fearful that the students and craftsmen headed off into the brush all together, in one group, instead of arguing amongst themselves or resorting to fisticuffs, which would have been the natural course of things.

Making our way through pine woods dense with fallen trees and underbrush and many bright yellow birches as well, we succeeded in crossing the border of Saxony, and by noon were in that city whose name, as the site of the greatest and most holy of events, I had heard proclaimed from all pulpits and rostra more sonorously than those of Bethlehem and Jerusalem and Corinth and Ephesus taken together . . .

The town seemed unusual to me because there was no entry gate for those coming from the north, and before I got to the Coswig Gate I had to walk through massive defensive walls and along the banks of the moat around half the town. And I must say, considering its extraordinarily great fame, Wittenberg is actually a rather small town. But then again, as is well known, there is nothing left of mighty Babylonia, while little Nazareth still flourishes, even though it is said to be a miserable and filthy place.

So I entered Wittenberg by way of the Coswig Gate and easily found the street called Fischergasse – it was between Cranach's houses and the Elbe Gate, along the town wall, on the river side – and, by the grace of God, Herr Sum was at home, in his small chamber in the master furrier's house, where I had been told he would be.

I knocked and entered upon his summons; he was sitting at his dinner, chewing on a goose leg, with a wine goblet in front of him, wearing fairly worn slippers of red Moroccan leather. I noticed them right away because his legs were comfortably stretched out, resting on a cushioned footstool. His round brown eyes glanced at me with some annoyance, and he asked as he chewed:

"Well – what is it?"

"Does Master Sum perhaps recall – from Tallinn . . . ?"

"Ohoo! Yes!" he cried out in recognition. "Balthasar! Balthasar, that means 'the one whom Baal should take under his protection.'" He looked me over with care, and his prematurely grey goatee widened with his smile. "In truth, it doesn't look as though Baal has been pampering you. Sit down. Eat. Talk to me."

I sat down and ate and unburdened my heart to him. And to tell the truth I was even a little disappointed at how lightly Herr Sum took the sin of my eleven-thaler debt and my secret flight.

"Ho-ho-ho!" Sum laughed, "and on account of this debt you are racing madly across Germany as if you'd been bitten by a gadfly! Let's take care of it. With interest. Naturally."

Of course, for someone like him, who reputedly had rich relatives in Hanover or Osnabrück, and possibly even a recently inherited manor, this eleven thalers was a mere trifle.

"And now that you're in Wittenberg, what do you want to do next?"

"What's the use of my wanting . . . anything?"

"Well . . . how about studying here for a semester or two?"

"Yes . . . but . . ."

"That could be arranged, too. If you're serious about it. And, after all, you . . ." Here Herr Sum paused, gave me an odd look, as if taking my measure, and then began to speak in Latin. I tried with all my might to work out how I had offended him, for I recalled my first conversation with Rector Wolff. But Herr Sum was as amiable as ever. After an hour of friendly conversation in Latin – which, thanks to the goose and the wine and my enormous sense of relief, became ever more fluent – Herr Sum sent me to the sauna. And even though German bathhouses don't hold a candle to the saunas in Tallinn – they do not know anything about making steam or using birch-branches, for example; all they do is splash about with hot and cold water – even so, afterwards I felt newly born. Though not in the sense, I must confess, of having been washed clean of sin. For I had already managed to arrange a meeting with the pretty sauna maid for that evening at eight, at the Augustinian monastery. Her name was Gertrud . . . she had a face like a little lamb's . . . Forgive me, Lord, that my first visit to those walls, where for so many years Doctor Luther lived and worked in Your service, should be for no more worthy a reason than this . . . But somehow I did not consider myself polluted afterwards, for we were both warm and clean from the sauna and smelt of resin soap. And Gertrud knew of a sheltered recess in the back wall of the monastery, thickly carpeted with dried beech leaves. And in the dark, these coal-black leaves, which I could not see, but knew to be bright red, rustled under us – almost, but not quite, like the hay in the loft at Kalamaja, when . . . Annika, now I'm rattling on to my big sister about my escapades with girls, and I can see clearly just how clouded your Madonna-like forehead has become . . . Ta-ta-ta-ta-taa . . .

Herr Sum's landlord, at his request, found lodgings for me right there in Fischergasse, with a blue-nosed tanner by the name of Manger. Herr Sum took me to meet Rector Fabricius, and from there I found the College of Theology on my own. He also sent off payment for my debt, the eleven thalers, to Rector Wolff, and arranged with the rector here to permit me to make tuition payments in instalments. He gave me a job which kept me from starving and which I could work at between lectures: that is, he employed me to make seven copies of the completed chapters of his *dissertatio*, so that his friends could read and discuss them before he dispatched them to the printer. I did this work in the evenings and at night, in between everything else. "Everything else" included prowling around Wittenberg's famous spots and listening to the celebrated preachers at the Town Church; it included the market shops and student festivals and the pubs of Piesteritz, the fishermen of Strengkolk and the boatmen of the Elbe – and Gertrud, and a thousand other things. And before noon I attended lectures by Pomeranus Junior son of the famous old Bugenhagen. The son looked like someone pulled out of a pit of rotting flax, and his stature derived more from his filial status than from any outstanding intellectual achievements of his own. But primarily – because Herr Sum recommended it – I attended the lectures of the small, hunchbacked Paulus Eberus, who was now, after the death of Philip Melanchthon, considered by all of reformed Germany to be one of the most important heirs to the great Philip's spiritual and intellectual authority – or whatever was still left of the severely plucked feathers of that authority. Eberus had apparently suffered an unlucky fall in his childhood which had left him hunchbacked. His little-boy face, with a fine fuzz of grey hair and a scrawny neck, was narrow and prematurely wrinkled; and when, on the infrequent occasion of an especially lofty, spirited, impassioned sermon, his fragile wrists inside his wide sleeves flashed into view and his black robes started to flap over his hump, he reminded one of a small injured bird that has fallen onto the floor of the lecture hall and been stepped

513

upon. I do not know how to assess how brilliant a man he actually was. But he was a man of goodwill; despite all the hopeless-seeming things of the world, he had in him more goodwill and benevolence than ten saints. From the creaking lectern where, a few decades earlier, Luther himself had thundered his hard and bitter truths, Eberus now preached tirelessly and persistently in his high, monotonous voice, that what mattered was not how the followers of Flacius claimed they differed from the views of Melanchthonites; what mattered was that which unified them as Lutherans. And if not from elsewhere, then it became clear to me from these lectures – though actually from elsewhere as well: from church, tavern, street, marketplace – that at least here, in Germany, the movement of the Cleansing of the Faith had conclusively been torn asunder, as old Rhoda in Stettin had already told us. But I did not think only of old Rhoda in all the muttering about "patching up torn breeches" at this university. My thoughts turned even more to someone else: to my friend Märten, whom I had misled a little and lost all contact with, Märten, with his wolf-cub face, whose birch carving I had lugged all this way to Wittenberg in my bag, either because I could not bring myself to leave it behind or because I was ashamed to. I thought of him and his unflagging contrariness: the way that his ideas, following upon others' unanimous opinions, had an effect like the diabolical screech of a knife scraping up left-over gravy in an empty pan after a Christian meal. In particular, I recalled what he said to me once when I asked him whether he believed that earth-gods really existed: "Of course they do. Why else would pastors, from every pulpit, insist that they don't!"

In any event, I had been at the university a month or so when I stopped in at Master Sum's, one afternoon, with fresh copies of his *dissertatio* under my arm. He took them from me and put them on the table, but instead of asking me to take off my coat and hang it up he pulled a cloak around his shoulders, put a beret on his head, and said: "Come, let's take a walk."

We walked along the bank of the canal towards the university, and I expected him to start telling me the news that I thought I had detected on his face earlier, in the candle-lit room. But instead, Herr Sum asked me suddenly: "Tell me, what is your position with regard to the question of our Saviour's Ubiquity?"

To tell the truth, I had no position on this matter. A bit taken aback, I was at a loss as to what to say, and then, as we walked over the paving stones, slippery with wet maple leaves and black in the dim light of evening, I remembered something: Yes, in the course of my readings, I had chanced upon a piece by a man named Timann. So, thank God, I knew in some detail what this question involved. It came down to the long-standing argument underlying the basic question of Communion: is the body of Christ present in all things, and consequently is the Communion wafer really His body, or only symbolically so? This is the question that the Flacians and Melanchthonites have been arguing with increasing rancour for over twelve years. But as far as my position is concerned . . . Well, there were times when I thought – not that I am incapable of delving to the bottom of this question, but I have just not managed to find time to pursue it – when I thought – and may God forgive me if this should be arrogant of me – that this question was very like one which made Doctor Luther laugh at the papal splitting of hairs over the question of whether one devil or seven thousand could fit on the point of a needle . . . times when I thought that the furious battle over this question was actually a battle over something entirely different which I have not had the time to work out.

We walked back to the town church. Its towers without their spires looked like two giant burnt-down candles, dark against a fading sunset sky that arched above the settlement outside the castle walls. (During Schmalkalden's war, the spires had been removed, so that cannons might be set on the flat surfaces of the towers, but now there were neither cannons nor spires.) I said:

515

"This same Timann writes," – even the title of his book had suddenly come back to me, and I cited it from sheer vanity, which I do try to overcome, but to which I succumbed once again – "Timann writes in his *Farrago senteniarum et caetera** that Christ sits at His Father's right hand, so that He – since God's right hand is everywhere is, *ergo*, also everywhere. Timann says in so many words that Christ is in each apple and pear . . ." We had just reached the edge of the marketplace, and as we walked across the square we passed a large pile of horse manure, black in the twilight, and I was terribly tempted to add, "and in each little mound of manure," but it seemed somehow impious, not with regard to Timann but to Christ – and in Herr Sum's presence, no less. So I said:

"But when it is written, 'And He sits at the right hand of His Father', I think there are two possible interpretations: either it does not mean anything – which clearly cannot be said of the Word of the Gospels – or it means that He does not sit at His Father's left hand at all! And how the gentlemen who insist on His omnipresence reconcile that contradiction, I would like very much to see. But since they have not shown me this, I believe that the Communion bread and wine are our Saviour's body and blood. But how they are these things – I try to keep from struggling too much with that question."

As I recall, Herr Sum was silent for a time after that, and I asked myself whether my answer, which I had blurted out without much thought, had perhaps displeased him. For when it comes to former teachers, one can never be entirely sure what they will tolerate. But then Herr Sum said:

"Balthasar, Büren, the Burgomaster of Bremen and the speakers of the church of St Ansgarius have asked me to become the preacher there."

"And . . . ?" I asked in a voice dull with shock.

* Various opinions and so forth (Latin).

"And I have decided to go there."

That was it, then, for the good life I had been leading, I thought. What a pity. A confounded pity! Just the week before I had worked out that if I managed to make it through three more semesters, I might even be able to complete my master's degree. And that would be a big plus, wherever I presented myself as a candidate for a pulpit . . . But now it was over. And I was not just eleven thalers in debt, but sixteen. Now, to Herr Sum.

"I cannot pay you back," I said grimly, but with a clear conscience.

"That's not what I wanted to talk to you about," Herr Sum s aid.

"And I have nothing more to say on the matter of Ubiquity," I said, vexed. God, forgive me, but not even in my dreams could I fathom your mysterious intentions!

"Balthasar, the gentlemen in Bremen have also written to say that I should find here, in Wittenberg, an assistant pastor for St Ansgarius' Church – a reasonable Melanchthonite."

I felt ashamed of the aggrieved tone I had taken – did I expect Herr Sum to stay in Wittenberg just to support me?! – and in an effort to make amends I tried to think through carefully which of the younger professors or the *lectores publici* at the university I might recommend to Herr Sum.

"Well, there should be any number of suitable men here . . ."

"I think I've already found a suitable man . . ."

"Do I know him?"

"A little, yes."

"Who is it?"

"You, yourself."

Dearest Annika, I will not deny it. I was speechless for some time – for fear that if I said anything it would turn out that I had misunderstood Herr Sum. Or that he was teasing me for some unknown reason. We walked back towards the castle church. The local jackdaws circled the tower, flapping and cawing. A ragged beggar came towards us and stretched out a trembling hand. Herr Sum did not notice him, but I dropped a halfpenny into his hand . . . Lord God, this has to be either an absurd misunderstanding or a miserable joke – and what have I done to deserve it? . . . Or . . . could it really be true? And in that case, what could I have done to deserve it?

And when Herr Sum continued, I realised that it was neither a misunderstanding nor a joke: Master Sum really had chosen me. "And why not?" he reasoned, making it sound so self-evident that after a while I began to believe it myself: And why not? I had a strong foundation from Tallinn's trivium school. I had studied for three years at the duke's Pedagogical Institute in Stettin. And there were not that many students who had finished with as broad a foundation of learning as I. And to that I could now add a semester, even though it was only half over, but a semester nonetheless, in Wittenberg. And actually we would not be going to Bremen until spring, and by then I would have completed, stretching it only a little, almost two Wittenberg semesters . . . And Herr Sum felt – in this I did not argue with him – that, compared with the average young pastor, I could manage to hold my own in most matters. As to my worries about ascending to the pulpit of "the most splendid church of Tallinn's famous mother-city", Herr Sum broke into hearty laughter:

"He-he-he-heh, tell me my friend, why is it always so, that young whelps from some *Ober-* or *Nieder-Viehland** can puff themselves up in the pulpits of St Olaf's or St Nicholas' in Tallinn – I am not, of course, referring to your dear brother-in-law, who came from Danzig, I believe. Why should not a youth from Tallinn, from Kalamaja village, be able, for once, to proclaim the Word of God from the pulpit of St Ansgarius Church in Bremen?! Let them listen! To the true, glorious Word! The

* Upper- or Lower-Cattle Country (German).

Word, containing the sap of life and redolent of the earth!" And he went on, so that I do not even remember right now exactly what he said or what I thought about it.

Dear sister, you understand, of course, that this long yarn up here in this steeple is not so much an explanation to you, who cannot hear it in any case, but rather a way of putting off a difficult and important decision. But now the damp northwest wind, summery though it may be, has blown away all that is secondary, and I will hurry to get to the heart of the matter.

Towards the end of April, when the brief winter snows had long since melted and the wetlands of the Elbe were tinged a blue-green, we set off for Bremen. From the harbour next to the great wooden bridge of Leipzig we set sail on a riverboat with a high mast and low decks, in a small cabin, in the company of a hoarse captain and deckhands smelling of tar. Some other time I will describe our long boat trip in detail: the castles and towns we sailed past, and all the barriers along the river, where the lancers of various counts and dukes stopped and inspected us and charged us tolls. There is one thing I have to tell you about, though: what I saw and heard in the town of Magdeburg. In Magdeburg we transferred to another ship, which was to take us on downriver, and we had a few days' wait there as the cargo was loaded on board. So that on Sunday morning I went to their grand cathedral to hear the famous Matthias Flacius, whom many prefer to call "infamous". He had been a professor in Jena for a number of years, until the duke dismissed him. Now, as the dispute over the doctrine of original sin was growing more heated, he had come to preach in his old church. Naturally, I could not miss an opportunity like that. I saw in Magdeburg, for the first time, that there were in fact towns larger and more imposing than Tallinn, and in this cathedral I realised that St Olaf's and St Nicholas' in Tallinn were not the world's most impressive churches . . . which I well knew, of course, but an honest man would not rush to such a concession until he had seen for himself. By the way, even when a man has seen it with his own eyes and uttered it with his own lips, he need not, in my opinion, bruit it about on every market square, if only out of self-respect. And then I heard Flacius' sermon.

Ten years earlier, Magdeburg Cathedral had always been so crowded for his sermons that, even at the furthest walls, in front of the image of the Mother of God standing on a dragon, and under the sculpted procession of the Wise and Foolish Virgins, people had been injured in the crush. But now the church was half empty, even though, during his rank tirades – on such themes as "Wittenberg's race of worms" and the "Dragon of Zwinglianism, which, with the shameful help of Melanchthon, has befouled the holy grave of Luther with its excrement", and so on. I saw many an eye catch fire at those rank words and many listeners' jaws clench in their shared hatred. For, in their opinion, they alone were faithful to Luther's teachings. And they considered Melanchthon worse than Judas, with his subtle arguments about human nature and its desires, and his interpretation of many sacred things as purely symbolic . . . But Flacius himself was a slight man, with bulging, cold brown eyes and a pock-marked face, and he spoke an oddly accented German, being from Illyria, and hammered out his remarks with a kind of dull insistence, so that I could not understand what there was about him that attracted people – other than his unshakeable Lutheranism and the fact that in the use of foul language he probably outdid Doctor Luther himself. For his entire sermon, especially when he started to talk of original sin . . . But Annika, I will not confuse you with Flacius' dogmatism . . . I will just say this: his sermon sounded as though neither Melanchthon nor Peucer nor Erasmus had ever lived. And as though Luther, the old thunderer, had said only those things which he uttered in his final, desperate, angry arguments. But when we came out of the church, and Herr Sum asked me what I had thought of Flacius' sermon, and I told him honestly, he squeezed my elbow with a "Shhh!"

I then continued, in a lower voice, to say that surely the duke had dismissed Flacius from his professorship, and Herr Sum replied, when we had emerged from the crowd of churchgoers:

"Dismissals can be handed out one day and recalled the next. And even in the case of a half-empty church . . . I believe you noticed the faces of Flacius' old guard?"

"I did."

"There you are – so the victory of the Melanchthonites is by no means certain in Germany . . ."

And I do have to admit: as we sailed down the ever-widening river towards Hamburg, in the midst of increasingly heavy boat traffic, and as I came up onto the deck in the early mornings – filling my lungs with the sweet-damp river air and seeing the dawn reddening over the right bank and listenening to the water sloshing at the stern and smelling the tarred cables and feeling the movement of the boat under the soles of my feet – I felt with my whole body and spirit that all that quarrelling, all those ups and downs of position and reputation, no matter how holy the issues, are not what matter most under God's heaven, even though I do not yet know what does matter most . . . But of course it was easy for me to come to that conclusion at a time when I myself was sailing towards my own undeserved and unexpected elevation in status.

And then we were there, in the most wonderful, welcoming town of Bremen, about which I have so much to relate that I will not even begin to do it here. Herr Putteman, a kind gentleman with a button nose and an apostle's tonsure, took us in to live in his grand house, and on the eleventh Sunday after Trinity I am to deliver my trial sermon here, in the church of St Ansgarius. With the help of Herr Sum and Herr Puttemann, we have chosen as its basis the eighteenth chapter of Luke, beginning with the ninth verse: "And He spake this parable unto certain which trusted in themselves that they were righteous, and despised others: Two men went up into the temple to pray; the one a Pharisee and the other a publican . . ." And now I am sitting here on a beam in the bell tower, and as I listen to the wind blowing over the bells I am reading your letter, which reached me this morning:

But in the meantime, both here in Tallinn and in the whole territory of Estonia, great changes have taken place, as you have perhaps heard and as I told you in the letter I sent to Stettin. On the fourth day of the month of June, last year, after long discussions in the Council, your acquaintance Herr Horn led the army of Erik, the new king of Sweden, off the ships and onto the shores of Tallinn, and the town and all of Harjumaa province ceremonially bowed down to this king, on which occasion a great many church bells were rung. But the castle of Toompea in Tallinn did not yield easily to the Swedes, so that Herr Horn was forced to mount cannons on the bastions and around the moats, and the cannons began to thunder to the accompaniment of the bells. The bell-ringers tired, but not the gunners. The terrible bombing continued day and night for two weeks, causing the plaster in our vaulted kitchen ceiling to rain down on us, and when the castle had been considerably damaged and the Stür den Kerl Tower destroyed, Herr Oldenbokkum surrendered himself and the castle to the Swedes and got safe passage for himself and all the soldiers of the Order (half of whom immediately hired themselves out to the Swedes), after which all the church bells rang again for three days, but at least the cannons finally fell silent. And now in Tallinn, those who were hoping for the Swedes are very happy, but many of those who were hoping for the Danes or Poles or some third power are even more outspoken and self-important than the supporters of the Swedes, and everywhere in the marketplace and in front of churches they loudly praise *"vår* *unge Majestet"** and *"våra träffliga officerare"*.† But the reason I am writing to you is that Father's inheritance, the part he left you, needs to be claimed. He bequeathed to me, as a widow without any wealth worthy of mention, half the money he had left, 150 marks in silver and this house – where you will always be welcome, and would have it to yourself at first, and if I move there later, to share with me, if its thatched roof be acceptable to you still. According to the will, your share is the rest of the money in the same amount aforementioned and all the rest of the movable goods: the contents of the house, the silver, the animals (horses, barnyard animals, hogs and heifers), everything which, taken together, Father considered to be of equal value with my share, as is the case. And now all this property is here awaiting the management of its owner.

So it is true, and I did not misunderstand it in my first hasty reading: I am free of debt! And that shabby old house, which I imagined crumbling into dust when I received Father's death notice, now rushes into being again in my mind's eye and rises there, under the willows swaying in the wind, against a grey sea of whitecaps – containing all its smells and sounds and all the things that once took place there. Its low door of weatherbeaten boards, with its twisted juniper-branch handle, is open . . . That door is still there . . . And I can, if I want . . . But this is of course a foolish thought. I am just about to ascend to the pulpit here. I will have no problem with my trial sermon. It is just a formality. That is the first point. And the second is that I will complete this formality to the delight and satisfaction of the entire cathedral chapter and all the gentlemen of the congregation. No doubt about that. Just a few months ago, they managed to struggle free of the tyranny of the famous Museus and of Flacius' followers in general. Now they want to be more

* Our young majesty (Swedish). † Our splendid officers (Swedish).

Melanchthonian than Melanchthon himself, and they will be grateful to me for presenting Luke's text on conciliation. For it is precisely in the spirit of conciliation that I have to interpret it – this is what the leadership of the cathedral chapter wish. Even though if it had to be Luke, I would have preferred, just between us, to preach on the text of the nineteenth chapter: "And he went into the Temple, and began to cast out them that sold therein, and them that bought . . ." Which text seems to me always appropriate in a large merchant town, but here, in addition, it could have been directed at the shameless greed of that Museus whom they have driven out, something all Bremen is still buzzing about – and to some extent it might have been a way for me to give voice to my own extended torment at living so long under a burden of debt . . . But when I proposed this text to the leadership of the congregation they all began to shake their heads and mutter objections, and even Herr Puttemann said: "Hmm . . . we think that will not be necessary . . ." And Herr Sum winked at me and agreed with them right away . . . But I immediately felt as though it were a case of them against me . . .

But of course I will get rooms in a house belonging *to the church*, on Sögestrasse. They showed me the rooms last week and they are considerably better than those allotted to you and Meus. Right now there are workmen whitewashing the ceiling and repairing the wooden wall panelling in the great-room. I will get the rooms and four hundred marks a year. The first hundred will be put into my hand right after the trial sermon has officially been pronounced acceptable. So that – and this is the most important thing, is it not? – I will actually be free of debt here too. Even before it happens there. Yes, both here and there . . . And maybe there even more completely somehow . . . I am not sure I can say in what way, but . . . Of course, if I were (ha-ha-ha-ha) to head back home, I could not hope for a miracle – they would not just whisk me up into the pulpit of St Olaf's or Holy Ghost . . . They would send me off somewhere into the countryside, to a dilapidated church and a congregation that had fled to the swamps, where I would live in a burnt-out parsonage, maybe not completely destroyed, such as one finds in ever-greater number in Livonia these days, with its walls leaning at all angles, its stoves in rubble, doors askew, windows shattered, rotting inside and out, its rafters like bones against the grey sky, its thatch roof in the stomachs of starving cows and the cows in the stomachs of the last plunderers . . . It would be a different story in Tallinn . . . But it would be dangerous for me to go there for the very reason you mention, and as I was reading your letter up here, looking out to sea, I jumped when I came to the mention of a certain distant village:

And then there's another curious story I want to write about. In my widowhood I have found occupation for my hands and sustenance for my heart in continuing those activities that I considered my duty as the wife of a pastor: that is, to lighten the suffering of the sick and the dying. And God has aided me in this Christian activity, for the relatives of the departed, as well as those who have recovered from their illnesses, have been satisfied with me and have recommended me to some of the finer families that were members of the parish under blessed Meus – the homes of Germans and even relatives of Council members. And thus I happened to the sickbed of our long-time acquaintance, Herr Vegesack, to which he took in the autumn and from which he did not rise again. And a few days before his death he told me that you, Balthasar, had been with the peasants during the great uprisings of '60, when they came to the Town Hall in Tallinn to seek support for the rebels. He claims to have seen you with his own eyes, standing with the rebels in front of the Council. And he was completely clear-headed when he told me this. And I said to him that his eyes must have deceived him, for your presence in Tallinn at that time was utterly impossible, just as it was impossible that you would have been involved with the peasants, even if you had somehow come to your homeland – something that, deep down, I do not actually consider so utterly impossible, given your singularly capricious and singularly stubborn spirit and the way you poke your nose into all kinds of things out of a kind of childish curiosity. But I remained silent on that, and Herr Vegesack said, and his old, sour, merchant smile spread over his yellowish face: "And it is best that it never happened at all," and he closed one eye, "even if it may have happened . . ." And in the few days that remained to him, he did not mention it again, and then he was called from this world and I have not known to this moment what to think about it. My heart is sad that you are so far away and will likely remain where you are, but it is also at peace about you.

Beloved sister, this almost sounds as though I should stay abroad for the sake of your peace of mind! . . . Or do you really think that to return home would mean rushing into unknown danger? But listen, whether I was there during the rebellion or not is de facto of no importance . . . A councilman mumbled something on his deathbed, and we do not know whether he has told anyone about it but you – for why would anyone else have been interested? – and now he is in the ground . . . But it is unbelievable that he recognised me that time . . . And is that a reason for me to keep away from Tallinn forever? What? To be acceptable in the marble pulpit of Bremen's St Ansgarius but not in the birch pulpits of Mary's Land? To tell the truth, I am tempted, sorely tempted, but . . . oh well . . .

Otherwise life goes on as usual, and although the situation outside the town walls is still quite unsettled, there's not much news to relate about our friends and relatives. The Kurgla folks were gone for a long time during and after the rebellion, but I've heard that they have returned again and Uncle Jakob has rebuilt his burnt-out house . . . I wonder whether the big fir at the corner of the stone fence was burned or is still standing? . . . with the help of Jürgen and a new farmhand – the farmhand from Kurgla, named Paavel, whom you remember perhaps, was apparently killed in the rebellion . . .

Paavel killed . . . That means that Epp is . . .

And in spite of all the dangers, Doctor Friesner rides constantly back and forth between Tallinn and Turku and Riga and Mitau, and Herr Horn is said to have stated that neither Herr Johann nor Gotthart can hoist him onto the gallows tree, for each one has to leave half of him to be hanged by the other. But Frau Katharina smiles sweetly as always . . .

Annika . . . look, I am getting up from this beam and walking along the balustrade, sun-wise, around the bells. Below me are the warm red roofs of this imposing foreign town. To my left are this land's wind and its cloud shadows and sparkling sunshine. To my right is the inaudible hum of the bells. And in my hand is your letter, fluttering in the wind like a living titmouse. And I confess to myself and to you, if God were to give me a sign right now, if His voice were to say to me up here: "Balthasar, why do you wish to cast anchor in this strange town, in this foreign land? Why do you want to get involved in the arguments foreign to you, simmering in this land? Even before you could open your mouth to say what you, deep in your heart, considered to be my will – yes, even before that – they came to tell you what they, in their view, thought you should believe it to be. Balthasar, you are twenty-five years old and ought to be thinking of both your father's grave and your children's cradle. Balthasar, take care to weigh carefully, in the scales of your heart, whether it is not sheer pride which makes this marble pulpit here, in this church, so desirable that you cannot ask yourself: How big a part of your desire to stay here is your enthusiasm to serve – me, yes, but also, silver – do not deny it – and how big a part is a betrayal of the many mute and distant things which are easier to renounce than me – and the silver . . . ? And consider carefully, are you really afraid to go home because of something said to your sister by a man now in his grave – and it could indeed be that it was said not only to your sister, so that, in staying here you are actually running away?! Balthasar – do you not believe at all any more in the power of that magic drink that you once swallowed in a tower higher than this one? . . . Balthasar . . . ?"

But there is no voice. There is only the wind whistling even louder. I have been making ever-smaller circles around the bells, as though I were trying to arrive somewhere more quickly. And then I pause in front of Big Boomer. I shut my eyes. I say: "Lord, if you were to open your mouth now to say to me: 'Balthasar'". . . There is no voice. But the bells hum more audibly. I open my eyes – Annika, there are such things as signs! – I open my eyes and read – in letters big as my thumb, directly in front of my eyes, in the bronze surface of the bell – maybe it is the name of the bellmaster of long ago. No matter:

BALTHASAR

Balthasar hurried down the steeple stairs and, without turning to look back, walked through the empty church of St Ansgarius. A little marble fellow, the one bowing over the stone likeness of Councilman Gröpening lying on his grave, looked at him with an uncomprehending half-grin.

That same evening at Herr Puttemann's house, Balthasar said to the council members and church leaders:

"My most kind lords and friends – for now at last I dare call you such – I cannot accept your most generous offer. God has decided otherwise. I have received a letter. My father has died in Tallinn. I must go home and claim my inheritance."

"That is a pity," Herr Sum said, and Balthasar was almost hurt at how casually he seemed to say it. "That is a pity, but of course you must go."

"*If* the inheritance is sufficiently large," Herr Puttemann said, "as I must assume it to be, although I am surprised."

The gentlemen did not ask how large the inheritance was, and Balthasar did not venture to tell them.

Herr Sum located a ship in the harbour for Balthasar, belonging to the merchants of Bremen. It was the *Neptune*, set to sail for the North Sea at noon the following day, aiming to get through the strait before King Christian closed it again to ships from Bremen, as he had threatened to do. Balthasar reached an agreement with the stout Captain Holt, and early the next morning he set out for the docks of Schlachte. And Herr Sum actually came to send off his young friend, which one would not have expected of him, given his way of treating most things with casual informality.

"I will send you what I owe, at the first opportunity," Balthasar said. "It comes to eighteen thalers, including my passage home."

"Fine, fine. At the first or second or third opportunity, yes. And give my regards to my Tallinn acquaintances – Tegelmeister, Balder and the others. And do well yourself. In truth, you should beg my forgiveness for taking off like this, but you are too stubborn for that . . ."

"But Herr Sum, it's true that my father . . ."

"Of course it's true. But still, you would not be leaving if you hadn't wanted to leave for other reasons. Maybe because, childishly, you hope to be able to decide more independently, at home, what God deems to be right. I saw clearly how your face tightened when we declared

529

your chosen text to be inappropriate. Well, this childish hope will pass with the years. And maybe it will be easier for you in that bear-town of yours, than it is here, to become the kind of man whose head everyone does not attempt to turn in his own direction. And evidently you have other reasons as well. I think women may play a role here, too. But probably most important is the fact that you are simply not yet German enough."

"How do you mean . . . ?"

"Not enough to feel at home in any and all the cities from Amsterdam to Narva and from Kraini to Bergen. But still, remember this: I will always be your friend. You are an unusual fellow, and among my pupils there has been none other like you. Well then . . ."

They had reached the dock and walked out to the nearest barges. The three-masted *Neptune*, heavily laden, was two hundred cubits away, in the middle of the river, its sails partly unfurled.

"Alright. It'll be some time before you cast off. God go with you. I'll walk back to town."

"And please give my regards to Herr Puttemann and thank him for me again."

"Fine, fine." Master Sum bestowed a brief smile on him and then disappeared behind a human chain of workmen unloading sacks of salt onto the pier from a nearby barge. Balthasar tried to keep him in view, but a two-and-a-half-pood sack was just then being passed from hand to hand and obscured Herr Sum for a stretch of twenty or thirty paces; and when it finally thudded onto the heap, he had disappeared between the stacks of wares.

Not until the barge carrying Balthasar, with his bundle and travel case – barely more baggage than he had once taken aboard the *Dolphin* – reached the middle of the river, did he realise that although he had thanked Herr Puttemann himself and then asked Herr Sum to thank him again, he had neglected entirely to thank Herr Sum!

"So be it. I'll remedy that in a letter from Tallinn."

The sight of the water widening at the stern, and of the town on the riverbank growing more distant as it unrolled past with its thousand windows – some dark, some bright, and the sudden realisation of the great length and many dangers of the voyage ahead all weighed on Balthasar's heart, pressing it against the insubstantial, tarred boards between him and the bottomless, gurgling river. And God's earth seemed so unfathomably enormous that the idea that one "thank-you" letter sent from beyond many lands and seas would actually arrive at its intended destination seemed possible only by means of a miracle . . . But just then Balthasar discovered that God's boundless world could, by His mysterious will, suddenly seem no larger than an anthill.

Balthasar paid the bearded bargeman his pennies and climbed up the wobbly rope ladder to the reassuringly wide deck of the *Neptune*.

"Well, well, so our distinguished pastor is on board," growled the copper-faced boatswain as they made their way, stepping over coils of rope, towards the stern, to greet the captain. "Well now, our worries are over! We'll be able to receive God's blessing even in the stomach of Skagen's sea serpent!"

If I don't reply to that, thought Balthasar, *he'll have the upper hand from now on*. And with complete seriousness he said:

"Yes you will. But only if you keep quiet, so that the monster doesn't fart you out too soon."

The boatswain responded with an appreciative, "Hmm . . ."

Captain Holt was sitting on a seal-oil barrel at the door of the stern cabin. A small table and stool, both with folding legs, had been set up directly in front of the cabin door. A middle-aged man, with bowl-cut, ash-grey hair, was sitting on the stool, his pen moving across the papers spread out on the table.

"Aha, the distinguished pastor," Holt murmured, looking searchingly at Balthasar. He apparently found that this man's profession (for

Herr Sum had told him, the day before yesterday, that he was a pastor from St Ansgarius) did not quite comport with his clothing and luggage – a simple and noticeably worn black coat, a clumsy wooden chest and a little bundle that the boatswain had put down beside him. So he said:

"The boatswain will show you to your cabin." But then this greeting suddenly seemed to him to be too curt – a man of the cloth, after all! – and he added in explanation: "I myself can't, as you see – I'm engaged with the notary, trying to secure an old debt. Long journey ahead . . ."

The notary raised his head from his papers and Balthasar recognised him instantly, with the sweet flash of recognition that always gave him pleasure. Maybe because he had noticed, in this regard, that he had better recall than most – including, it seemed, the notary. Even as he rummaged in his memory, trying to grab this man's name by the tail, he said:

"The esteemed notary does not recognise me? We've met. At Doctor Friesner's house in Tallinn. When the esteemed notary was the scribe for Herr Schmerten and had been injured by the Order's horses. In the summer of '58."

"Right. I did indeed go to see the Doctor there. But I do not remember you. Perhaps if I look at my notes. How long have you been away from Livonia?"

"I . . . umm . . . since the autumn of '58."

"Even longer than I have. I left there in the autumn of '60. Before the great peasant uprising. So that you cannot tell me the latest news?"

"The latest news? No."

When Balthasar had located his bunk next to the steersman's cabin and put his things away and returned – in the meantime the notary's name had come back to him – the man was sprinkling sand on his document. Captain Holt's notarised promissory note was complete.

"Herr Renner is now a notary in this town?" Balthasar asked.

"Just an alternative, for the time being. But you are returning to

Livonia, I've heard? It's true I was there only five or six years – wave to the walls of Toompea for me. Even though the Swedes are there now. And to the walls of Paide, too. If you should happen to visit them and anything's still standing."

The cables began to creak as the seamen, chanting in rhythm, weighed anchor. The notary climbed down the rope ladder in the stern and descended to a waiting boat. His folding table, stool and writing case were handed down to him.

And when the *Neptune* started downriver with the current, and the foresail opened and filled with wind, Notary Renner stood up in his boat – it is hard to say why, for he had lived but five or six years in Livonia and had not found his fortune there – and waved to the fair-haired, broad-shouldered young pastor standing at the ship's railing, setting sail for that unforgettable land.

Author's Afterword

The Story of Balthasar Russow owes its genesis to three circumstances. These now provide me with the welcome opportunity to express my sincere gratitude three times.

First (and unfortunately belatedly), to the departed Professor Paul Johansen, for his discovery of the records of Balthasar Russow's Estonian lineage. For with this documentation the figure of Russow attained a new prominence among the potential actors in Estonian historical literature.

Second, to academician Hans Kruus, for directing my attention to this discovery and also to its literary value.

Third, to the librarians of the rare manuscripts department of the Soviet Estonian Library of the Academy of Sciences, in particular, to comrades V. Miller and K. Robert, for their extraordinary helpfulness to me – far exceeding their official obligations – in examining all possible kinds of materials.

And finally, to the countless colleagues, too great in number to list here, in particular the historians whom I have pestered over the course of many years, at times with exceedingly bizarre questions in connection with my Balthasar.

J.K.
Tallinn, September 1969

Notes

23. "Honoured lords and ladies of the nobility." The original has the speaker using Low German: *"Ernveste hern und frawn von der adell."*

23. "Esteemed and gracious burghers!" The original has the speaker using Swedish: *"Förärade och nadigaste borgare!"*

23. Urgent summons: The original has "trilingual summons" because the crier summons the townspeople in the three main languages spoken by specific groups of people in this multi-ethnic town: Estonian for the craftsmen and the peasants; Low German for nobles, merchants and government officials; Swedish for the town burghers.

23. "Honourable Council! Beautiful women! Modest maidens!" The original has the speaker using Low German: *"Ein ersam raad! Schöne frawn! Tichtg junkfer!"*

24. Kalamaja: Name of the fishing village that Balthasar is from. Literal meaning: fish house.

25. "Fie, you little devil.": The original has the speaker using Low German: *"Fuu, du kleener deywel."*

25. Trivium School: The course of study here was based on the *trivium*, the elementary division of the seven liberal arts in medieval schools: grammar, rhetoric and logic. It is also referred to as town school and Latin school in the novel.

25. *Quarta*-level pupil: The grades in the town school begin with quarta, the fourth and lowest grade, being fourth from the top. It is followed by *tertia*, *secunda* and *prima*, which is the highest grade. The term primaner refers to a pupil in the graduating class. (There is also a level below the grades: the *infima* level, which is for pupils too young for *quarta*.)

26. Articles of Augsburg XVII to XIX: The Augsburg Confession (1530), one of the most important documents of the Lutheran Reformation, includes 28 articles of faith. Articles XVII to XIX concern Christ's return upon Judgement Day, Free Will and the Cause of Sin.

27. Athenaeus: Second/third- century A.D. Greek grammarian and rhetorician. Much of what we know about the ancient world and its writers we owe to him.

31. Paljassaare, Nairisaare, Salmesaare Islands in the Baltic Sea, off the coast of Livonia.

40. Mündrik-Mats: Bargeman-Mats.

45. Mary's Land: The territory of Old Livonia (present day Estonia and Latvia) was named Terra Mariana after the Livonian Crusade. From 1207 to 1215 it was a principality of the Holy Roman Empire. During the Livonian War, Terra Mariana ceased to exist.

46. The original in German:

> *Nicht vergebens sagt man:*
> *Liefflandt ist ein Blieflandt*
> *da sich gantz besonders jetzt*
> *mancher niedersetzt.*

46. Livland: German for Livonia.

46. Master Plettenberg: Wolter (or Walter) von Plettenberg (c.1450–February 28, 1535) was the Master (Landmeister) of the Livonian Order from 1494 to 1535 and one of the greatest leaders of the Teutonic Knights.

48. Melanchlaeni: A nomadic tribe, mentioned by Greek historian Herodotus, possibly referring to a people found in the vicinity of Lake Ladoga.

49. Church Treasury: The Estonian is *Jumalalaegas*, translated literally: "God's coffers". It was a fund established during the Reformation for the support of churches, schools and almshouses.

49. "Herr Frolink, as his name implied . . .": His name derives from the German word froh, meaning "happy".

51. *Symbolum Athanasianum*: Athanasian Creed, a Christian statement of belief, thought to have been written by Athanasius of Alexandria. Used by Christian churches since the sixth century.

55. *Primaner*: A student in the graduating class of the town school (Latin).

57. Blubber sheds: Where seal blubber was rendered.

67. Traani-Krõõt: wife of Traani-Andres. Names in Estonia could designate a number of things, among them, occupations. Andres is named Traani-Andres because he renders seal blubber and sells the oil, or *traan*.

73. "Free air of town": A serf who had escaped from or been released by his employer and had lived in town for a year and a day was considered a free man, officially under the protection of the town, and could no longer be legally claimed by the former employer.

78. *Ab urbe condita*: A monumental history of Rome by the historian Titus Livius, known as Livy.

94. Üksküll, Johan (also spelled Üxkyll, Yxkyll): A German noble who was executed because he tortured to death a peasant who had escaped from him and had been living in town. It was law that once a man had lived in "the free air of town" for a year and a day, he was officially under the protection of the town and could not be returned to servitude.

105. Barn-dwelling: The typical Estonian peasant dwelling was a long low building that combined a threshing barn at one end and two or three small chambers at the other, used for storage in winter and as bedrooms in summer. The central room was both the main living room and the kiln-room.

106. To burn-beat a field: To clear a plot of land for cultivation by clearing it of grasses, turf, trees and brush and then burning it all to enrich the soil.

106. Beestings: The first milk produced by a cow or similar animal immediately after giving birth. Alternative spelling: beastings

116. Would-be German: An Estonian who attempted to become Germanised to advance in society and sometimes stopped speaking Estonian, or spoke a blend of both languages.

119. Ruunaboy: He is called "*Ruunapoiss*" in Estonian. "*Ruun*" means gelding, "poiss" means boy. The poor chap is an object of contempt, viewed as sneaky, duplicitous, even traitorous. (His given name is Jürg . . . thus a namesake of Jürgen, Bal's cousin.)

127. Overseer: The overseer of peasants working on a manor was a peasant himself, the taskmaster or "enforcer" in charge of overseeing their output. The taskmasters were both feared and reviled.

135. Hooded chimney: A type of fireplace chimney harking back to the Middle Ages. The lower part of the chimney inside the house extended as a widening hood over the entire hearth and sometimes the surrounding kitchen area as well.

138. Peasant shoes: Of soft leather, without heels, fastened by laces wrapped around the calf.

142. *Cosmographia universalis*: Written by Sebastian Munster (1488–1552) in 1544. It is the earliest German description of the world and was one of the most successful and popular books of the sixteenth century, with twenty-four editions in a hundred years.

142. *Kannel*: Estonian folk instrument, similar to a "lap harp" or zither.

144. "Oh, would Her Ladyship please pardon me . . .": The original has her speaking German: "*Ach . . . wollen die Gnädigen mich entschuldigen . . .*"

146. *Magister utriusque medicinae*: Master of both healing arts (Latin).

147. The Peasant War (1524–25): A widespread revolt in the German-speaking areas of central Europe. About a hundred thousand peasants and farmers were slaughtered by the aristocrats.

152. *Hortus sanitatis*: Garden of Health (Latin).

152. *Liber pestilentialis:* Book of the Plague (Latin).

152. *Serratura*: Amputation (Latin).

157. Treaty of Pozvol: The peace treaty and defensive alliance concluded in September 1557 between the Livonian Confederation and Poland–Lithuania. It put Livonia under the protection of Poland–Lithuania. Some historians believe that it was a provocation for Ivan IV and the immediate cause of the Livonian War. Another cause often cited is the failure of the Livonians to pay a tribute that Ivan IV considered his due.

158. The Hansa: In the mid-thirteenth century, seafaring merchants of northern Germany established the Hanseatic League, a confederation of guilds for both defensive and economic purposes. Up to two hundred towns and cities throughout the North Sea and Baltic Sea regions were members of the League, as were several large trading houses. For over four hundred years, the Hanseatic League played a major role in the trade and politics of its members.

158. Bornholm's birch fungus: a fungus called chaga that grows on birch, alder and beech trees. It was and still is used to treat stomach and lung cancers and other stomach and intestinal ailments.

159. Apothecary: The Town Hall Apothecary in Tallinn (Estonian: *Raeapteek*). It has occupied the same building since the early fifteenth century.

166. *Klarett*: Popular beverage prepared of white wine, ginger and other spices.

206. Witch's broom: growth on some conifers and deciduous trees, with a great many shoots that look like a bundle of twigs.

214. Splint-flame (Estonian: *peerg*): The main source of light in farmhouses was a burning splint of wood, usually a thin length of pinewood or birch, clamped in an iron holder affixed either to a wall or to a wooden stand.

227. Monstrance: A receptacle for the Host.

227. The spirit of Augsburg: Refers to the Augsburg Confession, the primary confession of faith of the Lutheran Church and one of the most important documents of the Lutheran Reformation.

254. Mithridates' potion: An antidote to poisoning, also used in the Middle Ages to ward off plague. Consisted of as many as sixty-five ingredients. Mithridates was king of Pontus, 132–63 B.C.

271. Thalia: Muse of comedy and pastoral poetry, one of the Nine Muses in Greek mythology.

280. Now I have been christened . . . : Estonian: *Nüüd olen mina ristitud ja Isa omaks saanud* . . .

308. Woe is me . . . : Latin: *Heu me, qui dirrupta nobili femina bestiis obiectus* . . .

318. *Köster*: Assistant to a pastor. The *köster* provided religious instruction to pupils, taught singing and often also played the organ for services.

334. *Praeceptus Germaniae*: Germany's Schoolmaster (Latin). Honorary title bestowed upon Philipp Melanchthon by his followers.

338. "On the Universal Love of God": Latin: *De amore Dei universale*.

342. On the True Customs of Northern Peoples: Latin: *De gentium septentrionalium veris moribus*.

346. Reval: German name for Tallinn.

358. St Veronica: Moved to pity at the sight of Jesus carrying his cross, she handed him her veil that he might wipe his brow. When he handed it back to her, the image of his face was imprinted on it.

361. Fugger of the North: Jacob Fugger the Rich (1459–1525), a German banker who inherited his father's business of trading and expanded it to the Adriatic Sea via Venice. All four brothers were traders.

366. *Voevoda*: A Slavic term meaning military commander, warlord or warrior-governor.

377. *Oprichnina*: The state policy devised by Ivan the Terrible between 1565 and 1572. It included instituting secret police, public executions, mass repressions, confiscation of land from aristocrats in Russia. The land where the policy would be carried out would bear its name: Oprichnina.

377. St George's Night Uprising: On April 23, 1343, peasants in Estonia rose up against their German masters in attacks that began in Harjumaa, northern Estonia, and spread to other areas over the course of several months. The rebellion was crushed by the Teutonic and Livonian Knights by the end of the year on the mainland, but was not quelled on Saaremaa Island until the spring of 1345.

409. Half-pood peasants: Peasants who were obliged to deliver a half-pood (about 18 pounds) of grain to the manor.

410. Kulpsuu: means "Ladle-mouth" – for his drooping lower lip.

415. The masters will be ravens' rations . . . : *Sakstest saavad rongad rooga / tulemöll teeb môisad tuhaks, / mets ja maa jääb meitele* . . . (Estonian).

424. One-foot peasants: Poor peasants, usually younger sons, who were given very small plots of land and were obliged to work one day a week at the manor.

440. Aesop's fable: Balthasar cites Aesop here. The story is actually a fable by Ivan Krylov (1769–1844), Russian's best-known fabulist, who did base some of his fables on those of Aesop. The fable tells of three creatures attempting to move a loaded cart. They pull with all their might, the crayfish scrambling backwards, the swan straining upwards and the pike pulling towards the sea. "The cart is still there today" is the concluding line. The fable was very popular during the Soviet era.

441.

> *Ind Jar Vertein Hundert XXXIII do geschach*
> *In Meye op den elff ten dach,*
> *All Reuel brande und de Dom mede,*
> *Garden und Schünen buten der stede,*
> *Kercken und Clöster verbranden all.*
> *Orgeln, Klocken und Volck ane tall,*
> *Bidde wy Gott all unse dage*
> *Dat he uns bescherme vor sodan plage.*

468. Ovid's wise book: *Ars Amatoria* (The Art of Love).

469. If you have a voice, sing . . . etc.: *Si vox est, canta, si mollia brachia salata: et quecunque potes dote placere, place* . . . (Latin).

471. Potiphar's wife: Story from Genesis. Potiphar makes Joseph the head of his household. Potiphar's wife is enraged because Joseph does not agree to lie with her and she accuses him of attempted rape.

505. *Lector publicus*: Public lecturer (Latin).

APPENDIX TWO

Selected Historical Figures

Albert, Duke of Prussia: (1490–1568) The last Grand Master of the Teutonic Knights and the first European ruler to establish Lutheranism (thus Protestantism) as the official state religion.

Flacius, Matthias: (1520–75) Lutheran reformer from Croatia. He was student, friend and then colleague of Melanchthon's. Their relationship eventually became rancorous over deep disagreements concerning interpretations of Reformation theology and basic Lutheran beliefs.

Frederick II: (1534–88) King of Denmark. Reigned from 1559 until his death. In a conflict over land holdings with Duke Magnus of Holstein, his younger brother, he bought Saaremaa and installed Magnus there as bishop.

Fürstenberg, Johann Wilhelm: Master of the Livonian Order from 1557 to 1559. He was accused of cowardice and incompetence for retreating with his forces from the Kirumpää encampment, thus enabling sixty thousand troops under Prince Shuiski to march unimpeded to Tartu. He was replaced by Gotthart Kettler.

Henning, Salomon: (1528–89) Contemporary chronicler of the Livonian War, in particular of the exploits of his patron Gotthart Kettler. His chronicle was published posthumously in 1590. It tells the story from the perspective of the dukes of Courland and kings of Poland. His narrative is not the lively, colourful tale that is Russow's, but it does present another important viewpoint on the Livonian War.

Horn, Henrik Claesson: (1512–95) Principal counsellor to the Danish King's favourite son, Duke Johann, and his closest adviser between 1558 and 1563. He also served under Johan's half brother Erik XIV, King of Sweden from 1560 to 1568. Horn served as governor of Tallinn and of Livonia and as a high-ranking military commander during the Livonian Wars.

Johan, Duke of Finland: (1537–92) Ruled as Duke from 1556 to 1558 and as Johan III, King of Sweden, from 1568 to his death. His half-brother Erik XIV of Sweden had imprisoned Johan in 1563. After he was released Johan deposed Erik and took power.

Kettler, Gotthart/Gotthard: (1517–87) Coadjutor to Fürstenberg, Kettler was the last Master of the Livonian Order. In 1560 the Order was decisively defeated by the Muscovite. Kettler sought the protection of Sigismund II Augustus, King of Poland and Grand Duke of Lithuania, by entering into an alliance with him. He ousted Monninkhusen from his position as Commander of Tallinn and returned Tallinn to the Order.

Koell, Johann: (c.1500–40) From 1532 to 1540 Koell was chaplain of Holy Ghost Church and preacher to the Estonian-speaking congregation. The earliest printed book in Estonian is his translation of Simon Wanradt's German language catechism, published in 1535.

Magnus, Duke of Holstein: (1540–83) Younger brother of King Frederick II of Denmark. He was bishop of Saare-Lääne, bishop of Kurland and crowned King of Livonia by Ivan IV, a title he held from 1570 to 1578.

Melanchthon, Philipp: (1497–1560) German theologian and reformer, friend of Martin Luther. He wrote the Augsburg Confession (*Confessio Augustana*), which became the official statement of faith for the Lutheran Church. A humanist and educator, he helped to found and reform public schools in Germany.

Monninkhusen, Christopher/Christoph (aka Christoph von Münchhausen/ Munchhausen): (d.1565) Danish vicegerent in Estonia from 1558 to 1560. In July 1558 he declared that Tallinn should become subject to the Danish crown, but citizens of Tallinn objected. Monninkhusen was later ousted by Gotthart Kettler.

Osiander Andreas: (1498–1552) A German Lutheran theologian and Christian mystic who disputed some views of Luther and Calvin. **Joseph Funk**, his son-in-law, defended and propagated Osiander's opinions after his death.

Renner, Johannes: (1525–c.1583) Author of *The Livonian Chronicle 1556–61*, which recounts the rise of Ivan IV. He was a notary and secretary to Brent von Schmerten, a Bremen official and governor of Järvamaa. Renner thus had access to documents and correspondence and was in a position to learn first hand about the activities of political figures.

Segenhagen (Siegenhoven) Franz von, Nicknamed Goldbeak (Starling): The last official commander of Tallinn, serving from 1555 to 1558. Left for Denmark in 1558, handing command of the Toompea fortress to Monninkhusen, the advocate-protector of the bishopric of Saaremaa.

Sigismund II Augustus: (1520–72) King of Poland, Grand Duke of Lithuania. Formed the Polish–Lithuanian Commonwealth. Signed the Treaty of Pozvol in 1557 with the Livonian Order, putting the diminished Order under his protection.

APPENDIX THREE

Archaic Units of Measurement

Cubit: length from fingertip to elbow: about 18 in./0.5 m.

Fathom: widest length between fingertips of outstretched arms: c. 2yd/1.8 m.

League: the distance a person could walk in an hour, commonly defined as 3 miles/4.8 k.m.

Span: width of palm plus length of thumb: c. 6 in./15 c.m.

Pood: c. 36–40 lbs/16–16. 38 k.g.

APPENDIX FOUR

Names of streets, gates, towers, villages and bridges

The words in parentheses in the translated names are not part of the
Estonian names as listed, but are understood.

Härjapea: Oxhead (River)

Hobuveski: Horsemill (Gate)

Hongasaare: Old-Pine Island

Jahuvärav: Flour Gate

Jänese küla: Rabbit Village

Kalamaja: Fish House (Village)

Karja värav: Cattle Gate
(Herd Gate)

Kiriku: Church (Street)

Kivisild: Stone Bridge

Köismäe: Rope Hill.

Kolmapäeva värav: Wednesday Gate

Kuninga: King (Street)

Kureküla: Stork Village

Lai: Broad (Street).

Laitänav: Broad Street

Läänemaa: Lääne County
(lit: Western land)

Lasnamäe: Teal Hill

Lontmaaker: Rope-Maker (Rise)

Lossi: Castle (Street)

Munkade: Monks' (Street)

Müürivahe: Between-the-Walls
(Street)

Neitsimäe: Virgin's Hill

Nõelasilm: Needle's Eye (Passage)

Nunnavärav: Nun's Gate

Paks Margareeta: Fat Margaret
(Tower)

Pikk Hermann: Tall Hermann
(Tower)

Pikk: Long (Street)

Pikkjalg: Long Leg (Street)

Pikksild: Long Bridge

Pirita: St Bridget's (Convent)

Pühajõe: Holy River

Puusilla: Wooden Bridge

Rataskaevu: Wheel-well (Street)

Rüütli: Knight (Street)

Saiakang White Bread Way

Seppade: Blacksmiths' (Street)

Soesoo: Warm Marsh

Suur karja: Big Cattle (Street)

Suur-Paljassaare: Big Barren Island

Suursaare: Big Island

Toompea: Cathedral Hill (the
upper town)

Väike Rannavärav: Small Coast Gate

Väike Rataskaevu: Small Wheel-well
(Street)

Väike-Toomi: Small Dome (Street)

Varessaare: Crow Island

Veskivärav: Mill Gate

Viru värav: Viru Gate

ÅLAND

SWEDEN

50 MILES

STOCKHOLM

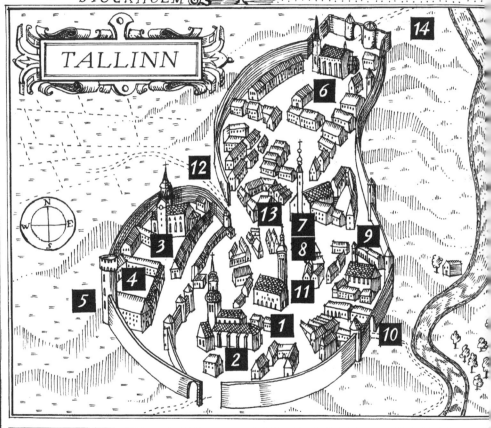

TALLINN

12

6

14

N
W E
S

3

13   7

8   9

4

5   11

1

10

2

1	BISHOP'S HOUSE & OLD MARKET	8	APOTHECARY
2	ST NICHOLAS' CHURCH	9	DOMINICAN MONASTERY
3	DOME CHURCH	10	VIRU GATE
4	TOOMPEA CASTLE	11	TOWN HALL
5	TALL HERMANN	12	NUN'S GATE
6	ST OLAF'S CHURCH	13	GREAT GUILD
7	HOLY GHOST CHURCH	14	GREAT COAST GATE